BEST OF THE
AKASHIC NOIR SERIES

USA NOIR

BEST OF THE
AKASHIC NOIR SERIES

USA NOIR

EDITED BY JOHNNY TEMPLE

Published by Akashic Books
©2013 Akashic Books
Copyright to the individual stories is retained by the authors.

Series concept by Tim McLoughlin and Johnny Temple
USA map by Aaron Petrovich

Hardcover ISBN-13: 978-1-61775-189-9
Paperback ISBN-13: 978-1-61775-184-4
Library of Congress Control Number: TK
All rights reserved

First printing

Akashic Books
PO Box 1456
New York, NY 10009
info@akashicbooks.com
www.akashicbooks.com

ALSO IN THE AKASHIC NOIR SERIES

FORTHCOMING

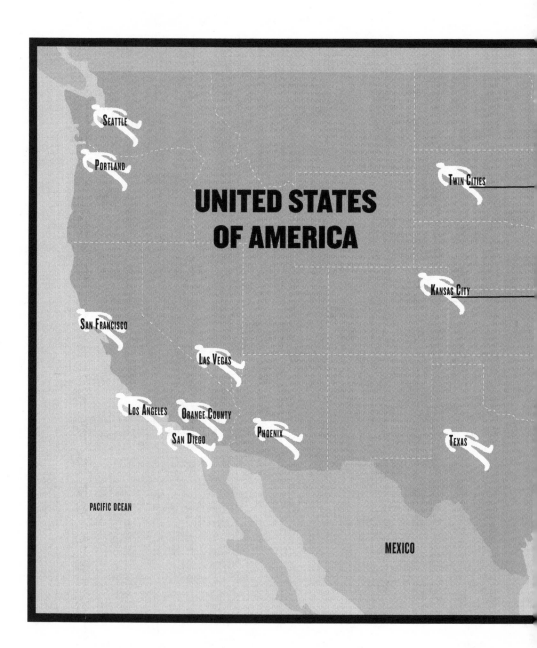

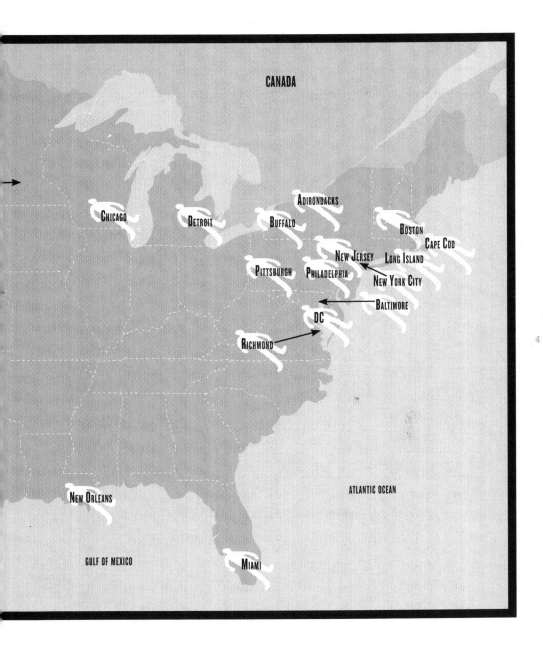

CANADA

Chicago

Detroit

Buffalo

Adirondacks

Boston

Cape Cod

New Jersey

Long Island

Pittsburgh

Philadelphia

New York City

Baltimore

DC

Richmond

ATLANTIC OCEAN

New Orleans

GULF OF MEXICO

Miami

TABLE OF CONTENTS

INTRODUCTION
Writers on the Run

I n my early years as a book publisher, I got a call one Saturday from one of our authors asking me to drop by his place for "a smoke." I politely declined as I had a full day planned. "But Johnny," the author persisted, "I have some *really good* smoke." My curiosity piqued, I swung by, but was a bit perplexed to be greeted with suspicion at the author's door by an unhinged whore and her near-nude john. The author rumbled over and ushered me in, promptly sitting me down on a smelly couch and assuring the others I wasn't a problem. Moments later, the john produced a crack pipe to resume the party I had evidently interrupted. This wasn't quite the smoke I'd envisaged, so I gracefully excused myself after a few (sober) minutes. I scurried home pondering the author's notion that it was somehow appropriate to invite his publisher to a crack party.

It may not have been appropriate, but it sure was noir.

From the start, the heart and soul of Akashic Books has been dark, provocative, well-crafted tales from the disenfranchised. I learned early on that writings from outside the mainstream almost necessarily coincide with a mood and spirit of noir, and are composed by authors whose life circumstances often place them in environs exposed to crime.

My own interest in noir fiction grew from my early exposure to urban crime, which I absorbed from various perspectives. I was born and raised in Washington, DC, and have lived in Brooklyn since 1990. In the 1970s and '80s, when violent, drug-fueled crime in DC was rampant, my mother hung out with cops she'd befriended through her work as a nearly unbeatable public defender. She also grew close to some of her clients, most notably legendary DC bank robber Lester "LT" Irby (a contributor to *DC Noir*), who has been one of my closest friends since I was fifteen, though he was incarcerated from the early 1970s until just recently. Complicating my family's relationship with the criminal justice system, my dad sued the police stridently in his work as legal director of DC's American Civil Liberties Union.

Both of my parents worked overtime. By the time my sister Kathy was nine and I was seven, we were latchkey kids prone to roam, explore, and occasionally break laws. Though an arrest for shoplifting helped curb my delinquent tendencies, the interest in crime remained. After college I worked with adolescents and completed a master's degree in social work; my focus was on teen delinquency.

Throughout the 1990s, my relationship with the urban underbelly expanded as I spent a great deal of time in dank nightclubs populated by degenerates and outcasts. I played bass guitar in Girls Against Boys, a rock and roll group that toured extensively in the US and Europe. The long hours on the road not spent on stage gave way to book publishing, which began as a hobby in 1996 with my friends Bobby and Mark Sullivan.

The first book we published was *The Fuck-Up*, by Arthur Nersesian—a dark, provocative, well-crafted tale from the disenfranchised. A few years later *Heart of the Old Country* by Tim McLoughlin became one of our early commercial successes. The book was widely praised both for its classic noir voice and its homage to the people of South Brooklyn. While Brooklyn is chock-full of published authors these days, Tim is one of the few who was actually born and bred here. In his five decades, Tim has never left the borough for more than five weeks at a stretch and he knows the place, through and through, better than anyone I've met.

In 2003, inspired by Brooklyn's unique and glorious mix of cultures, Tim and I set out to explore New York City's largest borough in book form, in a way that would ring true to local residents. Tim loves his home borough despite its flagrant flaws, and was easily seduced by the concept of working with Akashic to try and portray its full human breadth.

He first proposed a series of books, each one set in a different neighborhood, whether it be Bay Ridge, Williamsburg, Park Slope, Fort Greene, Bed-Stuy, or Canarsie. It was an exciting idea, but it's hard enough to publish a single book, let alone commit to a full series. After we considered various other possibilities, Tim came upon the idea of a fiction anthology organized by neighborhood, each one represented by a different author. We were looking for stylistic diversity, so we focused on "noir," and defined it in the broadest sense: we wanted stories of tragic, soulful struggle against all odds, characters slipping, no redemption in sight.

Conventional wisdom dictates that literary anthologies don't sell well, but this idea was too good to resist—it seemed the perfect form for exploring the whole borough, and we got to work soliciting stories. We batted around book titles, including *Under the Hood*, before settling on *Brooklyn Noir*. The volume came together beautifully and was a surprise hit for Akashic, quickly selling through multiple printings and winning awards. (See pages 548–550 for a full list of prizes garnered by stories originally published in the Noir Series.)

Having seen nearly every American city, large and small, through the windows of a van or tour bus, I have developed a deep fondness for their idiosyncrasies. So for me it was easy logic to take the model of *Brooklyn Noir*— sketching out dark urban corners through neighborhood-based short fiction— and extend it to other cities. Soon came *Chicago Noir, San Francisco Noir*, and *London Noir* (our first of many overseas locations). Selecting the right editor to curate each book has been the most important decision we make before assembling it. It's a welcome challenge because writers are often enamored of their hometowns, and many are seduced by the urban landscape's rough edges. The generous support of literary superheroes like George Pelecanos, Laura Lippman, Dennis Lehane, and Joyce Carol Oates, all of whom have edited series volumes, has been critical.

There are now fifty-nine books in the Noir Series. Forty of them are from American locales. As of this writing, a total of 787 authors have contributed 917 stories to the series and helped Akashic to stay afloat during perilous economic times. By publishing six to eight new volumes in the Noir Series every year, we have provided a steady venue for short stories, which have in recent times struggled with diminishing popularity. Akashic's commitment to the short story has been rewarded by the many authors—of both great stature and great obscurity—who have allowed us to publish their work in the series for a nominal fee.

I am particularly indebted to all sixty-seven editors who have cumulatively upheld a high editorial standard across the series. The series would never have gotten this far without rigorous quality control. There also couldn't be a Noir Series without my devoted and tireless (if occasionally irreverent) staff led by Johanna Ingalls, Ibrahim Ahmad, and Aaron Petrovich.

This volume serves up a top-shelf selection of stories from the series set in the United States. *USA Noir* only scratches the surface, however, and every single volume has more gems on offer.

When I set out to compile *USA Noir*, I was delighted by the immediate positive responses from nearly every author I contacted. The only author on my initial invitation list who isn't included here is one I couldn't track down: the publisher explained to me that the writer was "literally on the run." While I'm disappointed that we can't include the story, the circumstance is true to the Noir Series spirit.

And part of me—the noir part—is expecting a phone call from the writer, inviting me over for a smoke.

Johnny Temple
Brooklyn, NY
March 2013

PART I

TRUE GRIT

ANIMAL RESCUE

BY DENNIS LEHANE

Dorchester, Boston

(Originally published in *Boston Noir*)

Bob found the dog in the trash.

It was just after Thanksgiving, the neighborhood gone quiet, hungover. After bartending at Cousin Marv's, Bob sometimes walked the streets. He was big and lumpy and hair had been growing in unlikely places all over his body since his teens. In his twenties, he'd fought against the hair, carrying small clippers in his coat pocket and shaving twice a day. He'd also fought the weight, but during all those years of fighting, no girl who wasn't being paid for it ever showed any interest in him. After a time, he gave up the fight. He lived alone in the house he grew up in, and when it seemed likely to swallow him with its smells and memories and dark couches, the attempts he'd made to escape it—through church socials, lodge picnics, and one horrific mixer thrown by a dating service—had only opened the wound further, left him patching it back up for weeks, cursing himself for hoping.

So he took these walks of his and, if he was lucky, sometimes he forgot people lived any other way. That night, he paused on the sidewalk, feeling the ink sky above him and the cold in his fingers, and he closed his eyes against the evening.

He was used to it. He was used to it. It was okay.

You could make a friend of it, as long as you didn't fight it.

With his eyes closed, he heard it—a worn-out keening accompanied by distant scratching and a sharper, metallic rattling. He opened his eyes. Fifteen feet down the sidewalk, a large metal barrel with a heavy lid shook slightly under the yellow glare of the streetlight, its bottom scraping the sidewalk. He stood over it and heard that keening again, the sound of a creature that was one breath away from deciding it was too hard to take the next, and he pulled off the lid.

He had to remove some things to get to it—a toaster and five thick Yellow Pages, the oldest dating back to 2000. The dog—either a very small one or else a puppy—was down at the bottom, and it scrunched its head into its midsection when the light hit it. It exhaled a soft chug of a whimper and tightened its body even more, its eyes closed to slits. A scrawny thing. Bob could see its ribs. He could see a big crust of dried blood by its ear. No collar. It was brown with a white snout and paws that seemed far too big for its body.

It let out a sharper whimper when Bob reached down, sank his fingers into the nape of its neck, and lifted it out of its own excrement. Bob didn't know dogs too well, but there was no mistaking this one for anything but a boxer. And definitely a puppy, the wide brown eyes opening and looking into his as he held it up before him.

Somewhere, he was sure, two people made love. A man and a woman. Entwined. Behind one of those shades, oranged with light, that looked down on the street. Bob could feel them in there, naked and blessed. And he stood out here in the cold with a near-dead dog staring back at him. The icy sidewalk glinted like new marble, and the wind was dark and gray as slush.

"What do you got there?"

Bob turned, looked up and down the sidewalk.

"I'm up here. And you're in my trash."

She stood on the front porch of the three-decker nearest him. She'd turned the porch light on and stood there shivering, her feet bare. She reached into the pocket of her hoodie and came back with a pack of cigarettes. She watched him as she got one going.

"I found a dog." Bob held it up.

"A *what?*"

"A dog. A puppy. A boxer, I think."

She coughed out some smoke. "Who puts a dog in a barrel?"

"Right?" he said. "It's bleeding." He took a step toward her stairs and she backed up.

"Who do you know that I would know?" A city girl, not about to just drop her guard around a stranger.

"I don't know," Bob said. "How about Francie Hedges?"

She shook her head. "You know the Sullivans?"

That wouldn't narrow it down. Not around here. You shook a tree, a Sullivan fell out. Followed by a six-pack most times. "I know a bunch."

This was going nowhere, the puppy looking at him, shaking worse than the girl.

"Hey," she said, "you live in this parish?"

"Next one over. St. Theresa's."

"Go to church?"

"Most Sundays."

"So you know Father Pete?"

"Pete Regan," he said, "sure."

She produced a cell phone. "What's your name?"

"Bob," he said. "Bob Saginowski."

Bob waited as she stepped back from the light, phone to one ear, finger pressed into the other. He stared at the puppy. The puppy stared back, like, *How did I get* here? Bob touched its nose with his index finger. The puppy blinked its huge eyes. For a moment, Bob couldn't recall his sins.

"Nadia," the girl said and stepped back into the light. "Bring him up here, Bob. Pete says hi."

They washed it in Nadia's sink, dried it off, and brought it to her kitchen table.

Nadia was small. A bumpy red rope of a scar ran across the base of her throat like the smile of a drunk circus clown. She had a tiny moon of a face, savaged by pockmarks, and small, heart-pendant eyes. Shoulders that didn't cut so much as dissolve at the arms. Elbows like flattened beer cans. A yellow bob of hair curled on either side of her face. "It's not a boxer." Her eyes glanced off Bob's face before dropping the puppy back onto her kitchen table. "It's an American Staffordshire terrier."

Bob knew he was supposed to understand something in her tone, but he didn't know what that thing was so he remained silent.

She glanced back up at him after the quiet lasted too long. "A pit bull."

"That's a pit bull?"

She nodded and swabbed the puppy's head wound again. Someone had pummeled it, she told Bob. Probably knocked it unconscious, assumed it was dead, and dumped it.

"Why?" Bob said.

She looked at him, her round eyes getting rounder, wider. "Just because." She shrugged, went back to examining the dog. "I worked at Animal Rescue once. You know the place on Shawmut? As a vet tech. Before I decided it wasn't my thing. They're so hard, this breed . . ."

"What?"

"To adopt out," she said. "It's very hard to find them a home."

"I don't know about dogs. I never had a dog. I live alone. I was just walking by the barrel." Bob found himself beset by a desperate need to explain himself, explain his life. "I'm just not . . ." He could hear the wind outside, black and rattling. Rain or bits of hail spit against the windows.

Nadia lifted the puppy's back left paw—the other three paws were brown, but this one was white with peach spots. Then she dropped the paw as if it were contagious. She went back to the head wound, took a closer look at the right ear, a piece missing from the tip that Bob hadn't noticed until now.

"Well," she said, "he'll live. You're gonna need a crate and food and all sorts of stuff."

"No," Bob said. "You don't understand."

She cocked her head, gave him a look that said she understood perfectly.

"I can't. I just found him. I was gonna give him back."

"To whoever beat him, left him for dead?"

"No, no, like, the authorities."

"That would be Animal Rescue," she said. "After they give the owner seven days to reclaim him, they'll—"

"The guy who beat him? He gets a second chance?"

She gave him a half-frown and a nod. "If he doesn't take it," she lifted the puppy's ear, peered in, "chances are this little fella'll be put up for adoption. But it's hard. To find them a home. Pit bulls. More often than not?" She looked at Bob. "More often than not, they're put down."

Bob felt a wave of sadness roll out from her that immediately shamed him. He didn't know how, but he'd caused pain. He'd put some out into the world. He'd let this girl down. "I . . ." he started. "It's just . . ."

She glanced up at him. "I'm sorry?"

Bob looked at the puppy. Its eyes were droopy from a long day in the barrel and whoever gave it that wound. It had stopped shivering, though.

"You can take it," Bob said. "You used to work there, like you said. You—"

She shook her head. "My father lives with me. He gets home Sunday night from Foxwoods. He finds a dog in his house? An animal he's allergic to?" She jerked her thumb. "Puppy goes back in the barrel."

"Can you give me till Sunday morning?" Bob wasn't sure how it was the words left his mouth, since he couldn't remember formulating them or even thinking them.

The girl eyed him carefully. "You're not just saying it? Cause, I shit you not, he ain't picked up by Sunday noon, he's back out that door."

"Sunday, then." Bob said the words with a conviction he actually felt. "Sunday, definitely."

"Yeah?" She smiled, and it was a spectacular smile, and Bob saw that the face behind the pockmarks was as spectacular as the smile. Wanting only to be seen. She touched the puppy's nose with her index finger.

"Yeah." Bob felt crazed. He felt light as a communion wafer. "Yeah."

At Cousin Marv's, where he tended bar twelve to ten, Wednesday through Sunday, he told Marv all about it. Most people called Marv *Cousin* Marv out of habit, something that went back to grade school though no one could remember how, but Marv actually was Bob's cousin. On his mother's side.

Cousin Marv had run a crew in the late '80s and early '90s. It had been primarily comprised of guys with interests in the loaning and subsequent debt-repayal side of things, though Marv never turned his nose down at any paying proposition because he believed, to the core of his soul, that those who failed to diversify were always the first to collapse when the wind turned. Like the dinosaurs, he'd say to Bob, when the cavemen came along and invented arrows. Picture the cavemen, he'd say, firing away, and the tyrannosauruses all gucked up in the oil puddles. A tragedy so easily averted.

Marv's crew hadn't been the toughest crew or the smartest or the most successful operating in the neighborhood—not even close—but for a while they got by. Other crews kept nipping at their heels, though, and except for one glaring exception, they'd never been ones to favor violence. Pretty soon, they had to make the decision to yield to crews a lot meaner than they were or duke it out. They took Door Number One.

Marv's income derived from running his bar as a drop. In the new world order—a loose collective of Chechen, Italian, and Irish hard guys—no one wanted to get caught with enough merch or enough money for a case to go Federal. So they kept it out of their offices and out of their homes and they kept it on the move. About every two to three weeks, drops were made at Cousin Marv's, among other establishments. You sat on the drop for a night, two at the most, before some beer-truck driver showed up with the weekend's password and hauled everything back out on a dolly like it was a stack of empty kegs, took it away in a refrigerated semi. The rest of Marv's income derived from being a fence, one of the best in the city, but being a fence in their world (or a drop bar operator for that matter) was like being a mailroom clerk in the straight world—if you were still doing it after thirty, it was all you'd ever do. For Bob, it was a relief—he liked being a bartender and he'd hated that one time they'd had to come heavy. Marv, though, Marv still waited for the golden train to arrive on the golden tracks, take him away from all this. Most times, he pretended to be happy. But Bob knew that the things that haunted Marv were the same things that haunted Bob—the shitty things you did to get ahead. Those things laughed at you if your ambitions failed to amount to much; a successful man could hide his past; an unsuccessful man sat in his.

That morning, Marv was looking a hair on the mournful side, lighting one Camel while the previous one still smoldered, so Bob tried to cheer him up by telling him about his adventure with the dog. Marv didn't seem too interested, and Bob found himself saying "You had to be there" so much, he eventually shut up about it.

Marv said, "Rumor is we're getting the Super Bowl drop."

"No shit?"

If true (an enormous *if*), this was huge. They worked on commission— one half of one percent of the drop. A Super Bowl drop? It would be like one half of one percent of Exxon.

Nadia's scar flashed in Bob's brain, the redness of it, the thick, ropey texture. "They send extra guys to protect it, you think?"

Marv rolled his eyes. "Why, cause people are just lining up to steal from coked-up Chechnyans."

"Chechens," Bob said.

"But they're from Chechnya."

Bob shrugged. "I think it's like how you don't call people from Ireland *Irelandians*."

Marv scowled. "Whatever. It means all this hard work we've been doing? It's paid off. Like how Toyota did it, making friends and influencing people."

Bob kept quiet. If they ended up being the drop for the Super Bowl, it was because someone figured out no Feds deemed them important enough to be watched. But in Marv's fantasies, the crew (long since dispersed to straight jobs, jail, or, worse, Connecticut) could regain its glory days, even though those days had lasted about as long as a Swatch. It never occurred to Marv that one day they'd come take everything he had—the fence, the money and merch he kept in the safe in back, hell, the bar probably—just because they were sick of him hanging around, looking at them with needy expectation. It had gotten so every time he talked about the "people he knew," the dreams he had, Bob had to resist the urge to reach for the 9mm they kept beneath the bar and blow his own brains out. Not really—but close sometimes. Man, Marv could wear you out.

A guy stuck his head in the bar, late twenties but with white hair, a white goatee, a silver stud in his ear. He dressed like most kids these days—like shit: pre-ripped jeans, slovenly T-shirt under a faded hoodie under a wrinkled wool topcoat. He didn't cross the threshold, just craned his head in, the cold day pouring in off the sidewalk behind him.

"Help you?" Bob asked.

The guy shook his head, kept staring at the gloomy bar like it was a crystal ball.

"Mind shutting the door?" Marv didn't look up. "Cold out there."

"You serve Zima?" The guy's eyes flew around the bar, up and down, left to right.

Marv looked up now. "Who the fuck would we serve it to—Moesha?"

The guy raised an apologetic hand. "My bad." He left, and the warmth returned with the closing of the door.

Marv said, "You know that kid?"

Bob shook his head. "Mighta seen him around but I can't place him."

"He's a fucking nutbag. Lives in the next parish, probably why you don't know him. You're old school that way, Bob—somebody didn't go to parochial school with you, it's like they don't exist."

Bob couldn't argue. When he'd been a kid, your parish was your country. Everything you needed and needed to know was contained within it. Now that the archdiocese had shuttered half the parishes to pay for the crimes of the kid-diddler priests, Bob couldn't escape the fact that those days of parish dominion, long dwindling, were gone. He was a certain type of guy, of a certain half-generation, an almost generation, and while there were still plenty of them left, they were older, grayer, they had smokers' coughs, they went in for checkups and never checked back out.

"That kid?" Marv gave Bob a bump of his eyebrows. "They say he killed Richie Whelan back in the day."

"*They* say?"

"They do."

"Well, then . . ."

They sat in silence for a bit. Snow-dust blew past the window in the high-pitched breeze. The street signs and window panes rattled, and Bob thought how winter lost any meaning the day you last rode a sled. Any meaning but gray. He looked into the unlit sections of the barroom. The shadows became hospital beds, stooped old widowers shopping for sympathy cards, empty wheelchairs. The wind howled a little sharper.

"This puppy, right?" Bob said. "He's got paws the size of his head. Three are brown but one's white with these little peach-colored spots over the white. And—"

"This thing cook?" Marv said. "Clean the house? I mean, it's a fucking dog."

"Yeah, but it was—" Bob dropped his hands. He didn't know how to explain. "You know that feeling you get sometimes on a really great day? Like, like, the Pats dominate and you took the 'over,' or they cook your steak just right up the Blarney, or, or you just feel *good*? Like . . ." Bob found himself waving his hands again ". . . good?"

Marv gave him a nod and a tight smile. Went back to his racing sheet.

On Sunday morning, Nadia brought the puppy to his car as he idled in front of her house. She handed it through the window and gave them both a little wave.

He looked at the puppy sitting on his seat and fear washed over him. What does it eat? When does it eat? Housebreaking. How do you do that? How long does it take? He'd had days to consider these questions—why were they only occurring to him now?

He hit the brakes and reversed the car a few feet. Nadia, one foot on her bottom step, turned back. He rolled down the passenger window, craned his body across the seat until he was peering up at her.

"I don't know what to do," he said. "I don't know anything."

At a supermarket for pets, Nadia picked out several chew toys, told Bob he'd need them if he wanted to keep his couch. Shoes, she told him, keep your shoes hidden from now on, up on a high shelf. They bought vitamins—for a dog!—and a bag of puppy food she recommended, telling him the most important thing was to stick with that brand from now on. Change a dog's diet, she warned, you'll get piles of diarrhea on your floor.

They got a crate to put him in when Bob was at work. They got a water bottle for the crate and a book on dog training written by monks who were on the cover looking hardy and not real monkish, big smiles. As the cashier rang it all up, Bob felt a quake rumble through his body, a momentary disruption as he reached for his wallet. His throat flushed with heat. His head felt fizzy. And only as the quake went away and his throat cooled and his head cleared and he handed over his credit card to the cashier did he realize, in the sudden disappearance of the feeling, what the feeling had been: for a moment—maybe even a succession of moments, and none sharp enough to point to as the cause—he'd been happy.

"So, thank you," she said when he pulled up in front of her house.

"What? No. Thank *you*. Please. Really. It . . . Thank you."

She said, "This little guy, he's a good guy. He's going to make you proud, Bob."

He looked down at the puppy, sleeping on her lap now, snoring slightly. "Do they do that? Sleep all the time?"

"Pretty much. Then they run around like loonies for about twenty minutes. Then they sleep some more. And poop. Bob, man, you got to remember that—they poop and pee like crazy. Don't get mad. They don't know any better. Read the monk book. It takes time, but they figure out soon enough not to do it in the house."

"What's soon enough?"

"Two months?" She cocked her head. "Maybe three. Be patient, Bob."

"Be patient," he repeated.

"And you too," she said to the puppy as she lifted it off her lap. He came awake, sniffing, snorting. He didn't want her to go. "You *both* take care." She let herself out and gave Bob a wave as she walked up her steps, then went inside.

The puppy was on its haunches, staring up at the window like Nadia might reappear there. It looked back over its shoulder at Bob. Bob could feel its abandonment. He could feel his own. He was certain they'd make a mess of it, him and this throwaway dog. He was sure the world was too strong.

"What's your name?" he asked the puppy. "What are we going to call you?"

The puppy turned its head away, like, Bring the girl back.

First thing it did was take a shit in the dining room.

Bob didn't even realize what it was doing at first. It started sniffing, nose scraping the rug, and then it looked up at Bob with an air of embarrassment. And Bob said, "What?" and the dog dumped all over the corner of the rug.

Bob scrambled forward, as if he could stop it, push it back in, and the puppy bolted, left droplets on the hardwood as it scurried into the kitchen.

Bob said, "No, no. It's okay." Although it wasn't. Most everything in the house had been his mother's, largely unchanged since she'd purchased it in the '50s. That was shit. Excrement. In his mother's house. On her rug, her floor.

In the seconds it took him to reach the kitchen, the puppy'd left a piss puddle on the linoleum. Bob almost slipped in it. The puppy was sitting against the fridge, looking at him, tensing for a blow, trying not to shake.

And it stopped Bob. It stopped him even as he knew the longer he left the shit on the rug, the harder it would be to get out.

Bob got down on all fours. He felt the sudden return of what he'd felt when he first picked it out of the trash, something he'd assumed had left with Nadia. Connection. He suspected they might have been brought together by something other than chance.

He said, "Hey." Barely above a whisper. "Hey, it's all right." So, so slowly, he extended his hand, and the puppy pressed itself harder against the fridge. But Bob kept the hand coming, and gently lay his palm on the side of the animal's face. He made soothing sounds. He smiled at it. "It's okay," he repeated, over and over.

He named it Cassius because he'd mistaken it for a boxer and he liked the sound of the word. It made him think of Roman legions, proud jaws, honor.

Nadia called him Cash. She came around after work sometimes and she and Bob took it on walks. He knew something was a little off about Nadia—the dog being found so close to her house and her lack of surprise or interest in that fact was not lost on Bob—but was there anyone, anywhere on this planet, who wasn't a little off? More than a little most times. Nadia came by to help with the dog and Bob, who hadn't known much friendship in his life, took what he could get.

They taught Cassius to sit and lie down and paw and roll over. Bob read the entire monk book and followed its instructions. The puppy had his rabies shot and was cleared of any cartilage damage to his ear. Just a bruise, the vet said, just a deep bruise. He grew fast.

Weeks passed without Cassius having an accident, but Bob still couldn't be sure whether that was luck or not, and then on Super Bowl Sunday, Cassius used one paw on the back door. Bob let him out and then tore through the house to call Nadia. He was so proud he felt like yodeling, and he almost mistook the doorbell for something else. A kettle, he thought, still reaching for the phone.

The guy on the doorstep was thin. Not weak-thin. Hard-thin. As if whatever burned inside of him burned too hot for fat to survive. He had blue eyes so pale they were almost gray. His silver hair was cropped tight to his skull, as was the goatee that clung to his lips and chin. It took Bob a second to recognize him—the kid who'd stuck his head in the bar five, six weeks back, asked if they served Zima.

The kid smiled and extended his hand. "Mr. Saginowski?"

Bob shook the hand. "Yes?"

"Bob Saginowski?" The man shook Bob's large hand with his small one, and there was a lot of power in the grip.

"Yeah?"

"Eric Deeds, Bob." The kid let go of his hand. "I believe you have my dog."

In the kitchen, Eric Deeds said, "Hey, there he is." He said, "That's my guy." He said, "He got big." He said, "The size of him."

Cassius slinked over to him, even climbed up on his lap when Eric, unbidden, took a seat at Bob's kitchen table and patted his inner thigh twice. Bob couldn't even say how it was Eric Deeds talked his way into the house; he was just one of those people had a way about him, like cops and Teamsters—he wanted in, he was coming in.

"Bob," Eric Deeds said, "I'm going to need him back." He had Cassius in his lap and was rubbing his belly. Bob felt a prick of envy as Cassius kicked his left leg, even though a constant shiver—almost a palsy—ran through his fur. Eric Deeds scratched under Cassius's chin. The dog kept his ears and tail pressed flat to his body. He looked ashamed, his eyes staring down into their sockets.

"Um . . ." Bob reached out and lifted Cassius off Eric's lap, plopped him down on his own, scratched behind his ears. "Cash is mine."

The act was between them now—Bob lifting the puppy off Eric's lap without any warning, Eric looking at him for just a second, like, The fuck was that all about? His forehead narrowed and it gave his eyes a surprised cast, as if they'd never expected to find themselves on his face. In that moment, he looked cruel, the kind of guy, if he was feeling sorry for himself, took a shit on the whole world.

"Cash?" he said.

Bob nodded as Cassius's ears unfurled from his head and he licked Bob's wrist. "Short for Cassius. That's his name. What did you call him?"

"Called him Dog mostly. Sometimes Hound."

Eric Deeds glanced around the kitchen, up at the old circular fluorescent in the ceiling, something going back to Bob's mother, hell, Bob's father just before the first stroke, around the time the old man had become obsessed with paneling—paneled the kitchen, the living room, the dining room, would've paneled the toilet if he could've figured out how.

Bob said, "You beat him."

Eric reached into his shirt pocket. He pulled out a cigarette and popped it in his mouth. He lit it, shook out the match, tossed it on Bob's kitchen table.

"You can't smoke in here."

Eric considered Bob with a level gaze and kept smoking. "I beat him?"

"Yeah."

"Uh, so what?" Eric flicked some ash on the floor. "I'm taking the dog, Bob."

Bob stood to his full height. He held tight to Cassius, who squirmed a bit in his arms and nipped at the flat of his hand. If it came to it, Bob decided, he'd drop all six feet three inches and two hundred ninety pounds of himself on Eric Deeds, who couldn't weigh more than a buck-seventy. Not now, not just standing there, but if Eric reached for Cassius, well then . . .

Eric Deeds blew a stream of smoke at the ceiling. "I saw you that night. I was feeling bad, you know, about my temper? So I went back to see if the hound was really dead or not and I watched you pluck him out of the trash."

"I really think you should go." Bob pulled his cell from his pocket and flipped it open. "I'm calling 911."

Eric nodded. "I've been in prison, Bob, mental hospitals. I've been a lotta places. I'll go again, don't mean a thing to me, though I doubt they'd prosecute even *me* for fucking up a *dog.* I mean, sooner or later, you gotta go to work or get some sleep."

"What is *wrong* with you?"

Eric held out of his hands. "Pretty much everything. And you took my dog."

"You tried to kill it."

Eric said, "Nah." Shook his head like he believed it.

"You can't have the dog."

"I need the dog."

"No."

"I love that dog."

"No."

"Ten thousand."

"What?"

Eric nodded. "I need ten grand. By tonight. That's the price."

Bob gave a nervous chuckle. "Who has ten thousand dollars?"

"You could find it."

"How could I poss—"

"Say, that safe in Cousin Marv's office. You're a drop bar, Bob. You don't think half the neighborhood knows? So that might be a place to start."

Bob shook his head. "Can't be done. Any money we get during the day? Goes through a slot at the bar. Ends up in the office safe, yeah, but that's on a time—"

"—lock, I know." Eric turned on the couch, one arm stretched along the back of it. "Goes off at two a.m. in case they decide they need a last-minute payout for something who the fuck knows, but big. And you have ninety seconds to open and close it or it triggers two silent alarms, neither of which goes off in a police station or a security company. Fancy that." Eric took a hit off his cigarette. "I'm not greedy, Bob. I just need stake money for something. I don't want everything in the safe, just ten grand. You give me ten grand, I'll disappear."

"This is ludicrous."

"So, it's ludicrous."

"You don't just walk into someone's life and—"

"That *is* life: someone like me coming along when you're not looking."

Bob put Cassius on the floor but made sure he didn't wander over to the other side of the table. He needn't have worried—Cassius didn't move an inch, sat there like a cement post, eyes on Bob.

Eric Deeds said, "You're racing through all your options, but they're options for normal people in normal circumstances. I need my ten grand tonight. If you don't get it for me, I'll take your dog. I licensed him. You didn't, because you couldn't. Then I'll forget to feed him for a while. One day, when he gets all yappy about it, I'll beat his head in with a rock or something. Look in my eyes and tell me which part I'm lying about, Bob."

After he left, Bob went to his basement. He avoided it whenever he could, though the floor was white, as white as he'd been able to make it, whiter than it had ever been through most of its existence. He unlocked a cupboard over the old wash sink his father had often used after one of his adventures in paneling, and removed a yellow and brown Chock full o'Nuts can from the shelf. He pulled fifteen thousand from it. He put ten in his pocket and five back in the can. He looked around again at the white floor, at the black oil tank against the wall, at the bare bulbs.

Upstairs he gave Cassius a bunch of treats. He rubbed his ears and his belly. He assured the animal that he was worth ten thousand dollars.

Bob, three deep at the bar for a solid hour between eleven and midnight, looked through a sudden gap in the crowd and saw Eric sitting at the wobbly table under the Narragansett mirror. The Super Bowl was an hour over, but the crowd, drunk as shit, hung around. Eric had one arm stretched across the table and Bob followed it, saw that it connected to something. An arm.

Nadia's arm. Nadia's face stared back at Eric, unreadable. Was she terrified? Or something else?

Bob, filling a glass with ice, felt like he was shoveling the cubes into his own chest, pouring them into his stomach and against the base of his spine. What did he know about Nadia, after all? He knew that he'd found a near-dead dog in the trash outside her house. He knew that Eric Deeds only came into his life after Bob had met her. He knew that her middle name, thus far, could be Lies of Omission.

When he was twenty-eight, Bob had come into his mother's bedroom to wake her for Sunday Mass. He'd given her a shake and she hadn't batted at his hand as she normally did. So he rolled her toward him and her face was scrunched tight, her eyes too, and her skin was curbstone-gray. Sometime in the night, after *Matlock* and the ten o'clock news, she'd gone to bed and woke to God's fist clenched around her heart. Probably hadn't been enough air left in her lungs to cry out. Alone in the dark, clutching the sheets, that fist clenching, her face clenching, her eyes scrunching, the terrible knowledge dawning that, even for you, it all ends. And right now.

Standing over her that morning, imagining the last tick of her heart, the last lonely wish her brain had been able to form, Bob felt a loss unlike any he'd ever known or expected to know again.

Until tonight. Until now. Until he learned what that look on Nadia's face meant.

By one fifty, the crowd was gone, just Eric and Nadia and an old, stringent, functioning alcoholic named Millie who'd amble off to the assisted living place up on Pearl Street at one fifty-five on the dot.

Eric, who had been coming to the bar for shots of Powers for the last hour, pushed back from the table and pulled Nadia across the floor with him. He sat her on a stool and Bob got a good look in her face finally, saw something he still couldn't fully identify—but it definitely wasn't excitement or smugness or the bitter smile of a victor. Maybe something worse than all of that—despair.

Eric gave him an all-teeth smile and spoke through it, softly. "When's the old biddie pack it in?"

"A couple minutes."

"Where's Marv?"

"I didn't call him in."

"Why not?"

"Someone's gonna take the blame for this, I figured it might as well be me."

"How noble of—"

"How do you know her?"

Eric looked over at Nadia hunched on the stool beside him. He leaned into the bar. "We grew up on the same block."

"He give you that scar?"

Nadia stared at him.

"Did he?"

"She gave herself the scar," Eric Deeds said.

"You did?" Bob asked her.

Nadia looked at the bar top. "I was pretty high."

"Bob," Eric said, "if you fuck with me—even in the slightest—it doesn't matter how long it takes me, I'll come back for her. And if you got any plans, like Eric-doesn't-walk-back-out-of-here plans? Not that you're that type of guy, but Marv might be? You got any ideas in that vein, Bob, my partner on the Richie Whalen hit, he'll take care of you both."

Eric sat back as mean old Millie left the same tip she'd been leaving since Sputnik—a quarter—and slid off her stool. She gave Bob a rasp that was ten percent vocal chords and ninety percent Virginia Slims Ultra Light 100s. "Yeah, I'm off."

"You take care, Millie."

She waved it away with a, "Yeah, yeah, yeah," and pushed open the door.

Bob locked it behind her and came back behind the bar. He wiped down the bar top. When he reached Eric's elbows, he said, "Excuse me."

"Go around."

Bob wiped the rag in a half-circle around Eric's elbows.

"Who's your partner?" Bob said.

"Wouldn't be much of a threat if you knew who he was, would he, Bob?"

"But he helped you kill Richie Whalen?"

Eric said, "That's the rumor, Bob."

"More than a rumor." Bob wiped in front of Nadia, saw red marks on her wrists where Eric had yanked them. He wondered if there were other marks he couldn't see.

"Well then it's more than a rumor, Bob. So there you go."

"There you go what?"

"There you *go*," Eric scowled. "What time is it, Bob?"

Bob placed ten thousand dollars on the bar. "You don't have to call me by my name all the time."

"I will see what I can do about that, Bob." Eric thumbed the bills. "What's this?"

"It's the ten grand you wanted for Cash."

Eric pursed his lips. "All the same, let's look in the safe."

"You sure?" Bob said. "I'm happy to buy him from you for ten grand."

"How much for Nadia, though?"

"Oh."

"Yeah. Oh."

Bob thought about that new wrinkle for a bit and poured himself a closing-time shot of vodka. He raised it to Eric Deeds and then drank it down. "You know, Marv used to have a problem with blow about ten years ago?"

"I did not know that, Bob."

Bob shrugged, poured them all a shot of vodka. "Yeah, Marv liked the coke too much but it didn't like him back."

Eric drank Nadia's shot. "Getting close to two here, Bob."

"He was more of a loan shark then. I mean, he did some fence, but mostly he was a shark. There was this kid? Into Marv for a shitload of money. Real hopeless case when it came to the dogs and basketball. Kinda kid could never pay back all he owed."

Eric drank his own shot. "One fifty-seven, Bob."

"The thing, though? This kid, he actually hit on a slot at Mohegan. Hit for twenty-two grand. Which is just a little more than he owed Marv."

"And he didn't pay Marv back, so you and Marv got all hard on him and I'm supposed to learn—"

"No, no. He *paid* Marv. Paid him every cent. What the kid didn't know, though, was that Marv had been skimming. Because of the coke habit? And this kid's money was like manna from heaven as long as no one knew it was from this kid. See what I'm saying?"

"Bob, it's fucking one minute to two." Sweat on Eric's lip.

"Do you see what I'm saying?" Bob asked. "Do you understand the story?"

Eric looked to the door to make sure it was locked. "Fine, yeah. This kid, he had to be ripped off."

"He had to be killed."

Out of the side of his eye, a quick glance. "Okay, killed."

Bob could feel Nadia's eyes lock on him suddenly, her head cock a bit. "That way, he couldn't ever say he paid off Marv and no one else could either. Marv uses the money to cover all the holes, he cleans up his act, it's like it never happened. So that's what we did."

"You did . . ." Eric barely in the conversation, but some warning in his head starting to sound, his head turning from the clock toward Bob.

"Killed him in my basement," Bob said. "Know what his name was?"

"I wouldn't know, Bob."

"Sure you would. Richie Whelan."

Bob reached under the bar and pulled out the 9mm. He didn't notice the safety was on, so when he pulled the trigger nothing happened. Eric jerked his head and pushed back from the bar rail, but Bob thumbed off the safety and shot Eric just below the throat. The gunshot sounded like aluminum siding being torn off a house. Nadia screamed. Not a long scream, but sharp with shock. Eric made a racket falling back off his stool, and by the time Bob came around the bar, Eric was already going, if not quite gone. The overhead fan cast thin slices of shadow over his face. His cheeks puffed in and out like he was trying to catch his breath and kiss somebody at the same time.

"I'm sorry, but you kids," Bob said. "You know? You go out of the house dressed like you're still in your living room. You say terrible things about women. You hurt harmless dogs. I'm tired of you, man."

Eric stared up at him. Winced like he had heartburn. He looked pissed off. Frustrated. The expression froze on his face like it was sewn there, and then he wasn't in his body anymore. Just gone. Just, shit, dead.

Bob dragged him into the cooler.

When he came back, pushing the mop and bucket ahead of him, Nadia still sat on her stool. Her mouth was a bit wider than usual and she couldn't take her eyes off the floor where the blood was, but otherwise she seemed perfectly normal.

"He would have just kept coming," Bob said. "Once someone takes something from you and you let them? They don't feel gratitude, they just feel like you owe them more." He soaked the mop in the bucket, wrung it out a bit, and slopped it over the main blood spot. "Makes no sense, right? But that's how they feel. Entitled. And you can never change their minds after that."

She said, "He . . . You just fucking shot him. You just . . . I mean, you know?"

Bob swirled the mop over the spot. "He beat my dog."

The Chechens took care of the body after a discussion with the Italians and the Micks. Bob was told his money was no good at several restaurants for the next couple of months, and they gave him four tickets to a Celtics game. Not floor seats, but pretty good ones.

Bob never mentioned Nadia. Just said Eric showed up at the end of the evening, waved a gun around, said to take him to the office safe. Bob let him do his ranting, do his waving, found an opportunity, and shot him. And that was it. End of Eric, end of story.

Nadia came to him a few days later. Bob opened the door and she stood there on his stoop with a bright winter day turning everything sharp and clear behind her. She held up a bag of dog treats.

"Peanut butter," she said, her smile bright, her eyes just a little wet. "With a hint of molasses."

Bob opened the door wide and stepped back to let her in.

"I've gotta believe," Nadia said, "there's a purpose. And even if it's that you kill me as soon as I close my eyes—"

"Me? What? No," Bob said. "Oh, no."

"—then that's okay. Because I just can't go through any more of this alone. Not another day."

"Me too." He closed his eyes. "Me too."

They didn't speak for a long time. He opened his eyes, peered at the ceiling of his bedroom. "Why?"

"Hmm?"

"This. You. Why are you with me?"

She ran a hand over his chest and it gave him a shiver. In his whole life, he never would have expected to feel a touch like that on his bare skin.

"Because I like you. Because you're nice to Cassius."

"And because you're scared of me?"

"I dunno. Maybe. But more the other reason."

He couldn't tell if she was lying. Who could tell when anyone was? Really. Every day, you ran into people and half of them, if not more, could be lying to you. Why?

Why not?

You couldn't tell who was true and who was not. If you could, lie detectors would never have been invented. Someone stared in your face and said, *I'm telling the truth*. They said, *I promise*. They said, *I love you*.

And you were going to say what to that? Prove it?

"He needs a walk."

"Huh?"

"Cassius. He hasn't been out all day."

"I'll get the leash."

* * *

In the park, the February sky hung above them like a canvas tarp. The weather had been almost mild for a few days. The ice had broken on the river but small chunks of it clung to the dark banks.

He didn't know what he believed. Cassius walked ahead of them, pulling on the leash a bit, so proud, so pleased, unrecognizable from the quivering hunk of fur Bob had pulled from a barrel just two and a half months ago.

Two and a half months! Wow. Things sure could change in a hurry. You rolled over one morning, and it was a whole new world. It turned itself toward the sun, stretched and yawned. It turned itself toward the night. A few more hours, turned itself toward the sun again. A new world, every day.

When they reached the center of the park, he unhooked the leash from Cassius's collar and reached into his coat for a tennis ball. Cassius reared his head. He snorted loud. He pawed the earth. Bob threw the ball and the dog took off after it. Bob envisioned the ball taking a bad bounce into the road. The screech of tires, the thump of metal against dog. Or what would happen if Cassius, suddenly free, just kept running.

But what could you do?

You couldn't control things.

THE CONFIDENTIAL INFORMANT

BY GEORGE PELECANOS

Park View, NW, Washington, DC

(Originally published in *DC Noir*)

I was in the waiting area of the Veteran's Hospital emergency room off North Capitol Street, seeing to my father, when Detective Tony Barnes hit me back on my cell. My father had laid his head down on the crossbar of his walker, and it was going to be a while before someone came and called his name. I walked the phone outside and lit myself a smoke.

"What's goin' on, Verdon?" said Barnes.

"Need to talk to you about Rico Jennings."

"Go ahead."

"Not on the phone." I wasn't about to give Barnes no information without feeling some of his cash money in my hand.

"When can I see you?"

"My pops took ill. I'm still dealin' with that, so . . . make it nine. You know where."

Barnes cut the line. I smoked my cigarette down to the filter and went back inside.

My father was moaning when I took a seat beside him. Goddamn this and goddamn that, saying it under his breath. We'd been out here for a few hours. A girl with a high ass moving inside purple drawstring pants took our information when we came in, and later a Korean nurse got my father's vitals in what she called the triage room, asking questions about his history and was there blood in his stool and stuff like that. But we had not seen a doctor yet.

Most of the men in the waiting room were in their fifties and above. A couple had walkers and many had canes; one dude had an oxygen tank beside him with a clear hose running up under his nose. Every single one of them was wearing some kinda lid. It was cold out, but it was a style thing, too.

Everyone looked uncomfortable and no one working in the hospital seemed to be in a hurry to do something about it. The security guards gave you a good eye-fuck when you came through the doors, which kinda told you straight off what the experience was going to be like inside. I tried to go down to the cafeteria to get something to eat, but nothing they had was appealing, and some of it looked damn near dirty. I been in white people's hospitals, like Sibley, on the high side of town, and I know they don't treat those people the way they was treating these veterans. I'm saying, this shit here was a damn disgrace.

But they did take my father eventually.

In the emergency room, a white nurse named Matthew, redheaded dude with Popeye forearms, hooked him up to one of those heart machines, then found a vein in my father's arm and took three vials of blood. Pops had complained about being "woozy" that morning. He gets fearful since his stroke, which paralyzed him on one side. His mind is okay, but he can't go nowhere without his walker, not even to the bathroom.

I looked at him lying there in the bed, his wide shoulders and the hardness of his hands. Even at sixty, even after his stroke, he is stronger than me. I know I will never feel like his equal. What with him being a Vietnam veteran, and a dude who had a reputation for taking no man's shit in the street. And me . . . well, me being me.

"The doctor's going to have a look at your blood, Leon," said Matthew. I guess he didn't know that in our neighborhood my father would be called "Mr. Leon" or "Mr. Coates" by someone younger than him. As Matthew walked away, he began to sing a church hymn.

My father rolled his eyes.

"Bet you'd rather have that Korean girl taking care of you, Pops," I said, with a conspiring smile.

"That gal's from the Philippines," said my father, sourly. Always correcting me and shit.

"Whateva."

My father complained about everything for the next hour. I listened to him, and the junkie veteran in the next stall over who was begging for something to take away his pain, and the gags of another dude who was getting a stomach tube forced down his throat. Then an Indian doctor, name of Singh, pulled the curtain back and walked into our stall. He told my father that there was nothing in his blood or on the EKG to indicate that there was cause for alarm.

"So all this *bull*shit was for nothin'?" said my father, like he was disappointed he wasn't sick.

"Go home and get some rest," said Dr. Singh, in a cheerful way. He smelled like one them restaurants they got, but he was all right.

Matthew returned, got my father dressed back into his streetclothes, and filled out the discharge forms.

"The Lord loves you, Leon," said Matthew, before he went off to attend to someone else.

"Get me out this motherfucker," said my father. I fetched a wheelchair from where they had them by the front desk.

I drove my father's Buick to his house, on the 700 block of Quebec Street, not too far from the hospital, in Park View. It took awhile to get him up the steps of his row house. By the time he stepped onto the brick-and-concrete porch, he was gasping for breath. He didn't go out much anymore, and this was why.

Inside, my mother, Martina Coates, got him situated in his own wheelchair, positioned in front of his television set, where he sits most of his waking hours. She waits on him all day and sleeps lightly at night in case he falls out of his bed. She gives him showers and even washes his ass. My mother is a church woman who believes that her reward will come in heaven. It's 'cause of her that I'm still allowed to live in my father's house.

The television was real loud, the way he likes to play it since his stroke. He watches them old games on that replay show on ESPN.

"Franco Harris!" I shouted, pointing at the screen. "Boy was *beast*."

My father didn't even turn his head. I would have watched some of that old Steelers game with him if he had asked me to, but he didn't, so I went upstairs to my room.

It is my older brother's room as well. James's bed is on the opposite wall and his basketball and football trophies, from when he was a kid all the way through high school, are still on his dresser. He made good after Howard Law, real good, matter of fact. He lives over there in Crestwood, west of 16th, with his pretty redbone wife and their two light-skinned kids. He doesn't come around this neighborhood all that much, though it ain't but fifteen minutes away. He wouldn't have drove my father over to the VA Hospital, either, or waited around in that place all day. He would have said he was too busy, that he couldn't get out "the firm" that day. Still, my father brags on James to all his friends. He got no cause to brag on me.

I changed into some warm shit, and put my smokes and matches into my coat. I left my cell in my bedroom, as it needed to be charged. When I got downstairs, my mother asked me where I was going.

"I got a little side thing I'm workin' on," I said, loud enough for my father to hear.

My father kinda snorted and chuckled under his breath. He might as well had gone ahead and said, *Bullshit*, but he didn't need to. I wanted to tell him more, but that would be wrong. If my thing was to be uncovered, I wouldn't want nobody coming back on my parents.

I zipped my coat and left out the house.

It had begun to snow some. Flurries swirled in the cones of light coming down from the streetlamps. I walked down to Giant Liquors on Georgia and bought a pint of Popov, and hit the vodka as I walked back up Quebec. I crossed Warder Street, and kept on toward Park Lane. The houses got a little nicer here as the view improved. Across Park were the grounds of the Soldier's Home, bordered by a black iron, spear-topped fence. It was dark out, and the clouds were blocking any kinda moonlight, but I knew what was over there by heart. I had cane-pole fished that lake many times as a kid, and chased them geese they had in there, too. Now they had three rows of barbed wire strung out over them spear-tops, to keep out the kids and the young men who liked to lay their girlfriends out straight on that soft grass.

Me and Sondra used to hop that fence some evenings, the summer before I dropped out of Roosevelt High. I'd bring some weed, a bottle of screw-top wine, and my Walkman and we'd go down to the other side of that lake and chill. I'd let her listen to the headphones while I hit my smoke. I had made mix-tapes off my records, stuff she was into, like Bobby Brown and Tone-Loc. I'd tell her about the cars I was gonna be driving, and the custom suits I'd be wearing, soon as I got a good job. How I didn't need no high school diploma to get those things or to prove how smart I was. She looked at me like she believed it. Sondra had some pretty brown eyes.

She married a personal injury lawyer with a storefront office up in Shepherd Park. They live in a house in PG County, in one of those communities got gates. I seen her once, when she came back to the neighborhood to visit her moms, who still stays down on Luray. She was bum-rushing her kids into the house, like they might get sick if they breathed this Park View air. She saw me walking down the street and turned her head away, trying to act like she didn't recognize me. It didn't cut me. She can rewrite history in her mind if she wants to, but her fancy husband ain't never gonna have what I did, 'cause I had that pussy when it was new.

I stepped into the alley that runs north-south between Princeton and Quebec. My watch, a looks-like-a-Rolex I bought on the street for ten dollars, read 9:05. Detective Barnes was late. I unscrewed the top of the Popov and had a pull. It burned nice. I tapped it again and lit myself a smoke.

"Psst. Hey, yo."

I looked up over my shoulder, where the sound was. A boy leaned on the lip of one of those second-floor, wood back porches that ran out to the alley. Behind him was a door with curtains on its window. A bicycle tire was showing beside the boy. Kids be putting their bikes up on porches around here so they don't get stole.

"What you want?" I said.

"Nothin' you got," said the boy. He looked to be about twelve, tall and skinny, with braided hair under a black skully.

"Then get your narrow ass back inside your house."

"You the one loiterin'."

"I'm mindin' my own, is what I'm doin'. Ain't you got no homework or nothin'?"

"I did it at study hall."

"Where you go, MacFarland Middle?"

"Yeah."

"I went there, too."

"So?"

I almost smiled. He had a smart mouth on him, but he had heart.

"What you doin' out here?" said the kid.

"Waitin' on someone," I said.

Just then Detective Barnes's unmarked drove by slow. He saw me but kept on rolling. I knew he'd stop, up aways on the street.

"Awright, little man," I said, pitching my cigarette aside and slipping my pint into my jacket pocket. I could feel the kid's eyes on me as I walked out the alley.

I slid into the backseat of Barnes's unmarked, a midnight-blue Crown Vic. I kinda laid down on the bench, my head against the door, below the window line so no one on the outside could see me. It's how I do when I'm rolling with Barnes.

He turned right on Park Place and headed south. I didn't need to look out the window to know where he was going. He drives down to Michigan Avenue, heads east past the Children's Hospital, then continues on past North Capitol and then Catholic U, into Brookland and beyond. Eventually he turns around and comes back the same way.

"Stayin' warm, Verdon?"

"Tryin' to."

Barnes, a broad-shouldered dude with a handsome face, had a deep voice. He favored Hugo Boss suits and cashmere overcoats. Like many police, he wore a thick mustache.

"So," I said. "Rico Jennings."

"Nothin' on my end," said Barnes, with a shrug. "You?"

I didn't answer him. It was a dance we did. His eyes went to the rearview and met mine. He held out a twenty over the seat, and I took it.

"I think y'all are headed down the wrong road," I said.

"How so?"

"Heard you been roustin' corner boys on Morton and canvasing down there in the Eights."

"I'd say that's a pretty good start, given Rico's history."

"Wasn't no drug thing, though."

"Kid was in it. He had juvenile priors for possession and distribution."

"Why they call 'em priors. That was before the boy got on the straight. Look, I went to grade school with his mother. I been knowin' Rico since he was a kid."

"*What* do you know?"

"Rico was playin' hard for a while, but he grew out of it. He got into some big brother thing at my mother's church, and he turned his back on his past. I mean, that boy was in the AP program up at Roosevelt. Advanced Placement, you know, where they got adults, teachers and shit, walkin' with you every step of the way. He was on the way to college."

"So why'd someone put three in his chest?"

"What I heard was, it was over a girl."

I was giving him a little bit of the truth. When the whole truth came out, later on, he wouldn't suspect that I had known more.

Barnes swung a U-turn, which rocked me some. We were on the way back to Park View.

"Keep going," said Barnes.

"Tryin' to tell you, Rico had a weakness for the ladies."

"Who doesn't."

"It was worse than that. Girl's privates made Rico stumble. Word is, he'd been steady-tossin' this young thing, turned out to be the property of some other boy. Rico knew it, but he couldn't stay away. That's why he got dropped."

"By who?"

"Huh?"

"You got a name on the hitter?"

"Nah." Blood came to my ears and made them hot. It happened when I got stressed.

"How about the name of the girlfriend?"

I shook my head. "I'd talk to Rico's mother, I was you. You'd think she'd know somethin' 'bout the girls her son was runnin' with, right?"

"You'd think," said Barnes.

"All I'm sayin' is, I'd start with her."

"Thanks for the tip."

"I'm just sayin'."

Barnes sighed. "Look, I've already talked to the mother. I've talked to Rico's neighbors and friends. We've been through his bedroom as well. We didn't find any love notes or even so much as a picture of a girl."

I had the photo of his girlfriend. Me and Rico's aunt, Leticia, had gone up into the boy's bedroom at that wake they had, while his mother was downstairs crying and stuff with her church friends in the living room. I found a picture of the girl, name of Flora Lewis, in the dresser drawer, under his socks and underwear. It was one of them mall photos the girls like to get done, then give to their boyfriends. Flora was sitting on a cube, with columns around her and shit, against a background, looked like laser beams shooting across a blue sky. Flora had tight jeans on and a shirt with thin straps, and she had let one of the straps kinda fall down off her shoulder to let the tops of her little titties show. The girls all trying to look like sluts now, you ask me. On the back of the photo was a note in her handwriting, said, *How U like me like this? xxoo, Flora.* Leticia recognized Flora from around the way, even without the name printed on the back.

"Casings at the scene were from a nine," said Barnes, bringing me out of my thoughts. "We ran the markings through IBIS and there's no match."

"What about a witness?"

"You kiddin'? There wasn't one, even if there was one."

"Always someone knows somethin'," I said, as I felt the car slow and come to a stop.

"Yeah, well." Barnes pushed the trans arm up into park. "I caught a double in Columbia Heights this morning. So I sure would like to clean this Jennings thing up."

"You *know* I be out there askin' around," I said. "But it gets expensive, tryin' to make conversation in bars, buyin' beers and stuff to loosen them lips . . ."

Barnes passed another twenty over the seat without a word. I took it. The bill was damp for some reason, and limp like a dead thing. I put it in the pocket of my coat.

"I'm gonna be askin' around," I said, like he hadn't heard me the first time.

"I know you will, Verdon. You're a good CI. The best I ever had."

I didn't know if he meant it or not, but it made me feel kinda guilty, back-dooring him the way I was planning to do. But I had to look out for my own self for a change. The killer would be got, that was the important thing. And I would be flush.

"How your sons, detective?"

"They're good. Looking forward to playing Pop Warner again."

"Hmph," I said.

He was divorced, like most homicide police. Still, I knew he loved his kids.

That was all. It felt like it was time to go.

"I'll get up with you later, hear?"

Barnes said, "Right."

I rose up off the bench, kinda looked around some, and got out the Crown Vic. I took a pull out the Popov bottle as I headed for my father's house. I walked down the block, my head hung low.

Up in my room, I found my film canister under the T-shirts in my dresser. I shook some weed out into a wide paper, rolled a joint tight as a cigarette, and slipped it into my pack of Newports. The vodka had lifted me some, and I was ready to get up further.

I glanced in the mirror over my dresser. One of my front teeth was missing from when some dude down by the Black Hole, said he didn't like the way I looked, had knocked it out. There was gray in my patch and in my hair. My eyes looked bleached. Even under my bulky coat, it was plain I had lost weight. I looked like one of them defectives you pity or ridicule on the street. But shit, there wasn't a thing I could do about it tonight.

I went by my mother's room, careful to step soft. She was in there, in bed by now, watching but not watching television on her thirteen-inch color, letting it keep her company, with the sound down low so she could hear my father if he called out to her from the first floor.

Down in the living room, the television still played loud, a black-and-white film of the Liston-Clay fight, which my father had spoke of often. He was missing the fight now. His chin was resting on his chest and his useless hand was kinda curled up like a claw in his lap. The light from the television grayed his face. His eyelids weren't shut all the way, and the whites showed. Aside from his chest, which was moving some, he looked like he was dead.

Time will just fuck you up.

I can remember this one evening with my father, back around '74. He had been home from the war for a while, and was working for the Government Printing Office at the time. We were over there on the baseball field, on Princeton, next to Park View Elementary. I musta been around six or seven. My father's shadow was long and straight, and the sun was throwing a warm gold color on the green of the field. He was still in his work clothes, with his sleeves rolled up to his elbows. His natural was full and his chest filled the fabric of his shirt. He was tossing me this small football, one of them K-2s he had bought me, and telling me to run toward him after I caught it, to see if I could break his tackle. He wasn't gonna tackle me for real, he just wanted me to get a feel for the game. But I wouldn't run to him. I guess I didn't want to get hurt, was what it was. He got aggravated with me eventually, lost his patience and said it was time to get on home. I believe he quit on me that day. At least, that's the way it seems to me now.

I wanted to go over to his wheelchair, not hug him or nothing that dramatic, but maybe give him a pat on his shoulder. But if he woke up he would ask me what was wrong, why was I touching him, all that. So I didn't go near him. I had to meet with Leticia about this thing we was doing, anyway. I stepped light on the clear plastic runner my mother had on the carpet, and closed the door quiet on my way out the house.

On the way to Leticia's I cupped a match against the snow and fired up the joint. I drew on it deep and held it in my lungs. I hit it regular as I walked south.

My head was beginning to smile as I neared the house Leticia stayed in, over on Otis Place. I wet my fingers in the snow and squeezed the ember of the joint to put it out. I wanted to save some for Le-tee. We were gonna celebrate.

The girl, Flora, had witnessed the murder of Rico Jennings. I knew this because we, Leticia and me that is, had found her and made her tell what she knew. Well, Leticia had. She can be a scary woman when she wants to be. She broke hard on Flora, got up in her face and bumped her in an alley. Flora cried and talked. She had been out walking with Rico that night, back up on Otis, around the elementary, when this boy, Marquise Roberts, rolled up on them in a black Caprice. Marquise and his squad got out the car and surrounded Rico, shoved him some and shit like that. Flora said it seemed like that was all they was gonna do. Then Marquis drew an automatic and put three in Rico, one while Rico was on his feet and two more while Marquise was standing over him. Flora said Marquise was smiling as he pulled the trigger.

"Ain't no doubt now, is it?" said Marquise, turning to Flora. "You mine."

Marquise and them got back in their car and rode off, and Flora ran to her home. Rico was dead, she explained. Wouldn't do him no good if she stayed at the scene.

Flora said that she would never talk to the police. Leticia told her she'd never have to, that as Rico's aunt she just needed to know.

Now we had a killer and a wit. I could have gone right to Detective Barnes, but I knew about that anonymous tip line in the District, the Crime Solvers thing. We decided that Leticia would call and get that number assigned to her, the way they do, and she would eventually collect the $1,000 reward, which we'd split. Flora would go into witness security, where they'd move her to far Northeast or something like that. So she wouldn't get hurt, or be too far from her family, and Leticia and me would get five hundred each. It wasn't much, but it was more than I'd ever had in my pocket at one time. More important to me, someday, when Marquise was put away and his boys fell, like they always do, I could go to my mother and father and tell them that I, Verdon Coates, had solved a homicide. And it would be worth the wait, just to see the look of pride on my father's face.

I got to the row house on Otis where Leticia stayed at. It was on the 600 block, those low-slung old places they got painted gray. She lived on the first floor.

Inside the common hallway, I came to her door. I knocked and took off my knit cap and shook the snow off it, waiting for her to come. The door opened, but only a crack. It stopped as the chain of the slide bolt went taut. Leticia looked at me over the chain. I could see dirt tracks on the part of her face that showed, from where she'd been crying. She was a hard-looking woman, had always been, even when she was young. I'd never seen her so shook.

"Ain't you gonna let me in?"

"No."

"What's wrong with you, girl?"

"I don't want to see you and you ain't comin' in."

"I got some nice smoke, Leticia."

"Leave outta here, Verdon."

I listened to the bass of a rap thing, coming from another apartment. Behind it, a woman and a man were having an argument.

"What happened?" I said. "Why you been cryin'?"

"Marquise came," said Leticia. "Marquise made me cry."

My stomach dropped some. I tried not to let it show on my face.

"That's right," said Leticia. "Flora musta told him about our conversation. Wasn't hard for him to find Rico's aunt."

"He threaten you?"

"He never did, direct. Matter of fact, that boy was smilin' the whole time he spoke to me." Leticia's lip trembled. "We came to an understandin', Verdon."

"What he say?"

"He said that Flora was mistaken. That she wasn't there the night Rico was killed, and she would swear to it in court. And that if I thought different, I was mistaken, too."

"You sayin' that you're mistaken, Leticia?"

"That's right. I been mistaken about this whole thing."

"Leticia—"

"I ain't tryin' to get myself killed for five hundred dollars, Verdon."

"Neither am I."

"Then you better go somewhere for a while."

"Why would I do that?"

Leticia said nothing.

"You give me up, Leticia?"

Leticia cut her eyes away from mine. "Flora," she said, almost a whisper. "She told him 'bout some skinny, older-lookin' dude who was standin' in the alley the day I took her for bad."

"You gave me *up*?"

Leticia shook her head slowly and pushed the door shut. It closed with a soft click.

I didn't pound on the door or nothing like that. I stood there stupidly for some time, listening to the rumble of the bass and the argument still going between the woman and man. Then I walked out the building.

The snow was coming down heavy. I couldn't go home, so I walked toward the avenue instead.

I had finished the rest of my vodka, and dropped the bottle to the curb, by the time I got down to Georgia. A Third District cruiser was parked on the corner, with two officers inside it, drinking coffee from paper cups. It was late, and with the snow and the cold there wasn't too many people out. The Spring Laundromat, used to be a Roy Rogers or some shit like it, was packed with men and women, just standing around, getting out of the weather. I could see their outlines behind that nicotine-stained glass, most of them barely moving under those dim lights.

This time of night, many of the shops had closed. I was hungry, but Morgan's Seafood had been boarded up for a year now, and The Hunger Stopper, had those good fish sandwiches, was dark inside. What I needed was a beer, but Giant had locked its doors. I could have gone to the titty bar between Newton and Otis, but I had been roughed in there too many times.

I crossed over to the west side of Georgia and walked south. I passed a midget in a green suede coat who stood where he always did, under the awning of the Dollar General. I had worked there for a couple of days, stocking shit on shelves.

The businesses along here were like a roll call of my personal failures. The Murray's meat and produce, the car wash, the Checks Cashed joint, they had given me a chance. In all these places, I had lasted just a short while.

I neared the G.A. market, down by Irving. A couple of young men came toward me, buried inside the hoods of their North Face coats, hard of face, then smiling as they got a look at me.

"Hey, slim," said one of the young men. "Where you get that vicious coat at? *Baby* GAP?" Him and his friend laughed.

I didn't say nothing back. I got this South Pole coat I bought off a dude, didn't want it no more. I wasn't about to rock a North Face. Boys put a gun in your grill for those coats down here.

I walked on.

The market was crowded inside and thick with the smoke of cigarettes. I stepped around some dudes and saw a man I know, Robert Taylor, back by where they keep the wine. He was lifting a bottle of it off the shelf. He was in the middle of his thirties, but he looked fifty-five.

"Robo," I said.

"Verdon."

We did a shoulder-to-shoulder thing and patted backs. I had been knowing him since grade school. Like me, he had seen better days. He looked kinda under it now. He held up a bottle of fortified, turned it so I could see the label, like them waiters do in high-class restaurants.

"I sure could use a taste," said Robert. "Only, I'm a little light this evenin'."

"I got you, Robo."

"Look, I'll hit you back on payday."

"We're good."

I picked up a bottle of Night Train for myself and moved toward the front of the market. Robert grabbed the sleeve of my coat and held it tight. His eyes, most time full of play, were serious.

"Verdon."

"What?"

"I been here a couple of hours, stayin' dry and shit. Lotta activity in here tonight. You just standin' around, you be hearin' things."

"Say what you heard."

"Some boys was in here earlier, lookin' for you."

I felt that thing in my stomach.

"Three young men," said Robert. "One of 'em had them silver things on his teeth. They was describin' you, your build and shit, and that hat you always be wearin'."

He meant my knit cap, with the Bullets logo, had the two hands for the double l's, going up for the rebound. I had been wearing it all winter long. I had been wearing it the day we talked to Flora in the alley.

"Anyone tell them who I was?"

Robert nodded sadly. "I can't lie. Some bama did say your name."

"Shit."

"I ain't say *nothin'* to those boys, Verdon."

"C'mon, man. Let's get outta here."

We went up to the counter. I used the damp twenty Barnes had handed me to pay for the two bottles of wine and a fresh pack of cigarettes. While the squarehead behind the plexiglass was bagging my shit and making my change, I picked up a scratched-out lottery ticket and pencil off the scarred counter, turned the ticket over, and wrote around the blank edges. What I wrote was: *Marquise Roberts killed Rico Jennings.* And: *Flora Lewis was there.*

I slipped the ticket into the pocket of my jeans and got my change. Me and Robert Taylor walked out the shop.

On the snow-covered sidewalk I handed Robert his bottle of fortified. I knew he'd be heading west into Columbia Heights, where he stays with an ugly-looking woman and her kids.

"Thank you, Verdon."

"Ain't no thing."

"What you think? Skins gonna do it next year?"

"They got Coach Gibbs. They get a couple receivers with hands, they gonna be all right."

"No doubt." Robert lifted his chin. "You be safe, hear?"

He went on his way. I crossed Georgia Avenue, quick-stepping out the way of a Ford that was fishtailing in the street. I thought about getting rid of my Bullets cap, in case Marquise and them came up on me, but I was fond of it, and I could not let it go.

I unscrewed the top off the Night Train as I went along, taking a deep pull and feeling it warm my chest. Heading up Otis, I saw ragged silver dollars drifting down through the light of the streetlamps. The snow capped the roofs of parked cars and it had gathered on the branches of the trees. No one was out. I stopped to light the rest of my joint. I got it going, and hit it as I walked up the hill.

I planned to head home in a while, through the alley door, when I thought it was safe. But for now, I needed to work on my head. Let my high come like a friend and tell me what to do.

I stood on the east side of Park Lane, my hand on the fence bordering the Soldier's Home, staring into the dark. I had smoked all my reefer and drunk my wine. It was quiet, nothing but the hiss of snow. And "Get Up," that old Salt-N-Pepa joint, playing in my head. Sondra liked that one. She'd dance to it, with my headphones on, over by that lake they got. With the geese running around it, in the summertime.

"Sondra," I whispered. And then I chuckled some, and said, "I am high."

I turned and walked back to the road, tripping a little I stepped off the curb. As I got onto Quebec, I saw a car coming down Park Lane, sliding a little, rolling too fast. It was a dark color, and it had them Chevy headlights with the rectangle fog lamps on the sides. I patted my pockets, knowing all the while that I didn't have my cell.

I ducked into the alley off Quebec. I looked up at that rear porch with the bicycle tire leaning up on it, where that boy stayed. I saw a light behind the porch door's window. I scooped up snow, packed a ball of it tight, and threw it up at that window. I waited. The boy parted the curtains and put his face up on the glass, his hands cupped around his eyes so he could see.

"Little man!" I yelled, standing by the porch. "Help me out!"

He cold-eyed me and stepped back. I knew he recognized me. But I guess he had seen me go toward the police unmarked, and he had made me for a snitch. In his young mind, it was probably the worst thing a man could be. Behind the window, all went dark. As it did, headlights swept the alley and a car came in with the light. The car was black, and it was a Caprice.

I turned and bucked.

I ran my ass off down that alley, my old Timbs struggling for grip in the snow. As I ran, I pulled on trashcans, knocking them over so they would block the path of the Caprice. I didn't look back. I heard the boys in the car, yelling at me and shit, and I heard them curse as they had to slow down. Soon I was out of the alley, on Princeton Place, running free.

I went down Princeton, cut left on Warder, jogged by the front of the elementary, and hung a right on Otis. There was an alley down there, back behind the ball field, shaped like a T. It would be hard for them to navigate back in there. They couldn't surprise me or nothing like that.

I walked into the alley. Straight off, a couple of dogs began to bark. Folks kept 'em, shepherd mixes and rottweilers with heads big as cattle, for security. Most of them was inside, on account of the weather, but not all. There were some who stayed out all the time, and they were loud. Once they got going, they would bark themselves crazy. They were letting Marquise know where I was.

I saw the Caprice drive real slow down Otis, its headlights off, and I felt my ears grow hot. I got down in a crouch, pressed myself against a chain-link fence behind someone's row house. My stomach flipped all the way and I had one of them throw-up burps. Stuff came up, and I swallowed it down.

I didn't care if it was safe or not; I needed to get my ass home. Couldn't nobody hurt me there. In my bed, the same bed where I always slept, near my brother James. With my mother and father down the hall.

I listened to a boy calling out my name. Then another boy, from somewhere else, did the same. I could hear the laughter in their voices. I shivered some and bit down on my lip.

Use the alphabet, you get lost. That's what my father told me when I was a kid. Otis, Princeton, Quebec . . . I was three streets away.

I turned at the T of the alley and walked down the slope. The dogs were out of their minds, growling and barking, and I went past them and kept my eyes straight ahead. At the bottom of the alley, I saw a boy in a thick coat, hoodie up. He was waiting on me.

I turned around and ran back from where I came. Even with the sounds of the dogs, I could hear myself panting, trying to get my breath. I rounded the T and made it back to Otis, where I cut and headed for the baseball field. I could cross that and be on Princeton. When I got there, I'd be one block closer to my home.

I stepped up onto the field. I walked regular, trying to calm myself down. I didn't hear a car or anything else. Just the snow crunching beneath my feet.

And then a young man stepped up onto the edge of the field. He wore a bulky coat without a cap or a hood. His hand was inside the coat, and his smile was not the smile of a friend. There were silver caps on his front teeth.

I turned my back on him. Pee ran hot down my thigh. My knees were trembling, but I made my legs move.

The night flashed. I felt a sting, like a bee sting, high on my back.

I stumbled but kept my feet. I looked down at my blood, dotted in the snow. I walked a couple of steps and closed my eyes.

When I opened them, the field was green. It was covered in gold, like it gets here in summer, 'round early evening. A Gamble and Huff thing was coming from the open windows of a car. My father stood before me, his natural full, his chest filling the fabric of his shirt. His sleeves were rolled up to his elbows. His arms were outstretched.

I wasn't afraid or sorry. I'd done right. I had the lottery ticket in my pocket. Detective Barnes, or someone like him, would find it in the morning. When they found *me*.

But first I had to speak to my father. I walked to where he stood, waiting. And I knew exactly what I was going to say: I ain't the low-ass bum you think I am. I been workin' with the police for a long, long time. Matter of fact, I just solved a homicide.

I'm a confidential informant, Pop. Look at me.

THE GOLDEN GOPHER

BY SUSAN STRAIGHT

Downtown Los Angeles

(Originally published in *Los Angeles Noir*)

N obody walked from Echo Park to Downtown. Only a walkin fool. But in the fifteen years I'd lived in LA, I'd only met a few walkin fools. LA people weren't cut out for ambulation, as my friend Sidney would have said if he were here. But the people of my childhood weren't here. They were all back in Rio Seco.

The only walkin fools here were homeless people, and they walked to pass the time or collect the cans or find the church people serving food, or to erase the demons momentarily. They needed air passing their ears like sharks needed water passing their gills to survive.

But me—I'd been a walkin fool since I was sixteen and walked twenty-two miles one night with Grady Jackson, who was in love with my best friend Glorette. I'd been thinking about that night, because someone had left a garbled message on my home phone around midnight—something about Glorette. It sounded like my brother Lafayette, but when I'd listened this morning, all I heard was her name.

Grady Jackson and his sister were the only other people I knew from Rio Seco who lived in LA now, and I always heard he was homeless and she worked in some bar. I had never seen them here. Never tried to. That night years ago, when he stole a car, I'd wanted to come to LA, where I thought my life would begin.

But I had thought of Grady Jackson every single day of my life, sometimes for a minute and sometimes for much of the evening, since that night when I realized that we were both walkin fools, and that no one would ever love me like he loved Glorette.

I came out my front door and stepped onto Delta, then turned onto Echo Park Avenue. My lunch meeting with the editor of the new travel magazine *Immerse* was at one. I had drunk one cup of coffee made from my mother's beans, roasted darker than the black in her cast-iron pan. When I went home to Rio Seco, she always gave me a bag. And I had eaten a bowl of cush-cush like she made me when I was small—boiled cornmeal with milk and sugar.

All the things I'd hated when I was young I wanted now. I could smell the still-thin exhaust along the street. It smelled silver and sharp this early. Like wire in the morning, when my father and brothers unrolled it along the fence line of our orange groves.

All day I would be someone else, and so I'd eaten my childhood.

When I got close to Sunset, I saw the homeless woman who always wore a purple coat. Her shopping cart was full with her belongings, and her small dog, a rat terrier, rode where a purse would have been. She pushed past me with her head down. Her scalp was pink as tinted pearls.

At Sunset, I headed toward Downtown.

Downtown, receptionists and editors always said, "Parking is a bitch, huh?" I always nodded in agreement—I bet it was a bitch for them. If someone said, "Oh my God, did you get caught up in that accident on the 10?" I'd shake my head no. I hadn't.

And I never took the bus. Never. Walking meant you were eccentric or pious or a loser—riding the bus meant you were insane or masochistic and worse than a loser.

I had a car. Make no mistake—I had the car my father and brothers had bought me when I was twenty-two and graduating from USC. They wanted to make sure I came home to Rio Seco, which was fifty-five miles away. My father was an orange grove farmer and my brothers were plasterers. They drove trucks. They bought me a Chevy Corsica, and I always smiled to think of myself as a pirate.

I was like a shark too—or like the homeless people. I needed to walk every day, wherever I was, traveling for a piece or just home. I needed constant movement. And every time I walked somewhere, I thought of Grady Jackson. Now that I was thirty-five, it seemed like my mind placed those rememories, as my mother called them, into the days just to assure me of my own existence.

I'd have time in the Garment District before lunch. One thing about walkin fools—they had to have shoes.

I had on black low-heeled half-boots today, and flared jeans, and a pure white cotton shirt with pleats that I'd gotten in Oaxaca. It was my uniform, for when I had to move a long way through a city. Boots, jeans, and plain shirt, and my hair slicked back and held in a bun. Nothing flashy, nothing too money or too poor. A woman walking—you wanted to look like you had somewhere to go, not like you were rich and ready to be robbed, and not like a manless searching female with too much jewelry and cleavage.

Down Sunset, the movement in my feet and hips and the way my arms swung gently and my little leather bag bumped my side calmed me. My brain wasn't thinking about bills or my brother Lafayette, who'd just left his wife and boys, or that Al Green song I'd heard last night that made me cry because no one would ever sing that to me now and slide his hands across my back, like the boys did when we were at house parties back in Rio Seco. When we were young. "*I'm so glad you're mine*," Al sang, and his voice went through me like the homemade mescal I'd tried in Oaxaca, in an old lady's yard where only a turkey watched us.

No one I knew now, in this life, at all the parties and receptions and gallery openings, felt like that—like the boys with us back home, in someone's yard after midnight. Throats vibrating close to our foreheads, hands sliding across our shoulder blades. Girl, just— Just lemme get a taste now. Come on.

When I was home lately, I had trouble working. I looked at old things like my mother's clothespins and a canvas bag I used to wear across my shoulder when we picked oranges in my father's grove.

But walking, I was who I had become—a travel writer everyone wanted to hire.

I'd written about the Bernese Oberland for *Conde Nast*, about Belize for *Vogue*, about Brooklyn for *Traveler*.

I passed vacant lots tangled with morning glories like banks of silver-blue coins, and the sheared-off cliffs below an old apartment complex, where shopping carts huddled like ponies under the Grand Canyon.

I looked at my watch. Eight forty-five. I smelled all the different coffees wending through the air from doughnut shops and convenience stores. Black bars were slid aside like stiffened spiderwebs. Every morning in late summer, my mother and I would brush aside the webs from the trees in our yard, the ones made each night by desperate garden spiders. Here, everyone was desperate to get the day started and make that money.

My cell rang while I was waiting for the light at Beaudry.

"FX?" It was Rick Schwarz, the editor.

"Yup," I said.

"So what does that stand for?" He laughed. He was in his car.

"It stands for my name, Rick."

He laughed again. "We still on for one? Clifton's Cafeteria?"

"Sounds fine," I said.

"So—I don't know what you look like. You never have a contributor's photo."

"I look absolutely ordinary," I said, my body lined up with a statue in the window of a botanica. "See you at one."

I stood there for a minute, the sun behind me, tracing the outline of the Virgen de Soledad. These people must be from Oaxaca, because this virgin, with her black robe in a wide triangle covered with gold, her face severe and impassive, was their patron saint. I had prayed before her in a cathedral there, because my mother asked me to do so each place I went. My mother's house was full of saints.

Across Beaudry, I could see the mirrored buildings glinting like sequined disco dresses in the hot sun. My phone rang again.

"Fantine?"

"Yes, Papa," I said. I tried to keep walking, but then he was silent, and I had to lean against a brick building in the shade.

"That your tite phone?" he said. My little phone—my cell.

"Yes, Papa."

"You walk now?"

"I'm going downtown," I said. "Does Mama want something? Some toys?" I could stop by the toy district today, if my nephews wanted something special.

My father said, "Fantine. Somebody kill Glorette. You better come home, oui. Tomorrow. Pay your respect, Fantine."

Then he hung up.

No one ever called me by my name. I had been FX Antoine for ten years, since I decided to become a writer. Only my family and my Rio Seco friends knew my name at all.

That was why I'd always loved LA, especially Downtown. No one knew who I was. No one knew what I was. People spoke to me in Spanish, in Farsi, in French. My skin was the color of walnut shells. My hair was black and straight and held tightly in a coil. My eyes were slanted and opaque. I just smiled and listened.

But Glorette—even if she'd worn a sack, when she walked men would stare at her. They wanted to touch her. And women hated her.

Glorette had skin like polished gold, and purple-black eyes, and brows like delicate crow feathers, and her lips were full and defined and pink without lipstick. She was nearly iridescent—did that fade when blood stopped moving? Now she was dead.

I bit my lip and walked, along Temple and down to Spring Street, where crowds of people moved quickly, all of them with phone to ear, or they spoke into those mouthpieces like schizophrenics. And the homeless people were talking quietly to themselves or already shouting. Everyone was speaking to invisible people.

My father's voice had lasted only a few minutes. *I don't talk into no plastic and holes*, he always said. *Like breathin on a pincushion.*

He'd said Glorette was dead.

I stopped at the El Rey, one of the tiny shacks with a drop-down window that sold burritos and coffee. My father, when he came from Louisiana to California and began working groves, learned to eat burritos instead of biscuits and syrup. I wanted horrible coffee, not good coffee like my mother's, like Glorette's mother's, like all the women I'd grown up with on my small street. All of them from Louisiana, like my parents. The smell of their coffee beans roasting every morning, and the sound of the tiny cups they drank from even after dark, on the wood porches of our houses, when the air had cooled and the orange blossoms glowed white against the black leaves.

But the man who handed me the coffee smiled, and his Mayan face—eyes sharp and dark as oleander leaves, teeth square as Chiclets—looked down into mine. I put the coins in his palm. Pillows of callus there. I sipped the coffee and he said, "*Bueno, no?*"

So good—cinnamon and nighttime and oil. "*Que bueno*," I said. "*Gracias.*" He thought I was Mexican.

Then tears were rolling down my face, and I ducked into an alley. Urine and beer and wet newspaper. Glorette was dead. I closed my eyes.

Glorette—when we were fourteen, we walked two miles to high school, and her long stride was slow and measured as a giraffe's. Her legs long and thin, her body small, and the crescent of white underneath the purple-black iris that somehow made her seem as if she were sleepily studying everyone. Her hair to her waist, but every day I coiled it for her into a bun high on her skull. All day, men imagined her hair down along her back, tangled in their hands. I wore mine in a bun because I didn't want it in my way while I did my homework and wrote my travel stories about places I'd made up. Always islands, with hummingbirds and star fruit because I liked the name.

Every boy in Rio Seco loved her. But I talked too much smack. I couldn't wait to leave. If someone said, "Fantine, you think you butter, but your ass is Nucoa like everybody else," I'd say, "Yet all you deserve is Crisco."

Grady Jackson had fallen for Glorette so hard that he stole a car for her, and nearly died, but she felt nothing for him, and he'd never forgiven her.

* * *

Grady Jackson and his sister Hattie were from Cleveland by way of Mississippi. Grady. He hated his name. He was in my math class, though I was two years younger, and he wrote *Breeze* on top of his papers. Mr. Klein gave them back and said, "Write your proper name."

Grady said to me, "I want somebody call me Breeze. Say, I'm fittin to hat up, Breeze, you comin? Cause my mama name me for some sorry-ass uncle down in Jackson. Jackson, Missippi, and my name Jackson. Fucked up. And she in love with some fool name Detroit."

Glorette. We were freshmen, and a senior basketball player who had just moved here was talking to her every day. "Call me Detroit, baby. Where I'm from. Call me anything you want, cause you fine as wine and just my kind."

But Detroit had no car. Glorette smiled, her lips lifting only a little at the corners, and turned her head with the heavy pile of hair on top, her neck curved, and Detroit, who had reddish skin and five freckles on top of each cheek, said, "Damn, they grow some hella fine women out here in California."

He didn't even look at me.

That weekend, I was on my front porch when Grady Jackson pulled up in a car. My brothers Lafayette and Reynaldo had an old truck, and they jumped down from the cab. "Man, you got a Dodge Dart? Where the hell you get the money? You ain't had new kicks for a year. Still wearin them same Converse."

Grady looked up at me. "Glorette in your house? Her mama said she ain't home."

I saw his heavy brown cheeks, the fro that wouldn't grow no matter how he combed it out, and his T-shirt with the golden sweat stains under his arms. Should have just called himself *Missippi* and made fun of it, learned to rap like old blues songs and figured himself out. But Cleveland had already messed him up. I said, "She's home. She's waiting for Detroit to call her after his game."

He spun around and looked at Glorette's house, across the dirt street from mine, and said, "She think that fool gonna take her to LA? She keep sayin she want to go to LA. I got this ride, and I'm goin. You know what, Fantine? Tell her I come by here and I went to LA without her. Shit."

Then Lafayette said to him, "Grady, man, come in the barn and get a taste."

My brothers had hidden a few beers in the barn. When Grady went with them, I didn't even hesitate. I'd wanted to go to Los Angeles my whole life. I got into the Dart and lay down in the backseat.

When Grady started the car, he turned the radio up real loud, so Glorette could hear it, I figured, and then he spun the wheels and called out to my brothers, "Man, I'ma check out some foxy ladies in LA!" I could smell the pale beer when his breath drifted into the back. He played KDAY, some old Commodores, and then he talked to himself for a long time. I knew the car must be on the freeway, by the steady uninterrupted humming. I had never been on a freeway.

"She always talkin bout LA. Broadway. Detroit don't hear nothin. He don't know how to get to LA. He know Detroit. She coulda been checkin out a club. Checkin LA."

I fell asleep on the warm seat, and when the car jerked to a stop, I woke up. Grady was crying. His breath was ragged in his throat, I could smell the salt on his face, and his fists pounded the steering wheel. "There. I seen it, okay? And you didn't. You didn't see shit cause you waitin on some fool-ass brotha who just want to play you."

I sat up and saw Los Angeles. The city of angels. But it was just a freeway exit and some narrow streets with hulking black buildings. I remembered one said *Hotel Granada*, windows with smoke stains like black scarves flying from the empty sills.

Grady looked back and said, "Fantine? What the hell you doin in here?"

I walked down Broadway, where the butt models showed off curvier jeans than you'd see on Melrose or Rodeo. No mannequins in the doorways of some stores—just the bottom half, turned cheeks to shoppers. All the stereos blasting *ranchero* and *cumbia* and salesmen calling out and jewelry flashing fake gold.

LA. I had come here for college, and that was it. I wanted to live in an apartment with a fire escape so that I could see it all. See more than orange groves and my father's truck and the ten grove houses set along our street. I wanted to live above a restaurant, to watch people all day long, people who weren't related to me. I knew everyone's story at home, or I thought I did.

Now I lived in a lovely Mediterranean castle building, and I had a lunch meeting, and I wanted shoes. I wasn't going to think about Grady and Glorette. I walked along Broadway, turned on 8th, and then headed down Los Angeles toward the Garment District.

"No one shops downtown," people always said to me at receptions or parties in Hollywood or Westwood. When I was at a tapas party in Brentwood the week before, someone said, "Oh my God, I had to go downtown with my mother-in-law because her Israeli cousin works in the Jewelry District. I thought I would die. Then she wanted to see another cousin who sells jeans wholesale in some alley. Nobody speaks English, people can't drive, and we took a wrong turn and ended up in Nairobi. I swear. It was like Africa. All these homeless people on the street and they were all black."

"African American," someone else said smugly, holding up his martini glass.

"They were tribal. Living in cardboard boxes."

"But is that better than dung huts in Africa?" the same guy said. "Did you know that people are so resourceful they make houses out of crap?"

I drank my apple martini. The color of caterpillar blood. Had they ever cut a caterpillar in half after they pulled it off a tomato plant?

I said, "People made houses out of shit everywhere. Sod houses in the Great Plains—back then, there must have been old poop in that grass and earth. Adobe bricks—must have been some old mastodon shit in that. Dung houses just seem more unadulterated."

They looked at me. I thought, *Where did that word come from? No adult added?*

"Sorry. I'm—I'm Tom Jenkins," the guy said.

"FX Antoine," I said. Then the woman's face changed.

"You're FX Antoine? I love your stuff! I do ads for *Lucky*."

I smiled. I drank my caterpillar blood and turned gracefully away while she studied me, reaching for a crusty bread round spread with tapenade.

The sidewalks were wet here, as I passed the Flower District with gladiol spears in buckets, and carnations that didn't smell sweet. I still loved these streets, the doors sliding up to reveal roses and jeans and blankets. I slowed down in the Garment District, with rows of jeweled pointy-toed pumps everyone wanted now, and the glittery designer knockoff gowns. Usually everything looked like pirate treasure to me.

But today the voices were harsh. The men from Israel and Iran and China and Mexico hollering at the sales clerks and delivery guys, looking at me and dismissing me. I wore no veil, and I wasn't a buyer. They wanted wholesalers, not women who were headed to work, trying to get a bargain.

I ain't no blue-light special. Hattie had said that. I shop in Downtown LA, she bragged to us when she came home to Rio Seco once after she'd moved here to become an actress. That was Grady's sister's name. Hattie Jackson. She said she'd never go to Kmart again in her life. But I still hadn't seen her on television or in a movie.

I sat in one of the tiny burger places and called my brother. "Lafayette?"

"You heard?" he said. His radio was going, and my brother Reynaldo was singing. They must be on a job.

"Yeah."

"Man, Glorette was in this alley behind the taqueria, you remember that one close to here? She was in a shoppin cart. Her hair was all down. Somebody had been messin with her." He paused, but I didn't ask, and so he told me. "Look like she had a belt around her neck. But we don't know what got her. Or who."

Got gotted. I hadn't heard that for a while. She done got gotted. Damn. I said, "What about Grady Jackson?"

My brother said, "Who?"

"Grady. The one she was supposed to marry, after she got pregnant and that musician left her."

"What about Grady? That country-ass brotha been gone."

"I know, Lafayette," I said. Hamburgers hissed behind me. "He lives somewhere in LA. I should tell him."

"Sprung fool. Only one might know is his sister. Remember? She was gon be on TV. She worked in some place called Rat or Squirrel. Some bar. I remember she said it was just part-time while she was waitin for this movie about some jazz singer. I gotta go. Naldo callin me."

I walked back up Los Angeles Street toward Spring again. I didn't want shoes.

All these years, I had never wanted to look up Hattie Jackson in the phone book. I didn't really know if Grady was homeless or not—I'd just heard it when I was home in Rio Seco. Someone would say his cousin had heard Grady lived on the streets in a cardboard box, and all I could think of was being a child, in a box from my mother's new refrigerator, drawing windows with magic marker, Glorette sitting beside me.

I had left all that behind, and I didn't want to remember it—every memory made me feel good, for the smell of the oranges we kept in a bowl inside our box house, and then bad, for not being there to help my father during the harvest. I didn't want to see Hattie, or Grady.

Sprung fool. Growing up, I always heard my brothers and their friends talk about fools. *Man, that is one ballplayin fool. Don't do nothin but dribble. Damn, Cornelius is a drinkin fool.*

When I went to college, I heard Shakespeare. *The fool. Fool, make us laugh. Go tell the fool he is needed.* When I went to England, I saw the dessert Raspberry Fool. I closed my eyes, back then, tasting the cream and cake, thinking of Grady Jackson.

* * *

How you gon get sprung like that over one woman? That's what my brothers always said to him.

He came to the barn another night, and my brothers were working on a car. I stood in the doorway, watching him hold his right hand in a rag. Grady said to Lafayette, "She over there at her mama's? Glorette?"

Lafayette said, "Man, she told me she was movin in with Dakar soon as he got a record deal. Said they was gettin a place together. I don't keep track of that girl."

Grady said, "I heard him say it. Dakar. He was playin bass in a club, and I heard him tell somebody, 'I gotta book, man, I gotta get to LA or New York so I can get me a deal. Tired of this country-ass place.' So I hatted him up."

My brother said, "Damn, fool, your finger bleedin! He done bit off your finger?"

The red stain was big as a hibiscus flower on the dirty rag. Grady said, "He pulled a knife on me. Man, I kicked his ass and told him to go. He was gon come back and then book again, leave Glorette all the time. I just—I told him to stay away." He was panting now, his upper lip silver with sweat. "Forever."

He pushed past me and said nothing. I had already been accepted to college, and Glorette had told me she was pregnant with Dakar's child—I'd seen a swell high up under her breasts, awkward on her body like when we used to put pillows inside our shirts in that refrigerator house.

I left for college, and when I came back in the summer, my brothers told me what had happened. Grady had been driving a Rio Seco city trash truck for a year, made good money, and he rented a little house. When Dakar didn't come back, and Glorette had the baby—a boy—Grady took her in and said he'd marry her. But after a year of not loving him, of still loving a man who got ghost, she left him to get sprung herself—on rock cocaine—and she refused to ever love anyone again.

I walked through the Toy District again, the dolls and bright boxes and stuffed animals from China and Mexico. Glorette's son would be a teenager now.

Often my mother would call and say, "Marie-Therese and them wonder can you get a scooter. For her grandson. Out there in LA."

To everyone from back home, LA was one big city. They didn't know LA was a thousand little towns, entire worlds recreated in arroyos and strawberry fields and hillsides. And Downtown had canyons of black and silver glass, the Grand Central Market, Broadway, and its own *favela*.

That's where I was headed now. I was close to 3rd and Main. If you hadn't been to Brazil, and you hadn't seen a *favela*—that's what Skid Row looked like. The houses made of cardboard, the caves dug out under the freeway overpasses, the men sprawled out sleeping on the sidewalk right now, cheeks against the chain-link.

Were they all fools for something? Someone?

Would Grady Jackson still be on the street? Would he be alive?

All the men—sleeping with outstretched fingers near my heels, pushing carts, doing ballet moves between cars—black men with gray hair, heavy beards, bruise-dark cheeks, a Mexican man with a handlebar moustache and no teeth who grinned at me and said, "Hey, *payasa.*" A man my age, skin like mine, his hair dreaded up in a non-hip way. Like bad coral. He sat on the curb, staring at tires.

I kept moving. How would I find Grady among these thousands of people? And why would he still care about Glorette?

Sprung fool.

I glanced down an alley and saw a woman standing in the doorway of a porta potty. She lifted her chin at me. Her cheeks were pitted and scarred, her black hair like dead seaweed, and her knees gray as rain puddles. Then a man whispered in her ear and she pulled him inside by his elbow, and closed the door.

Glorette. She wanted to go wherever Sere Dakar went. He played the bass and the flute. He played songs for her. He left when she was seven months pregnant. Nothing mattered to her but living inside a cloud, and yet she was still beautiful. The bones in her face lovelier. She smoked rock all night, walked up and down the avenues like the guys who passed me now, their faces crack-gaunt.

A man waved and hollered high above me. Construction workers were gutting one of the old banks and an old SRO hotel. I saw the signs for luxury lofts on the building's roof. I turned on Spring Street.

Rat or Squirrel. What was Lafayette talking about? Hattie Jackson had a TV gig? I needed more coffee, and I needed to get myself together before meeting Rick, so I headed to Clifton's Cafeteria.

As I left Skid Row, the haunted men became fewer, like emissaries sent out among the rest of us. The other thousands and thousands of homeless people had packed their tents and boxes and sleeping bags and coats and melted into invisibility because now the day was truly the day.

* * *

I tried, but had no heart for it. Rick was short, and thin, and handsome, and funny. He held his tray like a shield, and then put soup and salad on it and laughed at the greenery in Clifton's. I put away the notebook where I'd tried to write about Oaxaca, and mole, and mescal.

Rick sat down and said, "So, since you're a world traveler, it's good to know where you're from."

"Here. Southern California."

"LA?"

"No." I picked up one fry. "Rio Seco."

"Really?" He studied me. "Where's that?"

"Have you been to Palm Springs?"

"Of course! I love mid-century."

"Well, it's on the way." I smiled slightly. I didn't know him well enough to explain. "Where are you from?"

Rick said, "Brooklyn."

"What part?"

He raised his eyebrows, like black commas. "Ah-hah. Fort Greene."

"Cool," I said. "Nice coffeehouse there. Tillie's."

He grinned, all the way this time. "But I live on Spring Street now. New loft. It's echoing, I've got so much space to fill."

I looked out the window at the shoulders bumping past. "Don't you worry about all the homeless people?"

"Worry?" He slanted his head.

"Do they bother you?"

"They keep to themselves," Rick said. "Everyone has parameters, and most people seem to respect those parameters."

I nodded and ate another fry. Like powder inside. Parameters and boundaries and demarcation. I could never explain that to my mother, or to Glorette.

Rick looked up under my lowered eyes. "But you know what? It's scary when you're walking past a guy and he looks dead. I mean really dead. Laid out on the sidewalk in a certain way."

Without any parameters, I thought. Not even curled up properly.

"And then you see him shiver or snore." He moved a piece of mandarin orange around on his plate. "Anyway."

Time for work. The way Rick put down his fork meant business. He said, "Let me tell you about *Immerse*. People don't want to just take a trip. They want immersion, journeys, a week or two that can change their lives. Change the way they feel about themselves and the world."

No, they didn't, I thought. I looked at the haze in the window. They wanted to read about me walking down an alley in Belize, me going to the Tuba City swap meet and eating frybread tacos and meeting an old woman who made turquoise jewelry. But they really just wanted a week-long cruise to Mazatlán where they never even got off the boat but once to buy souvenirs. A week in Maui where they swam on a black sand beach and then went to Chili's for dinner at the mall near the condo complex.

A woman paused to adjust her shopping bags, and she looked straight at me in the window and smiled.

I looked like anyone. A sista, a homegirl, a *payasa*. Belizean. Honduran. Creole.

"How about Brazil?" Rick said. "You look like you could be Brazilian, FX."

"Where in Brazil?"

"Not the usual. Find somewhere different."

He was challenging me. "Have you ever been in love?" I asked him, partly just to see what his face would do, but partly because editors realized I never mentioned any Handsome Gentleman or Nameless Boyfriend who accompanied me. I was clearly alone, and because of my adventurousness and initials, mysterious.

"Twice," Rick said, looking right at me. "In high school, and she dumped me for a football player. In college, and she dumped me for a professor. Now I'm in love with my apartment and my job."

None of us, at the parties or lunches, were ever in love. That was why we made good money and ate good food and lived where we wanted to. And yet Grady, and Glorette, had always been in love, and they'd never had anything but that love.

"My name is Fantine Xavierine," I said. I looked into his eyes—brown as coffee. Mine were lemon-gold. "I was named for a slave woman who helped my great-great-grandmother survive in Louisiana."

"Okay," he said. He glanced down, at his fork. "I like that. So you'll be fine in Brazil."

I walked with him for a block toward Spring Street. It was after two. I could head home now. Rick said, "You know, this place was worse than a ghost town a few years back, because the ghosts were real. But now all these hip places have shown up. There's a bar people in the office are going to lately—the Golden Gopher. I guess it was a dive before."

Rat. Gopher.

"Thanks, Rick," I said, and I touched his arm. Gym strong. He was shoulder to shoulder with me. "I'll call you."

I remembered it now. 8th and Olive. Grady had driven down dark streets for a long time, looking for it, and from the backseat, I was dizzy seeing the flashes of neon and stoplights. Then I saw through the back window a neon stack of letters. *Golden Gopher*.

I walked toward 8th. Grady had parked and then he'd seen me. He'd said, "I can't leave you here. Somebody get you, and your brothers kill me. Come on."

At Olive, I rounded the corner, and a film crew with three huge trucks and a parade of black-shirted young guys with goatees was swarming 8th Street. They didn't notice me. They were filming the tops of apartment buildings, where a young man was looking out the window of a place he would probably never live. A place probably meant to be New York or Chicago or Detroit.

There was no neon in this light. There was only a façade of black tile, and a door, and a sign that read *Golden Gopher*. It didn't open until five p.m.

The security guy noticed me now. A brother with cheeks pitted as a cast-iron pot. His badge glinted in the light from a camera. "Excuse me," he said.

"You're in the movies," I said, and I moved away.

Even I couldn't walk for another two hours. I looked for a Dunkin' Donuts or somewhere I could sit, and suddenly realized how much my feet hurt, how much my head hurt. I never felt like this in Belize or Oaxaca, because I'd be back in my hotel or in the bar, listening and watching. Now I was like a homeless person, just waiting, wanting to rest for a couple of hours.

I sat at a plastic-topped table and closed my eyes.

Hattie was twenty-two then, and Grady was eighteen, and I was only a freshman. He'd pulled me by the arm into the doorway of the club, past a knot of drunken men. One of them put his palm on my ass, fit his fingers around my jeans' pocket as if testing bread, and said, "How much?"

Grady jerked me away and up to the bar, and a man said, "You can't bring that in here. Underage shit."

A line of men sat at the bar, and someone knocked over a beer when he stood up. Then his sister spoke from behind the counter. She said, "Grady. What the hell."

Hattie was beautiful. Not like Glorette. Hattie's face was round and brown-gold and her hair straightened into a shining curve that touched her cheeks. Her lips were full and red. Chinese, I thought back then. Black Chinese. Her dress with the Mandarin collar.

She pushed three glasses of beer across the counter and someone reached past my neck and took them. Smoke and hair touched my cheek. I remembered. The bar was dark and smelled of spilled beer and a man was shouting in the doorway, "I'll fire you up!" and through an open back door I could hear someone vomiting in the alley.

"I wanted to come see you," Grady said. Sweat like burned biscuits at his armpits, staining his T-shirt. "See LA. The big city."

"Go home," Hattie said. "Right now, before somebody kicks your country ass. Take that Louisiana girl wit you."

I looked at Hattie, her contempt. She thought I was Glorette. I said, "I was born in California. I'm gonna live in LA myself. But I'm not gonna work in a bar."

I thought she'd be mad, but she said, "You probably not gonna work at all, babyface."

Grady pulled me back out the door, and this time the hand fit itself around my breast, just for a moment, and someone said, "Why buy the cow?"

Then we were driving again in the Dart, and Grady was murmuring to himself, "They got a bridge. She said."

He drove up and down the streets, and I said, "The full moon rises in the east. Papa said. Look."

He drove east, and the moon was like a dirty dime in front of us, and we took a beautiful bridge over the Los Angeles River, which raced along the concrete, not like our river. Grady said, "We can't get on the freeway again."

"Why not?"

"Shit, Fantine, cause I stole this car, and you ain't but fourteen. John Law see me, I'm goin to jail."

He drove down side roads along the freeway, past factories and small houses and winding around hills. The Dart ran out of gas in Pomona.

We were on Mission Boulevard, and Grady said, "You wanted to come. Now walk."

I walked slowly back toward 8th. It was nearly five and the sun was behind the buildings, but the sidewalks were still warm. I was carried along in a wave of people leaving work. Homeless men were already staking out sidewalk beds in alleys. Back at the bar, the blackness was like a cave, tile and door so dark it was as if someone had carved out the heart of the building. The film crew was gone. A pink curtain waved in an open window where they'd trained the camera.

A bucket slammed down on the sidewalk, and someone began to wash off the tile. A homeless guy. Green army coat, black sneakers glistening with fallen foam from his brush and rag, and black jeans shiny with wear and dirt. His hair was thin and nappy, and a brown spot showed on the side of his head, like the entrance to an anthill.

Grady. No. Uh-uh. Grady?

He'd had ringworm in Mississippi, when he was a kid, and he'd always combed his natural over that place. Grady. His hand moved back and forth over the tile, washing off fingerprints and smudges. He was missing the end of his right ring finger.

I couldn't do it. I pressed myself against the building across the street. *Hey, Grady, remember me? I wish I could get to know you again, have lunch, tapas or sushi, and then take a couple weeks before I tell you Glorette got killed by somebody in an alley, and she still only loved a guy who left her.*

I watched him for ten minutes. He washed the tile, wiped down the door, and polished the gold handle with a different rag. Then he stepped back and turned to look at something above my head.

I didn't move. His eyes crossed over me but didn't pause. He went inside, and he never came back out.

Other people stepped in now that the door was open. Two actors from *The OC.* Three young women wearing heels and carrying briefcases. A guy in a suit.

I crossed the street and went inside. This was not a dive. It looked like Liberace had decorated, with chandeliers and black pillars and even little lamps with gopher shades in gold. I squinted. The jukebox played Al Green. My eyes hurt from saltwater and darkness, and I didn't see Grady Jackson.

The bartender leaned forward and said, "You okay?" He had a two-tone bowling shirt on, and a porkpie and sideburns.

"Does Hattie Jackson work here?" I said. The bar was cool under my fingers.

"Who?"

"She's about forty. She was a bartender here."

A young woman—Paris Hilton–blond but with cool black roots, and a satin camisole—came up behind the bar and squinted. "She means Gloria, I'll bet."

Gloria was in an alcove to the side. It was like a little liquor store, and she was arranging bottles of Grey Goose and Ketel One. Her nails were red. But her lips were thin and brown. She looked old.

"Hattie?"

"Gloria Jones," she said to me. I leaned against the wall. My hips hurt, somehow. She knew me. She said, "When I came here, you had Pam Grier and Coffy and all them. My mama named me Hattie after the one in *Gone with the Wind*. Who the hell want to be a maid? I changed my name long time ago. After you was here with my fool-ass brother."

"Was that him? Outside?"

She nodded. "Comes to clean, and then he walks again. He got five, six routes a day. You know. He goes all the way along the river till Frogtown. Comes back later." She pushed the bottles around. "I don't get much tips over here. People don't buy this shit till they ready to go to a private party."

"You've been here all this time."

She shrugged. "Seem like not much longer." She wore a wig. The hairs were perfect. "After my senior year. I was fine as wine, but even the hookers in LA was something else. Hollywood was crazy. I came downtown to get me an apartment and wait for the right movie. Did the dancing place for a month."

"The dancing place?"

"Over on Olympic. The men dance with you for ten dollars and they gotta buy you them expensive drinks. But they smelled. Lord, they all smelled different, and some of them, the heat comin off their underarms and neck and you could smell it comin up from their pants. Even if they had cologne, just made it worse. I couldn't do it. I came here, and I was behind the counter forever serving drinks. The guys would tip me good, all the old drunks, and I went to the movies every night after work. Now the theaters are all Spanish. I just get me a video after work. And I sleep till I come in. I live next door."

I didn't know what to say. Her eyes were brown and muddy, as if washed in tea. "They were filming your building today."

She shrugged. "Always doin somethin. Now that Downtown is cool again. Grady can't even get his food in the alley now. Miss Thang at the bar like a hawk."

"He comes back for dinner?"

Gloria looked around and nodded. "I used to take my plate out there early, before we got started. Take me two enchiladas and rice. Hold a extra plate under there and gave him half. Used to have Mexican food in here. Not now." She glanced out over her counter. "Now the little old actors be out in the alley. Think they big time."

I walked away from her alcove, past the bar, the bowling-shirt watching me with a puzzled look—*What is she? Brazilian?*—and out to the alley. It must have been just a place to dump trash before—but now huge couches covered with velvet and pillows lay at each end, and the OC boys were already collapsed on one, with two girls. It was cool to be in a dive, in an alley, drinking Grey Goose martinis.

"Where does he eat now?" I whispered to Hattie, to Gloria, as she marked off bottles on a list.

"In the other alley. Next door," she said softly. "At six. Every night, I take me a smoke break out there. And I take my purse."

I waited for Grady there. I ignored the other homeless men, the drunks from down the street who stumbled past the Golden Gopher, the snide comments of one girl wearing a slinky dress who said, "Uh, the library is on 5th, okay?"

I saw him turn the corner and lope slowly toward me, steady, knees bending, arms moving easily at his sides. He stopped about ten feet from me and said, "Fantine?"

I nodded.

He said, "I been waiting for you. All this time."

His hands were rimmed with black, like my father's when he'd been picking oranges all night. His eyes were tiny, somehow, like sunflower seeds in the deep wrinkles around them. All that sun. All those miles.

"You told me you was gon come to LA. And you left for college. I married Glorette. I married her." His four top teeth were gone, like an open gate to his mouth. "Didn't nobody know. We went to the courthouse. Me and her."

I said, "Grady, I came to tell you—"

"I knew you was somewhere in LA. Me and Glorette went to the courthouse after Sere Dakar was gone. He played the flute. But he wasn't African. I seen his driver license one time. Name Marquis Parker. He was from Chicago. Call hisself *Chi-town* sometimes. Told me he was goin to LA and play in a band. Glorette was havin a baby."

"He'd be seventeen now," I said. "Her son."

But Grady stepped closer, the ripe sweet smell of urine and liquor and onions rising from his coat. "No. My son. I was gon raise him. Dakar was gon leave every time. So I got him in my truck."

I tried to remember. Grady had an old Pinto back then. "You didn't have a truck."

He trembled, and breathed hard through his mouth. "Fantine. All this time I waited to tell you. Cause I know you won't tell nobody. You never told nobody about the car. About Pomona."

I shook my head. My brothers would have beat his ass.

"I waited till Dakar came out that one bar where he played. I told him I had some clothes to sell. Then I busted him in the head and put him in the trash truck. It was almost morning. I took the truck up the hill. To the dump."

"Grady," Hattie said from behind me, "shut up." She dipped a hand in her purse and brought out a foil-wrapped package. "Eat your dinner and shut up. You ain't done nothin like that."

"I did."

"You a lie. You never said nothin to me."

"Fantine—you was at the barn that night." He held up his hand, as if to stop me, but he was showing me his finger. "Chicago had a knife. When I got to the dump and went to the back of the truck, he raised up and took a piece of me with him. But I had me a tire iron."

I looked up at the slice of sky between buildings. Missippi and Cleveland and Louisiana and Chicago—all in California. Men and fathers and fools.

Grady tucked the package against him then, like it was a football. "I was waitin on Fantine. She can tell Glorette he didn't leave. I disappeared his ass, and then I married her. But she left anyway. She still loved him. I don't love her now. I'm done." He brought the package to his lips and breathed in.

"You left him there?" I said. Sere Dakar—his real name something else. A laughing, thin musician with a big natural and green eyes. "At the dump?"

Grady threw his head up to the black sky and dim streetlamps. His throat was scaly with dirt. "The truck was full. I drove it up there and hit the button. Raised it up and dumped it in the landfill. Every morning, the bulldozer covered the layers. Every morning. It was Tuesday." He stepped toward me. "He had my finger in there with him. I felt it for a long time. Like when I was layin in the bed at night, with Glorette, my finger was still bleedin in Dakar's hand." His eyes were hard to see. "Tell her."

"She's dead, Grady. I came to tell you. Somebody killed her back in Rio Seco. In an alley. They don't know who. I'm going to see her tomorrow morning. Pay my respects." I pictured Glorette lying on a table, the men who would have to comb and coil her hair. Higher on her head than normal, because she couldn't lie on her back with all that hair gathered in a bun.

We'd always slept with our hair in braids. My eyes filled with tears, until the streetlamps faded to smears and I let down my eyelids hard. The tears fell on the sidewalk. When I looked down, I saw the wet.

Hattie went back inside without speaking to me, and she closed the black door hard. And Grady started to walk away, that familiar dipping lope that I'd watched for hours and hours while just behind him, that night.

I had to call a cab to get home. I went to Rio Seco the next morning in my Corsica. I thought I would see Grady Jackson there, or at the funeral, but I didn't.

My father said to me, "You goin to Brazil? That far?" He shook his head. "You never fall in love with none of them place. Not one, no."

I smiled and kissed him on the cheek. I sat all that night in my apartment, listening to Al Green, hearing the traffic on Echo Park Avenue, watching out my window as the palm fronds moved in the wind.

No one ever saw Grady Jackson again. I asked Hattie the following week, and the week after that, and then a month later. She was angry with me, and told me not to come back to the Golden Gopher. "You didn't have to tell him," she hissed.

"But he would have known someday," I said.

"You know what?" she said, her fingers hard as a man's on my wrist. "I loved my brother. I never loved nobody else in the world, but every day I saw my brother. I can't never go back home, but he came to me. And you done took that away. You don't know a damn thing about me or him."

The next time I went to the bar, she was gone too.

I knew him. I figured he just started walking one day and never went back to Skid Row. Maybe he walked to Venice and disappeared under the waves. Maybe he walked all the way to San Francisco, or maybe he had a heart attack or died of dehydration, still moving.

That night, when we were young, when Grady left the car in Pomona, we walked down Mission Boulevard, leaving behind the auto shops and tire places, moving past vacant lots and tiny motor courts where one narrow walk led past doors behind which we could hear muffled televisions. Junkyard dogs snarled and threw themselves against chain-link. And we moved easy and fast, me just behind Grady. Walking for miles, past strawberry fields where water ran like mercury in the furrows. Walking past a huge pepper tree with a hollow where an owl glided out, pumping wings once and then gone.

That night, we walked like we lived in the Serengeti, I realized all those years later when I watched Grady disappear down 8th into the darkness. Like pilgrims on the Roman roads of France. Like old men in England. Like Indians through rain forests, steady down the trail. Fools craving movement and no words and just the land, all the land, where we left our footprints, if nothing else.

THE BOOK SIGNING

BY PETE HAMILL

Park Slope, Brooklyn

(Originally published in *Brooklyn Noir*)

Carmody came up from the subway before dusk, and his eyeglasses fogged in the sudden cold. He lifted them off his nose, holding them while they cooled, and saw his own face smiling from a pale green leaflet taped to the wall. There he was, in a six-year-old photograph, and the words *Reading* and *Book Signing* and the date and place, and he paused for a moment, shivering in the hard wind. The subway was his idea. The publisher could have sent him to Brooklyn in a limousine, but he wanted to go to the old neighborhood the way he always did, long ago. He might, after all, never come this way again.

The subway stairs seemed steeper than he remembered and he felt twinges in his knees that he never felt in California. Sharp little needles of pain, like rumors of mortality. He didn't feel these pains after tennis, or even after speed-walking along the Malibu roads. But the pain was there now, and was not eased by the weather. The wind was blowing fiercely from the harbor, which lay off in the darkness to his right, and he donned his glasses again and used both gloved hands to pull his brown fedora more securely to his brow. His watch told him that he had more than a half hour to get to the bookstore. Just as he had hoped. He'd have some time for a visit, but not too much time. He crossed the street with his back to the place where the bookstore awaited him, and passed along the avenue where he once was young.

His own aging face peered at him from the leaflets as he passed, some pasted on walls, others taped inside the windows of shops. In a way, he thought, they looked like Wanted posters. He felt a sudden . . . what was the word? Not fear. Certainly not panic. *Unease.* That was the word. An uneasiness in the stomach. A flexing and then relaxing of muscles, an unwilled release of liquids or acids, all those secret wordless messages that in California were cured by the beach and the surf or a quick hit of Maalox. He told himself to stop. This was no drama. It was just a trip through a few streets where he had once lived but had not seen for decades. After seventeen novels, this would be his first signing in the borough that had formed him. But the leaflets made clear that here, in this neighborhood, his appearance might be some kind of big deal. It might draw many people. And Carmody felt apprehensive, nervous, wormy with unease.

"How does it feel, going back to Brooklyn?" Charlie Rose had asked him the night before, in a small dark television studio on Park Avenue.

"I don't know," Carmody said, and chuckled. "I just hope they don't throw books at me. Particularly my own books."

And wanted to add: *I've never really left.* Or to be more exact: *Those streets have never left me.*

The buildings themselves were as Carmody remembered them. They were old-law tenements, with fire escapes on the façades, but they seemed oddly comforting to Carmody. This was not one of those New York neighborhoods desolated by time and arson and decay. On the coast of California, he had seen photographs of the enrubbled lots of Brownsville and East New York. There were no lots here in the old neighborhood. If anything, the buildings looked better now, with fresh paint and clear glass on the street-level doors instead of hammered tin painted gray. He knew from reading the *New York Times* that the neighborhood had been gentrified, that most of the old families had moved away, to be replaced by younger people who paid higher rents. There was some unhappiness to all of that, the paper said, but still, the place looked better. As a boy he had walked these streets many times on nights like this, when most people retreated swiftly from the bitter cold to the uncertain warmth of the flats. Nights of piled snow and stranded streetcars. Now he noticed lights coming on in many of those old apartments, and shadows moving like ghosts behind drawn shades and curtains. He peered down a street toward the harbor, noticed some stubborn scabs of old snow, black between parked cars, and in the distance saw a thin scarlet band where the sun was setting in New Jersey. On this high slope, the harbor wind turned old snow into iron. But the sliver of sun was the same too. The day was dying. It would soon be night.

If the buildings were the same, the shops along the avenue were all different. Fitzgerald's bar was gone, where his father did most of his drinking, and so was Sussman's Hardware and Fischetti's Fruit and Vegetable and the Freedom Meats store and the pharmacy. What was the name of that drugstore? Right there. On that corner. An art supply store now. An art supply store! *Moloff's.* The drugstore was called Moloff's, and next door was a bakery. "Our Own" they called it. And now there was a computer store where a TV repair shop once stood. And a dry cleaner's where men once stood at the bar of Rattigan's, singing the old songs. All gone. Even the old clock factory had been converted into a condominium.

None of this surprised Carmody. He knew they'd all be gone. Nothing lasts. Marriages don't last. Ball clubs don't last. Why should shops last? Wasn't that the point of each one of his seventeen books? The critics never saw that point, but he didn't care. Those novels were not literature, even to Carmody. He would say in interviews that he wrote for readers, not for critics. And said to himself: I'm not Stendhal, or Hemingway, or Faulkner. He knew that from the beginning. Those novels were the work he did after turning forty, when he reached the age limit for screenwriting. He worked at the top of his talent, to be sure, and used his knowledge of movies to create plots that kept readers turning the pages. But he knew they were commercial products, novels about industries and how they worked, his characters woven from gossip and profiles in *Fortune* or *Business Week*. He had started with the automobile industry, and then moved to the television industry, and the sugar industry, and the weapons industry. In each of them the old was destroyed by the new, the old ruling families decayed and collapsed and newer, more ruthless men and women took their places. The new one was about the food industry, from the farms of California to the dinner plates of New York and Los Angeles. Like the others, it had no aspirations to be seen as art. That would be pretentious. But they were good examples of craft, as honest as well-made chairs. In each of them, he knew, research served as a substitute for imagination and art and memory. Three different researchers had filed memos on this last one, the new one, the novel he would sign here tonight, in the Barnes & Noble store five blocks behind him. He hoped nobody in the audience would ask why he had never once written about Brooklyn.

To be sure, he had never denied his origins. There was a profile in *People* magazine in 1984, when his novel about the gambling industry went to number one on the *New York Times* best seller list and stayed there for seventeen weeks. He was photographed on the terrace of the house in Malibu with the Pacific stretched out beyond him, and they used an old high school newspaper photograph showing him in pegged pants and a T-shirt, looking like an apprentice gangster or some variation on the persona of James Dean. The article mentioned his two ex-wives (there was now a third woman receiving his alimony checks), but the reporter was also from Brooklyn and was more intrigued by the Brooklyn mug who had become a best-selling author.

"You went west in 1957," the reporter said. "Just like the Dodgers."

"When they left, I left too, because that was the end of Brooklyn as I knew it," Carmody said. "I figured I'd have my revenge on Los Angeles by forcing it to pay me a decent living."

That was a lie, of course. One among many. He didn't leave Brooklyn because of the Dodgers. He left because of Molly Mulrane.

Now he was standing across the street from the building where both of them had lived. The entrance then was between a meat market and a fruit store, converted now into a toy store and a cell phone shop. Molly lived on the first floor left. Carmody on the top floor right. She was three years younger than Carmody and he didn't pay her much attention until he returned from the Army in 1954. An old story: She had blossomed. And one thing had led to another.

He remembered her father's rough, unhappy, threatening face when he first came calling to take her to the movies. Patty Mulrane, the cop. And the way he looked when he went out in his police uniform for a four-to-twelve shift, his gun on his hip, his usual slouch shifting as he walked taller and assumed a kind of swagger. And how appalled Patty Mulrane was when Carmody told him he was using the GI Bill to become a writer. "A writer? What the hell is that? I'm a writer too. I write tickets. Ha ha. A writer . . . How do you make a living with that? What about being a lawyer? A doctor? What about, what do they call it now, *criminology*? At least you'd have a shot at becoming a lieutenant . . ." The father liked his Fleischman's and beer and used the Dodgers as a substitute for conversation. The mother was a dim, shadowy woman who did very little talking. Molly was the youngest of the three children, and the only one still at home that summer. Her brother, Frankie, was a fireman and lived with his wife in Bay Ridge. There was another brother: What was his name? Sean. Seanie. Flat face, hooded eyes, a hard tank-like body. Carmody didn't remember much about him. There had been some kind of trouble, something about a robbery, which meant he could never follow his father into the police department, and Seanie had moved to Florida where he was said to be a fisherman in the Keys. Every Sunday morning, father, mother, and daughter went to mass together.

Now, on this frozen night, decades later, Carmody's unease rushed back. Ah, Molly, my Molly-O . . . The fire escapes still climbed three stories to the top floor where the Carmodys lived. But the building looked better, like all the others on the avenue. On the top floor right on this frozen night, the shades were up and Carmody could see ochre-colored walls, and a warm light cast by table lamps. This startled him. In memory, the Carmody flat was always cold, the windows rimmed with frost in winter, he and his sisters making drawings with their fingernails in the cold bluish light cast from a fluorescent ceiling lamp. His father was cold too, a withdrawn bitter man who resented the world and the youth of his children. His mother was a drinker, and her own chilly re-morse was relieved only by occasional bursts of rage. They nodded or grunted when Carmody told them about his ambitions, and his mother once said, in a slurred voice, "Who do you think you are, anyway?"

One Saturday afternoon in the Mulrane flat, he and Molly were alone, her parents gone off to see Frankie and his small child. Molly proudly showed him her father's winter uniform, encased in plastic from Kent's dry cleaners, and the medals he had won, and the extra gun, a nickel-plated .38 caliber Smith & Wesson, oiled and ready in a felt box. She talked to him about a book she was reading by A.J. Cronin and he told her she should read F. Scott Fitzgerald. She made him a ham and swiss cheese sandwich for lunch. They sipped tea with milk, thick with sugar. And then, for the first time, they went to bed together in her tiny room with its window leading to the fire escape. She was in an agony, murmuring prayers, her hands and arms moving in a jittery way to cover breasts and hair, trembling with fear and desire. *"Hold me tight,"* she whispered. *"Don't ever leave me."*

He had never written any of that, or how at the end of his first year of college, at the same time that she graduated from St. Joseph's, he rented the room near New York University, to get away from his parents and hers, and how she would come to him after work as a file clerk at Metropolitan Life and they would vanish into each other. He still went back to Brooklyn. He still visited the ice house of his parents. He still called formally in the Mulrane apartment to take Molly to the Sanders or the RKO Prospect. He was learning how to perform. But the tiny room had become their place, their gangster's hideout, the secret place to which they went for sin.

Now on this frozen night he stared at the dark windows of the first floor left, wondering who lived there now, and whether Molly's bones were lying in some frozen piece of the Brooklyn earth. He could still hear her voice, trembling and tentative: "We're sinners, aren't we?" He could hear her saying: "What's to become of us?" He could hear the common sense in her words and the curl of Brooklyn in her accent. "Where are we going?" she said. "Please don't ever leave me." He could see the mole inside her left thigh. He could see the fine hair at the top of her neck.

"Well, will ya lookit this," a hoarse male voice said from behind him. "If it ain't Buddy Carmody."

Carmody turned and saw a burly man smoking a cigarette in the doorway of a tenement. He was wearing a thick ski jacket and jeans, but his head was bare. The face was not clear in the obscure light but the voice told Carmody it was definitely someone from back then. Nobody had called him Buddy in forty-six years.

"How are ya?" Carmody said, peering at the man as he stepped out of the doorway. The man's face was puffy and seamed, and Carmody tried to peel away the flesh to see who had lived in it when they both were young.

"Couldn't stay away from the old neighborhood, could ya, Buddy?"

The unease was seething, but now Carmody felt a small stream of fear make its move in his stomach.

"It's been a long time," Carmody said. "Remind me, what's your name?"

"You shittin' me, Buddy? How could you figget my name?"

"I told you, man, it's been a long time."

"Yeah. It's easy to figget, for some people."

"Advanced age, and all that," Carmody said, performing a grin, glancing to his left, to the darkening shop windows, the empty street. Imagining himself running.

"But not everybody figgets," the man said.

He flipped his cigarette under a parked car.

"My sister didn't figget."

Oh.

Oh God.

"You must be Seanie," Carmody said quietly. "Am I right? Seanie Mulrane?"

"Ah, you remembered."

"How are you, Seanie?"

He could see Seanie's hooded eyes now, so like the eyes of his policeman father: still, unimpressed. He moved close enough so that Carmody could smell the whiskey on his breath.

"How am I? Huh. How am I . . . Not as good as you, Buddy boy. We keep up, ya know. The books, that miniseries, or whatever it was on NBC. Pretty good, you're doing."

Carmody stepped back a foot, as subtly as possible, trying to decide how to leave. He wished a police car would turn the corner. He trembled, feeling a black wind of negation pushing at him, backing him up, a small focused wind that seemed to come from the furled brow of Seanie Mulrane. He tried to look casual, turned and glanced at the building where he was young, at the dark first floor left, the warm top floor right.

"She never got over you, you prick."

Carmody shrugged. "It's a long time ago, Seanie," he said, trying to avoid being dismissive.

"I remember that first month after you split," Seanie said. "She cried all the time. She cried all day. She cried all night. She quit her job, 'cause she couldn't do it and cry at the same time. She'd start to eat, then, *oof,* she'd break up again. A million fuckin' tears, Buddy. I seen it. I was there, just back from the Keys, and my father wanted to find you and put a bullet in your head. And Molly, poor Molly . . . You broke her fuckin' heart, Buddy."

Carmody said nothing. Other emotions were flowing now. Little rivers of regret. Remorse. Unforgivable mistakes. His stomach rose and fell and rose again.

"And that first month? Hey, that was just the start. The end of the second month after you cut out, she tells my mother she's knocked up."

"No . . ."

"Yes."

"I didn't know that, Seanie. I swear—"

"Don't *lie,* Buddy. My old man told your old man. He pulled a gun on him, for Chrissakes, tryin' to find out where you was."

"I never heard any of this."

"Don't lie, Buddy. You lie for a livin', right? All those books, they're lies, ain't they? Don't lie to me."

"I didn't know, Seanie."

"Tell the truth: You ran because she was pregnant."

No: That wasn't why. He truly didn't know. He glanced at his watch. Ten minutes until the book signing. He felt an ache rising in his back.

"She had the baby, some place in New Jersey," Seanie said. "Catholic nuns or something. And gave it up. A boy it was. A son. Then she came home and went in her room. She went to mass every morning, I guess prayin' to God to forgive her. But she never went to another movie with a guy, never went on a date. She stood in her room, like another goddamned nun. She saw my mother die, and buried her, and saw my father die, and buried him, and saw me get married and move here wit' my Mary, right across the street, to live upstairs. I'd come see her every day, and try talkin' to her, but it was like, 'You want tea, Seanie, or coffee?'"

Seanie moved slightly, placing his bulk between Carmody and the path to Barnes & Noble.

"Once I said to her, I said, 'How about you come with me an' Mary to Florida? You like it, we could all move there. It's beautiful,' I said to her. 'Palm trees and the ocean. You'd love it.' Figuring I had to get her out of that fuckin' room. She looked at me like I said, 'Hey, let's move to Mars.'" Seanie paused, trembling with anger and memory, and lit another cigarette. "Just once, she talked a blue streak, drinkin' gin, I guess it was. And said to me, real mad, 'I don't want to see anyone, you understand me, Seanie? I don't want to see people holdin' hands. I don't want to see little boys playin' ball. You understand me?'" He took a deep drag on the Camel. "'I want to be here,' she says to me, 'when Buddy comes back.'"

Carmody stared at the sidewalk, at Seanie's scuffed black shoes, and heard her voice: *When Buddy comes back.* Saw the fine hair at the top of her neck. Thinking: Here I am, I'm back.

"So she waited for you, Buddy. Year after year in that dark goddamned flat. Everything was like it was when you split. My mother's room, my father's room, her room. All the same clothes. It wasn't right what you done to her, Buddy. She was a beautiful girl."

"That she was."

"And a sweet girl."

"Yes."

"It wasn't right. You had the sweet life and she shoulda had it with you."

Carmody turned. "And how did she . . . When did she . . ."

"Die? She didn't die, Buddy. She's still there. Right across the street. Waitin' for you, you prick."

Carmody turned then, lurching toward the corner, heading to the bookstore. He did not run, but his legs carried him in flight. Thinking: She's alive. Molly Mulrane is alive. He was certain she had gone off, married someone, a cop or a fireman or a car salesman, had settled in the safety of Bay Ridge or some far-off green suburb. A place without memory. Without ghosts. He was certain that she had lived a long while, married, had children, and then died. The way everybody did. And now he knew the only child she ever had was his, a son, and he was in flight, afraid to look back.

He could sense the feral pack behind him, filling the silent streets with howls. He had heard them often in the past few years, on beaches at dusk, in too many dreams. The voices of women, wordless but full of accusation:

wives, and girlfriends, and one-night stands in college towns; women his own age and women not yet women; women discarded, women used, women injured, coming after him on a foggy moor, from groves of leafless trees, their eyes yellow, their clothing mere patchy rags. If they could speak, the words would be about lies, treacheries, theft, broken vows. He could see many of their faces as he moved, remembering some of their names, and knew that in front, leading the pack, was Molly Mulrane.

Crossing a street, he slipped on a ridge of black ice and banged against the hood of a parked car. Then he looked back. Nobody was there.

He paused, breathing hard and deep.

Not even Seanie had come after him.

And now the book signing filled him with another kind of fear. Who else might come there tonight, knowing the truth? Hauling up the ashes of the past? What other sin would someone dredge up? Who else might come for an accounting?

He hurried on, the feral visions erased. He was breathing heavily, as he always did when waking from bad dreams. A taxi cruised along the avenue, its rooftop light on, as if pleading for a fare to Manhattan. Carmody thought: I could just go. Just jump in this cab. Call the store. Plead sudden illness. Just go. But someone was sure to call Rush & Malloy at the *Daily News* or Page Six at the *Post* and report the no-show. *Brooklyn Boy Calls It In.* All that shit. No.

And then a rosy-cheeked woman was smiling at him. The manager of the bookstore.

"Oh, Mr. Carmody, we thought you got lost."

"Not in this neighborhood," he said. And smiled, as required by the performance.

"You've got a great crowd waiting."

"Let's do it."

"We have water on the lectern, and lots of pens, everything you need."

As they climbed to the second floor, Carmody took off his hat and gloves and overcoat and the manager passed them to an assistant. He glanced at himself in a mirror, at his tweed jacket and black crew-collared sweater. He looked like a writer all right. Not a cop or a fireman or even a professor. A writer. He saw an area with about a hundred people sitting on folding chairs, penned in by walls of books, and more people in the aisles beyond the shelves, and another large group standing at the rear. Yes: a great crowd.

He stood modestly beside the lectern as he was introduced by the manager. He heard the words, "one of Brooklyn's own . . ." and they sounded strange. He didn't often think of himself that way, and in signings all over the country that fact was seldom mentioned. This store itself was a sign of a different Brooklyn. *Nothing stays the same. Everything changes.* There were no bookstores in his Brooklyn. He found his first books in the public library branch near where he lived, or in the great main branch at Grand Army Plaza. On rainy summer days he spent hours among their stacks. But the bookstores—where you could buy and own a book—they were down on Pearl Street under the El, or across the river on Fourth Avenue. His mind flashed on *Bomba the Jungle Boy at the Giant Cataract.* The first book he'd ever finished. How old was I? Eleven. Yes. Eleven. It cost a nickel on Pearl Street. That year, I had no bad dreams.

During the introduction, he peered out at the faces, examining them for hostility. But the faces were different too. Most were in their thirties, lean and intense, or prepared to be critical, or wearing the competitive masks of apprentice writers. He had seen such faces in a thousand other bookstores, out in America. About a dozen African-Americans were scattered through the seats, with a few standing on the sides. He saw a few paunchy men with six or seven copies of his books: collectors, looking for autographs to sell on eBay or some fan website. He didn't see any of the older faces. Those faces still marked by Galway or Sicily or the Ukraine. He didn't see the pouchy, hooded masks that were worn by men like Seanie Mulrane.

His new novel and five of the older paperbacks were stacked on a table to the left of the lectern, ready for signing, and Carmody began to relax. Thinking: It's another signing. Thinking: I could be in Denver or Houston or Berkeley.

Finally, he began to read, removing his glasses because he was nearsighted, focusing on words printed on pages. His words. His pages. He read from the first chapter, which was always fashioned as a hook. He described his hero being drawn into the mysteries of a grand Manhattan restaurant by an old college pal, who was one of the owners, all the while glancing up at the crowd so that he didn't sound like Professor Carmody. The manager was right: It was a great crowd. They listened. They laughed at the hero's wisecracks. Carmody enjoyed the feedback. He enjoyed the applause too, when he had finished. And then he was done, the hook cast. The manager explained that Carmody would take some questions, and then sign books.

He felt himself tense again. And thought: Why did I run, all those years ago? Why did I do what I did to Molly Mulrane?

I ran to escape, he thought.

That's why everybody runs. That's why women run from men. Women have run from me too. To escape.

People moved in the folding chairs, but Carmody was still. I ran because I felt a rope tightening on my life. Because Molly Mulrane was too nice. Too ordinary. Too safe. I ran because she gave me no choice. She had a script and I didn't. They would get engaged and he'd get his BA and maybe a teaching job and they'd get married and have kids and maybe move out to Long Island or over to Jersey and then—*I ran because I wanted something else. I wanted to be Hemingway in Pamplona or in a café on the Left Bank. I wanted to make a lot of money in the movies, the way Faulkner did or Irwin Shaw, and then retreat to Italy or the south of France. I wanted risk. I didn't want safety. So I ran. Like a heartless frightened prick.*

The first question came from a bearded man in his forties, the type who wrote nasty book reviews that guaranteed him tenure.

"Do you think if you'd stayed in Brooklyn," the bearded man asked, "you'd have been a better writer?"

Carmody smiled at the implied insult, the patronizing tone.

"Probably," he answered. "But you never know these things with any certainty. I might never have become a writer at all. There's nothing in the Brooklyn air or the Brooklyn water that makes writers, or we'd have a couple of million writers here . . ."

A woman in her twenties stood up. "Do you write on a word processor, in longhand, or on a typewriter?"

This was the way it was everywhere, and Carmody relaxed into the familiar. Soon he'd be asked how to get an agent or how he got his ideas and how do I protect my own ideas when I send a manuscript around? Could you read the manuscript of my novel and tell me what's wrong? The questions came and he answered as politely as possible. He drew people like that, and he knew why: He was a success, and there were thousands of would-be writers who thought there were secret arrangements, private keys, special codes that would open the doors to the alpine slopes of the best-seller lists. He tried to tell them that, like life, it was all a lottery. Most didn't believe him.

Then the manager stepped to the microphone and smiled and said that Mr. Carmody would now be signing books. "Because of the large turnout," the manager said, "Mr. Carmody will not be able to personalize each book. Otherwise many of you would have a long wait." Carmody thanked everybody for coming on such a frigid night and there was warm, loud applause. He sat down at the table and sipped from a bottle of Poland Spring water.

He signed the first three books on the frontispiece, and then a woman named Peggy Williams smiled and said, "Could you make an exception? We didn't go to school together, but we went to the same school twenty years apart. Could you mention that?"

He did, and the line slowed. Someone wanted him to mention the Dodgers. Another, Coney Island. One man wanted a stickball reference, although he was too young to ever have played that summer game. "It's for my father," he explained. There was affection in these people, for this place, this neighborhood, which was now their neighborhood. But Carmody began to feel something else in the room, something he could not see.

"You must think you're hot shit," said a woman in her fifties. She had daubed rouge on her pale cheeks. "I've been in this line almost an hour."

"I'm sorry," he said, and tried to be light. "It's almost as bad as the Department of Motor Vehicles."

She didn't laugh.

"You could just sign the books," she said. "Leave off the fancy stuff."

"That's what some people want," he said. "The fancy stuff."

"And you gotta give it to them? Come on."

He signed his name on the title page and handed it to her, still smiling.

"Wait a minute," she said, holding the book before him like a summons. "I waited a long time. Put in, 'For Gerry'—with a G—'who waited on line for more than an hour.'"

She laughed then too, and he did what she asked. The next three just wanted signatures, and two just wanted "Merry Christmas" and then a collector arrived and Carmody signed six first editions. He was weary now, his mind filling with images of Molly Mulrane and Seanie's face and injuries he had caused so long ago. All out there somewhere. And still the line trailed away from the table, into a crowd that, without his glasses, had become a multicolored smear, like a bookcase.

The woman came around from the side aisle, easing toward the front of the line in a distracted way. Carmody saw her whisper to someone on the line, a young man who made room for her with the deference reserved for the old. She was hatless, her white hair cut in girlish bangs across her furrowed brow. She was wearing a short down coat, black skirt, black stockings, mannish shoes. The coat was open, showing a dark rose sweater. Her eyes were pale.

Holy God.

She was six feet away from him, behind two young men and a collector. A worn leather bag hung from her shoulder. A bag so old that Carmody remembered buying it in a shop in the Village, next door to the Eighth Street Bookshop. He remembered it when it was new, and so was he.

He glanced past the others and saw that she was not looking at him. She stared at bookshelves, or the ceiling, or the floor. Her face had an indoor whiteness. The color of ghosts. He signed a book, then another. And the girl he once loved began to come to him, the sweet pretty girl who asked nothing of him except that he love her back. And he felt then a great rush of sorrow. For her. For himself. For their lost child. He felt as if tears would soon leak from every pore in his body. He heard a whisper of someone howling. The books in front of him were now as meaningless as bricks.

Then she was there. And Carmody rose slowly and leaned forward to embrace her across the table.

"Oh, Molly," he whispered. *"Oh, Molly, I'm so, so sorry."*

She smiled then, and the brackets that framed her mouth seemed to vanish, and for a moment Carmody imagined taking her away with him, repairing her in the sun of California, making it up, writing a new ending. Rewriting his own life. He started to come around the table.

"Molly," he said. "Molly, my love."

Then her hand reached into the leather bag and he knew what it now must hold. Passed down from her father. A souvenir of long ago.

Yes, he thought. Release me, Molly. Yes. Bring me your nickel-plated gift. Do it.

Her hand came out of the bag, holding what he expected.

RUN KISS DADDY

BY JOYCE CAROL OATES

Kittatinny Mountains

(Originally published in *New Jersey Noir*)

T ell Daddy hello! Run kiss Daddy."

He'd been gone from the lake less than an hour but in this new family each parting and each return signaled a sort of antic improvised celebration—he didn't want to think it was the obverse of what must have happened before he'd arrived in their lives—the Daddy departing, and the Daddy not returning.

"Sweetie, h'lo! C'mere."

He dropped to one knee as the boy ran at him to be hugged. A rough wet kiss on Kevin's forehead.

The little girl hesitated. Only when the mother pushed more firmly at her small shoulders did she spring forward and run—wild-blue-eyed suddenly, with a high-pitched squeal like a mouse being squeezed—into his arms. He laughed—he was startled by the heat of the little body—flattered and deeply moved, kissing the excited child on the delicate soft skin at her temple where—he'd only just noticed recently—a pale blue vein pulsed.

"What do you say to Daddy when Daddy comes back?"

The mother clapped her hands to make a game of it. This new family was so new to her too, weekends at Paraquarry Lake were best borne as a game, as play.

"Say *Hi Daddy!—Kiss-kiss Daddy!*"

Obediently the children cried what sounded like *Hi Daddy! Kiss-kiss Daddy!*

Little fish-mouths pursed for kisses against Daddy's cheek.

Reno had only driven into the village of Paraquarry Falls to bring back semi-emergency supplies: toilet paper, flashlight batteries, mosquito repellant, mouse traps, a gallon container of milk, a shiny new garden shovel to replace the badly rusted shovel that had come with the camp. Also, small sweet-fruit yogurts for the children though both he and the mother weren't happy about them developing a taste for sugary foods—but there wasn't much of a selection at the convenience store.

In this new-Daddy phase in which unexpected treats are the very coinage of love.

"Who wants to help Daddy dig?"

Both children cried *Me!*—thrilled at the very prospect of working with Daddy on the exciting new terrace overlooking the lake.

And so they helped Daddy excavate the old, crumbled-brick terrace a previous owner had left amid a tangle of weeds, pebbles, and broken glass, or tried to help Daddy—for a while. Clearly such work was too arduous for a seven-year-old, still more for a four-year-old, with play shovels and rakes; and the mild June air too humid for much exertion. And there were mosquitoes and gnats. Despite the repellant. For these were the Kittatinny Mountains east of the Delaware Water Gap in early June—that season of teeming buzzing fecundity—just to inhale the air is to inhale the smells of burgeoning life.

"Oh! Dad-dy!" Devra recoiled from something she'd unearthed in the soil, lost her balance, and fell back onto her bottom with a little cry. Reno saw it was just a beetle—iridescent, wriggling—and told her not to be afraid: "They just live in the ground, sweetie. They have special beetle work to do in the ground."

Kevin said, "Like worms! They have 'work' in the ground."

This simple science—earth science—the little boy had gotten from Reno. Very gratifying to hear your words repeated with child-pride.

From the mother Reno knew that their now-departed father had often behaved "unpredictably" with the children and so Reno made it a point to be soft-spoken in their presence, good-natured and unexcitable, predictable.

What pleasure in being *predictable!*

Still, Devra was frightened. She'd dropped her play shovel in the dirt. Reno saw that the little girl had enough of helping Daddy with the terrace for the time being. "Sweetie, go see what Mommy's doing. You don't need to dig anymore right now."

Kevin remained with Daddy. Kevin snorted in derision, his baby sister was so *scaredy.*

Reno was a father, again. Fatherhood, returned to him. A gift he hadn't quite deserved the first time—maybe—but this time, he would strive to deserve it.

This time, he was forty-seven years old. He—who'd had a very hard time perceiving himself other than *young, a kid.*

And this new marriage!—this beautiful new family small and vulnerable as a mouse cupped trembling in the hand—he was determined to protect with his life. Not ever *not ever* let this family slip from his grasp as he'd let slip from his grasp his previous family—two young children rapidly retreating now in Reno's very memory like a scene glimpsed in the rearview mirror of a speeding vehicle.

"Come to Paraquarry Lake! You will all love Paraquarry Lake."

The name itself seemed to him beautiful, seductive—like the Delaware River at the Water Gap where the river was wide, glittering and winking like shaken foil. As a boy he'd hiked the Appalachian Trail in this area of northeastern Pennsylvania and northwestern New Jersey—across the river on the high pedestrian walkway, north to Dunfield Creek and Sunfish Pond and so to Paraquarry Lake which was the most singular of the Kittitanny Ridge lakes, edged with rocks like a crude lacework and densely wooded with ash, elm, birch, and maples that flamed red in autumn.

So he courted them with tales of his boyhood hikes, canoeing on the river and on Paraquarry Lake, camping along the Kittatinny Ridge where once, thousands of years ago, a glacier lay like a massive claw over the land.

He told them of the Lenni Lenape Indians who'd inhabited this part of the country for thousands of years!—far longer than their own kind.

As a boy he'd never found arrowheads at Paraquarry Lake or elsewhere, yet he recalled that others had, and so spoke excitedly to the boy Kevin as if to enlist him in a search; he did not quite suggest they might discover Indian bones that sometimes came to the surface at Paraquarry Lake, amid shattered red shale and ordinary rock and dirt.

In this way and in others he courted the new wife Marlena, who was a decade younger than he; and the new son, Kevin; and the new daughter who'd won his heart the first glimpse he'd had of her—tiny Devra with white-blond hair fine as the silk of milkweed.

Another man's lost family. Or maybe *cast off*—as Marlena had said in her bright brave voice determined not to appear hurt, humiliated.

His own family—Reno had hardly cast off. Whatever his ex-wife would claim. If anything, Reno had been the one to be cast off by her.

Yet careful to tell Marlena, early in their relationship: "It was my fault, I think. I was too young. When we got married—just out of college—we were both too young. It's said that if you 'cohabit' before getting married it doesn't actually make any difference in the long run—whether you stay married, or get divorced—but our problem was that we hadn't a clue what 'cohabitation' meant—means. We were always two separate people and then my career took off . . ."

Took off wasn't Reno's usual habit of speech. Nor was it Reno's habit to talk so much, and so eagerly. But when he'd met a woman he believed he might come to seriously care for—at last—he'd felt obliged to explain himself to her: there had to be some failure in his personality, some flaw, otherwise why was he alone, unmarried; why had he become a father whose children had grown up largely without him, and without seeming to need him?

At the time of the divorce, Reno had granted his wife too many concessions. In his guilty wish to be generous to her though the breakup had been as much his wife's decision as his own. He'd signed away much of their jointly owned property, and agreed to severely curtailed visitation rights with the children. He hadn't yet grasped this simple fact of human relations—the more readily you give, the more readily it will be taken from you as what you owe.

His wife had appealed to him to be allowed to move to Oregon, where she had relatives, with the children; Reno hadn't wanted to contest her.

Within a few years, she'd relocated again—with a new husband, to Sacramento.

In these circuitous moves, somehow Reno was cast off. One too many corners had been turned, the father had been left behind except for child-support payments.

Trying not to feel like a fool. Trying to remain a gentleman long after he'd come to wonder why.

"Paraquarry Lake! You will all love Paraquarry Lake."

The new wife was sure, yes, she would love Paraquarry Lake. Laughing at Reno's boyish enthusiasm, squeezing his arm.

Kevin and Devra were thrilled. Their new father—new *Daddy*—so much nicer than the old, other Daddy—eagerly spreading out photographs on a tabletop like playing cards.

"Of course," the new Daddy said, a sudden crease between his eyes, "this cabin in the photos isn't the one we'll be staying in. This is the one—" Reno paused, stricken. It felt as if a thorn had lodged in his throat.

This is the one I have lost was not an appropriate statement to make to the new children and to the new wife listening so raptly to him, the new wife's fingers lightly resting on his arm.

These photographs had been selected. Reno's former wife and former children—of course, *former* wasn't the appropriate word!—were not shown to the new family.

Eleven years invested in the former marriage! It made him sick—just faintly, mildly sick—to think of so much energy and emotion, lost.

Though there'd been strain between Reno and his ex-wife—exacerbated when they were in close quarters together—he'd still insisted upon bringing his family to Paraquarry Lake on weekends through much of the year and staying there—of course—for at least six weeks each summer. When Reno couldn't get off from work he drove up weekends. For the "camp" at Paraquarry Lake—as he called it—was essential to his happiness.

Not that it was a particularly fancy place: it wasn't. Several acres of deciduous and pine woods, and hundred-foot frontage on the lake—*that* was what made the place special.

Eventually, in the breakup, the Paraquarry Lake camp had been sold. Reno's wife had come to hate the place and had no wish to buy him out—nor would she sell her half to him. In the woman's bitterness, the camp had been lost to strangers.

Now, it was nine years later. Reno hadn't seen the place in years. He'd driven along the Delaware River and inland to the lake and past the camp several times but became too emotional staring at it from the road, such bitter nostalgia wasn't good for him, and wasn't, he wanted to think, typical of him. So much better to think—to tell people in his new life, *It was an amicable split-up and an amicable divorce overall. We're civilized people—the kids come first!*

Was this what people said, in such circumstances? You did expect to hear, *The kids come first!*

Now, there was a new camp. A new "cabin"—an A-frame, in fact—the sort of thing for which Reno had always felt contempt; but the dwelling was attractive, "modern," and in reasonably good condition with a redwood deck and sliding glass doors overlooking both the lake and a ravine of tangled wild rose to the rear. The nearest neighbor was uncomfortably close—only a few yards away—but screened by evergreens and a makeshift redwood fence a previous owner had erected.

Makeshift too was the way in which the A-frame had been cantilevered over a drop in the rocky earth, with wooden posts supporting it; if you entered at the rear you stepped directly into the house, but if you entered from the front, that is, facing the lake, you had to climb a steep flight of not-very-sturdy wood steps, gripping a not-very-sturdy railing. The property had been owned by a half-dozen parties since its original owner in the 1950s. Reno wondered at the frequent turnover of owners—this wasn't typical of the Water Gap area where people returned summer after summer for a lifetime.

The children loved the Paraquarry camp—they hugged their new Daddy happily, to thank him—and the new wife who'd murmured that she wasn't an "outdoor type" conceded that it was really very nice—"and what a beautiful view."

Reno wasn't about to tell Marlena that the view from his previous place had been more expansive, and more beautiful.

Marlena kissed him, so very happy. For he had saved her, as she had saved him. From what—neither could have said.

Paraquarry Lake was not a large lake: seven miles in circumference. The shoreline was so distinctly uneven and most of it thickly wooded and inaccessible except by boat. On maps the lake was L-shaped but you couldn't guess this from shore—nor even from a boat—you would have to fly in a small plane overhead, as Reno had done many years ago.

"Let's take the kids up sometime, and fly over. Just to see what the lake looks like from the air."

Reno spoke with such enthusiasm, the new wife did not want to disappoint him. Smiling and nodding yes! What a good idea—"Sometime."

The subtle ambiguity of *sometime*. Reno guessed he knew what this meant.

In this new marriage Reno had to remind himself—continually—that though the new wife was young, in her mid-thirties, he himself was no longer that young. In his first marriage he'd been just a year older than his wife. Physically they'd been about equally fit. He had been stronger than his wife, he could hike longer and in more difficult terrain, but essentially they'd been a match and in some respects—caring for the children, for instance—his wife had had more energy than Reno. Now, the new wife was clearly more fit than Reno, who became winded—even exhausted—on the nearby Shawagunik Trail that, twenty years before, he'd found hardly taxing.

Reno's happiness was working on the camp: the A-frame that needed repainting, a new roof, new windows; the deck was partly rotted, the front steps needed to be replaced. Unlike Reno's previous camp of several acres, the new camp was hardly more than an acre and much of the property was rocky and inaccessible—fallen trees, rotted lumber, the detritus of years.

Reno set for himself the long-term goal of clearing the property of such litter and a short-term goal of building a flagstone terrace beside the front steps, where the earth was rocky and overgrown with weeds; there had once been a makeshift brick terrace or walkway here, now broken. Evidence of previous tenants—rather, the negligence of previous tenants—was a cause of annoyance to Reno as if this property dear to him had been purposefully desecrated by others.

During the winter in their house in East Orange, Reno had studied photos he'd taken of the new camp. Tirelessly he'd made sketches of the redwood deck he meant to extend and rebuild, and of the "sleeping porch" he meant to add. Marlena suggested a second bathroom, with both a shower and a tub. And a screened porch that could be transformed into a glassed-in porch in cold weather. Reno would build—or cause to be built—a carport, a new field-stone fireplace, a barbecue on the deck. And there was the ground-level terrace he would construct himself with flagstones from a local garden supply store, once he'd dug up and removed the old, broken bricks half-buried in the earth.

Reno understood that his new wife's enthusiasm for Paraquarry Lake and the Delaware Water Gap was limited. Marlena would comply with his wishes—anyway, most of them—so long as he didn't press her too far. The high-wattage smile might quickly fade, the eyes brimming with love turn tearful. For divorce is a devastation, Reno knew. The children were more readily excited by the prospect of spending time at the lake—but they were children, impressionable. And bad weather in what was essentially an outdoor setting—its entire raison d'être was *outdoors*—would be new to them. Reno understood that he must not make with this new family the mistake he'd made the first time—insisting that his wife and children not only accompany him to Paraquarry Lake but that they enjoy it—visibly.

Maybe he'd been mistaken, trying so hard to make his wife and young children *happy*. Maybe it's always a mistake, trying to assure the happiness of others.

His daughter was attending a state college in Sacramento—her major was something called communication arts. His son had flunked out of Cal Tech and was enrolled at a "computer arts" school in San Francisco. The wife had long ago removed herself from Reno's life and truly he rarely thought of any of them, who seemed so rarely to think of him.

But the daughter. Reno's daughter. *Oh hi, Dad. Hi. Damn, I'm sorry—I'm just on my way out.*

Reno had ceased calling her. Both the kids. For they never called him. Even to thank him for birthday gifts. Their e-mails were rudely short, perfunctory.

The years of child support had ended. Both were beyond eighteen. And the years of alimony, now that the ex-wife had remarried. How many hundreds of thousands of dollars . . . Though of course, Reno understood.

But the new children! In this new family!

Like wind rippling over the surface of Paraquarry Lake—emotion flooded into Reno at the thought of his new family. He would adopt the children—soon. For Kevin and Devra adored their new Daddy who was so kind, funny, patient, and—yes—predictable—with them; who had not yet raised his voice to them a single time.

Especially little Devra captivated him—he stared at her in amazement, the child was so *small*—tiny rib cage, collarbone, wrists—after her bath, the white-blond hair thin as feathers against her delicate skull.

"Love you—I love you—all—so much."

It was a declaration made to the new wife only in the dark of their bed. In her embrace, her strong warm fingers gripping his back, and his hot face that felt to him like a ferret's face, hungry, ravenous with hunger, pressed into her neck.

At Paraquarry Lake, in the new camp, there was a new Reno emerging.

It was hard work but thrilling, satisfying—to chop his own firewood and stack it beside the fireplace. The old muscles were reasserting themselves in his shoulders, upper arms, thighs. He was developing a considerable axe swing, and was learning to anticipate the jar of the axe head against wood which he supposed was equivalent to the kick of a shotgun against a man's shoulder—if you weren't prepared, the shock ran down your spine like an electric charge.

Working outdoors, he wore gloves that Marlena gave him—"Your hands are getting too calloused, scratchy." When he caressed her, she meant. Marlena was a shy woman and did not speak of their lovemaking but Reno wanted to think that it meant a good deal to her as it meant to him after years of pointless celibacy.

He was thrilled too when they went shopping together—at the mall, at secondhand furniture stores—choosing Adirondack chairs, a black leather sofa, a rattan settee, handwoven rugs, andirons for the fireplace. It was deeply moving to Reno to be in the presence of this attractive woman who took such care and turned to him continually for his opinion as if she'd never furnished a household before.

Reno even visited marinas in the area, compared prices: sailboats, Chris-Craft power boats. In truth he was just a little afraid of the lake—of how he might perform as a sailor on it. A rowboat was one thing, but even a canoe—he felt shaky in a canoe, with another passenger. With this new family vulnerable as a small creature cupped in the palm of a hand—he didn't want to take any risks.

The first warm days in June, a wading pool for the children. For there was no beach, only just a pebbly shore of sand hard-packed as cement. And sharp-edged rocks in the shallows. But a plastic wading pool, hardly more than a foot of water—that was fine. Little Kevin splashed happily. And Devra in a puckered yellow Spandex swimsuit that fit her little body like a second skin. Reno tried not to stare at the little girl—the astonishing white-blond hair, the widened pale-blue eyes—thinking how strange it was, how strange Marlena would think it was, that the child of a father not known to him should have so totally supplanted Reno's memory of his own daughter at that age; for Reno's daughter too must have been beautiful, adorable—but he couldn't recall. Terrifying how parts of his life were being shut to him like rooms in a house shut and their doors sealed and once you've crossed the threshold, you can't return. Waking in the night with a pounding heart Reno would catch his breath thinking, *But I have my new family now. My new life now.*

Sometimes in the woods above the lake there was a powerful smell—a stink—of skunk, or something dead and rotted; not the decaying compost Marlena had begun which exuded a pleasurable odor for the most part, but something ranker, darker. Reno's sinuses ached, his eyes watered, and he began sneezing—in a sudden panic that he'd acquired an allergy for something at Paraquarry Lake.

That weekend, Kevin injured himself running along the rocky shore—as his mother had warned him not to—falling, twisting his ankle. And little Devra, stung by yellow jackets that erupted out of nowhere—in fact, out of a hive in the earth that Reno had disturbed with his shovel.

Screaming! High-pitched screams that tore at Reno's heart. If only the yellow jackets had stung *him*—Reno might have used the occasion to give the children some instruction.

Having soothed two weeping children in a single afternoon, Marlena said ruefully, "Camp can be treacherous!" The remark was meant to be amusing but there was seriousness beneath, even a subtle warning, Reno knew.

He swallowed hard and promised it wouldn't happen again.

This warm-humid June afternoon shading now into early evening and Reno was still digging—"excavating"—the old ruin of a terrace. The project was turning out to be harder and more protracted than he had anticipated. For

the earth below the part-elevated house was a rocky sort of subsoil, of a texture like fertilizer; moldering bricks were everywhere, part-buried; also jagged pieces of concrete and rusted spikes, broken glass amid shattered bits of
red shale. The previous owners had simply dumped things here. Going back
for decades, probably. Generations. Reno hoped these slovenly people hadn't
dumped anything toxic.

The A-frame had been built in 1957—that long ago. Sometime later
there were renovations, additions—sliding glass doors, skylights. A sturdier
roof. Another room or two. By local standards the property hadn't been very
expensive—of course, the market for lakeside properties in this part of New
Jersey had been depressed for several years.

The new wife and the children were down at the shore—at their
neighbors' dock. Reno heard voices, radio music—Marlena was talking
with another young mother, several children were playing together. Reno
liked hearing their happy uplifted voices though he couldn't make out any
words. From where he stood, he couldn't have said with certainty which small
figure was Kevin, which was Devra.

How normal all this was! Soon, Daddy would quit work for the eve-
ning, grab a beer from the refrigerator, and join his little family at the dock.
How normal Reno was—a husband again, a father and a homeowner here at
Paraquarry Lake.

Of all miracles, none is more daunting than *normal*. To be—to become—
normal. This gift seemingly so ordinary is not a gift given to all who seek it.

And the children's laughter too. This was yet more exquisite.

With a grunt Reno unearthed a large rock he'd been digging and scraping
at with mounting frustration. And beneath it, or beside it, what appeared to
be a barrel, with broken and rotted staves; inside the barrel, what appeared to
be shards of a broken urn.

There was something special about this urn, Reno seemed to know. The
material was some sort of dark red earthenware—thick, glazed—inscribed
with figures like hieroglyphics. Even broken and coated with grime, the pieces
exuded an opaque sort of beauty. Unbroken, the urn would have stood about
three feet in height.

Was this an Indian artifact? Reno was excited to think so—remains of the
Lenni Lenape culture were usually shattered into very small pieces, almost
impossible for a nonspecialist to recognize.

With the shiny new shovel Reno dug into and around the broken urn,
curious. He'd been tossing debris into several cardboard boxes, to be hauled

to the local landfill. He was tired—his muscles ached, and there was a new, sharp pain between his shoulder blades—but he was feeling good, essentially. At the neighbors' dock when they asked him how he was he'd say, *Damn good! But thirsty.*

His next-door neighbor looked to be a taciturn man of about Reno's age. And the wife one of those plus-size personalities with a big smile and greeting. To them, Marlena and Reno would be a *couple.* No sign that they were near-strangers desperate to make the new marriage work.

Already in early June Reno was beginning to tan—he looked like a native of the region more than he looked like a summer visitor from the city, he believed. In his T-shirt, khaki shorts, waterstained running shoes. He wasn't yet fifty—he had two years before fifty. His father had died at fifty-three of a heart attack but Reno took care of his health. He had annual checkups, he had nothing to worry about. He would adopt the woman's children—that was settled. He would make them his own: Kevin, Devra. He could not have named the children more fitting names. Beautiful names for beautiful children.

The Paraquarry property was an excellent investment. His work was going well. His work was not going badly. His job wasn't in peril—yet. He hadn't lost nearly so much money as he might have in the recent economic crisis—he was far from desperate, like a number of his friends. Beyond that—he didn't want to think.

A scuttling snake amid the debris. Reno was taken by surprise, startled. Tossed a piece of concrete at it. Thinking then in rebuke, *Don't be ridiculous. A garter snake is harmless.*

Something was stuck to some of the urn shards—clothing? Torn, badly rotted fabric?

Reno leaned his weight onto the shovel, digging more urgently. A flash of something wriggling in the earth—worms—cut by the slice of the shovel. Reno was sweating now. He stooped to peer more closely even as the cautionary words came: *Maybe no. Maybe not a good idea.*

"Oh. God."

Was it a bone? Or maybe plastic? No, a bone. An animal bone?

Covered in dirt, yet a very pale bone.

A human bone?

But so small—had to be a child's bone.

A child's forearm perhaps.

Reno picked it up in his gloved hands. It weighed nothing—it might have been made of Styrofoam.

"It is. It really . . . is."

Numbly Reno groped amid the broken pottery, tossing handfuls of clumped dirt aside. More bones, small broken rib bones, a skull . . . A skull!

It was a small skull of course. Small enough to cup in the hand.

Not an animal skull but a child's skull. Reno seemed to know—*a little girl's skull.*

This was not believable! Reno's brain was struck blank, for a long moment he could not think . . . The hairs stirred at the nape of his neck and he wondered if he was being watched.

A makeshift grave about fifteen feet from the base of his house. And when had this little body been buried? Twenty years ago, ten years ago? By the look of the bones, the rotted clothing, and the broken urn, the burial hadn't been recent.

But these were not Indian bones of course. Those bones would be much older—badly broken, dim, and scarified with time.

Reno's hand shook. The small teeth were bared in a smile of sheer terror. The small jaws had fallen open, the eye sockets were disproportionately large. Of course, the skull was broken—it was not a perfect skull. Possibly fractured in the burial—struck by the murderer's shovel. The skeleton lay in pieces—had the body been dismembered? Reno was whispering to himself words meant to console—*Oh God. Help me, God. God!* As his surprise ebbed Reno began to be badly frightened. He was thinking that these might be the bones of his daughter—his first daughter; the little girl had died, her death had been accidental, but he and her mother had hurriedly buried her . . .

But no: ridiculous. This was another time, not that time.

This was another campsite. This was another part of Paraquarry Lake. This was another time in a father's life.

His daughter was alive. Somewhere in California, a living girl. He was not to blame. He had never hurt her. She would outlive him.

Laughter and raised voices from the lakeshore. Reno shaded his eyes to see—what were they doing? Were they expecting Daddy to join them?

Kneeling in the dirt. Groping and rummaging in the coarse earth. Among the broken pottery, bones, and rotted fabric faded to the no-color of dirty water, something glittered—a little necklace of glass beads.

Reno untangled it from a cluster of small bones—vertebrae? The remains of the child's neck? Hideous to think that the child skeleton might have been broken into pieces with a shovel, or an axe. An axe! To fit more readily into the urn. To hasten decomposition.

"Little girl! Poor little girl."

Reno was weak with shock, sickened. His heart pounded terribly—he didn't want to die as his father had died! He would breathe deeply, calmly. He held the glass beads to the light. Amazingly the chain was intact. A thin metallic chain, tarnished. He put the little glass-bead necklace into the pocket of his khaki shorts. Hurriedly he covered the bones with dirt, debris. Pieces of the shattered urn he picked up and tossed into the cardboard box. And the barrel staves . . . Then he thought he should remove the bones also—he should place them in the box, beneath the debris, and take the box out to the landfill this evening. Before he did anything else. Before he washed hurriedly, grabbed a beer, and joined Marlena and the children at the lakefront. He would dispose of the child's bones at the landfill.

No. They will be traced here. Not a good idea.

Frantically he covered the bones. Then more calmly, smoothing the coarse dirt over the debris. Fortunately there was a sizable hole—a gouged-out, ugly hole—that looked like a rupture in the earth. Reno would lay flagstones over the grave—he'd purchased two dozen flagstones from a garden supply store on the highway. The children could help him—it would not be difficult work once the earth was prepared. As bricks had been laid over the child's grave years ago, Reno would lay flagstones over it now. For he could not report this terrible discovery—could he? If he called the Paraquarry police, if he reported the child skeleton to county authorities, what would be the consequences?

His mind went blank—he could not think.

Could not bear the consequences. Not now, in his new life.

Numbly he was setting his work tools aside, beneath the overhang of the redwood deck. The new shovel was not so shiny now. Quickly then—shakily—climbing the steps, to wash his hands in the kitchen. A relief—he saw his family down at the shore, with the neighbors—the new wife, the children. No one would interrupt Reno washing the little glass-bead necklace in the kitchen sink, in awkward big-Daddy hands.

Gently washing the glass beads that were blue—beneath the grime a startling pellucid blue like slivers of sky. It was amazing, you might interpret it as a sign—the thin little chain hadn't broken in the earth.

Not a particle of dirt remained on the glass beads when Reno was finished washing them, drying them on a paper towel on the kitchen counter.

"Hey—look here! What's this? Who's this for?"

Reno dangled the glass-bead necklace in front of Devra. The little girl stared, blinking. It was suppertime—Daddy had cooked hamburgers on the outdoor grill on the deck—and now he pulled a little blue glass-bead necklace out of his pocket as if he'd only just discovered it.

Marlena laughed—she was delighted—for this was the sort of small surprise she appreciated.

Not for herself but for the children. In this case, for Devra. It was a good moment, a warm moment—Kevin didn't react with jealousy but seemed only curious, as Daddy said he'd found the necklace in a "secret place" and knew just who it was meant for.

Shyly Devra took the little necklace from Daddy's fingers.

"What do you say, Devra?"

"Oh Dad-dy—thank you."

Devra spoke so softly, Reno cupped his hand to his ear.

"Speak up, Devra. Daddy can't hear." Marlena helped the little girl slip the necklace over her head.

"Daddy, *thank you!*"

The little fish-mouth pursed for a quick kiss of Daddy's cheek.

Around the child's slender neck the blue glass beads glittered, gleamed. All that summer at Paraquarry Lake, Reno would marvel he'd never seen anything more beautiful.

STILL AIR

BY TERRANCE HAYES

East Liberty, Pittsburgh

(Originally published in *Pittsburgh Noir*)

The morning after Amp got killed our neighborhood was lit up with rumors. My mother and me, we barely even made the block before someone passing said, almost with a whistle, "You hear that nigga Amp got popped by some gangbangers?" Someone else said, carrying the news like a bag of bricks, "Sad what happened to that boy who got robbed last night." People who didn't know Amp or his kin said, "I know his mother." "I knew his pops." Rumors idled in the slow drag of the traffic, the rich Fox Chapellers and Aspinwallers who drove across the Allegheny River into what was our little moat of trouble: Penn Circle, the road looping East Liberty like a noose.

Lies, gossip, bullshit, half-truths spread out, carried in the school and city buses. Pompano heard it was two white guys, probably plainclothes cops, that took Amp out. Walking by with her girlfriends, Shelia said she heard gunshots and shouts. "Amp went out shooting shit up like a true thug," she cackled, pointing her finger at me like the barrel of a gun. Her girlfriends laughed like she wasn't talking about someone who'd actually been killed. I mean, Amp was dead and people was already kicking his name around like it never had any air inside it.

This is why I never wanted anybody to give me a nickname. Well, that ain't exactly true. Most people call me Demario, but I used to let Star call me Fish sometimes. My grandmother used to call me Fish. Her "little fish," even though I was taller than her by the time I was fourteen. I didn't even know Amp's real name. Maybe I heard a teacher say it when we was in preschool at Dilworth. *Anthony Tucker. Andrew Trotter.* By first grade the teachers, even Principal Paul with her thick-ass eyeglasses and that belt squeezed too tight around her gray pantsuit, called Amp "Amp." It was the only name he answered to.

I can't really say he was my friend, though, to tell you the truth. He was never really in class that much, and then he dropped out of high school junior year. Star said it was because he wanted to get a job as soon as he heard she was pregnant, but I think he'd have dropped out anyway. He spent his days on the corner behind Stanton Pharmacy. He was always there in jeans so new it looked like he hadn't even washed them yet. New sneakers, pro jerseys—people said he had a Steelers jersey for damn near every player. You'd think he'd be there waving his shit in my face or calling me a clown, but I don't think he ever even noticed me. He'd look right through me, call me *youngblood* even though we were the same age.

And once he sold me a hammer, I shit you not. It was in the book bag on my shoulders that morning. Even crazier, he sold my mother a big twenty-four-inch level. How he got her to buy it, I'll never know. But that's what he did—or what he'd been doing for the last couple of months. Word was out and people, mostly old dudes trying to make ends doing handy work or whatever in Highland Park, would buy shit from him. He'd take you around the corner to a grocery cart full of stuff. I saw he had a cordless drill and a circular saw one day. An empty paint bucket and a couple of utility knives the next. I bought the hammer for two dollars. It was big too. Practically a mallet. I doubt Amp kept what he didn't sell. He just wanted to get paid. Rumor was, he was stealing things from Home Depot, but I saw the shit. Most of it was used. None of it was useless but most of it was used.

You'd find him near Stanton Pharmacy with that dog that always followed him around, some scrawny watered-down pit bull he called Strayhorn. The dog always barked at me. It'd go to barking like it wanted to bite me in my kneecaps when I passed and wouldn't stop until I was down the street. For a long time I thought Amp was whispering *sic 'ems* in the dog's dull gray ears, but now I think he was just talking all kinds of mysterious shit to it. That's why Star liked him. Why she dumped me for him, I guess. She said he had poetry in him.

"I heard they killed the boy's dog too!" my mother said to her friend Miss Jean as we stood waiting for the 71A. This is what I tried to do every morning: walk my mother to her bus. It was the only time we got to talk since I was usually knocked out by the time she came home from work in the hospital kitchen. I know it sounds like I'm some kind of momma's boy or that I'm soft-hearted, but it was something my grandmother made me promise to do. In fact, I only started calling my mother "Mother," instead of "Marie" like I used to, after my grandmother died. I used to call my grandmother "Mother" and my mother "Marie," because when we all lived together in the East Mall projects, that's what I heard them call each other. You remember the East Mall?

The damn building used to straddle Penn Avenue, cars drove right beneath it. Now that that shit's been demolished, I almost can't believe we lived there. I mean, who puts a building right on top of the street? If Penn Circle was the moat, well, the East Mall was like one of its bankrupt castles. No, better yet, it was like an old drawbridge that couldn't be lowered. Anyway, we were on the fifth floor so I never heard any actual traffic, but when I looked out of my window, I could see the cars going and coming 24/7. I could see the houses in four neighborhoods at once: Shadyside, Friendship, East Liberty, I could see where Penn Avenue curved up the hill to Garfield.

If I had a better sense of Pittsburgh history, I could tell you all the stuff my grandmother used to tell me. I mean in detail. When the civic arena was built in the '50s, I think it was the '50s, a lot of blacks were driven from their homes in the Hill District. Some ended up in Homewood or on the North Side, some moved out this way. My grandmother could also tell you, gladly, about all the famous Pittsburgh Negroes from back in the day. Mary Lou Williams. George Benson. And Billy Eckstine, who grew up just a few blocks away in Highland Park. She would sing "Skylark," which is a song I think he must have made. If she had the record she would have played it all the time, no doubt. *Skylark, have you anything to say to me? Won't you tell me where my love can be? Is there a meadow in the mist, where someone's waiting to be kissed?* It went something like that.

"Yep. They killed the boy and his dog, I can't believe it," my mother said this time, bothering a white man with his dress shirt cuffs rolled up to his hairy forearms. He didn't have a single tattoo.

East Liberty had been plush once, that's what my grandmother always said. Decorated with big unvandalized houses. But then they dropped a lasso on the neighborhood in the late '60s. Homeowners moved across town and contracted their shabby cousins and uncles to convert their old places into shabby rental units. The living rooms were the size of bedrooms, the bedrooms the size of closets. Businesses left, the projects came. You know that little strip of Highland Park Avenue between Centre and East Liberty Boulevard that cuts through Penn Circle like the white line on a *DO NOT ENTER* sign? My grandmother hated it, but that's where everybody hung out. The blackest block for blocks. After they demolished all the projects and got a Whole Foods and Home Depot and a fancy bookstore, white people started calling it the East End. Fucking changed the name of the part of the neighborhood they wanted back. We still call it Sliberty, though.

My grandmother said the neighborhood was on white people's minds again. White people young enough to be the grown children of the people who'd left decades ago. Contractors were called to make the apartments houses again. They'd be corralling us like a bunch of Indians, my grandmother said. She said "Native Americans" but I knew what she was talking about. Reservations and Indian-giving and shit. I rarely heard her call people their real names. I once heard her ask this Mexican lady if she preferred "Latino" or "Hispanic." And sometimes, when she was being sarcastic, she might say "Negro," but I never heard her used the word "nigga." She said things like: "Look at these Negroes." The way she said it sounded worse than "nigga" to me. She was dead with cancer before she had a chance to see me and Marie living on our own for the first time.

"They ain't kill his dog, it wasn't that kind of thing," someone said behind me. It was Benny giving me the *wuzzup* nod and then flipping open his cell phone.

"People saying it was some plainclothes white cops, but I know it wasn't cops," I said to him.

"No, I heard it wasn't cops too, yo," he replied, assuming I'd heard it from the same place he had.

"Pranda said they was some old country-looking motherfuckers. Some old long-hair-and-plaid-vests shit. She was 'bout to call the cops about it, but I was like, *Them motherfuckers ain't even been caught yet! They find out you been talking to the PoPo, they coming for you.*" He shook his head while holding the cell phone to his ear. I couldn't tell if he was talking to me or the person on the other line. "I think they were drug dealers from down south," he said. "Some old meth heads or some shit. Naw, man, fuck no. I ain't going back over that bitch house until them motherfuckers get caught!" He laughed into the phone.

Marie. My mom, her bus showed up either just ahead of schedule or just behind it, depending on your perspective. It was never on time. She never said anything like, "Home right after school." She knew I'd be there. Homework done. Learning more from television than I ever did at school. She kissed me on my face the same way her mother used to kiss me and her. Then she whispered, "My little fish." I pretended I didn't hear it. Told her, "Goodbye. Be good."

I was supposed to walk to school, get there five or ten minutes before the first bell. But I was going to see Amp's people. His uncle Shag would want to know what I knew. Or I should say, if Shag heard I knew anything, I should see him before he sent someone to find me. Everybody said he was kind of crazy. He didn't sell drugs or anything, but he'd been in jail a few years for something. Nobody fucked with him.

I wanted to tell Shag what I knew, but first I went back to the alley where, the night before, I'd seen Amp running with the white men right behind him. There was a big old dumpster there. I let my hand rest for a moment on its lid before I opened it and looked inside. The smell crawled over my face. Black garbage bags, white garbage bags, little tiny plastic bags, muddy liquid rot, an old sneaker, a lawn chair—it was all sour. But there was no corpse. No dog, no tat-covered body. Amp had tattoos all along his neck and arms. On the back of each of his hands was his dad's name and *R.I.P.* in block letters. As if the man had died twice. Or as if Amp might forget him in the time it took him to look from one hand to the other. I heard he got Star's name tattooed over his heart as soon as she got pregnant, but I don't think that shit was true.

When I got to Amp's house nobody was there. I guess they could have been at the morgue. People said they'd seen the ambulance, the body bag. Everybody noticed when an ambulance or police cars blazed through the neighborhood. I pulled out my phone and looked down the block. New houses were being built along the streets I had passed walking to Amp's. They stood out like new cars in a junkyard next to the dumps around them. They were big odd-colored places. Light green, light blue, light red wood siding. They looked like empty dollhouses, even the one or two that actually had white people living inside. The *FOR SALE* signs called them *Historic District* houses and had prices with six digits. Like whoever was selling them wanted us to know we could never afford them. More old houses were being leveled and more new "historic" houses were being built on top of them. Construction workers, real estate agents, young families, white people were coming and going through the neighborhood's side streets. It wasn't a big deal. Nobody was scary or threatening or anything. Sometimes we'd wave when they passed us on the street.

And anyway, most of the guys I knew were truly minor criminals. Burglarizing the cars and backyards of Highland Park for chump change. No one who was really hardcore lasted long. Not because they got killed in a drive-by or something you see in a movie, though that happened occasionally, but because they usually got snatched by the police before they could do anything that was truly gangster. Everyone was happy when Chuck Ferry was off the streets, for example. He was just too dangerous for anybody's good. The streets were left more often than not to a mix of loiterers, dudes like Amp, and tired old men and boys who did little more than strut along the corners and back alleys. But when I passed them the morning after Amp was killed, everybody seemed nervous. I could feel it. Everybody was anxious to have the villains off the street so the neighborhood could be returned to itself.

"Heard ya boy got got," a dude said when he saw me sitting on Amp's steps. He was a few years older than me. I knew he was looking for some little bit of gossip he could take with him on down the road.

"Wasn't my boy," I said without looking him in the eye.

"Damn. That's some cold shit to say, youngblood." The dude stared until I looked at him. Then walked off with something like mild disgust flickering across on his face.

I've never been in a fight. I've never even broke up a fight. I'm the quiet dude that's always watching from the edge of the clash. Dude like me, always the first one people ask what happened. "You saw that shit, Demario? Who threw the first punch?" Usually I know, but I don't say. The conversations go faster that way. I got no problem with bystanding. One time Star sort of hinted that was my problem. I didn't think it was a put down at first.

Star. She is without a doubt the blackest person I know. Which is funny because she is also yellow as a brown banana. She didn't wear dashikis and all that Back-to-Africa shit, but she wore these white shells in her braids. And she knew everything there was to know about Malcolm X, M.L.K., W.E.B. Them famous Negroes whose names were initials. She still had an OBAMA '08 sign propped up in her bedroom window. I could see it whenever I stood across the street looking at her house. I never got, you know, to run my hands over her body and all that, but I know she had a little tattoo shaped like Africa somewhere under her clothes. She never showed it to me.

"What you doing?" I said with a flatness I meant to sound cool when I phoned her. I knew she wouldn't be at school. She was like eight months pregnant. She'd have the baby in a couple of weeks and be back to finish the last two months of our junior year at Peabody.

"I can't talk to you right now, Mario."

"Yeah, I know. I heard what happened to Amp."

She was quiet. Like she was holding her breath. I knew she'd been crying. After a long minute, she said, "I just don't know why this is happening." Damn. Then we were quiet a little while longer.

"I saw the dudes."

"Who? You saw the dudes that did it?"

"Don't worry, I'm gonna take care of it for you."

"Who'd you see?"

Amp wasn't dead yet when I saw him, I almost told her. I thought of how they had him pinned to a dumpster in an alley off Black Street. Two wiry, scruffy men. The dog, Strayhorn, was snapping at the pant leg of one of them. The guy gave the dog a frantic kick and then kicked at Amp in the same frantic way. They sort of snatched and poked at him. Amp's shirt had been ripped. He was bleeding. I could hear him saying, "I ain't got your shit. I ain't got your shit." Declaring it, really. Like he wasn't afraid. Like he was in charge even if they were the ones grabbing and shoving and delivering awkward blows. They could barely handle him. I knew they weren't gangsters. But I still did nothing.

"I'm gonna take care of this shit," I said to Star, half talking up my nerve. I didn't really know what I was saying.

"Don't go trying to be a hero, Mario."

"No, it ain't like that."

"Just go to the police."

"Police?"

"Or go by his house— Wait a minute," she said, putting me on hold.

I rubbed my brow. I thought for the first time that calling the police wasn't such a bad idea. I won't say I had plans to take care of Star, exactly. All the money I made working at the Eagle went to Marie. We lived in this little-ass apartment. My mother had been strange since her mother died. She was working long, lonely hours. She was my priority. And then Amp's death last night, well, I told you she kissed me like her mother used to: a peck on each cheek then on my nose. Shit was embarrassing. I jerked back just a bit, but then I relaxed. I knew she was sad.

The phone clicked back on: "Demario?"

"Yeah? Why you put me on hold?"

"Listen: go over to Amp's house and tell his uncle what you saw."

"I'm there now. Ain't nobody here."

"You there now? At Amp's house?"

"Yeah," I said. "Fuck is wrong with you, Star?"

"Don't cuss at me," she said.

"I want to see you."

She sighed. "No. You can't see me."

"I'm coming by."

"Just stay there. Wait for Shag . . . Come by after you speak to him."

So that's what I did. I sat on the steps with my hands in my pockets. Had there been no baby, maybe Star would have gotten back with me. Had there been no baby and no Amp, maybe she could have let herself fall for me. I ain't bad looking. Amp was just a little taller. But he had these long dreadlocks, where I just have this little nappy afro. Not even enough to braid into corn-rows. Once when we were hanging out at Highland Park, Star said she liked my Asiatic Black Man eyes. She grabbed my jaw and looked right into them like she was reading something. Fuck, I hadn't ever heard the word *Asiatic* before.

People thought my grandmother had some Asian in her. She had a pudgy face—before the cancer got at her—she had a pudgy face and these slanted eyes that made her look like she was just waking up. If you were on her bad side her face looked full of NotToBeFuckedWithness. I know dudes who just moved and nodded when they saw her walking their way. But if you were on her good side, the same face, the same expression, just seemed real mellow. She'd nod back to those brothers almost without moving her head. She really wasn't to be fucked with, though, that's for sure. She kept a fat switchblade in her bra. I got it now.

After thirty, forty minutes, Shag pulled up in an old gray sedan. He was a long skinny man. Going bald. He almost didn't have to lean over to roll down the passenger-side window.

"Who are you, boy? What you want?" He didn't seem all that fucked up over anything. Just suspicious as anyone who finds somebody on his porch in the middle of the day.

"I'm Demario. I used to go to school with your nephew Amp."

Shag didn't exit the car. I started thinking he wasn't as calm as I first thought. Seemed like he was figuring something out. Maybe he thought I had a gun or something. All I had was a few books and a hammer in my backpack. And my grandmother's blade. I had that in my back pocket.

"I saw what happened to him last night," I told Shag.

People were saying the dudes who'd killed Amp hadn't been caught, that was true for the moment. People were saying some sort of drug shit was in-volved, it didn't seem like that to me. I'd seen them but the stupid dog was the only one to notice me. He barked with the gray hair up on his neck. But it wasn't his usual wild, territorial bark. There was urgency in it. Fear. I probably imagined it. The whole thing couldn't have taken more than a minute or two.

I cleared my throat. "I think it was a couple of dudes who been renovating those houses on Euclid."

That was my theory. It should have felt good to tell him, but it didn't.

"Come here," he said, waving me to the car window. He glanced up and down the street in a way that made me nervous. But what else could I do? Couldn't run with him right there looking at me. I walked over to him with my hand stuffed in my pockets.

"What they do with him? You tell the cops?"

"I don't know what they did. That's why I came over. See how he doing." That was mostly true. I'd come hoping Amp was alive, hoping the rumors were lies. But really, I just didn't want Shag to ask why I hadn't helped his nephew survive. I'd seen Amp fighting back. The dog was barking at me. Like it was saying, *They're gonna kill him, they're gonna kill him, do something!* Amp broke free, running off into the darkness of the alley with the men behind him. Maybe his dog barked at me just a beat longer before it realized I wasn't going to do anything. It turned, running after them. I didn't follow.

"Well, he ain't here . . ." Shag said, getting out of the car.

"Okay." I could see it in his face, he was lying to see if I'd know he was lying.

"You should come in with me and wait for him, he'll be back soon probably," Shag said.

"No, I got some errands to run. I might come back by later."

Shag chuckled slightly and said, half to himself, "Nigga talking about *errands*." He was jingling his keys.

"I'll come back later."

"Man, come on in the house," he said. Then, a little bit softer: "I got something I want you to do."

"Amp ain't alive is he?" I said. Blurted.

"No, he ain't," he sighed. "He ain't."

He opened the door and I followed him up a flight of stairs to the second floor where he and Amp and Amp's mother lived. I don't know where she was. Bawling at the East Liberty precinct. Picking out caskets. I thought the air smelled funny. Damp, salty with grief maybe. She might have been locked in her bedroom dreaming her son was still alive. We moved down a tiny hallway to a tiny den. I recognized Amp in the wood-colored face of a boy on an end table. His first or second grade school portrait. His grin was so wide it showed every one of his teeth. He had a small gold stud in his ear. I remembered he'd been the first of the boys our age to get pierced. Instead of the white-collared shirts we were supposed to wear for our school uniforms at Dilworth, he wore a loose white T-shirt.

"Amp did that shit," Shag told me, pointing to where the thick blue carpet was yanked back revealing a perfect hardwood floor beneath it. "Told his momma he was going to fix this place up with his tools." Shag sat down on a plaid sofa that took up nearly all the space in the room. I saw the edge of a bedsheet spilling beneath it and figured it was where he slept.

"You want to smoke," he asked, pulling out a sandwich bag full of weed. He was settling in, I hadn't sat down yet.

"No," I said. Though I wanted to get high, really. What I really wanted was something to lift me from the ground. Up through the roof, up on above Penn Circle sitting like a bull's-eye in the middle of our neighborhood. Up on out of Pittsburgh. But I told him no and watched him roll a blunt.

"I told that nigga he was gone get jacked up for stealing them boys' shit," Shag said. He told me to sit down, but he didn't seem to care when I didn't. "I told his momma too. His room's full of their shit. Some dusty safety goggles, screwdrivers, dirty work gloves, dirty work boots, a fucking sliding T-bevel. You know what a T-bevel is? Amp didn't know either, but he got one in there."

Shag's phone buzzed on his hip but he didn't answer it.

"So I need you to do me a favor, youngblood. We need to ride over to where them motherfuckers are working and I need you to point them out to me."

"I didn't get a good look at them."

"That's all right. I want you to try. Just point in the right direction, know what I mean?"

He reached between the cushions of the sofa. I saw the butt of the gun just as his phone started buzzing again. This time he answered it. He smiled at me, then stood and walked from the room.

I sat down on the couch and touched the gun handle where it stuck out like the horn of an animal. I thought for a second about taking it and the bag of weed. Instead I got up, tipped to the hall, and listened. I could see into Amp's room. There were a pair of sneakers and a dog leash on his bed.

"No, I'll probably head to Newark. Atlanta. Somewhere with more black people than there are here." I could hear Shag taking a piss in the bathroom while he talked. "You ain't good for shit, you know that, right? No. No, nigga, just stay there. I got somebody here gonna ride over there with me."

I thought again of the gun. Shag would want me to drive while he shot from the window. Or worse, he'd drive while he made me shoot. Either way, what I'd seen meant I'd have to be a part of what was going to happen.

I tried to be quiet running out of the house. I kept thinking I could hear a dog barking behind me. Amp's dog. The ghost of his dog. I didn't look back until I was panting around the corner. I was a few blocks from Star's house. But I turned toward Euclid where the new houses were being built.

There was a young white woman working in her yard. Planting flowers or something. Trimming the hedges. She glanced at me, then stared as I walked up the steps of the big empty house standing next to hers. There was no one there. I rattled the doorknob looking through its window into the wide bare rooms. I glanced back at the white woman who was pulling off her gardening gloves and still watching me. I pulled the hammer Amp sold me from my book bag and used it to smash the window on the door. The woman rushed inside her house. I reached through and tried to grab the door latch, but couldn't. I walked across the porch and hammered at the pane of the living room window until it broke open like a mouth with its teeth knocked out. It was loud as hell. I didn't fucking care. I guess I got cut. My blood dripping on the shiny hardwood floors almost looked like a trail of pennies.

I wanted to carve Amp's name somewhere no one would find it. Not for another fifty years or so. Not until the house had been lived in by rich white people, then rented out to poor black people, then renovated for white people again. I wanted someone in the future to strip back the sheetrock and find Amp's named carved into a beam. There was nowhere to carve it, though. Nowhere discreet. The kitchen didn't have cabinets yet. The bathroom on the first floor had no toilet. Wires hung from the ceilings and walls. Just an empty house. My grandmother said—she used to say this all the time—that people, black or white, would always fight over dirt but nobody could ever really own it. She said the land could only belong to the land. The rivers belonged to the rivers. The air was still air no matter who claimed to own it.

On the second floor I stood at a window in the master bedroom. Brick and sky, metal and wood, concrete and dirt, you already know what I saw out there: all the shit that gives air something to lean on. I knew the cops were on their way. And I'd have to do something. Say something. I thought I could already hear the sirens. I thought I could hear dogs trying to match the sound. I sat in the middle of the floor with the hammer in my lap. I had blood on my shirt and pants. I wasn't crying. I was barely breathing.

When I dialed Star's number, the dial tones echoed around me. We'd talked on the phone, but I hadn't seen her in weeks. Wasn't that I was afraid of Amp or his fucking dog. I just kept thinking she'd ask me over eventually. Soon as Amp fucked up, I figured she'd want to see me. And really, when I heard he was dead, I thought it was a reason to see her. Pregnant or not. I was going to be there for her. I was going to be with her.

Star didn't speak a word when she answered. "Hey," I said after a few seconds. I said it just as I'd said it to my mother when we came home from my grandmother's funeral. Sort of like it was a question. Softly. Slowly. It embarrassed me the same way when I said it then. "Hey."

WHITE TRASH

BY JEROME CHARYN

Claremont/Concourse, The Bronx

(Originally published in *Bronx Noir*)

P rudence had escaped from the women's farm in Milledgeville and gone
on a crime spree. She murdered six men and a woman, robbed nine
McDonald's and seven Home Depots in different states. She wore a
neckerchief gathered under her eyes and carried a silver Colt that was more
like an heirloom than a good, reliable gun. The Colt had exploded in her face
during one of the robberies at McDonald's, but she still managed to collect
the cash, and her own willfulness wouldn't allow her to get a new gun.

She wasn't willful about one thing: she never used a partner, male or female. Women were more reliable than men; they wouldn't steal your money
and expect you to perform sexual feats with their friends. But women thieves
could be just as annoying. She'd had her fill of them at the farm, where they
read her diary and borrowed her books. Pru didn't appreciate big fat fingers
touching her personal library. Readers were like pilgrims who had to go on
their own pilgrimage. Pru was a pilgrim, or at least that's what she imagined.
She read from morning to night whenever she wasn't out foraging for hard
cash. One of her foster mothers had been a relentless reader, and Prudence
had gone right through her shelves, book after book: biographies, Bibles,
novels, a book on building terrariums, a history of photography, a history of
dance, and Leonard Maltin's *Movie Guide*, which she liked the best, because
she could read the little encapsulated portraits of films without having to
bother about the films themselves. But she lost her library when she broke out
of jail, and it bothered her to live without books.

The cops had caught on to her tactics, and her picture was nailed to the
wall inside post offices, supermarkets, and convenience stores; she might have
been trapped in a Home Depot outside Savannah if she hadn't noticed a state
trooper fidgeting with his hat while he stared at her face on the wall.

Pru had to disappear or she wouldn't survive her next excursion to Home
Depot or McDonald's. And no book could help her now. Travel guides
couldn't map out some no-man's land where she might be safe. But Emma

Mae, her cellmate at Milledgeville, had told her about the Bronx, a place where the cops never patrolled McDonald's. Besides, she hadn't murdered a single soul within five hundred miles of Manhattan or the Bronx. Pru wasn't a mad dog, as the bulletins labeled her. She had to shoot the night manager at McDonald's, because that would paralyze the customers and discourage anyone from coming after her.

She got on a Greyhound wearing eyeglasses and a man's lumber jacket after cutting her hair in the mirror of a public toilet. She'd been on the run for two months. Crime wasn't much of a business. Murdering people, and she still had to live from hand to mouth.

She couldn't remember how she landed in the Bronx. She walked up the stairs of a subway station, saw a synagogue that had been transformed into a Pentecostal church, then a building with a mural on its back wall picturing a paradise with crocodiles, palm trees, and a little girl. The Bronx was filled with Latinas and burly black men, Emma Mae had told her; the only whites who lived there were "trash"—outcasts and country people who had to relocate. Pru could hide among them, practically invisible in a casbah that no one cared about.

Emma Mae had given her an address, a street called Marcy Place, where the cousin of a cousin lived, a preacher who played the tambourine and bilked white trash, like Prudence and Emma. He was right at the door when Pru arrived, an anemic-looking man dressed in black, with a skunk's white streak in his hair, though he didn't have a skunk's eyes; his were clear as pale green crystals and burned right into Pru. She was hypnotized without his having to say a single syllable. He laughed at her disguise, and that laughter seemed to break the spell.

"Prudence Miller," he said, "are you a man or a girl?"

His voice was reedy, much less potent than his eyes.

Emma Mae must have told him about her pilgrimage to the Bronx. But Pru still didn't understand what it meant to be the cousin of a cousin. His name was Omar Kaplan. It must have been the alias of an alias, since Omar couldn't be a Christian name. She'd heard all about Omar Khayyam, the Persian philosopher and poet who was responsible for the *Rubaiyat*, the longest love poem in history, though she hadn't read a line. And this Omar must have been a philosopher as well as a fraud—his apartment, which faced a brick wall, was lined with books. He had all the old Modern Library classics, like *Anna Karenina* and *The Brothers Karamazov*, books that Pru had discovered in secondhand shops in towns that had a college campus.

"You'll stay away from McDonald's," he said in that reedy voice of his, "and you'd better not have a gun."

"Then how will I earn my keep, Mr. Omar Kaplan? I'm down to my last dollar."

"Consider this a religious retreat, or a rest cure, but no guns. I'll stake you to whatever you need."

Pru laughed bitterly, but kept that laugh locked inside her throat. Omar Kaplan intended to turn her into a slave, to write his own *Rubaiyat* on the softest parts of her flesh. She waited for him to pounce. He didn't touch her or steal her gun. She slept with the silver Colt under her pillow, on a cot near the kitchen, while Omar had the bedroom all to himself. It was dark as a cave. He'd emerge from the bedroom, dressed in black, like some Satan with piercing green eyes, prepared to soft-soap whatever white trash had wandered into the Bronx. He'd leave the apartment at seven in the morning and wouldn't return before nine at night. But there was always food in the fridge, fancier food than she'd ever had: salmon cutlets, Belgian beer, artichokes, strawberries from Israel, a small wheel of Swiss cheese with blue numbers stamped on the rind.

He was much more talkative after he returned from one of his pilferings. He'd switch off all the lamps and light a candle, and they'd have salmon cutlets together, drink Belgian beer. He'd rattle his tambourine from time to time, sing Christian songs. It could have been the dark beer that greased his tongue.

"Prudence, did you ever feel any remorse after killing those night managers?"

"None that I know of," she said.

"Their faces don't come back to haunt you in your dreams?"

"I never dream," she said.

"Do you ever consider all the orphans and widows you made?"

"I'm an orphan," she said, "and maybe I just widened the franchise."

"Pru the orphan-maker."

"Something like that," she said.

"Would you light a candle with me for their lost souls?"

She didn't care. She lit the candle, while Satan crinkled his eyes and mumbled something. Then he marched into his bedroom and closed the door. It galled her. She'd have felt more comfortable if he'd tried to undress her. She might have slept with Satan, left marks on his neck.

She would take long walks in the Bronx, with her silver gun. She sought replicas of herself, wanderers with pink skin. But she found Latinas with baby carriages, old black women outside a beauty parlor, black and Latino men on a basketball court. She wasn't going to wear a neckerchief mask and rob men and boys playing ball.

The corner she liked best was at Sheridan Avenue and East 169th, because it was a valley with hills on three sides, with bodegas and other crumbling little stores, a barbershop without a barber, apartment houses with broken courtyards and rotting steel gates. The Bronx *was* a casbah, like Emma Mae had said, and Pru could explore the hills that rose up around her, that seemed to give her some sort of protective shield. She could forget about Satan and silver guns.

She returned to Marcy Place. It was long after nine, and Omar Kaplan hadn't come home. She decided to set the table, prepare a meal of strawberries, Swiss cheese, and Belgian beer. She lit a candle, waiting for Omar. She grew restless, decided to read a book. She swiped *Sister Carrie* off the shelves—a folded slip of paper fell out, some kind of impromptu bookmark. But this bookmark had her face on it, and a list of her crimes. It had a black banner on top. *WANTED DEAD OR ALIVE.* Like the title of a macabre song. There were words scribbled near the bottom. *Dangerous and demented.* Then scribbles in another hand. *A real prize package. McDonald's ought to give us a thousand free Egg McMuffins for this fucking lady.* Then a signature that could have been a camel's hump. The letters on that hump spelled O-M-A-R.

She shouldn't have stayed another minute. But she had to tease out the logic of it all. Emma Mae had given her a Judas kiss, sold her to some supercop. Why hadn't Satan arrested her the second she'd opened the door? He was toying with her like an animal trainer who would point her toward McDonald's, where other supercops were waiting with closed-circuit television cameras. They meant to film her at the scene of the crime, so she could act out some unholy procession that would reappear on the six o'clock news.

A key turned in the lock. Pru clutched her silver Colt. Omar appeared in dark glasses that hid his eyes. He wasn't dressed like a lowlife preacher man. He wore a silk tie and a herringbone suit. He wasn't even startled to see a gun in his face. He smiled and wouldn't beg her not to shoot. It should have been easy. He couldn't put a spell on her without his pale green eyes.

"White trash," she said. "Is Emma Mae your sister?"

"I have a lot of sisters," he said, still smiling.

"And you're a supercop and a smarty-pants."

"Me? I'm the lowest of the low. A freelancer tied to ten different agencies, an undercover kid banished to the Bronx. Why didn't you run? I gave you a chance. I left notes for you in half my books, a hundred fucking clues."

"Yeah, I'm Miss Egg McMuffin. I do McDonald's. And I have no place to run to. Preacher man, play your tambourine and sing your last song."

She caught a glimpse of the snubnosed gun that rose out of a holster she hadn't seen. She didn't even hear the shot. She felt a thump in her chest and she flew against the wall with blood in her eyes. And that's when she had a vision of the night managers behind all the blood. Six men and a woman wearing McDonald's bibs, though she hadn't remembered them wearing those. They had eye sockets without the liquid complication of eyes themselves. Pru was still implacable toward the managers. She would have shot them all over again. But she did sigh once before the night managers disappeared and she fell into Omar Kaplan's arms like a sleepy child.

PART II

AMERICAN VALUES

ALICE FANTASTIC

BY MAGGIE ESTEP

Aqueduct Racetrack, Queens

(Originally published in *Queens Noir*)

I'd been trying to get rid of the big oaf for seventeen weeks but he just kept coming around. He'd ring the bell and I'd look out the window and see him standing on the stoop looking like a kicked puppy. What I needed with another kicked puppy I couldn't tell you, since I'd taken in a little white mutt with tan spots that my cousin Jeremy had found knocked up and wandering a trailer park in Kentucky. Cousin Jeremy couldn't keep the dog so he called me up and somehow got me to take the animal in. After making the vet give her an abortion and a rabies shot, Jeremy found the dog a ride up from Kentucky with some freak friend of his who routinely drives between Kentucky and Queens transporting cheap cigarettes. The freak friend pulled his van up outside my house one night just before midnight and the dog came out of the van reeking of cigarettes and blinking up at me, completely confused and kicked-looking. Not that I think the freak friend of Cousin Jeremy's actually kicked her. But the point is, I already had a kicked puppy. What did I need with a guy looking like one?

I didn't need him. But he'd ring the bell and I'd let him in, and, even if I was wearing my dead father's filthy bathrobe and I hadn't showered in five days, he'd tell me, *You look fantastic, Alice.* I knew he actually meant it, that he saw something fantastic in my limp brown hair and puffy face and the zits I'd started getting suddenly at age thirty-six. It was embarrassing. The zits, the fact that I was letting this big oaf come over to nuzzle at my unbathed flesh, the little dog who'd sit at the edge of the bed watching as me and Clayton, the big oaf, went at it.

My life was a shambles. So I vowed to end it with Clayton. I vowed it on a Tuesday at seven a.m. after waking up with an unusual sense of clarity. I opened my eyes to find thin winter sunlight sifting in the windows of the house my dead father left me. Candy, the trailer trash dog, was sitting at the edge of the bed, politely waiting for me to wake up because that's the thing with strays, they're so grateful to have been taken in that they defer to your schedule and needs. So, Candy was at the edge of the bed and sun was coming in the windows of my dead father's place on 47th Road in the borough of Queens in New York City. And I felt clear-headed. Who knows why. I just did. And I felt I needed to get my act together. Shower more frequently. Stop smoking so much. Get back to yoga and kickboxing. Stop burning through my modest profits as a modest gambler. Revitalize myself. And the first order of business was to get rid of the big oaf, Clayton. Who ever heard of a guy named Clayton who isn't ninety-seven years old, anyway?

I got into the shower and scrubbed myself raw, then shampooed my disgusting oily head. I took clean clothes out of the closet instead of foraging through the huge pile in the hamper the way I'd been doing for weeks. I put on black jeans and a fuzzy green sweater. I glanced at myself in the mirror. My semi-dry hair looked okay and my facial puffiness had gone down. Even my zits weren't so visible. I looked vaguely alive.

I took my coat off the hook, put Candy's leash on, and headed out for a walk along the East River, near the condo high-rises that look over into Manhattan. My dead father loved Long Island City. He moved here in the 1980s, when it was almost entirely industrial, to shack up with some drunken harlot, right after my mom kicked him out. Long after the harlot had dumped my father—all women dumped him all the time—he'd stayed on in the neighborhood, eventually buying a tiny two-story wood frame house that he left to me, his lone child, when the cancer got him last year at age fifty-nine. I like the neighborhood fine. It's quiet and there are places to buy tacos.

"Looking good, *mami*," said some Spanish guy as Candy and I walked past the gas station.

I never understand that *mami* thing. It sounds like they're saying *mommy*. I know they mean *hot mama* and, in their minds, it's a compliment, but it still strikes me as repulsive.

I ignored the guy.

As Candy sniffed and pissed and tried to eat garbage off the pavement, I smoked a few Marlboros and stared across at midtown Manhattan. It looked graceful from this distance.

The air was so cold it almost seemed clean and I started thinking on how I would rid myself of Clayton. I'd tried so many times. Had gotten him to agree not to call me anymore. But then, not two days would go by and he'd ring the bell. And I'd let him in. He'd look at me with those huge stupid brown eyes and tell me how great I looked. *Alice, you're fantastic*, he'd told me so many times I started thinking of myself as Alice Fantastic, only there really wouldn't be anything fantastic about me until I got rid of Clayton. When he would finally shut up about my fantasticness, I'd start in on the *This isn't going to work for me anymore, Clayton* refrain I had been trotting out for seventeen weeks. Then he'd look wounded and his arms would hang so long at his sides that I'd have to touch him, and once I touched him, we'd make a beeline for the bed, and the sex was pretty good, the way it can be with someone you are physically attracted to in spite of or because of a lack of anything at all in common. And the sex being good would make me entertain the idea of instating him on some sort of permanent basis, and I guess that was my mistake. He'd see that little idea in my eye and latch onto it and have *feelings*, and his *feelings* would make him a prodigious lover, and I'd become so strung out on sex chemicals I would dopily say *Sure* when he'd ask to spend the night, and then again dopily say *Sure* the next morning when he'd ask if he could call me later.

But enough is enough. I don't want Clayton convincing himself we're going to be an everlasting item growing old together.

Right now Clayton lives in a parking lot. In his van. This I discovered when, that first night, after I picked him up in the taco place and strolled with him near the water, enjoying his simplicity and his long, loping gait, I brought him home and sucked his cock in the entrance hall and asked him to fuck me from behind in the kitchen, and then led him to the bedroom where we lay quiet for a little while until he was hard again, at which point I put on a pair of tights and asked him to rip out the crotch and fuck me through the hole. After all that, just when I was thinking up a polite way of asking him to leave, he propped himself up on his elbow and told me how much he liked me: "I really like you. I mean, I *really* like you," looking at me with those eyes big as moons, and even though I just wanted to read a book and go to sleep, I didn't have the heart to kick him out.

All that night, he babbled at me, telling me his woes, how his mother has Alzheimer's and his father is in prison for forgery and his wife left him for a plumber and he's been fired from his job at a cabinet-making shop and is living in his van in a parking lot and showering at the Y.

"I've got to get out of Queens soon," he said.

"And go where?"

"Florida. I don't like the cold much. Gets in my bones."

"Yeah. Florida," I said. I'd been there. To Gulfstream Park, Calder Race Course, and Tampa Bay Downs. I didn't tell him that though. I just said, *Yeah, Florida*, like I wasn't opposed to Florida, though why I would let him think I have any fondness for Florida, this leading him to possibly speculate that I'd want to go live there with him, I don't know. I guess I wanted to be kind to him.

"Just a trailer is fine. I like trailers," Clayton said.

"Right," I said. And then I feigned sleep.

That was seventeen weeks ago. And I still haven't gotten rid of him.

Candy and I walked for the better part of an hour and then headed home, passing back by the gas station where the moron felt the need to repeat, *Looking good, mommy*, and I actually stopped walking and stared at him and tried to think of words to explain exactly how repulsive it is to be called *mommy* and how it makes me picture him fucking his own mother, who is doubtless a matronly Dominican woman with endless folds of ancient flesh, but I couldn't find the words and the guy was starting to grin, possibly thinking I was actually turned on by him, so I kept walking.

Once back inside my place, I gave Candy the leftovers from my previous night's dinner and sat down at the kitchen table with my computer, my *Daily Racing Form*, and my notebooks. I got to work on the next day's entries at Aqueduct. No matter how much I planned to change my life in the coming weeks, I still had to work. It wasn't much of a card, even for a Wednesday in February, so I figured I wouldn't be pushing a lot of money through the windows. But I would watch. I would take notes. I would listen. I would enjoy my work. I always do.

Several hours passed and I felt stirrings of hunger and glanced inside my fridge. Some lifeless lettuce, a few ounces of orange juice, and one egg. I considered boiling the egg, as there are days when there's nothing I love more than a hard-boiled egg, but I decided this wasn't one of those days. I would have to go to the taco place for take-out. I attached Candy's leash to her collar and threw my coat on and was heading to the door when the phone rang. I picked it up.

"Hi, Alice," came Clayton's low voice.

I groaned.

"What's the matter? You in pain?"

"Sort of."

"What do you mean? What hurts? I'll be right there."

"No, no, Clayton, don't. My pain is that you won't take *No* for an answer."

"No about what?"

"No about our continuing on like this."

There was dead silence.

"Where are you?" I asked.

"In the parking lot."

"Clayton," I said, "I know you think you're a nice guy, but there's nothing nice about coming around when I've repeatedly asked you not to. It's borderline stalking."

More silence.

"I need my peace and quiet."

After several moments: "You don't like the way I touch you anymore?"

"There's more to life than touching."

"Uh," said Clayton. "I wouldn't know since you won't ever let me do anything with you other than come over and fuck you."

Clayton had never said *fuck* before. Clayton had been raised in some sort of religious household. He wasn't religious himself, but he was reserved about cursing.

"My life is nothing. Clayton. I go to the racetrack. I make my bets and take my notes. I talk to some of the other horseplayers. I go home and cook dinner or I go to the taco place. I walk my dog. That's it. There's nothing to my life, Clayton, nothing to see."

"So let me come with you."

"Come with me where?"

"To the racetrack."

"I'm asking you to never call me again and get out of my life. Why would I want to take you to the racetrack?"

"Just let me see a little piece of your life. I deserve it. Think of it as alimony."

I couldn't see why I should do anything for him. But I agreed anyway. At least it got him off the phone.

I took the dog out to the taco place. Came home and ate my dinner, giving half to the dog.

I'd told Clayton to meet me the next morning at eleven and we'd take the subway. He offered to drive but I didn't trust that monstrous van of his not to break down en route. He rang the bell and I came downstairs to find him looking full of hope. Like seeing each other in daylight hours meant marriage and babies were imminent. Not that he'd asked for anything like that but he was that kind of guy, the kind of guy I seem to attract all too often, the want-to-snuggle-up-and-breed kind of guy. There are allegedly millions of women out there looking for these guys so I'm not sure why they all come knocking on my door. I guess they like a challenge. That's why they're men.

"Hi, Alice," he beamed, "you look fantastic."

"Thanks," I said. I *had* pulled myself together, was wearing a tight black knee-length skirt and a soft black sweater that showed some shoulder—if I ever took my coat off, which I wasn't planning to do as I figured any glimpsing of my flesh might give Clayton ideas.

"I'm just doing this 'cause you asked," I said as we started walking to the G train, "but you have to realize this is my job and you can't interfere or ask a lot of questions." I was staring straight ahead so I didn't have to see any indications of hurt in his eyes, because this was one of his ruses, the hurt look, the kicked puppy look, and I was damn well sick of it.

"Right," said Clayton.

We went down into the station and waited forever, as one invariably does for the G train, and all the while Clayton stared at me so hard I was pretty sure he would turn me to stone.

Eventually, the train came and got us to the Hoyt-Schermerhorn stop in Brooklyn where we switched to the far more efficient A train. I felt relief at being on my way to Aqueduct. Not many people truly love Aqueduct, but I do. Belmont is gorgeous and spacious and Saratoga is grand if you can stand the crowds, but I love Aqueduct. Aqueduct is down-on-their-luck trainers slumping in the benches, degenerates, droolcases, and drunks swapping tips, and a few seasoned pro gamblers quietly going about their business. My kind of place.

Thirty minutes later, the train sighed into the stop at Aqueduct and we got off, us and a bunch of hunched middle-aged white men, a few slightly younger Rasta guys, and one well-dressed suit-type guy who was an owner or wanted to pretend to be one.

"Oh, it's nice," Clayton lied as we emerged from the little tunnel under the train tracks.

The structure looks like the set for a 1970s zombie movie, with its faded grim colors and the airplanes headed for JFK flying so low you're sure they're going to land on a horse.

"We'll go up to the restaurant, have some omelettes," I told him once we were inside the clubhouse. "The coffee sucks but the omelettes are fine."

"Okay," said Clayton.

We rode the escalator to the top, and at the big glass doors to the Equestris Restaurant, Manny, the maître d', greeted me and gave us a table with a great view of the finish line.

Then Clayton started in with the questions. He'd never been a big question guy, wasn't a very verbal guy period, but suddenly he wanted to know the history of Aqueduct and my history with Aqueduct and what else I'd ever done for a living and what my family thought of my being a professional gambler, etc., etc.

"I told you, I have to work. No twenty questions. Here's a *Racing Form,*" I said, handing him the extra copy I'd printed out. "Now study that and let me think."

The poor guy stared at the *Form* but obviously had no idea how to read it. Sometimes I forget that people don't know these things. Seems like I always knew, what with coming here when I was a kid when Cousin Jeremy still lived in Queens and babysat me on days when my father was off on a construction job. I'd been betting since the age of nine and had been reasonably crafty about money-management and risk-taking since day one. I had turned a profit that first time when Jeremy had placed bets for me, and though I'd had plenty of painful losing days since, for the most part I scraped by. I'd briefly had a job as a substitute teacher after graduating from Hunter College, but I hated it. So I gambled and supplemented my modest profits with income from the garden apartment in my house. Not many people last more than a few years gambling for a living but, for whatever reason, I have. Mostly because I can't stand the thought of doing anything else.

I was just about to take pity on Clayton and show him how to read the *Form* when Big Fred appeared and sat down at one of the extra chairs at our table.

"You see this piece of shit Pletcher's running in the fifth race?" Fred wanted to know. Big Fred, who weighs 110 pounds tops, isn't one for pleasantries. He had no interest in being introduced to Clayton, probably hadn't even noticed I was with someone; he just wanted confirmation that the Todd Pletcher–trained colt in the fifth race was a piece of shit in spite of having cost $2.4 million at the Keeneland yearling sale and having won all three races he'd run in.

"Yeah," I said, nodding gravely. "He'll be 1-9."

"He's a flea," said Fred.

"Yeah. Well. I wouldn't throw him out on a Pick 6 ticket."

"I'm throwing him out."

"Okay," I said.

"He hasn't faced shit and he's never gone two turns. And there's that nice little horse of Nick's that's a closer."

"Right," I said.

"I'm using Nick's horse. Singling him."

"I wouldn't throw out the Pletcher horse."

"Fuck him," said Fred, getting up and storming off to the other end of the place, where I saw him take a seat with some guys from the *Daily Racing Form*.

"Friend of yours?" asked Clayton.

I nodded. "Big Fred. He's a good guy."

"He is?"

"Sure."

I could tell Clayton wanted to go somewhere with that one. Wanted to ask why I thought some strange little guy who just sat down and started cursing out horses was a good guy. Another reason Clayton had to be gotten rid of.

One of the waiters came and took our omelette order. Since I'd mapped out most of my bets, I took ten minutes and gave Clayton a cursory introduction to reading horses' past performances. I was leaning in close, my finger tracing one of the horse's running lines, when Clayton kissed my ear.

"I love you, Alice," he said.

"Jesus, Clayton," I said. "What the fuck?"

Clayton looked like a kicked puppy.

"I brought you here because I thought it'd be a nice way to spend our last day together but, fuck me, why do you have to get ridiculous?"

"I don't want it to end. You're all I've got."

"You don't have me."

"What do you mean?"

"Clayton, there's no future. *No mas*," I said.

"No who?"

"*No mas*," I repeated. "No more. Spanish."

"Are you Spanish?"

"No, Clayton, I'm not Spanish. Shit, will you let me fucking work?"

"Everything okay over here?"

I looked up and saw Vito looming over the table. Vito is a stocky, hairy man who is some kind of low-level mafioso or mafioso-wannabe who owns a few cheap horses and fancies himself a gifted horseplayer.

"Everything's fine," I said, scowling at Vito. Much as Clayton was pissing me off, it wasn't any of Vito's business. But that's the thing with these Vito-type guys at the track: What with my being a presentable woman under the age of eighty, a real rarity at Aqueduct, these guys get all protective of me. It might have been vaguely heartwarming if Vito wasn't so smarmy.

Vito furrowed his monobrow. He was sweating profusely even though it was cool inside the restaurant.

"I'm Vito," he said, aggressively extending his hand to Clayton, "and you are . . . ?"

"Clayton," said my soon-to-be-ex paramour, tentatively shaking Vito's oily paw.

"We all look out for Alice around here," Vito said.

Go fuck yourself, Vito, I thought, but didn't say. There might be a time when I needed him for something.

"Oh," said Clayton, confused, "that's good. I look out for her too."

Vito narrowed his already small eyes, looked from me to Clayton and back, then turned on his heels.

"See ya, Vito," I said as the tubby man headed out of the restaurant, presumably going down to the paddock-viewing area to volubly express his opinions about the contestants in the first race.

A few races passed. I made a nice little score on a mare shipping in from Philadelphia Park. She was trained by some obscure woman trainer, ridden by some obscure apprentice jockey, and had only ever raced at Philadelphia Park, so, in spite of a nice batch of past performances, she was being ignored on the tote board and went off at 14-1. I had $200 on her to win and wheeled her on top of all the logical horses in an exacta. I made out nicely and that put me slightly at ease and reduced some of the Clayton-induced aggravation that had gotten so severe I hadn't been able to eat my omelette and had started fantasizing about asking Vito to take Clayton out. Not *Take Him Out* take him out, I didn't want the guy dead or anything, just put a scare into him. But that would have entailed asking a favor of Vito and I had no interest in establishing that kind of dynamic with that kind of guy.

The fifth race came and I watched with interest to see how the colt Big Fred liked fared. The Todd Pletcher–trained horse Fred hated, who did in fact go off at 1-9, broke alertly from the six hole and tucked nicely just off the pace that was being set by a longshot with early speed. Gang of Seven, the horse Big Fred liked, was at the back of the pack, biding his time. With a quarter of a mile to go, Gang of Seven started making his move four wide, picking off his opponents until he was within spitting distance of the Pletcher horse. Gang of Seven and the Pletcher trainee dueled to the wire and both appeared to get their noses there at the same time.

"Too close to call," said the track announcer. A few minutes later, the photo was posted and the Pletcher horse had beat Big Fred's by a whisker.

"I'm a fucking idiot!" I heard Fred cry out from four tables away. I saw him get up and storm out of the restaurant, probably heading to the back patio to chain-smoke and make phone calls to twenty of his closest horseplaying friends, announcing his own idiocy.

"Guy's got a problem," Clayton said.

"No he doesn't," I replied, aggravated. While it was true that Big Fred had a little trouble with anger management, he was, at heart, a very decent human being.

I got up and walked away, leaving Clayton to stare after me with those dinner plate–sized eyes.

I went down to the paddock, hoping that Clayton wouldn't follow me. I saw Vito there staring out the big viewing window, his huge belly pressing against the glass. As I went to find a spot as far away from Vito as possible, I craned my neck just to check that Clayton hadn't followed me. He had. I saw him lumbering around near the betting windows, looking left and right. He'd find me at any minute.

So I did something a little crazy.

"Vito," I said, coming up behind him.

"Huh?" He turned around.

"Favor?" I asked.

His tiny black eyes glittered. "Anything, baby," he purred.

I already regretted what I was doing. "Can you scare that guy I was sitting with? Just make him a little nervous? Make him go home?"

Vito's tiny eyes got bigger, like someone had just dangled a bleeding hunk of filet mignon in front of him.

"You serious?" He stood closer to me.

I had a moment's hesitation. Then thought of Clayton's love pronouncements. "Yeah."

"Sure. Where is he?"

I glanced back and didn't see Clayton. "Somewhere around here, let's look."

Vito lumbered at my side. We searched all around the betting windows of the ground floor, but no Clayton. Then I glanced outside and spotted him standing near an empty bench, hunched and cold and lost-looking under the dove-gray sky.

"There," I said.

"You got it, baby," said Vito. Without another word, he marched outside. I saw him accost Clayton. I saw Clayton tilt his head left and right like a confused dog would. I thought of Candy. Later this afternoon, I'd go home to her and just maybe, thanks to Vito, I wouldn't have to worry about the big oaf turning up with his big eyes and his inane declarations. Me and Candy could have some peace and quiet.

Now Clayton and Vito had come back inside and were walking together. They passed not far from where I was standing. Where was Vito taking him? I figured he'd just say a few choice words and that would be that. But they seemed to be going somewhere.

I followed them at a slight distance. I didn't really care if Clayton saw me at this point. They went down the escalator and out the front door. Vito was only wearing a thin button-down shirt but he didn't seem to register the bite of the February air. Clayton pulled his coat up around his ears.

They headed over to the subway platform. I saw Clayton pull out his Me-troCard and go through the turnstile. Then he handed his card back to Vito, who went through after him.

What the fuck?

I stopped walking and stayed where I was in the middle of the ramp leading to the turnstiles. The two men were about a hundred yards in front of me but they had their backs to me. There wasn't anyone else on the platform.

They started raising their voices. I couldn't hear what was being said. There was wind and a big airplane with its belly low against the sky. Then the sound of an oncoming train and a blur of movement. A body falling down onto the tracks just as the train came. I braced myself for some sort of screeching of brakes. There wasn't any. The train charged into the station. The doors opened then closed. No one got on or off. The train pulled away. There was just one guy left standing on the platform. He was staring down at the tracks.

My fingers were numb.

I slowly walked up the platform. Found my MetroCard in my coat. Slid it in and went through the turnstile. I walked to the edge and looked down at the tracks. There was an arm separated from the rest of the body. Blood pouring out of the shoulder. The head twisted at an angle you never saw in life. I wasn't sure how the train conductor had failed to notice. The MTA has been very proud of its new one-person train operation system that requires just one human to run the entire train. Maybe that's not enough to keep an eye out for falling bodies.

I felt nauseated. I started to black out and then he steadied me, putting his hands at the small of my back.

"He was talking about you," said Clayton, staring down at Vito's big mangled body. "Said you were going to blow him in exchange for him getting rid of me. He was just trying to upset me but it was disrespectful to you. I wanted to scare him but he fell onto the tracks." Clayton spoke so calmly. "He was talking shit about you, Alice," he added, raising his voice a little.

"Well," I said, "that wasn't very nice of him, was it?"

Clayton smiled.

He really wasn't a bad-looking guy.

THE GOSPEL OF MORAL ENDS

BY BAYO OJIKUTU

77th & Jeffery, Chicago

(Originally published in *Chicago Noir*)

S wear I'm trying to keep up with Reverend this morning. Ain't so easy, not with the black angels crooning at his back, *alleluia,* and these *amens* rising in flocks from the Mount's bloody red carpet and gleaming pews, and the Payless heels square stomping up above my head until Calvary's balcony rocks in rhythm with the charcoal drum sergeant's skins. Seems the flock understands his sermon mighty fine, else why would they make all such noise in Mount Calvary? It's me then. I am the lost.

"Today is a good day, Church. Ain't it, Church? Always a good day for fellowshipping in the community of the Lord God, ain't it?"

The woman leaning on her walking stick across the aisle echoes loud as the speaker box boom.

"Amen!"

"We come in here on this good day looking for the righteous way to serve Him to bring manifest—y'all like that word, Church, that's a good word—let me say it again. We come in here to bring *man-i-fest* His glory in a world gone wicked, Church. We got this here fine church built on a mount—and we call it Calvary, like that hilltop where the Lord God sent His One Son to hang from a cross for us and save us from sin, deliver us from black death, Church. Make me so happy when I talk bout how the Savior came to this world to sacrifice His life for us, so happy, Church, all so we could come back here to the hilltop and build up a palace that'd shine bright in His city, so all would know. But all still ain't here celebrating the Good News, Church—no matter how loud I speak it, y'all sing it, and no matter the blazing beauty of this here Mount Calvary. City's wicked, Church, so wicked; we got folk look like us, talk like us, breathe like us out here. But them folk is confused, Church, lost out in concrete Gomorrah. Y'all know too much about that place already. That's right, the wicked place right outside the oak doors to our Mount Calvary. Right down there on 79th Street, where sin whirls among folk blind to the Good News."

Maybe my trouble understanding Reverend Jack comes from these tiny ears, a quarter of the space the Good Lord carved on either side of my head for hearing. Or maybe confusion comes from eyes gone pus-yellow driving Sunday sunrise fares out to the good places north, south, and west; far, far from the wicked, whirling city and never back into concrete Gomorrah a moment before seven o'clock the following Saturday night.

Or maybe I'm carrying the soul of a Black Jew up inside me. Not like the one-eyed Candy Man, or the musty shysters on the corner of State and Madison, their nappy heads hid underneath unraveling crochet hats. Sammy Davis was a happy half-monkey/half-rat, and the zero corner hustlers call themselves "Ethiopian Hebrews," selling their stinky incense sticks. I know I ain't no chimp dancing on a music box or no rat running into corners, or no shyster either. Ain't looking to get down with no big-boned Swedish honeys or start no funky sweet revolution. Just getting hold of this preacher's babble before salvation passes me by, trying to—Black Jews, you see, don't sing or dance God or shout *alleluia* in the temple. We read holy script in quiet. That way, we understand what the rabbi's spewing. We Black Jews get to know what the sermon means, Church.

My religion would explain this Scandinavian wanderer's nose misplaced on my Down-Deep-in-the-field face. I smell from it plenty good, better had what with this crooked beak jabbing from my head, stabbing and jabbing at the rearview mirror reflection as I pull on seeing holes to explore my rot. The nose's tip hooks down like those of the old olive diamond hawks underneath the tracks on Wabash Avenue, except that nostrils gape wide and jungle-black where cheeks meet. I breathe the stank of the Lord Jesus' celebration: this funk of salt, Walgreens makeup counter product, relaxer lye, and air panted from deep in guts filled with only starvation and desperation. Smelling lets my beak know something's ill in the reverend's Sunday spiel, and that knowledge means trouble on the Mount.

"But why's the world still so wicked if the Lord God sent His One Son down here to die and save us from sin? Let the Reverend explain the mystery to you—"

Reverend Jack's Satan changes every first and third Sunday. God is always the father, Jesus is his namesake son, and the Holy Ghost is that daytime creeping soul who slips inside the good Calvary Baptist lady in the satin dress, takes hold of her up in row ten after the reverend drops the sermon's main point. Twists her skull at the base of the neck, bends her in half, then snaps her holy rock-head front to back with the drum sergeant's beat; until the

Ghost is done with her and he tosses the top half of this lady free so the end of her spine slams into wood pew.

She never cries or screams in pain as the Holy Ghost works her fierce like so; saved lady just shouts in this thrusting rhythm, "Praise you in me, Holy Ghost. Stay up in me, Holy Ghost. Deep up in me, Holy Ghost. *Glory.* Praise you in me, Holy Ghost," and then again, before she hops into the aisle, mist rising from cocoa forehead, arms and legs flapping against each other while her neck snaps backwards without wood to interrupt the flow of ecstasy. There she goes with that sanctified chicken jig, same dance every other Sunday of the month.

Mount Calvary Missionary Baptist has sat just west of 77th and Jeffery Boulevard since the real Jews first let dark folks on these blocks fifty years back. Deep Down wanderers brought the Mount with them from Mobile County, Alabama, or some such burning place, so this is really Mount Calvary Second Baptist, too many words to get in before crooning an *alleluia* and interrupting the mission. The church used to be a rickety wood frame worship-shack blending in perfect with the houses leaned sideways by lake wind, siding smudged orange-brown by the burn of the wicked city's July sun, same as the Rothschild Liquor store across from the church parking lot. That old mud-weed lot where the Cadillac hearses parked whenever one of the Section C heads who sit under haberdashery and Easter brims passed on from this world to that better place prepared for them in the Kingdom.

But that old Deep Tuscaloosa–style shack didn't shine sufficient for the Good News. So Reverend sent me to the alderwoman's main ward office in the old Gold Medallion cab, carrying five large from Calvary's tithe right after Mayor Harold died. Handed the flock loot over to that elected bag lady in exchange for eminent domain over half the row of homes just east of Jeffery, and the mud-weed lot too. City crashed down them shacks that used to line 77th long before they swore in Gomorrah's new king. Then the church board started passing around a second collection pot on the second and fourth Sundays. They called it "the building reserve special blessing fund."

"Give what you can, Church," Reverend told the flock then. "Know times is rough for folk round here right round now, but sacrifice is remembered eternal—and remember, you sacrificing for the One who gave the greatest sacrifice, who made that path into Glory with His own blood. If you can't give to build up a new place for celebrating Him, there's still gon be a place for you on the Path, Church. I promise it. Still gon be a place for you in His new house. Somebody say *amen.*"

Before hardhats started pouring foundation to the new temple, Reverend had to pay out six weeks' worth of bingo proceeds to the bag lady, just so she'd change the title to this block of 77th Street to his name. Original paperwork claimed the Lord, or the Mount itself, or the flock, as the new church land's owner. "Naw, that ain't right," Reverend moaned back then. "All deeds got a price, Moral." Then he pointed me toward the bags of bingo gold, and watched as I piled them into my cab's trunk.

So the Church got to building its shining palace on the north side of 77th Street, foundation laid by the sacrifice of the flock, bricks stacked by the real big-time loot kicked back from DC in '93, after the reverend sent us around in the bingo vans and the hearse to collect all the living and dead souls, bring them on back to the rickety old shack to cast rightful vote for our good brother, slick Willie C. That honorary deacon on the Mount never would have sat on his high throne not for the tireless work we put in here in the city, and the new church never could've afforded its masonry not for the deacon's big payback.

Like the reverend say, "Rejoice and be exceedingly glad: for great is our reward in the Kingdom. That's from the Good News, Church." No trouble understanding that sermon, not even in my dwarf ears.

Today the wood pews in the Mount shine with fine finish, and you can't hear the high heels clicking as the Section C women prance about the vestibule cause this plush red carpet stretches front door to black angel choir bandstand to swallow the sharpest points. Drywall towers above us, spackled to match the floor, with stereo speakers built behind and up into the ceilings, too, so no matter whether you're sitting in row J on the second balcony or downstairs in the toilet stall, you hear his sermon in surround sound. My sweet Lord Jesus, don't forget those holy shining basement bowls below the Mount, porcelain from Taiwan with the automatic power flush, and the perfume shooting from vents as stall doors open and close. Just enough mist let loose so you never smell your own shit, no matter gaping nose holes.

Even if you arrive late to the eleven thirty and find the Mount packed through to the balconies with blue-black city souls, and you end up sitting in the last row of main floor pews—even then, you still see the reverend's pockmarked skin turn orange as he spews the Good News in front of a thousand furs and brims and palms and heels stomping. Last summer, Reverend had me install this camera here over the back row, lens set to beam him to the four movie screens at each corner of the service. Lens don't leave the podium until Reverend Jack's calligraphy-mustached grill crackles from his microphone as he dances one of his glory circles and drops the main point. I strung the camera cord up to stretch past the Mount's balconies and the rafters, just like he told me, and now this wire carries the sermon and the sight of its pinstriped deliverer out for broadcast someplace way beyond the flock.

"What we doing on this good day here on Mount Calvary?"

"*Celebratin'!*"

"All right then, y'all hearing me. Only one thing that word could mean after how I just told it to you—'I celebrate man.' You celebrating the Lord God sending His One Son in man form just to sacrifice that human life so that the souls of we men would be forever saved. If you bring manifest, Church, then you celebrating the Good News. See how warm that makes you, just saying it. I know it makes me warm. Say it with me together, Church, and feel the shower of His Glory. Celebrate the Good News . . . Celebrate the Good News . . ."

"*Celebrate the Good News!*"

"Well all right then, Church. You been hearing about this fellow Teddy Mann all about the streets, ain't you? If you ain't heard, Church, then best time you listened in close. You come in here on Sunday morning and you feel *sanctified* bout the way of your souls, sacrificing your time for the One—"

"*Amen,*" the church sister squeals short-throated on her cane.

"Yes siree, Reverend—" the drummer boy in his clean green fatigues answers before he two-stick slaps his cymbals.

"*Amen,*" some Low End woman in the first balcony says before stomping square heels together.

"Sing his name on high now, Church. But the minute you step back outside them oak church doors, we ain't on the Mount no more. You back in the world, Church, and it ain't so warm. Not with that icy wind whipping up from the concrete. Even your Mah-shall Fields wool ain't fine enough to keep you covered out there. Ain't nobody praying to Him at the liquor store counter, no sweet virgin voices humming hymns by the lotto machine. Ain't no Good Book studying in the battlefield, out there as one man spills his brother's blood over the wages of sin, Church. No Reverend Jack preaching the Word over the rivers of pain and lakes of broken glass. Them folk don't even know the Good Lord out there in the concrete world, do they, Church?"

"No sir," Deacon Nate responds. "They don't *even* know."

"Or maybe they got the facts all switched up. Cause out there, I hear children who look just like your good children talking about Teddy Mann like he himself is the Lord God Almighty. Say Teddy be making rainwater fall out the sky; Teddy, he feeds us with the warmth of his crack glory. He brings smiles to faces flush of ashy worry and worn wrinkles. Teddy do so it, cause he's the king of 79th Street, that concrete path. Folk swear they see him walking on top of the pond down by the Highlands. Strutting with the ducks just before he goes and turns that same water into wine, multiplies the fishes and loaves, cures the leper, and raises the dead. Breaks my heart to hear folk talking like so, Church, but I go on and listen to them desecrate and blaspheme Jesus' holy name. These are my people, even when they lost in their confusion. I know this place, don't I, Church?"

"Amen!"

All the flock, they did say *alleluia-amen* together, as Lucifer is a black angel fallen down from the choir, never the church board folk in Section C.

The Calvary ushers appear at the service hall's front door with their fake gold sashes draping right shoulder to left hip. "Mount Calvary Missionary" is scripted in sparkling letters along the diagonal of their chests, and they cradle collection pots between stomachs and clasped hands. Ushers always start with the back row. Such is the price for coming late to the eleven thirty. So I reach into my left pocket, palm brushing against the Good News just slightly, but find nothing save for lint and receipts from my weekend fares. The church sister on her cane stands and stares at me crooked-eyed, no matter that it was me who carted her to the Mount. Because of her, I was late this morning.

I left all my spare cash locked in the yellow cab's glove compartment, parked out in the new paved lot. Been leaving cash locked up since I accidentally dropped a hundred spot into the pot; that c-note earned carrying the serpent Teddy Mann from Cornell Avenue all the way out to O'Hare to catch his red-eye to the islands one Sunday morning. Tried to explain it to the usher, that longtime fellow flock member, how I'd made a mistake that good Sunday, tried to get my tip back from him. Missionary sash-wearing muthafucka just looked at me crooked-eyed as the church lady on her walking stick and strutted on to row twenty-four to continue collection rounds.

Ain't got nothing for them on this good day then, nothing but my Good News message. So I climb over the legs of the other late folk and dash for the service's corner door, holding on to my crotch like I've gotta go bad. Old church sister still stares at me though, I see her, and so does the reverend in the fourth corner movie screen, gray-black eyes beaming down. But I do make it to the red carpet stairs, and I let go of myself only as I touch the banister.

I walk up along the thick fiber instead of down to the basement toilet. Got plenty of time before the collectors make it up top. Takes them twenty minutes to finish rounding up the fellowship loot from Section C. Don't feel or hear a damn thing as I step into the blackness separating staircase from square stomp in the Payless balcony aisles. Nothing except for this Good News rubbing steel against my side and the reverend panting heavy into his podium mic.

Teddy Mann's got the finest honey mamma ever seen on the Mount. Kind so fine you want to call her "mamma" just so you can go on pretending like you remember sliding headfirst from her in the beginning. And maybe you would've held on to that joy somewhere had you been the one so blessed; sure know if you were born from between there, Church, you wouldn't need Reverend Jack to tell you a thing about Galilee.

Honey mamma looks to be some righteous mix of Humboldt Park Spaniard, Howard Street Jamaican rum, Magnificent Mile skyrising, and 95th Street sanctifying. Got slanted eyes, cold as Eskimo soles, and a fish-hook nose. Not a beak hook like mine, no, hers is curved upwards just so funk's gotta climb to seep into her. Her skin's the same color sand used to be on top of Rainbow Beach when I was little, but clean sand—only thing that shows against her smooth face is the peach fuzz barely sprouting from her pores. You only notice it if you're blessed enough to catch yourself daring to stare her way; of course, you're only so brave because Teddy Mann's never to be found in these balcony pews.

Her smile is just slightly yellowed from all the sugar breathed from bubble-gum lips. She's tall, not so tall to cast shadow over that sly serpent Teddy; but she stands high and regal like the queens who ruled history's pale make-believe lands. So fine and upright that when honey mamma reaches down to tap your shoulder, you know you're a hero just short of the gods in heaven.

Teddy must have claimed honey mamma after he turned to evildoing. Serpent served some 26th and California time after he first started playing with that dope—Burglary, Assault with Intent, some desperate something—and hooked up with the old-time concrete kings from Blackstone Avenue behind those bars. Vestibule says after his bid, Teddy returned to 79th Street and proved his soul in flowing blood and cash rolls, and before long the kings turned Sodom, Gomorrah, old Babylon Lounge off Stony Island, and the Zanzibar on the Isle, over to him. Almost twenty years later, he's still the king with all the paper ends and crooked angles covered. Must be the game that won her over, that same street player's game that lets the congregation know sly

Teddy is the king on Reverend's sin throne this third Sunday.

There his honey mamma goes, celebrating in Row D first balcony. The sweet mother of Jesus, halfway smiling in that faded yellow gleam, halfway smiling and halfway weeping, sharp bones jabbing through hands patted together soft in Reverend Jack's pauses. Purple shame just now fades from her cheeks and these slant eyes cut into slices so her pupils hide from the good day sermon. Reverend just told the Mount all about her man, like they ain't already heard the concrete tales. Yet honey mamma's still gotta go through these sermon motions. She may have lost Paradise and fallen down from the Mount, taken by Teddy Mann's sly way, but the fact that she's here seeking to celebrate His Good News only goes to prove Reverend Jack's main point about the iniquity of that black serpent, evildoing Satan.

Teddy told me this story about his lady while we rode out north to O'Hare. Her name is Eva, with the "a" from the reverend's "feast" tacked on for the sake of the celebration. Back in the beginning of their thing, baritone Deacon Nate, who was Teddy's cousin just up from Mississippi, long before he came about his saved seat in Row Two, he arrived in concrete Gomorrah and tried to convince the serpent how this heifer couldn't be about nothing special, how she'd bring him down from his throne like all them other fake-ass mixed-nut tricks be doing a nigga trying to get his money right. Spewing hatred's spittle, that's how Deacon Nate talked before he came to know Jesus.

Or maybe Nate was such a hater until Teddy took him for a ride along 79th Street in the purple custom Jaguar. They kept riding the strip until they found Eva, then they rolled half a block behind, following her sweet strides. The Jag's passenger seat and Teddy's cousin's Mississippi gabardines were all wet with shame, and Nate was babbling off at the mouth in baritone tongues as the light turned red at King Drive, praising the glory of His name and the wonder of His deeds. Then he begged the serpent for explanation.

"That's what this life in the game is all about, brother . . . What's your name?" Teddy's black eyes reached over the cab's sliding glass protector, burned into my dashboard ID card. "Moral? *Hah.* That's a good black man's name. That's what I tried to tell my bumblefuckin cousin sitting there all stiff-nutted staring at my lady; a black man goes and gets into this game, right, and sets himself up proper, I told the fool. Get hold of as much knowledge here, as much cash as a nigga can on this Earth. Not cause being a smart nigga means a goddamn thing, Moral, or cause calling your black ass rich is worth shit in the end. Black man follows the path to treasure so he can get himself something beautiful in this life. Get him something so fine he knows he's alive cause his

limbs is stirring with fresh blood. So fine, he believes there's a god somewhere, one who is good cause he gives life this purpose. A true god, not this quarter-wit bullshit they got ill pimps like Reverend Jack preaching up high on the Mount about, that bastard. Him and his cockamamie god standing on high with the kings, getting paid off lost souls. Ain't talking about no lie to make niggas feel good about the chitlins down deep in their guts and the stupidity sky high in their minds; a true and real god who creates sweet, beautiful things for human beings. That god leaves you humble with his mighty eye for making beauty, humble but proud at the same time to be alive. Can't help humble pride walking down 79th Street next to a living creation that fine, brother. Hear me? You gotta get that god knowledge so you grasp how to appreciate it. Gotta get that man's paper so you can afford her, cause the god rule say she costs. That's all we're in this cockamamie quarter-assed game for, Moral. Told my cousin this as he sat next to me—know what that buzzard went and did right afterwards? Country fuck went and got religion on the Mount with the pimp. Deacon's nuts ain't got stiff since. Punk-ass plantation retard. But *you* hear what I'm saying to you, don't you, Moral?"

"I hear you."

Sly Teddy reached his hairy black hand through the protection shield and dropped that Ben Franklin note into my lap, then he used the orange palm to slick down goatee waves on either side of his lips. He stared into the cab's rearview mirror all the while, checking me for doubt, fear, or worship, burning into these rot holes in search of my soul. But there wasn't no rhyme or revolution in me that good Sunday morning, Church. I wasn't but a gypsy cabbie, sore eyes running off into the Good Lord's purple sunrise.

Serpent squeezed my shoulder blade just a bit before pointing shaped nails at the fare meter: $48.50, the red bulbs blinked. I dug down in my pockets for change to return to him, without glancing in the rearview.

"Ain't got nothing smaller?" I asked. But before I could look up, he'd patted me on the left shoulder and propped open his back door as a United jet roared over my "For Hire" sign—couldn't even shake the serpent's hand cause I was busy unraveling the torn dollar bills from my pockets.

"What a friend we have in Jesus, hey Moral?" Teddy crooned in funky gospel rhythm as his steppers tapped against O'Hare's tar street. "You take it slow and easy and keep your eyes peeled ahead on that path riding home, will you?"

Sly serpent left the rest of his message in my backseat. Not another c-note, no, that there lump sitting snug up under the Saturday edition of the *Chicago Tribune* Metro section (y'all know sly Teddy's bout the only soul you'll still see round here reading the *Trib*, Church). I brushed the thin paper sheets to the floor, and there was his black steel, same one he wears underneath the flaps of his snakeskin leather as he slithers about the city, a cold killer .357 piece, chromed to shine in its camel pouch. Tried to call out the window to let him know he left it, I did, but that driver's-side glass wouldn't roll down. Swear, Church.

Been riding round the Mount three weeks now with this message and its thick holster right next to the spare cash in my glove compartment. The Metro section, I threw that away long before making it back to 79th Street for Reverend Jack's early service.

For as I passed by and beheld your devotions, I found an altar with this inscription: TO THE UNKNOWN GOD. *Whom therefore ye ignorantly worship, him declare I unto you. God that made the world all things therein, seeing that He is Lord of Heaven and Earth, dwelleth not in temples made with hands.*

This is what their Bible book says proper. I snatch the soft cover from the Row A pew before this crusty-lipped child hops about and screams with the Good News at the end of our days. Heist this scripture from the cross-eyed and the stupid to read the words of Acts as written by old dark fellow Hebrews. I've freed the bound holy book and tucked it into the chest pocket of my driving shirt. Because I need the word kept close to life, as I ain't one of these just-up-from-the-Down-Deep flock, bouncing mad about the Mount's pews and aisles as the reverend preaches his sermon.

"Am I my brother's keeper, Church? Y'all come on, come on and tell me now—"

"Yes, siree, Reverend," Deacon Nate replies, "that's what it say."

"*Well.* Somebody been coming to Bible study like they suppose to." Reverend Jack's gray-blacks cut to the choir bandstand. "Yes, Church, Good Book tell us we're our brother's keeper, indeed. Repeat it with me: *indeed*. It's on us to certify he ain't strayed from Paradise or off the Mount. Book don't tell us something though, Church—cause back there in Paradise, the answer was obvious. But today we've got to ask the question. Need to get some kind of resolution before we go out and *proselytize* in His holy name. Uh-oh, Reverend . . . y'all like the sound of that fancy word now, don't you? I'll break it down for you next week—y'all remind me, Church. What I got to know now before I send y'all out to do the good works, is who is 'my brother,' Church? *Hah.* Who is my brother?"

The drum sergeant lets cymbals quake as his foot pounds the bass drum pedal to cover the church's silence—yes, finally, silence from the flock—raining down from both balconies. Reverend Jack's eyes switch about holes in the movie screen pictures as he wipes the ballpoint end of his nose.

"We gotta know who our brother is if He expects us to be keeping him, don't we, Church? You gotta answer soon if You expect me to look out for him on our way to Your bosom. I'm gon listen to what You tell me, whatever it might be, Lord, but You gotta tell me something soon. We had a talk, me and the Lord. Know how I tell y'all bout getting down on humble knees and praying to the Most High for guidance, and mercy, and deliverance for the wicked? This time I got down to pray and asked Him for an answer, Church. Understanding's what I was after. Do y'all hear me?"

"*Amen, Reverend,*" the first balcony shouts, honey mamma Eva louder than all the rest, purple shame gone from her now. "*We hear ya. Go head on.*"

"But Church, in His benevolent wisdom, I'm still waiting out an explanation from on High, Church. It's one of them mysteries; Lord puts em down here for us sometimes, in this maze of concrete and glass. Lays rhyming riddles in the cracks of our lives. Like when He sent His son into the shadow of darkness to withstand the temptation of Beelzebub, Church—y'all remember that? Why'd He put His One Son through such tribulation? He don't never give us no questions we can't handle though, Church. Never an answer that'll break us."

"Glory, *ah-ley-lu-ya,*" the woman says down below before hobbling into her pew.

"He left me to think on it, amidst all this wicked darkness in the city Gomorrah. I sought for understanding, and I waited patient, Church. Is my brother the hustlers and the pimps and whores and crooks and killers scampering about like dark rats—is my brother Teddy Mann? Jesus the Son Himself kept even the most vile sinner close to Him as He spread the word of His coming. But that was back before Satan took over the living Earth and the minds of the lost. Lord didn't have to think on pandemic pestilence and Tech-Nines and poison powders in the mail and flaming terror wielded by the lost. Them Romans overran Judah long before Satan swallowed the minds of the wicked, you see. Not like now—we gotta be cautious on the Mount today. It's a good day for fellowshipping, yes it is, long as we stay cautious, Church. Y'all still with me?"

"*Amen!*"

Reverend Jack snatches the microphone from its stand and slides his wiggling Stacey Adams from the podium to spin inside the microphone cord's electric circle, and my camera follows him just below us, broadcasting Reverend's jig to the four corners and up above, too. The crusty-faced boy jumps wood pew to not-so-plush balcony carpet, and sweet Eva's face turns sun-kissed as she applauds, and the balcony folk praise him on high. I try to listen still. I'm patient as the flock, as the reverend beseeches us to be. No matter I may be one of those gypsy cab Jews with loss and confusion beating against my stolen holy book. Patient, because if Jesus came now I know he'd be a gold-medallion cabbie, taking folk where they asked to go because that's the job script, just waiting for his chance to save them from their requested destination. Church, don't you know that gypsy-cabbie Jesus would catch the lost way switching about those passengers' eye holes long before the ride's end?

"It's time for a cleansing, Church—a rapture—time for us to start preparing the path. As He prepped the way for us into His Father's Kingdom by shedding His own blood. We, brothers and sisters, must shed *wickedness*, so the city is purified for His coming. He's riding in on that pearl white horse of His, come again to destroy the most Wicked One and deliver His peace unto the chosen. *Well.* Y'all know I got mercy in me, Church, y'all know it—we gon go out there and give the wicked and the lost their fair chance with the two-step test. Those that pass, we gon keep them and wait for Him to ride on to the Mount and deliver us together. The rest of them, Church? Old preachers used to talk about forsaking immoral means on the way to righteousness. But when the ends we preparing for is His return, Church, I can't think of no means that qualify as *immoral.* Slick-tongued serpent lives a long, lavish life, if y'all let him do it. But it's time for us to go bout changing this city, getting it ready, Church. Time for lies and false righteousness and double-dealing and back-sliding and all such wickedness to be cast down from the Mount and out of the city, so we can start to make a way for salvation. Y'all hear me?"

"I hear you," I say, as Reverend's come to his main point in these tiny ears of mine. The answer rains with the heel stomping and the skin-pounding drum sergeant's celebration. Honey mamma Eva sings *alleluia* and jumps on the red carpet like the child in Row A, and she claps those pretty hands together, more than going through motions now.

The Reverend steps further left of the podium in the big movie screens, spinning and sliding and whirling without ever touching the cord that connects him to sound. He chants into the mic as clean sweat pours free along his brow, and the black angels sing with him. *"Celebrate the Good News. Celebrate the Good News."* Mount Calvary shakes with the power of His glory, and I know the path, Church.

Celebrate the Good News.

I walk toward the balcony ledge once, twice, until my waist bounces against drywall and the Good News' steel does feel so very mighty. Reverend Jack tells the truth about this, so very mighty, this message gripped in the left hand. Put it between his gray-black eyes, and the Mount is silent once again. Miracles do abound. Flock's quiet enough even for the reading of the Word hidden against my chest. Save for this bouncing boy screaming out because he ain't ready for the News like he thought he was gonna be when it was delivered all funked up in charcoal and war fatigue drummer skins and rhythm guitar strum, and those sweet black angel hymns. When it comes in silence, the Good News tears righteousness from the child until his eyes fill with yellow rot like mine. He is as lost as I was lost.

Underneath this obnoxious fear, the sound of pearl hooves sound near. *Klump. Ku-lump.* Since the drum sergeant must've lost his sticks, let the Good Lord's pony keep the rhythm for you. These boys is just scared is all, Church—don't pay them mind. Just ain't used to Good News without screaming in exaltation, *alleluia;* so feel their trepidation, *amen.*

I want to look over my shoulder at Eva, feast upon her glory one last time. Finest thing to ever set foot on Mount Calvary since they strung Him to that tree and drove in the spikes. Since the Lord called eminent domain over our salvation for the price of His Own Son's blood. Can't look back there though, for Teddy Mann's black steel has got me—and it's throbbing in its hot might, shining and reflecting the gray in Reverend Jack's movie screen eyes. I've never seen a yellow testifier with pupils this color; bet they never seen a Black Jew with eyes rotted yellow neither. *Wicked City.*

I let go the Good News' truth blasts, one, two, three times. For Father, Son, and Holy Ghost, though my real religion tells me to only believe in the First. Church, you hear this boy screaming wild still?

All the black angels run down from the bandstand. One of them, the curly-headed Alabama queer who bit into thick lips as Reverend damned the sodomites last month, he dashes to the podium in time to catch Reverend before his head's fallen from the circle, and this black angel cries as sacred life spills to turn the choir robe a darker red than Mount Calvary's carpet. Purple-crimson sea to swallow the main point in whole.

Celebrate the Good News, and hold on to it tight, Church, cause the wicked will make one last stand on this good day for fellowshipping, stand against the Mount until He comes to vanquish them. Yes, they must. Says so at the end of their holy book.

Before Eva turns away from the two-step test, I swear she shines that sugar-stained smile down my way. Still no shame in her glorious face. Honey mamma smiles and runs off to the darkness before the steps, going through glorious motions again with most of the rest. She runs quivering hips from me, Church, and my Down Deep gabardines soak wet at the crotch. The church has fallen from the Mount, and the mighty temple rises once more.

"Quit your screaming now, boy," I say. "Wanna hear the hooves coming near. That's the Holy Ghost almost in me."

Deacon Nate's baritone sounds down in Row Two. "It's him, that black Satan, Moral," he yells. "Good Lord of Mercy, Church, put him down now!"

The wicked do come for me, just like in their Book. But they ain't swift as the Holy Ghost or this blazing white horse riding in from Galilee.

I leap into their path. "Praise you in me, all up in me. You in me real good." I sing and dance my chicken dance, arms and legs and Good News flapping all about in the first balcony aisle. "Stay up in me. You my salvation, *Glory*. Praise you in me."

WHEN ALL THIS WAS BAY RIDGE

BY TIM MCLOUGHLIN

Sunset Park, Brooklyn

(Originally published in *Brooklyn Noir*)

S tanding in church at my father's funeral, I thought about being arrested on the night of my seventeenth birthday. It had occurred in the train yard at Avenue X, in Coney Island. Me and Pancho and a kid named Freddie were working a three-car piece, the most ambitious I'd tried to that point, and more time-consuming than was judicious to spend trespassing on city property. Two Transit cops with German shepherds caught us in the middle of the second car. I dropped my aerosol can and took off, and was perhaps two hundred feet along the beginning of the trench that becomes the IRT line to the Bronx, when I saw the hand. It was human, adult, and severed neatly, seemingly surgically, at the wrist. My first thought was that it looked bare without a watch. Then I made a whooping sound, trying to take in air, and turned and ran back toward the cops and their dogs.

At the 60th Precinct, we three were ushered into a small cell. We sat for several hours, then the door opened and I was led out. My father was waiting in the main room, in front of the counter.

The desk sergeant, middle-aged, black, and noticeably bored, looked up briefly. "Him?"

"Him," my father echoed, sounding defeated.

"Goodnight," the sergeant said.

My father took my arm and led me out of the precinct. As we cleared the door and stepped into the humid night he turned to me and said, "This was it. Your one free ride. It doesn't happen again."

"What did it cost?" I asked. My father had retired from the police department years earlier, and I knew this had been expensive.

He shook his head. "This once, that's all."

I followed him to his car. "I have two friends in there."

"Fuck'em. Spics. That's half your problem."

"What's the other half?"

"You have no common sense," he said, his voice rising in scale as it did in volume. By the time he reached a scream he sounded like a boy going through puberty. "What do you think you're doing out here? Crawling 'round in the dark with the niggers and the spics. Writing on trains like a hoodlum. Is this all you'll do?"

"It's not writing. It's drawing. Pictures."

"Same shit, defacing property, behaving like a punk. Where do you suppose it will lead?"

"I don't know. I haven't thought about it. You had your aimless time, when you got out of the service. You told me so. You bummed around for two years."

"I always worked."

"Part-time. Beer money. You were a roofer."

"Beer money was all I needed."

"Maybe it's all I need."

He shook his head slowly, and squinted, as though peering through the dirty windshield for an answer. "It was different. That was a long time ago. Back when all this was Bay Ridge. You could live like that then."

When all this was Bay Ridge. He was masterful, my father. He didn't say *when it was white*, or *when it was Irish*, or even the relatively tame *when it was safer*. No. When all this was Bay Ridge. As though it were an issue of geography. As though, somehow, the tectonic plate beneath Sunset Park had shifted, moving it physically to some other place.

I told him about seeing the hand.

"Did you tell the officers?"

"No."

"The people you were with?"

"No."

"Then don't worry about it. There's body parts all over this town. Saw enough in my day to put together a baseball team." He drove in silence for a few minutes, then nodded his head a couple of times, as though agreeing with a point made by some voice I could not hear. "You're going to college, you know," he said.

That was what I remembered at the funeral. Returning from the altar rail after receiving communion, Pancho walked passed me. He'd lost a great deal of weight since I'd last seen him, and I couldn't tell if he was sick or if it was just the drugs. His black suit hung on him in a way that emphasized his gaunt frame. He winked at me as he came around the casket in front of my pew, and flashed the mischievous smile that—when we were sixteen—got all the girls in his bed and all the guys agreeing to the stupidest and most dangerous stunts.

In my shirt pocket was a photograph of my father with a woman who was not my mother. The date on the back was five years ago. Their arms were around each other's waists and they smiled for the photographer. When we arrived at the cemetery I took the picture out of my pocket, and looked at it for perhaps the fiftieth time since I'd first discovered it. There were no clues. The woman was young to be with my father, but not a girl. Forty, give or take a few years. I looked for any evidence in his expression that I was misreading their embrace, but even I couldn't summon the required naïveté. My father's countenance was not what would commonly be regarded as a poker face. He wasn't holding her as a friend, a friend's girl, or the prize at some retirement or bachelor party; he held her like a possession. Like he held his tools. Like he held my mother. The photo had been taken before my mother's death. I put it back.

I'd always found his plodding predictability and meticulous planning of insignificant events maddening. For the first time that I could recall, I was experiencing curiosity about some part of my father's life.

I walked from Greenwood Cemetery directly to Olsen's bar, my father's watering hole, feeling that I needed to talk to the men that nearly lived there, but not looking forward to it. Aside from my father's wake the previous night, I hadn't seen them in years. They were all Irish. The Irish among them were perhaps the most Irish, but the Norwegians and the Danes were Irish too, as were the older Puerto Ricans. They had developed, over time, the stereotypical hooded gaze, the squared jaws set in grim defiance of whatever waited in the sobering daylight. To a man they had that odd trait of the Gaelic heavy-hitter, that—as they attained middle age—their faces increasingly began to resemble a woman's nipple.

The door to the bar was propped open, and the cool damp odor of stale beer washed over me before I entered. That smell has always reminded me of the Boy Scouts. Meetings were Thursday nights in the basement of Bethany Lutheran Church. When they were over, I would have to pass Olsen's on my way home, and I usually stopped in to see my father. He would buy me a couple of glasses of beer—about all I could handle at thirteen—and leave with me after about an hour so we could walk home together.

From the inside looking out: Picture an embassy in a foreign country. A truly foreign country. Not a Western European ally, but a fundamentalist state perennially on the precipice of war. A fill-the-sandbags-and-wait-for-the-airstrike enclave. That was Olsen's, home to the last of the donkeys, the white dinosaurs of Sunset Park. A jukebox filled with Kristy McColl and the Clancy Brothers and flyers tacked to the flaking walls advertising step-dancing classes, Gaelic lessons, and the memorial run to raise money for a scholarship in the name of a recently slain cop. Within three blocks of the front door you could attend a cockfight, buy crack, or pick up a streetwalker, but in Olsen's, it was always 1965.

Upon entering the bar for the first time in several years, I found its pinched dimensions and dim lighting more oppressive, and less mysterious, than I had remembered. The row of ascetic faces, and the way all conversation trailed off at my entrance, put me in mind of the legendary blue wall of silence in the police department. It is no coincidence that the force has historically been predominantly Irish. The men in Olsen's would be pained to reveal their zip code to a stranger, and I wasn't sure if even they knew why.

The bar surface itself was more warped than I'd recalled. The mirrors had oxidized and the white tile floor had been torn up in spots and replaced with odd-shaped pieces of green linoleum. It was a neighborhood bar in a neighborhood where such establishments are not yet celebrated. If it had been located in my part of the East Village, it would have long since achieved cultural-landmark status. I'd been living in Manhattan for five years and still had not adjusted to the large number of people who moved here from other parts of the country and overlooked the spectacle of the city only to revere the mundane. One of my coworkers, herself a transplant, remarked that the coffee shop on my corner was *authentic*. In that they served coffee, I suppose she was correct.

I sat on an empty stool in the middle of the wavy bar and ordered a beer. I felt strangely nervous there without my father, like a child about to be caught doing something bad. Everyone knew me. Marty, the round-shouldered bartender, approached first, breaking the ice. He spoke around an enormous, soggy stub of a cigar, as he always did. And, as always, he seemed constantly annoyed by its presence in his mouth; as though he'd never smoked one before, and was surprised to discover himself chewing on it.

"Daniel. It's good to see you. I'm sorry for your loss."

He extended one hand, and when I did the same, he grasped mine in both of his and held it for a moment. It had to have been some sort of signal, because the rest of the relics in the place lurched toward me then, like some nursing-home theater guild performing *Night of the Living Dead*. They shook hands, engaged in awkward stiff hugs, and offered unintelligible condolences.

Frank Sanchez, one of my father's closest friends, squeezed the back of my neck absently until I winced. I thanked them as best I could, and accepted the offers of free drinks.

Someone—I don't know who—thought it would be a good idea for me to have Jameson's Irish whiskey, that having been my father's drink. I'd never considered myself much of a drinker. I liked a couple of beers on a Friday night, and perhaps twice a year I would get drunk. I almost never drank hard liquor, but this crew was insistent, they were matching me shot for shot, and they were paying. It was the sort of thing my father would have been adamant about.

I began to reach for the photograph in my pocket several times and stopped. Finally I fished it out and showed it to the bartender. "Who is she, Marty?" I asked. "Any idea?"

The manner in which he pretended to scrutinize it told me that he recognized the woman immediately. He looked at the picture with a studied perplexity, as though he would have had trouble identifying my father.

"Wherever did you get such a thing?" he asked.

"I found it in the basement, by my father's shop."

"Ah. Just come across it by accident then."

The contempt in his voice seared through my whiskey glow, and left me as sober as when I'd entered. He knew, and if he knew they all knew. And a decision had been reached to tell me nothing.

"Not by accident," I lied. "My father told me where it was and asked me to get it."

Our eyes met for a moment. "And did he say anything about it?" Marty asked. "Were there no instructions or suggestions?"

"He asked me to take care of it," I said evenly. "To make everything all right."

He nodded. "Makes good sense," he said. "That would be best served by letting the dead sleep, don't you think? Forget it, son, let it lie." He poured me another drink, sloppily, like the others, and resumed moving his towel over the bar, as though he could obliterate the mildewed stench of a thousand spilled drinks with a few swipes of the rag.

I drank the shot down quickly and my buzz returned in a rush. I hadn't been keeping track, but I realized that I'd had much more than what I was used to, and I was starting to feel dizzy. The rest of the men in the room looked the same as when I walked in, the same as when I was twelve. In the smoke-stained bar mirror I saw Frank Sanchez staring at me from a few stools away. He caught me looking and gestured for me to come down.

"Sit, Danny," he said when I got there. He was drinking boilermakers. Without asking, he ordered each of us another round. "What were you talking to Marty about?"

I handed Frank the picture. "I was asking who the woman is."

He looked at it and placed it on the bar. "Yeah? What'd he say?"

"He said to let it lie."

Frank snorted. "Typical donkey," he said. "Won't answer a straight question, but has all kinds of advice on what you should do."

From a distance in the dark bar I would have said that Frank Sanchez hadn't changed much over the years, but I was close to him now, and I'd seen him only last night in the unforgiving fluorescent lighting of the funeral home. He'd been thin and handsome when I was a kid, with blue-black hair combed straight back, and the features and complexion of a Hollywood Indian in a John Wayne picture. He'd thickened in the middle over the years, though he still wasn't fat. His reddish brown cheeks were illuminated by the roadmap of broken capillaries that seemed an entrance requirement for "regular" status at Olsen's. His hair was still shockingly dark, but now with a fake Jerry Lewis sheen and plenty of scalp showing through in the back. He was a retired homicide detective. His had been one of the first Hispanic families in this neighborhood. I knew he'd moved to Fort Lee, New Jersey long ago, though my father said that he was still in Olsen's every day.

Frank picked up the picture and looked at it again, then looked over it at the two sloppy rows of bottles along the back bar. The gaps for the speed rack looked like missing teeth.

"We're the same," he said. "Me and you."

"The same, how?"

"We're on the outside, and we're always looking to be let in."

"I never gave a damn about being on the inside here, Frank."

He handed me the photo. "You do now."

He stood then, and walked stiffly back to the men's room. A couple of minutes later Marty appeared at my elbow, topped off my shot, and replaced Frank's.

"It's a funny thing about Francis," Marty said. "He's a spic who's always hated the spics. So he moves from a spic neighborhood to an all-white one, then has to watch as it turns spic. So now he's got to get in his car every day and drive back to his old all-spic neighborhood, just so he can drink with white men. It's made the man bitter. And," he nodded toward the glasses, "he's in his cups tonight. Don't take the man too seriously."

Marty stopped talking and moved down the bar when Frank returned. "What'd Darby O'Gill say to you?" he asked.

"He told me you were drunk," I said, "and that you didn't like spics."

Frank widened his eyes. "Coming out with revelations like that, is he? Hey, Martin," he yelled, "next time I piss tell him JFK's been shot!" He drained his whiskey, took a sip of beer, and turned his attention back to me. "Listen. Early on, when I first started on the job—years back, I'm talking—there was almost no spades in the department; even less spics. I was the only spic in my precinct, only one I knew of in Brooklyn. I worked in the seven-one, Crown Heights. Did five years there, but this must've been my first year or so.

"I was sitting upstairs in the squad room typing attendance reports. Manual typewriters back then. I was good too, fifty or sixty words a minute—don't forget, English ain't my first language. See, I learned the forms. The key is knowin' the forms, where to plug in the fucking numbers. You could type two hundred words a minute, but you don't know the forms, all them goddamn boxes, you're sitting there all day.

"So I'm typing these reports—only uniform in a room full of bulls, only spic in a room full of harps—when they bring in the drunk."

Frank paused to order another shot, and Marty brought one for me too. I was hungry and really needed to step outside for some air, but I wanted to hear Frank's story. I did want to know how he thought we were similar, and I hoped he would talk about the photo. He turned his face to the ceiling and opened his mouth like a child catching rain, and he poured the booze smoothly down his throat.

"You gotta remember," he continued, "Crown Heights was still mostly white back then, white civilians, white skells. The drunk is just another mick with a skinfull. But what an obnoxious cocksucker. And loud.

"Man who brought him in is another uniform, almost new as me. He throws him in the cage and takes the desk next to mine to type his report. Only this guy can't type, you can see he's gonna be there all day. Takes him ten minutes to get the paper straight in the damn machine. And all this time the goddamn drunk is yelling at the top of his lungs down the length of the squad room. You can see the bulls are gettin' annoyed. Everybody tells him to shut up, but he keeps on, mostly just abusing the poor fuck that brought him in, who's still struggling with the report, his fingers all smudged with ink from the ribbons.

"On and on he goes: 'Your mother blows sailors . . . Your wife fucks dogs . . . You're all queers, every one of you.' Like that. But I mean, really, it don't end, it's like he never gets tired.

"So the guy who locked him up gets him outa the cage and walks him across the room. Over in the corner they got one of these steam pipes, just a vertical pipe, no radiator or nothing. Hot as a motherfucker. So he cuffs the drunk's hands around the pipe, so now the drunk's gotta stand like this"— Frank formed a huge circle with his arms, as if he were hugging an invisible fat woman—"or else he gets burned. And just bein' that close to the heat, I mean, it's fuckin' awful. So the uniform walks away, figuring that'll shut the scumbag up, but it gets worse.

"Now, the bulls are all pissed at the uniform for not beatin' the drunk senseless before he brought him in, like any guy with a year on the street would know to do. The poor fuck is still typing the paperwork at about a word an hour, and the asshole is still at it, 'Your daughter fucks niggers. When I get out I'll look your wife up—again.' Then he looks straight at the uniform, and the uniform looks up. Their eyes lock for a minute. And the drunk says this: 'What's it feel like to know that every man in this room thinks you're an asshole?' Then the drunk is quiet and he smiles."

Marty returned then, and though I felt I was barely hanging on, I didn't dare speak to refuse the drink. Frank sat silently while Marty poured, and when he was done Frank stared at him until he walked away.

"After that," he continued in a low voice, "it was like slow motion. Like everything was happening underwater. The uniform stands up, takes his gun out, and points it at the drunk. The drunk never stops smiling. And then the uniform pulls the trigger, shoots him right in the face. The drunk's head like explodes, and he spins around the steam pipe—all the way—once, before he drops.

"For a second everything stops. It's just the echo and the smoke and blood on the wall and back window. Then, time speeds up again. The sergeant of detectives, a little leprechaun from the other side—must've bribed his way past the height requirement—jumps over his desk and grabs up a billy club. He lands next to the uniform, who's still holding the gun straight out, and he clubs him five or six times on the forearm, hard and fast, *whap-whap-whap*. The gun drops with the first hit but the leprechaun don't stop till the bone breaks. We all hear it snap.

"The uniform pulls his arm in and howls, and the sergeant throws the billy club down and screams at him: 'The next time . . . the next time, it'll be your head that he breaks before you were able to shoot him. Now get him off the pipe before there's burns on his body.' And he storms out of the room."

Frank drank the shot in front of him and finished his beer. I didn't move.

He looked at me and smiled. "The whole squad room," he said, "jumped into action. Some guys uncuffed the drunk; I helped the uniform out. Got him to a hospital. Coupla guys got rags and a pail and started cleaning up.

"Now, think about that," Frank said, leaning in toward me and lowering his voice yet again. "I'm the only spic there. The only other uniform. There had to be ten bulls. But the sergeant, he didn't have to tell anybody what the plan was, or to keep their mouth shut, or any fucking thing. And there was no moment where anybody worried about me seeing it, being a spic. We all knew that coulda been any one of us. That's the most on-the-inside I ever felt. Department now, it's a fucking joke. Affirmative action, cultural-diversity training. And what've you got? Nobody trusts anybody. Guys afraid to trust their own partners." He was whispering and starting to slur his words.

I began to feel nauseated. It's a joke, I thought. A cop's made-up war story. "Frank, did the guy die?"

"Who?"

"The drunk. The man that got shot."

Frank looked confused, and a bit annoyed. "Of course he died."

"Did he die right away?"

"How the fuck should I know? They dragged him outa the room in like a minute."

"To a hospital?"

"Was a better world's all I'm saying. A better world. And you always gotta stay on the inside, don't drift, Danny. If you drift, nobody'll stick up for you."

Jesus, did he have a brogue? He certainly had picked up that lilt to his voice that my father's generation possessed. That half-accent that the children of immigrants acquire in a ghetto. I had to get out of there. A few more minutes and I feared I'd start sounding like one of these tura-lura-lura motherfuckers myself.

I stood, probably too quickly, and took hold of the bar to steady myself. "What about the picture, Frank?"

He handed it to me. "Martin is right," he said slowly, "let it lie. Why do you care who she was?"

"Who she *was*? I asked who she *is*. Is she dead, Frank? Is that what Marty meant by letting the dead rest?"

"Martin . . . Marty meant . . ."

"I'm right here, Francis," Marty said, "and I can speak for myself." He turned to me. "Francis has overindulged in a few jars," he said. "He'll nap in the back booth for a while and be right as rain for the ride home."

"Is that the way it happened, Frank? Exactly that way?"

Frank was smiling at his drink, looking dreamily at his better world. "Who owns memory?" he said.

"Goodnight, Daniel," Marty said. "It was good of you to stop in."

I didn't respond, just turned and slowly walked out. One or two guys gestured at me as I left, the rest seemed not to notice or care.

I removed the picture from my pocket again when I was outside, an action that had taken on a ritualistic feel, like making the sign of the cross. I did not look at it this time, but began tearing it in strips, lengthwise. Then I walked, and bent down at street corners, depositing each strip in a separate sewer along Fourth Avenue.

He'd told me that he'd broken his arm in a car accident, pursuing two black kids who had robbed a jewelry store.

As I released the strips of paper through the sewer gratings, I thought of the hand in the subway tunnel, and my father's assertion that there were many body parts undoubtedly littering the less frequently traveled parts of the city. Arms, legs, heads, torsos; and perhaps all these bits of photo would find their way into disembodied hands. A dozen or more hands, each gripping a strip of photograph down in the wet slime under the street. Regaining a history, a past, that they lost when they were dismembered, making a connection that I never would.

...e. The pot of rice was one sticky clod. I dumped it into the sink.
...d two beers and ordered a pizza. While we waited, we went out
...cony. We drank our beers and watched the pool where a lone pink
...loated.

...is, Mimi," he said. "The house I was at today, it also has a three-
...Three fucking cars! And there's just one dude who lives there,
...ds."

...e's the wife?" I asked, taking a swig.

...ook his head. "Died from cancer or something—and not long ago.
...cking art all over the place and expensive dishes are stacked in a
...abinet the length of our living room wall. His brats have these little
...cars they drive around the neighborhood. They live on this dead
...l de sac. Old money Costa Mesa, looks like. People have got serious
...r there. More than they need."

...e people have all the luck."

...deserve that kind of life," he said.

...ryone thinks they do."

...we really do. His fucking housecleaner knows more about his stuff
...t he has than he does. He has so much crap he wouldn't miss a few
...isappearing."

...ate it when you sound stupid," I said. "You think you can just help
...? Is that what you're saying?"

...i shrugged, took a long pull off the bottle, and slipped out of his red
...cowboy boots, setting them inside our apartment doorway. He pulled
...T-shirt. He was still that sleek boy, a beauty. His curly brown hair was
...d blond and he had just the right amount of growth on his face. His
...vere white-white and his bare feet were perfect. He could be a model,
...how handsome he was. Feet and teeth, I always say, have got to be su-
...His physique made me overlook the fact that he wasn't the brightest
...n the room.

...Shepard needs a nanny for his kids, pretty much right away," Levi said.
...eone smart enough to tutor. He's running an ad but says he can't find
...ght person."

...I'm a teacher," I reminded him, "not a nanny."

...But you could be a nanny . . . for a time. Then we'd both be working
...:."

..."You think he'd go for a fricken handyman and his older girlfriend both
...ing for him? Please."

CRAZY FOR YOU

BY BARBARA DeMARCO-BARRETT

Costa Mesa, Orange County, California
(Originally published in *Orange County Noir*)

When I moved into Levi's apartment in the converted motel on Placentia Avenue, the blue neon "i" of the *Placent_a Arms* sign was burned out. I worried it was an omen, a feng shui gaffe. It made me think too damn much of placenta, birthing, that whole entire mess—not a good thing when the sight of blood makes you faint. I've grown used to most things, and I figured I'd grow used to the sign, if I didn't leave Levi or go crazy first. But I hadn't grown used to it, and I was still here. It was going on three months and my feeling of foreboding had only increased.

The Arms, a chipping aqua U-shaped construction, was clean enough, but Levi's apartment above the fray on the second story, right-hand corner, was growing smaller and duller by the day. So was Westside Costa Mesa, once idyllic cattle grazing land, then an agricultural haven. Now, about the only things that grew wildly were the illegal immigrant population, low-income housing, and Latino gangs. So different from where I was from. If I spoke the language it might be different, or if I was brunette. But I was blond, the only gringa in our apartment complex.

I pulled a folding chair onto the balcony and lit a hand-rolled cigarette, the only tobacco I could afford these days. In the Arms' courtyard just below sat a square swimming pool that had seen better days. Sorry little children with loser parents—why else would they be living at the Placent_a Arms?—splashed in its murky depths. Even the mourning doves inhabiting the adjacent kumquat tree seemed weary of the pool, but then Southern California was mired in a ubiquitous drought and the pool must've been better than nothing, I suppose. Although you can make yourself believe pretty much anything if your life depends on it.

At night, after a drink or two, as you watched the lights beneath the water, all blue and tropical, it was easy to trick yourself into thinking you were at some lush Orange County resort and were one of the beautiful people. The reverie never lasted long, though, because one drunk resident or another would start singing off-key—Barry Manilow, Aerosmith, pop Latino—reminding you that you were *not* in posh Newport Beach, the next city over, or in Laguna Beach, just down the coast, but in lovely Costa Misery. My sister Leonora, a nurse, left home back east to work for a plastic surgeon—the perks included discounted *enhancements*—and I followed when I quit my teaching job, all because of Levi.

Levi was sixteen when we met, seventeen when we started spending time together—backstage, on the football field, in cars. I was Levi's drama teacher, thirty-three years old, but young-looking for my age. My friends called him jailbait, this sleek pretty boy with sea-foam green eyes and abs to die for. I lusted after the kid, but when my soon-to-be-ex husband caught us in my car in the parking lot outside Bob's Big Boy and threatened to have me fired, I decided I needed my job teaching more than I needed Levi, resigned, and moved here. I saw what happened to other teachers who crossed the line, who forgot they were teachers and not teenagers.

A year later, when Levi turned eighteen, he quit school and found me. He was of age, but still too young for me. I was still living with Leonora and her three dogs, substitute teaching in Costa Misery, along bus routes. The trip cross-country had killed my beater and I let my driver's license expire. The better school districts never seemed to have an opening and I didn't want a full-time gig at just any school. Levi had already rented the furnished apartment at the Arms and I planned on spending just a few days, thinking this would help to get him out of my system. But he guilt-tripped me into moving in, said he wouldn't even be out here if not for me.

"Mimi, the guy's a loser," Leonora said. "You can do better." But I was addicted to Levi's body, his skin that felt like silk, and tired of being one of Leonora's pack.

My stomach growled. I lit another cigarette and looked at my watch. Five o'clock. Levi would be home soon. I went inside to throw something together for dinner.

Levi worked as a handyman. Ten bucks an hour, sometimes more. Not what he thought he was worth, but it paid the rent, bought the beer. He told me stories about the rich people's houses where he spent his days—brushing the walls of a nursery with designer paint or retiling a hot tub. He described how, at one home, the outdoor pool connected with the interior of the house through a manmade cave with faux boulders you had to swim through. So Orange County.

Another client owned two houses side by side—one of them they lived in

and the other one was the kids' playhouse. [...] up at church soup kitchens and lived in parks [...] was indeed unfair. And I was a little envious. [...] had too much, while others had so damn little[...]

On the west side, everyone—the Latinos, [...] the dogs—was, for the most part, lackluster. The [...] I suppose, but every day I read the police files i[...] of the crime in coastal Orange County happene[...] Here were the factories, auto shops, taquerías, an[...] us were scraping by, but on the east side that bo[...] where the real money was, that's where the Orang[...] ined and fantasized about resided. I'd been to Di[...] they called it the Happiest Place on Earth, not with[...] and tourists with blue-white legs and lunky cam[...] But a house on the east side, now that would make[...]

Levi came home from installing shelves in wh[...] kitchen of a TV cooking show: marble—not gran[...] stovetop, a fridge the size of our bathroom. He ramb[...] meowner didn't even have a wife. I was standing at t[...] rice, adding vegetable broth every few minutes, to ma[...] for at a restaurant when you order risotto is not the i[...] it takes for some sadly underpaid restaurant worker to[...] plumplike. Biscuits, which I had flattened with my m[...] most prized kitchen implement—and baked in the doll[...] a stovetop that only had three working burners, were c[...]

Levi could see I was down, so he kissed my cheek [...] arms around me from behind. After a day among kids [...] teachers like dog doo, Levi's touch was heaven. He snak[...] my skirt and found my sweet spot. I wanted to shoo h[...] leave risotto for *one minute*—but once Levi got on a cert[...] no stopping him.

Levi liked to give me pleasure, or maybe he knew this [...] he had to offer, so he got on his knees and buried his fac[...] about went nuts, but kept stirring until I just couldn't tak[...] the spoon clatter to the counter and dropped to the aqua an[...] I pulled Levi down with me. It didn't take us long, which is an[...] about Levi—he wasn't one of those guys who needed to linger [...]

We finished, and I washed my hands before returning to[...]

it was too l[...] Levi crack[...] onto the b[...] inner tube [...] "Get t[...] car garage[...] with his k[...] "Whe[...] He sl[...] There's f[...] monster [...] motorize[...] end—a c[...] funds ov[...] "Sor[...] "We[...] "Ev[...] "Bu[...] and wh[...] things [...] "I [...] yoursel[...] Le[...] leathe[...] off his[...] streak[...] teeth [...] that's [...] perio[...] bulb [...] "Sor[...] the [...] the[...] wo[...]

"Don't call me a handyman," he snapped.

"That's what you are, babe."

He looked hurt. "I aspire to more."

"Sure you do," I said. "I just don't like where you're headed with this." I stroked his chest and tickled his nipples, which always put him in a good mood.

"Shepard would like you, Mimi. I told him about you. He seems lonely. I mean, who wouldn't be, your wife up and dies and leaves you with little kids? But once he sees a pretty young thing like you, his day's suddenly gonna seem a lot brighter. Don't you want to brighten up a widower's day?"

"I'm not that young."

"You're the sexiest thing going," he said, running his fingers along my collarbone. "We could both be working there."

"And then?"

"Who knows? But you deserve better'n this," he said, his hands describing an arc about him, his voice going low. "You think all the rich fucks in this town work for what they have? A lot of them got old money. Inheritances. Bank accounts handed down. Or they have great gigs, businesses that haul ass. We weren't lucky that way. Shit, Shepard has an entire goddamn library! He's old, Mimi, but he has money."

"Levi, you're scaring me."

"Don't be scared, baby. How about I just introduce you to him?" He put his hands on my shoulders and looked down at me with his seawater eyes. "C'mon, Mimi. As long as you don't like him *that* way, and why would you?— he's not *me*—it could be fun."

"Ripping off your employer . . . fun, huh?"

He shrugged. "Like I said, it'd be better'n this."

We turned our attention back to the pool and that pink inner tube bobbing about when a pizza boy came whistling into the courtyard, looking like a waiter holding a tray with that flat box poised on his fingers.

"We'd need a plan," I said, as the pizza boy looked up, trilled the fingers of his other hand like we were in some Hollywood musical, and headed for the cement stairway.

"Mims, I'm all about planning," Levi replied, pulling a twenty from his pocket.

The stinking economy, even here in glorious Orange County, had pushed substitute teaching gigs further and further apart, so the next day, around lunchtime, I was sitting on the balcony smoking a hand-rolled and scanning the classifieds. A cherry pie cooled on the counter. I had to do something fast to rescue my financial situation. Levi's truck skidded in. He threw a veggie bologna sandwich together—white bread from Trader Joe's, Dijon mustard, and four slices of fake lunchmeat—and said he was taking me with him to Shepard's house, ten minutes away.

I climbed into his truck, a major gas hog, which you just about needed a ladder to get into. As we passed Latinas with long black braids that touched their waists who pushed strollers, and homeless guys wearing tattered backpacks, he said, "Um, by the way, Shepard thinks you're my older sister, so just play it cool."

"Excuse me?"

"I decided he wouldn't like the idea of you being my girlfriend."

"Sometimes you fucking make me wonder."

He nodded, keeping his eyes fixed on the road. "I just thought of it. Brilliant, huh?"

"Yeah, right. Incredible genius you got goin' in that head of yours."

But as we crossed over Newport Boulevard, leaving the not-so-good side of town for the lush, moneyed side where tall eucalyptus swayed in the faint ocean breeze, Costa Misery segued to Piece of Heaven, California, with its cute cottages, palm trees, rosebushes, magenta bougainvillea, and Jaguars, BMWs, and hybrids.

We pulled into his boss's driveway. A tall husky guy in khakis and a polo shirt, with short graying hair, futzed in the garage. He was a bit thick in the middle and wore conservative beige shoes.

"You owe me big time," I said, pushing open the door as Mr. Orange County Republican approached us.

"That a promise?" he responded, as I jumped from the cab.

The guy had probably been a hottie once and was handsome in an almost-fifty way, but he was so not my type. He held out his hand. "You must be Levi's sister," he said, giving me a warm handshake. "He didn't tell me you were so pretty."

"He's been forgetting to take his ginkgo biloba," I countered, playing it off, but I was charmed. And it takes a lot to charm me.

Levi laughed as if I were the funniest older sister in the entire universe.

"You two get acquainted," said Levi. "The back fence is calling me."

Shepard gave him the thumbs-up sign and said, "Shall we go inside?" His eyes were friendly as he gestured me in and hit the electric garage door button. "The kids are at school, but I'll show you around so you can see where you'd be spending your days."

I forced a smile, tried to look interested.

"School's out tomorrow," he said. "I need someone who can be a nanny *and* a teacher. Only occasional sleepovers, when I'm out of town." He had a gap between his front teeth, which were white and even. I had a boyfriend once with a gap I loved to tongue.

"Your brother said you're a teacher."

Brother? Then I remembered.

"I was, back east," I said. "Taught drama and English. I've been substitute teaching since I moved here. Not a lot of work these days for teachers without seniority."

"That's too bad," he said, touching my shoulder to direct me into the living room. He must have noticed how my gaze fell on the baby grand because he said, "You play?"

"Used to."

"Like riding a bicycle, don't you think? You're welcome to . . ." He nodded toward it.

"Ah, no, maybe another time." Being able to play piano impressed people, but it didn't impress me. You could learn anything if you wanted to.

"Your brother said you like to bake."

"I'm obsessed with making pies." When we have extra money, I almost added.

"You're welcome to bake here, anytime. I can't remember the last time a pie came out of that oven. Just give me a list; I'll buy you what you need."

If it were possible to fall in love with a house, I was falling—hard—especially for the kitchen. With that kitchen, I could bake a million pies and never grow bored.

"Like something? Coffee? A soda?" he asked, sticking a glass into the opening of the fridge's front panel. He pushed a button. Ice dropped and chinked into the glass.

"Diet Coke?"

"Sure thing," he said, taking one from the fridge. He moved toward the cabinet.

"No glass," I said, so he tore a paper towel from the roll and wiped the top of the can clean before handing it to me. No one had ever done that before, and I swear, he looked different after that. Charming.

We talked about my background and his needs, and an hour later, when the kids were dropped off, he gave them big bear hugs and introduced us. "Bella and Dante, this is Mimi. She might be helping out. Want to show her your rooms?" The kids appraised me like I was a new piece of furniture, and then Bella took my hand.

"My room first," she said. Her little brother led the way, running his Hot Wheels police car along the wall.

They showed me their rooms and I liked them. Levi stuck in his head and said he had to run off for a while, and when he returned at five, he seemed hyper, strange, and rushed me to go.

As we pulled away from the curb and headed down the tree-lined street, Levi said: "He's not bad, right?"

"He was fine," I replied, almost adding, *He was more than fine.* "And you're lowdown." I had never felt so cold toward Levi. But he didn't seem to notice.

"He tell you what he does for a living? I think he's a developer or something."

"Something like that," I said.

"Major bucks."

"Construction's taking a dive."

"He tell you that? Don't believe it," he said, turning onto a street with houses behind high walls, pulling over and putting the truck in park. He scooched over to me, took me in his arms, and started kissing my neck. Melted me every time. Stupid guys who were cute made the best lovers. It was the truly smart ones you had to watch out for, who could fracture your heart with one skewered word.

"C'mon, baby, don't be mad. It's a way for us to get ahead."

"But his kids weren't brats. They were sweet."

He pulled a blanket from under the seat, covered us as he pushed me down with kisses, and said, "After this, we'll go eat. I'm starving."

We sat across from each other at Wahoo's Fish Tacos, a popular haunt on Placentia, down the street from where we lived. The exterior was covered with chipping teal paint. Surf stickers smattered the windows. The menu offered Mexican entrees that weren't gourmet, but were good enough, priced for artists and people on limited incomes, and for rich Orange Countians who wanted to feel they were getting away with something. As he talked about what we'd do with the money—a new truck for him, a kitchen for me—you'd think I was one hungry fish, the way I went for it. I must have been beyond bored. We'd go slow and easy, figure things out, and when we had all the pieces, we'd make our play, he said. But I had a bad feeling.

Levi started staying up late, figuring out where we'd escape to once we had a few of Shepard's more high-end belongings that Levi would give to a friend of a friend who would split the proceeds. I did a bit of research and learned that Shepard had paintings and antiques worth thousands. He had one Chagall lithograph, *The Artist with a Goat, #1026,* that was worth thirty grand. Even inane simple drawings of dolphins that lined the hallway by that overrated Laguna Beach artist, Wyland, sold for three grand apiece. Levi's idea was we'd leave Costa Misery for Mexico. No one can find you down there, he said.

A week into my new nannyhood, as Levi and I were wrapping it up for the day and I was saying goodbye to the children, Shepard said, "The kids are going to their aunt's. Why don't I take you out to dinner, my thanks for coming to our rescue."

Levi didn't miss a beat. "Go ahead, sis," he said. "It'd be fun for you."

Sis?

I scanned what I was wearing—jeans, a purple pullover, lowtop red Converse. "I'm not exactly dressed up."

"You'd look gorgeous in a flour sack," said Shepard.

Levi winked at me. I shrugged. "Okay, then."

Levi hurried off a little too quickly with a nonchalant wave.

"Let's have a taste before we go," said Shepard. "Pick anything you like from the wine cellar and I'll meet you out by the pool."

The cellar was a converted closet off the kitchen with a slate floor and thermostat that said fifty-three degrees. I chose a 1987 Tondonia because I liked the name. He carried our glasses to the back patio that overlooked the pool. This pool was a million times better than the one at the Arms.

"I could get used to this," I said, after we clinked glasses.

"I hope you do," he said, his voice all syrupy and warm, like the wine.

Soon Shepard and I were in his Jag cruising up Newport Boulevard to Habana, a Cuban restaurant in a funky open-air mall with an oil-drum waterfall and tattooed, pierced hipsters. Habana was dark, lit only with candles. You could barely see who was sitting next to you, but the waiter could see well enough to recognize Shepard and make a big deal, and it was different being with someone before whom people groveled.

Shepard ordered a bottle of Barolo red, which he explained was the king of wines. We toasted and he said to order whatever tickled my fancy. Those were his words. During dinner, a second bottle of wine arrived and for dessert we shared a Cuban flan. Our fingers brushed against one another.

"We're delighted you came to us, Mimi. The children like you very much."

"They're sweethearts," I said.

"Actually, to be honest, I'm the happiest." He stroked my arm and focused on it as if it were a great treasure. "You've got great skin."

"This light would make anyone look good," I said, feeling guilty over how much I enjoyed his attention. Then I thought, *What the hell. Levi got me into this*, and I gave in. Right then and there I felt myself loosen and open to Shepard. When his hand found mine, I let it. And when he brought my hand to his lips, I let him. We left the restaurant and returned to his Jag, his arm laced around my shoulder. He opened the passenger door and I slid onto the butter-soft leather seats that reclined at the touch of a button. He got in and buzzed down the windows. He turned to kiss me and I kissed him back, tongued that gap in his front teeth. The wine was talking; I've always been an easy drunk. His hand found its way under my pullover and then he was in my jeans. I pressed against his fingers and before long I shuddered. Who cared if he was a conservative and a bit too husky—he had the touch of an angel and I liked how sweet and considerate he was. He was different from anyone I'd ever been with. Maybe older guys with money could afford to be patient, considerate.

"What about you?" I asked into his neck, rubbing him down there.

"There's time for that," he said, gently removing my hand and kissing it.

When I got home, Levi wanted to know where we went and what we did. He wasn't so laid-back about it anymore. I didn't tell him everything, and I distracted him with sex. It always worked. I had to keep my OC Republican a secret for now.

But things had changed and Levi knew it. Now when we arrived at work in the morning, there was no mistaking the glimmer in Shepard's eyes. He'd hang around the house to have coffee with me before taking off. On occasion, when everyone was out of the house, we'd fool around.

"The dude fucking likes you," Levi said a week later, his eyes flashing. We were in his truck, at a stop light.

"What are you talking about?"

"He's been asking me all about you. He's in love with you."

"He can't be," I said, secretly wishing it were so.

"Hey, it could be good for us," he scowled.

"What do you mean?"

"Shit, what could be better for us than if he wanted to marry you?"

"Excuse me?"

"It wouldn't have to change things between us. No one's as great for you as I am. You'd never go for someone that old. And if you did, I'd kill you." He laughed, then added, "You'd just have to live with him for a time. It would help us pull off our plan."

"You're talking too crazy for me," I said, as we crossed over Newport Boulevard and Piece of Heaven turned back into Costa Misery, with its pawnshops, its dive bars. But that night, after Levi went back out to do who knows what—he wouldn't say—I stood on the balcony and smoked a hand-rolled. As the lit murky water below pulled my focus, the sounds of the compound drew close—TV, a neighbor singing off-key, kids screaming—and my own version of an old Animals song spun an endless loop in my brain: *I gotta get outa this place, if it's the last thing I ever do.*

The next day, after Shepard's sister picked up his kids for an overnight, he said, "Let me take you to the fair. You've been to the Orange County Fair, right?"

"Um, no," I answered. I'd left Bumfuck where "hooptedoodle" was a favorite expression, and I had no desire to return.

"Then you got to let me take you."

"Fairs are a Republican thing."

"Pshaw!" he said, tucking in his turquoise polo shirt with a tiny alligator over the left breast.

"Shouldn't you take your kids?"

"They've been, and I'll take them again before it ends. Tonight it will be just you and me. How about it?"

I said yes. I said yes to everything—to Levi and his schemes, now to Shepard.

I went to freshen up.

Levi called from another job while I was in the bathroom; Shepard had run out of work for him. I told him I had to work late. I'd been spending more and more time at Shepard's and less and less time at our sorry excuse for a home. It was getting to Levi. I knew because when he talked about Shepard, he no longer used his name.

"The motherfucker tell you anything interesting?" or "What's up with the motherfucker?" I found a bindle with white powder in Levi's things. His skin was becoming all mottled and he was losing weight. He denied using crank, said he had gotten it for a friend, but he was short-tempered and negative. Now I just wanted to escape with Shepard, go someplace where Levi couldn't find me.

Shepard and I walked hand in hand to his dusty blue Jag and moments later were gliding down Broadway to Newport and up to Del Mar, his hand on my knee, my hand on his thigh, to where the dark sky was lit up all red from the lights on the rides and the midway. The Ferris wheel spun lazily around, its colorful, happy life temporary—like mine, I feared. This happiness wouldn't last—it couldn't; it hadn't been a part of the plan for me to fall for an Orange County Republican. Levi would never let me have Shepard. I wanted to confess and tell him what Levi was planning, but I didn't know how I could put it where he wouldn't just fire me and tell me to be on my way.

We parked and walked toward the lights, toward the Tilt-a-Whirl and the rollercoaster with purple neon cutting the black sky, teenagers on all sides of us running amok, clutching cheap stuffed animals and stalks of cotton candy. Shepard bought us caramel apples, fried Twinkies, and roasted corn on the cob. We got wristbands and drank draft beer.

It was going on eleven and the fairgoers were pouring through the gates, probably to get a jump on the freeways. Shepard and I moved against the flow, heading toward the livestock area, past Hercules, the giant horse, llama stalls, and a corral where the pig races took place. He said he'd been coming here since he was a kid. Fair diehards moseyed about. My phone rang—Levi's ringtone—but I ignored it, and I feared it. Levi said he could always find me. Something about the GPS positioning on my phone and how he'd rigged it. Cell phones didn't make you freer—they made your whereabouts known, and I didn't like it one bit, this hold Levi had on me.

Couples lingered in the shadows. Shadows scared me. I worried Levi might be hiding in them. Lately everything got on his nerves and he suspected everyone. He'd screamed at the next-door neighbor to quit his fool singing. He'd even pierced the pink inner tube in the pool because he no longer liked seeing it floating there.

Shepard directed me to the metal bleachers around the cattle arena. He picked me up, set me on one so our faces were level, and kissed me. "You make me so happy," he said.

This tall bulky man had grown on me. He pulled a little robin's egg–blue box from his pocket and flipped it open. A diamond solitaire.

He took the ring from the box and slid it on my finger. "You will, won't you?" he said. "Marry me?"

* * *

Levi was leaning over the railing of the balcony, smoking with one of his low-life loser buddies, when I arrived home at midnight. I'd taken off the ring and sequestered it at the bottom of my tampon holder.

The light from the water bounced off Levi and his buddy whose name I forgot. I gave them a half-hearted wave. Levi nodded and smiled his lizard-cold smile.

"Where've you been?" he asked, flicking his cigarette butt down into the pool as his buddy took off.

"Had to stay with the kids until Shepard got home." I took a cigarette from Levi's pack on the cement floor.

"Fuck you did," he said.

I gave him a long look. It was always better to say less than more.

"Where's the ring?" he said.

"What ring?"

"Mimi, this'll only work if you're straight with me about the motherfucker."

I went to go into the apartment, but he grabbed my arm. "I'm gonna tell him all about you, Mimi. You weren't supposed to fall in love with the asshole. You love *me*, remember?"

I wrenched my arm away and hurried inside. I poured a glass of water, trying to think.

Levi hurried in behind me. "Don't fucking walk away from me, Mimi."

"I'll do what I want."

"Fuck you will." He pulled me to him, pressed his mouth against mine, hiked his hand up my top. "C'mon, baby, what happened to us?"

I pulled free. "Leave me alone, you asshole."

"I own you," he said. "I came all the way out here to find you and claim you and now you're mine."

"Whatever drug you're doing, it's making you crazy."

"Crazy for you," he said, grabbing me with one hand and undoing his belt buckle with the other.

I'd never given in to a man forcing me and I wasn't about to now. I tried pushing him away, but his grip on my arm only grew tighter.

"You always liked it with me before," he said. "Mr. OC motherfucker better'n me now, Mimi?" His face looked strained, a Halloween mask. "He won't want you when I tell him who you really are, when I tell him everything you planned. He'll take his ring back and then where will you be?"

"What *I* planned?"

He jammed his hand down my pants and hurt me and that's when something snapped. My prized marble roller sat on the counter behind me, where it always was. I felt for it with my free hand and almost had it, but it slipped away. My hand landed on Levi's hammer. I brought it around and cracked it against his skull as hard as I could. His sea-foam green eyes went wide, as if he were seeing me for the first time. Then he crumpled to the linoleum. A trickle of blood issued from his ear.

"Levi!" I gasped. "Shit!"

The way his eyes gazed into the living room without blinking gave him a peaceful look I had never seen.

I tried to think. Should I pack up my things, including my pastry roller, and split? I considered cleaning my fingerprints off everything in the apartment, but I wouldn't be able to get rid of every little hair, every little cell of mine that had flaked off. I knew about DNA. I could be easily tied to Levi, even without a car or California driver's license. Even without my name on the month-to-month lease or on bills; I still received my mail at Leonora's. To the mostly Latino transient residents, I must've looked like any other gringa. But I talked to Levi on my cell phone all the time. I could even be tied to him through Shepard. They would visit Levi's former employer and find me there, loving my new life.

No, I couldn't simply leave.

I pulled down the shades and locked the door. I wiped my fingerprints off the hammer after placing it near Levi. I turned on the shower as hot as I could stand, peeled off my clothes, and stepped in. This would calm me and help me think.

As the scalding water poured down my face, it came to me, what I would say and do: *I came home, Levi was here with a drug-dealing buddy, I took a shower and heard something. When I got out of the shower, I found my boyfriend on the floor.*

I turned off the water, wrapped myself in a towel, and jumped into my role. I hurried out to the kitchen, as if I'd heard something bad and found Levi hurt on the kitchen floor. I bent down to see what was wrong. Water puddled about me and mixed with Levi's blood. I ran screaming from the apartment onto the balcony. As I started down the steps, the towel slipped from my body, and I let it. I was a crazy naked lady. Residents—men in underwear and T-shirts and women in nightgowns—started emerging from their hovels.

"Call the police!" I made a good hysteric. Someone had done my poor boyfriend in.

Women called in Spanish to each other. More than once I heard the word "loco." A short dark woman with gold front teeth wrapped me in a Mexican blanket, patted my wet hair, and cooed to me in Spanish. The sirens grew closer. A crowd had gathered around us and upstairs at the doorway to the apartment.

There would be an investigation, but after a while I would be cleared. No one ever saw us fight. There was no insurance settlement coming. Why would I kill my boyfriend? The authorities would search instead for the lowlife who did him—or not. Probably not. Who cared about one more druggie dude going bye-bye? My first chance I would call Shepard, tell him details about what happened that he would have heard about on the news. I would tell him how Levi made me say I was his sister, had threatened my life even, had never wanted me to fall for him. I would remind Shepard that I loved him, every inch of him. Shepard believed in me, would never think I could do something like this.

I knew how to be patient. Shepard and Piece of Heaven, California, would eventually be mine, and before long, the ring would be back on my finger.

MASTERMIND

BY REED FARREL COLEMAN
Selden, Long Island
(Originally published in *Long Island Noir*)

J eff Ziegfeld was always the exception to the rule: the dumb Jew, the blue-collar Jew, the tough Jew. No matter the Zen of the ethnic group the wheel of fortune got you born into, dumb and poor was the universal formula for tough. And he had to be tough because it's hard to be hard when your name is Jeffrey Ziegfeld. Didn't exactly make the kids on the block shit their pants when someone said, "Watch out or Ziggy'll kick your ass." He was extra tough because his dad liked to smack him around for the fun of it, all the time saying, "Remember, dickhead, no matter how strong you get, I'll always be able to kick your ass. I grew up the last white kid in Brownsville. And where'd you grow up? Lake Grove, a town with no lake and no grove. What a fucking joke. Kinda like you, huh, kid?"

J-Zig, as one of the other inmates at the jail in Riverhead had taken to calling him, could trace what had gone wrong with his life back to before he was born. Neither one of his parents had ever gotten out of high school or over moving out of Brooklyn. Long Island was a rootless, soulless place where everyone except the Shinnecock, the East End farmers, and the fishermen came from Northern Boulevard or the Grand Concourse or Pitkin Avenue. And even the natives were trading in their roots and souls for money. All the goddamned Indians wanted to do was run slot machine and bingo parlors. The working farms had been converted into condos, McMansions, and golf courses that no one like J-Zig could afford to play. Not that J-Zig knew a rescue club from a lob wedge. The fishermen? Well, they'd become the cause célèbre of Billy Joel, Long Island's king of schlock'n'roll. Billy Joel, born and bred in Hicksville. Hicksville, indeed.

J-Zig's head was somewhere else as he sat on the ratty Salvation Army couch in his dank basement apartment in Nesconset. Nesconset, a stone's throw from his mom's house in Lake Grove. It might just as well have been a million miles away for all he saw of his mom since she'd remarried. He had plenty of reasons to hate his real father, but he hated O'Keefe, his mom's new husband, even more and that was really saying something. His stepfather, a retired city fireman with a belly like a beach ball and the manners of a hyena, was a drunk and more than a little anti-Semitic. J-Zig didn't let that get to him. O'Keefe— if the moron had a first name, J-Zig didn't know it—hated everybody, himself most of all. Jews were probably only fourth or fifth on his list. Besides, O'Keefe's opinion of him was nothing more than the buzzing of mosquito wings. There was only one man J-Zig ever cared enough about to want to impress.

J-Zig had a terminal case of yearning exacerbated by persistent bouts of resentment. But he was a lazy son of a bitch and about as ambitious as a dining room chair. There'd be no pulling himself up by his bootstraps—whatever the fuck bootstraps were, anyhow—not for this likely lad. One way or the other he was a man destined to be a ward of the taxpaying public. He'd already tried on three of the state's myriad options: jail, welfare, and the old reliable unemployment insurance. Truth was, he found none of them very much to his liking. The food and company at the jail sucked. Welfare was okay as far as it went, but since he and the wife and her bastard son by another man's drunken indiscretion had split, he no longer qualified. He liked unemployment fine, but the bitch of it was you had to work for a while to qualify and J-Zig wasn't keen on that aspect of the equation. So he sold fake Ecstasy outside clubs and stolen car parts to pay the bills.

When he wasn't making do with the drugs or the hot car parts, he worked as muscle, doing collections for a loan shark and fence named Avi Ben-Levi. Ben-Levi was a crazy Israeli who put cash on the street and charged major vig to his desperate and pathetic clients. Avi might have been a madman, but J-Zig admired the shit out of him. He admired him not only because Avi was only a few years older than him and had everything J-Zig wanted—a big house in King's Point, a gull-wing Mercedes, and the hottest pussy this side of the sun—but because of how Avi got it.

"Balls, Jeffrey, balls. That's what counts in this world. I came to this coun-try five years ago with three words of English and these," Avi would say, grab-bing his own crotch. "Look at me. I am a plain-looking bastard with a high school education. I even got kicked out of the IDF. Not easy getting kicked out of the Israeli army, but I did it. And here I am. Do you have the balls to make good, Jeffrey? Do you have them?"

That was a question J-Zig sometimes asked himself until it was the only thing in his head. Still, as much as J-Zig yearned for Avi's approval, he hated being muscle. Well, except when it came to gamblers.

He had no respect for gamblers. They'd borrow the money and blow it that day and then, when J-Zig would come to collect, they'd squeal and beg like little girls. He liked to hear them scream when he snapped their bones like breadsticks. It was the business types he felt sorry for. All sorts of people borrowed money from Avi, but as broke as he could be at times, J-Zig knew better than to dip into a loan shark's well. Once they had you, they had you by the balls and then they squeezed and squeezed and squeezed until they milked you dry. Thing was, Ben-Levi didn't do the milking himself. It was always left to the muscle like J-Zig. It had been a few months since he'd worked for Ben-Levi because the Israeli had wounded J-Zig's pride. Isn't it always the way: the people whose love you want hurt you the most? He'd come to the loan shark with an excellent idea about how to streamline Ben-Levi's business.

"What, are you a mastermind all of a sudden? Listen, Jeffrey, never confuse muscle with balls, okay? You are good muscle, but show me your balls. Until you do, just do your job, get paid, and shut up." He'd waved his hand in front of J-Zig's face. "This ring and watch are worth more money than you will ever see in your life, so please, either go to Wharton or keep your genius ideas to yourself."

Mastermind. The word had been stuck in J-Zig's head ever since. He burned to prove the Israeli wrong, to repay Avi for mocking him. He wanted to shove Avi's sarcasm so far up his ass that they'd be able to see it in Tel Aviv. It didn't seem to matter what J-Zig did or how hard he tried to please, because his father du jour would always shit on him. He could never remember a time when his real dad had anything but disdain for him. His dad's pet name for J-Zig was the Little Idiot, as in, *Where the fuck is that little idiot?* or *What did the little idiot get on his report card this term?* That's how J-Zig still saw himself—a little idiot. Then there were all the other men who had passed through J-Zig's front door on the way to his mother's bed. Most of them ignored him. The ones who didn't treated him like a case of the crabs. *Hey, can't you ditch the kid? I can't fuck if I know the kid's listening to you squeal through the wall.* Compared to them, O'Keefe was a fucking prince among men. But it was Avi more than any of them he burned to prove wrong.

But J-Zig couldn't figure out how to do it. He hadn't hit upon the right idea just yet, though he knew the right idea was out there waiting for him to find it. He could feel it sometimes like an itch on the bottom of his foot that he couldn't quite get to. If he could only reach it, J-Zig was sure he could finally escape the weight of the gravity that had held him down his entire miserable life.

Then it happened in a flash: the idea hit him like a Taser. When he re-traced his steps that day, he even understood the genesis of it. This in itself was a near miracle. Deductive reasoning and introspection weren't usually dishes on J-Zig's menu. The day had started out like most others. Maybe a little better than recent days because he'd fallen into some stolen airbags at dirt-cheap prices. God love tweakers. Meth heads didn't haggle, they just wanted enough cash to keep themselves buzzing for the next few weeks. Sometimes they got a little violent, but violence was something J-Zig could handle. He was better at it than most anyone stupid enough to take him on. He was empathetic to the tweakers' plight. Shit, who wouldn't get edgy when his world was spinning that much faster than everyone else's? Who wouldn't get wound up tight after not sleeping for days on end?

J-Zig had found a body shop in Selden willing to buy the boosted airbags at a fair price. Getting goods cheap didn't mean dick if you couldn't find some-one to take them off your hands. The exchange of the airbags for cash went smoothly and the gelt in his pocket meant his expenses were covered for the next two months with a little something left over. Mick, his connection at the body shop, told J-Zig that they could handle as much merchandise as he could bring in. In a tough economy everyone was looking to cut corners. This new connection and the cash were cool, but it wasn't his way to prove himself. What it was, was a big weight off his shoulders and that helped clear his head.

For the first time in a long while, he had a little mad money and room to breathe. He decided to head a few miles west, straight down Middle Country Road, for the Smith Haven Mall. In Saudi Arabia, they have Mecca and Me-dina. On Long Island they have Roosevelt Field and the Smith Haven Mall. Who needs God when you've got the Gap? Everybody on the island, even lowlife mutts like Jeff Ziegfeld, prayed at the temple of conspicuous consump-tion. *Say hallelujah. Say amen.*

The second piece of the grand scheme planted its seed in J-Zig's brain as he turned left out of the body shop's driveway and toward the mall. A com-mercial came on the radio for Island World Gold and Jewelry Exchange—Long Island's biggest and most generous gold and jewelry exchange, so the announcer claimed, with branches in Floral Park, Bethpage, Massapequa, Mastic, Selden, Yaphank, and Riverhead. *Selden!* And there it was right in front of him, directly across Middle Country Road from the body shop—Island World Gold and Jewelry Exchange. Funny how he never noticed it before. A sign in the window read: *MORE CASH ON HAND THAN ANY THREE OF OUR COMPETITORS COMBINED.* Still, it didn't quite register. The only thing he was thinking about was checking out the high school girls parading around the mall in skintight pants cut so low you could see the waistbands of their thongs peeking out the back. J-Zig was pretty successful with high school girls who had a thing for bad boys with good bodies. But when he got close to the mall, thoughts of teenage girls and their silky thongs went right out of his head.

There were two white-and-blue Suffolk County Police cruisers blocking the Middle Country Road entrances to the mall. The cops were out of their units, motioning for approaching cars to turn around and leave. J-Zig noticed the vast parking lots were empty and that there were Suffolk County PD cars all over the place, their cherry tops lit up like Times Square on New Year's Eve. There were fire engines and ambulances too.

"Excuse me, officer, what's going on?" he asked one of the cops, slowing his car to a crawl. J-Zig's tone was utterly respectful. He'd learned the hard way how to talk to cops. If you kissed their asses and licked their boots a little, they might tell you what you wanted to know.

"Prank," the cop said. "Some stupid kid called in a bomb threat. Okay, now let's keep it moving."

That's when it all clicked. *Eu-fucking-reka!*

It was week seven of his master plan and so far everything was going smoothly. If everything continued going that way—and he had no reason to think it wouldn't—he would hit Island World Gold and Jewelry Exchange in Selden that coming Thursday at two p.m. J-Zig got stiff just thinking about what he'd been able to manage completely on his own. He was proudest of exhibiting three qualities he wasn't exactly known for: diligence, patience, and calm. He had written out the entire plan, step by step. He'd made a list of the equipment he needed and the research he had to do before even thinking about pulling the job. He went over the lists again and again and again.

First thing he did was get ahold of the meth head who'd gotten him the airbags, because J-Zig needed a steady flow of funds to help finance the job. He promised the tweaker better prices for his merchandise if he could keep the supply of car parts coming. Mick at the body shop was good to his word and said he would pay top dollar for anything J-Zig could deliver. Greed and drugs were great motivators, and within twenty-four hours the tweaker was knocking on J-Zig's door and J-Zig was in turn knocking on the body shop's door. Everybody was happy.

Over the following weeks, whenever he went to the body shop for a transaction, he scoped out the external security setup at Island World. By his third trip, he was totally confident he hadn't missed anything. It was pretty basic stuff: a camera on the front door, one on the back door, one on the parking lot, one on the side street. He spent days in the abandoned Taco Bell parking lot with a pair of binoculars fixed on Island World. It got so he recognized the employees, their cars, the times they went to lunch. Most importantly, he took note that the armored car pickup came at two fifteen p.m. every day of the week.

Next thing he did was turn some of his car-part profits into used gold jewelry at a flea market in Sayville. He knew that the stuff was gaudy crap, but that wasn't the point. He needed something to use as an excuse to scope out Island World from the inside. Unlike with the outside security, J-Zig would only get one shot, two at most, to survey the internal security. There would be cameras inside, some he knew he wouldn't be able to see, but that would sure as shit see him. He couldn't risk making too many scouting trips. One, his being there a lot would raise suspicions that he was in fact scouting out the place for a job. Two, he was a convicted felon. Admittedly, a low-class felon, but a felon nonetheless. If Island World's security company was thorough, they might identify him and suspect he was using them to dispose of hot jewelry. He meant to set off some alarm bells, but not that way and not just yet.

He'd convinced a local commercial real estate broker that he was interested in a stand-alone building not unlike the one that housed Island World Gold and Jewelry Exchange. "For coins and other collectibles," he told the broker, who was then only too happy to give J-Zig the keys for a look-see.

When the rep from the same firm that did Island World's security met him at the vacant building, J-Zig realized he shouldn't have wasted time worrying about them being thorough. The rep was so eager to land the account, he volunteered more information than J-Zig could have hoped for.

"We do security for a client right down the road from here in Selden that does sort of what you have in mind for this place. It's roughly the same size and we can do the same setup."

The schmuck practically tripped over his own penis giving out details. And in an attempt to sell an even more elaborate system, the sales rep listed the pitfalls of the Island World setup and explained how a very clever criminal might defeat the system entirely. Some of it was beyond J-Zig's capabilities, but he didn't need to defeat the whole system, just part of it. He thanked the salesman, took his card, and told him he'd be in touch.

The other part of the plan was trickier and more dangerous because it directly involved the police. At random times and on different prepaid Walmart cell phones, he called in various emergencies at the Smith Haven Mall. One Monday it was a car fire. One Wednesday it was a robbery. One Thursday it was a heart attack. One Friday it was a bomb threat. Bomb threat won in a landslide. The police response was incredible. Every cruiser in the 4th Precinct and half the fire departments on the North Shore of Suffolk County showed up at the mall. That would take care of the cops to his west. J-Zig was smart enough not to repeat the phone-threat routine in the 6th Precinct, the one responsible for Selden, but he was willing to bet they would respond to a bomb threat at the local high school with the same sort of vigor the 4th Precinct cops responded to a bomb threat at the mall. When J-Zig pulled the job, the cops would be so preoccupied they wouldn't know what hit them.

What made this especially cool was how, for the first time in his whole fucked-up life, all the parts were falling into place. The stars had finally aligned for him. All of it, from the bad economy to the kid's bomb prank, from the tweaker to Mick, from the radio commercial to Island World being right across the street from the body shop, had made it pretty easy. But now Thursday was here and the easy stuff was done. It was time to go to work.

He'd made all the calls as he pulled into the body shop's parking lot. When he stepped into the shop to greet Mick, the firehouse claxons erupted, calling for the volunteer firemen to get their asses to the firehouse. Then, as he walked to the back room of the body shop to use the bathroom and establish his alibi, J-Zig heard the police sirens wailing. By the time he slid out the back door, all hell had broken loose. Emergency vehicles were flying down Middle Country Road in both directions: fire engines and ambulances and police cars, lots and lots of police cars. With all of the activity no one noticed him dash across the street. Certainly no one saw him slip into the latex gloves and Obama mask in the shadows along the back edge of Island World's parking lot. He had no doubt that Island World's two female employees were too busy to notice him. Every day at this time, they assembled their cash take and jewelry for the armored car pickup at two-fifteen. It was only when J-Zig threw the brick, lit road flares, and a smoke grenade—much easier to get than he thought it would be—through the side window of Island World Gold and Jewelry Exchange that the employees would sense something was terribly wrong. By then it would be too late.

It was magic. When the two women came screaming and coughing out the back door, he ran in and scooped up the two bags. Before leaving, he checked out the back door and he couldn't believe his eyes. The two women were still running and hadn't bothered looking back. He was out of there and at the edge of the lot, out of sight of the cameras. He slipped the deposit bags, gloves, and his mask into the gym bag he had hidden there the night before with the brick, road flares, and grenade. If anything, the activity on Middle Country Road had intensified. Now there were news and police helicopters in the air. Getting back across the street was no easy thing, but he made it. He tossed the gym bag in the trunk of his car, walked through the body shop's back door—which he had made sure to keep slightly ajar with a small stone— hurried to the bathroom, and flushed. He looked at his watch. 2:06 p.m. The stars were still aligned, but that wasn't the beauty part of the deal, not by a long shot.

The sweetness was that J-Zig was going to get the chance to shove Avi Ben-Levi's own words up his ass after all. He had arranged for Ben-Levi, a man with all the right connections in the wrong world, to fence the jewelry. That's why J-Zig had taken the gold and diamonds and not just the cash—so he could get the chance to face Ben-Levi and gloat. He had fantasized about how the meeting would go for nearly seven weeks. After shaking hands with Mick to reestablish his alibi, he was going to head straight from the body shop to meet with Ben-Levi at his office in Great Neck. And as a kind of subtle and final fuck you to his former employer, J-Zig had purchased a ticket on EL AL for a flight to Israel. Israel was where he needed to go. He wished he could see the look on Avi's face when he opened the letter J-Zig would send him explaining how he'd pulled off the job at Island World Gold and Jewelry Exchange. He would sign the letter *Mastermind*.

J-Zig slammed the toilet door loud enough to be heard over the sirens and then stepped back into the shop itself. Mick was there waiting for him.

"We were gonna send a search party in there after you, for fuck's sake. What the fuck were you doing?" Mick asked.

"Stomach's been bothering me." J-Zig winked. "I wouldn't go in there for a while unless you get battle pay."

"I consider myself warned."

"What the fuck's going on out here anyway?" he asked, as innocent as a spring lamb, while a few more police cruisers flew by. "I heard all the commotion when I was in the can."

"Fuck if I know. Come on in the office, there's some friends I want you to meet."

J-Zig looked at his watch again. "Maybe another time, I've got—"

"Look, man, for what I've been paying you, you owe me this small favor."

178 // USA Noir

It was tough to argue Mick's point, so he didn't bother. "Lead the way."

He was in the office, the door shut at his back, before he could quite make sense of what was going on. Even after seeing the shields hanging on chains around the necks of Mick's three friends and the 9mms strapped to their belts, it almost didn't register. Then he heard Mick, who was still behind him, say: "Jeffrey Ziegfeld, you're under arrest." J-Zig felt Mick tug his wrists and slap on the cuffs. "You have the right to remain silent. Anything you say can and will be used against you in a court of law. You have the right to an attorney. If you cannot afford an attorney, one will be provided to you. Do you understand these rights?"

J-Zig didn't answer the question, but asked one of his own: "What are the charges?"

"*What are the charges*, he asks," said the fierce-looking detective standing directly in front of J-Zig. "Are you fucking kidding me or what? Hey, this guy missed his calling. He shoulda done standup."

J-Zig repeated the question: "What are the charges?"

"This guy can't be this dumb, can he?" the detective asked the cops behind him. Then he spoke directly to J-Zig. "Are you really that stupid?"

J-Zig repeated the question again: "What are the charges?"

"Okay, rocket scientist, let me give you a clue. My name is Detective Robert Ferraro and we're from the Suffolk County PD Auto Crime Task Force. You think maybe now you can figure it out, or do I have to draw you a picture with crayons?"

J-Zig heard someone laughing. It took a second or two until he realized it was himself.

"Mick, can you believe this guy? He's facing like a ten spot in prison and he's laughing his head off. Hey, shithead, what's so funny?" asked Ferraro.

"I am," said J-Zig.

"You wanna let us in on the joke?" Ferraro asked.

"The punch line won't be as funny to you if I just tell you, but you'll find out soon enough."

"Whatever. Mick, get this moron outta here."

Later that afternoon, when J-Zig's impounded car had been towed to the 6th Precinct, Mick and Ferraro searched it for more stolen parts. Nobody at the precinct paid the two auto crime task force detectives much mind. Who gave a fuck about some dumb-ass skell who was selling car parts to a police sting operation? They were too busy looking for the guy who jerked around half the first responders in Suffolk County, ripped off Island World Gold and Jewelry Exchange, and then disappeared into thin air. After a minute or two, Ferraro found the gym bag with the money, the jewelry, the gloves, and the Obama mask.

"Holy fuck, Mick!"

"What is it?"

"The punch line."

When J-Zig was arraigned the next morning at the courthouse in Central Islip, he seemed utterly calm. He turned and smiled at the crush of media squeezed into the courtroom. After the long list of charges were read, the judge asked for J-Zig's plea.

"Tell Avi Ben-Levi to go fuck himself!" is what he answered.

J-Zig knew it really didn't matter what he said. He was going to spend a lot of his now somewhat less miserable life in prison.

THE CLOWN AND BARD

BY KAREN KARBO

SE *Twenty-Eighth Avenue, Portland*

(Originally published in *Portland Noir*)

harlotte is sprawled on the bathroom floor of my apartment on Southeast Ankeny, the one I rented because I thought she'd like it. Rundown but arty, with forced-air heat and bad plumbing. High ceilings, creaking stairs, walls plastered in thick, sharp stucco. The lobby smells like mold and cantaloupe two days past its prime. The couple downstairs has a pirate flag tacked over their front window, and the landlord is twenty-three and walks around her apartment in a red thong and T-shirt. The building is shaped like a V, so I can easily see into her windows. She has a small wrought-iron balcony where she grows orange flowers in green plastic pots.

Since Charlotte deceived me with the film critic, I've done pretty much whatever I've wanted to do. Free rein is what I've got. She bombed the country and I'm just looting the shops. She would say I mixed my metaphors right there. That's what being married to Charlotte got me. Now I know about mixed metaphors, and how it really is possible to feel someone pull your heart straight out of your chest like in *Indiana Jones and the Temple of Doom*, then stomp on it.

I drop the toilet lid—*bang!*—and sit down. It's possible Charlotte's not dead. This is just the sort of thing she would do to make me feel bad. Like all chicks, she's a drama queen. I stare down at her head, angled like she's trying to lay her ear on her shoulder. Blood trickles out of one perfectly round nostril. There's no blood coming out of her ears that I can see. Most likely she's just conked out.

Charlotte thought she had the right to have an affair with the film critic because I occasionally found myself associating with Lorna, my ex-wife, the mother of my son. Once in a blue moon, after I'd taken Ray Jr. to the zoo or the Malibu Grand Prix, I'd return him to Lorna's apartment and we'd knock one out for old time's sake. It was like looking through a photo album. Associating with someone after you've been married is not the same as meeting a film critic at the bar in Esparza's, where you share a plastic wooden bowl of chips and hot sauce and listen to Patsy Cline and comment on the stuffed armadillos hanging on the ceiling and then share an order of ostrich tacos, all the while talking arty crap.

The film critic has more hair than I do.

Once, when Charlotte refused to show me respect by answering whether she was in love with the film critic, I was forced to shove her into a bookcase, so she knew we weren't just having one of our usual arguments. I meant business.

I said, "This thing with the film critic is a dalliance, right? There's nothing to it, right? Answer me. Yes or no."

She said, "He's actually more of a film *reviewer*."

She bruised her back on the edge of the shelf. It wasn't that bad. What's a little bruise? She's hardy. Skis and rides horses and takes kick-boxing classes. Most of the top row of books rained down upon her head and neck. They were only paperbacks. Still, she bitched to anyone who would listen, her herd of sympathetic friends, her therapist, her divorce lawyer, and of course the ostrich taco–loving film critic. Charlotte wouldn't touch an ostrich taco when she was with me. Now it's the new white meat.

Now Charlotte's lying on my bathroom floor, wedged between the hot water pipe and the toilet. Is it laying or lying? Charlotte would know. She has a master's degree and a daily subscription to the *New York Times*. The hot water pipe serves the whole building, and why it goes through my apartment I don't know. At night it's hot enough to leave a blister. Charlotte hit it on the way down, which caused her to twist her body, which caused her to lose her balance and hit her head on the edge of the tub. I stare at her head. Her curly hair is coming out of its scrunchie. She doesn't look like she's breathing. I stare at her tits. I wonder if she still wears an underwire.

It's possible she's holding her breath just to piss me off, to punish me for going to Prague.

She acted like I planned this. That's what Charlotte never *got*. I'm a simple guy. I take life as it comes. When I mentioned going to Prague I was just talking, just filling the air with my words. She should know how it is. She's fucking a film critic.

It was the last week in August. The leaves hung exhausted on the trees. I was still living over on Northeast Sandy. We met for dinner at the Kennedy School. The critic was at a film festival. I told her the next time we met he had to be in town, for her to prove to me there was still hope for us.

"I don't think there's any real hope for us," she said.

"Then why are you here?" I asked.

"I wonder that myself," she said. She ordered a gin and tonic.

"That's what he drinks, gin and tonic? *Tanqueray* and tonic?"

"Sometimes in the summer I've been known to order a gin and tonic," she said. "Jesus."

She lied. She was a liar.

She used to love me. Now she picked fights. Like about the gin and tonic. I buttered a piece of bread and put it in front of her. She folded her arms and looked out the window at the parking lot. A guy wearing a red plaid skirt pushed a shopping cart full of empty bottles. I could tell she was itching to get out of there. The back of my neck got hot, the way it did when she was pissing me off.

Suddenly, I said I had something to tell her. She looked back at me, but it was polite. She was so polite. I'd been fired from the pest control company out on Foster Road and was now working at a place that made clamps, couplings, screws, and knobs. They also made a really nice brass drawer pull. The week before, in the break room, one of the machinists was talking about quitting and moving to Prague, and then the HR chick, who'd never looked at this guy once, was practically in his lap. She said she'd always wanted to go to Prague.

"I'm going to Prague," I said.

"Prague? What's in Prague?"

"It's something I've always wanted to do."

"You have?" Her green eyes were on me. She leaned forward on her pale forearms. I could smell her grapefruity perfume, something called Happy I'd given her one Christmas. This was where she should have said, *Ray, you are so full of shit.* This is where her master's degree failed her, where all her books and snooty left-wing websites let her down.

Did I say she worked in R&D at Intel, designing stuff she wasn't allowed to talk about? Something to do with microchips and biology. When I met her I didn't know what R&D was. She used words like *ebullient* just to make me feel stupid. Who was the stupid one now? Yeah, I'm off to Prague. The only foreign place I'd ever been before was Ensenada.

"Is this work-related? Like when they sent you to Chelyabinsk?"

"Sure," I said. "A business trip."

I'd forgotten I told Charlotte I'd done a business trip to Chelyabinsk.

Last year Donnie, a guy at the knob company, had found a terrific and extremely hot Russian wife on the Internet. Her name was Olga but she liked to be called Bootsie. She was a great gal. Once Donnie surprised Bootsie with a subscription to *Self* and she fell to her knees and sobbed with gratitude. She wrapped her hands around his heels and laid her forehead on his shoes. She then gave him the best blowjob he'd ever had, after which she went into the kitchen and whipped up a roast.

Donnie had given me the name of the website where he got his wife and I thought, *Why not?* Charlotte didn't love me anymore. She was off drinking gin and tonics with the film critic. So one night after work, after I'd had a few beers, I typed in Charlotte's height, weight, hair, and eye color, and out came Agnessa Fedoseeva.

She was studying to be something called an esthetician, but was hoping to find a big strong man she could love and kiss with enthusiasm. She was anxious to inquire if I was a big strong man. She was curious how many flat-screen TVs I had. She sent me a videotape of herself dressed in a red, white, and blue teddy and high heels, dancing around her living room with a sparkler sizzling in each hand.

I put the trip to Chelyabinsk on a credit card, and told Charlotte I was being sent there by the knob company, to set up a new factory.

"But why are they sending *you?*" Charlotte had wanted to know. "I think it's great. Really exciting, and really good for you. You need to have the dust of the world on your feet. But you don't speak Russian."

"They're impressed with my work ethic."

"You do work hard," said Charlotte. "When you have a job."

I'm tired of staring at Charlotte laying or lying on the bathroom floor, playing passed out, milking the situation, doing her best to make me look like the bad guy.

I walk back down the long hallway to the kitchen. I sit in the dark at my kitchen table. Outside, the streetlights shine on the snow, filling my front rooms with that weird aquarium light. I look out the window at the Laurelhurst Theater marquee. They're showing *Alien* and *Meatballs*. Charlotte would think that was funny. Agnessa spoke no English, but she'd laugh anyway.

Charlotte will come out of the bathroom eventually. For being so smart, she is so predictable. That's how she works. If I stand over her and wonder whether she's dead, she'll act dead on purpose, just to piss me off. But if I turn my back on her, leave the room, she'll come marching out and wonder what's going on.

The back of my neck feels hot. None of this would have happened if she had let the Prague business go. It was just something I'd said to get her attention. Then I found myself saying I was moving in September, just after Labor Day, and would be there for at least six months.

"Six months?" she said, eyes big.

"Maybe a year."

I thought she'd forget about it. She'd go home to the film critic and they'd open a bottle of merlot and discuss the early films of Martin Scorsese.

Charlotte started e-mailing me. Where would I be living in Prague? Did I know Prague was settled in the fourth century? Prague Castle was the largest castle in the world. There was also an entire wall of graffiti dedicated to John Lennon. I should definitely check out the museum of the Heydrich assassination. She sent me links to websites, and guidebooks she'd ordered on Amazon. She gave me books by Czechoslovakian writers. Who the fuck is Kafka? She signed the e-mails with *xo*.

Agnessa read romance novels. She loved stuffed animals. She was thirty-one and still lived with her mother, who needed new teeth and an operation. I'd sent her an international calling card and she rang me every evening. She confessed she had two other men who wanted to marry her, one who lived in Indiana and had four flat-screen TVs, and one who lived in Florida and had three flat-screen TVs. Did I know how dear I was to her, that she was still interested in me even though I only had one TV?

Charlotte and I started meeting on Wednesdays for coffee at a place that served stale pastries and had too many free newspapers. Every so often I'd take Ray Jr. out of school for the morning and bring him along, just to remind Charlotte what a good dad I could be. Being a good single dad is better than having a pit bull puppy when it comes to attracting women. I made Ray drink his orange juice and study his spelling words. Charlotte said she was really going to miss me.

One day I got her to go with me to Hawthorne to shop for presents to give to the family who would be putting me up in Prague, before I had my own apartment.

"Who exactly are we shopping for?" she asked. We nosed around a crowded shop that sold expensive journals, massage oil, and funny greeting cards. The rain had started. The shop smelled like wet dog and patchouli.

"There's a thirty-one-year-old living at home, a girl who loves stuffed animals."

"Is she . . ." Charlotte looked at me, narrowed one eye a little like she does. I could feel my pulse in my forehead. She was going to ask me if there was something going on with this girl, if somehow I was going to Prague to see her. It was all over her face. Behind her a woman was trying to get at the wire card rack. I just looked at her. *Go ahead, ask me.* I waited. ". . . mentally disabled or something?"

I thought of Agnessa and her living room sparkler dance.

"It's possible," I said.

Charlotte picked out a hand lotion that smelled like apple pie and a stuffed panda.

I sent them to Agnessa, who loved the gifts. I loved Agnessa, for being so easy to please. I spent entire paychecks sending her shampoo, socks, Levi's and one of those mesh bags girls stick their underwear in before it goes in the washing machine. I sent her some Happy too. Fuck Charlotte.

I gave notice on the apartment I was living in off Northeast Sandy. I told the landlady I was moving to Prague. Elaine was a chick with cats who worked in a bookstore and had a stack of books on Wicca beside her bed. She believed in the power of crystals and Match.com. I struck up an association with Elaine. It was an association of convenience. She was lonely. She liked helping me define just how evil Charlotte was, how slutty and duplicitous. Elaine volunteered to put a spell on Charlotte. I told her to stop; I wasn't looking for a commitment. When I told Elaine I was moving to Prague she smirked, "Prague, Minnesota?"

"Uh, no," I said.

"Where are you really going?"

"I got a new place on Southeast Ankeny, across from that yuppie wine bar."

"Noble Rot, where wine is a meal."

When Charlotte kicked me out she said I could take anything I wanted, so I did. The heavy stainless steel pots and pans we got as a wedding present. All the DVDs we'd watched together, and what the hell, the DVD player. The books she told people were her favorites. The flannel duvet cover with the roses. A black sweater that smelled of Happy, and a few pairs of her underpants, fished out of the dirty clothes hamper. Our wedding album, and from the freezer, the top layer of our wedding cake. It looked like a hat wrapped in waxed paper.

Elaine showed up on a Saturday afternoon to help me pack my stuff. She'd brought some empty boxes from the bookstore and started on the kitchen. The only things in the freezer were a few blue plastic ice cube trays, a pair of chilled beer glasses—a trick Charlotte taught me—and that damn frozen wedding cake. Elaine said I should toss it, didn't know why I was holding on to it. I said, "I'm a good guy, I got a sentimental streak a mile wide, so sue me."

Charlotte took me out for American food the day before I left. Before meeting her I had a sighting of Extremo the Clown's art car, parked near the Starbucks on Burnside. The art car looks like a Mayan temple on wheels with hundreds of heads sculpted into the sides and a pyramid-altar thing rising from the roof. It's well known that an art car sighting means good luck. I'm luckier than most people, but as I passed by I touched one of the open-mouthed heads on the trunk. The leaves on the maples were red and gold. I found myself wondering what the weather would be like in Prague, even though I wasn't going to Prague.

Charlotte took me to Esparza's. I'm sure she enjoyed the irony, bringing her ex to the same restaurant where she betrayed him with another, but I was having my own private last laugh—my new place was just across the parking lot. I could see into my new kitchen on the second floor. I could see my box of pots and pans sitting on the kitchen table.

I could be in R&D too. I could have my own secret projects.

After we ordered margaritas she pulled out a red suede pouch. Her hands shook as she unsnapped it. She pulled out her engagement ring, the one we'd bought together, the one she'd paid for, technically, since at the time I was between jobs. I'd said anything less than a single karat was hardly worth the effort and she'd agreed, and there it was and she was giving it to me, saying she wanted me to have it, to take it to Prague, to keep it in a safe place, and to think of her.

"I'm just really proud of you, taking this big step. I'm sorry we didn't work out. I really am. But this is better. You're going to really see the world."

She cried. Her mascara ran. I made an old joke, about how she needed to get another brand of mascara, one that didn't run every time she cried. Every T-shirt I owned had a smudgy black stain on the shoulder. I could have definitely gotten some that night, but there was nowhere to take her. My flight was leaving in the morning, and I'd told her that I was sleeping on Elaine's fold-out couch. I liked to drop Elaine's name now and then, just to make sure she was paying attention.

A week passed, then two. I went to work at the knob factory, where my job was quality control. I sat on a tall stool in a room with no windows, making sure our wall brackets had the right amount of screw holes. At night I drank Czechvar beer and played World of Warcraft and kept an eye on the parking lot of Esparza's Tex-Mex to see if Charlotte and the film critic ever showed up.

I didn't tell Agnessa I'd moved to Prague, though I did give her my new address and phone number at Southeast Ankeny. Agnessa was getting impatient. Her other suitors were starting to tug at her heart ropes. She was running out of Happy.

One cold night the server crashed and I couldn't get back onto WoW, so I called up Agnessa and told her she should apply for a fiancée visa. What the hell. I'd spied Extremo the Clown's art car again that day, parked in the lot at Wild Oats. Lucky me, and lucky Agnessa. I figured at least I could get her to Portland. Get her out of Chelyabinsk, where her family thought nothing of eating moldy bread spread with rancid butter. I liked this idea, saving Agnessa from her difficult life. A fiancée visa lasted for ninety days. I figured then I could decide whether to ship her back or not.

"Oh, Ray!" she breathed. "Thank you, I love you, thank you."

"We'll get the fiancée visa and then let's give it a shot. Let's send the engagement up the flagpole and see who salutes. Let's take the idea of us out for a test drive."

"Ray? Ray—I—uh—I . . ." I could hear her moist gasps of confusion.

"We'll give it the ol' college try," I said.

Smoke and mirrors, smoke and mirrors. I admit I misled Agnessa, but she'd get over it. And I'm actually a good guy. To make things right I bought a black velvet box at Fred Meyer's, and sent her Charlotte's diamond, Federal Express. Agnessa called when she received the ring and wept. I should hope so. That ring cost Charlotte four grand. She sent me another sparkler video and some Russian chocolate. In the video, she showed off the ring and threw kisses into the camera.

Prague is eight hours ahead of Portland, or maybe it's nine. I e-mailed Charlotte at one a.m. so she would think I was writing to her first thing in the morning, when I arrived at the knob factory. The factory was in a suburb of Prague. I told her I had to take a bus to get there, along with the other workers. I even had a lunch pail, filled with sandwiches made with dark bread. In the evenings I strolled along the Charles Bridge. I saw the world famous astronomical clock (Wikipedia has a good picture) and discovered a great bar called the Clown and Bard, where the barmaid admired my tattoo and served me some dill soup, on the house.

Charlotte started writing, *Love, C,* at the bottom of her e-mails.

One rainy night after work I went to Holman's, around the corner from my apartment. The storm drains were clogged with soggy Cornflake-looking leaves.

My Vans got soaked. I ordered a patty melt and a Bud Light. A woman a few tables over was wearing Happy. I smelled it over the cheap disinfectant and grilled onions. Ah, hell. I used my calling card to call Charlotte from the pay phone.

She answered on the first ring. I told her I was calling from the Clown and Bard.

"Ray, are you all right?"

I loved that concern in her voice. I said I was fine, while making sure I didn't sound fine at all. I wanted her to think that maybe I'd had some food poisoning. Maybe a worker on the bus beat me up for being an American. Maybe I was dying of loneliness. Anything could happen in Prague.

"It's three thirty in the morning. I thought you didn't have a phone in your flat."

"You were being missed," I said. A roar went up from the bar. Monday Night Football on the TV. "I'm at the Clown and Bard. They're watching football. You know, soccer."

She didn't understand what I was doing at a bar at three thirty a.m. I told her I couldn't sleep.

"So, what, you've just been out walking the streets?"

"I was hungry."

There was a long pause, as if she'd never heard anything so ridiculous in her life. I covered my mouth so I wouldn't laugh. Then it all went bad. It was the beginning of how I find myself at this moment, with her laying unconscious on my bathroom floor.

"Is it that woman?" she asked. "The one with the learning disability? Is that why you're out so late? You've been out with her?"

"What are you talking about?" What was she talking about?

"The one you sent the hand lotion to?"

I forgot I'd told her Agnessa lived in Prague.

The more I denied seeing Agnessa while I was in Prague, the more Charlotte believed I was lying. I said, "I haven't seen her. And anyway, we're non-touching friends." Charlotte went batshit crazy when I said that. It was true. I'm a good man. I don't lie unless I have to. When I was in Chelyabinsk, Agnessa let me hold her elbow when we crossed the street. Donnie said that's how these Russian women are. Until they receive a victory rock, there's no hope of any action.

"I haven't seen Ag in months," I said. "She's a friend. She reminds me of you. She's got that sense of humor, but not so cutting. And answer me this, why are Slavic women either as short as they are wide, or supermodels?"

"She's a supermodel?"

"It's usually the really old ones who are short and fat. The ladies who sweep the streets."

"Ray, just tell me. Is there anything going on with this woman or not?"

"Did you know they serve patty melts at the Clown and Bard? Bizarre, huh?"

Charlotte hung up on me. I paid for my half-eaten melt and walked home. If I left the lights off I could sit in the living room and drink a beer and watch my landlady paint her nails in her thong and T-shirt. Charlotte had given me an idea. As soon as Agnessa's fiancée visa came through I'd tell Charlotte my work in Prague was finished. I'd tell her I was coming home with my friend Agnessa, who wanted to start a new life in the States. Of course, she would stay with me until she found a place of her own. Charlotte would lose her mind. Maybe Agnessa and I could double date with Charlotte and the film critic. It would be fun.

My calls to Charlotte started going to voice mail, my e-mails went unanswered. My landlady got curtains. I took Ray Jr. to IMAX to see a movie about coral reefs. He vomited into my lap. I was counting on associating with Lorna a little, but she clapped her hand over her nose and told me to go home. There was a message on my voice mail from Agnessa, wondering whether I'd made her airplane reservations. Nothing from Charlotte after two full weeks.

I decided it was time to come home.

The forced-air heat comes on. Outside, big messy snowflakes blow out of the sky. From my window I can see across the snowy street into the Noble Rot, where wine is a meal. Once Charlotte stops playing possum and gets up off the bathroom floor I can take her right over there. Show there are no hard feelings. She thinks I am a vengeful type, controlling, but she has me all wrong.

Playing possum. I have to laugh. It is how we met, how she fell for me. I was still at the pest control company out on Foster Road. One spring morning she'd called up fairly hysterical. There was a dead possum in her tulips. A few of us were in the break room, shaking the snack machine to see if we could free a half-released bag of Doritos. The supervisor came in and thought we might want to draw straws. Charlotte lived in Lake Oswego, where the ladies tend to have nothing better to do than go to yoga, get their nails done, and flirt with the hired hands. Sometimes you can even get lucky.

Charlotte came to the door wearing baggy shorts and a University of Michigan T-shirt. Reading glasses on her head and a pen and sheaf of papers in one hand. Mint-green toenail polish. She held the back door open for me.

"I would have just tossed him in the trash but the garbage isn't until next Wednesday. That didn't seem very, I don't know, hygienic."

But when we got to the side yard where the tulips grew there were only a few flattened stalks, a petal or two strewn about.

"He was just here," she said, then whirled on her heel and startled me by punching me in the arm. She had a great loud laugh. "He was playing possum. Oh my God."

She offered me a beer for my trouble, and I told her that possums don't actually play dead, that they're so frightened they fall into a real coma. Then, after a few hours, they rouse themselves and go on their way. Charlotte thought that was fascinating. She made me sit down at her kitchen table and tell her more.

Not many women have ever looked at me that way.

Tonight she came over to my apartment uninvited. I'd sent her an e-mail two days ago telling her I was home from Prague, in case she cared. I didn't tell her where I live. I figured I'd let it slip next week, after Agnessa arrives from Chelyabinsk.

"Hello!" she said, stomping the snow off her red cowboy boots before coming right on in. She walked around my front room. Touched the DVDs stacked on top of the TV, picked up the empty Czechvar bottle on the desk beside the computer. Flipped through a stack of mail on the end table beside the couch.

"You settled right in here, didn't you?"

"It's good to see you," I said. It was good to see her. She wasn't wearing any perfume.

"I got your new address from Elaine," she said. "How's the jet lag?"

"Who?" I knew who. Elaine was the only person who was aware I'd moved to Southeast Ankeny.

"I had a dream about you last night." I didn't know where I was going with this, but chicks always liked to hear that you had a dream about them.

"I came to get my ring back," she said. She was in one of those moods. Fine.

"Why don't you sit down and I'll get it."

She pulled her hair out of its scrunchie and pulled it back up on top of her head. She didn't sit down.

I took my time. I walked down the long hallway to my bedroom. I sat on the bed in the dark. It occurred to me that Agnessa was going to need some-place to put her clothes. I didn't have a bureau, but instead used the top two shelves in the closet. I walked back down the hallway. Charlotte wasn't there. From the kitchen I could hear the freezer door open, then Charlotte's loud laugh. *Ha!*

I stood in the middle of my front room, stared at a poster I'd taken from our old house, black-and-white, a young couple kissing on a Paris street. It had some name in French.

"This wasn't something I wanted to tell you over the phone, but one night someone broke into my flat in Prague and stole your ring," I called into the kitchen. I was glad not to have to look her in the eye. "They took my wallet too. And my passport."

She came back into the living room holding the frozen top layer of our wedding cake. "I can't believe this."

"It's our wedding cake," I said.

"Yeah, I know what it is. How is it you still have it?"

"You said I could take anything I wanted."

"What did you do with it for the two months you were in Prague?"

"I got a sentimental streak a mile wide, so sue me."

She started shaking her head. She shook her head and laughed. Laughing and crying, mascara running. "At first I thought Elaine was the nut job, but it's you! I didn't believe her when she said you didn't even go to Prague. It was impossible. No one is that crazy. She said if I didn't believe her to check the freezer."

"Elaine is a nut job," I said. "She thinks she's a witch."

"Stop, Ray, just stop."

"She wanted to put a spell on you but I wouldn't let her."

"You're out of your mind."

"The guys broke into my flat when I was out one night with Agnessa," I said. "You wanted the truth and this is the truth. I'm in love with Agnessa."

"The girl who lives with her parents and likes stuffed animals?" She put the wedding cake on the table so she could cross her hands over her chest like she does and throw her head back, the better to laugh her guts out. She was lucky I didn't throttle her right there and then.

I said that I strolled across the Charles Bridge with Agnessa, and admired the astronomical clock with Agnessa, and that Agnessa's family actually owned the Clown and Bard.

She said, "God, Ray, could you be a bigger loser?"

I stared at her. She wasn't supposed to say that.

"That's a rhetorical question, by the way."

She stalked down the hall to the bathroom to find some tissue to wipe her eyes. I followed her, and when she turned around I grabbed her by the neck and gave her a good shake. Grabbing a woman by the arm is a loser's game. They throw your hand off and shriek, "Don't touch me!" and act as if you're some low-life abuser. I just needed her to shut her up, and the neck is the pipeline to the mouth. I will admit that after she got quiet, I tossed her against that scalding-hot water pipe just to get my point across. So sue me.

Back in the kitchen, I put the frozen wedding cake back into the freezer. I looked out the window. Down on the street a girl rode past on her bike, the flakes settling on her hot-pink bike helmet. Portland is cold enough to invite snow but too warm to keep it. It has something to do with the Japanese current. Charlotte could tell you, but she isn't coming out of the bathroom anytime soon.

The snow stops like I said it would. I put on my Vans and locate my passport in the top drawer of my desk. Outside, the air feels good on my arms. The back of my neck is nice and cool. The forced-air heat was way too much in that place. In the parking lot I pull the plates off my truck, crunch across the snow, and stuff them into the dumpster behind Esparza's. Just as I'm closing the lid, I hear the slow koosh-koosh of bald tires on snow and look up to see the art car rolling down the street. I tell you, I've always been lucky.

At PDX I call the phone company to turn off my service. I'm doing Agnessa a favor. I only want the best for her and it's best for her to go with the guy with the multiple TVs. Then I call 911 and report an intruder. I give my address and tell them it's right across the street from Noble Rot, where wine is a meal. Then I buy a ticket for the next plane out. Like I said before, I'm a simple guy. I take life as it comes.

PART III

Road Rage

MULHOLLAND DIVE

BY MICHAEL CONNELLY

Mulholland Drive, Los Angeles

(Originally published in *Los Angeles Noir*)

Burning flares and flashing red and blue lights ripped the night apart. Clewiston counted four black-and-whites pulled halfway off the roadway and as close to the upper embankment as was possible. In front of them was a firetruck and in front of that was a forensics van. There was a P-one standing in the middle of Mulholland Drive ready to hold up traffic or wave it into the one lane that they had open. With a fatality involved, they should have closed down both lanes of the road, but that would have meant closing Mulholland from Laurel Canyon on one side all the way to Coldwater Canyon on the other. That was too long a stretch. There would be consequences for that. The huge inconvenience of it would have brought complaints from the rich hillside homeowners trying to get home after another night of the good life. And nobody stuck on midnight shift wanted more complaints to deal with.

Clewiston had worked Mulholland fatals several times. He was the expert. He was the one they called in from home. He knew that whether the identity of the victim in this case demanded it or not, he'd have gotten the call. It was Mulholland, and the Mulholland calls all went to him.

But this one was special anyway. The victim was a name and the case was going five-by-five. That meant everything about it had to be squared away and done right. He had been thoroughly briefed over the phone by the watch commander about that.

He pulled in behind the last patrol car, put his flashers on, and got out of his unmarked car. On the way back to the trunk, he grabbed his badge from beneath his shirt and hung it out front. He was in civies, having been called in from off-duty, and it was prudent to make sure he announced he was a detective.

He used his key to open the trunk and began to gather the equipment he would need. The P-one left his post in the road and walked over.

"Where's the sergeant?" Clewiston asked.

"Up there. I think they're about to pull the car up. That's a hundred thousand dollars he went over the side with. Who are you?"

"Detective Clewiston. The reconstructionist. Sergeant Fairbanks is expecting me."

"Go on down and you'll find him by the— Whoa, what is that?"

Clewiston saw him looking at the face peering up from the trunk. The crash test dummy was partially hidden by all the equipment cluttering the trunk, but the face was clear and staring blankly up at them. His legs had been detached and were resting beneath the torso. It was the only way to fit the whole thing in the trunk.

"We call him Arty," Clewiston said. "He was made by a company called Accident Reconstruction Technologies."

"Looks sort of real at first," the patrol officer said. "Why's he in fatigues?"

Clewiston had to think about that to remember.

"Last time I used Arty, it was a crosswalk hit-and-run case. The vic was a marine up from El Toro. He was in his fatigues and there was a question about whether the hitter saw him." Clewiston slung the strap of his laptop bag over his shoulder. "He did. Thanks to Arty we made a case."

He took his clipboard out of the trunk and then a digital camera, his trusty measuring wheel, and an eight-battery Maglite. He closed the trunk and made sure it was locked.

"I'm going to head down and get this over with," he said. "I got called in from home."

"Yeah, I guess the faster you're done, the faster I can get back out on the road myself. Pretty boring just standing here."

"I know what you mean."

Clewiston headed down the westbound lane, which had been closed to traffic. There was a mist clinging in the dark to the tall brush that crowded the sides of the street. But he could still see the lights and glow of the city down to the south. The accident had occurred in one of the few spots along Mulholland where there were no homes. He knew that on the south side of the road the embankment dropped down to a public dog park. On the north side was Fryman Canyon and the embankment rose up to a point where one of the city's communication stations was located. There was a tower up there on the point that helped bounce communication signals over the mountains that cut the city in half.

Mulholland was literally the backbone of Los Angeles. It rode like a snake along the crest of the Santa Monica Mountains from one end of the city to the other. Clewiston knew of places where you could stand on the white stripe and look north across the vast San Fernando Valley and then turn around and look south and see across the west side and as far as the Pacific and Catalina Island. It all depended on whether the smog was cooperating or not. And if you knew the right spots to stop and look.

Mulholland had that top-of-the-world feel to it. It could make you feel like the prince of a city where the laws of nature and physics didn't apply. The foot came down heavy on the accelerator. That was the contradiction. Mulholland was built for speed but it couldn't handle it. Speed was a killer.

As he came around the bend, Clewiston saw another firetruck and a tow truck from the Van Nuys police garage. The tow truck was positioned sideways across the road. Its cable was down the embankment and stretched taut as it pulled the car up. For the moment, Mulholland was completely closed. Clewiston could hear the tow motor straining and the cracking and scraping as the unseen car was being pulled up through the brush. The tow truck shuddered as it labored.

Clewiston saw the man with sergeant's stripes on his uniform and moved next to him as he watched.

"Is he still in it?" he asked Fairbanks.

"No, he was transported to St. Joe's. But he was DOA. You're Clewiston, right? The reconstructionist."

"Yes."

"We've got to handle this thing right. Once the ID gets out, we'll have the media all over this."

"The captain told me."

"Yeah, well, I'm telling you too. In this department, the captains don't get blamed when things go sideways and off the road. It's always the sergeants and it ain't going to be me this time."

"I get it."

"You have any idea what this guy was worth? We're talking tens of millions, and on top of that he's supposedly in the middle of a divorce. So we go five-by-five-by-five on this thing. *Comprende*, reconstructionist?"

"It's Clewiston and I said I get it."

"Good. This is what we've got. Single car fatality. No witnesses. It appears the victim was heading eastbound when his vehicle, a two-month-old Porsche Carrera, came around that last curve there and for whatever reason didn't straighten out. We've got treads on the road you can take a look at. Anyway, he went straight off the side and then down, baby. Major head and torso injuries. Chest crushed. He pretty much drowned in his own blood before the FD could get down to him. They stretchered him out with a chopper and transported him anyway. Guess they didn't want any blowback either."

"They take blood at St. Joe's?"

Fairbanks, about forty and a lifer on patrol, nodded. "I am told it was clean."

There was a pause in the conversation at that point, suggesting that Clewiston could take whatever he wanted from the blood test. He could believe what Fairbanks was telling him or he could believe that the celebrity fix was already in.

The moonlight reflected off the dented silver skin of the Porsche as it was pulled up over the edge like a giant beautiful fish hauled into a boat. Clewiston walked over and Fairbanks followed. The first thing Clewiston saw was that it was a Carrera 4S. "Hmmmm," he mumbled.

"What?" Fairbanks said.

"It's one of the Porsches with four-wheel drive. Built for these sort of curves. Built for control."

"Well, not built good enough, obviously."

Clewiston put his equipment down on the hood of one of the patrol cars and took his Maglite over to the Porsche. He swept the beam over the front of the high-performance sports car. The car was heavily damaged in the crash and the front had taken the brunt of it. The molded body was badly distorted by repeated impacts as it had sledded down the steep embankment. He moved in close and squatted by the front cowling and the shattered passenger-side headlight assembly.

He could feel Fairbanks behind him, watching over his shoulder as he worked.

"If there were no witnesses, how did anybody know he'd gone over the side?" Clewiston asked.

"Somebody down below," Fairbanks answered. "There are houses down there. Lucky this guy didn't end up in somebody's living room. I've seen that before."

So had Clewiston. He stood up and walked to the edge and looked down. His light cut into the darkness of the brush. He saw the exposed pulp of the acacia trees and other foliage the car had torn through.

He returned to the car. The driver's door was sprung and Clewiston could see the pry marks left by the jaws used to extricate the driver. He pulled it open and leaned in with his light. There was a lot of blood on the wheel, dashboard, and center console. The driver's seat was wet with blood and urine.

The key was still in the ignition and turned to the "on" position. The dashboard lights were still on as well. Clewiston leaned further in and checked the mileage. The car had only 1,142 miles on the odometer.

Satisfied with his initial survey of the wreck, he went back to his equipment. He put the clipboard under his arm and picked up the measuring wheel. Fairbanks came over once again. "Anything?" he asked.

"Not yet, sergeant. I'm just starting."

He started sweeping the light over the roadway. He picked up the skid marks and used the wheel to measure the distance of each one. There were four distinct marks, left as all four tires of the Porsche tried unsuccessfully to grip the asphalt. When he worked his way back to the starting point, he found scuff marks in a classic slalom pattern. They had been left on the asphalt when the car had turned sharply one way and then the other before going into the braking skid.

He wrote the measurements down on the clipboard. He then pointed the light into the brush on either side of the roadway where the scuff marks began. He knew the event had begun here and he was looking for indications of cause.

He noticed a small opening in the brush, a narrow pathway that continued on the other side of the road. It was a crossing. He stepped over and put the beam down on the brush and soil. After a few moments, he moved across the street and studied the path on the other side.

Satisfied with his site survey, he went back to the patrol car and opened his laptop. While it was booting up, Fairbanks came over once again.

"So, how'z it look?"

"I have to run the numbers."

"Those skids look pretty long to me. The guy must've been flying."

"You'd be surprised. Other things factor in. Brake efficiency, surface, and surface conditions—you see the mist moving in right now? Was it like this two hours ago when the guy went over the side?"

"Been like this since I got here. But the fire guys were here first. I'll get one up here."

Clewiston nodded. Fairbanks pulled his rover and told someone to send the first responders up to the crash site. He then looked back at Clewiston.

"On the way."

"Thanks. Does anybody know what this guy was doing up here?"

"Driving home, we assume. His house was in Coldwater and he was going home."

"From where?"

"That we don't know."

"Anybody make notification yet?"

"Not yet. We figure next of kin is the wife he's divorcing. But we're not sure where to find her. I sent a car to his house but there's no answer. We've got somebody at Parker Center trying to run her down—probably through her lawyer. There's also grown children from his first marriage. They're working on that too."

Two firefighters walked up and introduced themselves as Robards and Lopez. Clewiston questioned them on the weather and road conditions at the time they responded to the accident call. Both firefighters described the mist as heavy at the time. They were sure about this because the mist had hindered their ability to find the place where the vehicle had crashed through the brush and down the embankment.

"If we hadn't seen the skid marks, we would have driven right by," Lopez said.

Clewiston thanked them and turned back to his computer. He had everything he needed now. He opened the Accident Reconstruction Technologies program and went directly to the speed and distance calculator. He referred to his clipboard for the numbers he would need. He felt Fairbanks come up next to him.

"Computer, huh? That gives you all the answers?"

"Some of them."

"Whatever happened to experience and trusting hunches and gut instincts?"

It wasn't a question that was waiting for an answer. Clewiston added the lengths of the four skid marks he had measured and then divided by four, coming up with an average length of sixty-four feet. He entered the number into the calculator template.

"You said the vehicle is only two months old?" he asked Fairbanks.

"According to the registration. It's a lease he picked up in January. I guess he filed for divorce and went out and got the sports car to help him get back in the game."

Clewiston ignored the comment and typed *1.0* into a box marked *B.E.* on the template.

"What's that?" Fairbanks asked.

"Braking efficiency. One-oh is the highest efficiency. Things could change if somebody wants to take the brakes off the car and test them. But for now I am going with high efficiency because the vehicle is new and there's only twelve hundred miles on it."

"Sounds right to me."

Lastly, Clewiston typed 9.0 into the box marked C.F. This was the subjective part. He explained what he was doing to Fairbanks before the sergeant had to ask.

"This is coefficient of friction," he said. "It basically means surface conditions. Mulholland Drive is asphalt base, which is generally a high coefficient. And this stretch here was repaved about nine months ago—again, that leads to a high coefficient. But I'm knocking it down a point because of the moisture. That mist comes in and puts down a layer of moisture that mixes with the road oil and makes the asphalt slippery. The oil is heavier in new asphalt."

"I get it."

"Good. It's called trusting your gut instinct, sergeant."

Fairbanks nodded. He had been properly rebuked.

Clewiston clicked the enter button and the calculator came up with a projected speed based on the relationship between skid length, brake efficiency, and the surface conditions. It said the Porsche had been traveling at 41.569 miles per hour when it went into the skid.

"You're kidding me," Fairbanks said while looking at the screen. "The guy was barely speeding. How can that be?"

"Follow me, sergeant," Clewiston said.

Clewiston left the computer and the rest of his equipment, except for the flashlight. He led Fairbanks back to the point in the road where he had found the slalom scuffs and the originating point of the skid marks.

"Okay," he said. "The event started here. We have a single-car accident. No alcohol known to be involved. No real speed involved. A car built for this sort of road is involved. What went wrong?"

"Exactly."

Clewiston put the light down on the scuff marks.

"Okay, you've got alternating scuff marks here before he goes into the skid."

"Okay."

"You have the tire cords indicating he jerked the wheel right initially and then jerked it left trying to straighten it out. We call it a SAM—a slalom avoidance maneuver."

"A SAM. Okay."

"He turned to avoid an impact of some kind, then over-corrected. He then panicked and did what most people do. He hit the brakes."

"Got it."

"The wheels locked up and he went into a skid. There was nothing he could do at that point. He had no control because the instinct is to press harder on the brakes, to push that pedal through the floor."

"And the brakes were what were taking away control."

"Exactly. He went over the side. The question is why. Why did he jerk the wheel in the first place? What preceded the event?"

"Another car?"

Clewiston nodded. "Could be. But no one stopped. No one called it in."

"Maybe . . ." Fairbanks spread his hands. He was drawing a blank.

"Take a look here," Clewiston said.

He walked Fairbanks over to the side of the road. He put the light on the pathway into the brush, drawing the sergeant's eyes back across Mulholland to the pathway on the opposite side. Fairbanks looked at him and then back at the path.

"What are you thinking?" Fairbanks asked.

"This is a coyote path," Clewiston said. "They come up through Fryman Canyon and cross Mulholland here. It takes them to the dog park. They probably wait in heavy brush for the dogs that stray out of the park."

"So your thinking is that our guy came around the curve and there was a coyote crossing the road."

Clewiston nodded. "That's what I'm thinking. He jerks the wheel to avoid the animal, then overcompensates, loses control. You have a slalom followed by a braking skid. He goes over the side."

"An accident, plain and simple." Fairbanks shook his head disappointedly. "Why couldn't it have been a DUI, something clear-cut like that?" he asked. "Nobody's going to believe us on this one."

"That's not our problem. All the facts point to it being a driving mishap. An accident."

Fairbanks looked at the skid marks and nodded. "Then that's it, I guess."

"You'll get a second opinion from the insurance company anyway," Clewiston said. "They'll probably pull the brakes off the car and test them. An accident means double indemnity. But if they can shift the calculations and prove he was speeding or being reckless, it softens the impact. The payout becomes negotiable. But my guess is they'll see it the same way we do."

"I'll make sure forensics photographs everything. We'll document everything six ways from Sunday and the insurance people can take their best shot. When will I get a report from you?"

"I'll go down to Valley Traffic right now and write something up."

"Good. Get it to me. What else?"

Clewiston looked around to see if he was forgetting anything. He shook his head. "That's it. I need to take a few more measurements and some photos, then I'll head down to write it up. Then I'll get out of your way."

Clewiston left him and headed back up the road to get his camera. He had a small smile on his face that nobody noticed.

Clewiston headed west on Mulholland from the crash site. He planned to take Coldwater Canyon down into the Valley and over to the Traffic Division office. He waited until the flashing blue and red lights were small in his rearview mirror before flipping open his phone. He hoped he could get a signal on the cheap throwaway. Mulholland Drive wasn't always cooperative with cellular service.

He had a signal. He pulled to the side while he attached the digital recorder, then turned it on and made the call. She answered after one ring, as he was pulling back onto the road and up to speed.

"Where are you?" he asked.

"The apartment."

"They're looking for you. You're sure his attorney knows where you are?"

"He knows. Why? What's going on?"

"They want to tell you he's dead."

He heard her voice catch. He took the phone away from his ear so he could hold the wheel with two hands on one of the deep curves. He then brought it back.

"You there?" he asked.

"Yes, I'm here. I just can't believe it, that's all. I'm speechless. I didn't think it would really happen."

You may be speechless, but you're talking, Clewiston thought. *Keep it up.*

"You wanted it to happen, so it happened," he said. "I told you I would take care of it."

"What happened?"

"He went off the road on Mulholland. It's an accident and you're a rich lady now."

She said nothing.

"What else do you want to know?" he asked.

"I'm not sure. Maybe I shouldn't know anything. It will be better when they come here."

"You're an actress. You can handle it."

"Okay."

He waited for her to say more, glancing down at the recorder on the center console to see the red light still glowing. He was good.

"Was he in pain?" she asked.

"Hard to say. He was probably dead when they pried him out. From what I hear, it will be a closed casket. Why do you care?"

"I guess I don't. It's just sort of surreal that this is happening. Sometimes I wish you never came to me with the whole idea."

"You rather go back to being trailer park trash while he lives up on the hill?"

"No, it wouldn't be like that. My attorney says the prenup has holes in it."

Clewiston shook his head. Second guessers. They hire his services and then can't live with the consequences.

"What's done is done," he said. "This will be the last time we talk. When you get the chance, throw the phone you're talking on away like I told you."

"There won't be any records?"

"It's a throwaway. Like all the drug dealers use. Open it up, smash the chip, and throw it all away the next time you go to McDonald's."

"I don't go to McDonald's."

"Then throw it away at The Ivy. I don't give a shit. Just not at your house. Let things run their course. Soon you'll have all his money. And you double dip on the insurance because of the accident. You can thank me for that."

He was coming up to the hairpin turn that offered the best view of the Valley.

"How do we know that they think it was an accident?"

"Because I made them think that. I told you, I have Mulholland wired. That's what you paid for. Nobody is going to second guess a goddamn thing. His insurance company will come in and sniff around, but they won't be able to change things. Just sit tight and stay cool. Say nothing. Offer nothing. Just like I told you."

The lights of the Valley spread out in front of him before the turn. He saw a car pulled over at the unofficial overlook. On any other night he'd stop and roust them—probably teenagers getting it on in the backseat. But not tonight. He had to get down to the traffic office and write up his report.

"This is the last time we talk," he said to her.

He looked down at the recorder. He knew it would be the last time they talked—until he needed more money from her.

"How did you get him to go off the road?" she asked.

He smiled. They always ask that. "My friend Arty did it."

"You brought a third party into this. Don't you see that—"

"Relax. Arty doesn't talk."

He started into the turn. He realized the phone had gone dead.

"Hello?" he said. "Hello?"

He looked at the screen. No signal. These cheap throwaways were about as reliable as the weather.

He felt his tires catch the edge of the roadway and looked up in time to pull the car back onto the road. As he came out of the turn, he checked the phone's screen one more time for the signal. He needed to call her back, let her know how it was going to be.

There was still no signal.

"Goddamnit!"

He slapped the phone closed on his thigh, then peered back at the road and froze as his eyes caught and held on two glowing eyes in the headlights. In a moment he broke free and jerked the wheel right to avoid the coyote. He corrected, but the wheels caught on the deep edge of the asphalt. He jerked harder and the front wheel broke free and back onto the road. But the back wheel slipped out and the car went into a slide.

Clewiston had an almost clinical knowledge of what was happening. It was as if he was watching one of the accident recreations he had prepared a hundred times for court hearings and prosecutions.

The car went into a sideways slide toward the precipice. He knew he would hit the wooden fence—chosen by the city for aesthetic reasons over function and safety—and that he would crash through. He knew at that moment that he was probably a dead man.

The car turned 180 degrees before blowing backwards through the safety fence. It then went airborne and arced down, trunk first. Clewiston gripped the steering wheel as if it was still the instrument of his control and destiny. But he knew there was nothing that could help him now. There was no control.

Looking through the windshield, he saw the beams of his headlights pointing into the night sky. Out loud, he said, "I'm dead."

The car plunged through a stand of trees, branches shearing off with a noise as loud as firecrackers. Clewiston closed his eyes for the final impact. There was a sharp roaring sound and a jarring crash. The airbag exploded from the steering wheel and snapped his neck back against his seat.

Clewiston opened his eyes and felt liquid surrounding him and rising up his chest. He thought he had momentarily blacked out or was hallucinating. But then the water reached his neck and it was cold and real. He could see only darkness. He was in black water and it was filling the car.

He reached down to the door and pulled on a handle but he couldn't get the door to open. He guessed the power locks had shorted out. He tried to bring his legs up so he could kick out one of the shattered windows but his seat belt held him in place. The water was up to his chin now and rising. He quickly unsnapped his belt and tried to move again but realized it hadn't been the impediment. His legs—both of them—were somehow pinned beneath the steering column, which had dropped down during the impact. He tried to raise it but couldn't get it to move an inch. He tried to squeeze out from beneath the weight but he was thoroughly pinned.

The water was over his mouth now. By leaning his head back and raising his chin up, he gained an inch, but that was rapidly erased by the rising tide. In less than thirty seconds the water was over him and he was holding his last breath.

He thought about the coyote that had sent him over the side. It didn't seem possible that what had happened had happened. A reverse cascade of bubbles leaked from his mouth and traveled upward as he cursed.

Suddenly everything was illuminated. A bright light glowed in front of him. He leaned forward and looked out through the windshield. He saw a robed figure above the light, arms at his side.

Clewiston knew that it was over. His lungs burned for release. It was his time. He let out all of his breath and took the water in. He journeyed toward the light.

James Crossley finished tying his robe and looked down into his backyard pool. It was as if the car had literally dropped from the heavens. The brick wall surrounding the pool was undisturbed. The car had to have come in over it and then landed perfectly in the middle of the pool. About a third of the water had slopped over the side with the impact. But the car was fully submerged except for the edge of the trunk lid, which had come open during the landing. Floating on the surface was a lifelike mannequin dressed in old jeans and a green military jacket. The scene was bizarre.

Crossley looked up toward the crestline to where he knew Mulholland Drive edged the hillside. He wondered if someone had pushed the car off the road, if this was some sort of prank.

He then looked back down into the pool. The surface was calming and he could see the car more clearly in the beam of the pool's light. And it was then that he thought he saw someone sitting unmoving behind the steering wheel.

Crossley ripped his robe off and dove naked into the pool.

OUR EYES COULDN'T STOP OPENING

BY MEGAN ABBOTT

Alter Road, Detroit

(Originally published in *Detroit Noir*)

S he always wanted to go and there was no stopping her once she got it in her head. Her voice was like a pressure in the car, Joni's mother's Buick, its spongy burgundy seats and the smell forever of L'Air du Temps.

Joni was game for it and I guess we all were, we liked Keri, you see, we admired her soft and dangerous ways. So lovely with her slippery brown hair lashed with bright highlights (all summer spent at the Woods Pool squeezing lemons into her scalp), so lovely with her darted skirts, ironed jeans, slick Goody barrettes. She was Harper Woods but, you see, she transcended that, so we let her slide, we let her hang with us, even let her lead us sometimes, times like this. Her mother put every dime of her Hutzel Hospital nurse's salary into her daughter's clothes, kept Keri looking Grosse Pointe and Keri could pass, pass well enough to snare with her pearl-pink nails, fingers spread, a prime tow-headed, lacrosse-playing Grosse Pointe South boy, Kirk Deegan, hair as blond as an Easter chick and crisp shirts with thin sherbet-colored stripes and slick loafers, ankles bare with the fuzz of downy boy hair. Oh my, did she hit the jackpot with him. Play her cards right, she could ride him any-where she wanted to go.

None of us, not even anyone we knew, was supposed to cross Alter Road, even get near Alter Road, it was like dropping off the face of the Earth. Worse even than that. The things that happened when you slipped across that burn-ing strip of asphalt, the girl a few years older than us—someone's cousin, you didn't know her—who crossed over, ended up all the way over on Connor, they found her three days later in a field, gangbanged into a coma at some crack house and dumped for dead, no, no, it was three weeks later and some-one saw her taking the pipe and turning tricks in Cass Corridor. No, no, it was worse, far worse . . . and then it'd go to whispers, awful whispering, what could be worse, you wondered, and you could always wonder something even worse.

But there Keri would be, nestled in the backseat, glossy lips shining in the dark car, fists on the back of the passenger seat, saying, *Let's go, let's go. C'mon. What's here, there's nothing here. Let's go.*

How many nights, after all, could be spent sloshing long spoons in our peanut butter cup sundaes at Friendly's, watching boys play hockey at Community Ice, huddling down in seats at Woods Theater, popcorn sticky on our fingers, lips, driving around trying to find parties, any parties, where new boys would be, boys we'd never met, but our boys, they all wore their letter jackets and all had the same slant in their hair, straight across the forehead, sharp as ice, and the same conversation and the same five words before your mouth around the beer can begging for the chance to not talk, to let the full-mouthed rush of music flood out all the talk and let the beer do its work so this boy in front of you might seem everything he wasn't and more—how many nights of that, I ask you?

So when Keri said, *Let's go,* maybe we let ourselves unsnide our tones, let our tilted-neck looks loosen a bit, unroll our eyes, curl into her quiet urging and *go, go, go.*

When he was around, Joni's brother, he'd buy us beer, wine coolers, and she'd hide them in the hedgerow underneath her bedroom window until we needed them. But he was at Hillsdale most of the time, trying to get credits enough to graduate and start working at Prudential for his dad. So there was Bronco's, right off the Outer Drive exit, and you could buy anything you wanted there, long as you were willing to drop twelve dollars for a four-pack of big-mouth Mickey's, or a tall 40 of Old Style, the tang of it lingering in your mouth all night.

Bronco's, it was a kick, the street so empty and the fluorescent burst of its sign rising like a beacon, a shooting star as you came up the long slope on I-94. Sometimes it made your heart beat, stomach wiggle, vibrate, flip, like when the manager—a big-bellied white guy with a greasy lower lip—made Keri go in the back with him, behind the twitchy curtain. But he only wanted to turn her around, only wanted to run his fingers studded with fat gold over her chest and backside, and what did any of us care? It was worth the extra bottle of Boone's Farm Strawberry Hill he'd dropped in our paper bag. Hell, you always pay a price, don't you? Like Keri said, from the dark of the backseat, how different was it from letting the Blue Devils football starters under your bra so you'd get into the seniors' party on Lakeshore where the parents had laid out for six cases of champagne before heading to Aruba for the weekend? How different from that? Very different, we said, but we knew it wasn't.

And it wasn't only Bronco's. Bronco's was just how it started. Next, it was leaving a party on Windmill Pointe, hotted up on beer and cigarettes and feeling our legs bristling tight in our jeans and Keri saying, *Let's go that way, yes, that way*, and before we knew it, we'd tripped the fence.

Goddamn, Alter Road a memory.

We pitched over the shortest curl of a bridge, over a sludgy canal not twelve feet across, and there we were. But it wasn't like over by Bronco's. It was just as deserted, but it didn't look like a scarred patch of city at all. The smell of the water and trailers backed up onto the canal, abandoned trailers, one after another, rutted through with shimmering rust, quivering under streetlamps, narrow roads filled with rotting boats teetering on wheels, mobile homes with windows broken out, streets so narrow it was like being on the track of a funhouse ride and then, suddenly, all the tightness giving way to big, empty expanses of forlorn, overgrown fields, like some kind of prairie. Never saw anything like it, who of us had? And our breath going fast in the car because we'd found something we'd never seen before. And it was like our eyes couldn't stop opening.

We'd let the gas pedal surge, vibrate, take us past sixty, seventy on the side streets, take the corners hard, let the tires skid, what did we care? There was no one here. There was no one on the streets. All you could see was shivering piles of trash, one-eyed cats darting. What did it matter? There was no one left. I tell you, it was ours.

But Keri, she kept finding new streets and her voice, soft and lulling, the Grosse Pointe drawl, bored-sounding even when excited, hot under the eyes, all that. She'd say—and who were we to decline?—she'd say, *Turn left, turn left, Joni, there, Joni, there*, and we'd find ourselves further in, further in, down the river, the slick brew of the canals long past now, and trembling houses cooing to us as the wind gasped through their swelling crevices, their glassless windows, their dark glory. That's the thing Keri showed us. She showed us that.

It's beautiful, she said without even saying it.

If we'd all been speaking out loud, we'd have never had the guts to say it.

And eventually, we saw people.

First, a stray cluster of figures, young men, walking together. A man alone, singing softly, we could hear, our windows open, radio off, we wanted to hear. Do you see? We wanted to hear. He was singing about a lady in a gold dress.

A woman, middle-aged, clapping her hands at her dog, calling him toward her, the dog limping toward her, howling, wistful.

But mostly small fits of young men standing around, tossing cigarette embers glowing into the street.

At first, Joni'd pick up speed whenever she saw them, chattering high-pitched and breathless, about how they'd try to jack her mother's car and take it to a chop shop—there's hundreds of them all over the city, there are—and in twenty minutes her mother's burgundy Buick Regal would be stripped to a metal skeleton. *That's how it works*, she'd say. *That's what they do.*

None of us said anything. We felt the car hop over a pothole, our stomachs lifting, like on the Gemini at Cedar Pointe.

Then, Keri: *This time, Joni, go slow. Come on, Joni. Let's see what they're doing. Let's see.* And Joni would teeth-chatter at us about white girls raped in empty fields till they bled to death, and we let her say it because she needed to say it, had to get it out, and maybe we had to hear it, but we knew she'd go slower, and she did.

And then we'd be long past Alter, past Chalmers even, into that hissing whisper that was, to us, Detroit. Detroit. Say it. Hard in your mouth like a shard of glass. Glittering between your teeth and who could tell you it wasn't terrifying and beautiful all at once?

His voice was low and rippled and yeah, I'll say it, his skin was dark as black velvet, with a blue glow under the streetlamp, and he was talking to his friends from the sidewalk and we could almost hear them and God we wanted to and there was Keri and she had her hands curled around the edges of the top of the car door, window down, and he was looking at her like he knew her, and how could he? He didn't, but he couldn't miss that long spray of hair tumbling out the window as she craned to get a better look, to hear, to get meaning.

"You lost, honey?" is what he said, and it was like glass shattering, or something stretched tight for a thousand miles suddenly letting loose, releasing, releasing.

"Yes," was all she managed to whisper back before Joni had dropped her foot down on the gas hard and we all charged away, our hearts hammering . . .

. . . and Keri still saying, *Yes, yes, yes* . . .

You have to understand, we didn't know anything. We didn't know anything at all about conditions, history, the meanings of things. We didn't know anything. We were seeing castles in ruin like out of some dark fairy tale, but with an edge of wantonness, like all the best fairy tales.

Keri, by the lockers Monday a.m., doors clattering, pencils rolling down polished halls, she leans toward me, cheek pressed on the inside of my locker door, swinging it, rocking it. She says, *Remember when Joni drove the car real slow and let us get our eyeful and he looked at me and in his eyes I could see he knew more than any of us, more than all the teachers at school, all the parents too, he knew more in that flashing second than all the rest of everyone, all of them sleeping through forever in this place, this marble-walled place. In his eyes, what I could see was he was someone more than I could ever be.*

Keri, she tells us, first date with Kirk Deegan, he resplendent in Blue Devils jacket and puka shell necklace from a December trip to Sanibel Island, he winds his way from his hulking colonial on Rivard to her faded one-story in Harper Woods, can smell the pizza grease from the deli on the corner and he won't come inside. No, he stands one foot on the bottom porch step, Ray-Bans propped, and says, "Nah, where would I fit?"

I should've seen it coming because who wanted to keep doing the same thing, which was fun at first, but where could it go, in the end? You couldn't get out of the car. It was for kicks and you did it until the kicks stopped. This time, it worked like this: Joni started dating a De La Salle boy and he had a car anyway and evenings were now for him and I was starting up tennis and there were new parties and Keri, we saw her more like a long-haired flitter in the corner of our eye. We barely saw her at all. She was there in the Homecoming Court, glowing in her floral dress, smiling brightly, waving at everyone and standing ramrod straight, face perfect and still. Face so frozen for all the flashing cameras, for all the cheering faces, for all of us, for everybody.

It was her last of everything that year. It was her last. You could kind of see it then, couldn't you? It was there somehow, making everything more special, more like *something*, at least.

Later, at the dance, willowing around Kirk Deegan, he towering over her with that bright wedge of hair, the blackwatch plaid vest and tie, that slit-eyed cool, he who never let another boy come near, even touch her shoulder, even move close. What boy ever kept me so tight at hand? What boy? I ask you. He loved her that much, everyone said it. He loved her that much.

Sidling up to me in study hall, eyes fluttering, red, Keri's voice tired, slipping into my ear. *How was the party?* she's asking. *Was Stacey mad I didn't go?* I just smiled because of course Stacey was mad, because Keri was supposed to come and bring Kirk, because if Kirk came, so would Matt Tomlin, and she was angling for Matt Tomlin, was so ready for him she could barely stand it.

Where'd you guys go? I asked. And she gave me a flicker of a smile and she didn't say anything. And I said, Did you and Kirk . . . and she shook her head fast.

I didn't see him. It wasn't that.

And she told me Kirk was too wasted to go anywhere, showing off some old scotch of his father's and then drinking three inches of it, passing out on the leather armchair like some old guy. So she took his Audi and went for a drive and before she knew it she was long past Alter Road, long past everything. Even the Jefferson plant, the Waterworks. She said she drove all around in his car and saw things and ended up getting lost down by some abandoned railroad.

She was crazy to be doing it and I told her so and she nodded like she agreed, but I could tell by the way she looked off in the other direction that she didn't agree at all and that all she'd realized was that she wouldn't bother telling me about it anymore. But she didn't stop going. You could feel her rippling in her own pleasure over it. Like she was someone special who got to do things no one else did.

I met some people a few weeks ago, she said. They invited me to a party at this big old house, I don't even know where. You could see the big Chrysler plant. That was all you could see. The house, it had turrets like a castle. Like a castle in a fairy tale. I remember I wanted to go to the top and stand in the turret like a lost princess and look out on the river, waving a long handkerchief like I was waiting for a lover to come back from the sea.

I didn't know what she was talking about. I never heard anyone talk like this. I think it was the most I ever heard her talk and it didn't make any more sense than Trig class to me.

The house was empty, she said. The floors were part broken through. My foot slid between the boards and this boy, he had to lift me out and he was laughing. They were playing music and speakers were all over the house, one set up on an old banister thick as a tree trunk and everyone dancing and beer and Wild Irish Rose, wine so red like bloodshot eyes and smoking, getting high, and the whole place alive and I danced, one of them danced with me, so dark and with a diamond in his ear and he said he'd take me to Fox Creek, near the trailers, and we'd shoot old gas tanks, and I said I would, and he sang in my ear and I could feel it through my whole body, like in lab when Mr. Muskaluk ran that current through me in front of the class, like that, like that. It was this. I could do anything, no one cared. I could do anything and no one stopped me.

"What did you do, Keri?" I asked, my voice sounded funny to me. Sounded fast and gasping. "What did you do?"

Anything, she whispered, voice breathless and dirty. *Anything*.

Did I have time for that, for that kind of trashiness? Don't you see, Joni said, she's Harper Woods. She may look Grosse Pointe, she may have one on her arm. But that's a flash, a trick of the eye. Deep down, she's five blocks from the freeway. It all comes back. You can fight it, but it comes back.

So we dropped her and it was just as well because lots of things were happening, with boys' hockey starting and everyone's parents taking trips to Florida and so there were more parties and there was the thing with the sophomore girl and the senior boy and the police and things like that that everyone talked about. Other stuff happened too—I'd dropped out of tennis and then dropped back in—there was a boy for me with a brush of brown hair and the long, Adam's-appled neck of a star basketball player, which he was, and I took him to the Sadie Hawkins dance and he took me to parties and to parents' beds in upstairs rooms at parties and slid his tongue fast into my dry mouth and his hands fumbling everywhere, and his car, it smelled like him, Polo and new sneakers and Stroh's, and when it was over and I smelled those things, which you could smell on a dozen boys a day, it was him all over again, but then before I knew it, it was gone. He was gone, yeah, but the feeling that went with it too. Just like that.

Please, please can you drop me somewhere? Keri said, and we were in the school parking lot and her eyes rung wide and fingers gripped the top of the car door.

Okay, I said, even after barely seeing her for months, a quick hello in the hallways, a flash in the locker room, me on my way in, she on her way out. To Kirk's? I asked.

She said no. She said no and shook her head, gaze drifting off to the far end of the parking lot. Further than that. Further than that.

And then I knew and I told her it was my father's car and if I got a scratch, he'd never buy me the Fiero come graduation and she promised it would be okay and I said yes. Against everything, I said yes.

So she was next to me and the sky was orange, then red as the sun dropped behind the Yacht Club, its gleaming white bell tower soaring—when I was a kid I thought it was Disneyland—I was going to take her. I felt somehow I had to.

Where are we going? I'd say, and she'd chew her gum and look out the window, fingers touching, breath smoking the glass. She was humming a song and I didn't know it. It wasn't a song any of us would know, a song we sang along with on WHYT, a song we all shouted out together in cars. It was something else all together. Plaintive and funny and I thought suddenly: Who does she think she is in my father's car singing songs I don't know in her white Tretorns and her pleated shirt and hair brushed to silk, whirling gold hoops hanging from her ears? And she thinks she can just go wherever she wants, do things in other places, touch more than the surface of things, and then keep it all inside her and never let anyone see in. Never let any of us.

You can drop me here, she was saying. We were at the foot of Windmill Pointe.

You just want me to leave you here? I asked, looking around, seeing not a soul. In Grosse Pointe, especially these its most gleamy stretches, the streets were always empty, like plastic pieces from a railroad set.

Yes, she said, and waved as she began walking toward the water, toward the glittering lighthouse.

Wait, Keri, I said, opening my door so she could hear me. Where are you going?

And she half-turned and maybe she smiled, maybe she even said something, but the wind took it away.

When I saw her in school, I asked her. I said, Where did you go? What were you doing there? She was putting on her lipgloss and shaking her hair out. I watched her eyes in the mirror magnet on the inside of her locker door. I thought maybe I'd see something, see something in there.

She watched me back, eyes rimmed with pale green liner, and I knew she had to tell someone, didn't she? What did it count to run off the rails if you didn't tell a soul? I looked at her with the most simpering face I could manage to make her see she could tell me, she could tell me.

But she didn't now, did she? And that was the last time, see? It was the last of that flittering girl.

"Her cousin's letting her drive her Nova, you should see it," Joni was telling me. "I saw her in it. Do you think she's taking it there? Next thing you know, we'll be driving down Jefferson to go see the Red Wings game and she'll be rolling with some black guys." Joni was telling me this as we squeezed together on the long sofa at a party, beers in hand, Joni's face sweaty and flushed, bangs matted to foreheads, chests heaving lightly.

I said I didn't think she went at all anymore. I told Joni she wasn't going at all. I didn't want her to know. It was something between us. And, truth told, if she'd asked me, I'd've gone with her still. But she didn't ask me, did she?

* * *

It was in the aching frost of February and I was coming out of a party on Beaconsfield and I saw her drive by. I saw the blue Nova and I saw her at the wheel and I saw which way she was headed and maybe my head was a little clogged from the beers, but I couldn't help it and I was in my dad's car and I headed toward Alter Road. She was long gone, but I kept driving and I thought maybe I'd see the car again, especially once I hit the ghostly pitch over the bridge at Alter and Korte Street. How many beers was it, I thought I could hear the squeal of her tires. The only sound at all, other than the occasional sludge of water against the creaking docks over the canal, were those tires. I thought it had to be her and I stopped my car, rolled down my windows, couldn't hear anything so figured she stopped. Did she stop? I edged past the side streets and ended up back at that shell of a trailer court, those aluminum and wood carcasses, like plundered ships washed to shore. And that was when I thought I saw her, darting around the bowed trees, darting along like some kind of wood nymph in a magic forest, and yet it was this.

I could admit, if I let myself, there was a beauty in it, if you squinted, tilted your head. If you could squeeze out ideas of the kind of beauty you can rest in your palm, fasten around your neck, never have an unease about, a slip of cashmere, one fine pearl, a beauty everyone would understand and feel safe with. But I wouldn't really do that, not for more than a second, and Keri, she would. It was like this place she'd found was Broadway, Hollywood, Shangri-La, and she would make it hers.

I parked my car and got out, the wind running in off the lake and charging at me, but I went anyway. That beer foaming my head, I just kept going. Who was going to stop me? I was going to see, see the thing through. I wasn't going to tell, but I was going to see it for myself.

Wading through the golden rod, studded with scrap metal, with shredded firecrackers, flossy crimps of insulation foam, there I was. The trailers all edged in rust like frills peeking from under a dress, but as you got closer, it wasn't so dainty and there was a feel in the air of awfulness. All of it, it reminded me of places you're not supposed to be, they're just not for you, like when we went to that house, when we were in Girl Scouts, to deliver the Christmas presents to the family on Mt. Elliott, and everyone told us, Just watch, they'll have a big TV and a VCR and they'll be lying around collecting welfare with tons of kids running around, and that wasn't what happened at all, and remember how the baby wouldn't stop shaking and the look in the mother's eyes like she'd long ago stopped being surprised at anything, and the plastic on the windows and the leaking refrigerator, we weren't supposed to be there at all, now, were we?

This, it was like that, but different, because this had that lostness but then too in place of sad there was this hard current of nastiness and dirtiness and badness, sweaty, gun-oil, mattress-spring coil throbbing, stains spreading. My eyes skating over the abandoned trailers and thinking of the things happening behind the bulging screens, the pitted aluminum. The sky so black and the vague sound of music and the feeling of teetering into something and then it getting inside you, feeding off you, making you its own.

There was a laugh then and it struck me hard right through the swirling muzz in my head, but it was warm, rippling, and it broke up some of the nastiness for me, but not enough.

Coming from one of the trailers, a faded red one with a rolling top, like a curling tongue. There was something glowing inside and there was music.

I felt my ankle twist on a bottle curved deep into the earth. I could hear the music, a thud-thud, bass tickling me, promising things, and I walked closer, I just did.

I walked closer like I could, like I was allowed, even as this was no place for me. That tickling laugh kept rolling itself out, felt like long fingers uncoiling just shy of me, just shy of my body, hot and itchy under my coat, aching for the cold wind ripping off the water and instead this runny canal, a ditch swelling.

And then there it was.

Soft, high, sweet, Keri's own laugh.

Like when we watched a funny movie or when we watched Joni make cross-eyes or when we danced in our bedrooms, singing, singing until we thought our lungs would burst.

But then turning, turning like a dial and the laugh got lower, throatier, and I could feel it prickling under my skin, then sinking through me, down my legs, along the twitching pain in my ankle, straight into the ground.

Reaching under my feet.

And in my head, I could see her face and she's lying on a stripped mattress, hair spread out beneath, a windmill, and she's laughing and twisting and squirming, her head tilting back, neck arching, and who knew what was happening, what was happening to draw that throaty laugh from her, pump that bursting flush into her cheeks, face, God, Keri, God, all kinds of dark hands on her, she at the center of some awful white-girl gangbang. All those hands touching her white white-girl skin. These are the things I thought, I won't claim otherwise.

* * *

I was standing ten seconds, a minute, who knew, the cold snaking around me but not touching. I could've stood forever, twenty feet from that trailer, watching. But then. But then. The sound.

A hinge struck and I could hear and there it was, I could see they weren't in the trailer but on the other side of it and there I was, back to the mangled sheet metal, sidling around, and that's when I saw the bonfire that made the glow and I hid behind the tinsely branches of a half-fallen tree and I watched and I saw everything, or figured I did.

There were two black guys and a white guy and there was a tall black girl with a dark jacket on and I could see it had gold print struck in it and then I saw it was a letter jacket, Keri's letter jacket from volleyball, and the girl was climbing on the picnic table and that was where Keri was and she was dancing. She was dancing to the music from the radio they'd brought and one of the black guys, Keri was saying something to him as she danced, and he was laughing and watching her and I could tell he was the one she was with, you could see it in his eyes and hers, it was vibrating between them.

She was there in the Homecoming Court, resplendent in her floral dress, smiling brightly, waving at everyone and standing ramrod straight, face perfect and still.

And the black girl joined Keri and the girl had a can of beer and so did Keri and the guys, they were shouting and they were lightly rocking the table, and the white guy was tipping a bottle of something into his mouth and singing about how some girl was his twilight zone, his Al Capone, and I could smell the pot and a lot was going on like at any party and it seemed like maybe more, but I was watching Keri and Keri's face, it was lit from the fire and it was a crazy orange flaring up her cheeks and she was wearing her long cashmere muffler from Jacobson's, coiled around her neck, flapping tight in the wind, and she was dancing and the fire lit her hair and I could see her face and it was like I'd never seen it before and never would again because things made sense even if they didn't because there was something there that I felt twenty years too young to understand, no, not too young, because I couldn't understand it because she was fathoms deep and I would be driving along Kercheval in fifteen minutes, driving to my family's three-bedroom colonial and tucking myself in and hoping the boy would call and thinking about the next party and here was Keri and she was fathoms deep and I was . . .

I couldn't have known, watching her there, watching her dancing and looking like that, feeling that way, that she would be gone by finals, by junior prom even. I never said a word about what I saw and I never told her to watch out either, even though, the way I was, I could only see it as she was going for broke and it could turn out any number of ways but most of them bad. But even if I had tried to warn her, to hold her back, it wouldn't have mattered because I would've told her to watch out for the wrong things, the wrong places. I couldn't have known, watching her there, that two weeks later she'd be driving a drunken Kirk Deegan home late after a postgame party, driving him in his Audi and coming into the Deegan garage too close to the wall and shearing off the sideview mirror. I couldn't have known Kirk Deegan would get so mad and push her so hard against the garage wall and her head hitting that pipe and then turning and hitting the edge of the shovel hanging and what must have been a sickening crack and her falling and her dying and her dying there on the floor of his garage. Her dying on the floor of his garage and him there, too dumbstruck to call the police, an ambulance, his parents, anyone, for a half hour while she was there, hair spread on the cement floor like a windmill and then gone forever. I couldn't have known that. But one way or another I did.

PUBLIC TRANSPORTATION

BY LEE CHILD

Chandler, Arizona

(Originally published in *Phoenix Noir*)

H e said he wouldn't talk to me. I asked him why. He said because he was a cop and I was a journalist. I said he sounded like a guy with something to hide. He said no, he had nothing to hide.

"So talk to me," I said, and I knew he would.

He scuffed around for a minute more, hands on the top of the bar, drumming his fingers, moving a little on his stool. I knew him fairly well. He was edging out of the summer of his career and entering the autumn. His best years were behind him. He was in the valley, facing a long ten years before his pension. He liked winning, but losing didn't worry him too much. He was a realistic man. But he liked to be sure. What he hated was not really knowing whether he had won or lost.

"From the top," I said.

He shrugged and took a sip of his beer and sighed and blew fumes toward the mirror facing us. Then he started with the 911 call. The house, out beyond Chandler, south and east of the city. A long low ranch, prosperous, walled in, the unlit pool, the darkness. The parents, arriving home from a party. The silence. The busted window, the empty bed. The trail of blood through the hallway. The daughter's body, all ripped up. Fourteen years old, damaged in a way he still wasn't prepared to discuss.

I said, "There were details that you withheld."

He asked, "How do you know?"

"You guys always do that. To evaluate the confessions."

He nodded.

I asked, "How many confessions did you get?"

"A hundred and eight."

"All phony?"

"Of course."

"What information did you withhold?"

"I'm not going to tell you."

"Why not? You not sure you got the right guy?"

He didn't answer.

"Keep going," I said.

So he did. The scene was clearly fresh. The parents had gotten back maybe moments after the perpetrator had exited. Police response had been fast. The blood on the hallway carpet was still liquid. Dark red, not black, against the kid's pale skin. The kid's pale skin was a problem from the start. They all knew it. They were in a position to act fast and heavy, so they were going to, and they knew it would be claimed later that the speed was all about the kid being white, not black or brown. It wasn't. It was a question of luck and timing. They got a fresh scene, and they got a couple of breaks. I nodded, like I accepted his view. Which I did. I was a journalist, and I liked mischief as much as the next guy, but sometimes things were straightforward.

"Go on," I said.

There were photographs of the kid all over the house. She was an only child. She was luminous and beautiful. She was stupefying, the way fourteen-year-old white Arizona girls often are.

"Go on," I said.

The first break had been the weather. There had been torrential rain two days previously, and then the heat had come back with a vengeance. The rain had skimmed the street with sand and mud and the heat had baked it to a film of dust, and the dust showed no tire tracks other than those from the parents' vehicle and the cop cars and the ambulance. Therefore the perpetrator had arrived on foot. And left on foot. There were clear marks in the dust. Sneakers, maybe size ten, fairly generic soles. The prints were photographed and e-mailed and everyone was confident that in the fullness of time some database somewhere would match a brand and a style. But what was more important was that they had a suspect recently departed from a live scene on foot, in a landscape where no one walked. So APBs and be-on-the-lookouts were broadcast for a two-mile radius. It was midnight and more than a hundred degrees and pedestrians were going to be rare. It was simply too hot for walking. Certainly too hot for running. Any kind of sustained physical activity would be close to a suicide attempt. Greater Phoenix was that kind of place, especially in the summer.

Ten minutes passed and no fugitives were found.

Then they got their second break. The parents were reasonably lucid. In between all the bawling and screaming they noticed their daughter's cell phone was missing. It had been her pride and joy. An iPhone, with an AT&T

contract that gave her unlimited minutes, which she exploited to the max. Back then iPhones were new and cool. The cops figured the perp had stolen it. They figured the kind of guy who had no car in Arizona would have been entranced by a small shiny object like an iPhone. Or else if he was some kind of big-time deviant, maybe he collected souvenirs. Maybe the cache of photographs of the kid's friends was exciting. Or the text messages stored in the memory.

"Go on," I said.

The third break was all about middle-class parents and fourteen-year-old daughters. The parents had signed up for a service whereby they could track the GPS chip in the iPhone on their home computer. Not cheap, but they were the kind of people who wanted to know their kid was telling the truth when she said she was sleeping over at a girlfriend's house or riding with a buddy to the library. The cops got the password and logged on right there and then and saw the phone moving slowly north, toward Tempe. Too fast for walking. Too fast for running. Too slow to be in a car.

"Bike?" one of them said.

"Too hot," another answered. "Plus no tire tracks in the driveway."

The guy telling the story next to me on his stool had been the one who had understood.

"Bus," he said. "The perp is on the bus."

Greater Phoenix had a lot of buses. They were for workers paid too little to own cars. They shuttled folks around, especially early in the morning and late at night. The giant city would have ground to a halt without them. Meals would have gone unserved, pools uncleaned, beds unmade, trash not collected. Immediately all the cops as one imagined a rough profile. A dark-skinned man, probably small, probably crazy, rocking on a seat as a bus headed north. Fiddling with the iPhone, checking the music library, looking at the pictures. Maybe with the knife still in his pocket, although surely that was too much to ask.

One cop stayed at the house and watched the screen and called the game like a sports announcer. All the APBs and the BOLOs were canceled and every car screamed after the bus. It took ten minutes to find it. Ten seconds to stop it. It was corraled in a ring of cars. Lights were flashing and popping and cops were crouching behind hoods and doors and trunks and guns were pointing, Glocks and shotguns, dozens of them.

The bus had a driver and three passengers aboard.

The driver was a woman. All three passengers were women. All three were elderly. One of them was white. The driver was a skinny Latina of around thirty.

"Go on," I said.

The guy beside me sipped his beer again and sighed. He had arrived at the point where the investigation was botched. They had spent close to twenty minutes questioning the four women, searching them, making them move up and down the street while the cop back at the house watched for GPS action on the screen. But the cursor didn't move. The phone was still on the bus. But the bus was empty. They searched under the seats. Nothing. They searched the seats themselves.

They found the phone.

The last-but-one seat at the back on the right had been slit with a knife. The phone had been forced edgewise into the foam rubber cushion. It was hidden there and bleeping away silently. A wild goose chase. A decoy.

The slit in the seat was rimed with faint traces of blood. The same knife.

The driver and all three passengers recalled a white man getting on the bus south of Chandler. He had seated himself in back and gotten out again at the next stop. He was described as neatly dressed and close to middle age. He was remembered for being from the wrong demographic. Not a typical bus rider.

The cops asked, "Was he wearing sneakers?"

No one knew for sure.

"Did he have blood on him?"

No one recalled.

The chase restarted south of Chandler. The assumption was that because the decoy had been placed to move north, then the perp was actually moving south. A fine theory, but it came to nothing. No one was found. A helicopter joined the effort. The night was still dark but the helicopter had thermal imaging equipment. It was not useful. Everything single thing it saw was hot.

Dawn came and the helicopter refueled and came back for a visual search. And again, and again, for days. At the end of a long weekend it found something.

"Go on," I said.

The thing that the helicopter found was a corpse. White male, wearing sneakers. In his early twenties. He was identified as a college student, last seen the day before. A day later the medical examiner issued his report. The guy had died of heat exhaustion and dehydration.

"Consistent with running from a crime scene?" the cops asked.

"Among other possibilities," the medical examiner answered.

The guy's toxicology screen was baroque. Ecstasy, skunk, alcohol.

"Enough to make him unstable?" the cops asked.

"Enough to make an elephant unstable," the medical examiner answered.

The guy beside me finished his beer. I signaled for another.

I asked, "Case closed?"

The guy beside me nodded. "Because the kid was white. We needed a result."

"You not convinced?"

"He wasn't middle-aged. He wasn't neatly dressed. His sneakers were wrong. No sign of the knife. Plus, a guy hopped-up enough to run himself to death in the heat wouldn't have thought to set up the decoy with the phone."

"So who was he?"

"Just a frat boy who liked partying a little too much."

"Anyone share your opinion?"

"All of us."

"Anyone doing anything about it?"

"The case is closed."

"So what really happened?"

"I think the decoy indicates premeditation. And I think it was a double bluff. I think the perp got out of the bus and carried on north, maybe in a car he had parked."

I nodded. The perp had. Right then the car he had used was parked in the lot behind the bar. Its keys were in my pocket.

"Win some, lose some," I said.

TOO NEAR REAL

BY JONATHAN SAFRAN FOER

Princeton, New Jersey

(Originally published in *New Jersey Noir*)

On the first day of my forced sabbatical, I noticed a car driving down Nassau Street with a large spherical device extending from its top. It looked like the past's vision of the future. I assumed it was part of some meteorology or physics or even psychology experiment—another small contribution to our charming campus atmospherics—and I didn't give it much thought. I probably wouldn't have even noticed it in the first place had I not been taking my first walk for walk's sake in years. Without a place to get to, I finally was where I was.

A few weeks later—exactly a month later, I was to learn—I saw the vehicle again, this time crawling down Prospect Avenue. I was stopped at a corner, not waiting for the light to change, not waiting for anything that might actually happen.

"Any idea what that is?" I asked a student who was standing at the curb beside me. Her quick double-take suggested recognition.

"Google," she said.

"Google what?" I asked, but wanting far more to know what she thought of me, and how other students on campus were talking about and judging me.

"Street view."

"Which is what?"

She sighed, just in case there was any doubt about her reluctance to engage with me. "That thing above the car is a camera with nine lenses. Every second it takes a photograph in each direction, and they're stitched together into a map."

"What kind of map?"

"It's 3-D and can be navigated."

"I thought you used a map *for* navigating."

"Yeah, well."

She was finished with me, but I wasn't ready to let her go. It's not that I cared about the map—and if I had, I could have easily found better answers elsewhere. But her reluctance to speak with me—even to be seen standing beside me—compelled me to keep her there.

I asked, "No one minds having all of these pictures taken all the time?"

"A lot of people mind," she said, rummaging through her bag for nothing.

"But no one does anything about it?"

The light changed. I didn't move. As the student walked away, I thought I heard her say, "Fucking pig." I'm virtually positive that's what she said.

A few days earlier, while eating pasta out of the colander, I'd heard an NPR piece about something called "the uncanny valley." Apparently, when we are presented with an imitation of life—a cartoon, a robot-looking robot—we are happily willing to engage with it: to hear its stories, converse with it, even empathize. (Charlie Brown's face, characterized by only a few marks, is a good example.) We continue to be comfortable with imitations as they more and more closely resemble life. But there comes a point—say, when the imitation is 98 percent lifelike (whatever *that* means)—when we become deeply unsettled, in an interesting way. We feel some repulsion, some alienation, some caveman reflex akin to what happens when nails are run down a blackboard.

We are happy with the fake, and happy with the real, but the near real—the too near real—unnerves us. (This has been demonstrated in monkeys as well. When presented with near-lifelike monkey heads, they will go to the corners of their cages and cover their faces.) Once the imitation is fully believable—100 percent believable—we are again comfortable, even though we know it is an imitation of life. That distance between the 98 percent and 100 percent is the uncanny valley. It was only in the last five years that our imitations of life got good enough—movies with digitally rendered humans, robots with highly articulated musculature—to generate this new human feeling.

The experience of navigating the map fell, for me, into the uncanny valley. Perhaps this is because at forty-six I was already too old to move comfortably within it. Even in those moments when I forgot that I was looking at a screen, I was aware of the finger movements necessary to guide my journey. To my students—my former students—I imagine it would be second nature. Or first nature.

I could advance down streets, almost as if walking, but not at all like walking. It wasn't gliding, or rolling or skating. It was something more like being stationary, with the world gliding or rolling or skating toward me. I could turn my "head," look up and down—the world pivoting around my fixed perspective. It was *too much* like the world.

Google is forthright about how the map is made—why shouldn't they be?—and I learned that the photos are regularly updated. (Users couldn't tolerate the dissonance of looking at snow in the summer, or the math building that was torn down three months ago. While such errors would put the map safely on the far side of the uncanny valley, it would also render it entirely uninteresting—if every bit as useful.) Princeton, I learned, is reshot on the fourth of every month.

I wanted to walk to the living room, find my wife reading in her chair, and tell her about it.

The investigation never went anywhere because there was nowhere for it to go. (It was never even clear just *what* they were investigating.) I'd had two previous relationships with graduate students—explicitly permitted by the university—and they were held up as evidence. Evidence of *what*? Evidence that past the appropriate age I had sexual hunger. Why couldn't I simply repress it? Why did I have to have it at all? My persistent character was my character flaw.

The whole thing was a farce, and as always it boiled down to contradictory memories. No one on a college campus wants to stand up to defend the right of an accused harasser to remain innocent until proven guilty. The university privately settled with the girl's family, and I was left with severely diminished stature in the department, and alienated from almost all of my colleagues and friends. I believed they believed me, and didn't blame them for distancing themselves.

I found myself sitting in coffee shops for hours, reading sections of the newspaper I never used to touch, eating fewer meals on plates, and for the first time in my adult life, going for long, directionless walks.

The first night of my forced freedom, I walked for hours. I left the disciplinary committee meeting, took rights and lefts without any thought to where they might lead me, and didn't get back to my house until early the next morning. My earphones protected me from one kind of loneliness, and I walked beyond the reach of the local NPR affiliate—like a letter so long it switches from black pen to blue, the station became country music.

At some point, I found myself in the middle of a field. Apparently I was the kind of person who left the road, the kind of person who walked on grass. The stars were as clear as I'd ever seen them. *How old are you?* I wondered. *How many of you are dead?* I thought, for the first time in a long while, about my parents: my father asleep on the sofa, his chest blanketed with news that was already ancient by the time it was delivered that morning. The thought entered my mind that he had probably bought his last shirt. Where did that thought come from? Why did it come? I thought about the map: like the stars, its images are sent to us from the past. And it's also confusing.

I thought that maybe if I took a picture of the constellations, I could e-mail them to my wife with some pithy thumb-typed sentiment—*Wish you were here*—and maybe, despite knowing the ease and cheapness of such words, she would be moved. Maybe two smart people who knew better could retract into the shell of an empty gesture and hide out there for at least a while.

I aimed the phone up and took a picture, but the flash washed out all of the stars. I turned off the flash, but the "shutter" stayed open for so long, trying to sip up any of the little light it could, that my infinitesimally small movements made everything blurry. I took another picture, holding my hand as still as I could, but it was still a blur. I braced my arm with my other hand, but it was still a blur.

On the fourth of the next month, I waited on the corner of Nassau and Olden. When the vehicle came, I didn't wave or even smile, but stood there like an animal in a diorama. I went home, opened my laptop, and dropped myself down at the corner of Nassau and Olden. I spun the world, so that I faced northwest. There I was.

There was something exhilarating about it. I was in the map, there for anyone searching Princeton to see. (Until, of course, the vehicle came through again in four weeks, replacing the world like the Flood.) Sitting at my kitchen counter, leaning into the screen of a laptop I bought because, like everybody else, I liked the way it looked, I felt part of the physical world. The feeling was complicated: simultaneously empowering and emasculating. It was an approximate feeling had by someone unable to locate his actual feelings.

I asked myself: Should I go on a trip?

I asked: Should I try to write a book?

Should I apologize? To *whom* should I apologize? I'd already apologized to my wife in every way possible. To the girl's parents? What was there to apologize *for*? Would an apology retroactively create a crime?

There were the problems of shame and anger, of wanting to avoid and manufacture encounters like the one with the student at the streetlight. I needed to be away from judgment, and I needed to be understood. There was nothing keeping me. I'd never been enthusiastic about teaching, but I'd lost my enthusiasm for *everything*. I felt, in the deepest sense, uninspired, deflated. I'd lost my ability to experience urgency, as if I thought I was never going to die.

I took a left on Chestnut, and suddenly heard something beautiful. *Heard*, so I wasn't in the map. This was real. The music was coming from someone's earphones, a student's. She was wearing sweatpants, like the athletes do after their showers after practice. It was a beautiful song, so beautiful it made me ecstatic and depressed. I didn't know how I felt. I didn't know how to ask what the song was. I didn't want to interrupt her, or risk a condemnatory look. I kept a fixed distance. She entered a dorm. There was nothing to do.

Afraid of forgetting the tune, I called my phone, and left myself a message, humming the bit I could remember. And then I forgot about it, and after seven days my phone automatically erased saved messages. And then, too late, I remembered. So I took my phone to the store where I bought it and asked if there was any way to recover an erased message. The clerk suggested I send the SIM card to the manufacturer, which I did, and seven weeks later I was e-mailed a digital file with every message I'd received since buying the phone. I found nothing remarkable in this, felt no even small thrill in the confirmation that nothing is ever lost. I was angered or saddened by its inability to impress me.

This was the first message:

Hi. It's Julie. Either you're hearing this, and therefore deserve to be congratulated on having entered the modern world, or—and this seems equally likely—you have no idea what the blinking red light means, and my voice is hanging in some kind of digital purgatory . . . If you don't call me back, I'll assume the latter. Anyway, I just walked out of your office, and wanted to thank you for your generosity. I appreciate it more than you could know. You kept saying, "It goes without saying," but none of it went without saying. As for dinner, that sounds really nice. At the risk of inserting awkwardness, maybe we should go somewhere off campus, just to, I don't know, get away from people? Awkward? Crazy? You wouldn't tell me. Maybe you would. It goes without saying that I loathe awkwardness and craziness. And the more I talk about it, the worse it gets. So I'm going to cut my losses. Call me back and we can make a plan.

That was how it began. Dinner was my suggestion, going off campus was hers. It was a pattern we learned to make use of: I asked if she wanted something to drink, she ordered wine; I wiped something nonexistent from her cheek, she held my hand against her face; I asked her to stay in the car to talk for another few minutes . . .

The final message was me humming the unknown song to myself.

I went to Venice in the map. Never having been to actual Venice, I have no idea how the experience measured up. Obviously there were no smells, no sounds, no brushing shoulders with Venetians, and so on. (It is only a matter of time before the map fills out with such sensations.) But I did walk across the Bridge of Sighs, and I did see Saint Mark's Basilica. I walked through Piazza San Marco, read Joseph Brodsky's tombstone on San Michele, window-shopped the glass factories of the Murano islands (bulbs of molten glass held in place at the ends of those long straws until the next month). I looked out at the digital water, its unmoving current holding vaporettos in place. I tried to keep walking, right out onto the water. And I did.

Only someone who hasn't given himself over to the map would scoff at the deficiency of the experience. The deficiency is the fullness: removing a bit of life can make life feel so much more vivid—like closing your eyes to hear better. No, like closing your eyes to remember the value of sight.

I went to Rio, to Kyoto, to Capetown. I searched the flea markets of Jaffa, pressed my nose to the windows of the Champs-Élysées, waded with the crows through the mountains at Fresh Kills.

I went to Eastern Europe, visiting, as I had always promised her I would, the village of my grandmother's birth. Nothing was left, no indication of what had once been a bustling trading point. I searched the ground for any remnant, and was able to find a chunk of brick. I download images of the brick from a number of perspectives, and sent them to a friend in the engineering department. He was able to model the remnant, and fabricate it on a 3-D-rendering printer. He gave me two of them: one I kept on my desk, the other I sent to my mother to place on my grandmother's grave.

I went to the hospital where I was born. It has since been replaced with a new hospital.

I went to my elementary school. The playground had been built on to accommodate more students. Where do the children play?

I went to the neighborhood in which my father grew up. I went to his house. My father is not a known person. There will never be a plaque outside of his childhood home letting the world know that he was born there. I had a plaque made, mailed it to my younger brother, and asked him to affix it with

Velcro on the sixteenth of the following month. I returned to his house that afternoon and there it was.

Instead of dropping myself back down in Princeton, I decided to walk all the way home. It is quicker to walk in the map, as each stride can cover a full city block, but I knew it would take me most of the night. I didn't mind. I wanted it that way. The night had to be filled. Halfway across the George Washington Bridge I looked down.

Nothing ever happens because nothing *can* happen, because despite the music, movies, and novels that have inspired us to believe that the extraordinary is right around the corner, we've been disappointed by experience. The dissonance between what we've been promised and what we've been given would make anyone confused and lonely. I was only ever trying to inch my imitation of life closer to life.

I can't remember the last time I didn't pause halfway across a bridge and look down. I wanted to call out, but to whom? Nobody would hear me because there's no sound. I was there, but everyone around me was in the past. I watched my braveness climb onto the railing and leap: the suicide of my suicide.

On the fourth of the next month, I walked beside the vehicle. It was easy to keep pace with it, as the clarity of the photographs depends on the car moving quite slowly. I took a right down Harrison when the car did, and another right on Patton, and a left on Broadmead. The windows were tinted—apparently the drivers have been subject to insults and arguments—so I didn't know if I was even noticed. The driver certainly didn't adjust his driving in any way to suggest so. I walked beside him for more than two hours, and only stopped when the blister on my right heel became unbearable. I had wanted to outlast him, catch him on his lunch break, or filling up at the gas station. That would have been a victory, or at least a kind of intimacy. What would I have said? *Do you recognize me?*

I went home and turned on my computer. Everywhere you looked in Princeton, there I was. There were dozens of me.

Hi, it's me. I know I'm not supposed to call, but I don't care. I'm sad. I'm in trouble. Just with myself. I'm in trouble with myself. I don't know what to do and there's no one to talk to. You used to talk to me, but now you won't. I'm not going to ruin your life. I don't know why you're so afraid of that. I've never done anything to make you think I'm in any way unreliable. But

I have to say, the more you act on your fear that I will ruin your life, the more compelled I feel to ruin it. I'm not a great person, but I've never done anything to you. I know it's all my fault, I just don't know how. What is it? I'm sorry.

I was spending more time each day inside of the map, traveling the world—Sydney, Reykjavik, Lisbon—but mostly going for walks around Princeton. I would often pass people I knew, people I would have liked to say hello to or avoid. The pizza in the window was always fresh, I always wanted to eat it. I wanted to open all of the books on the stand outside the bookshop, but they were forever closed. (I made a note to myself to open them, facing out, on the fourth of the next month, so I would have something to read inside the map.) I wanted the world to be more available to me, to be touchable.

I was puzzled by my use of the map, my desire to explore places that I could easily explore in the world itself. The more time I spent in the map, the smaller the radius of my travels. Had I stayed inside long enough, I imagine I would have spent my time gazing through my window, looking at myself looking at the map. The thrill or relief came through continual reencounters with the familiar—like a blind person's hands exploring a sculpture of his face.

Unable to sleep one night—it was daytime in the map, as always—I thought I'd check out the progress on the new dorms down by the water. Nothing could possibly be more soul-crushing than campus construction: slow and pointless, a way to cast off money that had to either be spent or lost. But the crushing of the soul was the point. It was part of my exile inside of the map inside of my house.

As I rotated the world to see the length of the scaffolding, something caught my attention: a man looking directly into the camera. He was approximately my age—perhaps a few years older—wearing a plaid jacket and Boston Red Sox hat. There was nothing at all unusual about someone looking back at the camera: most people who notice the vehicle are unable to resist staring. But I had the uncanny sense that I'd seen this person before. Where? Nowhere, I was sure, and yet I was also sure somewhere. It didn't matter, which is why it did.

I dropped myself back down on Nassau Street, drifted its length a few times, and finally found him, standing outside the bank, again looking directly into the camera. There was nothing odd about that, either—he could have simply walked from one location to the other, and by chance crossed paths with the vehicle. I rotated the world around him, examined him from all sides, pulled him close to me and pushed him away, tilted the world to better see him. Was he a professor? A townie? I was most curious about my curiosity about him. Why did his face draw me in?

I walked home. It had become a ritual: before closing the map, I would walk back to my front door. There was something too dissonant about leaving it otherwise, like debarking a plane before it lands. I crossed Hamilton Avenue, wafted down Snowden, and, one giant stride at a time, went home. But when I was still several hundred feet away, I saw him again. He was standing in front of my house. I approached, shortening my strides so that the world only tiptoed toward me. He was holding something, which I couldn't make out for another few feet; it was a large piece of cardboard, across which was written: *YOU WON'T GET AWAY WITH IT.*

I ran to the actual door and opened it. He wasn't there. Of course he wasn't.

As computing moves off of devices and into our bodies, the living map will as well. That's what they're saying. In the clumsiest version we will wear goggles onto which the map is projected. In all likelihood, the map will be on contact lenses, or will forgo our eyes altogether. We will literally live in the map. It will be as visually rich as the world itself: the trees will not merely look like trees, they will feel like trees. They will, as far as our minds are concerned, *be* trees. Actual trees will be the imitations.

We will continuously upload our experiences, contributing to the perpetual creation of the map. No more vehicles: *we* will be the vehicles.

Information will be layered onto the map as is desired. We could, when looking at a building, call up historical images of it; we could watch the bricks being laid. If we crave spring, the flowers will bloom in time lapse. When other people approach, we will see their names and vital info. Perhaps we will see short films of our most important interactions with them. Perhaps we will see their photo albums, hear short clips of their voices at different ages, smell their shampoo. Perhaps we will have access to their thoughts. Perhaps we will have access to our own.

On the fourth of the next month, I stood at my door, waiting for the vehicle, and waiting for him. I was holding a sign of my own: *YOU DON'T KNOW ME.* The vehicle passed and I looked into the lens with the confidence of innocence. He never came. What would I have done if he had? I wasn't afraid of him. Why not? I was afraid of my lack of fear, which suggested a lack of care.

Or I was afraid that I *did* care, that I wanted something bad to happen.

I missed my wife. I missed myself.

I did an image search for the girl. There she was, posing on one knee with her high school lacrosse team. There she was, at a bar in Prague, blowing a kiss to the camera—to *me*, three years and half a globe away. There she was, holding on to a buoy. Almost all of the photos were the same photo, the one the newspapers had used. I pulled up her obituary, which I hadn't brought myself to read until then. It said nothing I didn't know. It said nothing at all. The penultimate paragraph mentioned her surviving family. I did an image search for her father. There he was.

I entered the map. I looked for him along Nassau Street, and at the construction site where I'd first seen him. I checked the English department, and the coffee shop where I so often did my reading. What would I have said to him? I had nothing to apologize for. And yet I was sorry.

It was getting late. It was always the middle of the day. I approached my house, but instead of seeing myself holding the sign, as I should have, I saw my crumpled body on the ground in front of the door.

I went up to myself. It was me, but wasn't me. It was my body, but not me. I tilted the world. There were no signs of any kind of struggle: no blood, no bruises. (Perhaps the photo had been taken in between the beating and the appearance of bruises?) There was no way to check for a pulse in the map, but I felt sure that I was dead. But I couldn't have been dead, because I was looking at myself. There is no way to be alive and dead.

I lifted myself up and put myself back down. I was still there. I pulled all the way back to space, to the Earth as a marble filling my screen in my empty house. I dove in, it all rushed to me: North America, America, the East Coast, New Jersey, Princeton Borough, Princeton Township, my address, my body.

I went to Firestone Library to use one of the public computers. I hadn't been to the library since the investigation, and hadn't even thought to wonder if my identity card was still activated. I tried to open the door, but I couldn't extend my arm. I realized I was still in the map.

I got up from my computer and went outside. Of course my body wasn't there. Of course it wasn't. When I got to Firestone, I extended my arm—I needed to see my hand reaching in front of me—and opened the door. Once inside, I swiped my ID, but a red light and beep emitted from the turnstile.

"Can I help you?" the security guard asked.

"I'm a professor," I said, showing him my ID.

"Lemme try that," he said, taking my card from me and swiping it again.

Again the beep and red light.

He began to type my campus ID into his computer, but I said, "Don't worry about it. It's fine. Thanks anyway." I took the ID from him and left the building.

I ran home. Everyone around me was moving. The leaves flickered as they should have. It was all almost perfect, and yet none of it was right. Everything was fractionally off. It was an insult, or a blessing, or maybe it was precisely right and I was fractionally off?

I went back into the map and examined my body. What had happened to me? I felt many things, and didn't know what I felt. I felt personally sad for a stranger, and sad for myself in a distanced way, as if through the eyes of a stranger. My brain would not allow me to be both the person looking and being looked at. I wanted to reach out.

I thought: I should take the pills in the medicine cabinet. I should drink a bottle of vodka, and go outside, just as I had in the map. I should lay myself down in the grass, face to the side, and wait. Let them find me. It will make everyone happy.

I thought: I should fake my suicide, just as I had in the map. I should leave open a bottle of pills in the house, beside my laptop opened to the image of myself dead in the yard. I should pour a bottle of vodka down the drain, and leave my wife a voicemail. And then I should go out into the world—to Venice, to Eastern Europe, to my father's childhood home. And when the vehicle approaches, I should run for my life.

I thought: I should fall asleep, as I had in the map. I should think about my life later. When I was a boy, my father used to say the only way to get rid of a pestering fly is to close your eyes and count to ten. But when you close your eyes, you also disappear.

RIDE ALONG

BY JAMES W. HALL

Coconut Grove, Miami

(Originally published in *Miami Noir*)

J umpy was reaching for the door handle to get out when Guy took hold of his arm, saying, "Nothing weird this time. Promise me."

Jumpy took a few seconds to turn his head and look at Guy.

"Define weird."

He had a point. It was more than weird already, an oddball pair like them out on a Sunday morning, four a.m., parked in a gravel lane next to a boarded-up house, with the orange sulfur lights from Douglas Road flickering like sky-fire through the big banyans. Three blocks north was the rubble and peeling paint of the Coconut Grove ghetto, three blocks the other way the mansions rose like giant concrete hibiscus blooms, pink and yellow, surrounded by high fortress walls, video cams, and coconut palms. The have-nots getting the exhaust fumes from Dixie Highway, the haves taking nice sweet hits on the ocean breezes.

Thirty feet in front of where Guy was parked, standing next to a battered Oldsmobile, two black dudes were fidgeting while Guy and Jumpy stayed inside the white Chevy with the headlights off. Been there two, three minutes already. Doing deals with fidgety folks wasn't Guy's idea of good business practice.

"The soul train must have a station around here," Jumpy said.

"You're jacking yourself up, man. I told you. You freak out this time, it's over, I walk."

"I don't like dreadlocks," Jumpy said.

"It's a hairstyle is all," Guy told him. "A Rastafarian thing from Jamaica. Same as a crew cut is to you."

"I never did like dreadlocks. It's a gut reaction."

"Okay, so you don't like dreadlocks. But a little fashion incompatibility, that isn't going to keep us from doing our business, right?"

"It looks dirty," Jumpy said. "Unkempt."

"Yeah, well, then let's forget it. Start the car, get the hell out of here."

"You losing your nerve, teach? Get right up close to the devil, feel his warm breath on your face, then you back away?"

"Nothing weird, okay? That's all I'm asking."

Jumpy was 6'4", skinny as a greyhound, pasty-skinned, all knuckles and Adam's apple. Kind of muscles that were easy to miss in that string bean body, like the braided steel cables holding a suspension bridge together. From what Guy had been able to learn, Jumpy had a couple of years of college, then he'd shipped out as a Marine for two hitches, then a lone-wolf mercenary for a while, off in Rwanda and Venezuela, spent a few years in a federal pen in Kansas, now he was on the prowl in Miami. Whatever unspeakable shit he'd been into never came up directly in conversation. Guy didn't ask, Jumpy didn't say. But it was there like a bad smell leaking from a locked room. The man was dangerous, and Guy loved it. Got a little tipsy from the proximity. So much to learn, so much to bring back to his own safe world. Riding the knife blade of violence, ever so careful not to get cut.

Jumpy didn't pump up his past. Very understated, even flip. Guy considered that a form of extreme cool, like those muscle-bound bodybuilders who only wore loose clothes. Tight shirts were for showboat assholes.

Jumpy didn't have to flaunt. There was a halo around him nobody could miss, a haze of androgen and pheromones that could turn a barroom edgy in a blink. Guy had seen nights when the bad boys lined up for a chance at Jumpy, pool cue in one hand, switchblade in the other, one by one coming at him like twigs into a wood chipper. Going in solid, coming out a spew of sawdust.

Trouble was, in Jumpy's line of work, nuance might be a better strategy than overwhelming force. But try to tell that to Jumpy. Dialing back that guy's throttle, even for Guy, a silver-tongued specialist, a man Jumpy respected, it could present a challenge. Not that Guy was morally opposed to violence. In the abstract, inflicting pain and drawing blood was fine. He'd written about it for years, described it in excruciating detail. But putting it into flesh-and-blood action, no, that wasn't his instinctive first choice like it was with Jumpy.

"So we cool on this?" Guy said. "Do your deal and walk. No crazy-ass banter, no stare-downs. Right?"

Jumpy kept his lasers fixed on the two dreadlocks.

"I need some signal of agreement, Jumpy. A grunt is enough."

Jumpy turned his head and blinked. That was all Guy was getting.

They got out and Guy tried to match Jumpy's casual saunter over to the Olds.

The two gangstas insisted on patting Guy down, then after a moment's indecision, they did a hurry-up job frisking Jumpy and stepped away like they'd burned their hands. The tall one went around to the trunk of the Olds and popped the lid.

Guy stayed a couple of steps behind Jumpy while the tall dude, wearing a black T-top and baggy shorts, showed off the Squad. His dreadlock buddy stood by the driver's door watching. His right hand fiddling around his shirttail, ready to quick-draw if things went bad.

Dreadlock One was extolling the merits of the Squad Automatic Weapon, otherwise known as SAW. Eight hundred–meter range, lightweight, just over twenty pounds with the two hundred–round magazine. Talking straight English with a little Bahamian singsong, none of the hip-hop, we-badass bullshit.

When Dreadlock One paused, Guy said, "You want to hold it, Jumpy? Inspect it?"

Jumpy was silent.

"One of you should check that shit, man, we don't want no pissing and moaning later on."

"Let me know when the sales pitch is over," Jumpy said. "I'll get the cash."

Dreadlock One shifted his angle, moving for a better view of Guy.

"What're you looking at?"

"That's what I'm asking myself," he said.

"Do that again?" Guy said.

"Who'm I doing business with," Dreadlock One asked, "man or woman? From across the way, you look like a dude; up close like this, you could be a bull-dyke bitch."

Guy felt Jumpy shift closer to him.

"Happens all the time," Guy said. "It's the haircut."

Guy had blond shoulder-length Jesus hair, slender hips, and sleek Scandinavian features. A man of long smooth planes. Not feminine so much as asexual. A floater. Hovering between the sexes. Some women found him sexy, and just about as many men.

"More than the freaking haircut. It's your whole entire weird-ass self."

Jumpy stepped between Guy and Dreadlock One and said, "Why don't you reach down my partner's pants and find out?"

The second dreadlock cackled, then grinned a big gold smile. "Yeah, Willie, do it, man, reach your hand in there and squeeze."

"I was just curious," Willie said. "It don't matter. Forget it."

"Don't be shy," said Jumpy. "Reach in, take a handful, make yourself happy. Guy's cool with that, aren't you, Guy?"

Willie stared at Guy's face for a few ticks, then shook his dreads.

Jumpy took two quick steps and grabbed Willie's hand, took a grip on Guy's belt buckle, pulled it out, and jammed the dude's spidery fingers down the front of Guy's pants.

The other dread had his pistol out and was aiming at Jumpy, ordering him to step the fuck away from his partner, let him go, stop that shit.

Jumpy released Willie's hand and the man yanked it out of Guy's pants.

"So what am I?" Guy said.

Willie didn't say anything. He turned and saw his partner with the pistol out.

"Put that shit away, man. Put it away."

"So what am I?" Guy said. "Did your field trip enlighten you?"

"Two thousand for the SAW. Five hundred for the loaded magazine. Take it or leave it, no negotiating."

"Two for the whole caboodle or I'm outta here. Starting now. Ten, nine, eight, seven . . ."

"Two'll do," Willie said.

"Hard bargainer," Jumpy said. "Tough nut."

Jumpy and Guy walked back over to the stolen Chevy, Jumpy getting into the passenger seat. Staying there for a minute, another minute with Guy standing back by the trunk waiting, watching, recording.

Jumpy's door was swung wide open, the overhead light on.

The two dreadlocks were talking near their Olds Ciera, but after a while they started shooting looks over. Willie held the SAW in one hand.

Jumpy sat there and sat there and sat some more until finally the head dread came strolling. Dumbass carrying the SAW one-handed.

"You got the bread or you fucking with me?"

"It's stuck," Jumpy said. "Fucking glove box is stuck."

"Stuck?"

Jumpy leaned back in the seat, gestured toward the glove compartment. Willie leaned in the door, peered through the darkness.

"You got a screwdriver," Jumpy said, "something that can pry it open?"

Willie craned another inch forward and Jumpy took a grip on the padded handle and slammed the door closed on the dreadlock's neck. Opened it and slammed it again and then a third time. Then one more for good luck and pushed the dread out of the way and reached down to the gravel and took hold of the SAW and aimed it out the crook of the open door at Dreadlock Two, who was trotting over with a big-ass chrome .45 in his right hand.

Guy was frozen. It was a freaking movie streaming around him. Every outrageous, amazing second of it. Hand down the pants and all.

The SAW kicked against Jumpy's shoulder. Jumpy fired again over Dreadlock Two's head, yelling at him to drop his weapon. Which he did. Not giving it a second thought, just tossing it into the gravel.

The downed dread struggled to his feet. Jumpy aimed the SAW at his chest.

"So what're we going to have here? Two dead assholes?"

"No, man. Don't be doing that. Ain't no need. We just get the fuck up and be gone."

"Sounds like a plan," Jumpy said. He fired the SAW into the air and the two men sprinted off toward the neighborhood where lights were coming on in bedrooms.

Jumpy got out of the Chevy and walked over to the Oldsmobile. "We got about ten seconds. You coming? Or you want to stay here and get the police point of view on things?"

Guy trotted over to the Oldsmobile and got in.

Jumpy pitched the SAW onto the backseat. Guy could smell its oily warmth. Jumpy must've used nearly forty rounds. Which left one-sixty still in the magazine.

Guy started the car. Put the shifter into drive and made a U-turn.

"Can you use any of that?" Jumpy said when they were five blocks away, cruising down Douglas Road into the ritzy jungle shadows of Coconut Grove.

"Think I can," Guy said. "Yes sir. I think I most certainly can."

Guy dug the little Sony from his front pocket and found the record button and he started to speak into the miniature device. Jumpy smiled and took them south toward the condo parking lot where he'd left his old Civic.

Sirens filled the night like the wails of predatory beasts circling their night's meal.

"What's this mean?" Jumpy held up a sheaf of papers.

He was standing in the doorway of Dr. Guy Carmichael's tiny windowless cubicle. Guy's office hours were from four till six. At six fifteen his evening graduate fiction workshop started and ran till nine forty. At the moment it was five thirty, so at worst he'd have to deal with Jumpy for fifteen minutes before he could claim he had to rush off to class.

"Could you be more precise? What does *what* mean?"

"Okay," Jumpy said. "What the fuck is this? A fucking C minus on my story."

"Did you read my comments? Is there something you're confused about?"

Jumpy looked down the hall, then checked the other direction. He was wearing a white button-down shirt and blue jeans and loafers without socks. Trying to fit in with some preppy image of a college student still surviving from his first fling at higher education back in the early '70s.

"I wrote what happened. You were there. You saw it. This is what happened. And that's all it's worth? Not even a fucking C? What've I got to do, kill somebody to get an A?"

"It's the writing," Guy said. "Not the events you describe."

"On my paper you said—shit, where is it?" Jumpy started fumbling through the typed pages, looking for Guy's tiny scrawl.

Jumpy used a battered Royal typewriter and he whited out his mistakes with big glops smeared across paragraph-sized portions of his paper. Guy admired his stamina, hunched over the tiny machine, those enormous fingers drilling letter after letter onto the white page. Stamina was one thing. Talent was another. Guy had tried hard with Jumpy, made him a special project, devoted hours and hours to one-on-ones in his office and in a bar on Biscayne. But after a minute or two of anything short of unadulterated praise, Jumpy glazed over and slid back into the murky grotto inside his bulletproof skull.

Jumpy found the comment he'd been searching for and put a finger on Guy's words as he read.

"*It's not credible that two such dissimilar men would pair up for such an effort.* That's what I mean. *Not credible.* But we did. We paired up. So why in fuck's name is that a C minus?"

"You have to convince the reader it's credible."

"You're the reader, Guy. You were fucking there. You were fucking standing right there pissing your fucking Dockers. And you don't believe what happened right in front of your fucking eyes? I'm missing something here."

One of Guy's grad students, Mindy Johnston, stuck her head in the doorway and said, "Ooops. Didn't mean to interrupt."

Mindy was a poet, aggressively ethereal. Wispy red hair, enormous breasts that defeated her every attempt to conceal them.

"I just came by to drop off my assignment. I can't be in class tonight. Migraine's acting up."

Guy accepted the paper and told Mindy he hoped she felt better soon.

"Try a pop of heroin," Jumpy said. "Blow that migraine right away."

Jumpy's gaze was fixed on Mindy's bosom. A smile slathered on his lips.

"Heroin?" Mindy said.

242 // USA Noir

"Say the word, and I'll drop a couple of hits off at your apartment. Special delivery. First two are free."

She squinched up her face into something between a smile and a scream.

"That's a joke, right?" Mindy backed out of the office and floated quickly down the hallway.

"Inappropriate," Guy muttered.

Jumpy said, "You got anything going Saturday night?"

Guy drummed the nub of his red ink pen against his desktop.

"Not more gun dealing," Guy said. "I've had my fill of that."

"I got so much shit going on I gotta get a bigger appointment book," Jumpy said. "Name your poison. Something that'll get me an A this time."

"I remember one time you mentioned organized crime. That caught my attention. There's a place in the book I'm working on, I could use some details."

"The mob," Jumpy said. Then he looked around Guy's office at the framed diplomas, the photographs of his kids and wife and two little dogs.

"Might could arrange something," Jumpy said. "I'll give you a call."

"And about that C minus," Guy said.

"Yeah?"

"I'll read it again. Maybe I missed something the first time."

"That's cool," said Jumpy. "Maybe you did."

Jumpy picked Guy up in the Pink Pussycat parking lot at one a.m. on Saturday. He was driving a green Jaguar convertible, top down. Chrome wraparound sunglasses and a black aloha shirt with red martini glasses printed on it.

Guy got in, and without a word or look in his direction, Jumpy peeled out, slashed into traffic on Biscayne. Once they'd settled down into the flow of vehicles, Guy smoothed his hand across the leather seat. His long blond hair tangling in the wind.

"Car yours?"

"It is tonight."

"A loaner," Guy said, smiling, trying to get with the lingo.

Jumpy looked over. His expression was dead tonight, maybe he was working himself up, or he was nervous, Guy couldn't tell. That had been his biggest challenge, trying to capture the interior life of a man like Jumpy. Was he constantly on drugs and so blitzed there was no coherent thought rolling through his head? Or was he dumb, just incapable of nuanced feelings or thought? Based on the writing Guy had seen, he was tilting toward the dumb option. Jumpy couldn't string two sentences together without making half a dozen errors of grammar, syntax, or logic. By the end of a paragraph, Jumpy's ideas were so insufferably scrambled, making sense of his story was impossible.

Guy was getting good detail from these ride-alongs, some nice asshole-puckering moments of violence, but overall, Jumpy wasn't giving away a lot about his psychodynamics. What pushed the man's buttons? Who the hell could tell?

After tonight, Guy figured he'd bail on this whole enterprise. He'd had enough of the street for a while. A night or two like the gun buy last week could keep Guy satiated for a good long time. His wife, Shelly, had no idea what he was up to. But she could smell the fear on him when he returned, the stink of sweat and cigarette smoke and the prickly tang of danger. And she was beginning to make irritable noises.

So after tonight Guy was done. Cash out, walk away with his winnings. Spend the rest of the semester using this brief immersion in the back-alley world of Jumpy Swanson to fuel his imagination for one more crime novel.

He didn't know how Jumpy would take it, him making his exit. Or what quid pro quo Jumpy was expecting. C minus was already a mercy grade. And Guy wasn't about to fudge on his own academic values as payback for a half dozen adventures on the South Florida streets. There would come a day, Guy was pretty sure, when Jumpy would stomp out of his office disgusted with Guy's failure to give him the secret key to the kingdom Jumpy so passionately and unaccountably wanted. Jumpy Swanson, an author? Oh, get serious.

Jumpy headed north off Biscayne into neighborhoods Guy didn't recognize. Residential, middle-class, or maybe edging down to lower-middle. The cars in the driveways were mostly midsize, newer models. The houses were dark, probably retirees or working-class folks who'd had their fill of TV movies for the evening and had headed off to the sack.

It wasn't the sort of neighborhood Guy had been expecting. Though Jumpy had revealed only that his mob friends were eager to meet Guy, a professional writer. Guy assumed the gangsters had the customary overinflated sense of their own glamour and the resulting ambition to have their lives portrayed on the screen, or on the pages of some runaway best seller.

Guy was always ambivalent about being introduced as a writer. On the one hand, it embarrassed him to be the object of admiration to people who had no inkling what the artistic endeavor was all about. It felt silly to get the little bows of courtesy from illiterates. On the other hand, in an instance like tonight, meeting men for whom crime was a way of life, having some professional connection with the larger world was, to Guy's way of thinking, like wearing Kevlar. Sure, he was a snitch. But it was all in the open, and for commercial, not legal gains. He'd make sure these guys got a copy of the next book, maybe even put their nicknames on the acknowledgment page. Johnny "The Nose." Frank "Hatchet Breath" Condilini.

Jumpy wheeled into a yard that was crowded with cars. They were parked in every direction: beaten-up compacts, a brand-new white Cadillac, a couple of BMWs, a pickup truck from the '60s. Hard to decipher the demographics, but the haphazard parking jobs suggested the occupants had arrived in haste and under the influence of dangerous substances.

There was a peephole in the front door. A cliché that Guy saw instantly he would be unable to use. The man whose face appeared was fat and his greasy skin danced with colored lights. Guy could feel the throb of bass music rising up from the sidewalk, a beat that was as hypnotically slow and primitive as the heartbeat of a dying man.

"Who's the pussy?"

"I told Philly I was bringing him. He's the guy, the writer."

"What's he write?" the thug said. "Parking tickets?"

"Open the fucking door, Moon."

The door opened and the wall of music rushed like dark wind from the house. Guy waded past Moon. The man was at least four hundred pounds and he moved with a sluggish wobble like a deep-sea diver running low on air.

"What is this place?" Guy spoke an inch from Jumpy's ear but wasn't sure he heard. Jumpy made no response, just led the way across the room.

The living room stretched half the length of the house and through sliding doors looked out on an empty swimming pool and a dark canal. The strobes were covered with colored lenses and Guy was almost instantly seasick. No furniture, no rugs on the terrazzo. Half a dozen mattresses sprawled around the room, where knots of naked people squirmed in the flickering light.

"You brought me to a freaking sex party, Jump?"

The music cut off halfway through his question and Guy's voice echoed through the room. Someone tittered and there was a muffled groan. A second later, as Guy was still processing his embarrassment, the music restarted, something faster and even louder, and the strobes picked up their pace as well. The air was tainted with chemical smells, booze and weed and other compounds he could only guess at.

Guy followed Jumpy over to a makeshift bar, a long picnic table laid out with iced buckets full of longnecks and pints of gin and bourbon. Jumpy mixed a gin and tonic in a clear plastic cup and handed it to Guy.

"Relax you, put you in the mood."

He made his own drink, then held up the plastic cup for a clink.

"To improving my grade," Jumpy said.

"To creating credible characters." Guy wasn't backing down on his values for some quick tour of a sleazy hashish den.

Jumpy gulped his drink and Guy followed suit, *mano a mano*.

Jumpy led Guy deeper into the house, down a long narrow corridor. This was architecture Guy had seen in dozens of Florida tract homes built in the '60s. Three bedrooms down that tight corridor, a single bath. Sliding doors on the closets and hard surfaces in every direction. He had never considered such spaces forbidding, but given the present circumstance Guy held back a few paces behind Jumpy, and started to consider his options for escape.

At the end of the hall, the music had softened to a thudding growl. Jumpy halted before a closed door and tapped four times and a voice answered from within.

Jumpy opened the door, then looked at Guy hanging back. "You wanted to meet my people, right? Get down and dirty. Isn't that the idea?"

Guy felt his fear collapsing into something more extreme. A dark knot of dread. He was not up to this. He felt suddenly trapped, cornered by Jumpy. Conned into deeper water than he'd bargained for. A wave of paranoia rolled and crashed in his gut.

"Philly, meet Guy. Guy, Philly."

The man was bald and short and his stomach was as tight and perfectly round as a bowling ball. He wore striped undershorts or perhaps pajama bottoms, but was otherwise naked. The room was lit with a vague blue light as though rare mushrooms might be growing in long trays somewhere nearby. It was the master bedroom and was probably half the size of the living room. Its sliding glass door had a view across the canal, looking into the patio of a house where an elderly couple were slow-dancing under paper lanterns.

Philly shook Guy's limp hand and stepped back to size him up.

"This is Mr. High-and-Mighty? Pardon me, Jump, but he looks like a fucking twit."

Guy was turning to leave, to run back the way he'd come, jog all the way home if it came to that, when a hand touched his bare ankle, the fingers sliding around the knobby bone and taking a strong grip.

Down in the blue haze on the bedroom floor he saw the girl, naked, with enormous breasts. Her wispy red hair was tangled and dirty, and there was a sloppy grin on her face as if Mindy Johnston had finally entered the gossamer stratosphere she was always writing about.

Guy staggered away from her touch and lost his balance. He shot out a hand to steady himself, but the wall beside him moved away. As Guy lurched toward it, the wall moved again. He flapped his arms like a clumsy tightrope walker, and after another moment found his equilibrium.

The gin and tonic was spinning inside his skull.

"You son of a bitch." Guy turned and stepped into Jumpy's face. "What the fuck have you done?"

"Hey, professor, come on in, the water's fine." It was a woman's voice he vaguely recognized.

He turned back to the mattress and saw beside Mindy was Paula Rhodes, a new grad student who'd been struggling to find her place in the program. A bit more mature than the others, a woman who'd written for New York travel magazines and already had a Master's degree. She, like Mindy, wanted, for some ungodly reason, to write poetry. To sing the body electric.

She had risen up to her knees and was reaching out to Guy with her unloosened breasts wobbling and her eyes on fire with some chemical enthusiasm. Around the room, he made out at least four other students from the program, all of them tangling and untangling like a nest of snakes.

"Hey, I want to thank you, professor," Philly said. "You got us hooked up with a better class of consumer than we been seeing lately. I owe you, man."

Moon, the bull-necked gatekeeper, appeared in the doorway. He too was now wearing only his underwear. Saggy white briefs with dark hair coiling out around the edges. In one hand he was holding a silver tray with syringes and rubber straps, and an array of other nefarious equipment that Guy didn't recognize. In the other he gripped the barrel of the SAW. Eight hundred–meter range, lightweight, just over twenty pounds with the two hundred–round magazine.

Moon presented the hors d'oeuvre tray to Guy, poking him in the sternum with its corner.

"A little hit of research, Guy?" Jumpy said.

The walls of the bedroom were breathing in and out and the lights had invaded the interior of Guy's chest.

"You used me. You son of a bitch, you used me to take advantage of these kids."

"I used *you*, Guy? I fucking used *you?*"

Mindy Johnston's hand snaked inside the leg of Guy's trousers, her fingers trickling up his calf. Her voice a swoon.

"Come on, professor. Come on, it's fun. It's so wild."

Guy looked across the canal and saw the old couple still fox-trotting to some melody that didn't pass beyond their walls. He thought of Shelly, his wife of ten years, the way they used to dance in their own living room. Languorous steps, drifting around their barren house for hours at a time.

Jumpy edged to the door, slipping past Moon into the hallway. Moon slid sideways like the bars of a cell locking into place between Guy and the world he'd known.

"Hey, Guy, enjoy yourself, man. Moon'll show you the ropes, won't you, big fellow?"

Moon had stashed the tray and gun somewhere and now had a grip on Guy's right bicep and was injecting some clear solution into a bulging vein in the crook of Guy's arm. The room was bigger than Guy had originally thought. The ceiling was no ceiling. Where the roof should have been, there were stars, whole galaxies exposed, comets shooting from left and right. A cool solar wind swirling down from the heavens.

"This is what you wanted, right?" Jumpy said from the hall. "Up close and personal."

There were bare hands on his ankles drawing him down to the quicksand mattress, down into a pit of flesh and crazy-colored lights, a world he'd written about before. But he'd gotten it all wrong. All completely wrong.

SECOND CHANCE

BY ELYSSA EAST

Buzzards Bay, Cape Cod
(Originally published in *Cape Cod Noir*)

Cunningham said that he had set up the reform school on Penikese Island so we could have a clean break with our pasts. We couldn't walk home from out here in the middle of nowhere Buzzards Bay. Couldn't hitch or swim here, either. Even boaters considered the currents dangerous where we were, twelve miles out from the Cape, past the islands of Nonamesset, Veckatimest, Uncatena, Naushon, the Weepeckets, Pasque, and Nashawena, just north of Cuttyhunk. There was no Cumbie Farms, no Dunkin' Donuts, no running water, Internet, or cell service here. Not even any trees. Just a house made from the hull of an old wooden ship that had run aground. Me and six other guys, all high school age, who were lucky to be here instead of in some lockup, lived with Cunningham and the staff, most of whom were also our teachers. The school had a barn, chicken coop, wood-shop, and outhouse. The only other things were the ruins of a leper colony, a couple of tombstones that Cunningham liked to call a cemetery, and the birds. Lots of birds. Seagulls, all of them, that hovered over this place like a screeching, shifting cloud that rained crap and dove at our heads all day.

This was our clean slate, a barren rock covered in seagull shit.

We had to leave most of our things behind on the mainland when we were shipped out here on a rusty lobster boat called *Second Chance*, but our pasts couldn't help but follow us here anyway. We were always looking over our shoulders and finding them there. Depending on the time of day, we were either chasing the shadows of our pasts or being chased by them. We cast them out over the water with our fishing nets. They were with us when we hoed the garden, split wood, and changed the oil to keep *Second Chance*, the school's only boat, in working order. We watched them tackle and collide and fall to the ground next to us while we played football and beat the shit out of each other much like the waves that endlessly pounded this rock. I just wondered when our pasts would pick themselves up, dust themselves off, and walk away. You could say that's what we all wanted them to do. Least that's what I wanted for mine.

* * *

I never meant to be in the car that killed that girl. It was like that was someone else, not me. Like I wasn't even there. But I was.

Mr. Riaf, my court-appointed lawyer, had said that the hardest thing out here
on Penikese was figuring out how to survive the other guys. "Someone always
cracks," he said. "Don't let it be you, kid."

Freddie Paterniti said that when DYS told him he could go to school on an
island for a year instead of being thrown back in the can, he thought he was
gonna be spending his days jet skiing. Everybody gave Freddie a load of shit
for being such a stupid fuck though they had all thought the same thing. Me,
I never admitted to knowing better.

Instead of jet skis, cigarette boats, and chicks in bikinis, we got Cunningham, the school's founder, an ex-Marine who fought in Vietnam and looked
like Jean-Claude Van Damme crossed with Santa Claus. Cunningham believed that our salvation lay in living like it was 1800, but the lesson wasn't
about history: "You boys were chosen to ride *Second Chance* here because
you have shown a demonstrated capacity for remorse for your crimes. We're
here to teach you that your actions literally create the world around you. By
creating everything you need with your own bare hands, you can re-form the
person you are deep within. And you can take that second chance all the way
back to a new place inside."

That's why we carried water, slopped pigs, caught fish, dug potatoes, gathered eggs, and built tables and chairs, and if we didn't, we wouldn't have had
anywhere to sit and nothing to eat.

We chopped a lot of firewood that was brought in on *Second Chance* from
Woods Hole. If we got pissed off—which was often—we were sent out to chop
more. At first our muscles ached for days. The feel of the axe ricocheted up
our elbows, into our shoulders, our skulls. But we got stronger. Soon we split
wood and dreamed of splitting the take, splitting open girls' thighs, splitting
this place, this life.

We were constantly making our world in this nowhere place, chopping
it to bits, and redoing it all over again, but we couldn't remake what we had
done to earn our way here.

"Boys," Tiny Bledsoe would say when we made the cutting boards that
were sold in a fancy Falmouth gift shop to help fund the school, "consider
yourselves to be in training for Alcatraz. Soon you'll graduate to making li-

cense plates and blue jeans!" Each time Tiny said this Freddie hit the wood-shop floor, laughing.

Freddie and Tiny were an odd couple. Freddie: sixteen, short, oily, wall-eyed, with the whiniest high-pitched Southie voice you could imagine. Tiny: seventeen, a lumbering, club-footed giant who came from East Dennis. They were nothing like me and my big brother Chad, but they reminded me of us in their own way. They both claimed to have killed people. That was their thing. Their special bond. Something that Chad and me have now too.

That girl's mother sent me a picture of her, lying in her casket. It looked like one of those jewelry boxes lined in pink satin with a little ballerina that spins while the music plays. All you have to do is turn the key and that ballerina comes to life, but there's no key on a casket. Just some motor at the gravesite that lowers the box into the ground. My little sister Caroline had one of those jewelry boxes. There was nothing in it but some rings she got out of those grocery store things you put a quarter in. The rings weren't worth anything, but Chad convinced me to steal her jewelry box anyway.

Freddie and Tiny. It was never Tiny and Freddie, though Tiny was a foot taller. Even Cunningham and our teachers caught on, always saying "Freddie and Tiny" like "I got Freddie's and Tiny's homework here!" "Freddie and Tiny are going to lead us in hauling traps!" "Freddie and Tiny . . ."

One day early in the year, Ryan Peasely was rolling his eyes in mechanics class and mumbling behind Cunningham's back, "Freddie and Tiny sucked my cock. Freddie and Tiny ate my ass." It seemed like no one could hear him other than me, but Tiny had sonar for ears. He clamped down on Ryan with a headlock in no time flat. Freddie then whispered into Ryan's ear that he would kill him by running a set of battery chargers off *Second Chance*'s engine block up his ass.

Ryan is from Wellesley. Just cause he used to sell dope to his private school buddies he thinks he's better than all of us, but Ryan just about shit his pants that day. Cunningham punished Freddie and Tiny by making them clean out the outhouse, but Freddie didn't seem to care. He nearly died from laughing so hard.

When Freddie laughs he sounds like the trains that went through the woods down the road from the cul-de-sac where I grew up back in Pocasset: "A-Huh-a-huh-a-huh-a-huh. A-Huh-a-huh-a-huh-a-huh."

* * *

It was also Chad's idea to take Caroline's jewelry box and set it on the train tracks. Bits of that doll went flying everywhere. You could still hear the music playing long after the train left.

Caroline cried so hard after she saw her jewelry box was missing, I went out and gathered up all the pieces of the ballerina that I could find. I wanted to give them to Caroline and make her feel better, but Chad shook his head and said, "What people don't know can't hurt them."

I threw the pieces of the ballerina in the yard later on. I still remember watching the bits of pink plastic and white gauze fly from my hand.

Chad came into the room we shared later that night and said, "You're a real man now, you know that, kid?"

I was only eight, and he was thirteen but he had started shaving. He knew what it meant to be grown up.

Learning how to be a man is part of Penikese's chop-wood-carry-water philosophy. Penikese isn't like being in jail, boot camp, or even regular school, though we can earn our GED and learn a couple of trades like fishing and woodworking. It's some of all of these things in an Abe-Lincoln-in-a-log-cabin kind of way. Cunningham leads us on walks and tells us stories about the island and calls it history. Wood shop is where Mr. Da Cunha teaches us how to make furniture, which is also his way to con us into measuring angles and calling it geometry. We whittle pieces of wood along with the time; we're stuck here for a year unless we fuck up, which means getting shipped off to juvie, which none of us wants though there is something about this place that makes everything bad we've ever done seem impossible to escape. Like the fact that the house where we're living is a ship going nowhere.

At night we sit by kerosene lanterns and do homework around the kitchen table or play pool, except for Bobby Pomeroy who spends a lot of time in the outhouse where we're all convinced he's busy beating wood.

Bobby grew up on a farm somewhere in Western Mass., where he was busted for assault and date-raping some girl. Cause he's a farm boy, he teaches us things that even Cunningham doesn't know. Useful things. Like how to hypnotize a chicken.

We'd only been here for a few weeks when Bobby grabbed the smallest chicken in the coop by its feet and lifted it, so it was hanging upside down. The chicken was squawking and clucking, but as soon as Bobby starting swinging it around and around it quieted down. "That'll learn ya," Bobby said, then set the chicken back on the ground. Next thing you knew that chicken was walking in circles and bumping into things, like it was drunk. We all laughed our asses off, but for Tiny and DeShawn.

"That's not fucking funny," Tiny said.

"Whassamattuh?" Freddie said.

"It's just a little chicken."

"You feckin' killed some girl and you're getting ya panties in a wad over some dumb chicken that's gonna end up in a pot pretty soon heyah?" Freddie said.

"Just make it stop," Tiny replied. His eyes were turning red, his lower lip quivering, but the chicken was still spinning around bumping into things. We couldn't stop cracking up.

"Fucking knock it off, you assholes!" Tiny yelled.

Then the chicken lay down and stopped moving altogether. The chickens in the coop went quiet too. All we could hear was the wind whistling like a boiling kettle.

"That's fucking sick," Kevin Monahan said. "You're sick, Tiny. Killing your own girlfriend and defending some stupid chicken." Kevin was in for burning down an apartment building in Springfield while cooking up meth with his father. Some old lady's cat died in the fire.

"Arson ain't no big thing compared to killing a pretty little girl, pansy," Freddie said.

Bobby snapped his fingers over the bird, which rolled onto its feet and started walking again.

"That's like some voodoo or something," DeShawn said, moving away from Bobby like he was a man possessed.

Bobby had power over that chicken just like Freddie had power over Tiny and Chad had power over me.

Chad and me used to be like Freddie and Tiny: inseparable. I followed Chad everywhere, did whatever he did, and whatever he wanted me to do. Now he's doing time on a twenty-year sentence on account of our accident. On account of me.

Sometimes we got Saturday afternoon passes to Woods Hole on the mainland. Saturdays in "the Hole" were good until Freddie convinced Tiny to steal *Second Chance* and take it over to Osterville where they said they were going to break into some boats cause Ryan Peasely told them how much money he cleared dealing from his dad's summer house out thataway.

As we ferried over that late September day, Tiny said, "I ain't doin' it." Stubby Knowles, our mechanics and fisheries teacher who also captained *Second Chance*, was inside the wheelhouse and couldn't hear us over the sound of the engine, the wind, and the squawking gulls.

"Whassamattah? You chickenin' out?" Bobby asked.

"Fuck you," Tiny shot back.

Tiny didn't like Bobby much. After the chicken-swinging incident, Tiny asked if taking care of the chickens could be his chore and his alone, like he wanted to keep the birds safe from Bobby. No one fought him for the honor.

"Bawk!" Bobby said. Freddie snorted with laughter. They high-fived.

Tiny stared so hard at Bobby he could have burned two holes straight through him with his eyes. Bobby shrank. Tiny was twice his size and could have easily snapped him in two.

Tiny started to laugh that kind of laugh that sounds weirdly close to crying. "Fooled yas, I did," Tiny said. But Tiny hadn't fooled anyone. He was only staying in because he didn't want Bobby to take his place as Freddie's best.

As soon as we stepped off the boat, Freddie said, "Listen, homies, we gonna bust this shit up like something real," like we were a bunch of brothers who had escaped Rikers on some wooden raft and sailed our way up to the Cape to terrorize all the rich people.

"DeShawn, my nigga, you reel in da hos for me."

Freddie always talked like a gangsta rapper to DeShawn, so did Bobby. Two boys, as white as they come. Even Freddie, though he's Italian, as pale as the moon. Tiny just stood to the side looking confused, waiting for them to get it over with and talk like their old selves again.

Bobby and Freddie worshipped DeShawn cause he's black and from Dorchester. DeShawn wouldn't say anything about why he was here, but you could always see wheels turning behind his eyes, going somewhere way the fuck far away and running us over on his way there.

Whenever DeShawn got that look on Freddie always said, "Like, De-Shawn my man, you and me relate, homes, cuz your shit is real, brother, just like my shit is real, a'ight?"

Freddie never seemed to notice the look that came over DeShawn's eyes when he talked to him. Then again, if he did notice he didn't seem to care. It's kind of like Chad saying what you don't know can't hurt you, only with Freddie it was pretending that you don't know, like pretending that DeShawn didn't hate him would help keep him from getting his ass kicked all over the Hole.

* * *

The night of the accident, back in August, I pretended everything was okay.

"Dudes," Chad had said to some friends of his who pulled up next to us in front of the Cumbie Farms, "I bet you a thousand dollars my little brother and I can jack a car faster than you."

It had been a long time since Chad and me had broken into a car and I doubted he and his friends had any money, unless they were dealing, which they probably were, but I didn't want to know. I hadn't seen much of Chad in three years, not since he had turned eighteen and joined the Army.

"Why you wanna go fight the war?" I asked him before he left.

Chad pointed to his head and said, "Gotta be easier than fighting the war inside."

It wasn't that Chad was a bad guy, it was that he was good at things you weren't supposed to do, like breaking into places and stealing shit. And Chad had this ability to not get caught, which, in a twisted way, made me and Caroline think he was going to do well being off in the Army fighting terrorists. But not even Mom could explain why Chad was eventually discharged and came back from Afghanistan with scripts for all kinds of things, except to say, "It's as if your brother has taken lots of bullets inside his heart, Tommy. You can't actually see the place that got hurt, but if you could, you'd know how badly he's suffering." Sometimes I could see it written all over his face, though, like that night sitting and drinking in the car at Cumbie's.

"Remember how good it used to be?" Chad asked. "You and me, droppin' it like it's hot?" He took a swig from his beer and wiped his mouth.

I remembered how it was, letting Chad talk me into sneaking into someone else's garage, their car, their house, riding away on their bikes with PlayStations and laptops stuffed into our backpacks. It was everything I had wanted to forget about myself, but for Chad. Once he left, I started trying to clean up my act, but now Chad was back and he had a thousand dollars riding on my back.

"Yeah, that was cool," I said as we finished off our beers before heading out to find a new ride for the night. Maybe it's cause we grew up without a dad, but it was easier to lie than to admit that I never wanted to do any of that stuff, I had just wanted to be with Chad. "Welcome home, bro," I said. "It's good to have you back."

Chad passed me another bottle of beer. As he steered the car onto the dark road, I felt myself move back to that place I had been trying to get beyond, but now that Chad was home safe I knew I had never wanted to leave.

We parked behind the valet parking booth next to the Pocasset Golf Club clubhouse. Chad took a lumpy sock out of a military duffle bag and tucked it inside his jean jacket. "BRB, dude," he said, and got out of the car and went inside the booth.

The booth sat there, dark, motionless, silent, with a blue glow coming through the blinds. I sat and downed another beer, tasting its bitterness, waiting for fifteen minutes, maybe more, for Chad to emerge.

Chad got into the car and held up a set of keys to a '66 Mustang.

"Whoa, so how did you do that?" Like I needed to ask.

"Just a little barter. This way we get the sweet ride, we gas 'er, and return 'er by eleven. Ain't no need to go breakin' no law."

Chad texted his friends: *Got the ride boyz. Where U @?*

In Woods Hole, we all gathered back at the dock at five, like always. Stubby was yelling into his cell phone, pacing back and forth. *Second Chance* was gone.

Freddie and Tiny never made it to Osterville. A coast guard patrol boat picked them up near Popponesset where the boat had run out of gas. They said they had planned to bring it back in time and would have filled it up, but they didn't have any money because of school policy so it wasn't their fault *Second Chance* ran out of gas.

The Mustang at the golf club had a full tank. So did Chad. Whatever he had done in that booth had shot his eyes through with blood.

We drove to where his friends were sliding a slim jim into the door of some shit Toyota.

"Well, I guess you won," one of his friends said and gawked at our ride.

Chad and I had a few beers left, but his friends were out so Chad thought it would be cool to race to the liquor store over on the other side of the Bourne Bridge.

"The old Bridge Over Troubled Waters, ha ha ha," his friend, the one who was driving, said.

"Whoever gets there last is buying," Chad commanded, then laid down enough rubber to leave them behind in a cloud of smoke.

The more fucked up and dangerous Chad's idea was, the more likely it was that he could pull it off. That's what set him apart. That's why I loved him and feared him all the same. Why I thought he was going to come home a hero. Why we were going to beat his friends across that bridge and they were gonna be buying us a case of Bud and a bottle of Goldschläger, suckahs.

Later on, the cops kept asking me what I said to try and stop Chad from "stealing" the Mustang or from cooking up Ritalin and Talwin—which, they explained, is as good as mixing coke and heroin—in that valet booth, or even putting back half a case of beer while driving. They made a big deal out of the drinking and driving as if everyone else around here didn't do it. But I never said anything to stop Chad. It wasn't just because I knew there was no stopping him once he set his mind to a thing, or that I knew how badly he needed to win at something since coming back home. It was that I had wanted us to win together.

Cunningham ended up revoking Saturday privileges because we all knew that Freddie and Tiny were planning to steal the boat and never said anything about it.

Bobby tried to reason with Cunningham: "But if you had never known about it you never would've gotten upset, so you don't need to punish us because there was no reason to tell you. Besides, Tiny had been talking about stealing *Second Chance* for weeks. Until they didn't come back, nothing bad had happened, so what was there to say?"

Freddie and Tiny were punished with extra wood chopping. Bobby had to shovel shit all week.

I still remember what it felt like going over the bridge in that Mustang. All I could feel was how high and fast we were, Chad and me together, set free from something inside.

"Pop me another cold one," Chad said.

I reached into the backseat, grabbed one of our beers, and cracked open the bottle as we were nearing the exit. But we were in the left-hand lane and the exit ramp was already in sight. Chad's friends were right behind us. Chad floored the Mustang to get ahead of an SUV next to us and ferry over straight onto the ramp. But the SUV driver gave us the finger and accelerated too, cutting us off from the lane. Chad slammed on the brakes. My head whipped forward. The beer went flying out of my hand. The bottle sailed into the windshield and exploded. A spray of beer stung Chad's eyes. He lifted his hands off the wheel. Shards of glass cut his face, his hands.

My shoulder hit the window. The seat belt cut into my neck. And the Mustang slammed into the driver's-side door of a Honda Civic that was trailing the SUV.

Katelyn Robichard, UMass Dartmouth freshman and Corsairs striker, 2009 Little East Conference Women's Soccer Offensive Player of the Year, was at the wheel of the Honda. Her seat belt stayed secured, but her airbag didn't inflate. And pretty little Katelyn Robichard snapped forward at her waist, just like a jack-in-the-box that sprung up out of its lid and collapsed.

Freddie and Tiny were out doing their time, chopping a forest full of wood for the third day in a row, when a periwinkle shell flew out of the clouds and pelted Freddie in the head.

"Muthahfeckah," Freddie muttered and slammed his axe down on a piece of wood.

Another shell came hurling toward him. He swung at the clouds with his axe and yelled, "Come down here, you bitches! You want a piece of me? I'll show you a piece of me, ya shit-eating birds."

The sky filled with cackles, like God was slapping his thigh at the sight of Freddie blowing his top.

A gull dive-bombed his head and tore at his hair. A shrieking Freddie covered his head with his one free hand and continued swinging his axe overhead. More gulls flew at him. Tiny started throwing pieces of wood into the sky.

We hated those giant, hungry clouds of birds, but we hated Freddie and Tiny more for getting us all in trouble.

Except for Bobby, who was in the outhouse, we were all inside supposedly doing homework and chores. But we got up to watch the big show out the kitchen window. Freddie was swinging his axe around like some murderous fuck. "I'm wicked pissa sick o' bein' out here with all these birds shitting on me all the goddamned time!"

"It's not the birds that're causing the problem," Cunningham said. He stood on the porch, the picture of calm. His voice sounded out low and deep, like a horn through the fog.

Tiny could always tell when Cunningham was about to deliver one of his living-like-a-homesteader-is-good-for-you lectures. "Astern, astern! Eye-roller coming on!" he would shout, like a rogue wave that only he could see was moving through Cunningham. But for now, Tiny was still throwing pieces of wood in the air at the gulls. Da Cunha came busting out the back door and beelined straight for Tiny, throwing him down in a hammerlock.

"It's you, Freddie," Cunningham said. "The birds are just birds. You're the one choosing to see it as an attack. Life is full of people and things, situations that are going to dump shit on you. You can't control that. You can only control your reaction to it. You have to learn your Pukwudgies."

"Feck you and your fekwudgees!" Freddie shouted. "I'm sick of getting it in the ass from you pricks." The gulls shrieked and laughed as they followed Freddie, who stormed off toward the water with that axe.

Da Cunha still had a grip on Tiny, who turned limp as he watched Freddie disappear. "It's not fair!" Tiny sobbed. "It's not fair. It wasn't my idea to steal the boat. I didn't want to take it. It's all Freddie's fault."

It was true. It had been Freddie's idea, but Bobby had tried to paint it like it was Tiny's doing. Cunningham said it didn't matter whose idea it was. They had stolen *Second Chance* together.

Da Cunha released Tiny, who rolled on the ground. Stubby appeared. He and Da Cunha went out toward the water, after Freddie.

"What's a Pukwudgie?" DeShawn asked.

"Come on," Cunningham said. "Time for a little island history lesson." Cunningham gave Tiny a hand, helping him up. He wrapped his arm around Tiny, and led the rest of us up the hill. As we rounded the graveyard we could hear Freddie's shouts of "Feck you, you feckin' narc, Tiny!" go by on the wind.

The stone ruins of the leper colony looked like the bones of a giant that had been buried there and gradually unearthed. As soon as we passed them for the windward side of the island, the seagulls that had been trailing us dropped off. The wind started to howl and whine.

Ryan and Kevin went back cause they were on the evening's cook shift. DeShawn gave me a look like he didn't want to walk back with Ryan, who was nothing but a snot-nosed pain in the ass, or Kevin, who was bound to do something stupid like walk us off a cliff. Maybe he was also scared that Freddie was still running around with that axe. No matter. I could tell by the way Cunningham had his arm around Tiny that he wasn't going to let him go anywhere. This walk was for Tiny. Maybe I knew it was also for me.

I put up my hands as we crashed into that girl's car, but I could still see her face. Her body jackknifing. Her head and chest flying over the steering wheel, toward the windshield.

They call it safety glass because when your head hits the windshield it shatters but stays in place so that it catches you, like a net. If that fails, and you're airborne, it crumbles like a cookie so you don't get cut. But chunks of metal went flying. That girl didn't stand a chance.

Sometimes I feel as if I'm made of safety glass, as if everything inside me has shattered yet somehow stays intact. But Chad was all cut up inside, like that broken beer bottle, which sliced up his face.

Everything would've been okay if I hadn't handed Chad that beer.

Cunningham took us to a crumbling stone courtyard that gave us a little protection from the wind. Me, Tiny, and DeShawn sat down on some old stone benches where we could see the water and some lights from New Bedford, on the other side of the bay. Cunningham cleared his throat, like he had been practicing some speech he'd prepared.

"After the leper colony closed, a caretaker lived out here with his wife and two sons. They were the only people on the island. Then one of the kids killed the other. They said it was a freak accident, but anyone who knew this place and that family knew the truth. It was because of the Pukwudgies.

"The Pukwudgies were these little demons, no bigger than your hand, that made the Wampanoags' lives miserable. They broke their arrows, bored holes in their canoes, and ruined their crops. It would not be inaccurate to say they were the Wampanoag equivalent to having a seagull defecate on your head, but as tiny as they were, they had great power over the Wampanoag giant Moshup and his sons." When he said "giant," Cunningham shot Tiny a meaningful look.

"One day, Moshup declared war against the Pukwudgies. He gathered his sons and set out across the Cape to hunt them down. At night, while Moshup and his boys were sleeping, the Pukwudgies snuck up on Moshup's sons, blinded them, and stabbed them to death. Moshup buried his sons along the shoreline. He was so aggrieved he covered their gravesites with rocks and soil to create enormous funerary mounds. In time the ocean rose, carrying the mounds—and the boys' remains—to here. All the islands here in Buzzards Bay—Naushon, Pasque, Nashawena, Cuttyhunk, and Penikese—are what remains of the great giant's sons."

The wind was threading its way through the holes in the stonework, curling itself around us, sliding across the backs of our necks.

"You mean we're sitting on some Indian grave?" DeShawn asked.

Cunningham nodded. DeShawn shuddered.

In the silence, you could hear the ocean churning underneath the wind. That was when I heard what sounded like a small mewling thing. I looked around. DeShawn caught my eye and nudged his head over toward Tiny who started bubbling up like a hot two-liter that had just been cracked open. "She-she-she—"

DeShawn scratched at the ground with a rock. It smelled like fresh dirt.

"I didn't mean to hurt her," Tiny gurgled. "I loved her."

260 // USA Noir

Tiny was now going like a geyser. I just kept watching the water, the blackness moving out there, flashing like silver in the moonlight.

"I liked her so much."

DeShawn looked like he wanted to dig his way to China with that rock, anything to get out of there. Then he suddenly stopped, like he remembered he was digging on someone's grave. He sat on his hands and glanced away.

Tiny curled up in a ball and put his hands over his head, as if he was scared he was gonna get hit. Cunningham scooped him up like Santa Claus picking up some big fat kid who was crying because he wanted a new fire truck, only it wasn't a truck Tiny wanted. It was a new life. That was all Tiny wanted. At age seventeen.

The world is full of people like us. Floating out here like these half-sunk islands covered in shit. We're drifting through your city, your town, cutting across your backyard, walking up your fire escape, sliding a slim jim between your car window and door, slipping into your leather bucket seats that smell like money—your money. We're wiring your ignition, busting your satellite radio, rifling through your shit, tossing out manuals and hand sanitizer, tissues, registration, and pens, until we find that emergency envelope full of freshly printed twenties. We coast along your streets, caught up in the current of something swirling inside us, riding swells of blacktop anger with the wind at our backs. We don't really want your car, your daughter, your jewelry, your things. Just like with you, that shit helps us forget why it can hurt to be alive, but only for a little while.

We snuck away, DeShawn and me, leaving Tiny to be lectured by Cunningham about "crossing the treacherous waters," "a new day dawning," and "making the journey called Second Chance." Somewhere behind us on that dark path, we could hear Tiny say he wanted to be different, but he just didn't know how. He just didn't know how, he repeated again and again, the sound of his voice echoing in the wind.

Later that night, we could hear Tiny crying himself to sleep, rocking back and forth. It was like we were all at sea, rolling through the waves of regret crashing around inside him.

"Feckin' A," Freddie said. "Feckin' knock it off, you pansy." Freddie had calmed down since earlier. At dinner that night he was so cool it was spooky, like Stubby and Da Cunha had worked him up something good.

"Shut up," DeShawn said. "I'm sick of you and your freak-ass shit."

"Yo, homes," Freddie said. "I didn't mean nuthin' by it. You and me, we're cool, a'ight?"

"No," DeShawn answered. "We ain't never been cool."

We had all been pretending to be asleep, just waiting for Tiny to knock it off, which he did, eventually. Then the house slowly quieted down as the other guys stopped tossing and turning and dozed off for real. But after all of Tiny's tears, that silence kept me awake.

I stared out the window and watched the moon rise higher like a giant eyeball staring out over the hill where the leper cemetery was. In the silence, I could tell someone else was awake and knew I was up too. And he—or it—was just waiting for that moment when I would fall asleep. I lay as still as possible and listened to the waves against our island rock. It was like we were part of some cycle of nature, meant to crash up against things forever.

Eventually, I fell asleep.

In the morning, I could hear Cunningham racing down the stairs. Tiny screaming. Voices coming in from outside. DeShawn and me flew out of bed at the same time, put on our jeans and boots, and ran downstairs. Ryan, Kevin, and Bobby came stumbling out of bed behind us.

Opening the door, I heard it. Like so many little creatures, Pukwudgies maybe, sobbing or laughing—I couldn't tell which—in the wind. I looked around for them, but I didn't see anything. DeShawn pointed to the chicken coop.

Cunningham, Da Cunha, and Stubby just stood and stared. Tiny was on his knees, inside the coop. No one was saying a word.

The chickens, which were usually running all over the place by the morning, crowing and cock-a-doodle-dooing, were trying to stand on their little chicken legs, but as soon as they got halfway up, they fell over. Someone or something had come in the middle of the night and broken all their legs, just snapped them like twigs. The chickens kept trying to stand, flopping over, and crying out. Lying there, dying, but wanting to live.

At least twenty pairs of beady little eyes looked up at us for help, looked at us for nothing cause there was nothing we could do but put them out of their misery.

Tiny was running his fingers through the dirt, tears streaming down his face. Even Bobby looked like someone had just punched him in the gut.

Freddie was the last person to come out of the house. He strolled up to the chicken yard and didn't even try not to laugh.

Tiny picked up one of the littlest birds. I couldn't tell if it was the same chicken Bobby had hypnotized. They had all grown some in the past couple of weeks and most of them had looked the same to me anyway. But Tiny held that chicken close to him and rocked it like it was a baby he was going to do everything in his power to try and save.

Sometimes I wish I could have cried like Tiny did. After Chad and me hit that car, I didn't even realize there were tears streaming down my cheeks. There were sirens and lights. Cops and paramedics sawing through car doors with their Jaws of Life.

The last thing I remember was Chad sitting there, patting the dashboard of the Mustang and saying, "Guess we're gonna have to take this one out and shoot it."

The next day we all watched the fog swallow *Second Chance* whole. Freddie was onboard, being shipped out to "Plymouth Rock"—*Plymouth County Correctional Facility*, as it reads on the books, where all the child murderers go.

Tiny was different after that. I guess DeShawn and me changed too. We helped Tiny dig a grave and bury all the chickens. Cunningham showed us some books in the school library where we read up on Indian funerary mounds. We gathered up some rocks and soil and covered the birds' grave the Wampanoag way.

Tiny, DeShawn, and me never talked about the chickens or how we became friends, if that's what we really were. We didn't talk about much. But we did our chores or whatever, and never said anything, which was like saying a lot because it wasn't like being with someone you can talk to but don't. It was pretty much all right.

PART IV

HOMELAND SECURITY

AFTER THIRTY

BY DON WINSLOW
Pacific Beach, San Diego
(Originally published in *San Diego Noir*)

1945

Charlie Decker is a hard case.

Ask anybody—his shipmates, his captain, his family back in Davenport if they'll talk to you about him. They'll all tell you the same thing.

Charlie's no good.

He's trouble and always has been. Drunkenness, absent-without-official-leave, brawling, gambling, insubordination—three stretches in the navy and Charlie's been in and out of the brig and up and down the ranks. The navy probably would have thrown him out if there wasn't a war on and they didn't need a man who knew how to make an engine run. Give Charlie Decker thirty minutes and a wrench and he can fix anything, but you also know that he can wreck anything too, and just as easily.

People tried to tell Millie this, but she wouldn't listen. Her roommates saw it clear as day. One good look in Charlie's eyes, that cocky smirk of his, and you knew. They told her but it went through one ear and out the other. Now she opens her eyes, looks at the clock on her bed table, and slaps him on the butt. "Charlie, get up."

"What?" he mumbles, happy in his sweet, warm sleep. They sat up and drank when she came home from her night shift at Consolidated, and then they did it and then drank some more, so he don't want to get up.

She shakes his shoulders. "It's thirty *days.*"

Millie knows the navy—up to thirty days it's AWOL, after thirty it's desertion. He's been shacked up with her for almost a month now. Almost a month in the little bungalow that was already crowded with four other girls, and he said he was going back before the thirty days were up.

But now he mumbles, "To hell with that." And closes his eyes.

"You're going to get in big trouble," Millie says. AWOL, he would get a captain's mast, but probably no time in the brig because he's set to ship out soon anyway. But for desertion he's going to get a court-martial, maybe *years* in the brig, and then a DD.

"Charlie, get *up*."

He rolls over, kisses her, and then shows her what trouble is. That's the thing—she knows he's bad news but he's just so damn handsome and so good in the sack. She knew from the moment they met at Eddie's Bar that she couldn't keep her legs shut with Charlie.

Charlie makes her see fireworks.

Charlie rolls off her, reaches for the green pack of Lucky Strikes by the bed, finds his Zippo, and lights one up.

"Go fix us some breakfast," he says.

"What do you want?"

"Eggs?"

"*Try* buying eggs, Charlie."

"We got any coffee left?"

"A little."

Like everything else, it's rationed. Coffee, sugar, meat, cigarettes, chocolate, gasoline of course. The girls swap ration coupons but there's only so much and she doesn't like it when Charlie deals in the black market. She tells him it's unpatriotic.

Charlie doesn't give a damn. He figures he's done his patriotic duty all over the Pacific, most recently on a tin can in the cordon line off Okinawa, and he deserves a little coffee and sugar.

The first cigarette of the day is always the best.

Charlie sucks the smoke into his lungs and holds it before letting it out his nose. It makes him feel good, relaxed, at ease with the decision he has to make.

"Then after breakfast you'll go back," Millie is saying.

"I thought you loved me," Charlie says, flashing his smile. He's proud of the smile—his teeth are white and even.

"I do." She does love him, despite everything. That's why she doesn't want to see him get into a really bad jam. He's always going to get in a little trouble, Millie knows, that's part of what she loves about him.

"Then why do you want me to go?" Charlie teases. "You know we're shipping out."

"I know."

"Will you wait for me?" he asks.

"Of course I will."

He knows she won't. Millie needs it, like most women. The story is that men need it and women just put up with it, but Charlie knows better. Maybe not virgins, maybe they don't, but once a woman's had it, she wants it again. And Millie wants it. Takes a couple of drinks to loosen her up enough to admit it, but after that, hell, look out.

If he ships out she'll be with another guy by the time he gets back. He knows this for a fact because she was cheating on some poor jerk when she went to bed with *him*. Anyway, Charlie knows she won't wait and tells himself that's why he's not going back. She'll find another guy to sleep with, another guy's back to scratch with her nails, another guy to tell that he makes her helpless to stop him.

That's what he tells himself most of the time, and when that story doesn't sell—usually in those cold gray hours of the early morning when he's so drunk he's almost sober—he tells himself a different story—that he doesn't want to go back to the brig.

Charlie has felt an SP's baton in the kidneys, along with the metallic taste of his own blood when they decided it was more fun to bust up his face, and he don't want any more of it. They do whatever they want to do to you in the brig, and then hose it down like that washes it all away. Thirty days AWOL, the captain might send him to the brig and it's not a chance he wants to take.

That's what Charlie tells himself, anyway.

Now he watches Millie walk into the kitchen and likes the way she looks in the little white silk robe he bought her.

Millie's a looker, all right.

That Saturday night he had liberty and headed down to Eddie's because he heard that's where the factory girls go. The ship had just limped back for repairs so they had a lot of free time, and after what they'd been through they were all ready to for it too. The scuttlebutt was that Eddie's was the place to go, so he skipped the usual dives in the Gaslamp and headed to Pacific Beach. The joint was crowded with sailors and Marines all after the same thing, but he saw her and gave her that smile and she smiled back.

Charlie went up to her and talked and then she let him buy her a drink and then another and they talked and he asked her a lot of questions about herself and found out she came out from a little town in North Dakota because she'd always wanted to see the ocean and she wanted an adventure.

"I heard there were jobs for women in San Diego," she said. "So I got on a train and here I am."

"Here you are," Charlie smiled.

"In Pacific Beach, California," she said.

"Do you like it?"

She nodded. "I like the money and it's fun living with the other girls most of the time."

They talked some more and then he asked if they could get out of there and she said okay but where did he want to go?

"Can't we just go to your place?" he asked. "You said you have a place."

"I do," she said, "but I don't want to go right away. A girl likes a little romance, you know."

Oh, hell, he knew. He was just hoping this one girl didn't. But if she didn't, she'd be the first ever. At least of the ones you didn't pay. The whores, they didn't want romance, they just wanted you to get your business over with as soon as possible so they could get on with theirs. It was like eating on a ship—hurry up and finish because there's a sailor waiting for your chair.

But Millie, she looked at him with those dark blue eyes and he decided that a walk along the beach would be just the thing. You expected blue eyes with a blond girl, but Millie's hair was jet black, and cut short, and she had these cute lips that made you think of Betty Boop. When he walked close to her she smelled like vanilla, because, she told him, perfume was hard to get.

But the vanilla smelled good behind her ear, in her hair. She was small, what did she call it—petite—and fit nice under his arm as they walked on the sand under the pier. A radio was playing somewhere and they stood and danced under the pier and he held her tight.

"You feel nice," he said, because it was all he could think of to say and because it was true too.

"So do you," she responded.

Now he remembers how nice she smelled and how good she felt under his arm and how life was the way he always hoped it would be. There were no flames that night, no acrid smoke that burned his nose, no screams that seared his brain, and the waves touched the beach like kisses, and if he told the truth he would have stayed there forever with her on Pacific Beach and not even taken her back to her place and her bed.

But he did and they made love and he slept through his liberty. He meant to go back that day, he really did, while it was still no big deal, but it was just too good with her in the little bungalow.

Millie shared the bedroom with another girl from the factory, a girl named Audrey from Ohio, and they'd run a rope across the room and draped a blanket over it for a little privacy. Sometimes Millie didn't want to make love if Audrey was home because she felt shy with the other girl just across from the blanket. But Audrey worked the day shift and was gone a lot of nights with an airman, and sometimes Millie did it anyway with Audrey there and Charlie suspected she liked it because it made her feel dirty.

The bungalow was crowded, but so was all of Pacific Beach since they built the factories and all the people came for work. There was hardly any place to lie down—some people lived in tents in backyards—so Millie felt lucky to stay there even though it was hard to get into the bathroom sometimes and there were two girls sleeping in the living room.

Charlie liked it there too, that was the problem, even though it often felt as crowded as a ship. But it was quiet in the morning with the girls gone on their shifts, and he and Millie got up late and had the kitchen to themselves and they'd take their coffee and cigarettes out into the tiny yard and enjoy the sun.

Audrey had a car and sometimes they'd drive down to Oscar's for hamburgers, or go to Belmont Park and ride the roller coaster, and Millie would scream and hold on tight to his arm and he liked that. One time when Millie got paid they went to the Hollywood Theater downtown to see the burlesque and she dug her elbow into his ribs when he gawked at Zena Ray, and they both laughed at Bozo Lord even though his jokes were corny. And afterward he got her to admit she thought the girls were pretty, and she was a pistol in bed that night.

On the nights she worked, he'd stay home or hit the bars on Garnet or Mission Boulevard, keeping a sharp eye out for the SPs even though there were a lot of guys walking around in civvies—the 4Fs, sure, but mostly men who had served their bit, or been wounded, or were on leave. So the SPs didn't look at him too hard and anyway they were busy keeping an eye on the sailors and marines who flooded the sidewalks and had fistfights that spilled into the street.

Charlie would make sure he arrived back to the bungalow before she got home, tired from work but too jazzed up to go to sleep, and he thought it was funny that this tiny girl was building PBYs and B-24s.

"You've probably killed more Japs than I have," he said to her one morning.

"I don't like to think about that," she said.

The nights were fun but the days were the best. Most days they'd sleep in late, then have breakfast and walk down to Pacific Beach and swim, or just sit or lie down on the sand and take naps, or walk along the boardwalk and maybe stop someplace to have a beer, and the days just went by and now July has become August, and he has a tough decision to make.

Charlie comes into the kitchen in his skivvies and a T-shirt and sits down at the table.

"Aren't you going to put some clothes on?" she asks.

"The other girls are all at work, aren't they?" he asks.

She pours him a cup of coffee and sets it down in front of him. Then she puts a little margarine in a pan, waits for it to bubble, and throws in two slices of bread and fries them.

He can feel her impatience and aggravation. He hasn't done a damn thing but hang around for a month, and even though she says it's all right with her, he knows it isn't. Women can't stand a man not working. Just a fact of life—it was that way with his mother and his old man and it's the same way with Millie and him now. She knows he can't get a job, knows he can't ever get a job with a DD on his record, so she's wondering how long he plans on living off her and he knows that's what's on her mind.

Has been for the past couple of weeks, if you want to know the truth. Since that night he woke up with Millie shaking his shoulder, telling him he was having a bad dream.

"It's okay, baby," she was saying. "It's okay. You're having a nightmare."

He didn't want to tell her it wasn't a nightmare but real life, and she asked him, "Where were you?"

"None of your damn business," was all he said, and he felt that his cheeks were wet with tears and then he remembered that he'd been crying and moaning, over and over again, "I don't want to go back, I don't want to go back . . ."

She asked him, "Where? Where don't you want to go back to, Charlie?"

"I told you it was none of your damn business," he said, and slapped her across her pretty little Betty Boop mouth. When she came back in from the kitchen she had ice in a towel pressed against her lower lip and there was a little streak of blood on her chin and she said, "You ever hit me again, I'll call the SPs and turn you in."

But she didn't throw him out.

She knew he had no place to go, no money, and would probably get picked up by Shore Patrol. So she pressed the ice to her lips and let him stay, but nothing was ever as good between them after that and he knows that he broke something between them that he can't fix.

Now she sets the plate down just a little hard.

"What?" he asks, even though he knows.

"What are you going to do?" she asks.

"Eat my breakfast," he answers.

"And then what?"

He almost says, *Slap that look off your puss if it's still there.* Instead he shoves a piece of fried bread into his mouth and chews it deliberately. A woman should let a man have his coffee and breakfast before she starts in on him. The day is going to be hot—the summer sun is already pounding the concrete outside—and she should just let things slide so they can go down to the beach and enjoy the breeze and the water, maybe walk down to the end of the pier.

But she won't let it go. She sits down, folds her forearms on the table, and says, "You have to go, Charlie."

He gets up from the table, goes back into the bedroom, and finds last night's bottle. Then he returns to the kitchen, pours some of the cheap whiskey into his coffee, sits down, and starts to drink.

"Oh, that will help," she says. "You showing up drunk."

Charlie doesn't want to listen to her yapping. He wants to get drunk even though he knows that no amount of booze can wash away the truth that no man can stand to know about himself.

That he's *afraid* to go back.

Since that moment the Jap planes came crashing onto the deck, spewing fuel and flame, and he saw his buddies become running torches and smelled them burning and he can't never get that smell out of his nose. Can't get it out of his head, either, because it comes in his sleep and he wakes up shaking and crying and moaning that he doesn't want to go back, please don't make him go back.

Charlie knows what they say about him, that he's no good, that he's a hard case, but he knows he ain't hard. Maybe he used to be, though now he knows he's as broken as the spine of the ship.

But the ship is repaired now and will be steaming out across the Pacific, this time to the Japanese home islands, and if they think Okinawa was bad, that was nothing compared to what it's going to be.

It ain't the thought of the brig and it ain't even the thought of losing her, because the truth is he's already lost her. He can take the brig and he can take losing her, but he can't take going back.

Something in him is broken and he can't fix it.

Now what he wants to do is get drunk, stay drunk, and lay on the beach, but she won't shut up.

"You have to go back, Charlie," she says.

He stares into his cup and takes another drink.

"If you go back today it will be all right."

He shakes his head.

Then she says it. "It's okay to be afraid."

Charlie throws the cup at her. He doesn't really know if he meant to hit her or not, but he does. The cup cuts her eye and splashes coffee all over her face and she screams and stands up. She wipes the coffee out of her eyes and feels the blood and then stares at him for a second and says, "You son of a bitch."

Charlie doesn't answer.

"Get out," Millie says. "Get out."

He doesn't move except to grab the bottle, take a drink directly from it, and lean back into the chair.

Millie watches this and says, "Fine. I'll get you out."

She heads for the door.

That gets him out of the chair because now he remembers what she said she'd do if he hit her again, and he did hit her again, and Millie is the kind of girl who does what she says she'll do, and he can't let her go and call Shore Patrol.

Charlie grabs her by the neck, pulls her into his chest, and then wraps his arms around and lifts her up, and she wriggles and kicks as he carries her toward the bedroom because he thinks maybe it can end that way. But when drops her on the bed she spits in his face and claws at his eyes and says, "You're real brave with a woman, huh, Charlie? Aren't ya?"

He hauls off and pops her in the jaw just to shut her up, but she won't shut up and he hits her again and again until she finally lays still.

"Now will you behave?" he asks her, but there's blood all over the pillow and even on the wall and her neck is bent like the broken spine of a ship and he knows he can't fix her.

She's so small, what do they call it—petite.

Charlie staggers into the bathroom, pushes past the stockings that hang from cords, and washes his bloody hands under the tap. Then he goes back into the bedroom, where Millie is lying with her eyes open, staring at the ceiling. He puts on the loud Hawaiian shirt he bought at Pearl, the one Millie liked, and a pair of khaki pants, and then sits down next to her to put on his shoes.

He thinks he should say something to her but he doesn't know what to say, so he just gets up, goes back into the kitchen, finds the bottle, and drains it in one long swallow. His hands shake as he lights a cigarette, but he does get it lit, takes a long drag, and heads out the door.

The sun is blinding, the concrete hot on his feet.

Charlie doesn't really know where to go, so he just keeps walking until he finds himself at the beach. He walks along the boardwalk, which is crowded with people, mostly sailors and their girls out for a stroll. He pushes his way through and then goes down the steps to the sand and under the pier where him and her held each other and danced to the radio.

Maybe it's the same radio playing now as he stands there listening to the music and looks out at the ocean and tries to figure out what to do next. They'll be looking for him soon, they'll know it was him, and if they catch him he'll spend the rest of his life in the brig, if they don't hang him.

Now he wishes he had just gone back like she told him to.

But it's too late.

He stares at the water, tells himself he should run, but there's nowhere to run to, anyway, and the music is nice and he thinks about that night and knows he should never have left the beach.

Then the music stops and a voice comes on and the voice is talking like he's real excited, like the radio did that day the Japs bombed Pearl Harbor.

Charlie turns around to look up at the boardwalk and all the people are just standing there, standing stock-still like they're photographs or statues. Then suddenly they all start to move, and whoop and yell, and hug each other and kiss and dance and laugh.

Charlie walks to the edge of the boardwalk.

"What's going on?" he asks this sailor who has his arm around a girl. "What's going on?"

"Didn't you hear?" the sailor answered, swinging the girl on his hip. "We dropped some kind of big bomb on Japan. They say it's the end of the war. They say the war is over!" Then he forgets about Charlie and bends the girl back and kisses her again.

And all along Pacific Beach people are hugging and kissing, laughing and crying, because the war is over.

Charlie Decker, the hard case, goes and sits in the sand.

He peers across the ocean toward a city that has burst into flame and people burn like torches and he knows he will never get the smell out of his nose or the pictures out of his brain. Knows that he will wake up crying that he can never go back.

Ask anybody—his shipmates, his captain, his family back in Davenport if they'll talk to you about him. They'll all tell you the same thing.

Charlie's no good.

Now, broken, he sinks back onto Pacific Beach.

MISSING GENE

BY J. MALCOLM GARCIA

Troost Lake, Kansas City

(Originally published in *Kansas City Noir*)

Evening

Fran's at night school studying for her associate's degree. I don't feel like watching TV so I get out the knife one of the interpreters gave me in Kandahar and start throwing it at the wall. He said he got it off the body of a bad guy who blew himself up laying an IED in the road, but I think he stole it off one of our guys, because it's a Gerber and it doesn't look like it was in any explosion. The terp could throw it and stick it every time. I'm not that good, but I throw it at the wall anyway. I can do it for hours.

I was a contractor over in Kandahar. Electrician. Worked there for twelve months. When my year was up, I flew home to Kansas City and took up with Fran and a couple of months later moved in with her. Mr. Fix It, the soldiers called me. Did some plumbing too. A little out of my league, but at two hundred tax-free grand a year I was more than willing to say I could do anything. I got used to the noise: mortars, sniper fire, return fire, .50 calibers, AKs, generators grinding all night, guys living on top of each other telling dead baby and fag jokes. Awful quiet now that I'm back. Behind Fran's house, I hear buses turn off Prospect and onto 39th Street, drone past and slice into the night until I don't hear anything again. The knife helps. I like the steady repetition of tossing it. The precision of it. Like fly fishing. Gene understood. He fought in Korea.

The trick with the knife, I told Gene, is you got to establish a rhythm. You do that and the silence becomes part of the flow and the *plink* the knife makes when it enters the wall interrupts the silence, and the small suck sound it makes when you pull it out, and then the silence again until you throw it, again and again.

Right, Gene said.

Next day

This is the third week I haven't seen Gene at Mike's Place. Out of all the regulars, he's the only one missing.

Melissa isn't here but we all know where she is. A public defender, Melissa has a court case this afternoon. I overheard her tell Lyle yesterday she would be working late. And Lyle? He may have a job painting or installing a countertop or a new floor or fixing someone's shitter. What I'm saying is, Lyle's around. He's a handyman. He'll be in later, as will his buddy Tim.

Bill's here. He's retired from working construction and basically sits at the bar all day drinking up his disability. And Mike, of course. It's his bar. The floor dips and the stools wobble, all of them, and the top of the pool table's got a big slash in it and someone walked off with the cue ball, but it's a good place—cheap, and it's only a couple of blocks from Fran's.

Then there's Gene. Or was. He drove off is how I look at it. Flew the coop, as they say. Well, that's it. I'm leaving too. Montana is what I'm thinking. I've been considering a move for a while. I mentioned Montana to Gene. He thought it was a good idea.

Wide open, no people, he said.

Absolutely, I said.

I'll tell Fran tonight.

Evening

What's on at seven?

Golden Girls reruns.

Oh.

You've had beer.

I was at Mike's.

Well, you missed my mother.

Oh . . . yeah?

Yeah. It's all right. I wasn't expecting her.

Fran's mother does that; drops by without calling. She's divorced and bored. Good thing Fran was here instead of me. Her mother nags me when Fran's not around. She knows I'm not going out on many jobs. I've told her we're okay. I earned a bundle in Afghanistan. She thinks I should have stayed another year and made even more.

I'm going to Montana.

Montana?

Yeah.

When?

I don't know.

Oh.

I play solitaire, spreading the cards across the blanket of our bed. I tell Fran not to move her legs beneath the blankets and disturb the cards but she does anyway.

Why Montana?

It's wide open.

Fran doesn't look up from her book, *The General and the Spy*. A man on the cover wears an open red tunic and some tight-ass white pants a real guy'd never wear. His skin's the color of a dirty penny and he has no hair on his chest. A woman's got her hands on his stomach, ready to rip into those pants I bet.

Fran folds the corner of a page, closes the book, and wipes tears from her eyes.

Nobody cries over those kinds of books, I tell her.

Montana?

I'm thinking about it. Gene's missing.

Who?

A guy I know.

Fran goes, Let's change the channel. Then let's talk.

Go ahead. Change it.

I changed it last time.

What do you want to watch? I ask.

I don't know.

She picks up her book and puts it down again. We stare at the TV, the remote between us.

Next day

Bill sits beside me at Mike's, buys me a beer. Crass old fucker Bill. Bald as a post and bug-eyed. He's always hunched over and rocks back and forth and makes these sick jokes about his neck being so long he can lick his balls like a dog. Deaf as Stevie Wonder is blind.

Hey, Bill, Tim says.

What you say? Bill asks.

Fuck you, Bill, Tim says.

What you say?

Tim laughs. Laughs loud and talks loud like we're all deaf as Bill. He sits at the end of the bar where Gene always stood, wipes his hands on his sweatshirt and jeans. Tim works in a warehouse in the West Bottoms. Refrigeration parts. Something like that. Comes in grimed in grease and oil. Starts at five in the morning and works all the time, weekends too. With jobs the way they are, is he going to say no when his boss offers him extra hours? I don't think so. Not with paying out child support to his ex.

His money being so tight is why he killed his dog's puppies. At least that's how he explains it. The dog, a brown and white mix between this and that, had a litter of seven. He put six of them in a pillow case and dropped them in Troost Lake. Then he shot the dog. Easier than getting her fixed. I stopped sitting next to Tim when I heard about the puppies.

Every time I think of them, I'm reminded of these Afghan laborers in Kandahar. One afternoon they found some puppies when they were collecting trash. A trash fire was burning and they threw the puppies into the fire. You want to hear some screaming, listen to puppies being barbecued. I hear them now. I ball up my fist and right hook my temple once, twice, three times, waiting for what I call *relief pain* to wrap my skull and take their shrieks out of my head. Tim and Bill look at me. I open my fist.

Fucking mosquito, I say and smack the side of my face again.

Big-ass mosquito, Tim says, still looking at me.

It's strange seeing him in Gene's spot at the end of the bar. Gene never sat, just stood. No matter how cold, he always wore shorts, a T-shirt, and a windbreaker. Brown shoes and white socks. Legs skinny and pale as a featherless chicken. Wore a cap that had the dates of the Korean War sewn in it. He told me that Kansas City winters didn't compare to a winter in Korea.

I saw frozen bodies stacked like cord wood covered with ice, Gene said. Some of them I put there.

It got cold in Afghanistan too, I said.

I remember one time when this truck driver got to Kandahar in December. Brand new. Just off the bus. He was so wet behind the ears I had to tell him where the chow hall was. He kept rubbing his hands together and I pointed out the PX where he could buy some gloves. He went on his first convoy an hour later. This guy, he got in his rig, took off, but realized he was in the wrong convoy. He turned back to the base and approached the gate fast because he was out in no man's land by himself. You didn't approach the gate fast. You didn't do that. But he was scared. Some Australians shot him five times with a .50 cal. I mean, he was obliterated. They had to check his DNA to figure out who he was. Less than two hours after I showed him the chow hall, I saw them put his body pieces in bags.

Evening

Fran tells me what I'm planning is called a *geographic*. Moving to get a new start somewhere else in the mistaken belief you'll leave your bad habits behind is how she puts it. She studied psychology last fall and thinks she can pick apart my mind now.

I mean it. I'm gone, I say.

She goes, When you decide to do it, just go. Don't bother telling me because I'm not going with you. Men have left me before. I survived. I'll survive you. Leave before I come home. Make it easy on us both.

I will, I say. I can do that.

Okay, she goes, okay.

Next day

Just me in here this afternoon.

What's the latest on Gene? I ask Mike.

Haven't heard a thing, he says.

Mike has owned Mike's for ten years. He was in a band, got married, and had a kid. In other words, time to get a real job. So he bought the bar and named it after himself. He's divorced now, sees the kid every two weeks, plays gigs occasionally, and runs this place. Says if he ever sells it, the buyer will have to keep the name. Years from now nobody will know who the hell Mike was but his name will be here. A piece of himself nobody will know and can't shake off. That's one way to make an impression.

I first came to Mike's by chance. I used to drink at another bar on the Paseo but one night it was packed. After Kandahar, I couldn't handle crowds, so I left. On my way home, I stopped at Mike's. Some lights on but barely anyone in it. I had a few beers and came back the next night. Two nights in a row and Mike figured he had himself a new regular. He bought me a beer and said his name was Mike. We shook hands. Sealed the deal, as they say.

I met Fran here. She was shooting pool by herself. Bent over the table, her ass jutted high and round against her jeans, and any man with a nut sack would have known that if she looked that nice from behind she'd be more than tolerable face-to-face. And, if she wasn't, so what with an ass like that. But she was fine all the way around.

She had light brown hair and a determined look. My glance moved down past her chin and rested on a set of perky tits that pressed just hard enough against her T-shirt that my imagination did not have to strain too hard to know what would be revealed when she undressed. I asked to shoot pool with her and we got to chitchatting. One thing led to another is what I'm saying.

I'm not sure when I noticed Gene. I just did. I remember seeing this old man at the end of the bar and thinking how solitary he looked, how he was off in his own world. He had one of those faces that sort of collapsed when he didn't talk, mouth and chin merging into a flat, frowning pond. When he took off his hat, the light shined on his bald, freckled head. He'd still be standing in his spot when I left a couple of hours later, the same bottle of Bud he had when I first came in half-empty and parked in front of him. He barely said a word to me in those days. Just nodded if we looked each other's way. But then as I began showing up every night, he started saying hello and I'd say hello back.

Evening

Fran and I drop our plates onto the crumb-graveled carpet for our beagle to lick. Partly chewed pizza crust, orange grease. Slobbered up in seconds. I reshuffle the cards.

I'm going to sleep, Fran says.

Say what?

Turn the TV off.

I'm still up.

Turn it down then.

It's not loud.

Please.

But it's not.

Shhh.

I shut off the TV, go out to the living room. I sit in the dark fingering my knife. The way Gene has vanished, an eighty-year-old man. I can't help but notice the empty space at the bar. Like a radiator turned off. All that dead air, dead space.

Funny what you learn about a guy after he's gone. For instance, Tim and Lyle said that Gene would come to Mike's at eleven in the morning. He would stay all day and apparently be pretty toasted by the time he left at closing. Really, he never seemed messed up to me. Maybe he kicked in and drank like a horse after I left.

One night, Gene told me he had taken his landlord to court. It wasn't clear to me why. I believed him, and whatever the reason, he made it seem like he'd won the case. After he disappeared, Bill told me Gene lived in his car. There never had been a court case or a landlord. Bill had put him up in his place but not for long. Said Gene wandered around the house with nothing on but his skivvies. I couldn't have that, Bill said. Not with my wife in the house and the grandkids coming over. I don't care if he is a vet.

Next day

Hey, Lyle, Mike says.

Mike, Lyle says, and takes a seat near Tim. He has his hair roped back in a ponytail and wears an army fatigue jacket that hangs well past his hands. His feet dangle off the bar stool and tap the air. He reeks of pot.

I was just getting ready to leave, Tim says.

No you're not, Lyle says.

He turns to me.

What's going on? Working?

Absolutely, I tell him. Staying busy.

You were in Afghanistan, weren't you? How was that?

Good. It was good.

That's good.

Actually, it was kind of crazy.

Crazy can be good, Lyle says, and he and Tim laugh.

Mike, I'll have another, Tim says.

I notice Melissa come in the back door.

Hi, Melissa, Mike says.

Hey, Melissa, Lyle says.

Melissa, what's up, Tim says.

Hey, Melissa says.

She sits next to Lyle and orders a Bud Light and a shot of Jack. She has on heels, gray slacks, gray jacket, and a white blouse.

Won my case, she says. Got him off.

Since none of us know who she's talking to, we all nod at the same time. Melissa smiles. She starts talking about the first time she came in here as she always does. I don't know why it bears repeating. I mean, I've got the story memorized. But she likes telling it. Maybe it gives her a sense of seniority. After Lyle she has been coming here longer than the rest of us. Like it makes her feel she belongs is what I'm saying.

It was just before closing, Melissa says. Mike and Lyle were shooting pool. Gene was in his usual spot. She remembers Mike saying he was about to close. Then he let her stay and the four of them had beers and got stoned after Mike locked up.

Gene got stoned? I say.

Yeah, Melissa says.

I hadn't heard that part before.

Evening

Fran tells me that instead of doing a geographic, I should go with her to visit her sister in St. Louis. It would be cheap, she says. No hotel or eating-out expenses.

Sounds okay, I say.

Did you order a pizza?

Not yet, I say. I'm tired of pizza.

What do you want?

I don't know. Shit, what's up with all the questions?

Fran goes into the kitchen. I hear her making herself a drink. I try calling Gene. I gave Gene my cell number one night. He called me a few times before he disappeared but I could never make out what he was saying. He had a sandpaper voice that came at you like radio static. What's that? What's that, Gene? I'd say, and then he'd hang up. I'd call him right back but he'd never pick up. He doesn't pick up now. I get one of those female computer-generated voices telling me to leave a message. I'd like to talk to Gene, I say, and hang up.

Next day

Anybody hear anything about Gene? I ask.

Lyle shakes his head. Melissa and Tim look at Lyle and shrug.

Getting to be awhile, Lyle says.

Yeah, awhile, Mike says.

I shout in Bill's ear and ask him what he knows. Well, he says, speaking like he's got a mouth full of cotton, I spoke to one of his sons in San Antone. Yes, San Antone it was. Gene gave me his number when he stayed with me. An emergency contact, he had said. Well, let's hope this isn't an emergency because Gene's son wants nothing to do with him. One of those kind of deals, if you know what I mean. Still a lot of water under that bridge, I guess. Anyway, I told his son, I just want you to know your father is missing. We haven't seen him for the longest. Maybe he's headed your way. But his boy said again he wanted nothing to do with him. What can you do?

He doesn't expect an answer and I don't give him one because, well, what can you do? Melissa, Tim, and Lyle go out back to smoke. Mike steps into the kitchen. Bill stares at his glass. I tell him that today for no good reason I was reminded of this private, a young gal. We got mortared and she got all messed up. She lay on the ground, her right arm ripped to shit like confetti.

Some medics put her on a stretcher and got an IV in her, and her shirt rose up exposing her flat stomach and full tits and despite all her screaming I thought she was beautiful. I went over to see if I could help and she looked at me wide-eyed and said, Am I going to die? No, I said. You're fine. You're going to make it.

Do I know if she did? No, I don't. That bothers me.

What you say? Bill says.

Evening

I call Fran from the union hall on Admiral Boulevard, shouting above the traffic noise of cars backed up overhead in the tangled mess that is I-70 and I-29 looping around one another. I only worked a few hours this afternoon, I tell her. I stuck around for something else to come up but nothing did. Can you pick me up?

Okay, she says.

By the time she gets me, I'm pissed off. Pissed I had only four hours of work today, pissed I couldn't get a ride home, pissed I had to wait around until Fran got off her job at Walgreens to get me. I was 360 degrees pissed off is what I'm saying.

I get in the car, ball my hand into a fist, and press my knuckles against Fran's right temple. She tilts her head away and I keep pushing with my fist until her head is against the window and I feel the vein in her temple pulse against my knuckles.

Stop it, you're hurting me, she says.

Next day

Mike, I'll have another one, Melissa says.

She's dating this gal, Rhonda, a school teacher. I don't know how old. Younger, I'd say by the look of her in a photo Melissa passed around. I don't care that she's gay. I mean lesbian. She corrected me one time. Men are gay, women are lesbian. Okay. What do I do with that bit of knowledge? Keep my mouth shut is what I'm saying.

Melissa talks about how nice it is to be involved with a woman who doesn't trip when Melissa has to work late. Doesn't ask a thousand questions to make sure that nothing is wrong. It's nice to be with someone who's an adult, Melissa says. She says that a lot. Nice to be involved with an adult. Like she's trying to convince herself that it's nice. Like maybe the confidence of her lover makes Melissa wonder what she's doing.

I'm going home, Tim says. Make some dinner.

What're you going to have? Lyle says.

I don't know.

What you say? Bill says.

Fuck you, Bill, Tim says, and he and Lyle laugh. It's not as funny as the first time he said it. It's starting to get old but I can't help smiling a little.

Gene and I had dinner together one night. I met him in the parking lot behind the Sun Fresh Market off Southwest Trafficway. I didn't know then that he was sleeping in his car. Just ran into him there and he asked me if I was hungry. Come to think of it, I said.

A bunch of clothes were heaped in the backseat of his station wagon. An old rusty job with wood paneling peeling off the doors. He had rigged a towel to take the place of a window that would no longer roll up. Laundry day, he said, explaining away the clothes.

We drove out of the parking lot to Mill Street and followed the curve into Westport to a little joint called The Corner. Some bums who might have been hippies years ago stood on Broadway wiping down car windows at a red light while the drivers waved them off. Gene and I sat down and a waitress cleared our table. I ordered a burger. Gene had the meatloaf special.

The Corner closed not long after that. A big *For Rent* sign hangs above the front door along with the name of some real estate company. I went by it the other day and noticed the table where Gene and I had sat surrounded by other empty tables made all the more empty by the emptiness of the place.

Evening

Fran's mother sits with me in the kitchen. Her perfume gives me a headache. I stare at her hair all puffy and piled up on her head and bleached so blond it's almost white. She twirls the lazy Susan with a finger, touches the corner of her mouth, and then goes back to spinning the lazy Susan, her finger skating along on a film of lipstick she rubbed off.

What's it taste like, your lipstick?

Why would you want to know? What kind of question is that for a man to ask?

I don't know, it just came to me, I want to say, but don't. One night, I was walking to the shitter and mortars started coming in. We were always being mortared. This is the real deal, baby! someone yelled. And then, the blasts lifted an eighteen-year-old private into the air, tossing him backward like a rag into all this dirt and noise and smoke; his blood sprayed over my face. I can still taste it.

Where's Fran? her mother says.

School, I say.

Have you thought of going back to school?

No.

Is it your plan for Fran to do all the work while you sit around? Fran's mother says. Have you thought about being more than an electrician?

No, Mrs. Lee, I haven't.

Well, it shows.

I apply a piece of Scotch tape to a corner above the cabinets where the wallpaper is peeling.

Fran's mother gets up and walks to the sink. I listen to the linoleum creak beneath her shoes.

When do you plan to clean these? she says of the dishes. Or are you waiting for them to pile up to the ceiling?

I throw the tape down and face her. She steps back, a little aren't-I-clever smirk on her face, and I turn the hot water on in the sink and pour in some soap. I find a sponge beneath the sink and start wiping down a plate. My fingertips turn white from squeezing the plate so hard. A littler harder and it would break. I want to feel it break but I ease up; put the plate on the rack. I start cleaning another one.

You two should get married, Fran's mother goes.

I keep washing the plate.

You're living together, she says. Not having a job hasn't stopped you from doing that. Married, you'd at least be official. It would show responsibility. Now wouldn't that be something?

I rinse the plate, set it on the rack. I lean on the sink, arms stiff.

I'm leaving, I say.

You're leaving. Where you going?

Montana.

Montana. What are you going to do in Montana?

Work.

Work. Work here for a change. You think some cowgirl is going to put up with you?

I raise my hand before she says anything more. There's this nasal termite sound to her voice that chisels into my head. I press my fingers against my eyes. My neck feels hard as a tree trunk.

Fran's mother stands beside me. I ignore her, work on another plate. She runs a finger over the dishes in the rack and shows me a spongy speck of pizza crust glued to her fingertip.

You can't do any better than that? she says.

I smash the plate on the edge of the sink and throw the jagged piece still in my hand against the wall. Fran's mother steps back, her eyes betraying panic, her finger still poised accusingly, and I grab her finger with a fury that fills me with a terrible heat and force it back until she kneels, screaming. A pasty white color washes through her face when the bone breaks, and I feel something break in me and I keep pressing back on her ruined finger, until the bone tears through the skin and into my palm. Her eyes swell like something wide and deep rising out of the ground, bubbling tears, and her screams take on a new level.

I let go of her hand and jam my knee into her solar plexus and put all my weight on her chest. She gags and spits up whatever she ate this morning. I rise up and then drop my knee into her chest, and her neck and face go all purple, and I do it again until I feel ribs crack under my knee. I sink into her chest and down to her spine like falling through ice. Blood geysers out of her mouth and then her eyes roll back. Her tongue lolls out of her mouth like a slug and I smell her bowels. I push myself off her and sit at the table. The silence is almost as loud as her screams. I focus on the hum of the refrigerator. White noise. I take up my knife. My hands shake and at first my throws are way off. Then my breathing steadies and I get my rhythm back and throw it once, twice, three times into the baseboards, the refrigerator humming behind me.

Next day

Rhonda's not answering, Melissa says, looking at her iPhone. Why isn't she answering?

The front door swings open.

Hey, Heidi, Mike says.

Hi, Mike, Heidi says.

She plops down beside Lyle, her mop of curly red hair flouncing on her shoulders. The two of them started dating not too far back. She tends bar here on the weekends. Has two kids. Their daddy dealt drugs and got busted. Lyle sells drugs, but hasn't been busted. I think she can do better. I bought books for her five-year-old daughter. I figured she'd appreciate that. Little picture books. But she started seeing Lyle and I quit the book thing. Maybe books weren't what I should have been giving her in the first place. But I was with Fran so books seemed appropriate. Neutral. Not too over-the-top is what I'm saying.

I force a smile at Heidi but I don't strike up a conversation. I'm not really here. Yesterday seems far away and today doesn't feel like today. I hear Heidi and Lyle talking but it's all background noise to Fran's mother dying. That's how I look at it. She died. She was in the wrong place at the wrong time. Something snapped inside me and she died. It was not me who killed her but something working through me I can't define. That something left me afterward as suddenly as it had come on and I almost fell asleep in the kitchen throwing my knife. But then the old me came back and I knew I had to clean up the mess left by that something else.

I carried Fran's mother into the garage and put her in the trunk of my car and covered her with a blanket. Finding a mop, I returned to the kitchen and washed the floor. Back in the garage, I looked for a box of five-, ten-, and twenty-pound weights Fran had bought at a yard sale when she got it into her head she was going to exercise. Dust and cobwebs covered the weights and clung to the hair on my arms, and I felt each hair released when I wiped the cobwebs off.

I put some rope and the weights in the trunk and drove to Troost Lake. Clouds sealed the sky so that no stars shone. I followed Troost Avenue to the turnoff into the lake, and the road narrowed and wound around the lake and my car lights skimmed over the oil blackness of the water and the wet stone walk where old men fished during the day. I parked the car under some trees, opened the trunk, and trussed Fran's mother up with the rope. She wasn't too heavy even with the weights I'd wedged beneath the rope. I held her and listened to what I thought was an owl. Shadows rose and dipped above me and then darted away and I could only assume they were bats. I waited for the owl to stop calling. In the vacancy left by its silence, I rolled Fran's mother down a hill and she splashed into the water and was absorbed into its darkness leaving only ripples that spread into nothingness.

Evening

When I'm with Fran, I think of her mother. I don't need that. I sit alone in the kitchen while Fran sleeps and punch my temples until my head feels like it will explode and thoughts of Mrs. Lee shatter into bits. I think of Gene and what he would say.

The last time I saw him, he was standing in front of a Church's Chicken near Gillham Plaza and 31st Street. It was hot and the wind blew trash and some napkins were pinned against Gene's knobby white knees. We said hello and he offered me a ride but I told him I had my car. I'm getting some coffee, I said.

When I went back outside, he was still there. I looked at him and he gave me a knowing wink like we were both in on something no one else would understand. I don't know what that might have been. But I'm thinking now he might have done some awful things in Korea besides killing gooks and letting their bodies freeze, and I think he saw in me the ability to do some awful things too, and then Fran's mother died and he was proved right. I'm just saying. I don't know. Gene didn't say and I never saw him again.

Next day

Okay, Mike, I'm outta here, Tim says. After one more.

I'll do one more too, Mike, Lyle says.

What you say?

Fuck you, Bill.

Lyle and Tim stand and walk outside to smoke. Melissa follows them tapping a number into her iPhone. Heidi looks at me and smiles. She asks Mike for a cigarette. Watch my purse, she says. Then she goes outside too. Mike puts two bottles of beer on the bar for Tim and Lyle. I wave him off when he looks at me. I feel all hemmed in. The beer congests me. It's difficult to breathe.

I'll pay up, Mike, I say.

Evening

In bed Fran rolls over with her back to me, her head on my right arm. I grit my teeth. Her touch sends shock waves through me and I get all jittery. I edge away from her. She says she has called her mother a few times but no one answers. It's not like her, she says. Her mother doesn't have an answering machine so Fran is going to go by the house in the morning.

That settles it. I'm out of here. When Fran leaves for work I'll be right behind her but headed in another direction. It will still be dark. I'll take 39th to Broadway and hang a right by the Walgreens and drive into downtown. A few blocks east, I'll see the glow from the Power & Light District keeping the sky open like an illumination mortar, and I'll cross the Broadway Bridge and get on I-29 north until I reach I-90 and then it's a direct shot west to Montana and wherever.

I feel my arm falling asleep beneath the weight of Fran's head. I curl it to get some circulation and realize I could choke her no problem. I drop my arm and slide it out from beneath her head and punch my temples with both fists until the pain overwhelms my thoughts.

I kick off my blankets; get my legs out from under the sheets. I long for a breeze. I imagine Fran's mother at the bottom of Troost Lake. I think of Tim's puppies and then I think of Kandahar and of other things I've seen. My head throbs. I shut my eyes against the room closing in on me, get up, and go sit in the kitchen. I find my knife, hands shaking. I start tossing it but can't establish a rhythm.

I drop the knife, think of Gene and of dead Koreans calling to him. I imagine he is sitting in his car miles away parked beneath a streetlight unable to sleep. Moths bounce against the windows. Flies strike the windshield. Beetles scuttle across the hood. I tell him that when I was a boy, my friends and I would drop grasshoppers into empty trash barrels and then we'd scream into the barrels and listen to our voices ping-pong against the sides like shrapnel, crumbling antennae, wings, legs. We'd pluck the grasshoppers out barely alive and bury them. I see them now, their jaws working furiously, filling with dirt. Hear the crunch-scrape of seeking mouths sucking air.

LOOT

BY JULIE SMITH
Garden District, New Orleans
(Originally published in *New Orleans Noir*)

Mathilde's in North Carolina with her husband when she hears about the hurricane—the one that's finally going to fulfill the prophecy about filling the bowl New Orleans is built in. Uh-huh, sure. She's been there a thousand times. She all but yawns.

Aren't they all? goes through her mind.

"A storm like no one's ever seen," the weather guy says, "a storm that will leave the city devastated . . . a storm that . . ."

Blah blah and blah.

But finally, after ten more minutes of media hysteria, she catches on that this time it might be for real. Her first thought is for her home in the Garden District, the one that's been in Tony's family for three generations. Yet she knows there's nothing she can do about that—if the storm takes it, so be it.

Her second thought is for her maid, Cherice Wardell, and Cherice's husband, Charles.

Mathilde and Cherice have been together for twenty-two years. They're like an old married couple. They've spent more time with each other than they have with their husbands. They've taken care of each other when one of them was ill. They've cooked for each other (though Cherice has cooked a good deal more for Mathilde). They've shopped together, they've argued, they've shared more secrets than either of them would be comfortable with if they thought about it. They simply chat, the way women do, and things come out, some things that probably shouldn't. Cherice knows intimate facts about Mathilde's sex life, for instance, things she likes to do with Tony, that Mathilde would never tell her white friends.

So Mathilde knows the Wardells plenty well enough to know they aren't about to obey the evacuation order. They never leave when a storm's on the way. They have two big dogs and nowhere to take them. Except for their two children, one of whom is in school in Alabama, and the other in California, the rest of their family lives in New Orleans. So there are no nearby relatives to shelter them. They either can't afford hotels or think they can't (though twice in the past Mathilde has offered to pay for their lodging if they'd only *go*). Only twice because only twice have Mathilde and Tony heeded the warnings themselves. In past years, before everyone worried so much about the disappearing wetlands and the weakened infrastructure, it was a point of honor for people in New Orleans to ride out hurricanes.

But Mathilde is well aware that this is not the case with the Wardells. This is no challenge to them. They simply don't see the point of leaving. They prefer to play what Mathilde thinks of as Louisiana roulette. Having played it a few times herself, she knows all about it. The Wardells think the traffic will be terrible, that they'll be in the car for seventeen, eighteen hours and still not find a hotel because everything from here to kingdom come's going to be taken, even if they could afford it.

"That storm's not gon' come," Cherice always says. "You know it never does. Why I'm gon' pack up these dogs and Charles and go God knows where? You know Mississippi gives me a headache. And I ain't even gon' *mention* Texas."

To which Mathilde replied gravely one time, "This is your life you're gambling with, Cherice."

And Cherice said, "I think I'm just gon' pray."

But Mathilde will have to try harder this time, especially since she's not there.

Cherice is not surprised to see Mathilde's North Carolina number on her caller ID. "Hey, Mathilde," she says. "How's the weather in Highlands?"

"Cherice, listen. This is the Big One. This time, I mean it, I swear to God, you could be—"

"Uh-huh. Gamblin' with my life and Charles's. Listen, if it's the Big One, I want to be here to see it. I wouldn't miss it for the world."

"Cherice, listen to me. I know I'm not going to convince you—you're the pig-headedest woman I've ever seen. Just promise me something. Go to my house. Take the dogs. Ride it out at my house."

"Take the dogs?" Cherice can't believe what she's hearing. Mathilde never lets her bring the dogs over, won't let them inside her house. Hates dogs, has allergies, thinks they'll pee on her furniture. She loves Mathilde, but Mathilde is a pain in the butt, and Cherice mentions this every chance she gets to anyone who'll listen. Mathilde is picky and spoiled and needy. She's good-hearted, sure, but she hates her precious routine disturbed.

Yet this same Mathilde Berteau has just told her to *promise* to take the dogs to her immaculate house. This is so sobering Cherice can hardly think what to say. "Well, I *know* you're worried now."

"Cherice. Promise me."

Cherice hears panic in Mathilde's voice. *What can it hurt?* she thinks. The bed in Mathilde's guest room is a lot more comfortable than hers. Also, if the power goes out—and Cherice has no doubt that it will—she'll have to go to Mathilde's the day after the storm anyhow, to clean out the refrigerator.

Mathilde is ahead of her. "Listen, Cherice, I *need* you to go. I need you to clean out the refrigerator when the power goes. Also, we have a gas stove and you don't. You can cook at my house. We still have those fish Tony caught a couple of weeks ago—they're going to go to waste if you're not there."

Cherice is humbled. Not about the fish offer—that's just like Mathilde, to offer something little when she wants something bigger. That's small potatoes. What gets to her is the refrigerator thing—if Mathilde tells her she needs her for something, she's bringing out the big guns. Mathilde's a master manipulator, and Cherice has seen her pull this one a million times—but not usually on *her*. Mathilde does it when all else fails, and her instincts are damn good—it's a lot easier to turn down a favor than to refuse to grant one. Cherice knows her employer like she knows Charles—better, maybe—but she still feels the pull of Mathilde's flimsy ruse.

"I'll clean your refrigerator, baby," Cherice says carefully. "Don't you worry about a thing."

"Cherice, goddamnit, I'm worried about *you!*"

And Cherice gives in. "I know you are, baby. And Charles and I appreciate it, we really do. Tell you what—we gon' do it. We gon' go over there. I promise." But she doesn't know if she can actually talk Charles into it.

He surprises her by agreeing readily as soon as she mentions the part about the dogs. "Why not?" he says. "We can sleep in Mathilde and Tony's big ol' bed and watch television till the power goes out. Drink a beer and have the dogs with us. Ain't like we have to drive to Mississippi or somethin'. And if the roof blows off, maybe we can save some of their stuff. That refrigerator ain't all she's got to worry about."

"We're *not* sleepin' in their bed, Charles. The damn guest room's like a palace, anyway—who you think you is?"

He laughs at her. "I know it, baby. Jus' tryin' to see how far I can push ya."

So that Sunday they pack two changes of clothes, plenty for two days, and put the mutts in their crates. The only other things they take are dog food and beer. They don't grab food for themselves because there's plenty over at Mathilde's, which they have to eat or it'll go bad.

The first bands of the storm come late that night, and Charles does what he said he was going to—goes to bed with a beer and his dogs. But after he's asleep, Cherice watches the storm from the window of the second-floor living room. The power doesn't go off until early morning, and when the rain swirls, the lights glint on it. The wind howls like a hound. Big as it is, the house shakes. Looking out, Cherice sees a building collapse, a little coffee shop across the street, and realizes how well built the Berteaus' house is. Her own is not. She prays that it will make it. But she knows she will be all right, and so will Charles and the dogs. She is not afraid because she is a Christian woman and she trusts that she will not be harmed.

But she does see the power of God in this. For the first time, she understands why people talk about being God-fearing instead of God-loving, something that's always puzzled her. You *better* have God on your side, she thinks. You just better.

She watches the transformers blow one by one, up and down the street, and goes to bed when the power goes out, finding her way by flashlight, wondering what she's going to wake up to.

The storm is still raging when she stirs, awakened by the smell of bacon. Charles has cooked breakfast, but he's nowhere to be found. She prowls the house looking for him, and the dogs bark to tell her: *third floor.*

"Cherice," he calls down. "Bring pots."

She knows what's happened: leaks. The Berteaus must have lost some shingles.

So she and Charles work for the next few hours, putting pots out, pushing furniture from the path of inrushing water, gathering up wet linens, trying to salvage and dry out papers and books, emptying the pots, replacing them. All morning the wind is dying, though. The thing is blowing through.

By two o'clock it's a beautiful day. "Still a lot of work to do," Charles says, sighing. "But I better go home first, see how our house is. I'll come back and help you. We should sleep here again tonight."

Cherice knows that their house has probably lost its roof, that they might have much worse damage than the Berteaus, maybe even flooding. He's trying to spare her by offering to go alone.

"Let's make some phone calls first," she says.

They try to reach neighbors who rode out the storm at home, but no one answers, probably having not remembered, like Cherice and Charles, to buy car chargers. Indeed, they have only a little power left on their own cell phone, which Cherice uses to call Mathilde. The two women have the dodged-the-bullet talk that everyone in the dry neighborhoods has that day, the day before they find out the levees have breached.

Though they don't yet know about the levees, Cherice nonetheless feels a terrible foreboding about her house, acutely needs to see how badly it's damaged. She doesn't have much hope that the streets will be clear enough to drive, but she and Charles go out in the yard anyhow to remove broken limbs from the driveway.

"Let's listen to the car radio, see if we can get a report," Cherice says, realizing they've been so preoccupied with saving the Berteaus' possessions, they've forgotten to do this.

She opens the car door, is about to enter, when she feels Charles tense beside her. "Cherice," he says.

She turns and sees what he sees: a gang of young men in hooded sweatshirts walking down the street, hands in their pockets. Looking for trouble.

Charles says, "You go on back in the house."

Cherice doesn't need to be told twice. She knows where Tony keeps his gun. She means to get it, but she's so worried about Charles she turns back to look, and sees that he's just standing by the car, hands in pockets, looking menacing. The young men pass by, but she goes for the gun anyway.

By the time she gets back, Charles is back inside, locking the door. "Damn looters," he says. "Goddamn looters." And his face is so sad Cherice wants to hug him, but it's also so angry she knows better. "Why they gotta go and be this way?" he says.

They listen to the Berteaus' little battery-powered radio and learn that there's looting all over the city, crime is out of control. "Ain't safe to go out," Charles says grimly. "Can't even get home to see about our property."

She knows he's sorry they came, that they didn't stay home where they belonged. "I'm gon' fix some lunch."

So they eat and then go out in the backyard and clean it up the best they can, even try to get some of the debris out of the swimming pool, but this is a losing battle. After a while they abandon the project, realizing that it's a beautiful day and they have their dogs and they're together. Even if their house is destroyed.

So they live in the moment. They try to forget the looting, though the sound of sirens is commonplace now. Instead of Tony's fish, they barbecue some steaks that are quickly defrosting, and Cherice fixes some potato salad while the mayonnaise is still good. Because they got so little sleep the night before, and because there's no electricity, they go to bed early.

Sometime in the night they awaken to a relentless thudding—no, a pounding on the Berteaus' door. "I'm goin'," Charles says grimly, and Cherice notices he tucks Tony's gun into the jeans he pulls on.

She can't just stay here and wait to see what happens. She creeps down the stairs behind him.

"Yeah?" Charles says through the door.

"I'm the next-door neighbor," a man says. "I've got Tony on the phone."

Charles opens the door and takes the man's cell phone. He listens for a while, every now and then saying, "Oh shit." Or, "Oh God. No." Cherice pulls on his elbow, mouthing *What?* to him, terrified. But he turns away, ignoring her, still listening, taking in whatever it is. Finally, he says, "Okay. We'll leave first thing."

Still ignoring Cherice, he gives the phone back to the neighbor. "You know about all this?" he says. The man only nods, and Cherice sees that he's crying. Grown man, looks like an Uptown banker, white hair and everything, with tears running down his cheeks, biting his lip like a little kid.

She's frantic. She's grabbing at Charles, all but pinching him, desperately trying to get him to just finish up and tell her what's going on. Finally, he turns around, and she's never seen him look like this, like maybe one of their kids has died or something.

He says only, "Oh, baby," and puts his arms around her. She feels his body buck, and realizes that he's crying too, that he can't hold it in anymore, whatever it is. Has one of their kids died?

Finally, he pulls himself together enough to tell her what's happened—that the city is flooded, their neighborhood is destroyed, some of their neighbors are probably dead. Their own children thought *they* were dead until they finally got Tony and Mathilde.

Cherice cannot take this in. She tries, but she just can't. "Eighty percent of the city is underwater?" she repeats over and over. "How can that be?"

They live in a little brick house in New Orleans East, a house they worked hard to buy, that's a stretch to maintain, but it's worth it. They have a home, a little piece of something to call their own.

But now we don't, Cherice thinks. *It's probably gone. We don't have nothin'.*

In the end, she can't go that way. She reasons that an entire neighborhood can't be destroyed, *something's* got to be left, and maybe her house is. She wants to go see for herself.

296 // USA NOIR

"Cherice, you gotta pay attention," Charles says. "Only way to go see it's to swim. Or get a boat maybe. There's people all over town on rooftops right now, waitin' to be rescued. There's still crazy lootin' out there. The mayor wants everybody out of town."

"That's what he said *before* the storm."

"He's sayin' it again. We goin' to Highlands tomorrow."

"Highlands?"

"Well, where else we gon' go? Mathilde and Tony got room for us, they say come, get our bearings, then we'll see. Besides, Mathilde wants us to bring her some things."

There it is again—Mathilde asking a favor to get them to leave. So that's how serious it is. Well, Cherice knew that, sort of. But it keeps surprising her, every time she thinks about it.

"How we gon' get out with all that lootin' goin' on?" she says. "Might even be snipers."

"Tony says the best way's the bridge. We can just go on over to the West Bank—we leavin' first thing in the morning. And I mean *first* thing—before anybody's up and lootin'. Let's try to get a few more hours sleep."

Cherice knows this is impossible, but she agrees because she wants to be close to Charles, to hold him, even if neither of them sleeps.

De La Russe is in the parking lot at the Tchoupitoulas Wal-Mart, thinking this whole thing is a clusterfuck of undreamed-of proportions, really wanting to break some heads (and not all of them belonging to looters), when Jack Stevens arrives in a district car. Sergeant Stevens is a big ol' redhead, always spewing the smart remarks, never taking a damn thing seriously, and today is no different.

"Hey, Del—think it's the end of the world or what?"

De La Russe is not in the mood for this kind of crap. "There's no goddamn chain of command here, Jack. Couple of officers came in, said they got orders to just let the looters have at it, but who am I s'posed to believe? Can't get nobody on the radio, the phones, the goddamn cell phones—" He pauses, throws his own cell across the concrete parking lot. It lands with something more like a mousy skitter than a good solid thud.

He has quite a bit more to say on the subject, but Stevens interrupts. "What the hell you do that for?"

"Why I need the goddamn thing? Nobody's gonna answer, nobody fuckin' cares where I am, nobody's where they're supposed to be, and I can't get nothin' but a fuckin' busy anyhow. Nothing around here . . . fuckin' . . . *works!* Don't you . . . fuckin' . . . get it?"

"Del, my man, you seem a little stressed."

De La Russe actually raises his nightstick.

"Hey. Take it easy; put that down, okay. Ya friend Jack's here. We gon' get through this thing together. All right, man?"

For a moment, De La Russe feels better, as if he isn't alone in a world gone savage—looters busting into all the stores, proclaiming them "open for business"; whole families going in and coming out loaded down with televisions and blasters and power tools (as if there's gonna be power anytime soon), right in front of half the police in the parish. Sure, De La Russe could follow procedure, order them out of there, holler, *Freeze, asshole!* like a normal day, but which one of 'em's gonna listen? In the end, what's he gonna do, shoot the place up? It's not like he's getting any backup from his brother officers and, as he's just told Stevens, it's not like he can get anybody on the goddamn phone anyway. Or the radio. Or anyhow at all.

"Now, first thing we're gon' do is go in there and get you another phone," Stevens says.

De La Russe knows what he means, and he's not even shocked. What's going on here is nothing short of the breakdown of society, and he thinks he's going to have to roll with it. Something about having Stevens with him is kind of reassuring; he *is* a sergeant—not Del's sergeant, but still, if he heard right, a sergeant in the New Orleans Police Department has just told him to go into Wal-Mart and loot himself a phone.

Just to be sure, he tries something out: "Loot one, you mean."

"Hell no! We're gonna *commandeer* you one." And Stevens about kills himself laughing.

They hitch their trousers and push past several boiling little seas of people, seemingly working in groups, helping themselves to everything from baby food to fishing poles. Nobody even glances at their uniforms.

"Why are we bothering with the goddamn phone?" De La Russe asks. "Damn things don't work anyhow."

"Yeah, you right," Stevens says. "But just in case." He turns to the busy knot of looters on the small appliances aisle and grabs himself one at random—a woman. Just shoves an arm around her, gets up under her chin, and pulls her against his body. De La Russe sees her pupils dilate, her eyeballs about pop out of her head with fear. Stevens whispers something in her ear and she nods.

When he lets her go, she reaches in the pocket of her jeans and comes out with a cell phone, which she hands over, meek as you please. Stevens passes it to De La Russe. "Now ya back in business." He swings his arms wide. "Anything else ya need?"

De La Russe feels sweat break out on his forehead. His scalp starts to prickle, and so do his toes. His heart speeds up a little. Weirdest part of all, he's actually having a sexual reaction; he's getting hard. Not all the way hard, just a little excited, like when he sees a woman he likes, maybe lights a cigarette for her, brushes her thigh, but that's all, no kiss or anything. A woman who isn't his wife but someone who's not supposed to get him excited. This is how he feels now, except with sweat and prickles. Because he's pretty sure this is not an idle question Stevens is asking. Thing about Stevens, there's rumors about him. About how he makes stuff disappear from the property room, shakes suspects down for drugs, little stuff that tells you a lot.

Thing about De La Russe, he's not above the same kind of thing. And he doesn't need rumors, he's been disciplined and everybody knows it. Yeah, he's been clean since then, but he's starting to feel this is something else again, this thing he's looking at. This thing that's nothing less than the breakdown of the social contract. It's just occurring to him that people are going to profit from this, and they're not just gonna be the Pampers-and-toothpaste thieves. He decides to get right down to it.

"What are you saying, sergeant?"

"Hell, Del, it's the end of the world and you're callin' me sergeant—what's up with that shit?" But he knows perfectly well.

De La Russe smiles. "I was just wondering if I heard you right." He waits for an answer, not allowing the smile to fade. Keeping his teeth bared.

"Remember that little eBay bi'ness you told me you and ya wife was runnin'? How she goes to garage sales and finds things she can sell to collectors? And then you photograph 'em and get 'em on up online? Y'all still doin' that?"

"Yeah. We still doin' that. Why?"

Stevens looks at him like he's nuts. "Why? Think about it, Del. You can sell just about anything on eBay." He pauses, does the wide-open this-could-all-be-yours thing again. "And we got access to just about anything."

De La Russe is getting his drift. His mind's racing, going instantly to the problems and working on solutions. He shrugs. "Yeah? Where would we store it?"

"Glad you axed, bro. Just happens I already hooked up with a lieutenant who's got a room at the Hyatt." The Hyatt has become the department's temporary headquarters. "He's got access to a couple other rooms we could use. And I don't mean hotel rooms. Storage rooms. Pretty big ones. We keep it there for now and when things get back to normal, somebody's garage, maybe."

De La Russe narrows his eyes. "What lieutenant?"

"Joe Dougald."

The patrolman almost does a double take. "Joe Dougald? You're dreaming. Guy's a boy scout."

Stevens hoots. "Yeah? Ya think so? I been doin' deals with Joe for fifteen years. Trust me. We can trust him."

De La Russe isn't sure if he even trusts Stevens, much less Dougald, but what the hell, the regular rules just don't seem to apply now that the apocalypse, or whatever this is, has come crashing in on them. And he's got two kids in Catholic school, with college looming. *That's* not going away.

He assesses the place. "Let's start with little stuff that's easy to carry. iPods, video games, stuff like that. Electronics, small appliances. Hey, do they have jewelry here?" He gives a little snort. Wal-Mart jewelry isn't going to make them rich, even if it exists. "Watches, maybe?"

Stevens smiles as if he likes the way De La Russe is getting into this. "This ain't the only store in town, ya know. And stores ain't the only sources we got. You're from the Second District, right? People there got real nice taste."

De La Russe decides he's just fallen into a real deal. Here they are, right this minute, he and Stevens, policing Wal-Mart and helping themselves while they're at it. He sees how he can patrol his own district, get credit for coming to work, arrest a few of the real looters—the street guys—and help himself to whatever he wants while everybody's still out of town. How come he hadn't thought of it first?

It's early the next day when De La Russe sees the black couple—oh, excuse *him*, the two African-Americans—packing up their car in front of the biggest-ass goddamn house in the Garden District, or so near it doesn't matter. What the hell are they thinking? There aren't any cops around here? He decides he's really going to enjoy this.

He parks his car and strolls up all casual, like he's just gonna talk to 'em. "How y'all?" Dicking with them.

They go rigid though. They know from the get-go he's trouble, and it has to be because of their guilty little consciences. "What y'all doing?"

"Leavin'," the man says. "Gettin' out of town quick as we can. You want to see some ID? My wife works here and the owners are in North Carolina. So we rode out the storm here." He starts to put his hand in his pocket, maybe to get the ID, and that gives De La Russe an excuse to slam him up against the car, like he thinks the guy's going to go for a weapon.

He pats the man down, and sure enough, there is one. Doesn't *that* just sweeten this whole deal. Worth a lot to a couple guys he knows. "You got a permit for this?"

The guy doesn't answer, but his wife pipes up: "It's not ours. It belongs to Tony. My employer. When the looters came . . ."

De La Russe smiles. ". . . ya thought it might be okay to steal ya boss's gun, huh? You know how pathetic that story sounds? Know who I think the looters are? Yeah. Yeah, I guess ya do. Let's see what else ya got here."

The woman says, "My boss, Mathilde . . . she asked me to bring—"

"Mrs. Berteau," the man says. "My wife works for Mathilde Berteau."

"Right," says De La Russe. "Y'all get in the backseat for a while."

"What about . . . ?" The woman's already crying, knowing exactly what's in store for her. He grabs her by the elbow and rassles her into the car, shoving her good, just for the fun of it.

"What about what?"

"Nothin', I just . . ."

The husband is yelling now. "Listen, call the Berteaus. All you have to do is call 'em, goddammit! Just call 'em and let 'em tell you."

"Like there was the least chance of that," Cherice says ten months later. The encounter had led to the misery and indignity of incarceration for three days and two nights, plus the humiliation of being accused of looting—almost the hardest part to bear. But she has survived, she and Charles, to tell the story at a Fourth of July barbecue.

"Know why I was wastin' my breath?" Charles chimes in. "'Cause that peckerwood was enjoyin' himself. Wasn't about to ruin his own good time."

She and Charles are living in Harvey now, in a rental, not a FEMA trailer, thank God, until they decide what to do about their gutted house. Their families have all heard the story many times over, but they've made new friends here on the West Bank, people they haven't yet swapped Katrina yarns with. Right now they have the rapt attention of Wyvette Johnson and her boyfriend Brandin. Cherice didn't catch his last name.

Wyvette gets tears in her eyes. "Mmmm. Mmmm. What about those poor dogs?"

This annoys Cherice, because it's getting ahead of the way she usually tells it. But she says, "I nearly blurted out that they were there at the last minute . . . before he took us away. But I thought they'd have a better chance if he didn't know about 'em. *Last* thing I wanted was to get my dogs stole by some redneck cop." Here she lets a sly smile play across her face. "Anyhow, I knew once Mathilde knew they was still in the house, that was gon' give her a extra reason to come get us out."

"Not that she needed it," Charles adds. "She was happy as a pig in shit to hear we'd been dragged off to jail. I mean, not jail, more like a chain-link cage, and then the actual Big House. I ended up at Angola, you believe that? The jail flooded, remember that? And then they turned the train station into a jail. Oh man, that was some third world shit! Couldn't get a phone call for nothin', and like I say, they put you in a cage. But one thing—it was the only damn thing in the city that whole week that worked halfway right. Kept you there a couple days, shipped you right out to Angola. But they got the women out of there just about right away. So Cherice was up at St. Gabriel—you know, where the women's prison is—in just about twenty-four hours flat. And after that, it wasn't no problem. 'Cause they actually had working phones there."

Wyvette is shaking her silky dreads. "I think I'm missin' somethin' here—did you say Mathilde was *happy* y'all were in jail?"

"Well, not exactly," Cherice says. "She was *outraged*— 'specially since I'd been there for two days when they finally let me make the call. It's just that outrage is her favorite state of mind. See, who Mathilde is—I gotta give you her number; every black person in Louisiana oughta have it on speed dial—who Mathilde is, she's the toughest civil rights lawyer in the state. That's why Charles made sure to say her name. But that white boy just said, 'Right,' like he didn't believe us. Course, we knew for sure she was gon' hunt him down and fry his ass. Or die tryin'. But that didn't make it no better at the time. In the end, Mathilde made us famous though. Knew she would."

"Yeah, but we wouldn't've got on CNN if it hadn't been for you," Charles says, smiling at her. "Or in the *New York Times* neither."

Wyvette and Brandin are about bug-eyed.

"See what happened," Charles continues, "Cherice went on eBay and found Mathilde's mama's engagement ring, the main thing she wanted us to bring to Highlands. Those cops were so arrogant they just put it right up there. In front of God and everybody."

"But how did you know to do that?" Wyvette asks, and Cherice thinks it's a good question.

"I didn't," she says. "I just felt so bad for Mathilde I was tryin' anything and everywhere. Anyhow, once we found the jewelry, the cops set up a sting, busted the whole crime ring—there was three of 'em. Found a whole garage full of stuff they hadn't sold yet."

Brandin shakes his head and waves his beer. "Lawless times. Lawless times we live in."

And Cherice laughs. "Well, guess what? We got to do a little lootin' of our own. You ever hear of Priscilla Smith-Fredericks? She's some big Hollywood producer. Came out and asked if she could buy our story for fifteen thousand dollars, you believe that? Gonna do a TV movie about what happened to us. I should feel bad about it, but those people got *way* more money than sense."

Right after the holiday, Marty Carrera of Mojo Mart Productions finds himself in a meeting with a young producer who has what sounds to him like a good idea. Priscilla Smith-Fredericks lays a hand on his wrist, which he doesn't much care for, but he tries not to cringe.

"Marty," she says. "I *believe* in this story. This is an important story to tell—a story about corruption, about courage, about one woman's struggle for justice in an unjust world. But most of all, it's the story of two women, two women who've been together for twenty-two years—one the maid, the other the boss—about the love they have for each other, the way their lives are inextricably meshed. In a good way.

"I want to do this picture for *them* and . . . well . . . for the whole state of Louisiana. You know what? That poor state's been screwed enough different ways it could write a sequel to the *Kama Sutra*. It's been screwed by FEMA, it's been screwed by the Corps of Engineers, it's been screwed by the administration, it's been screwed by its own crooked officials . . . *Everybody's* picking carrion off its bones. And those poor Wardells! I want to do this for the Wardells. Those people have a house to rebuild. They need the money and they need the . . . well, the lift. The *vindication*."

Marty Carrera looks at the paperwork she's given him. She proposes to pay the Wardells a $15,000 flat fee, which seems low to him. Standard would be about $75,000, plus a percentage of the gross and maybe a $10,000 "technical consultant" fee. He shuffles pages, wondering if she's done what he suspects.

And yes, of course she has. She's inflated her own fee at the expense of the Wardells. She thinks she should get $100,000 as an associate producer, about twice what the job is worth. And not only that, she wants to award the technical consultant's fee to herself.

Marty is genuinely angry about this. She's roused his sympathy for the wrongfully accused couple, and even for the beleaguered state, and he too be-lieves the Wardells' story—or more properly, Mathilde and Cherice's story—would make a great movie for television.

However, he thinks Ms. Smith-Fredericks is a species of vermin. "After looking at the figures," he says, "I think I can honestly say that you seem uniquely qualified to do a piece on looting."

But she doesn't catch his meaning. She's so full of herself all she hears is what she wants to hear. She sticks out her hand to shake.

Well, so be it, Marty thinks. *I tried to warn her.*

His production company doesn't need her. So what if she found the story and brought it to him? He's not obligated to . . . Well, he is, but . . .

"Marty," she says, "we're going to be great together."

He shakes her hand absentmindedly, already thinking of ways to cut her out of the deal.

THE PRISON

BY DOMENIC STANSBERRY
North Beach
(Originally published in *San Francisco Noir*)

It was 1946, and Alcatraz was burning. I had just got back into town and stood in the crowd along the seawall, looking out toward the island. The riot at the prison had been going on for several days, and now a fire had broken out and smoke plumed out over the bay. There were all kinds of rumors running through the crowd. The prisoners had taken over. Warden Johnston was dead. Capone's gang had seized a patrol boat and a group of escapees had landed down at Baker Beach. The radio contradicted these reports, but from the seawall you could see that a marine flotilla had surrounded Alcatraz Island and helicopters were pouring tracer fire into the prison. The police had the wharf cordoned off but it didn't prevent the crowds from gathering. The off-duty sailors and Presidio boys mixing with the peace-time johnnies. The office girls and Chinese skirts. The Sicilians with their noses like giant fish.

In the crowd were people I knew from the old days. Some of them met my eyes, some didn't. My old friend Johnny Maglie stood in a group maybe ten yards away. He gave me a nod, but it wasn't him I was looking at. There was a woman, maybe twenty-five years old, black hair, wearing a red cardigan. Her name was Anne but I didn't know this yet. Her eyes met mine and I felt something fall apart inside me.

My father had given me a gun before I left Reno. He had been a figure in North Beach before the war—an editor, a man with opinions, and he used to carry a little German revolver in his vest pocket. The gun had been confiscated after Pearl Harbor, but he'd gotten himself another somewhere along the way and pressed it into my hand in the train station. A gallant, meaningless gesture.

"Take this," he said.

"I don't need a gun."

"You may be a war hero," he said, "but there are people in North Beach who hate me. Who have always hated me. They will go after you."

I humored the old man and took the gun. Truth was, he was ill. He and

Sal Fusco had sent me to borrow some money from a crab fisherman by the name of Giovanni Pellicano. More than that, though, my father wanted me to talk with my mother. He wanted me to bring her on the train back to Reno.

Johnny Maglie broke away from his little group—the ex-soldiers with their chests out and the office janes up on their tiptoes, trying to get a glimpse of the prison. Maglie was a civilian now, looking good in his hat, his white shirt, his creases. My old friend extended his hand and I thought about my father's gun in my pocket.

I have impulses sometimes, ugly thoughts.

Maybe it was the three years I'd spent in the Pacific. Or maybe it was just something inside me. Still inside me.

Either way, I imagined myself sticking the gun in my old friend's stomach and pulling the trigger.

"So you're back in town," said Maglie.

"Yeah, I'm back."

Maglie put his arm around me. He and I had grown up together, just down the street. We had both served in the Pacific theater, though in different divisions. He had served out the campaign, but I'd come back in '44—after I was wounded the second time around, taking some shrapnel in my chest. This was my first time back to The Beach. Johnny knew the reason I had stayed away, I figured, but it wasn't something we were going to talk about.

"We fought the Japs, we win the goddamn war—but it looks like the criminals are going to come back and storm the city."

I had liked Maglie once, but I didn't know how I felt about him anymore.

"You going to stick around town for a while?"

"Haven't decided," I said.

"How's your mom?"

"Good."

He didn't mention my father. No one mentioned my father.

"You know," he stuttered, and I saw in his face the mix of shame and awkwardness that I'd seen more than once in the faces of the people who'd known my family—who'd moved in the same circles. And that included just about everybody in The Beach. Some of them, of course, played it the other way now. They held their noses up, they smirked. "You know," he said, "I was getting some papers drawn up yesterday—down at Uncle's place—and your name came up . . ."

He stopped then. Maybe it was because he saw my expression at the mention of his uncle, the judge. Or maybe it was because the cops were herding us away, or because a blonde in Maglie's group gave a glance in his direction.

"Join us," he said. "We're going to Fontana's."

I was going to say no. And probably I should have. But the girl in the red cardigan was a member of their group.

For twenty years, my father had run the Italian-language paper, *Il Carnevale*. He had offices down at Columbus, and all the Italian *culturatti* used to stop by when they came through the city. Enrico Caruso. The great Marconi. Even Vittorio Mussolini, the aviator.

My father had been a public man. Fridays, to the opera. Saturdays, to Cavelli's Books—to stand on the sidewalk and listen to Il Duce's radio address. On Tuesdays, he visited the Salesian school. The young boys dressed in the uniforms of the Faciso Giovanile, and my father gave them lectures on the beauty of the Italian language.

I signed up in December, '41.

A few weeks later my father's office was raided. His paper was shut down. Hearings were held. My father and a dozen others were sent to a detention camp in Montana. My mother did not put this news in her letters. Sometime in '43 the case was reviewed and my father was released, provided he did not take up residence in a state contiguous to the Pacific Ocean. When I came home, with my wounds and my letters of commendation, my stateside commander suggested it might a good idea, all things considered, if I too stayed away from the waterfront.

But none of this is worth mentioning. Anyway, I am an old man now and there are times I don't know what day it is, what year. Or maybe I just don't care. I look up at the television, and that man in the nice suit, he could be Mussolini. He could be Stalin. He could be Missouri Harry, with his show-me smile and his atomic bomb. This hospital, there are a million old men like me, a million stories. They wave their hands. They tell how they hit it big, played their cards, made all the right decisions. If they made a mistake, it wasn't their fault; it was that asshole down the block. Myself, I say nothing. I smell their shit. Some people get punished. Some of us, we get away with murder.

"You on leave?"

Anne had black hair and gray eyes and one of those big smiles that drew you in. There was something a bit off about her face, a skewed symmetry—a nose flat at the bridge, thin lips, a smile that was wide and crooked. The way she looked at you, she was brash and demure at the same time. A salesman's daughter, maybe. She regarded me with her head tilted, looking up. Amused, wry. Something irrepressible in her eyes. Or almost irrepressible.

"No, no," I said. "I've been out of the service for a while now."

She glanced at my hand, checking for the ring. I wasn't wearing one— but she was. It was on the engagement finger, which she tucked away when she saw me looking. What this meant, exactly, I didn't know. Some of the girls wore engagement rings the whole time their fiancés were overseas, then dumped the guy the instant he strolled off the boat. Anne didn't look like that type, but you never knew.

As for me, like I said, I wasn't wearing any kind of ring—in spite of Julia Fusco, back in Reno. We weren't married, but . . .

"I grew up here."

"In The Beach?"

"Yes."

She smiled at that—like she had known the answer, just looking.

"And you?"

"I've been out East for a while," she said. "But I grew up here, too."

"But not in The Beach?" I asked, though I knew the answer, the same way she had known about me.

"No, no. Dolores Heights."

The area out there in the Mission was mostly Irish those days, though there were still some German families up in the Heights. Entrepreneurs. Jews. Here before the Italians, before the Irish. Back when the ships still came around the horn.

"Where did you serve?"

I averted my eyes, and she didn't pursue it. Maybe because I had that melancholy look that says *don't ask any more*. I glanced at a guy dancing in front of the juke with his girlfriend, and I thought of my gun and had another one of my ugly moments. I took a drink because that helped sometimes. It helped me push the thoughts away. The place was loud and raucous. Maglie and his blonde were sitting across from me, chatting it up, but I couldn't hear a word. One of the other girls said something, and Anne laughed. I laughed too, just for the hell of it.

I took another drink.

Fontana's had changed. It had used to be only Italians came here, and you didn't see a woman without her family. But that wasn't true anymore. Or at least it wasn't true this night. The place had a fevered air, like there was something people were trying to catch on to. Or maybe it was just the jailbreak.

Maglie came over to my side and put his arm around my shoulders once again. He had always been like this. One drink and he was all sentimental.

"People don't know it," he said. "Even round the neighborhood, they don't know it. But Jojo here, he did more than his share. Out there in the Pacific."

"People don't want to hear about this," I said. There was an edge in my voice, maybe a little more than there should have been.

"No," said Maglie. "But they should know."

I knew what Maglie was doing. Trying to make it up to me in some way. Letting me know that whatever happened to my father, in that hearing, it wasn't his idea. And to prove it, I could play the hero in front of this girl from The Heights with her cardigan and her pearls and that ring on her finger.

I turned to Anne.

"You?" I asked. "Where were you during the war?"

She gave me a little bit of her story then. About how she had been studying back East when the war broke out. Halfway through the war, she'd graduated and gotten a job with the VA, in a hospital, on the administrative side. But now that job was done—they'd given it to a returning soldier— and she was back home.

The jukebox was still playing.

"You want to dance?"

She was a little bit taller than me, but I didn't mind this. Sinatra was crooning on the juke. I wanted to hold her closer, but I feared she'd feel the gun in my pocket. Then I decided I didn't care.

I glanced at the ring on her finger, and she saw me looking.

"Where is he?" I asked.

"Berlin."

I didn't say anything. Frank went on crooning. Some of my father's friends, I remembered them talking about the Berlin of the old days. About the cabarets and the bigmouthed blondes with husky voices who made the bulge in their pants grow like Pinocchio's nose.

"He, my fiancé—he's a lieutenant," she said. "And there's the reconstruction. He thought it was important, not just to win the war. Not just to defeat them. But to build it back."

"He's an idealist."

"Yes."

I wondered how come she had fallen for him. I wondered if she had known him long. Or if it had been one of those things where you meet somebody and you can't escape. You fall in a whirlwind.

* * *

At that moment, inside Alcatraz, Bernie Coy and five other convicts were pinned down in the cellblock. None of us in the bar knew that yet, or even knew their names. If you wanted to know what was going on inside Alcatraz, the best you could do was climb up a rooftop and listen to the radio—but it was too far to see, and the radio was filtered by the military. Anyway, prison officials weren't talking. They were too busy to talk. Later, though, it came out how Bernie Coy was the brains. He knew the guards' routines. He'd managed to crow apart the bars and lead a handful of prisoners into the gun room. He and his buddies had clubbed the guards, taken their keys, and headed down the hall to the main yard; but the last door in the long line of doors would not open. The keys were not on the ring. They had all the ammunition in the world, but they could not get past that door. Now they were pinned down, cornered by the fire on one side and the guards on the other. So they fought, the way men in a foxhole fight. Our boys in Normandy. The Japanese in those bloody caves. The floodlights swept the shore and the tracer bullets lit the sky, and they fought the way desperate men fight, creeping forward on their bellies.

Sinatra was winding it up now, and I pulled Anne a little closer. Then I noticed a man watching us. He was sitting at the same table as Maglie and the rest. He was still watching when Anne and I walked back.

He put his arm around Anne, and they seemed to know each other better than I would like.

"This is Davey," Anne said.

"Mike's best friend," he said.

I didn't get it at first, and then I did. Mike was Anne's fiancé, and Davey was keeping his eye out.

Davey had blue eyes and yellow hair. When he spoke, first thing, I thought he was a Brit, but I was wrong.

"London?" I asked.

"No, California," he smiled. "Palo Alto. Educated abroad."

He had served with Anne's fiancé over in Germany. But unlike Mike, he had not re-enlisted. Apparently he was not quite so idealistic.

"Part of my duties, far as my best friend," he said, "are to make sure nothing happens to Anne."

The Brit laughed then. Or he was still the Brit to me. A big man, with a big laugh, hard to dislike, but I can't say I cared for him. He joined our group anyway. We ate then and we drank. We had antipasti. We had crabs and shrimp. We had mussels and linguini. Every once in a while someone would come in from the street with news. *At the Yacht Harbor now . . . three men in a rowboat . . . the marines are inside, cell-to-cell, shooting them in their cots.* At some point, Ellen Pagione, Fontana's sister-in-law, came out of the kitchen to make a fuss over me.

"I had no idea you were back in town." She pressed her cheek against mine. "This boy is my favorite," she said. "My goddamn favorite."

Part of me liked the attention, I admit, but another part, I knew better. Ellen Pagione had never liked my father. Maybe she didn't approve of what had happened to him, though, and felt bad. Or maybe she had pointed a finger herself. Either way, she loved me now. Everyone in North Beach, we loved one another now.

Anne smiled. Girl that she was, she believed the whole thing.

A little while later, she leaned toward me. She was a little in her cups maybe. Her cheeks were flush.

"I want to take you home."

Then she looked away. I wondered if I'd heard correctly. The table was noisy. Then the Brit raised his glass, and everyone was laughing.

After dinner, Johnny Maglie grabbed me at the bar. I was shaking inside, I'm not sure why. Johnny wanted to buy me a beer, and I went along, though I knew I'd had enough. There comes a time, whatever the drink is holding under, it comes back up all of a sudden and there's nothing you can do. At the moment, I didn't care. I caught a glimpse of Anne. Some of the others had left, but she was still at the table. So was the Brit.

"How's your mom?" It was the same question Johnny had asked before, out on the street, but maybe he'd forgotten.

"She's got her dignity," I said.

"That's right. Your mama. She's always got her head up." He was a little drunk and a smirk showed on his face.

I knew what people said about my mother. Or I could guess, anyway. She was a Northern Italian, like my father, from Genoa. Refinement was important to her. We were not wealthy, but this wasn't the point. My father had only been a newspaperman, but it had been a newspaper of ideas, and the *prominenti* had respected him. Or so we had thought. My mother had tried for a little while to live in Montana, outside the camp where he was imprisoned, but it had been too remote, too brutal. So she had gone back to North Beach and lived with her sister. Now the war was over, and the restrictions had been lifted, but my father would not return. He had been disgraced, after all. And the people who could have helped him then—the people to whom he had catered, people like Judge Molinari, Johnny Maglie's uncle—they had done nothing for him. Worse than nothing.

"Are you going to stay in The Beach?" Johnny asked.

I didn't answer. My father worked in one of the casinos in Reno now, dealing cards. He lived in a clapboard house with Sal Fusco and Sal's daughter, Julia. Julia took care of them both.

About two months ago something had happened between Julia and me. It was the kind of thing that happens sometimes. To be honest, I didn't feel much toward her other than loyalty.

"So what are you going to do?"

I glanced toward Anne. The Brit had slid closer and was going on in that big-chested way of his.

"I don't know."

But I did know. There was a little roadhouse on the edge of Reno with some slots and card tables. Sal Fusco wanted my father and I to go into business with him. To get the loan, all I had to do was shake hands with Pellicano, the crab fisherman. But my father, I knew, did not really care about the roadhouse. All he wanted was for my mother to come to Reno.

I had spoken to my mother just hours before.

"If this is what you want, I will do it," she said.

"It's not for me. It's for him."

"Your father can come back here. The war is over."

"He has his pride."

"We all have our shame. You get used to it. At least here, I can wear my mink to the opera."

"There is no opera anymore."

"There will be again soon," she said. "But if this is what you want, I will go to Reno. If this is what my son wants . . ."

I understood something then. She blamed my father. Someone needed to take blame, and he was the one. And part of me, I understood. Part of me didn't want to go back to Reno either.

"It's what I want," I said.

Johnny Maglie looked at me with those big eyes of his. He wanted something from me. Like Ellen Pagione wanted. Like my father wanted. Like Julia Fusco. For a minute, I hated them all.

"I know how you used to talk about going into law," Johnny said. "Before all this business."

"Before all what business?"

"Before the war . . ." he stammered. "That's all I meant. I know you wanted to be an attorney."

"Everything's changed."

"My uncle—he said he would write a letter for you. Not just any school. Stanford. Columbia. His recommendation, it carries weight."

I would be lying if I said I didn't feel a rush of excitement—that I didn't sense a door opening and a chance to walk into another life.

"Is it because he feels guilty?" I asked. "Because of what happened to my father? He was at the hearing, wasn't he?"

Johnny looked at me blankly, as if he didn't understand.

"I saw Jake yesterday."

Jake was Judge Molinari's boy. He was a sweet-faced kid. His father's pride and joy. He'd done his tour in Sicily and distinguished himself, from what I heard.

"How's he doing?"

"Getting married."

"Good for him."

Back at the table, the Brit raised another glass. Beside him, Anne was beautiful. The way the Brit was looking at her, I didn't guess he was thinking about his buddy overseas.

I was born circa 1921. The records aren't exact. It doesn't matter. Like I said, there are times, these days, when I can't place the current date either. It is 1998, maybe. Or 2008. The nurse who takes care of me—who scoots me up off my ass and empties my bedpan—she was born in Saigon, just before the fall. 1971, I think. French Vietnamese, but the French part doesn't matter here in the States. Either way, she doesn't give a fuck about me. Outside the sunlight is white, and I glimpse the airplanes descending. We have a new air-port, a new convention center. Every place, these days, has a new convention center. Every place you go, there are airplanes descending and signs advertising a casino on the edge of town.

I close my eyes. The Brit gets up all of a sudden, goes out into the night. I see Anne alone at the table. I see my father dealing cards in Reno. I see Julia Fusco in my father's kitchen, fingers on her swollen belly.

My kid. My son.

A few days ago, for recreation, they wheeled us to the convention center. We could have been anywhere. Chicago. Toronto. I spotted a couple in the hotel bar, and it didn't take a genius to see what was going on.

You can try to fuck your way out. You can work the slot. You can run down the long hall but in the end the door is locked and you are on your belly, crawling through smoke.

No one escapes.

The nurse comes, rolls me over.

Go to sleep, she says. *Go to fucking sleep.*

"I was on Guam." Anne and I were outside now, just the two of us. The evening was all but over. "The Japanese were on top of the hill. A machine-gun nest."

One of the marine choppers was overhead now, working in a widening gyre. The wind had shifted and you could smell the smoke from the prison.

"Is it hard?"

"What?"

"The memories?"

"Of the war, you mean."

"Yes, the war."

I didn't know what to say. "A lot of people on both sides," I made a vague gesture. "Us or them. Sometimes, the difference, I don't know." I felt the confusion inside of me. I saw the dead Japs in their nest. "I don't know what pulls people through."

She looked at me then. She smiled. "Love."

"What?"

She was a little shier now. "Something greater than themselves. A dedication to that. To someone they love. Or to something."

"To an idea?"

"Yes," she said. "An idea."

What she said, it didn't explain anything, not really, but it was the kind of thing people were saying those days—in the aftermath of all the killing. I felt myself falling for it, just like you fall for the girl in the movie. For a moment, she wasn't Anne anymore, the girl from The Heights. She was something else, her face sculpted out of light.

She smiled.

"I'm old-fashioned," she said. "Why don't you get me a taxi?"

Then I had an idea. I didn't have to go to Reno. I could just walk up Columbus with Anne. We could catch a taxi. And we could keep going. Not out to Dolores Heights, or Liberty Heights, or wherever it was she lived. But beyond the neighborhoods . . . beyond the city . . . out through the darkened fields . . . carried along on a river of light.

Then from behind came a loud voice. It belonged to the Brit and it boomed right through me.

"Anne," he said. "I have gotten us a taxi."

I felt her studying me, reading my face. I felt her hand on my back. The Brit opened the taxi door.

My legs were shaking as I headed down the alley. I could hear the copters still, and the sirens along the waterfront. As I walked deeper into the neighborhood, I heard the old sounds too. An aria from an open window. Old men neighing. Goats on a hillside. I was drunk. At some point I had taken my father's gun out of my pocket. It was a beautiful little gun. I could have gotten into the taxi, I supposed. Or I could find Anne tomorrow. But I knew that wasn't going to happen. I had other responsibilities. I hadn't been in The Beach for a while, and I was disoriented. The alley was familiar and not familiar. Rome, maybe. Calabria. An alley of tradesmen, maybe an accountant or two, in the offices over the street. I saw a figure ahead, coming out of a door, and I recognized the corner. Judge Molinari had his office upstairs. Had for years. But this was a younger man. He turned to lock the door. Go the other way, I thought. Don't come toward me. But on he came. Jake Molinari, the judge's son. With the war behind him and a bride waiting. I hadn't planned to be here, but here I was. There are things you don't escape. In the dark, he was smiling to himself. Or I thought he was. He raised his eyes. He saw me. He saw the gun in my hand and his mouth opened. I thought of my father and Julia Fusco, and I shot him. He fell against the alley wall. Then all I could see was Anne. Her face was a blinding light. A flash in the desert. The man lay at my feet now. I shot him again.

At the top of the hill, I paused to look back. I knew how it was but I looked anyway. The sky over the bay was red. Alcatraz was still burning.

HELPER

BY JOSEPH BRUCHAC

Adirondacks, New York
(Originally published in *Indian Country Noir*)

T he one with the missing front teeth. He's the one who shot me. Before his teeth were missing.

Getting shot was, in a way, my fault. I heard them coming when they were still a mile away. I could've run. But running never suited me, even before I got this piece of German steel in my hip. My Helper. Plus I'd been heating the stones for my sweat lodge since the sun was a hand high above the hill. I run off, the fire would burn down and they'd cool off. Wouldn't be respectful to those stones.

See what they want, I figured. Probably just deer hunters who'd heard about my reputation. You want to get a trophy, hire Indian Charley.

Yup, that was what it had to be. A couple of flatlanders out to hire me to guide them for the weekend. Boys who'd seen the piece about me in the paper, posing with two good old boys from Brooklyn and the twelve-pointer they bagged. Good picture of me, actually. Too good, I realized later. But that wasn't what I was thinking then. Just about potential customers. Not that I needed the money. But a man has to keep busy. And it was better in general if folks just saw me as a typical Indian. Scraping by, not too well educated, a threat to no one. Good old Indian Charley.

Make me a sawbuck or two, get them a buck or two. Good trade.

I was ready to say that to them. Rehearsing it in my head. For a sawbuck or two, I'll get you boys a buck or two. Good trade. Indian humor. Funny enough to get me killed.

I really should have made myself scarce when I heard their voices clear enough to make out what the fat one was saying. It was also when I felt the first twinge in my hip. They were struggling up the last two hundred yards of the trail. That's when I should have done it. Not ran, maybe. But faded back into the hemlocks.

Son of a bidgin' Indin, the heavy-footed one said. And kept on saying it in between labored breaths and the sound of his heavy feet, slipping and dislodging stones. The other one, who wasn't so clumsy but was still making more noise than a lame moose, didn't say anything.

I imagined Heavy Foot was just ticked off at me for making my camp two miles from the road and the last of it straight up. It may have discouraged some who might've hired me. But it weeded out the weaker clientele. And the view was worth it, hills rolling away down to the river that glistened with the rising sun like a silver bracelet, the town on the other side that turned into a constellation of lights mirroring the stars in the sky above it at night.

The arrowhead-shaped piece of metal in my flesh sent another little shiver down the outside of my thigh. I ignored it again. Not a smart thing to do, but I was curious about my visitors.

Curiosity killed the Chippewa, as my grampa, who had also been to Carlisle, used to joke.

For some reason the picture of the superintendent's long face the last day I saw him came to mind. Twenty years ago. He was sitting behind his desk, his pale face getting red as one of those beets I'd spent two summers digging on the farm where they sent me to work for slave labor wages—like every other Indian kid at the school. The superintendent got his cut, of course. How many farmhands and housemaids do you need? We got hundreds of them here at Carlisle. Nice, civilized, docile little Indian boys and girls. Do whatever you want with them.

That was before I got my growth and Pop Warner saw me and made me one of his athletic boys. Special quarters, good food and lots of it, an expense account at Blumenthal's department store, a share of the gate. Plus a chance to get as many concussions as any young warrior could ever dream of, butting heads against the linemen of Harvard and Syracuse and Army. I also found some of the best friends I ever had on that football squad.

It was because of one of them that I'd been able to end up here on this hilltop—which, according to my name on a piece of paper filed in the county seat, belonged to me. As well as the other two hundred acres all the way down to the river. I'd worked hard for the money that made it possible for me to get my name on that deed. But that's another story to tell another time.

As Heavy Foot and his quieter companion labored up the last narrow stretch of trail, where it passed through a hemlock thicket and then came out on an open face of bedrock, I was still replaying that scene in the superintendent's office.

You can't come in here like this.

I just did.

I'll have you expelled.

I almost laughed at that one. Throw an Indian out of Carlisle? Where some children were brought in chains? Where they cut our hair, stole the fine jewelry that our parents arrayed us in, took our clothes, changed our names, dressed us in military uniforms, and turned us into little soldiers? Where more kids ran away than ever graduated?

You won't get the chance. I held up my hand and made a fist.

The super cringed back when I did that. I suppose when you have bear paw hands like mine, they could be a little scary to someone with a guilty conscience.

I lifted my little finger. First, I said, I'm not here alone. I looked back over my shoulder where the boys of the Carlisle football team were waiting in the hall.

I held up my ring finger. Second, I talk; you listen.

Middle finger. Third, he goes. Out of here. Today.

The super knew who I meant. The head disciplinarian of the school. Mr. Morissey. Who was already packing his bags with the help of our two tackles. Help Morissey needed because of his dislocated right shoulder and broken jaw.

The super started to say something. But the sound of my other hand coming down hard on his desk stopped his words as effectively as a cork in a bottle. His nervous eyes focused for a second on the skinned knuckles of my hand.

Fourth, I said, extending my index finger. No one will ever be sent to that farm again. No, don't talk. You know the one I mean. Just nod if you understand. Good.

Last, my thumb extended, leaning forward so that it touched his nose. You never mention my name again. You do not contact the agent on my reservation or anyone else. You just take me out of the records. I am a violent Indian. Maybe I have killed people. You do not ever want to see me again. Just nod.

The super nodded.

Good, I said. Now, my hand patting the air as if I was giving a command to a dog, stay!

He stayed. I walked out into the hall where every man on the football squad except for our two tackles was waiting, including our Indian coach. The super stayed in his office as they all shook my hand, patted me on the back. No one said goodbye. There's no word for goodbye. Travel good. Maybe we see you further down the road.

The super didn't even come out as they moved with me to the school gate, past the mansion built with the big bucks from football ticket sales where Pop Warner had lived. As I walked away, down to the train station, never looking back, the super remained in his seat. His legs too weak with fear for him to stand. According to what I heard later in France—from Gus Welch, who was my company commander and had been our quarterback at Carlisle—the superintendent sat there for the rest of the day without moving. The football boys finally took pity on him and sent one of the girls from the sewing class in to tell him that Charles, the big dangerous Indian, was gone and he could come out now.

Gus laughed. You know what he said when she told him that? Don't mention his name. That's what he said.

I might have been smiling at the memory when the two men came into view, but that wasn't where my recollections had stopped. They'd kept walking me past the Carlisle gate, down the road to the trolley tracks. They'd taken me on the journey I made back then, by rail, by wagon, and on foot, until I reached the dark hills that surrounded that farm. The one more Carlisle kids had run away from than any other. Or at least it was reported that they had run away—too many of them were never seen again.

That had been the first time I acted on the voice that spoke within me. An old voice with clear purpose. I'd sat down on the slope under an old apple tree and watched, feeling the wrongness of the place. I waited until it was late, the face of the Night Traveler looking sadly down from the sky. Then I made my way downhill to the place that Thomas Goodwaters, age eleven, had come to me about because he knew I'd help after he told me what happened there. Told me after he'd been beaten by the school disciplinarian for running away from his Outing assignment at the Bullweather Farm. But the older, half-healed marks on his back had not come from the disciplinarian's cane.

Just the start, he'd told me, his voice calm despite it all, speaking Chippewa. They were going to do worse. I heard what they said they'd done before.

I knew his people back home. Cousins of mine. Good people, canoe makers. A family peaceful at heart, that shared with everyone and that hoped their son who'd been forced away to that school would at least be taught things he could use to help the people. Like how to scrub someone else's kitchen floor.

He'd broken out the small window of the building where they kept him locked up every night. It was a tiny window, but he was so skinny by then from malnourishment that he'd been able to worm his way free. Plus his family were Eel People and known to be able to slip through almost any narrow place.

Two dogs, he said. Bad ones. Don't bark. Just come at you.

But he'd planned his escape well. The bag he'd filled with black pepper from the kitchen and hidden in his pants was out and in his hand as soon as he hit the ground. He'd left the two bad dogs coughing and sneezing as he ran and kept running.

As his closest relative, I was the one he had been running to before Morissey caught him.

You'll do something, Tommy Goodwaters said. It was not a question. You will help.

I was halfway down the hill and had just climbed over the barbed wire fence when the dogs got to me. I'd heard them coming, their feet thudding the ground, their eager panting. Nowhere near as quiet as wolves—not that wolves will ever attack a man. So I was ready when the first one leaped and latched its long jaws around my right forearm. Its long canines didn't get through the football pads and tape I'd wrapped around both arms. The second one, snarling like a wolverine, was having just as hard a time with my equally well-protected left leg that it attacked from the back. They were big dogs, probably about eighty pounds each. But I was two hundred pounds bigger. I lifted up the first one as it held on to my arm like grim death and brought my other forearm down hard across the back of its neck. That broke its neck. The second one let go when I kicked it in the belly hard enough to make a fifty-yard field goal. Its heart stopped when I brought my knee and the full weight of my body down on its chest.

Yeah, they were just dogs. But I showed no mercy. If they'd been eating what Tommy told me—and I had no reason to doubt him—there was no place for such animals to be walking this Earth with humans.

Then I went to the place out behind the cow barn. I found a shovel leaned against the building. Convenient. Looked well-used. It didn't take much searching. It wasn't just the softer ground, but what I felt in my mind. The call of a person's murdered spirit when their body has been hidden in such a place as this. A place they don't belong.

It was more than one spirit calling for help. By the time the night was half over I'd found all of them. All that was left of five Carlisle boys and girls who'd never be seen alive again by grieving relatives. Mostly just bones. Clean enough to have had the flesh boiled off them. Some gnawed. Would have been no way to tell them apart if it hadn't been for what I found in each of those unmarked graves with them. I don't know why, but there was a large thick canvas bag for each of them. Each bag had a wooden tag tied to it with the name and, God love me, even the tribe of the child. Those people—if I can call them that—knew who they were dealing with. Five bags of clothing, meager possessions and bones. None of them were Chippewas, but they were all my little brothers and sisters. If I still drew breath after that night was over, their bones and possessions, at least, would go home. When I looked up at the moon, her face seemed red. I felt as if I was in an old, painful story.

I won't say what I did after that. Just that when the dawn rose I was long gone and all that remained of the house and the buildings were charred timbers. I didn't think anyone saw me as I left that valley, carrying those five bags. But I was wrong. If I'd seen the newspapers from the nearby town the next day—and not been on my way west, to the Sac & Fox and Osage Agencies in Oklahoma, the Wind River Reservation in Wyoming, the lands of the Crows and the Cheyennes in Montana, the Cahuilla of California—I would have read about the tragic death by fire of almost an entire family. Almost.

I blinked away that memory and focused on the two men who paused only briefly at the top of the trail and then headed straight toward me where I was squatting down by the fire pit. As soon as I saw them clearly I didn't have to question the signal my Helper was giving me. I knew they were trouble.

Funny how much you can think of in the space of an eyeblink. Back in the hospital after getting hit by the shrapnel. The tall, skinny masked doctor bending over me with a scalpel in one hand and some kind of shiny bent metal instrument in the other.

My left hand grabbing the surgeon's wrist before the scapel touched my skin.

It stays.

The ether. A French accent. You are supposed to be out.

I'm not.

Oui. I see this. My wrist, you are hurting it.

Pardon. But I didn't let go.

Why?

It says it's going to be my Helper. It's talking to me.

They might have just given me more ether, but by then Gus Welch had pushed his way in the tent. He'd heard it all.

He began talking French to the doctor, faster than I could follow. Whatever it was he said, it worked.

The doctor turned back to me, no scalpel this time.

You are Red Indian.

Mais oui.

A smile visible even under the mask. Head nodding. *Bien*. We just sew you up then.

Another blink of an eye and I was back watching the two armed men come closer. The tall, lanky one was built a little like that doctor I'd last seen in 1918. No mask, though. I could see that he had one of those Abraham Lincoln faces, all angles and jutting jaw—but with none of that long-gone president's compassion. He was carrying a Remington .303. The fat one with the thick lips and small eyes, Heavy Foot for sure, had a lever-action Winchester 30-06. I'd heard him jack a shell into the chamber just before they came into view.

Good guns, but not in the hands of good guys.

Both of them were in full uniform. High-crowned hats, black boots, and all. Not the brown doughboy togs in which I had once looked so dapper. Their khaki duds had the words *Game Warden* sewed over their breast pockets.

They stopped thirty feet away from me.

Charley Bear, the Lincoln impersonator, said in a flat voice: We have a warrant for your arrest for trespassing. Stand up.

I stayed crouching. It was clear to me they didn't know I owned the land I was on. Not that most people in the area knew. After all, it was registered under my official white name of Charles B. Island. If they were really serving a warrant from a judge, they'd know that. Plus, there was one other thing wrong.

Game wardens don't serve warrants, I said.

They said he was a smart one, Luth, Heavy Foot growled.

Too smart for his own good.

My Helper sent a wave of fire through my whole leg and I rolled sideways just as Luth raised his gun and pulled the trigger. It was pretty good for a snap shot. The hot lead whizzed past most of my face with the exception of the flesh it tore off along my left cheekbone, leaving a two-inch wound like a claw mark from an eagle's talon.

As I rolled, I hurled sidearm the first of the baseball-sized rocks I'd palmed from the outside of the firepit. Not as fast as when I struck out Jim Thorpe twice back at Indian school. But high and hard enough to hit the strike zone in the center of Luth's face. Bye-bye front teeth.

Heavy Foot had hesitated before bringing his gun up to his shoulder. By then I'd shifted the second stone to my throwing hand. I came up to one knee and let it fly. It struck square in the soft spot just above the fat man's belly.

Ooof!

His gun went flying off to the side and he fell back clutching his gut.

Luth had lost his .303 when the first rock struck him. He was curled up, his hands clasped over his face.

I picked up both guns before I did anything else. Shucked out the shells and then, despite the fact that I hated to do it seeing as how guns themselves are innocent of evil intent, I tossed both weapons spinning over the edge of the cliff. By the time they hit the rocks below, I had already rolled Heavy Foot over and yanked his belt out of his pants. I wrapped it around his elbows, which I'd pulled behind his back, cinched it tight enough for him to groan in protest.

I pried Luth's hands from his bloody face, levered them behind his back, and did the same for him that I'd done for his fat buddy. Then I grabbed the two restraining belts, one in each hand, and dragged them over to the place where the cliff dropped off.

By then Luth had recovered enough, despite the blood and the broken teeth, to glare at me. But Heavy Foot began weeping like a baby when I propped them both upright at the edge where it wouldn't take more than a push to send them over.

Shut up, Braddie, Luth said through his bleeding lips, his voice still flat as stone. Then he stared at me. I've killed people worse than you.

But not better, I replied.

A sense of humor is wasted on some people. Luth merely intensified his stare.

A hard case. But not Braddie.

Miss your gun? I asked. You can join it.

I lifted my foot.

No, Braddie blubbered. Whaddaya want? Anything.

A name.

Braddie gave it to me.

I left them on the cliff edge, each one fastened to his own big rock that I'd rolled over to them. The additional rope I'd gotten from my shack insured they wouldn't be freeing themselves.

Stay still, boys. Wish me luck.

Go to hell, Luth snarled. Tough as ever.

But he looked a little less tough after I explained that he'd better hope I had good luck. Otherwise I wouldn't be likely to come back and set them loose. I also pointed out that if they struggled too much there was a good chance those delicately balanced big stones I'd lashed them to would roll over the edge. Them too.

I took my time going down the mountain—and I didn't use the main trail. There was always the chance that Luth and Braddie had not been alone. But their truck, a new '34 Ford, was empty. An hour's quiet watch of it from the shelter of the pines made me fairly certain no one else was around. They'd thoughtfully left the keys in the ignition. It made me feel better about them that they were so trusting and willing to share.

As I drove into town I had even more time to think. Not about what to do. But how to do it. And whether or not my hunch was right.

I parked the car in a grove of maples half a mile this side of the edge of town. Indian Charley behind the wheel of a new truck would not have fit my image in the eyes of the good citizens of Corinth. Matter of fact, aside from Will, most of them would have been surprised to see I knew how to drive. Then I walked in to Will's office.

Wyllis Dunham, Attorney at Law, read the sign on the modest door, which opened off the main street. I walked in without knocking and nodded to the petite, stylishly dressed young woman who sat behind the desk with a magazine in her nicely manicured fingers.

Maud, I said, touching my knuckles to my forehead in salute.

Charles, she drawled, somehow making my name into a sardonic remark the way she said it. What kind of trouble you plan on getting us into today?

Nothing we can't handle.

Why does that not make me feel reassured?

Then we both laughed and I thought again how if she wasn't Will's wife I'd probably be thinking of asking her to marry me.

What happened to your cheek? Maud stood up, took a cloth from her purse, wetted it with her lips, and brushed at the place where the bullet had grazed me and the blood had dried. I stood patiently until she was done.

Thanks, nurse.

You'll get my bill.

He in?

For you. She gestured me past her and went back to reading *Ladies' Home Journal*.

I walked into the back room where Will sat with his extremely long legs propped up on his desk, his head back against a couch pillow, his eyes closed.

Before you ask, I am not asleep on the job. I am thinking. Being the town lawyer of a bustling metropolis such as this tends to wear a man out.

Don't let Maud see you with your feet up on that desk.

His eyes opened at that and as he quickly lowered his feet to the floor he looked toward the door, a little furtively, before recovering his composure. Though Will had the degree and was twice her size, it was Maud who laid down the law in their household.

He placed his elbows on the desk and made a pyramid with his fingers. The univeral lawyer's sign of superior intellect and position, but done with a little conscious irony in Will's case. Ever since I had helped him and Maud with a little problem two years back, we'd had a special relationship that included Thursday night card games of cutthroat canasta.

Wellll? he asked.

Two questions.

Do I plead the Fifth Amendment now?

I held up my little finger. First question. Did George Good retire as game warden, has the Department of Conservation started using new brown uniforms that look like they came from a costume shop, and were two new men from downstate sent up here as his replacement?

Technically, Charles, that's three questions. But they all have one answer. No?

Bingo. He snapped his fingers.

Which was what I had suspected. My two well-trussed friends on the mountaintop with their city accents were as phony as their warrant.

Two. I held up my ring finger. Anybody been in town asking about me since that article in the Albany paper with my picture came out?

Will couldn't keep the smile off his face. If there was such a thing as an information magnet for this town, Will Dunham was it. He prided himself on quietly knowing everything that was going on—public and private—before anyone else even knew he knew it. With another loud snap of his long fingers he plucked a business card from his breast pocket and handed it to me with a magician's flourish.

Voilà!

The address was in the State Office Building. The name was not exactly the one I expected, but it still sent a shiver down my spine and the metal spearpoint in my hip muscle twinged. Unfinished business.

I noticed that Will had been talking. I picked up his words in mid-sentence.

. . . so Avery figured that he should give the card to me, seeing as how he knew you were our regular helper, what with you taking on odd jobs for us now and then. Repair work, cutting wood . . . and so on. Of course, by the time he thought to pass it on to me Avery'd been holding on to it since two weeks ago which was when the man came into his filling station asking about you and wanting you to give him a call. So, did he get tired of waiting and decide to look you up himself?

In a manner of speaking.

Say again?

See you later, Will.

The beauty of America's trolley system is that a man could go all the way from New York City to Boston just by changing cars once you got to the end of town and one line ended where another picked up. So the time it took me to run the ten miles to where the line started in Middle Grove was longer than it took to travel the remaining forty miles to Albany and cost me no more than half the coins in my pocket.

I hadn't bothered to go back home to change into the slightly better clothes I had. My nondescript well-worn apparel was just fine for what I had in mind. No one ever notices laborers. The white painter's cap, the brush, and the can of Putnam's bone-white that I borrowed from the hand truck in front of the building were all I needed to amble in unimpeded and take the elevator to the sixteenth floor.

The name on the door matched the moniker on the card—just as fancy and in big gold letters, even bigger than the word *INVESTMENTS* below it. I turned the knob and pushed the door open with my shoulder, backed in diffidently, holding my paint can and brush as proof of identity and motive. Nobody said anything, and when I turned to look I saw that the receptionist's desk was empty, as I'd hoped. Five o'clock. Quitting time. But the door was unlocked, the light still on in the boss's office.

I took off the cap, put down the paint can and brush, and stepped through the door.

He was standing by the window, looking down toward the street below.

Put it on my desk, he said.

Whatever it is, I don't have it, I replied.

He turned around faster than I had expected. But whatever he had in mind left him when I pulled my right hand out of my shirt and showed him the bone-handled skinning knife I'd just pulled from the sheath under my left arm. He froze.

You? he said.

Only one word, but it was as good as an entire book. No doubt about it now. My Helper felt like a burning coal.

Me, I agreed.

Where? he asked. I had to hand it to him. He was really good at one-word questions that spoke volumes.

You mean Mutt and Jeff? They're not coming. They got tied up elsewhere. You should be dead.

Disappointing. Now that he was speaking in longer sentences he was telling me things I already knew, though he was still talking about himself when I gave his words a second thought.

You'd think with the current state of the market, I observed, that you would have left the Bull at the start of your name, Mr. Weathers. Then you might have given your investors some confidence.

My second attempt at humorous banter fell as flat as the first. No response other than opening his mouth a little wider. Time to get serious.

I'm not going to kill you here, I said. Even though you deserve it for what you and your family did back then. How old were you? Eighteen, right? But you took part just as much as they did. A coward too. You just watched without trying to save them from me? Where were you?

Up on the hill, he said. His lips tight. There was sweat on his forehead now.

So, aside from investments, what have you been doing since then? Keeping up the family hobbies?

I looked over at the safe against the wall. You have a souvenir or two in there? No, don't open it to show me. People keep guns in safes. Sit. Not at the desk. Right there on the windowsill.

What are you going to do?

Deliver you to the police. Along with a confession. I took a pad and a pen off the desk. Write it now, starting with what you and your family did at your farm and including anyone else you've hurt since then.

There was an almost eager look on his weaselly face as he took the paper and pen from my hands. That look grew calmer and more superior as he wrote. Clearly, he knew he was a being of a different order than common humans. As far above us as those self-centered scientists say modern men are above the chimpanzees. Like the politicians who sent in the federal troops against the army of veterans who'd camped in Washington, DC this past summer asking that the bonuses they'd been promised for their service be paid to them. Men I knew who'd survived the trenches of Belgium and France, dying on American soil at the hands of General MacArthur's troops.

The light outside faded as the sun went down while he wrote. By the time he was done he'd filled twenty pages, each one numbered at the bottom, several of them with intricate explicatory drawings.

I took his confession and the pen. I placed the pad on the desk, kept one eye on him as I flipped the pages with the tip of the pen. He'd been busy. Though he'd moved on beyond Indian kids, his tastes were still for the young, the weak, those powerless enough to not be missed or mourned by the powers that be. Not like the Lindbergh baby, whose abduction and death had made world news this past spring. No children of the famous or even the moderately well-off. Just those no one writes about. Indians, migrant workers, Negro children, immigrants . . .

He tried not to smirk as I looked up from the words that made me sick to my stomach.

Ready to take me in now?

I knew what he was thinking. A confession like this, forced at the point of a knife by a . . . person . . . who was nothing more than an insane, ignorant Indian. Him a man of money and standing, afraid for his life, ready to write anything no matter how ridiculous. When we went to any police station, all he had to do was shout for help and I'd be the one who'd end up in custody.

One more thing, I said.

You have the knife. His voice rational, agreeable.

I handed him back the pad and pen.

On the last page, print *I'm sorry* in big letters and then sign it.

Of course he wasn't and of course he did.

Thank you, I said, taking the pad. I glanced over his shoulder out the window at the empty sidewalk far below.

There, I said, pointing into the darkness.

He turned his head to look. Then I pushed him.

I didn't lie, I said, even though I doubt he could hear me with the wind whistling past his face as he hurtled down past floor after floor. I didn't kill you. The ground did.

And I'd delivered him to the police, who would be scraping him up off the sidewalk.

Cap back on my head, brush and paint can in hand, I descended all the way to the basement, then walked up the back stairs to leave the building from the side away from where the first police cars would soon arrive.

I slept that night in the park and caught the first trolley north in the morning. It was mid-afternoon by the time I reached the top of the trail.

Only one rock and its human companion stood at the edge of the cliff. Luth had stayed hard, I guessed. Too hard to have the common sense to sit still. But not as hard as those rocks he'd gotten acquainted with two hundred feet below. I'd decide in the morning whether to climb down there, so far off any trail, and bury him. Or just leave the remains for the crows.

I rested my hand on the rock to which the fat man's inert body was still fastened. I let my gaze wander out over the forested slope below, the open fields, the meandering S of the river, the town where the few streetlights would soon be coming on. There was a cloud floating in the western sky, almost the shape of an arrowhead. The setting sun was turning its lower edge crimson. I took a deep breath.

Then I untied Braddie. Even though he was limp and smelled bad, he was still breathing. Spilled some water on his cracked lips. Then let him drink a little.

Don't kill me, he croaked. Please. I didn't want to. I never hurt no one. Never. Luth made me help him. I hated him.

I saw how young he was then.

Okay, I said. We're going back downhill. Your truck is there. You get in it. Far as I know it's yours to keep. You just drive south and don't look back.

I will. I won't never look back. I swear to God.

I took him at his word. There's a time for that, just as there's a time when words end.

EASY AS A-B-C

BY LAURA LIPPMAN
Locust Point, Baltimore
(Originally published in *Baltimore Noir*)

Another house collpased today. It happens more and more, especially with all the wetback crews out there. Don't get me wrong. I use guys from Mexico and Central America, too, and they're great workers, especially when it comes to landscaping. But some other contractors aren't as particular as I am. They hire the cheapest help they can get and the cheapest comes pretty high, especially when you're excavating a basement, which has become one of the hot fixes around here. It's not enough, I guess, to get the three-story rowhouse with four bedrooms, gut it from top to bottom, creating open, airy kitchens where grandmothers once smoked the wallpaper with bacon grease and sour beef. It's not enough to carve master bath suites from the tiny middle rooms that the youngest kids always got stuck with. No, these people have to have the full family room, too, which means digging down into the old dirt basements, sending a river of mud into the alley, then putting in new floors and walls. But if you miscalculate by even an inch—*boom*. You destroy the foundation of the house. Nothing to do but bring the fucker down and start carting away the bricks.

It's odd, going into these houses I knew as a kid, learning what people have paid for sound structures that they consider mere shells, all because they might get a sliver of a water view from a top-floor window or the ubiquitous rooftop deck. Yeah, I know words like ubiquitous. Don't act so surprised. The stuff in books—anyone can learn that. All you need is time and curiosity and a library card, and you can fake your way through a conversation with anyone. The work I do, the crews I supervise, that's what you can't fake because it could kill people, literally kill them. I feel bad for the men who hire me, soft types who apologize for their feebleness, whining: *I wish I had the time*. Give those guys a thousand years and they couldn't rewire a single fixture or install a gas dryer. You know the first thing I recommend when I see a place where the "man of the house" has done some work? A carbon monoxide detector. I couldn't close my eyes in my brother-in-law's place until I installed one, especially when my sister kept bragging about how handy he was.

The boom in South Baltimore started in Federal Hill twenty-five years ago, before my time, flattened out for a while in the '90s, but now it's roaring again, spreading through south Federal Hill and into Riverside Park and all the way up Fort Avenue into Locust Point, where my family lived until I was ten and my grandparents stayed until the day they died, the two of them, side by side. My grandmother had been ailing for years and my grandfather, as it turned out, had been squirreling away various painkillers she had been given along the way, preparing himself. She died in her sleep and, technically, he did, too. A self-induced, pharmaceutical sleep, but sleep nonetheless. We found them on their narrow double bed, and the pronounced rigor made it almost impossible to separate their entwined hands. He literally couldn't live without her. Hard on my mom, losing them that way, but I couldn't help feeling it was pure and honest. Pop-pop didn't want to live alone and he didn't want to come stay with us in the house out in Linthicum. He didn't really have friends. Mee-maw was his whole life and he had been content to care for her through all her pain and illness. He would have done that forever. But once that job was done, he was done, too.

My mother sold the house for $75,000. That was a dozen years ago and boy did we think we had put one over on the buyers. Seventy-five thousand! For a house on Decatur Street in Locust Point. And all cash for my mom, because it had been paid off forever. We went to Hausner's the night of the closing, toasted our good fortune. The old German restaurant was still open then, crammed with all that art and junk. We had veal and strawberry pie and top-shelf liquor and toasted grandfather for leaving us such a windfall.

So imagine how I felt when I got a referral for a complete redo at my grandparents' old address and the real estate guy tells me: "She got it for only $225,000, so she's willing to put another hundred thousand in it and I bet she won't bat an eyelash if the work goes up to $150,000."

"Huh," was all I managed. Money-wise, the job wasn't in my top tier, but then, my grandparents' house was small even by the neighborhood's standards, just two stories. It had a nice-size backyard, though, for a rowhouse. My grandmother had grown tomatoes and herbs and summer squash on that little patch of land.

"The first thing I want to do is get a parking pad back here," my client said, sweeping a hand over what was now an overgrown patch of weeds, the chain-link fence sagging around it. "I've been told that will increase the value of the property ten, twenty thousand."

"You a flipper?" I asked. More and more amateurs were getting into real estate, feeling that the stock market wasn't for them. They were the worst of all possible worlds, panicking at every penny over the original estimate, riding my ass. You want to flip property for profit, you need to be able to do the work yourself. Or buy and hold. This woman didn't look like the patient type. She was young, dressed to the nines, picking her way through the weeds in the most impractical boots I'd ever seen.

"No, I plan to live here. In fact, I hope to move in as quickly as possible, so time is more important to me than money. I was told you're fast."

"I don't waste time, but I don't cut corners," I said. "Mainly, I just try to make my customers happy."

She tilted her head, gazing at me through naturally thick, black eyelashes. It was the practiced look of a woman who had been looking at men from under her eyelashes for much of her life, sure they would be charmed. And, okay, I was. Dark hair, cut in one of those casual, disarrayed styles, darker eyes that made me think of kalamata olives, which isn't particularly romantic, I guess. But I really like kalamata olives. With her fair skin, it was a terrific contrast.

"I'm sure you'll make me very happy," was all she said.

I guess here is where I should mention that I'm married, going on eighteen years and pretty happily, too. I realize it's a hard concept to grasp, especially for a lot of women, that you can be perfectly happy, still in love with your wife, maybe more in love with your wife than you've ever been, but it's been eighteen years and a young, firm-fleshed woman looks up at you through her eyelashes and it's not a crime to think: *I like that.* Not: *I'd like to hit that,* which I hear the young guys on my crews say. Just: *I like that, that's nice, if life were different I'd make time for that.* But I had two kids and a sweet wife, Angeline, who'd only put on a few pounds and still kept her hair blond and long, and was pretty appreciative of the life my work had built for the two of us. So I had no agenda, no scheme going in. I was just weak.

But part of Deirdre's allure was how much she professed to love the very things whose destruction she was presiding over, even before I told her that the house had belonged to my grandparents. She exclaimed over the wallpaper in their bedroom, a pattern of tiny yellow roses, even as it was steamed off the walls. She ran a hand lovingly over the banister, worn smooth by my younger hands, not to mention my butt a time or two. The next day it was gone, yanked from its moorings by my workers. She all but composed an ode to the black-and-white tile in the single full bath, but that didn't stop her from meeting with Charles Tile Co. and choosing a Tuscany-themed medley for what was to become the master bath suite. (Medley was their word, not mine. I just put the stuff in.)

She had said she wanted the job fast, which made me ache a little, because the faster it went, the sooner I would be out of her world. But it turned out she didn't care about speed so much once we got the house to the point where she could live among the ongoing work—and once her end-of-the-day inspections culminated with the two of us in her raw, unfinished bedroom. She was wilder than I had expected, pushing to do things that Angeline would never have tolerated, much less asked for. In some part of my mind, I knew her abandon came from the fact that she never lost sight of the endpoint. The work would be concluded and this would conclude, too. Which was what I wanted as well, I guess. I had no desire to leave Angeline or cause my kids any grief. Deirdre and I were scrupulous about keeping our secret, and not even my longtime guys, the ones who knew me best, guessed anything was up. To them, I bitched about her as much as I did any client, maybe a little more.

"Moldings?" my carpenter would ask. "Now she wants moldings?" And I would roll my eyes and shrug, say: "Women."

"Moldings?" she asked when I proposed them.

"Don't worry," I told her. "No charge. But I saw you look at them."

And so it was with the appliances, the countertops, the triple-pane windows. I bought what she wanted, billed for what she could afford. Somehow, in my mind, it was as if I had sold the house for $225,000, as if all that profit had gone to me instead of the speculator who had bought the house from my mother and then just left it alone to ripen. Over time, I probably put ten thousand of my own money into those improvements, even accounting for my discounts on material and my time, which was free. Some men give women roses and jewelry. I gave Deirdre a marble bathroom and a beautiful old mantle for the living room fireplace, which I restored to the wood-burning hearth it had never been. My grandparents had one of those old gas-fired logs, but Deirdre said they were tacky, and I suppose she was right.

Go figure—I've never had a job with fewer complications. The weather held, there were no surprises buried within the old house, which was sound as a dollar. "A deck," I said. "You'll want a rooftop deck to watch the fireworks." And not just any deck, of course. I built it myself, using teak and copper accents, helped her shop for the proper furniture, outdoor hardy but still feminine, with curvy lines and that *verdi gris* patina she loved so much. I showed her how to cultivate herbs and perennials in pots, but not the usual wooden casks. No, these were iron, to match the décor. If I had to put a name to her style, I guess I'd say Nouvelle New Orleans—flowery, but not overly so, with genuine nineteenth-century pieces balanced by contemporary ones. I guess her taste was good. She certainly thought so and told me often enough.

"If only I had the pocketbook to keep up with my taste," she would say with a sigh and another one of those sidelong glances, and the next thing I knew I'd be installing some wall sconce she simply had to have.

One twilight—we almost always met at last light, the earliest she could leave work, the latest I could stay away from home—she brought a bottle of wine to bed after we had finished. She was taking a wine-tasting course over at this restaurant in the old foundry. A brick foundry, a place where men like my dad had once earned decent wages, and now it housed this chichi restaurant, a gallery, a health club, and a spa. It's happening all over Locust Point. The old P&G plant is now something called Tide Point, which was supposed to be some high-tech mecca, and they're building condos on the old grain piers. The only real jobs left in Locust Point are at Domino and Phillips, where the red neon crab still clambers up and down the smokestack.

"Nice," I said, although in truth I don't care much for white wine and this was too sweet for my taste.

"Vigonier," she said. "Twenty-six dollars a bottle."

"You can buy top-shelf bourbon for that and it lasts a lot longer."

"You can't drink bourbon with dinner," she said with a laugh, as if I had told a joke. "Besides, wine can be an investment. And it's cheaper by the case. I'd like to get into that, but if you're going to do it, you have to do it right, have a special kind of refrigerator, keep it climate controlled."

"Your basement would work."

And that's how I came to build her a wine cellar, at cost. It didn't require excavating the basement, luckily, although I was forever bumping my head on the ceiling when I straightened up to my full height. But I'm 6'3" and she was just a little thing, no more than 5'2", barely one hundred pounds. I used to carry her to bed and, well, show her other ways I could manipulate her weight. She liked me to sit her on the marble counter in her master bath, far forward on the edge, so I was supporting most of her weight. Because of the way the mirrors were positioned, we could both watch, and it was a dizzying infinity, our eyes locked into our own eyes and into each other's. I know guys who call a sink fuck the old American Standard, but I never thought of it that way. For one thing, there wasn't a single American Standard piece in the bathroom. And the toilet was a Canadian model, smuggled in so she could have the bigger tank that had been outlawed in interest of water conservation. Her shower was powerful, too, a stinging force that I came to know well, scrubbing up afterwards so Angeline couldn't smell where I had been.

The wine cellar gave me another month—putting down a floor, smoothing and painting the old plaster walls. My grandparents had used the basement for storage and us cousins had played hide-and-seek in the dark, a made-up version that was particularly thrilling, one where you moved silently, trying to get close enough to grab the others in hiding, then rushing back to the stairs, which were the home-free base. As it sometimes happens, the basement seemed larger when it was full of my grandparents' junk. Painted and pared down, it was so small. But it was big enough to hold the requisite refrigeration unit and the custom-made shelves, a beautiful burled walnut, for the wines she bought on the advice of the guy teaching the course.

I was done. There was not another improvement I could make to the house, so changed now it was as if my family and its history had been erased. Deirdre and I had been hurtling toward this day for months and now it was here. I had to move on to other projects, ones where I would make money. Besides, people were beginning to wonder. I wasn't around the other jobs as much, and I also wasn't pulling in the kind of money that would help placate Angeline over the crazy hours I was working. Time to end it.

Our last night, I stopped at the foundry, spent almost forty bucks on a bottle of wine that the young girl in the store swore by. Cakebread, the guy's real name. White, too, because I knew Deirdre loved white wines.

"Chardonnay," she said, wrinkling her nose.

"I noticed you liked whites."

"But not Chardonnay so much. I'm an ABC girl—Anything But Chardonnay. Dennis says Chardonnay is banal."

"Dennis?"

She didn't answer. And she was supposed to answer, supposed to say: *Oh, you know, that faggot from my wine-tasting class, the one who smells like he wears strawberry perfume.* Or: *That irritating guy in my office.* Or even: *A neighbor, a creep. He scares me. Would you still come around, from time to time, just to check up on me?* She didn't say any of those things.

She said: "We were never going to be a regular thing, my love."

Right. I knew that. I was the one with the wife and the house and the two kids. I was the one who had everything to lose. I was the one who was glad to be getting out, before it could all catch up with me. I was the one who was careful not to use the word love, not even in the lighthearted way she had just used it. Sarcastic, almost. It made me think that it wasn't my marital status so much that had closed off that possibility for us, but something even more entrenched. I was no different from the wallpaper, the banister, the garden. I had to be removed for the house to be truly hers.

My grandmother's parents had thought she was too good for my grandfather. They were Irish, shipworkers who had gotten the hell out of Locust Point and moved uptown, to Charles Village, where the houses were much bigger. They looked down on my grandfather just because he was where they once were. It killed them, the idea that their precious youngest daughter might move back to the neighborhood and live with an Italian, to boot. Everybody's got to look down on somebody. If there's not somebody below you, how do you know you've traveled any distance at all in your life? For my dad's generation, it was all about the blacks. I'm not saying it was right, just that it was, and it hung on because it was such a stark, visible difference. And now the rules have changed again, and it's the young people with money and ambition who are buying the houses in Locust Point, and the people in places like Linthicum and Catonsville and Arbutus are the ones to be pitied and condescended to. It's hard to keep up.

My hand curled tight around the neck of the wine bottle. But I placed it in its berth in the special refrigerator, gently, as if I were putting a newborn back in its bed.

"One last time?" I asked her.

"Of course," she said.

She clearly was thinking it would be the bed, romantic and final, but I opted for the bathroom, wanting to see her from all angles. Wanting her to see me, to witness, to remember how broad my shoulders are, how white and small she looked when I was holding her against my chest.

When I moved my hands from her hips to her head, she thought I was trying to position her mouth on mine. It took her a second to realize that my hands were on her throat, not her head, squeezing, squeezing, squeezing. She fought back, if you could call it that, but all her hands could find was marble, smooth and immutable. Yeah, that's another word I know. Immutable. She may have landed a few scratches, but a man in my work gets banged up all the time. No one would notice a beaded scab on the back of my hand, or even on my cheek.

I put her body in a trash bag, covering it with lime leftover from a landscaping job. Luckily, she hadn't been so crazed that she wanted a fireplace in the basement, so all I had to do was pull down the fake front I had placed over the old hearth, then brick her in, replace the fake front. It wasn't planned, not a moment of it, but when it happened, I knew what to do, as surely as I know what to do when a floor isn't level or a soffit needs to be closed up so birds can't get in.

Her computer was on, as always, her e-mail account open because she used cable for her Internet, a system I had installed. I read a few of her sent messages, just to make sure I aped her style, then typed one to an office address, explaining the family emergency that would take me out of town for a few days. Then I sent one to "Dennis," angry and hate-filled, accusing him of all kinds of things, telling him not to call or write. Finally, I cleaned the house best I could, especially the bathroom, although I didn't feel I had to be too conscientious. I was the contractor. Of course my fingerprints would be around. The last thing I did was grab that bottle of Chardonnay, took it home to Angeline, who liked it just fine, although she would have fainted if she knew what it cost.

Weeks later, when Deirdre was officially missing and increasingly presumed dead according to the articles I read in the *Sunpapers*, I sent a bill for the projects that I had done at cost, marked it "Third and Final Notice" in large red letters, as if I didn't know what was going on. She was just an address to me, one of a half-dozen open accounts. Her parents paid it, even apologized for their daughter being so irresponsible, buying all this stuff she couldn't afford. I told them I understood, having kids of my own, Joseph Jr. getting ready for college next year. I said I was so sorry for what had happened and that I hoped they found her soon. I do feel sorry for them. They can't begin to cover the monthly payments on the place, so it's headed toward foreclosure. The bank will make a nice profit, as long as the agents gloss over the reason for the sale; people don't like a house with even the hint of a sordid history.

And I'm glad now that I put in the wine cellar. Makes it less likely that the new owner will want to dig out the basement. Which means there's less chance of a collapse, and less likelihood that they'll ever find that little bag of bones in the hearth.

THE ROSE RED VIAL

BY PIR ROTHENBERG

Museum District, Richmond

(Originally published in *Richmond Noir*)

W hen I got inside I called her name. My house was dark and quiet, and although nothing appeared altered I felt that something had happened since I'd left for the museum's summer gala. There was a note on the kitchen table. I scanned it and it made no sense. I stuffed it into my pocket, took back a shot of whiskey, and walked the narrow hallway into the living room. I thought of the note; the words were going to make sense in a moment. I was sure of it, and felt so much like a balloon steadily expanding that I held my breath and winced at the inevitable explosion.

One month prior, in a storage room below the Virginia Historical Society, I sat before an empty glass cabinet preparing the lamps I would mount on the shelves. There were to be six items of Edgar Allan Poe memorabilia here, among them a lock of dark hair taken off the poet's head after his death; the key to the trunk that accompanied Poe to Baltimore, where he spent the final few days of his life; and a walking stick, which Poe left here in Richmond ten days before his death. The items were on loan from the Poe Museum across town for the city's celebration of the poet's bicentennial, as yet seven months away.

I took a pull from the small metal flask I kept in my utility belt. When I noticed I wasn't alone, it was too late to hide it. It was the new intern, a dark-haired girl with a small scar across her lower lip.

"Sorry," she said. "Didn't mean to scare you."

"You didn't," I said, and took another swig before recapping the flask.

She'd started at the museum on Monday, but I'd seen her the weekend before in my neighbors' backyard. The Hamlins had installed a six-foot privacy fence years ago, but by the unobstructed view from an upstairs window I'd watched the young woman standing like the very portrait of boredom, hand on the flare of her hip, as Barb Hamlin pointed out the trained wisteria and the touch-me-nots in her garden. She'd had one leg stretched into a band of sunlight when she glanced up and noticed me.

I went back to work on the lamps. "They give you something to do in here?"

"Rebecca," she said, strolling through the makeshift aisles of cases and boxes. Her dark hair fell in angles around her face and she wore a white summer dress unsuitable for an intern's duties. "And I wish they *would*. This room is why I'm here."

"Poe fan, huh?"

"You too," she said. "Or so Uncle Lou tells me."

I chuckled softly but did not look up. I was well acquainted with "Uncle Lou," former captain of the 3rd Precinct, famous for his supposed paternal brand of policing. Really, he'd never been more than a squat old tyrant. We'd been neighbors for a decade and the only thing that kept our peace was that six-foot fence. Now I was humbled to learn that "Uncle" was not a total misnomer; Lou, who'd sired no offspring, had a pretty young niece from Cincinnati.

"Maybe you could ask them to give me an assignment back here," Rebecca said.

I told her I was just a lighting technician, contracted, not even staff.

"But you know John," she said. John was the head curator. "You two are friends."

I thought she ought to ask Lou, a patron of the museum whose connections had likely procured her the internship in the first place. But I agreed to put in a word, if only to end the conversation: nothing good could come from associating with Hamlin kin—much less from upsetting one with a refusal. Yet it excited me too, the thought of Lou's scowling displeasure were he to discover Rebecca and I chumming around at the museum. *Displeasure* was a euphemism; he'd put his wife's garden shears through my skull.

Still, when she asked for a drink, I handed her the flask.

At sunset she was at my front door. I glanced toward Lou and Barb's house. Rebecca told me not to worry, they'd gone to play bridge with friends.

"So," she said, wandering into my living room, "do you have any first editions?"

"What?"

"Of Poe," she said.

"Did your uncle tell you that too?"

Glancing into corners, trailing her fingers along windowsills, she smiled. "I was hoping that a Poe aficionado—who works in a museum, no less—would have an artifact lying around."

"What," I said, "just lying around like junk mail?"

"Don't be nasty," she said, then picked up a green glass ashtray. "Like this," she said, holding it to the light. "It'd be great if you could say, 'And this is Poe's ashtray, recovered from his writing desk at his last residence at Fordham.'"

"That was my grandfather's."

She set it down. "Lou would like that. History buff."

Yeah, I thought. He had a hard time letting go of it.

"All sorts of Civil War memorabilia everywhere. Ever been inside?"

This was beginning to feel like a game. "What do you think?"

"How should I know where you've been?"

I told her she'd better not let Lou see us together.

"Together?" she said, hiding a smile.

"You know what I mean."

"Why, doesn't he like you?"

Now I just sat back and looked at her.

"Oh, I *know*," she said, grinning. "He told me to stay away from you."

Then she asked for a drink, even though, by the way she'd cringed earlier, I could tell she'd hated it. I was disappointed. She was only there with me for a little rebellion against the stuffy uncle and aunt.

So be it. I went to get the whiskey.

I spoke with John. I owed my job at the VHS—my very livelihood in this city—solely to him. By the end of the week Rebecca was putting in shifts assisting me in preparing the illumination of over 1,500 objects for the bicentennial exhibits. John and the staff unpacked items every day and created layout plans. It was my job to determine how best to light those books, paintings, and curios they wanted in cases, mounted upon walls, or perched on podiums. Rebecca was happy the hour or two a day she worked with me—rather, with the objects, to which her full attention was devoted. She was ecstatic watching the items emerge from their boxes, or gazing into the cases once the lighting was complete, all the pieces illuminated perfectly before they went back into their boxes for safekeeping. The lights from the displays would strike her face full on, or under her chin like a flashlight beam, or sidelong as in a Rembrandt painting. I wanted to pose her and arrange the light so as to expose every molecule of her simple beauty.

On my back, my head inside a case, I heard Rebecca gasp.

"Wow," she called, "have you seen this?"

When I stood up Rebecca was crouched by a case that John and I'd worked on that morning and had yet to finalize. She moved aside and looked at me, leaving one finger pressed to the glass.

"The perfume?" I said.

It was a small red vial, chipped along the lip—like Rebecca, with that nick running the width of her own. The original cork stopper, disintegrated long ago, had been replaced by a plastic facsimile.

Rebecca read from the placard: "*The essence of rose, believed given by Poe to Virginia the year of their marriage, 1836.*" She looked to me again, this time with a lusty sort of gaze. "Can you open the case?"

Although I was technically disallowed, as I was not a member of staff, I did have a key. John gave it to me for the sake of convenience—and because he trusted me. But I couldn't shake her eyes and thought, What the hell, the museum had better let her touch anything she wanted if they liked her uncle's money. I opened the case, then cradled the vial in my palms.

"If this breaks," I told her solemnly, "that's it. The end of us both."

I felt her warm fingers coax the vial free from my hold, and noted the light that shone from the case upon her thin nose and lean cheeks, a cool, sterile light that was all wrong. Then, with a move of her thumb, off came the stopper and my heart kicked like a horse.

"Rose," she said ecstatically, the vial beneath her nose.

I took a whiff. "Yup—now be care—"

She flipped the vial over upon her finger, then dragged the scent across her neck desperately, back and forth. I paled, took the bottle as forcefully as I dared, replaced the stopper, and put it away. She was grinning, her fingers down her dress top.

"Jesus, Rebecca!"

"Emery," she said softly, almost pityingly, "you knew I was going to do that."

I heard her call me in the parking lot behind the Historical Society. I didn't stop, but slowed. We walked together into a long, thin park of magnolia trees that bordered Sheppard Street. The humidity was palpable and a damp wind was gathering strength. I turned into an alley and Rebecca followed, eyeing the flask when I took it from my belt.

"You don't even like it," I snapped.

The evening light on her face reminded me of the light that shines upon generals or angels in classic paintings: the exultant yellows and oranges bleeding through churning clouds. I reminded her how quickly I'd be fired if anyone discovered what had happened, then plopped the flask into her hand.

To avoid being seen together, we stuck to the alleys, hopping over streets—Stuart, Patterson, Park—and cutting through the neighborhood diagonally. Below our feet the cobblestones were mashed together like crooked teeth, and on either side crowded slim garages, wooden fences, bushes and woody shrubs, and walls of ancient brick. Green plumes of foliage, heavy with flowers and fruit, alive with the frenetic song of mockingbirds, spilled over everything like lush curtains; and the ivy-draped limbs of mammoth tulip trees wound intricately overhead like the soft arms of giants. It awed me how wild and vivacious the wilderness could be on these nameless roads. It was hard to imagine that a city existed beyond the houses we walked behind.

"Here once, through an alley Titanic," intoned Rebecca, "Of cypress, I roamed with my Soul—Of cypress, with Psyche, my Soul."

She watched me for a reaction.

"That's Poe," she said, as if to a very slow child.

The trees were loud in the wind and I caught the distinct scent of rose.

"You've got to wash it off as soon as you get home."

"No one's going to know, Emery."

I glowered at her. A large, bulbous rain began to fall and rattle the magnolia leaves.

"I'm sorry," she said. "I didn't think it was that big a deal. I'll wash it off tonight." Then she threw her arm around my neck and pulled me down to her. "But just smell. Isn't it nice?"

I tensed, restrained for a moment, then drew in the scents—the deep rose, the sticky warm skin of her neck, the rain—and shivered. She leapt away and screamed with delight at the storm, and ran the length of the alley for her house. I didn't hurry. When I reached my back gate, I saw the blurry shape of Lou in his kitchen window, looking out.

That night I dreamed Rebecca was breaking into my house through a loose window. It was dark but there was a spotlight on her and she was naked. I spent the following morning distracted, preparing for work and wanting to see Rebecca. Wanting to see her in a particular light.

On my way to the museum, I found Lou in the alley breaking fallen tree branches for the trash. He was a stout, wiry man, white-haired and mustachioed, with a thick, soggy cigar between his teeth and sweet blue smoke clinging to his face. He cracked a limb under his knee and I imagined my bones making a similar sound. I felt sure that he'd seen me in the alley the previous night, that he already suspected something. But he said nothing, and did nothing more than nod curtly.

At the museum Rebecca and another intern were sanding walls in an empty exhibit room. When our paths crossed—Rebecca sweaty, covered in white dust, looking unhappy—I smelled the rose perfume. I eyed her, but said nothing. Lou's lack of reaction had me on guard, probably more so than if he'd clocked me. That, at least, would've been in character.

Once alone, I asked if she'd showered, and caught the image of her slick body in steam.

She played indignant, then laughed. "Maybe it's my natural scent."

I smelled rose the next day too. It lingered in the replica wood cabin where she'd worked. I followed it through the Story of Virginia exhibit, down thousands of years of history, from the Early Hunters of 14,000 BC to the Powhatan Indians to the Belmont Street Car. Was it a game? Had she bought some cheap spray from the drugstore to irk me? But the odor of an imitation would be like a candy apple compared to the earthy fruit I'd smelled upon her in the rain. I went into the storage room. I found the box where the perfume had been repacked, but it wasn't inside. Even its placard had vanished. I took a swig from my flask and found that I wasn't much surprised.

On Saturday evening Rebecca knocked on my door. She'd told her uncle she would be at Trina's, an intern she ate lunch with sometimes.

"What will you and Trina do?"

"I don't know," she said, shrugging. "Paint our nails. Talk about boys."

"Try on perfume?"

She spun around, swore the stuff simply hadn't washed off, that she had on a different perfume, that I was imagining things. I hadn't alerted John about the theft because I needed to get the perfume back myself. As much as I wanted to know how she'd done it, I'd already decided confronting her would get me nowhere. But now she was blinking. Big-eyed, disarming blinks. It infuriated me, this show of innocence while the scent of rose was so potent my eyes were practically watering.

"Perfumed from an unseen censer," she said, raising a brow.

"Poe," I said. "I know." Then I took her arm and pulled her up the stairs. She played nonchalant but I could feel her legs resisting. I moved her into the bathroom and sat her on the edge of the bathtub.

"What the *hell* are you doing?" she said.

I turned on the hot water in the sink and lathered a washcloth with soap. If she was having so much trouble ridding her neck of the scent, I told her, I was going to help. Rebecca's angry eyes grew challenging, playful. I kneeled, brought the cloth to her skin, and started scrubbing.

"That's hot," she said, but she acquiesced, tilting her head.

I wrung the washcloth, soaped it again, and resumed on the other side, taking hold of the back of her neck to steady her. This was a task, this was work—or so I told myself as I watched the soapy rivulets streak her skin. I felt her gaze on me, cool and calm now, and I didn't look up before kissing her. I tasted rose and chalky soap, and saw red behind my eyelids, pulsing in time with my chest.

Rebecca was curled on one end of the couch and asleep. The whiskey had knocked her out. I put a blanket over her and sat on the opposite end, staring into shadows. A breeze moved my hair and disturbed Rebecca's purse. I saw her keys in the purse. I took them, went barefoot into the Hamlins' yard, and let myself in.

I did this all as though in one unthinking movement, and only when I heard snoring did I note my own thrashing heart. For Lou, shooting intruders was dinner conversation. I found Rebecca's bedroom. Clothing was scattered in piles, and the tangled covers upon her bed made a fossilized impression of her body. On a dresser I fingered through a few trinkets, some cash and letters, then opened the top drawer. Here I found the girl's undergarments, which, perhaps for posterity, were the only items she'd stowed out of sight. I ran my hands through the silky contents, inhaled the scent of fabric soap and rose. Feeling into the corners I came upon a small, smooth object: the red vial with the chipped lip. I crept out of the house, flooded with excitement and pleasure.

That was Saturday; I didn't see Rebecca again until Monday afternoon, when I came in for a half-day shift. She was reading a magazine in the break room, a mug of tea below her chin.

"Rose hips?" I said, a sparkle in my voice.

"Chamomile."

"Yeah," I said. "It doesn't smell like rose."

She gave a small smile but didn't look up. I left and headed toward the storage room. The glass vial bulged in my pocket. When I arrived, the door was already open and John was inside with several other staff members. They were unpacking boxes. The room was a disaster.

"Ah," John said. "Just the fellow I was waiting for."

My stomach dropped. John explained: he'd been working in storage with Rebecca that morning when she noticed a loose placard; when they tried to return it to the item it described—a red perfume bottle, of course—they discovered it missing. Did I remember it? Did I know anything about it? I made a series of noncommittal noises, difficult as it was to think straight, much less be clever. Rebecca's little smile danced vividly to mind.

"We're ass-deep in here the rest of the day making sure it's really missing, not just misplaced." I offered to help; I could produce the vial from the first box I unpacked and *voila*! Case closed. But John refused. Staff only for now. "You know," he said, "to avoid any confusion."

"Why would you *do* that?" I said, nearly shouting.

"Why would *you* creep into my room and steal it?"

I scoffed. "You're accusing *me* of stealing!"

We stood facing each other under the magnolias. Rebecca stared off petulantly.

I took a few long breaths. "Do you want to know why 'Uncle Lou' doesn't like me?"

Rebecca's lips parted as if to speak, but she said nothing. She wanted to see what I'd say first, the crafty girl. I didn't care at that point, so I told her.

"He thinks I stole a painting." I laughed. "From a museum, no less."

"*Francis Keeling Valentine Allan*," Rebecca replied. "The portrait by Thomas Sully. Stolen in 2000 from the Valentine Museum. I know."

I watched her fixedly. By the end of this revelation, her eyes had drifted down the row of magnolias, her gaze light and airy.

She continued: "Poe said she loved him like her own child. It's a beautiful painting too, not that I've seen it in person."

"Did Lou also happen to tell you he and a squadron of police burst through my door and tore apart my house eight years ago? That if it wasn't for John choosing to trust me I'd have been blacklisted from working in any museum in this city again?"

Rebecca returned my stare; she looked ready to play rough. "He told me he saw you with a painting—covered by a sheet. He saw it in your hands the night of the burglary. You were trying to get it from your car to your back door. He *saw* you, Emery."

I shook my head and laughed. "So, you're Lou's little spy? Looking for lost treasure?"

"Lou is a horse's ass," she said. "Anyway, would I find it?"

"It was a storm window, for Christ's sake. Kid put a baseball through the old one a few days before. Once the cops were done demolishing my house, they were kind enough to look into it. Your uncle hates me because he made a fool of himself at the end of his career. He went out a laughingstock."

Rebecca shrugged. "He thinks you have it. Still."

"Do *you* think I have it?"

"You have my perfume," she said. "And I want it back."

Rebecca avoided me the next few days, which was fine, as the restrictions placed upon the non-staff made my job difficult enough. Gone was my key to the storage rooms and cases; gone the days I could work without staff watching over my shoulder. Rebecca had sealed her own fate too; she was back sanding walls all day. John hadn't ruled it theft, but neither did he believe the missing perfume an inventory list blunder. He simply called it "Missing." I could feel the growing weight in his eyes when he looked at me.

Lou found out about the perfume through his museum connections. That's what Rebecca told me a week later, when she appeared at my door again. She'd heard Lou speaking of it on the phone, invoking my name more than once to John and others she didn't know. I listened to her, weighing the veracity of what she said. I doubted Rebecca would tell Lou or John about my having the perfume; she wanted it for herself, and ratting me out wouldn't accomplish that. No, given the opportunity, she would steal back the perfume. Probably it was the only reason she was here now. I told her as much.

"I won't have to resort to that," she said, stepping close. "I think you'll give it back."

"Why, because John and your uncle are hot on my heels?" I said, cockily.

She considered it. "Maybe because you like me?"

I watched her eyes for sarcasm, but she closed them and burrowed her face into my neck, running me through with chills.

"And because I like you," she added.

One thing nagged me: if Lou had spoken with John and learned of the perfume, wasn't it likely he'd also heard of Rebecca working with me in the storage room? Uncle Lou knew plenty of the staff—hadn't *anyone* put his niece with me? We were careful, but there's only so much one can do. It's a small city. By Rebecca's account, though, Lou was clueless about us.

In bed we made love. She pressed herself close and said, "Smell. Not as nice, is it?"

I smelled rose, but it was sugary and cheap. She wanted the real stuff, just a drop—a molecule.

When I took the perfume from my dresser drawer, she said, "Not much of a hiding spot."

"That's what I thought of yours."

Then she grabbed for it. I held tight and we crashed back onto the bed. She was giving me a good fight, biting my ribs, pulling my hair. When exhaustion wore us down, I tipped the vial onto my finger and applied it to her neck. We lay in bed deep into the night, the perfume high upon the dresser. She was in my arms, and I knew I had to hide the vial before I fell asleep. Then I heard her voice, low and hypnotic.

"I'm going to turn you in."

I roused, tightened my embrace as though it was lovers' talk.

"You can't. I didn't steal it."

"But you have it."

"Darling," I said, "if you turn me in, I'll tell them the real story. Then John knows you're a thief, and your kindly uncle knows you've been cavorting with the likes of me. You lose both ways—and you don't get the perfume."

"If I turn you in, your life becomes a living hell."

I pinned her, gripped her neck with my hands. "I could kill you now," I said. "And that would be the end of this nonsense."

There was a flash of real fear in her eyes, but only a flash—something had come to her. "I'm at Trina's tonight," she said. "When I don't come home, Lou calls Trina."

"And?"

"And then Trina tells him about you."

I was suddenly so pleased with her, with her cunning and forethought, her tenacity. I lowered my head to kiss her, all the while feeling that I was losing myself to her, about to give her something she hadn't even asked for. I snatched the perfume and took her to the basement, where I pulled boxes away from the wall. When I removed a section of the fake wood paneling with a screwdriver, she laughed and said, "So, you're going to brick me up back there. I should have figured."

Then she saw the vault. She stood wide-eyed, the sheets in which she'd wrapped herself slinking down her shoulders. The dial spun swiftly under my fingers, right-left, left-right, and then there was the clean, cold click of the lock giving way. The massive door opened noiselessly. I reached into the darkness and drew out what was inside.

"I knew it!" she screamed. "You sneaky bastard!" She hurled a string of delightful profanity at me, then reached out to touch the painting. She held it while I flicked on a series of mounted spotlights that came together on the opposite wall. I hung the portrait in that pool of radiance—it was alive now, the woman who raised Edgar Allan Poe. She was depicted young, and had a small nose and mouth, large dark eyes and roseate cheeks; her black hair was pulled up, and long strands of it curled past the edges of her eyes down to her jaw. There was a ghostly light about her long neck and her gauzy white dress.

I lost track of how long we stared into it.

Eventually, Rebecca asked, "What's the point? I mean, it just sits in there. In the dark."

"What should I do," I said, "put it up in the living room? Rebecca, having this painting in the vault is dangerous enough. But it's worth it. It does something to me. Every morning I wake up and remember what's here, in my house. I'm sitting upon a great secret, and it makes everything . . . vibrate. But it's a *crime*." I brought my fingers to her neck. "And you don't wear your crime."

I put the painting back and the perfume in with it—now she couldn't rat me out without exposing herself as an accomplice who knew where the secret vault was. I swung the door shut and met Rebecca's contemptuous gaze. She apparently got the point.

"I want to trust you, Rebecca. And you to trust me. This assures that trust."

"That's not trust," she said. "That's mutually assured destruction."

The longer the perfume stayed missing, the more my hours diminished. The museum's auxiliary technicians were increasingly around, assigned to projects that ordinarily would have gone to me. I was not outright expelled, but more like a child faced into the corner. The cloud of suspicion that had loomed over me eight years before was above me again, and it was dark.

When I confronted John, he said, "Emery, there's just a lot of talk."

"Since when do you believe talk?"

"Let's give it some time," he said, "let it blow over."

"Is it Hamlin? Are you listening to Lou Hamlin now?"

"Emery," he said sharply, "you were the last one with the . . . People are suspicious."

Christ, I thought, he defends me when I'm guilty, and condemns me when I'm not—not completely, anyway.

The only bright thing in my life was the source of my troubles. I found it strange that Rebecca's uncle didn't try leashing her. Was he duped so easily, believing she spent all her nights at Trina's? In the basement I'd retrieve the perfume from the safe and trace the oil along her curves. We'd sleep upon the daybed with rose and sweat in the air. Rebecca was surprisingly agreeable to the situation, washing off the perfume dutifully before she left my house each morning, not arguing when I put it back in the safe. If we didn't make love, or study the painting, Rebecca would pose and I'd manipulate the lights so that I'd swear she floated in them, my treasure.

Rebecca's internship was nearly complete; she'd be leaving for Cincinnati in a matter of days. It struck me hard, and maybe her too, but neither of us spoke about it. Following my first day of work in four days, Rebecca, walking home beside me in the alleys, presented me with an idea.

"Would things be better for you if they found the perfume?"

I supposed they would, but the small red vial had been so long in our possession, and become so important to us, that I couldn't imagine being without it.

"I want you to give me the perfume," she said evenly. "I'll plant it in a box in one of the storage rooms."

Her face was confident and serene, and I wanted to kiss the little notch upon her lip for her offer. But it was too dangerous—besides, neither of us had access to the rooms. Then she handed me an envelope. Inside was a key she'd stolen, copied, and returned the day before.

I held onto the key. "It's too dangerous, Rebecca. If they catch you . . ."

"Then what? They send me home?"

"Or prison."

There was the Summer Celebration gala the next night, a fund-raising party for members, staff, and interns. I could do it then, slip in and out amidst the crowd.

"Why do you suddenly want to get rid of it?"

"For you."

I looked all around at the alley we were in, one of a thousand veins through which coursed the blood of our city to its heart, where a great and mysterious history seemed preserved for us.

"Poe should have died here," I said, "in these alleys. Not on some bench in Baltimore."

That night was our last with the perfume.

* * *

We took my car. At the museum, Memorial Hall was bustling with ritzy summer gowns and tuxedoed bartenders, colorful spreads of hors d'oeuvres, live jazz. Rebecca and I spent only a few minutes together—the Hamlins were expected shortly—and gulped down our wine in a corner. She was especially striking, having spent so long with her compact mirror as we dressed in the basement, painting on her dark eyes, making her face radiant.

"Rebecca . . ."

"You have to," she said. "You can't lose everything because of me."

"No, I mean, will you still . . ."

I was conflicted, afraid that returning the perfume was tossing away the only card I had, tossing away Rebecca herself. I couldn't finish, but she seemed to know what I meant, because she pulled me to her by my waist and gave me a slow, full-hearted kiss.

"Do it soon," she said. "I'll meet you later. Goodbye." And she disappeared into the crowd.

I waited, put crackers into my dry mouth, said quick hellos, then made my move. I was fueled with wine, sliding through back hallways, full of love for Rebecca. It wasn't fair that we couldn't keep it—I hadn't been fair, keeping it from her. Wouldn't it all blow over sooner or later? The old case of the missing perfume, just like the painting, which was by now a tired page on an FBI website. In the storage room I stood still, feeling the weight of the vial in my jacket pocket, and Rebecca's hands still around my waist. I had my treasure—not the painting anymore, but Rebecca. And she, such the devoted student of Poe, deserved to have the perfume. If it was time to return anything, it was the painting. With a wild surge of clarity and elation I rejoined the throngs of people, who had begun dancing as if to emulate my joy. I couldn't wait to tell Rebecca, to see her face; I'd have liked to see her uncle's too, just to show him my pleasure and confidence. But I found neither. Someone tugged at my elbow. It was Trina.

"You looking for Rebecca, Mr. Vance? She left a little while ago."

I stared at her, baffled, then said, "No, Trina. I'm not looking for Rebecca."

The row of magnolias was empty so I circled back to the parking ramp. She'd be waiting for me, my getaway driver. At my parking spot I discovered three things almost simultaneously: Rebecca wasn't there, my car was gone, and my keys were no longer in my jacket pocket. I ran home through the alleys trying to keep my mind blank, trying not to remember that last embrace with

Rebecca, her hands snaking around my waist. Lou's house was dark, as was mine. My door was unlocked. Inside I called her name.

Then I read the note:

Please forgive me. But you must see the bright side. The cloud of suspicion above you is lifted—evermore.
R.

I had my shot of whiskey, felt my body shudder, and then it came, the mean bang of fists against my door and the wave of blue uniforms through the halls. I heard my name from the lips of one officer, a young sergeant, who explained his warrant for search and seizure. I saw John in his suit, straight from the gala, and Lou Hamlin dressed in black like some prowler.

The young sergeant said solemnly, "Mr. Vance, is there a safe in your basement?"

I managed to ask if that was illegal.

"What you've got in it *is*," said Lou, sneering.

They ushered me into my basement and Lou coughed with laughter when he saw the safe in plain view. The sergeant tried the handle.

"Open it up, shitbird," said Lou.

The sergeant raised a finger to quiet Lou—this pleased me—and said, "You'll have to open the safe, Mr. Vance. That, or it'll be opened in the lab."

I felt my cold body rise and fall with my breath; I waited, but nothing came to me: no idea, no plan of escape. I was done.

"No need for that," I said, and went to open it.

"No," said the sergeant, blocking me. "Just recite the combination."

It was an unoriginal set of numbers, the poet's birthday: 01-19-18-09. As I recited them I remembered spinning the dial earlier in the evening to retrieve the perfume, Rebecca behind me on the bed doing her makeup, mirror in hand. The click of the lock woke me. The flashlights came out like swords and the beams ferreted through the dark, but where the light should have by now found the black hair, the thin nose, the quiet eyes, there was nothing but more dark, and more light chasing in until the beams struck the rear wall of the safe.

All eyes—and the beams of flashlights—turned upon me.

"Where is the painting, Mr. Vance?" asked the sergeant.

I looked at Lou's face, white and fishy, and kept my eyes on him when I said, "What painting?" It came out weak, unconvincing, but what did it matter? The empty safe was proof—the empty safe would hide my crime. Only John was touching the brackets on the opposite wall, and looking at the spotlights.

Lou erupted, snatching me by the collar and heaving me into the wall for some of his paternal policing. He got in one blow to my face before he was restrained by the officers. He fought at them too, and when he was finally subdued and handcuffed on the floor he was nearly foaming at his white mustache.

"She *said!*" Lou spat. "She said the painting was here! She saw it!"

Rebecca. His spy all along. I let this sit on my thoughts for a moment, as if seeing how long I could hold an ember.

The sergeant looked beat. He shook his head at Lou. Then his face brightened. "Mr. Hamlin, where *is* your niece?"

"She doesn't have it," he said. "She made this *happen!*"

Oh, treacherous Rebecca! But her note was coming into focus. She'd duped me good, but she'd gone to great lengths to dupe her uncle too, and leave me protected.

The sergeant peered at me. "Where is Rebecca? Does she have the painting?"

I said nothing.

That's when I heard John: "Rose. I smell rose."

Suddenly, I could smell it too, as if it had exploded in my pocket; it was all over me, all over the bed and the walls and the safe. I looked away from John.

"Mr. Vance," the sergeant continued, "if you can help us, it'll be good for you."

John leveled his gaze at me. "The perfume is here. I smell it. I smell the rose perfume!"

The sergeant patted me down and found the vial. He took a disinterested sniff, handed it to John, and turned back to me.

"Now there's this," he said, like a tired parent. "We could forget *this* altogether if you cooperate."

I looked at the sergeant and at Lou and I savored it, my chance to turn the tables on her, to beat her at her own game. And then I let it go. "Sergeant," I said, "Mr. Hamlin. Respectfully, I don't know where Rebecca is and I have no idea what painting you're talking about."

"Arrest him," Lou barked, sandwiched between officers. "Arrest him for the perfume!"

And they might have. But there was John again, the vial in his hand. "This isn't it."

"What?" I shouted, unable to stop myself.

John held up the vial and pointed to an unblemished lip. "No chip," he said. "Anyway, smell it. Putrid!" He placed the vial on a cabinet and made sure I saw the great disappointment in his eyes.

I was berated for another hour by the officers. What kind of game are you playing with us? Do you think you've gotten away with it? Don't you know it's just a matter of time? Do you really think this is going to end here, tonight? I just stared into a corner, hardly listening. I was thinking of Rebecca on westbound 64, driving fast with my car into the night. The questions weren't for me; they were for her. And when I found her, I would make sure she heard them.

When I was at last alone, I found the forged bottle where John had set it. Rebecca must've made the switch during our final night together. The vial rolled around on my palm. I was so disappointed that she'd forgotten to add the chip, I didn't have the heart to remove the cork and smell the candy spray she'd put inside.

PART V

UNDER THE INFLUENCE

AMAPOLA

BY LUIS ALBERTO URREA
Paradise Valley, Phoenix
(Originally published in *Phoenix Noir*)

H ere's the thing—I never took drugs in my life. Yes, all right, I was the champion of my share of keggers. Me and the Pope. We were like, Bring on the Corona and the Jäger! Who wasn't? But I never even smoked the chronic, much less used the hard stuff. Until I met Pope's little sister. And when I met her, she was the drug, and I took her and I took her, and when I took her, I didn't care about anything. All the blood and all the bullets in the world could not penetrate that high.

The irony of Amapola and me was that I never would have gotten close to her if her family hadn't believed I was gay. It was easy for them to think a gringo kid with emo hair and eyeliner was *un joto*. By the time they found out the truth, it was too late to do much about it. All they could do was put me to the test to see if I was a stand-up boy. It was either that or kill me.

You think I'm kidding.

At first, I didn't even know she existed. I was friends with Popo. We met in my senior year at Camelback High. Alice Cooper's old school back in prehistory—our big claim to fame, though the freshmen had no idea who Alice Cooper was. VH1 was for grandmothers. Maybe Alice was a president's wife or something.

You'd think the freak factor would remain high, right? But it was another hot space full of Arizona Republicans and future CEOs and the struggling underworld of auto mechanics and hopeless football jocks not yet aware they were going to be fat and bald and living in a duplex on the far side drinking too much and paying alimony to the cheerleaders they thought could never weigh 298 pounds and smoke like a coal plant.

Not Popo. The Pope. For one thing, he had more money than God. Well, his dad and his Aunt Cuca had all the money, but it drizzled upon him like the first rains of Christmas. He was always buying the beer, paying for gas and movie tickets and midnight runs to Taco Bell. "Good American food," he called it.

He'd transferred in during my senior year. He called it his exile. I spied him for the first time in English. We were struggling to stay awake during the endless literary conversations about A *Separate Peace*. He didn't say much about it. Just sat over there making sly eyes at the girls and laughing at the teacher's jokes. I'd never seen a Beaner kid with such long hair. He looked like some kind of Apache warrior, to tell you the truth. He had double-loops in his left ear. He got drogy sometimes and wore eyeliner under one eye. Those little Born Again chicks went crazy for him when he was in his devil-boy mode.

And the day we connected, he was wearing a Cradle of Filth T-shirt. He was staring at me. We locked eyes for a second and he nodded once and we both started to laugh. I was wearing a Fields of the Nephilim shirt. We were the Pentagram Brothers that day, for sure. Everybody else must have been thinking we were goth school shooters. I guess it was a good thing Phoenix was too friggin' hot for black trenchcoats.

Later, I was sitting outside the vice principal's office. Ray Hulsebus, the nickelback on the football team, had called me "faggot" and we'd duked it out in the lunch court. Popo was sitting on the wooden bench in the hall.

"Good fight," he said, nodding once.

I sat beside him.

"Wha'd you get busted for?" I asked.

He gestured at his shirt. It was originally black, but it had been laundered so often it was gray. In a circle were the purple letters, *VU*. Above them, in stark white, one word: *HEROIN*.

"Cool," I said. "Velvet Underground."

"My favorite song."

We slapped hands.

"The admin's not into classic rock," he noted. "Think I'm . . . advocating substance abuse."

We laughed.

"You like *Berlin?*" he asked.

"Berlin? Like, the old VH1 band?"

"Hell no! Lou Reed's best album, dude!"

They summoned him.

"I'll play it for ya," he said, and walked into the office.

And so it began.

Tía Cuca's house was the bomb. She was hooked up with some kind of Lebanese merchant. Out in Paradise Valley. The whole place was cool floor tiles and suede couches. Their pool looked out on the city lights, and you could watch roadrunners on the deck cruising for rattlers at dusk. Honestly, I didn't know why Pope wasn't in some rich private school like Brophy or Phoenix Country Day, but apparently his scholastic history was "spotty," as they say. I still don't know how he ended up at poor ol' Camelback, but I do know it must have taken a lot of maneuvering by his family. By the time we'd graduated, we were inseparable. He went to ASU. I didn't have that kind of money. I went to community college.

Pope's room was the coolest thing I'd ever seen. Tía Cuca had given him a detached single-car garage at the far end of the house. They'd put in a bathroom and made a bed loft on top of it. Pope had a king-size mattress up there, and a wall of CDs and a Bose iPod port, and everything was Wi-Fi'd to his laptop. There was a huge Bowie poster on the wall beside the door—in full Aladdin Sane glory, complete with the little shiny splash of come on his collarbone. It was so retro. My boy had satellite on a flat screen, and piles of DVDs around the slumpy little couch on the ground floor. I didn't know why he was so crazy for the criminal stuff—*Scarface* and *The Godfather*. I was sick of Tony Montana and Michael Corleone! Elvis clock—you know the one, with the King's legs dancing back and forth in place of a pendulum.

"Welcome," Pope said on that first visit, "to Disgraceland."

He was comical like that when you got to know him.

He turned me on to all that good classic stuff: Iggy, T. Rex, Roxy Music. He wasn't really fond of new music, except for the darkwave guys. Anyway, there we'd be, blasting that glam as loud as possible, and it would get late and I'd just fall asleep on his big bed with him. No wonder they thought I was gay! Ha. We were drinking Buds and reading *Hustler* mags we'd stolen from his Uncle Abdullah or whatever his name was. Aunt Cuca once said, "Don't you ever go home?" not mean like. Friendly banter, I'd say. But I told her, "Nah—since the divorce, my mom's too busy to worry about it." And in among all those excellent boys' days and nights, I was puttering around his desk, looking at the *Alien* figures and the Godzillas, scoping out the new copy of *El Topo* he'd gotten by mail, checking his big crystals and his antique dagger, when I saw the picture of Amapola behind his stack of textbooks. Yes, she was a kid. But what a kid.

"Who's this?" I said.

He took the framed picture out of my hand and put it back.

"Don't worry about who that is," he said.

Thanksgiving. Pope had planned a great big fiesta for all his homies and hench-men. Oh, yes. He took the goth-gansta thing seriously, and he had actual "hit

358 // USA Noir

men" (he called them that) who did errands for him, carried out security at his concerts. He played guitar for the New Nouveau Nuevos—you might remember them. One of his "soldiers" was a big Irish kid who'd been booted off the football team, Andy the Tank. Andy appeared at our apartment with an invitation to the fiesta—we were to celebrate the Nuevos' upcoming year, and chart the course of the future. I was writing lyrics for Pope, cribbed from Roxy Music and Bowie's *The Man Who Sold the World* album. The invite was printed out on rolled parchment and tied with a red ribbon. Pope had style.

I went over to Tía Cuca's early, and there she was—Amapola. She'd come up from Nogales for the fiesta, since Pope was by now refusing to go home for any reason. He wanted nothing to do with his dad, who had declared that only gay boys wore long hair or makeup or played in a band that wore feather boas and silver pants. Sang in English.

I was turning eighteen, and she was fifteen, almost sixteen. She was more pale than Popo. She had a frosting of freckles on her nose and cheeks, and her eyes were light brown, almost gold. Her hair was thick and straight and shone like some liquid. She was kind of quiet too, blushing when I talked to her, shying away from all us males.

The meal was righteous. They'd fixed a turkey in the Mexican style. It was stuffed not with bread or oysters, but with nuts, dried pineapple, dried papaya and mango slices, and raisins. Cuca and Amapola wore traditional Mexican dresses and, along with Cuca's cook, served us the courses as we sat like members of the Corleone family around the long dining room table. Pope had seated Andy the Tank beside Fuckin' Franc, the Nuevos' drummer. Some guy I didn't know but who apparently owned a Nine Inch Nails–type synth studio in his garage sat beside Franc. I was granted the seat at the end of the table, across its length from Pope. Down the left side were the rest of the Nuevos—losers all.

I was trying to keep my roving eye hidden from the Pope. I didn't even have to guess what he'd do if he caught me checking her out. But she was so fine. It wasn't even my perpetual state of horniness. Yes it was. But it was more. She was like a song. Her small smiles, her graciousness. The way she swung her hair over her shoulder. The way she lowered her eyes and spoke softly . . . then gave you a wry look that cut sideways and made savage fun of everyone there. You just wanted to be a part of everything she was doing.

"Thank you," I said every time she refilled my water glass or dropped fresh tortillas by my plate. Not much, it's true, but compared to the Tank or Fuckin' Franc, I was as suave as Cary Grant.

"You are so welcome," she'd say.

It started to feel like a dance. It's in the way you say it, not what you say. We were saying more to each other than Cuca or Pope could hear.

And then, I was hit by a jolt that made me jump a little in my chair.

She stood behind me, resting her hands on the top of the chair. We were down to the cinnamon coffee and the red grape juice toasts. And Amapola put out one finger, where they couldn't see it, and ran her fingernail up and down between my shoulder blades.

Suddenly, supper was over, and we were all saying goodnight, and she had disappeared somewhere in the big house and never came back out.

Soon, Christmas came, and Pope again refused to go home. I don't know how Cuca took it, having the sullen King Nouveau lurking in her converted garage. He had a kitsch aluminum tree in there. Blue ornaments. "Très Warhol," he sighed.

My mom had given me some cool stuff—a vintage Who T-shirt, things like that. Pope's dad had sent presents—running shoes, French sunglasses, a .22 target pistol. We snickered. I was way cooler than Poppa Popo. I had been over to Zia Records and bought him some obscure '70s CDs: Captain Beyond, Curved Air, Amon Duul II, the Groundhogs. Things that looked cool, not that I'd ever heard them. Pope got me a vintage turntable and the first four Frank Zappa LPs; I couldn't listen to that shit. But still. How cool is that?

Pope wasn't a fool. He wasn't blind either. He'd arranged a better gift for me than all that. He'd arranged for Amapola to come visit for a week. I found out later she had begged him.

"Keep it in your pants," he warned me. "I'm watching you."

Oh my God. I was flying. We went everywhere for those six days. The three of us, unfortunately. Pope took us to that fancy art deco hotel downtown—the Clarendon. That one with the crazy neon lights on the walls outside and the dark gourmet eatery on the ground-floor front corner. We went to movie matinees, never night movies. It took two movies to wrangle a spot sitting next to her, getting Pope to relinquish the middle seat to keep us apart. But he knew it was a powerful movement between us, like continental drift. She kept leaning over to watch me instead of the movies. She'd laugh at everything I said. She lagged when we walked so I would walk near her. I was trying to keep my cool, not set off the Hermano Grande alarms. And suddenly he let me sit beside her, and I could smell her. She was all clean hair and sweet skin. Our arms brushed on the armrest, and we let them linger, sweat against each other. Our skin forming a thin layer of wet between us, a little of her and a little of me mixing into something made of both of us. I was aching. I could have pole-vaulted right out of the theater.

She turned sixteen that week. At a three o'clock showing of *The Dark Knight*, she slipped her hand over the edge of the armrest and tangled her fingers in mine.

This time, when she left, Pope allowed us one minute alone in his garage room. I kissed her. It was awkward. Delicious. Her hand went to my face and held it. She got in Cuca's car and cried as they drove away.

"You fucker," Popo said.

I couldn't believe she didn't Facebook. Amapola didn't even e-mail. She lived across the border, in Nogales, Mexico. So the phone was out of the question, even though her dad could have afforded it. When I asked Pope about his father's business, he told me they ran a duty-free import/export company based on each side of the border, in the two Nogaleses. Whatever. I just wanted to talk to Amapola. So I got stamps and envelopes. I was thinking, what is this, like, 1980 or something? But I wrote to her, and she wrote to me. I never even thought about the fact that instant messages or e-mail couldn't hold perfume, or have lip prints on the paper. You could Skype naked images to each other all night long, but Amapola had me hooked through the lips with each new scent in the envelope. She put her hair in the envelopes. It was more powerful than anything I'd experienced before. Maybe it was voodoo.

At Easter, Cuca and her Lebanese hubby flew to St. Thomas for a holiday. Somehow, Pope managed to get Amapola there at the house for a few days. He was gigging a lot, and he was seeing three or four strippers. I'll admit, he was hitting the sauce too much—he'd come home wasted and ricochet around the bathroom, banging into the fixtures like a pinball. I thought he'd break his neck on the toilet or the bathtub. The old man had been putting pressure on him—I had no idea how or what he wanted of Pope. He wanted the rock 'n' roll foolishness to end, that's for sure.

"You have no idea!" Pope would say, tequila stink on his breath. "If you only knew what they were really like. You can't begin to guess." But, you know, all boys who wear eyeliner and pay for full-sleeve tats say the same thing. Don't nobody understand the troubles they've seen. I just thought Pope was caught up in being our Nikki Sixx. We were heading for fame, world tours. I thought.

And there she was, all smiles. Dressed in black. Looking witchy and magi-cal. Pope had a date with a girl named Demitasse. Can you believe that? Because she had small breasts or something. She danced at a high-end club that catered to men who knew words like "demitasse." She had little silver vials full of "stardust," that's all I really knew. It all left Pope staggering and blind, and that was what I needed to find time alone with my beloved.

We watched a couple of DVDs, and we held hands and then kissed. I freed her nipple from the lace—it was pink and swollen, like a little candy. I thought it would be brown. What did I know about Mexican girls? She pushed me away when I got on top of her, and she moved my hand back gently when it slipped up her thigh.

Pope came home walking sideways. I had no idea what time it was. I don't know how he got home. My pants were wet all down my left leg from hours of writhing with her. When Pope slurred, "My dad's in town," I didn't even pay attention. He went to Cuca's piano in the living room and tried to play some arrangement he'd cobbled together of *Tommy*. Then there was a silence that grew long. We looked in there and he was asleep on the floor, under the piano.

"Shh," Amapola said. And, "Wait here for me." She kissed my mouth, bit my lip.

When she came back down, she wore a nightgown that drifted around her legs and belly like fog. I knelt at her feet and ran my palms up her legs. She turned aside just as my hands crossed the midpoint of her thighs, and my palms slid up over her hip bones. She had taken off her panties. I put my mouth to her navel. I could smell her through the thin material.

"Do you love me?" she whispered, fingers tangled in my hair.

"Anything. You and me." I wasn't even thinking. "Us."

She yanked my hair.

"Do," she said. "You. Love me?"

Yank. It hurt.

"Yes!" I said. "Okay! Jesus! Love you!"

We went upstairs.

"Get up! Get up! Get the fuck up!" Popo was saying, ripping off the sheets. "Now! Now! Now!"

Amapola covered herself and rolled away with a small cry. Light was blasting through the windows. I thought he was going to beat my ass for sleeping with her. But he was in a panic.

"Get dressed. Dude—get dressed now!"

"What? What?"

"My dad."

He put his fists to his head.

"Oh shit. My dad!"

She started to cry.

I was in my white boxers in the middle of the room.

"Guys," I said. "Guys! Is there some trouble here?"

Amapola dragged the sheet off the bed and ran, wrapped, into the bathroom.

"You got no idea," Pope said. "Get dressed."

We were in the car in ten minutes. We sped out of the foothills and across town. Phoenix always looks empty to me when it's hot, like one of those sci-fi movies where all the people are dead and gone and some vampires or zombies are hiding in the vacant condos, waiting for night. The streets are too wide, and they reflect the heat like a Teflon cooking pan. Pigeons might explode into flame just flying across the street to escape the melting city bus.

Pope was saying, "Just don't say nothing. Just show respect. It'll be okay. Right, sis?"

She was in the backseat.

"Don't talk back," she said. "Just listen. You can take it."

"Yeah," Pope said. "You can take it. You better take it. That's the only way he'll respect you."

My head was spinning.

Apparently, the old man had come to town to see Pope and meet me, but Pope, that asshole, had been so wasted he forgot. But it was worse than that. The old man had waited at a fancy restaurant. For both of us. You didn't keep Big Pop waiting.

You see, he had found my letters. He had rushed north to try to avert the inevitable. And now he was seething, they said, because Pope's maricón best friend wasn't queer at all, and was working his mojo on the sweet pea. My scalp still hurt from her savage hair-pulling. I looked back at her. Man, she was as fresh as a sea breeze. I started to smile.

"Ain't no joke," Pope announced.

We fretted in silence.

"Look," he said. "It won't seem like it at first, but Pops will do anything for my sister. Anything. She controls him, man. So keep cool."

When we got there, Pope said, "The bistro." I had never seen it before, not really traveling in circles that ate French food or ate at "bistros." Pops was standing outside. He was a slender man, balding. Clean-shaven. Only about five-seven. He wore aviator glasses, that kind that turn dark in the sun. They were deep gray over his eyes. He was standing with a Mexican in a uniform. The other guy was over six feet tall and had a good gut on him. What Pope called a "food baby" from that funny movie everybody liked.

The old man and the soldier stared at me. I wanted to laugh. That's it? I mean, really? A little skinny bald guy? I was invincible with love.

Poppa turned and entered the bistro without a word. Pope and Amapola followed, holding hands. The stout soldier dude just eyeballed me and walked in. I was left alone on the sidewalk. I followed.

They were already sitting. It was ice cold. The way I liked it. I tried not to see Amapola's nipples. But I noticed her pops looking at them. And then the soldier. Pops told her, "Tápate, cabrona." She had brought a little sweater with her, and now I knew why. She primly draped herself.

"Dad . . ." said Pope.

"Shut it," his father said.

The eyeglasses had only become half-dark. You could almost see his eyes.

A waiter delivered a clear drink.

"Martini, sir," he said.

It was only about eleven in the morning.

Big Poppa said, "I came to town last night to see you." He sipped his drink. "I come here, to this restaurant. Is my favorite. Is comida Frances, understand? Quality." Another sip. He looked at the soldier—the soldier nodded. "I invite you." He pointed at Pope. Then at her. Then at me. "You, you, and you. Right here. Berry expensive." He drained the martini and snapped his fingers at the waiter. "An' I sit here an' wait." The waiter hurried over and took the glass and scurried away.

"Me an' my brother, Arnulfo."

He put his hand on the soldier's arm.

"We wait for you."

Popo said, "Dad . . ."

"Callate el osico, chingado," his father breathed. He turned his head to me and smiled. He looked like a moray eel in a tank. Another martini landed before him.

"You," he said. "Why you dress like a girl?" He sipped. "I wait for you, but you don't care. No! Don't say nothing. Listen. I wait, and you no show up here to my fancy dinner. Is okay. I don't care." He waved his hand. "I have my li'l drink, and I don't care." He toasted me. He seemed like he was coiled, steel springs inside his gut. My skin was crawling and I didn't even know why.

"I wait for you," he said. "Captain Arnulfo, he wait. You don't care, right?

Is okay! I'm happy. I got my martinis, I don't give a shit."

He smiled.

He pulled a long cigar out of his inner pocket. He bit the end off and spit it on the table. He put the cigar in his mouth. Arnulfo took out a gold lighter and struck a blue flame.

The waiter rushed over and murmured, "I'm sorry, sir, but this is a non-smoking bistro. You'll have to take it outside."

The old man didn't even look at him—just stared at me through those gray lenses.

"Is hot outside," he said. "Right, gringo? Too hot?" I nodded—I didn't know what to do. "You see?" the old man said.

"I must insist," the waiter said.

"Bring the chef," the old man said.

"Excuse me?"

"Get the chef out here for me. Now."

The waiter brought out the chef, who bent down to the old man. Whispers. No drama. But the two men hurried away and the waiter came back with an ashtray. Arnulfo lit Poppa's cigar.

He blew smoke at me and said, "Why you do this violence to me?"

"I . . ." I said.

"Shut up."

He snapped his fingers again, and food and more martinis arrived. I stared at my plate. Snails in garlic butter. I couldn't eat, couldn't even sip the water. Smoke drifted to me. I could feel the gray lenses focused on me. Pope, that chickenshit, just ate and never looked up. Amapola sipped iced coffee and stared out the window.

After forty minutes of this nightmare, Poppa pushed his plate away.

"Oye," he said, "tú."

I looked up.

"Why you wan' fock my baby daughter?"

Sure, I trembled for a while after that. I got it, I really did. But did good sense overtake me? What do you think? I was full-on into the Romeo and Juliet thing, and she was even worse. Parents—you want to ensure your daughters marry young? Forbid them from seeing their boyfriends. Just try it.

"Uncle Arnie," as big dark Captain Arnulfo was called in Cuca's house, started hanging around. A lot. I wasn't, like, stupid. I could tell what was what—he was sussing me out (that's a word Pope taught me). He brought

Bass Pale Ale all the time. He sidled up to me and said dumb things like, "You like the sexy?" Pope and I laughed all night after Uncle Arnie made his appearances. "You make the sexy-sexy in cars?" What a dork, we thought.

My beloved showered me with letters. I had no way of knowing if my own letters got to her or not, but she soon found an Internet café in Nogales and sent me cyber-love. Popo was drying up a little, not quite what you'd call sober, but occasionally back on the Earth, and he started calling me "McLovin." I think it was his way of trying to tone it down. "Bring it down a notch, homeboy," he'd say when I waxed overly poetic about his sister.

It was a Saturday when it happened. I was IM-ing Amapola. That's all I did on Saturday afternoons. No TV, no cruising in the car, no movies or pool time. I fixed a huge vat of sun tea and hit my laptop and talked to her. Mom was at work—she was always at work or out doing lame shit like bowling. It was just me, the computer, my distant girlie, and the cat rubbing against my leg. I'll confess to you—don't laugh—I cried at night thinking about her.

Does this explain things a little? Pope said I was whipped. I'd be like, that's no way to talk about your sister. She's better than all of you people! He'd just look at me out of those squinty Apache eyes. "Maybe," he'd drawl. "Maybe . . ." And I was just thinking about all that on Saturday, going crazier and crazier with the desire to see her sweet face every morning, her hair on my skin every night, mad in love with her, and I was IM-ing her that she should just book. Run away. She was almost seventeen already. She could catch a bus and be in Phoenix in a few hours and we'd jump on I-10 and drive to Cali. I didn't know what I imagined—just us, in love, on a beach. And suddenly the laptop crashed. Just gone—black screen before Amapola could answer me. That was weird, I thought. I cursed and kicked stuff, then I grabbed a shower and rolled.

When I cruised over to Aunt Cuca's, she was gone. So was Pope. Uncle Arnie was sitting in the living room in his uniform, sipping coffee.

"They all go on vacation," he said. "Just you and me."

Vacation? Pope hadn't said anything about vacations. Not that he was what my English profs would call a reliable narrator.

Arnie gestured for me to sit. I stood there.

"Coffee?" he offered.

"No, thanks."

"Sit!"

I sat.

I can't relate the conversation very clearly, since I never knew what the

F Arnie was mumbling, to tell you the truth. His accent was all bandido. I often just nodded and smiled, hoping not to offend the dude, lest he freak out and bust caps in me. That's a joke. Kind of. But then I'd wonder what I'd just agreed to.

"You love Amapola," he said. It wasn't a question. He smiled sadly, put his hand on my knee.

"Yes, sir," I said.

He nodded. Sighed. "Love," he said. "Is good, love."

"Yes, sir."

"You not going away, right?"

I shook my head. "No way."

"So. What this means? You marry the girl?"

Whoa. Marry? I . . . guess . . . I was going to marry her. Someday.

Sure, you think about it. But to say it out loud. That was hard. Yet I felt like some kind of breakthrough was happening here. The older generation had sent an emissary.

"I believe," I said, mustering some balls, "yes. I will marry Amapola. Someday. You know."

He shrugged, sadly. I thought that was a little odd, frankly. He held up a finger and busted out a cell phone, hit the speed button, and muttered in Spanish. Snapped it shut. Sipped his coffee.

"We have big family reunion tomorrow. You come. Okay? I'll fix up all with Amapola's papá. You see. Yes?"

I smiled at him, not believing this turn of events.

"Big Mexican rancho. Horses. Good food. Mariachis." He laughed. "And love! Two kids in love!"

We slapped hands. We smiled and chuckled. I had some coffee.

"I pick you up here at seven in the morning," he said. "Don't be late."

The morning desert was purple and orange. The air was almost cool. Arnie had a Styrofoam cooler loaded with Dr. Peppers and Cokes. He drove a bitchin' S-Class Benz. It smelled like leather and aftershave. He kept the satellite tuned to BBC Radio 1. "You like the crazy maricón music, right?" he asked.

". . . Ah . . . right."

It was more like flying than driving, and when he sped past Arivaca, I wasn't all that concerned. I figured we were going to Nogales, Arizona. But we slid through that little dry town like a shark and crossed into Mex without slowing down. He just raised a finger off the steering wheel and motored along, saying, "You going to like this."

And then we were through Nogales, Mexico, too. Black and tan desert. Saguaros and freaky burned-looking cactuses. I don't know what that stuff was. It was spiky.

We took a long dirt side road. I was craning around, looking at the bad black mountains around us.

"Suspension makes this road feel like butter," Arnie noted.

We came out in a big valley. There was an airfield of some sort there. Mexican army stuff—trucks, Humvees. Three or four hangars or warehouses. Some shiny Cadillacs and SUVs scattered around.

"You going to like this," Arnie said. "It's a surprise."

There was Big Poppa Popo, the old man himself. He was standing with his hands on his hips. With a tall American. Those dark gray lenses turned toward us. We parked. We got out.

"What's going on?" I asked.

"Shut up," said Arnie.

"Where's the rancho?" I asked.

The American burst out laughing.

"Jesus, kid!" he shouted. He turned to the old man. "He really is a dumbshit."

He walked away and got in a white SUV. He slammed the door and drove into the desert, back the way we had come. We stood there watching him go. I'm not going to lie—I was getting scared.

"You marry Amapola?" the old man said.

"One day. Look, I don't know what you guys are doing here, but—"

"Look at that," he interrupted, turning from me and gesturing toward a helicopter sitting on the field. "Huey. Old stuff, from your Vietnam. Now the Mexican air force use it to fight las drogas." He turned to me. "You use las drogas?"

"No! Never."

They laughed.

"Sure, sure," the old man said.

"Ask Amapola!" I cried. "She'll tell you!"

"She already tell me everything," he said.

Arnie put his arm around my shoulders. "Come," he said, and started walking toward the helicopter. I resisted for a moment, but the various Mexican soldiers standing around were suddenly really focused and not slouching and were walking along all around us.

"What is this?" I said.

"You know what I do?" the old man asked.

"Business?" I said. My mind was blanking out, I was so scared.

"Business." He nodded. "Good answer."

We came under the blades of the big helicopter. I'd never been near one in my life. It scared the crap out of me. The Mexican pilots looked out their side windows at me. The old man patted the machine.

"President Bush!" he said. "DEA!"

I looked at Arnie. He smiled, nodded at me. "Fight the drogas," he said.

The engines whined and chuffed and the rotor started to turn.

"Is very secret what we do," said the old man. "But you take a ride and see. Is my special treat. You go with Arnulfo."

"Come with me," Arnie said.

"You go up and see, then we talk about love."

The old man hurried away, and it was just me and Arnie and the soldiers with their black M16s.

"After you," Arnie said.

He pulled on a helmet. Then we took off. It was rough as hell. I felt like I was being pummeled in the ass and lower back when the engines really kicked in. And when we rose, my guts dropped out through my feet. I closed my eyes and gripped the webbing Arnie had fastened around my waist. "Holy God!" I shouted. It was worse when we banked—the side doors were wide open, and I screamed like a girl, sure I was falling out. The Mexicans laughed and shook their heads, but I didn't care.

Arnie was standing in the door. He unhooked a big gun from the stanchion where it had been strapped with its barrel pointed up. He dangled it in the door on cords. He leaned toward me and shouted, "Sixty caliber! Hung on double bungees!" He slammed a magazine into the thing and pulled levers and snapped snappers. He leaned down to me again and shouted, "Feel the vibration? You lay on the floor, it makes you come!"

I thought I heard him wrong.

We were beating out of the desert and into low hills. I could see our shadow below us, fluttering like a giant bug on the ground and over the bushes. The seat kicked up and we were rising.

Arnulfo took a pistol from his belt and showed me.

"Amapola," he said.

I looked around for her, stupidly. But then I saw what was below us, in a watered valley. Orange flowers. Amapola. Poppies.

"This is what we do," Arnulfo said.

He raised his pistol and shot three rounds out the door and laughed. I put my hands over my ears.

"You're DEA?" I cried.

He popped off another round.

"Is competition," he said. "We do business."

Oh my God.

He fell against me and was shouting in my ear and there was nowhere I could go. "You want Amapola? You want to marry my sobrina? Just like that? Really? Pendejo." He grabbed my shirt. "Can you fly, gringo? Can you fly?" I was shaking. I was trying to shrink away from him, but I could not. I was trapped in my seat. His breath stank, and his lips were at my ear like hers might have been, and he was screaming, "Can you fly, chingado? Because you got a choice! You fly, or you do what we do."

I kept shouting, "What? What?" It was like one of those dreams where nothing makes sense. "What?"

"You do what we do, I let you live, cabrón."

"What?"

"I let you live. Or you fly. Decide."

"I don't want to die!" I yelled. I was close to wetting my pants. The Huey was nose-down and sweeping in a circle. I could see people below us, running. A few small huts. Horses or mules. A pickup started to speed out of the big poppy field. Arnulfo talked into his mike and the helicopter heaved after it. Oh no, oh no. He took up the .60 caliber and braced himself. I put my fingers in my ears. And he ripped a long stream of bullets out the door. It was the loudest thing I'd ever heard. Louder than the loudest thing you can imagine. So loud your insides jump, but it all becomes an endless rip of noise, like thunder cracking inside your bladder and your teeth hurt from gritting against it.

The truck just tattered, if metal can tatter. The roof of the cab blew apart and the smoking ruin of the vehicle spun away below us and vanished in dust and smoke and steam.

I was crying.

"Be a man!" Arnulfo yelled.

We were hovering. The crew members were all turned toward me, staring.

Arnie unsnapped my seat webbing.

"Choose," he said.

"I want to live."

"Choose."

You know how it goes in *Die Hard* movies. How the hero kicks the bad guy out the door and sprays the Mexican crew with the .60 and survives a crash landing. But that's not what happened. That didn't even cross my mind. Not even close. No, I got up on terribly shaky legs, so shaky I might have pitched out the open door all by myself to discover that I could not, in fact, fly. I said, "What do I do?" And the door gunner grabbed me and shoved me up to the hot gun. The ground was wobbling far below us, and I could see the Indian workers down there. Six men and a woman. And they were running. I was praying and begging God to get me out of this somehow and I was thinking of my beautiful lover and I told myself I didn't know how I got there and the door gunner came up behind me now, he slammed himself against my ass, and he said, "Hold it, lean into it. It's gonna kick, okay? Finger on the trigger. I got you." And I braced the .60 and I tried to close my eyes and prayed I'd miss them and I was saying, *Amapola, Amapola,* over and over in my mind, and the gunner was hard against me, he was erect and pressing it into my buttocks and he shouted, "For love!" and I squeezed the trigger.

THE TIK

BY JOHN O'BRIEN

Scotch 80s, Las Vegas

(Originally published in *Las Vegas Noir*)

P art of me wished that I had asked the cab to wait. I hadn't. I stared up at the big double doors, weathered from the desert sun, yes, but still so imposing that you half-expected to see a muscled bodyguard when they opened. The doorbell didn't work. It never had. I felt the familiar quiver begin in the back of my neck as twice I dropped the ornate knocker, an upside-down black iron cross. I peered over my back to see if the cab was still in sight. The long drive was empty.

Despite the impending nightfall, I noticed the German shepherd asleep on the grass, his white face a beacon in the otherwise black lawn. I knew this dog and wondered if he would remember me. I walked over to nudge him awake.

When I had last left this house over ten years ago, I was certain that I was through with this all-consuming part of my life, but as I bent over to pet the dog, it was clear this place was far from finished with me; rather, like the dog, it was merely lying in wait for some new awakening. The shepherd lifted his head and growled, but whether the snarl was for me or something else, I did not know. I followed his gaze and was startled to find that I was being watched by a tall slim figure, standing where only moments before the closed doors had been.

"Timmers, you're back," she said, not at all surprised to see me.

I cringed at her easy, reflexive use of my nickname; at her prosaic manner of observation, as if I'd just returned from a short walk—when in fact I had been gone for a decade. This meeting was nothing less than heart-stopping for me.

"Melinda, I . . . I didn't hear the door open. You startled me . . ." So much so, in fact, that I couldn't remember anything that I had planned to say. "You sound as if you've been expecting me." She ignored this.

"Come in," she said.

As I followed her through the foyer and into the heart of the house, I began to feel a sort of resignation; a feeling that, now that I had set things in motion, I could sit back and relax, free from the burden of decision making. It was not an unpleasant outlook.

"Christ," I said as we walked into the living room, its windowed ceiling a full twenty feet above me. "I'd forgotten how damn big this place is."

"I doubt that," she responded. "Still drink bourbon?"

"Finally a question. Apparently there is at least one thing that you're not sure of." I was starting to feel cocky. How else could I feel? I'd come this far into the house, into my past. The less I thought about it, the better it felt. I was comfortable here. Melinda understood me in a way that no one else could.

"Not really, Timmers." She reached into an antique Spanish sideboard and extracted a dusty bottle of Wild Turkey.

"My brand, even. I'm impressed." I narrowed my eyes and grinned at her. Her presence was making me giddy. I was excited—this was so easy. She knew why I was here. It was like being in a cathouse—no pretense. You ask for sex and they give it to you. But a cathouse would seem like a church compared to this place.

"Your bottle, actually," she said.

"Fuck it," I said. "We can drink all we want later."

Without missing a beat she set down the bottle, picked up my hand, and turned silently toward the staircase. I willingly followed her determined walk and flowing silk robe. This was the beginning of the end of ten years' anxiety. It seemed as if I'd barely been away. Right now nothing seemed less relevant than my time away from her.

But I did have that time, and I had to remember that. I had to remember the futile years of trying to ignore this hidden life, with Melinda and this extravagant house standing at the center. I had to remember why I was here.

Why was I here?

What if I did like it? Liking it—living it—had been the whole point. I was back now and it was time to unlearn compassion and let Melinda take me again.

We climbed the staircase to her bedroom; ten years since it had been *our* bedroom and yet it looked exactly the same to me. Perhaps it would always be our bedroom. Melinda dropped my hand and turned to face me. She stepped back and looked into my eyes as she untied her robe and let it fall to the floor. I was amazed at her perfection. Though life had left its many marks on my body, she was just as I remembered—flawless, still possessing all the curves and textures of a nineteen-year-old showgirl.

She unbuttoned my shirt and in a moment I, too, was naked. Melinda wrapped herself around me. I lifted her onto the bed, the raw heat rising inside of me. It was exactly as I remembered. I ran my hands along her thighs, stopping short of the cleft of her. Her nipples were hard and brown. I took one between my teeth, one between thumb and finger, and bit and pinched with exacting pressure. Melinda cried out, but did not move to stop me. She was open beneath me, ready. It was time. I licked and tasted her until her legs quivered on the brink. I stopped short of her orgasm and lay on top of her, breathing in the intermission. Finally, I pushed into her. She climaxed in waves, acute bursts of pleasure. I was close behind, teetering on that exquisite edge.

Melinda sensed this, as I knew she would, and stopped all her motion. At once my imminent climax was completely in her control. She slid from beneath me and sat up on the side of the bed. She opened the nightstand drawer. I waited, trembling, as she extracted a stainless steel tray and with slick efficiency prepared the injection. The glowing black fluid filled the syringe. My hardness raged. I swallowed against it all, my throat dry.

At that moment it was impossible for me to understand how I had stayed away from this drug—we called it "The Tik"—for all those years. I had never heard of it outside this room and had never looked for it elsewhere. Somehow I knew that it existed nowhere but here. This place was as much a part of The Tik as I, moments before, had been a part of Melinda. She lived here in a desert oasis with it, and the whole scene had always been one great, indivisible, seductive, eternal entity to me. I had once believed that I could escape it by running. Now I had run back, and was going to try to escape another way.

Melinda tapped the needle of the syringe with a long red fingernail. The sexual tension and my own anticipation had my heart nearly beating out of my chest. My bloodstream was primed to rush the drug to my brain. Melinda turned, ready with the needle. I closed my eyes and offered my arm.

The beautiful pinch.

As the hot fluid rushed through my veins, Melinda prepared another hypo and injected herself. Then she dropped the syringe onto the tray and kicked it, lunging into me. As the stainless steel and empty vial clattered to the floor, Melinda clutched my waist and took me into her mouth. The heat of The Tik inside of me and the heat of Melinda's tongue outside of me combined into that perfect euphoria I'd known only within these walls. She held me on the brink for as long as she could. Then I yelled out, pumping into her.

The feeling of being alive poured over me, elemental and singular. We were finally together again.

The Tik.

We blinked in the aftermath, verifying it was real. I lay on my back, Melinda's head on my stomach. Then she reared up and playfully bit me. I laughed and pushed her off. Full of new energy, I bounded out of the bed and down the stairs, returning with the bottle of bourbon. Melinda already had her panties on and was rolling up her fishnets. I sucked the bottle as I watched her dress. She grabbed it from me and took a big swallow.

"I have a surprise for you," she said. She shoved the bottle back into my hand and pulled open the door of what had been my closet. I was stunned. Before me hung all my old clothes, just as I had left them.

I laughed. "Unfuckingbelievable. Do you still have the Jag too?"

"In the garage," she said.

Nothing had changed.

Melinda and the drug were working in perfect harmony. My head spun with satisfaction and lust. I grinned wildly and shook on the leather jacket that had always fit me like a second skin. It still did. My boots, my jeans, everything was in place. I gulped some more bourbon and pounced on Melinda. We fell onto the bed and I ripped off the black lace bra she had just put on. She laughed as the zipper on my jacket scratched her. We fucked again, more perfunctorily this time, then got dressed.

After finishing the bottle of bourbon we went down to the garage. Melinda's vintage Jag, a black 1967 XKE, was still in perfect shape, just as I, by now, expected everything to be. The car had also fit me. I slid into the driver's seat and palmed the bulb of the stick shift. Melinda's perfume blended with the smell of leather and night air. We squealed down the driveway and onto the moneyed side street. The ragtop was down and the wind blew Melinda's hair all around. I flew through a red light. We vanished into the night.

We headed for the Strip, battling traffic. I didn't mind. I basked in the stares this beautiful woman and car garnered beneath the streetlights and neon.

"Let's go to the Barbary Coast," I said.

"The Barbary Coast? You've got to be kidding," said Melinda. "Why?"

"Dunno," I said, shrugging my shoulders. "The $3.99 prime rib dinner?"

Melinda laughed, throwing her head back. "Oh, Timmers," she said. "I'd forgotten how you make me laugh."

We parked off the Strip and started walking hand in hand through the crowd. The Tik pulsed inside me and mixed with the bourbon. Melinda was on my arm. I was ten feet tall.

Overweight Midwesterners stared at the two of us, wishing they could be us. We were the Las Vegas they came to see. A middle-aged man in Bermuda shorts eyed Melinda's long legs.

"Loosest slots on the Strip," I said to him with a conspiratorial nod as we passed. Completely stunned, he looked up at me, his mouth agape. Melinda and I folded with laughter, then broke into a run.

After a few minutes, Melinda stopped, breathless, and turned to me. She squeezed my hand. Her nails broke the skin.

"It feels so good to have you back, Tim," she said.

I pushed her against the cold brick wall and put my mouth on hers while pressing my thigh between her legs.

"I love you," I whispered. My hand was sticky with blood.

She returned my kiss, our tongues rolling together until Melinda pulled back.

"Why then," she said, "are you going to make me go in there?" She nodded toward the billowing entrance of the Coast.

"Come on," I said. "I feel so good. I feel like slumming. And if we don't find any action in there"—I indicated the space in front of me with a grandiose sweep of my arm—"the entire Strip awaits us." We stepped through the forced air plenum and into the clanging miasma of the casino.

A semi-attractive blonde with a very large chest caught my attention. She was sitting alone at a blackjack table.

"I'm going to the girls' room," Melinda shouted over the cacophony of bells and chimes that rang from the slot carousels. "I'll catch up to you in a couple of minutes."

I nodded and watched her meander off, as did most of the people she passed. The fishnet stockings had that effect.

I sat down next to the blonde and threw a hundred dollars on the table. The dealer set a short stack of chips in front of me as a cocktail waitress in a bad pirate costume appeared at my elbow.

"A double bullshot," I said, placing a chip on her tray.

"What's that?" said the blonde as she slurped at a frothy blender drink.

"It's beef bouillon and vodka," I said, peering at my cards.

She wrinkled her nose into a grimace. "Ewww! Why are you drinking *that?*" The end of her straw was coated in waxy orange lipstick.

"I'm hungry," I said. After all, I was. I nodded yes to a hit from the dealer.

"That's so gross," she said.

"Fuck you," I said. Maybe semi-attractive was too generous a description for her, stacked or not. The bad casino lighting wasn't shoring up her odds either. "Now shut up and finish your snow cone."

"Okay, I will," she said. "And then you can."

"I can what?" I said, rolling my eyes. The waitress set down my drink with exactly the speed a pre-tip buys. I placed another chip on her tray and turned back to the blonde.

"You can fuck me," she said as the dealer flipped over his jack and ace.

"Who the fuck are you?" With characteristically perfect timing and an equally perfect brunette, led by the hand, Melinda intervened. The blonde sized up the two women and picked up her drink. "I'm more than you could handle anyway," she said, then collected her remaining chips and walked away, flipping us off.

"Tim, this is Teena," said Melinda, not even looking after the blonde. "She's new in town. Just got a job as a waitress over at the Peppermill."

"After I finish the training course," said Teena. "Of course," she added, giggling at her own quip.

"Right," said Melinda. "After you finish the training course." She wrapped an arm around Teena's waist and turned to me. "She's coming home with us for a nightcap." One look at Teena and I could see that Melinda had bribed her with the coke she always kept in her purse.

"Hi, Tim. I saw you walk in and thought you were really cute. I'm really glad to meet you," said Teena. She seemed like a willing little lamb, naïve and very sexy. Exactly what I'd had in mind.

"With that perky attitude," I said, "my bet is you'll sail right through that training course." Teena gave me a prom queen smile. Perfect, just like everything else so far.

"So what do you say, Tim?" asked Melinda, though she already knew the answer. "Nightcaps at our place?"

Our place. "That sounds just fine," I said. "First let's have a drink for the road." I pushed a chip toward the dealer and steered the girls around to the bar. "Will you be riding with us, Teena, or do you have your own car?"

"Teena will follow us out to the house," said Melinda, lifting an eyebrow down the bar.

I smiled at Teena.

"What can I get for you?" said the bartender, one eye eclipsed by a fake black eye patch.

Melinda looked at me. "Make a wish," she said.

* * *

I motioned Teena to park next to the Jag in the garage. Melinda took Teena inside to show her around while I looked over Teena's Honda and then locked up the garage. I went in the back door of the house and found Melinda and Teena necking in the kitchen. I didn't seem to disturb them.

"Save some for me, Mel," I said. "Anyone want a drink?"

"Tequila," said Melinda.

"Got any champagne?" asked Teena.

I headed for the sideboard to crack open a new bottle of bourbon.

"Join us upstairs when you're ready, Timmers," Melinda shouted down the hall. She was anxious despite her cool veneer. It had been a long time for her too. I was eager to do a number on Teena, but something vague seemed to be holding me back. *Fuck that,* I thought, and took the longest drink of bourbon in my life.

By the time I got up to the bedroom, Melinda's face was buried between Teena's legs. Teena seemed a little dazed but was holding up her end quite well, no doubt aided by the small mountain of coke next to her on the night-stand. Melinda saw me and bolted upright. She was covered with sweat.

"Fuck her, Tim," she said. "Fuck her proper."

Teena rolled over and did another line, then she lay back on the bed. "Yeah, fuck me," she said.

I did. I was rough but she took it. When I got off her, bruises started to form on the insides of her thighs. I reached for the bourbon and watched her and Melinda work on each other. I felt strange. The Tik still moved through me, though now at an even keel. I drank more bourbon.

I drank for a long time.

Melinda screamed and dug her nails into Teena's skin. Teena threw her head back on the pillow. Melinda rolled over and beckoned me. My head was spinning. I placed my hands on Teena's knees and opened her as Melinda reached for the nightstand. I centered all my consciousness on Teena. I fo-cused my whole body on my mouth, and my mouth on her. Melinda moved on the bed. I heard a whisper of rushing air. Teena stiffened and bucked under me. A hot spray rained across my back. Something clinked against the wall. I squeezed Teena's waist with all my strength. Tears came to my eyes. Teena's body went limp.

I lay hugging her, my breath so fast. The room was quiet. After a time I looked up at Melinda. She smiled and wiped the blood from her eyes. She got off the bed and picked up the straight razor, which she had thrown against the wall. She dropped it in the nightstand drawer.

"You okay, Timmers?" she asked. "I know it's been awhile." She paused, then reached back into the drawer. "Maybe it's time for another shot."

"No," I said. "Not yet."

I picked up the bourbon and had a sip. Melinda closed the drawer and turned toward the bathroom.

"Suit yourself, but we shouldn't wait too long," she said. "I'm going to clean up. Will you take care of that?" She nodded at the blood-soaked bed and the still body, naked and staring wide-eyed at the ceiling.

"Of course I will," I said. "Don't I always?"

I finished the bourbon as Melinda closed the bathroom door behind her. Out the window, dawn announced itself quietly with a barely perceptible change of color in the east. A car started off in the distance and I reflexively glanced at the garage door. It was still locked. I really didn't worry. Melinda and I had always led a charmed existence. I sighed and put on my pants.

"Wash my back, Tim," Melinda called from the shower when she heard me enter the bathroom. I opened the curtain and soaped up my hands. I massaged her back as I washed it.

"Ahhh, that feels good," she said. "Get in here. I'm ready for a good fucking."

She put her cheek against the wall and closed her eyes. I pulled her razor from my back pocket. With one motion I grabbed her hair and drew the blade across her throat. For an instant she stretched her neck out, exposing it even more, and then she slumped quietly to the bottom of the tub. I turned off the water and went into the bedroom, dropped the razor into her nightstand.

I cleaned up and finished dressing in the clothes that I had arrived in the day before. I kissed Teena's forehead. I kissed Melinda's hand and held it to my mouth for a long time.

Downstairs I lit a small fire on the love seat in the living room, then went to the kitchen and turned on all the gas jets. On my way out to the garage I stopped and, as an afterthought, picked up my leather jacket.

I backed the Jag out of the drive and looked for but did not see the German shepherd. It suddenly occurred to me how very old he must have been. As I put the Jag into gear, my eyes paused at the mailbox, an unlikely witness. I pulled away and, driving down the road, watched it disappear in the rearview mirror. I thought about how badly I needed to sleep.

LIGHTHOUSE

BY S.J. ROZAN

St. George, Staten Island

(Originally published in *Staten Island Noir*)

I
t sucked to be him.

Paul huffed and wheezed up Lighthouse Avenue, pumping his bony legs and wiping sweat from his face. His thighs burned and his breath rasped but he knew better than to ask if he could stop. One more uphill block, he figured, then he'd turn and head back down. That would be okay. That would take him past the mark one more time, even though there wasn't much to see from the street. A wall with a couple of doors, a chain-link fence, raggedy bright flags curling in the autumn breeze. The building itself, the little museum, nestled into the hillside just below. Paul didn't really have to see it. He didn't have to do this run at all, truth be told. He'd been there a bunch of times, inside, in that square stone room. He used to go just to stand in the odd cool stillness, just to look at those peculiar statues with all their arms and their fierce eyes. Long time ago, of course, before The Guys came, but the place hadn't changed and he already knew all he had to know about it. Alarm, yes; dog, no. Most important, people in residence: no.

He kept climbing, closing in on the end of the block. Paul liked it here. Lighthouse Hill was easy pickings.

It always had been, back from when he was a kid. The first B&E he pulled, he boosted a laptop from the pink house on Edinboro. Years ago, but he remembered. The planning, the job, his slamming heart. The swag. Everything.

It was good he did, because The Guys liked to hear about it. While he was planning a job they liked to help, and then when it was done they liked to hear the story over and over. Even though they'd been there. They wanted him to compare each job to other jobs so they could point out dumb things he did, and stuff that went right. That used to piss Paul off, how they made him go over everything a million times. Turned out, though, it was pretty worthwhile to listen to them, even though in the beginning he'd wondered what a bunch of stupid aliens knew about running a B&E. He was right about Roman too. Roman really was stupid. He never knew anything about anything. Paul had to be careful when and where he said that, even just thought it, because if Roman was listening he could do that kick thing and give Paul one of those sonuvabitch headaches. There was a way he'd found where he could sometimes think about stuff, sort of sideways and not using words, and The Guys didn't notice. But the thing was, even if Roman did catch Paul thinking about how stupid he was, it didn't matter; it was still true.

Larry and Stoom, though, they were pretty sharp. "You mean, for aliens?" Stoom asked once, with that sneer he always had. Paul thought for sure he was curling his lip, like in a cartoon. That was how he knew they must have lips, because of Stoom's sneer. Stoom was the only one who still used his alien name, and he was the nastiest (but not as pig-eyed mean as Roman). He was always ragging on Paul, telling him what a loser he was.

"Then why'd you pick me?" Paul yelled back once, a long time ago. "I didn't invite you. Why don't you just go the fuck back where you came from?"

Stoom said it was none of his business and then *whammo*, the headache.

But as far as the sharp-for-aliens thing, Stoom and Larry were actually pretty sharp for anybody. It was Larry who suggested Paul do his preliminary reconnaissance ("Casing the joint!" Roman bawled. "Call it casing the joint!") in sweats, jogging past a place a couple of times, at different hours. That was good for a whole bunch of reasons. For one thing, Larry was right: no one noticed a jogger, except other joggers, who were only interested in sizing you up, figuring if they were better or you were better. If they could take you. Of course, if it came to it, any of them could take Paul and he knew it. Real runners were all muscle and sinew. Paul looked like them, lanky, with short hair and sunken cheeks, but his skinniness was blasted out of what he used to be, drained by junk. As though the needles in his arm had been day by day drawing something out instead of pumping it in.

But he still laced up his running shoes and made himself circle whatever neighborhood it was, every time he was ready to plan a job. Which was pretty much every time the rent was due or the skag ran out. Even if he had the whole job ready to go in his head and didn't need to, like now, he still ran the streets around it. For one thing, The Guys liked that he did it this way, and as awful as the wheezing and the fire in his legs were, the headaches when they got mad were always worse.

Another thing: suiting up and going by a couple times over a couple days stretched out the planning part. That was Paul's favorite. He liked to learn stuff about his marks: who they were, how they lived, what they liked to do.

"Oh, please," said Stoom, about that. He sounded like he was rolling his eyes, though Paul didn't know if they had eyes, either. He'd asked once, what they looked like, but that turned out to be another thing that was none of his business. "You're a crook," Stoom went on. "You're a junkie. You're a loser with aliens in your head. All you need to know about people is what they have and when they won't be home."

"Maybe he wants to write a book about them," Larry suggested, in a bored and mocking voice. "Maybe he's going to be a big best-selling author."

That had burned Paul up, because that was exactly what he'd wanted before The Guys showed up. He always had an imagination; he was going to grow up and be a writer.

He never talked about The Guys anymore. He had, at first. It took him awhile to figure out no one else could hear them and everyone thought he was nuts. "There are no aliens, Paul. It's all in your head. You need to get help." Stuff like that.

Well, that first point, that was completely wrong. Paul used to argue, say obvious things like, "You can't see time either, but no one says it isn't there." All people did was stare and back away, so he stopped saying anything.

The second point, though, was completely right. That's where The Guys lived: in Paul's head. Where they'd beamed when they came to Earth on some kind of scouting mission, Paul didn't know what for. Or from where. They never did tell him why, but Stoom had told him from where. It's just, it was some planet he'd never heard of circling some star he'd never heard of in some galaxy really, *really* far away. *Magribke* was the closest Paul could come to pronouncing it. The Guys laughed at him when he said it that way, but they didn't tell him how to really say it. They didn't talk about their home planet much. Mostly, they just told Paul the Loser what to do.

They first showed up when he was fourteen. He supposed he'd been a peculiar kid—God knows his mom always thought so—but he wasn't a loser then. ("Oh, of course you were," Stoom said, but Paul knew he was wrong.) It was them, making him do weird shit, distracting him so he started flunking out, giving him those kick headaches—they were the ones who screwed him all up.

And the third point, get help? He'd tried. What did people think, he liked it like this, these bastards giving him orders, making him hurt really bad when he didn't do what they said? When he was sixteen and he knew for sure The Guys weren't leaving, he went looking for someone who could tell him what to do. Somebody at NASA or something. But NASA didn't answer his e-mails and his mom dragged him to a shrink. The shrink said she believed Paul about

The Guys, but she didn't. She gave him drugs to take but the drugs made the world all suffocating and gray, and they didn't make The Guys go away, it just made it so Paul couldn't hear them. They were still there, though, and he knew they were getting madder and madder, and when the drugs stopped working he'd be in bad trouble. So he stopped taking the drugs, and The Guys were so pleased he'd done it on his own that they only gave him a little kick headache, not even a whole day long.

What The Guys liked best was Paul breaking into places and boosting stuff, so that's what he started to do.

He didn't live at home anymore, not since he stopped seeing the shrink and taking her drugs. He knew his mom was relieved when he moved out, even though she pretended like she wanted him to stay. He still went home to see her sometimes. She acted all nervous when he was there, which she tried to hide, but he knew. She especially got nervous when he talked to The Guys. He'd asked them to just please shut up while he was with his mom, but of course they didn't. So he still went, but not so often.

He had a basement apartment in St. George. It had bugs and it smelled moldy but it was cheap and no one bothered him and it was easy to get to whatever neighborhood The Guys wanted him to hit next. It was also easy to get to his dealer, and it was a quiet, dark place to shoot up.

The first year after he moved out was the worst of his life. The Guys wouldn't shut up, and they were really into the headaches that whole year. It was part of some experiment they were doing for their planet. Even sometimes when Paul did exactly what they told him, they'd just start kicking. Sometimes he thought they wanted to kick his brains out from the inside.

Sometimes he wished they would.

That year it especially sucked to be him—until he discovered heroin.

Damn, damn, damn, what a find! The only bad thing: he hadn't thought of it years ago. Shooting up wasn't like taking the shrink's drugs. The Guys liked it. A needle of black tar, and everyone just relaxed, got all laid-back. Made him laugh the first time, the idea of a bunch of wasted aliens nodding out inside his head. He was a little afraid right after he laughed, but while they were high The Guys didn't care, didn't get mad, were so quiet they might as well not have been there at all.

It was the only time anymore that things were that way, the only time Paul could even pretend it was like it used to be before The Guys came, when he could do what he wanted and not what he was being told to do.

He reached the top of the hill and turned around. His long, loping strides down were such a relief after the pain of fighting his way up that he almost cried. He guessed that was another thing Larry was right about, though. If The Guys didn't make him do it this way, he'd be just another junkie passed out on a stinking mattress with a needle in his arm. He wouldn't be pulling B&E's, he'd be mugging old ladies when he got desperate for a few bucks to buy the next fix. The running kept him in some kind of shape, kept his muscles working, and cleared his head for planning his jobs.

"Well, sure. Glad to help. Because I don't think you really want to go to prison, do you?" Larry asked as Paul passed the bright line of flags again. Paul didn't answer. Larry's questions were never supposed to get answers. "There's no heroin in jail, you know."

Paul knew, and that was enough to make the idea terrifying. No skag, and for sure The Guys would come with him. How shitty would that be? If he thought they wouldn't, he'd let his ass get picked up in a New York minute, but no such luck and he knew it.

Though on his bad days—and what day wasn't bad, really?—he wondered how long he'd be able to stay out anyway. He had an arrest record, had been fingered twice for B&E's, but he was good ("We're good," Stoom said. "Whose idea was the surgical gloves?") and the cops were way overworked and no one had gotten hurt either time, so they cut him loose. But lately there was a new problem.

Lately, The Guys had started liking for people to get hurt.

The first time he'd hurt someone it was by accident. Well, all three times it was. But that first time, it was a year ago and fucked if Paul wasn't as scared as she was. He'd just slipped into the garage window of a square brick house in Huguenot, and like he knew it would be, the car was gone; and like he expected, the door to the kitchen had this cheesy old lock. ("Even you can pick that," Stoom said. Roman whined, "Oh, come on, kick it in," but Paul hadn't. He didn't have to do what Roman said if one of the others said something different.) The lady who lived there never came home before noon on Tuesdays. Paul wondered where she went, to the gym, to a class or something, and if it was a class, what did she like to learn about? The Guys jeered at that but no one kicked him, and he jiggled the credit card down the doorjamb and got in.

The girl at the kitchen counter dropped the coffee pot and screamed.

Paul almost pissed himself. He'd never seen her before. She didn't live there. Curly brown hair, brown eyes, she looked like the lady, maybe a sister or something, maybe visiting, shit, what did it matter? Good thing he was wearing the ski mask. He backed toward the door, was trying to run but she threw a plate, brained him, and he went down, slipping in all that spilled coffee. He thrashed around trying to get up and she whacked at him with the broom, so he had to grab it and pull at it and she wouldn't let go. He yanked really hard and she slipped too, went down with a thud, and then gave a loud moan and a lot of, "Ow-ow-ow!" Rolling around on the floor clutching her arm. Paul sped back through the window and ran down the street, ripping the mask and gloves off as he went, shoving them into a dumpster behind the bagel place, where he stopped and threw up.

As he was wiping his mouth he realized with a chill that The Guys were laughing.

Not at him; they did that all the time and he was used to it. But with each other, like he and his buddies used to (when he was a kid and had buddies) when they'd ring old lady Miller's doorbell and run away, or when they'd boost a couple of chocolate bars from Rifkin's. It wasn't the thing, the event itself: it was the rush. That's why they'd done it, and laughed like hell afterward, from the relief of not getting caught, and the rush. That's the kind of laughing The Guys were doing now.

"Glad you thought that was funny," he said, straightening up. "You like it that she clobbered me, huh?"

"Seriously? Who gives a shit?" Roman cracked up again. "Did you hear her screaming? *Ow-ow-OW!* I bet you broke her arm!"

"I enjoyed that face she made," Larry said. "When she screamed. I didn't know people's mouths could open that wide. That was very interesting."

Even Stoom was chortling, though he didn't have anything to say. Paul couldn't wait to get home, get his works, shoot up.

It was more than six months after that before the next person got hurt because Paul was in their house. Another accident, same kind of thing, a man coming home early, Paul barely getting out, The Guys close to hysterics. The one after that, just last month: the same but not the same. Paul had a bad feeling that time. He liked the house, full of small, fenceable stuff, he liked the layout—lots of trees and shrubs, once you got to the back door you were seriously hidden—but the lady who lived there had this funny schedule, you couldn't trust her not to come home. He was thinking maybe he should look for somewhere else but then Larry chimed in. The Guys never had an opinion before on where he should hit—at least, they'd never expressed one—but this time Larry said Paul should just go ahead and do it. Paul wanted to explain why not, but Roman started chanting, "Do it! Do it! Do it!" and when Stoom said, "I think it's a good idea too," Paul knew he was sunk. He did everything he could to be sure the lady would be away, and she was when he broke in and she was while he emptied her jewelry box into his backpack and shoved a laptop in with it and a nice little picture from the wall that might bring a few bucks, but before he could go back down the hall toward the stairs he heard her car crunch gravel in the driveway. He flashed on different ideas—hide in the closet, go out the window—but they were all stupid and he slammed down the hallway and flew down the stairs hoping he could get out while she was still wide-eyed staring and thinking, *What the fuck?* He didn't, though. She was like the girl the first time, this lady, she came right at him, screaming and cursing, smashing at him with her handbag, her fists, she was like a crazy lady. "Just move!" he yelled at her. "Just let me out of here!" But she wouldn't, so he pushed her. She stumbled backward and fell, banged her head on the floor. She made a long, low, sad/angry sound, tried to get up, couldn't get up. She pushed at the floor and flopped back, just glaring at Paul with eyes full of hate. When she tried to get up and he thought she'd be able to, he grabbed for something from the coat rack, it was just an umbrella but it was a big heavy one, and he raised it over his head.

Two things happened.

One: the lady's eyes got wide, her face went white, and she froze like a lying-down statue.

And two: Larry said mildly, "Hit her."

Paul froze too. Two frozen statues staring at each other. He dropped the umbrella and backed away, stumbled past the lady, yanked open the door, and ran. The Guys started kicking him even before he got the ski mask off. By the time he arrived back at his place his whole head was pounding, even his nose and his cheeks, like they were trying to kick his face off. It was one of the worst headaches ever and it took a long time to go away, partly because it was so bad he could hardly see to light the match and melt his tar.

When the smack wore off The Guys kicked him some more—they were really mad Paul didn't do what Larry said—so he had to have another fix. After that one, though, they calmed down for a while. By nighttime Paul was able to move his shaky self out of the apartment, get a cup of coffee and a slice.

The next day he felt okay enough to do some business. The lady's jewelry pawned pretty well, and he sold the laptop for some nice bucks. The picture, it turned out, wasn't worth shit, but his fence gave him a little for the frame, and for a couple of weeks Paul could spend the days running, eating pizza and Chinese, and shooting up. The Guys stayed pretty mellow, not like they weren't there, but it was just a lot of bullshit ragging on him, no headaches, no stupid ideas like the time they told him to jump off the ferry and he had to squeeze the rail so hard he thought he'd break his fingers. That time, they finally told him okay, he didn't have to, and then they laughed and laughed. Nothing like that now, and he relaxed a little and got into a rhythm. He saw his mom, and things were as close to good as they ever were, since The Guys had come.

Eventually, though, it got to be time to plan another job.

Paul had this idea, thinking about it only in that no-words way so The Guys wouldn't catch on. The little museum on Lighthouse Avenue, the Tibetan Museum, it had a lot of art in it, small statues, some made of gold or silver, some even with jewels on them. He told The Guys about them, how easy they'd be to fence and how much he could get for them, as long as he took them into Manhattan. He knew The Guys would like that, they liked that trip, which sometimes Paul made for skag if his dealer was in jail or something. He told them about the skylight into the square room and the alarm that even if it went off—and he didn't think the skylight was wired up, but even if it was—no one lived there and the precinct was at least five minutes away. Paul could stuff half a dozen, maybe even more, of those strange statues into his backpack and be out the door and sliding down the overgrown hill out back before the cop car ever pulled up in front. The police would walk around for a while with their flashlights, anyway. They'd try the doors in the wall, and by the time someone came to let them in, Paul would be home stashing the statues under the bed and breaking out his works.

The best part of the plan was the part he wasn't thinking in words. No one lived at the museum. No one would stop him. There'd be no one for him to hurt.

Long ago some people used to live there. Long, *long* ago the lady who built the museum lived next door, and the gardens were connected and she'd have come running. But there was a wall there now and the people who lived in her house didn't even like the museum all that much. He wasn't worried about them. And in the hillside below there were two little caves, for monks and nuns to meditate in. When Paul was a kid and used to come here, sometimes there'd be one of them in a cave for a few days, just sitting and thinking with their eyes closed. They used to leave their doors open and Paul would tiptoe over and hide behind the bushes and peek at them. Once, one of the nuns opened her eyes and saw him and he thought she'd be mad but she just smiled at him, nodded like she was saying hi, like she knew him already, and closed her eyes again. The nuns didn't look like the ones he was used to. He'd never seen real monks, only in Robin Hood comics, but they didn't look like this either. These monks and nuns had shaved heads—all of them, the nuns too—and gray robes and big brown beads, like rosary beads but not. He liked the way they seemed so calm and peaceful, though. That's why he liked to watch them. Even when he was a kid, even before The Guys came, he'd never been calm and peaceful like that.

But that was a long time ago. No one had used those caves for ten years, maybe more. The museum stopped having monks and nuns come and no one was ever there when the place was closed, and thinking without words Paul knew this was a good idea.

Even though he also knew he didn't have a good idea for next time.

He wasn't worrying about that now, as he finished his run and swung onto a bus for St. George. He couldn't. He needed to go get himself together. He'd have loved to get high but there was no way he could shoot up now and still be able to do this job when it got dark. So he went back to his basement apartment, pushed some pizza boxes and takeout cartons out of the way to find his black shirt and pants. He took a shower, even though the clothes were filthy, and then lay down, rolled himself in his blanket, and slept. He hoped The Guys would give him a break; sometimes they liked to scream and yell and wake him just as he was falling asleep. He was braced for it but they didn't and he slipped away.

When he woke up it was just after sunset. Excellent. He took his black backpack and stuffed his ski mask and his gloves into it, plus a rope, and a hammer and a pry bar for the skylight. He stuck in a light-blue sweatshirt too, for afterward when they'd be looking for a guy all in black. If anyone saw him to describe him to the cops. But no one would see him; that was the beauty of this plan.

At the bodega he bought two coffees, lots of cream and sugar, and threw them both back before he got to the bus stop. Now he was buzzed; good. He took the bus up to the corner past the museum and walked down. It was dark, with yellow squares of light glowing in people's windows, the kind of people who had normal lives and no aliens in their heads. Except for one dog walker, no one was out. The dog walker had gone around the corner by the time Paul got to the fence. He climbed it easily, trying to avoid the flags. He didn't know much about them but they were called prayer flags so he thought it was probably bad to step on them. He slid a little on the wet leaves on the north side of the building but he was completely hidden there from both the street and the next house. Because the building was buried in the hillside he was only maybe ten feet below the roof, and the rope tossed around a vent pipe took care of that. ("Lucky you're a broken-down skinny-ass runt or that pipe would've busted," Stoom pointed out. Paul didn't answer.) The skylight, like he figured, was some kind of plastic, and the panels were even easier to pry loose than he'd hoped. He lifted a panel out, laid it aside, and waited. Right about that too: no alarm. He grabbed on to the edge, slipped over, and he was in.

He dropped lightly into the center of the square stone room, almost the same spot on the floor he used to sit on when he was a kid and came in just to stare. The lady who sold the tickets thought it was neat that a little kid kept coming around, and didn't make him pay anything. Sometimes if he'd boosted some candy bars he'd bring her one, and she always took it with a big smile and a thank you.

He slipped the headlamp on and turned slowly, watching the beam play over the room. The place hadn't changed much, maybe not at all. On the side built into the hill a couple of stone ledges stepped back. Most of the statues sat on them, lined up in rows. A bunch more were in cases against the other three walls. Two of the cases stood one on either side of the door out to the balcony. The space smelled cool and damp, like it was one of those caves where the nuns and monks used to stay. It was still and silent, but not the heavy silence of the shrink's drugs or the skag. Those made him feel like everything was still there, he was just shutting it out. This, it was a quiet like everything had stopped to rest.

"What a lovely little trip down Memory Lane," Larry said acidly. "Can we get to work now?"

Paul swung the backpack off, opened it, and stepped up to the shelves, leaning over each statue. He wanted them all, wanted to take them and put them in his basement room just to stare around at them, but that wasn't why he was here and no matter how many he took that wasn't what would happen to them. He reached out. This one, it was gold. He held it, let the headlamp glint off it. Then into the pack. That one was beautiful but it was iron. Leave it. The two there, with jewels and coral, into the pack. The silver one. That little candlestick, it too. That was all the best from the ledges. Now for the cases on the walls. Paul turned his head, sweeping the light around.

There she was.

Just like the first time, the girl in the kitchen, Paul almost pissed himself. A nun, in gray robes, big brown beads around her neck. She smiled softly and Paul's mouth fell open. It was the same nun, the one from the cave, smiling the same smile.

"You—you—you're still here?" he managed to stammer.

"I've always been here," she replied. Her eyes twinkled, and she stood with her hands folded in front of her. When she smiled she looked like the lady he used to give candy bars to. He'd never noticed that before, that they looked alike. "Paul," she said, "you know you can't take those."

His voice had rung oddly off the stone walls. Hers didn't disturb the sense that everything was resting.

"How do you know my name?" This time he whispered so he wouldn't get the same echo.

"You came here when you were a little boy."

He nodded. "I used to watch you sitting there. Meditating."

"I know. I thought perhaps you'd join me sometime."

"I—"

Larry interrupted him, barking, "Paul! Get back to work."

He said, "Just give me—"

"No!"

That was Roman. The kick was from him too. Paul's head almost cracked. The pain was blinding, and he barely heard the nun calmly say, "Roman, stop that."

The kicking stopped instantly. Paul stared at the nun. "You can hear them?"

She smiled. "You don't have to do what they say, you know."

Paul swallowed. "Yes, I do."

"Yes, he does," Larry said.

"Yes! He does!" Roman yelled.

"No," said the nun.

"I can't get them to leave." Paul was suddenly ashamed of how forlorn he sounded. Like a real loser. He heard Larry snicker.

"Even so," she said.

He wasn't sure how to answer her, but he didn't get the chance. "Paul?" That was Stoom, sounding dark. When Stoom got mad it was really, really bad. "Do what you came for, and do it now. Remember, Paul: no swag, no skag." It was one of those times Paul could hear Stoom's sneer.

Paul looked at the nun, and then slowly around the room. The headlamp picked out fierce faces, jeweled eyes. "There's lots of places I could hit," he said to The Guys. "Doesn't have to be here. This was a dumb idea. You know, like my ideas always are. How about I just—"

"No," said Stoom.

"No," said Larry.

And Roman started kicking him, chanting, "No swag, no skag! No swag, no skag!" Then they were all three chanting and kicking, chanting and kicking.

Paul staggered forward, toward a statue of a person sitting cross-legged like the nun did. Pearls and coral studded its flowing gold robes. He reached for it but the nun moved smoothly in front of it. She said nothing, just smiled.

"No," Paul heard himself croak. "Please. You have to let me."

She shook her head.

"Paul!" Stoom snapped. "You moron loser. Push her out of the way."

"No. I'll get a different one."

"I want THAT one!" Roman whined.

Paul swung his head around. The headlamp picked out a glittering statue with lots of arms, over in a case by the door. He turned his back on the nun and lurched toward it. By the time he got there she was standing in front of it, hands folded, smiling. He hadn't seen her move.

"Paul," she said, "this life has been hard for you. I don't know why; I think, though, that the next turn of the wheel will be far better."

He didn't know what she was talking about. Wheel, what wheel? All three of The Guys were kicking him now, Roman the hardest, trying to pop his right eye out. "Please," he said. "Get out of the way."

She said nothing, just smiled the ticket lady's smile and stood there.

Paul took two steps over to the next cabinet.

There she was.

"Please!" he shouted at her. "Stop it!" His head pounded, the pain so searing he thought he might throw up. He could barely see but he knew she was still standing between him and the statues. "*Please!*"

"Hit her." That was Larry. Paul barely heard him through the pain. He tried to pretend he didn't hear him at all but Larry laughed. "Hit her. With a statue."

Paul's hands trembled as he reached into the backpack, took out the gold statue. "Please," he whispered to the nun–ticket lady. "Please move."

She just stood and smiled.

Paul lifted the statue way high. As he brought it down on her shaved head he realized he was screaming.

He felt the impact on her skull, felt it all the way up to his shoulders, his back. The nun crumpled to the floor without a sound. Blood flowed from the smashed-in place, started to pool under her face. Paul dropped the statue; it fell with a splash into the puddle of blood. "Oh my God," he whispered. "Oh my God oh my God oh my God."

"Oh my God is right!" Larry roared a grand, triumphant laugh. "You killed her!"

"Killed her! Killed her!" shrieked Roman.

"You know what happens now, don't you?" Larry said. "You go to jail. Prison, you loser, you go to prison where there's no smack and we go too! Oh, will that be fun!"

"No." Paul could barely get the word out. "I didn't. She's not dead."

"Really?" said Stoom. "Can you wake her up?"

Paul kneeled slowly, put out his hand, shook the nun gently. She still had that little smile, the ticket lady's smile, but she didn't respond at all.

"Look at all that blood," Stoom said. "You're stupid if you think anyone could be still alive with all their blood on the floor like that. You're stupid anyway, but she's dead and you killed her."

"Prison!" Roman bellowed. "Killed her! Prison!"

"No." Paul stood slowly, shaking his head. "No."

"Oh, yes, yes," Larry said. "Oh, yes."

Paul took one more look at the nun, then staggered toward the exit door. An alarm shrieked as he pushed it open. He ran across the terrace, slipping on the autumn leaves. When he got to the railing he stared down; the headlamp shone on branches and bushes growing out of the wall beneath him but couldn't reach all the way to the street below.

He grabbed the rail, ready to vault over.

"No," said Stoom in that very hard voice. "No, you're staying."

Paul felt his grip tighten on the rail, like The Guys were controlling his fingers. He heard a siren wail. That would be the cops, because of the door alarm. If he was still here when they came, he'd go to prison for sure.

"That's right," Larry said with satisfaction. "Prison for sure."

Paul took a slow, deep breath. "No," he whispered. "She told me I don't have to do what you say."

The Guys yelled, they bellowed and kicked, but Paul loosened his fingers one by one. He climbed over the railing, stood for a minute on the edge of the wall. Then he dove. His last thought was the hope that The Guys wouldn't have time to clear out of his head before he smashed it to bits on the pavement.

The impact, the thud of a body landing forty feet below, didn't penetrate very far into the square stone room. It barely disturbed the resting stillness, didn't echo at all past the golden Buddha in the middle of the floor. The statue lay on its side on a smooth dry stone tile, beside a backpack full of other statues. Except for the statue and the backpack, and the single panel removed from the skylight, nothing was out of place. The calm silence in the room continued, and would continue once the statues had been replaced in their proper spots by the museum's new director.

She would be pleased that something had scared off the thief, though greatly saddened that he'd fallen to his death over the railing at the terrace. As advised by the police, she'd add an alarm to the skylight. She had much to do, as she was all the staff the museum had. She guided visitors, and also sold the tickets, the ticket lady having retired years ago. She didn't mind the work. She was hoping, even, to soon reopen the meditation caves, to perhaps make the museum not just a serene spot, but a useful one, as it once had been: a beacon for poor souls with troubled minds.

SECRET POOL

BY Asali Solomon

West Philadelphia

(Originally published in *Philadelphia Noir*)

I learned about the University City Swim Club around the same time things started disappearing from my room. First I noticed that I was missing some jewelry, and then the old plaid Swatch I'd been saving for a future *Antiques Roadshow*. I didn't say anything to my mother, because they say it's dangerous to wake a sleepwalker. But then I felt like we were all sleepwalkers when Aja told me about the pool, hiding in plain sight right up on 47th Street in what looked like an alley between Spruce and Pine.

"You don't know about the University City Swim Club?" she said, pretending shock. It was deep August and I sat on the steps of my mother's house. Aja was frankly easier to take during the more temperate months, but since my summer job had ended and there were two and a half more weeks before eleventh grade, I often found myself in her company.

Aja Bell and I had been friends of a sort since first grade, when we'd been the only two black girls in the Mentally Gifted program, though there couldn't have been more than thirty white kids in the whole school. Aja loved MG because there was a group of girls in her regular class who tortured her. Then in sixth grade, I got a scholarship to the Barrett School for Girls and Aja stayed where she was. Now she went to Central High, where she was always chasing these white city kids. It killed her that I went to school in the suburbs with real rich white people, while her French teacher at Central High was a black man from Georgia. Despite the fact that I had no true friends at my school and hated most things about my life, she was in a one-sided social competition with me. As a result, I was subjected to Aja's peacocking around about things like how her friend Jess, who lived in a massive house down on Cedar Avenue, had invited her to go swimming with her family.

"Come off it, Aja. I just said I didn't know about it."

"I just think if you live right here . . . maybe your mom knows about it?"

"Look, is there a story here?"

"Well, it's crazy. There's this wooden gate with a towing sign on it like it's just a parking lot, but behind it is this massive pool and these brand-new lockers and everything. And it was so crowded!"

"Any black people there?"

"Zingha, why you have to make everything about black and white?"

"Maybe because people are starting all-white pools in my neighborhood." She sighed. "There was a black guy there."

"Janitor?"

"I think he was the security guard."

I snorted.

We watched a black Range Rover crawl down the block. The windows were tinted, and LL Cool J's "The Boomin' System" erupted from the speakers.

"Wow," I said, in mock awe. "That's boomin' from his boomin' system."

"So ghetto," said Aja.

"Um, because this is the ghetto," I said, though my mother forbade me to use the word.

"He spoke to me," Aja said suddenly. "The pool security guard. He wasn't that much older than us."

"Was he cute?" I asked without much interest.

"Tell you the truth, he's a little creepy. Like maybe he was on that line between crazy and, um, retarded."

I laughed and then she did too.

"So you been hanging out with Jess a lot this summer?" Jess, a gangly brunette with an upturned nose, was Aja's entry into the clique to which she aspired. But Jess sometimes ignored Aja for weeks at a time, and had repeatedly tried to date guys who Aja liked.

"Well, not a lot. She was at tennis camp earlier," Aja said, glancing away from my face. She could never fully commit to a lie. I imagined my older brother Dahani a couple of nights ago, spinning a casual yarn for my mom about how he'd been at the library after his shift at the video store. He said he was researching colleges that would accept his transfer credits. Dahani had been home for a year, following a spectacular freshman-year flameout at Oberlin. That memory led me to a memory from seventh grade when Dahani said he'd teach me how to lie to my mother so I could go to some unsupervised sleepover back when I cared about those things. I practiced saying, "There will be parental supervision," over and over. Dahani laughed because I bit the inside of my cheek when I said my line.

"You mean the pool at the Y?" my mom asked me later that night. We had just finished eating the spaghetti with sausage that she had cooked especially for my brother. She had cracked open her nightly can of Miller Lite.

"Not that sewer," I said.

"Poor Zingha, you hate your fancy school and you hate your community too. Hard being you, isn't it?"

"Sorry," I muttered, rather than hearing again about how I used to be a sweet girl who loved to hug people and cried along with TV characters.

Dahani, who used to have a volatile relationship with our mother, was now silent more often than not. But he said, "I know what you're talking about, Zingha. Up on 47th Street." Then he immediately looked like he wanted to take it back.

"You been there?" I asked.

"Just heard about it," my brother said, tapping out a complicated rhythm on the kitchen table. When he was younger it meant he was about to go to his room. Now it meant he was trying to get out of the house. I wasn't even sure why he insisted on coming home for dinner most nights. Though of course free hot food was probably a factor.

"So what are you up to tonight?" my mother asked him brightly.

"I was gonna catch the new Spike Lee with Jason," he said.

My mother's face dimmed. She always hoped that he'd say, *Staying right here.* But she rallied. "You liked that one, didn't you, Zingha?"

I looked at Dahani. "Sure, watch Wesley Snipes do it with a white woman and stick me with the dishes."

"Oh, I'll take care of the dishes," my mother snapped, managing to make me feel petty. Turning to Dahani she asked, "How *is* Jason?"

"Just fine," Dahani said, in a tight voice. I followed his eyes to the clock above the refrigerator. "Movie starts at seven."

My brother kissed my mom and left, just like he did every night since he'd come home in disgrace. I went upstairs so I wouldn't have to listen to the pitiful sound of her cleaning up the kitchen. After that she would doze in front of the TV for a couple of hours, half waiting for Dahani to come home. She always wound up in bed before that.

I went up into my brother's room. I didn't find my things, but I helped myself to a couple of cigarettes I knew I'd never smoke, and an unsoiled *Hustler* magazine.

It happened after I had done the deed with a couple of contorting blondes who must have made their parents proud. I had washed up for bed and was about to put on my new headphones, which would lull me to sleep.

I realized that my Walkman was gone.

Understand this. I did not care about the mother-of-pearl earrings from my aunt that even my mother admitted were cheap. I did not care about the gold charm bracelet that my mother gave me when I turned sixteen—the other girls in my class had been collecting tennis racket and Star of David charms since they were eight. And of course the future value of nonfunctioning Swatches was just a theory. But Dahani, who had once harangued my mother into buying him seventy-five-dollar stereo headphones, understood what my Walkman meant to me.

Every summer since eighth grade, the nonprofit where my mom worked got me an office job with one of their corporate "partners." I spent July and part of August in freezing cubicles wearing a garish smile, playing the part of Industrious Urban Youth. This summer it had been a downtown bank, where the ignoramus VPs and their ignoramus secretaries crowed over my ability to staple page one to two and guide a fax through the machine. If you think I was lucky I didn't have to handle french fries or the public, you try staying awake for six hours at a desk with nothing to do except arrange rubber bands into a neat pile. It was death.

Most of the money I made every summer went for new school uniforms and class trips. The only thing I bought that I cared about was the most expensive top-of-the-line Walkman. I had one for each summer I'd worked, and all three were gone. I turned on my lamp, folded my arms, and decided that I could wait up even if my mother couldn't.

The next day I hovered around the living room window waiting for Aja to appear on my block and also hoping that she wouldn't. I needed to tell someone about my brother. But on the other hand, Aja had the potential to be not so understanding. She had two parents: a teacher and an accountant who never drank beer from cans. They went to church and had a Standard Poodle called Subwoofer. It was true that sometimes we were so lonely that we told each other things. I had told her that I liked my brother's dirty magazines and she told me that she didn't like black guys because once her cousin pushed her in a closet and pulled out his dick. But whenever we made confessions like these, the next time we met up it was like those mouthwash commercials where couples wake up next to each other embarrassed by their breath. Besides, I didn't want her to pronounce my crack-smoking brother "ghetto," not even with her eyes.

He lied, he lied, he lied. Dahani, who used to make up raps with me and record them, who comforted me the one time we met our father, who seemed bored and annoyed, and once, back when we were both in public school, beat up a little boy for calling me an African bootyscratcher. *That* brother, said calmly, "I didn't take any of your stuff, Nzingha. What are you thinking?"

"I'm thinking: what the hell is going on? I'm thinking: where are my Walkmans? I'm thinking: where are you all the time?"

"I'm out. You should go there sometimes." He laughed his high-pitched laugh, the one that said how absurd the world is.

"Okay, so you supposedly went to the movies tonight, right? What happens to Gator at the end of *Jungle Fever*?" I asked.

"Ossie Davis shoots him."

"That's right. The crackhead dies. Remember that," I said.

"Crackhead?" Dahani sounded his laugh again. I didn't realize how angry I was until I felt the first hot tear roll down my cheek.

I stomped out, leaving his door open. That was an old maneuver, something we did to piss each other off when we lost a fight. But then I thought of something and went back in there. He wouldn't admit that he'd taken my things. But he agreed that if I didn't say anything to our mother, he'd take me to the pool. He could only take me at night after it closed, and only if I kept my mouth shut about going.

That night, a Friday, we made our mother's day by convincing her we were going to hang out on South Street together. Then, as it was getting dark, Dahani and I walked silently toward 47th Street. A clump of figures looked menacing at the corner until we got close and saw that they couldn't have been more than fifth graders. We slowed down to let a thin, pungent man rush past us. Even though the night air was thick enough to draw sweat, the empty streets reminded me that summer was ending.

"Is anybody else coming?" I asked finally. "Jason?"

"I haven't seen that nigger in months. Ever since he pledged, he turned into a world-class faggot." Jason, my brother's best friend from Friends Select, the only other black boy in his class, had started at Morehouse the same time my brother had gone to Oberlin.

"So it's just going to be us and the security guard?" I had worn a bathing suit under my clothes, but felt weird about stripping down in front of the character Aja described.

"Look," my brother said, "be cool, okay?"

"Cool like you?"

"You know, Nzingha, this is not the best time of my life either."

"But it could be. You could go back to school," I said, teetering on the edge of a place we hadn't been.

"It's not that fucking easy! Do you understand everything Mom's done for me already?"

"Don't talk to me like that."

"Let's just go where we're going."

We passed under a buzzing streetlight that could die at any moment. I had a feeling I knew from nightmares where I boarded the 42 bus in the daytime and got off in the dark. In the dreams I heard my sneakers hit the ground and I thought I would die of loneliness.

We finally reached the tall wooden gate with its warning about getting towed. In a low voice that was forceful without being loud, Dahani called out to someone named Roger. The gate opened and Dahani nearly pushed me into a tall, skinny man with a tan face and eyes that sparkled even in the near-dark.

"Hey man, hey man," he kept saying, pulling my brother in for a half-hug.

"What's up, Roger?" said Dahani. "This is my sister."

"Hey, sister," he said and tried to wink, but the one eye took the other with it.

I looked around. It was nicer than the dingy gray tiles and greenish walls at the Y pool, but to tell the truth, it was nothing special. I'd been going to pool parties at Barrett since sixth grade and I'd seen aqua-tiled models, tropical landscaping, one or two retractable ceilings. This was just a standard rectangle bordered by neat cream-colored asphalt on either side. There were a handful of deck chairs on each side and tall fluorescent lamps. This is what they were keeping us out of?

A bunch of white guys with skater hair and white-boy fades drank 40s and nodded to a boombox playing A Tribe Called Quest at the deep end near the diving board. Then nearby enough to hover but not to crowd, were the girls, who wore berry-colored bikinis. I thought of my prudish navy-blue one-piece. There was a single black girl sitting on the edge of the pool in a yellow bathing suit, dangling her feet in the water.

"Aja?" I called.

"Nzingha?" she replied, sounding disappointed.

Then I recognized Jess, who seemed not to see me until I was practically standing on top of her. Actually, this happened nearly every time we met. "Hey," she said finally. "I thought that was you." She always said something like that.

"What are you doing here?" Aja asked.

"My brother brought me."

"That's your brother?" Jess gestured with her head to Dahani, who stood with his hands in his pockets while Roger pantomimed wildly.

"You know him?" I asked.

"He's down with my boys," she said. I tried not to wince. "Speaking of which, hey, Adam! Can you bring Nzingha something to drink?"

We looked toward the end of the pool with the boys and the boombox. One of them, with a sharp-looking nose and a mop of wet blond hair sweeping over his eyes, yelled back: "Get it for her yourself!"

Jess's face erupted in pink splotches. "He's an incredible asshole," she said.

"And this is news?" said one of the other girls. She had huge breasts, a smashed-in face, and a flat voice. Suddenly I remembered the name Adam. Aja had a flaming crush on him for nearly a year, and then Jess had started going out with him on and off. Last I heard they were off, but now Aja liked to pretend she'd never mentioned liking him.

"I don't want anything to drink anyway," I said.

Aja asked if I was going to swim and I don't remember what I said because I was watching my brother walk down to the end of the pool where the boys were, trading pounds with wet hands. He reached into a red cooler and pulled out a 40. Roger stayed at the tall wooden gate.

"They think they're gangsters," Jess said, rolling her eyes in their general direction. "They call themselves the Gutter Boys. All they do is come here and smoke weed."

"That's not all," the girl with the smashed-in face said with a smirk.

"Is my brother here a lot?" I asked.

"I've only seen him once. But this is only the third time I've been here, you know, after hours."

My brother didn't seem interested in swimming. I didn't even know if he was wearing trunks. Instead he walked with a stocky swaggering boy toward the darkness of the locker room. *Don't go back there*, I wanted to scream. But all I did was stand there in my street clothes at the water's edge.

Adam cried out, "Chickenfight!"

"Not again," said smashed-in face. "I'm way too fucked up."

Adam swam over to us. "Look, Tanya, you'll do it again if you wanna get high later."

Tanya's friend murmured something to her quietly. Tanya laughed and said, "Hey, Adam, what about this?" Then she and her friend began kissing. At first just their lips seemed to brush lightly, and then the quiet girl pulled her in fiercely. I stepped back, feeling an unpleasant arousal. The boys became a cursing, splashing creature moving toward us. "Day-ummm!" called Roger, who began running over.

"Keep your eye on the gate, dude!" yelled one of the boys.

"Okay, you big lesbians get a pass," said Adam when they finally broke apart. Then he turned to Jess. "What can you girls do for me?"

"I think we're going to stick with the chickenfight," said Aja, giggling. She still liked him. I could not relate.

While they sorted out who would carry whom, my brother emerged from the locker room. I waited until he and the stocky boy had parted ways before I began walking over.

"Dahani," I called in a sharp voice.

"You ready to go?" he asked. I examined him. He didn't seem jittery and he wasn't sweating. This was what I knew of smoking crack from the movies.

"What are you looking at?" he asked.

I glanced back at the pool, where Adam, laughing, held Jess under the water. Aja sat forlornly on the shoulders of a round boy with flame-colored hair waiting for the fight to start. "I'm ready to go," I said.

When Roger closed the gate the pool disappeared, and though "Looking at the Front Door" sounded raucous bouncing off the water, I couldn't hear anything at all.

"Are you smoking crack?" I blurted.

Dahani came to a full stop and looked at me. "This is the last time I think I'm going to answer that dumb-ass question. No."

"Are you selling it?"

He sighed in annoyance. "Nzingha. No."

"But something isn't right."

"No, nothing is right," Dahani said. "But this is where I get off." We had reached my mother's house. He kept walking up the dark street.

It wasn't until a couple of nights later that Dahani didn't show up for dinner. My mother, who barely touched the pizza I ordered, kept walking to the front window and peering out.

When it began getting dark, I slapped my forehead. "Oh my God!" I said.

My mother looked at me with wild round eyes. "What?"

Without biting the inside of my cheek, I said, "I totally forgot. He said to tell you he wouldn't be home until really late."

"Where is he?"

"Don't know."

My mother folded her arms. "Thanks for almost letting me have a heart attack."

"Mom, he's a grown man."

"Nzingha," she said, "what is this thing with you and your brother?"

I didn't answer.

"You don't seem to realize that he's having a really hard time. I mean I'm the one stuck with loans from his year at college. I'm the one supporting his grown ass now and I'm the one who's going to have to take out more loans to send him back. So what's *your* issue?"

"Nothing," I said. "Can I go upstairs?"

"You really need to change your attitude. And not just about this."

"Can I go upstairs?" I said again.

My mother and I sometimes had strained conversations. It was she and Dahani who had fireworks. But now she looked so angry she almost shook. "Go ahead and get the hell out of my sight!" And I did, hating this.

That night I wasn't sure if I was sleeping or not. I kept imagining the nightmare-bright scene at the pool, those girls kissing, my brother disappearing into the back. Night logic urged me that I had to go back there. After my mother was in bed with her TV timer on, I climbed out of bed and dressed. Then excruciatingly, silently, I closed the front door. I plunged into darkness and walked the three blocks as fast as I could.

"Roger," I called at the gate, trying to imitate my brother's masculine whisper. I tapped the wood. There was a pause and then the tall gate wrenched open.

"Where's Dahani?" Roger said, waving me inside. His clothes were soaked and he was in stocking feet. "Oh God. You didn't bring Dahani?"

I felt my legs buckle, and only because Roger's sweaty hand clamped over my mouth was I able to swallow a scream. I had seen only one dead body in real life, at my great-grandmother's wake. Though with her papery skin and tiny doll's limbs, she'd never seemed quite alive. I'd never seen a dead body floating in water, but I knew what I was seeing when I saw Jess's naked corpse bob up and down peacefully. I ran to the water's edge near the diving board. There was a wet spot of something on the edge of the pool that looked black in the light.

Roger began pacing a tiny circle, moaning.

"Did you call 911?" I asked him.

"It was an accident. They're gonna think—"

"What if she's alive?" I said.

Roger suddenly loomed in front of me with clenched fists. "No cops! And she's not alive! Why didn't you bring Dahani?"

In the same way I knew things in dreams, I knew he hadn't done it. Not even in a Lenny in *Of Mice and Men* way. But I needed to get away from his panic. I spoke slowly. "It's okay. I'll go get him."

"You'll bring him here?"

Before I let myself out through the tall gate, I watched Roger slump to the side of the pool and sit Indian-style with his head in his hands. I took one last look at Jess. Later I wished that I hadn't.

I found myself at Aja's house. It was after midnight, but I rang the bell, hoping somehow that she might answer the door instead of her parents. I heard the dog barking and clicking his long nails excitedly on the floor.

Aja's dad, a short yellow man with a mustache and no beard, answered the door. "Zingha? Now you know it's too late. Does your mom know—"

"Mr. Bell, I really need to see Aja."

"Are you serious, girl?" Then he started pushing the door shut. The dog was going crazy.

"Aja!" I screamed.

Her mother appeared. She grabbed Subwoofer's collar with one hand and pulled him up short. He whimpered and I felt bad for him. All I'd ever known him to attack with was his huge floppy tongue.

"Shut up and get in here," she said.

Aja's father moved off to the side but he wasn't happy about it. "What the hell do you think you're doing?" he asked her.

"Quiet, you!" she responded. She was nearly a head taller than he was, with eggplant-colored lips and very arched eyebrows.

"Look, Nzingha," she said, "Aja's not here. We don't know where she is."

I shook my head frantically. "We have to find her! You don't know what's going on. There's a—"

"Stop talking and listen," she said, getting louder. "If anyone comes around asking where my daughter is, tell them the truth. That she has disappeared and that we are very worried. Mr. Bell will walk you home."

Mr. Bell fumed as he escorted me. "I guess there's no point in any more stupid fucking shit happening," he muttered. I didn't answer; he wasn't talking to me.

I let myself in as quietly as I had left, shocked by the thick silence of the house. I tried not to imagine Jess's closed eyes, her blood on the asphalt. I had to remind myself that she was dead, so she couldn't be as cold as she looked. I tried to tell myself that her floating body, Dahani, and Aja were in another world.

But the next morning I learned that my mother hadn't been home. She'd been down at the precinct with my brother.

By the time the police had arrived at the pool, Roger was nearly dead. He had tried to drown himself. He couldn't answer questions about Jess from his coma, but the police knew he hadn't done it.

It seemed to me, from what I managed to read before my mother started hiding the papers, that Jess's death had been an accident. But her dad was a lawyer and Aja was dragged back from an aunt's house in Maryland to do eighteen months in the Youth Detention Center. I went to visit her once that winter, in the dim, echoing room that reminded me of the cafeteria at our elementary school. I didn't tell my mother where I was going. She hadn't let me go to the trial.

Aja and I made painful small talk about how the food was destroying her stomach and about her first encounter with a bed bug. She said *fuck* more than usual and her skin looked gray.

Then she blurted, "I didn't do it."

"I know," I said.

"Things just got crazy." She told me about that night. Everyone had been drinking, including her, and Adam called for another chickenfight.

"First I fought that girl Tanya and I beat her easy. Then it was me and Jess. But I had won the time before, the night you came, you remember?"

I nodded, though I hadn't seen her victory.

"So she was really getting rough. And then she fucking—"

"We don't have to talk about this anymore," I said, trying to be the sweet girl my mother remembered.

"She pulled my top down. I kept telling them I wanted to stop. But they were yelling so loud. And Adam was cheering me on. It was so—" Aja's voice seemed to swell with tears, but her eyes remained empty.

"It doesn't matter," I said, and we were quiet for a moment. The din of the visiting room filled the space between us.

"But Jess was my best friend," she said. I had come to be good to her, yet I wanted to shake her by the shoulders until her teeth chattered.

My brother was able to convince the police that he hadn't done it. But he not only needed an alibi, he also had to rat out the Gutter Boys, with whom he'd apparently tried to go into business. Tried, I say, because he was such a crummy drug dealer that he had to steal to make up for what he couldn't sell. Dahani told the police what he knew about the small operation, and after that, a couple of Jeeps slowed down when he crossed the street, but he didn't turn up in the Schuylkill or anything. He got his old job at the video store back, but he got fired after a couple of months, and then our VCR disappeared. After two weeks in a row when he didn't come home, and my mom had called the police about sixteen times, she changed the locks and got an alarm system.

Sometime after that she looked at me over a new tradition—a second nightly beer—and said, "Nzingha, I know we should have talked about this as soon as I knew what was going on with your brother. But I didn't want to say anything because I know that you love him."

The scandal didn't break the pool. They held a floating memorial service for Jess and hired a real security company. The scandal did, however, break the news of the pool to the neighborhood. But at $1,400 a year, none of the black folks we knew could afford to join it anyway.

BUMS

BY WILLIAM KENT KRUEGER
West Side, St. Paul
(Originally published in *Twin Cities Noir*)

K id showed up at the river in the shadow of the High Bridge with a grin on his face, a bottle of Cutty in his hand, and a twenty-dollar bill in his pocket. Kid was usually in a good mood, but I'd never seen him quite so happy. Or so flush. And I couldn't remember the last time I'd seen a bottle of good scotch.

It was going on dark. I had a pot of watery stew on the fire—rice mostly, with some unidentifiable vegetables I'd pulled from the dumpster behind an Asian grocery store.

I held up the Cutty to the firelight and watched the reflection of the flames lick the glass. "Rob a bank?"

"Better." Kid bent over the pot and smelled the stew. "Got a job."

"Work? You?"

"There's this guy took me up on my offer."

Most days Kid stood at the top of the off-ramp on Marion Street and I-94 where a stoplight paused traffic for a while. He held up a handmade sign that read, *Will Work For Food.* He got handouts, but he'd never had anyone actually take him up on his offer.

"What kind of work?"

"Chopping bushes out of his yard, putting new bushes in. This yard, Professor, I tell you, it's big as a goddamn park. And the house, Jesus."

He called me Professor because I have a small wire-bound notepad in which I scribble from time to time. Why that translated into Professor, I never knew.

I wanted badly to break the seal on the bottle, but it wasn't my move.

Kid sat down cross-legged in the sand on the riverbank. He grinned up at me. "Something else, Professor. He's got a wife. A nice piece of work. The whole time I'm there, she's watching me from the window."

"Probably afraid you were going to steal something."

"No, I mean she's looking at me like I'm this stud horse and she's a . . . you know, a girl horse."

"Filly."

"That's it. Like she's a filly. A filly in heat."

I watched the gleam in Kid's eye, the fire that danced there. "You already have yourself a few shots of something?"

"It's the truth, swear to God. And get this. The guy wants me back tomorrow."

"Look, are we just going to admire this bottle?" I finally asked.

"Crack 'er open, Professor. Let's celebrate."

Kid and I weren't exactly friends, but we'd shared a campfire under the High Bridge for a while, and we trusted each other. Trust is important. Even if all you own can fit into an old gym bag, it's still all you own, and when you close your eyes at night, it's good to know the man on the other side of the fire isn't just waiting for you to fall asleep. Kid had his faults. For a bum, he thought a lot of himself. That came mostly from being young and believing that circumstance alone was to blame for his social station. I'd tried to wise him up, pointing out that lots of folks encounter adversity and don't end up squatting on the bank of a river, eating out of other people's garbage cans, wearing what other people throw away. He was good-looking, if a little empty in the attic, and had the kind of physique that would probably appeal to a bored rich woman. He was good companionship for me, always eager and smiling, kind of like a having a puppy around. I didn't know his real name. I just called him Kid.

The next evening when he came back from laboring in the rich man's yard, he explained to me about his plans for the guy's wife.

"She's got this long black hair, all shiny, hangs down to her hips, swishes real gentle over the top of her ass when she walks. Paints her nails red like little spots of blood at the end of her fingers and toes. Talks with this accent, I don't know what kind, but it's sexy. And she's hot for me, Professor. Christ, she's all over me."

Dinner that evening was fish, a big channel cat I'd managed to pull from the river with a chunk of moldy cheese as bait. I was frying it up in the pan I used for everything.

"If this woman is all you say she is, she could have any man she wants, Kid. What does she want with a bum?"

That offended him.

"I'm not like you, Professor. The booze don't have me by the throat. One break and I'm outta here."

"Dallying with a bored rich woman? How's that going to change your luck?"

Kid peered up from watching the fish fry. "I got inside today, looked the place over. They got all this expensive crap lying around."

"And you're what, just going to waltz in and help yourself?"

His looked turned coy. "She let me inside today when her old man took off to get a bunch of bushes from the nursery. Asked if I wanted some cold lemonade. Starts talking kind of general, you know. Where I'm from, do I got family, that kind of thing. Then, get this, she tells me her husband's not a man for her. No lightning in the rod, you know? I tell her that's a damn shame, all her good looks going to waste. She says, 'You think I'm pretty?' I tell her she's the prettiest goddamn thing I've ever seen. Then you know what, Professor? She invites me back tonight. Her old man's going out of town and she's all alone. Doesn't want to be lonely. Know what I'm saying? When it's dark, I'm heading over."

"You're spending the night?"

"Not the whole night. She don't want me around in the morning for the neighbors to see sneaking off."

"You sure you're not on something?"

"Proof, Professor," he said with a sly grin. "I got proof."

From his pants pocket he took a small ball of black fabric. He uncrumpled it and held it toward me with both hands, as if he were holding diamonds. "Her panties."

Thong panties, barely enough material to cover a canary.

"She gave you those?"

"Reached up under her skirt and slipped 'em off where she stood. Said they'd tide me over until tonight."

He went to his things and rolled the panties in his blanket.

"Hungry?" I asked.

"Naw. I'm going to the Y, slip inside and wash up. I want to smell good tonight. Don't wait up for me, Dad," he said with a grin, and he walked off whistling.

He didn't come back that night. I figured he'd got what he wanted from the rich man's wife and the rich man's house and I'd seen the last of him. What did I care? People come into your life and they go. You can't cry over them all.

So why did I feel so low the next day? All I wanted was to get drunk. Finally, I headed to the plasma center on University, let them siphon off a little precious bodily fluid, and I walked out with cash. I headed to the Gopher Bar for an afternoon of scintillating conversation with whoever happened to be around. It was a place where Kid and I had sometimes hung out together, and I hoped he might be there.

Laci was tending bar. A hard, unpretty woman with a quick mind. She sized me up as I sat on a stool. "Starting the wake, Professor?"

"You lost me," I said.

She threw a bar towel over her shoulder and came my way. "I figured you were planning to tip a few to the memory of your buddy. Not that a piece of crap like him deserves it."

"Kid? Piece of crap? What are you talking about?"

"You don't know?"

"Know what?"

She turned, took a bottle of Old Grand-Dad down from the shelf, and poured me a couple of fingers' worth. "This one's on the house."

Then she told me about Kid. It was all over the news.

The night before, he'd been shot dead in the rich man's house, but not before he beat the guy's wife to death with a crowbar.

"Funny." She shook her head. "I never figured him to be the violent kind. But anybody beats a woman to death deserves what he gets. Sorry, Professor, that's how I see it."

I swallowed the whiskey she'd poured, but instead of sticking around to get drunk, I walked back to the river.

That night I didn't bother putting together a fire, just sat on the riverbank below the High Bridge, listening to the sound of occasional traffic far above, thinking about Kid. At one point I pulled out my notepad, intending to write. I don't know what. Maybe a eulogy, something to mark his passing. Instead, I picked up a stick and scratched in the sand. A few minutes later a barge chugged past and the wake washed away what I'd written. I ended up crying a little, which almost never happens when I'm sober.

Two years ago I had a wife, a good job as a reporter with the *Star Tribune*, a house, a car. Then Deborah left me. She said it was the drinking, but it was me. I was never reliable. The drinking only made it worse. Not long after that I lost my job because I was happier sitting at the bar than at my desk trying to meet deadline. Everything pretty much went downhill from there. Somebody tells you they drink because they're a failure, it ain't so. They're a failure because they drink. And they drink because it's so damn hard not to. But as long as they have a bottle that isn't empty, they never feel far from being happy.

That's me, anyway.

Near dawn, I stood up from the long night of grieving for Kid. I was hungry. I walked the empty streets of downtown St. Paul to Mickey's Diner, got there just as the sun was coming up, ordered eggs, cakes, coffee. I picked up a morning paper lying on the stool next to me. Kid and what he'd done was still front-page news.

He had a name. Lester Greene. He had a record, spent time in St. Cloud for boosting cars. He had no permanent address. He was a bum. And he'd become a murderer.

The woman he'd killed was Christine Coyer, president and CEO of Coyer Cosmetics. Deborah used to ask for Coyer stuff every Christmas. All I remember about it was that it was expensive. According to the paper, she'd just returned from visiting family in New York City. Her husband had picked her up at the airport, brought her home, and while he parked the car in the garage, she'd gone into the house ahead of him. Apparently, she surprised Kid, who'd broken in with a crowbar, which he proceeded to use to crack her skull. He attacked her husband too, but the guy made it upstairs where he kept a pistol for protection. Kid followed and the rich man put four bullets in him in the bedroom. He was dead when the cops arrived. The husband knew the assailant. A bum on whom he had taken pity. A mistake he now regretted.

The story was continued on page 5A with pictures. I could tell already the whole thing smelled, but when I turned to the photos I nearly fell off my stool. There was the dead woman. She was fiftyish, nicely coiffed, but not with long black hair that brushed the top of her ass. She was a little on the chubby side, matronly even. Not at all the kind of figure a pair of thong panties would enhance.

If the article was correct, she'd been in the Big Apple when Kid had been given that delicate little sexual appetizer. So, if Christine Coyer didn't give it to him, who did?

During my college days, my clothing came from the Salvation Army. I shopped there in protest against consumerism and conformity. I shop there now out of necessity. For ten bucks I picked up a passable gray suit, a nearly white shirt, and a tie that didn't make me puke. I washed up in the men's room of a Super America on 7th, changed into the suit, and hoofed it to the address on Summit Avenue given in the newspaper story.

Like a big park, Kid had described the place. His perspective was limited. It was the fucking Tuileries Gardens, a huge expanse of tended flower beds and sculpted shrubbery with a château dead center. The cosmetics business had been very good to Ms. Coyer. And to her husband, no doubt. So good, in

410 // USA Noir

fact, one had to wonder why a man would do any of the dirty landscape work himself. Or hire someone like Kid to help.

I knocked on the door, a cold call, something I'd often done in my days as a journalist. I had my notepad and pen out, in case I needed to pretend to be a reporter.

A woman answered. "Yes?"

I told her I was looking for Christine Coyer's husband.

"He's not here," she informed me. "Do you have an appointment?"

No, just hoping to get lucky, I told her.

"Would you like to leave a message?"

I didn't. I thanked her and left.

I headed back to the river thinking the woman's accent was French, but not heavily so. Quebec, maybe. Her black hair when let down would easily reach her ass. And that body in thong panties would be enough to drive any man to murder.

What to do?

I could go to the police. Would they believe me? If I produced the panties, they might be inclined to look more skeptically on the rich man's story.

I could go to an old colleague. I still knew plenty of press people who'd take the story and dig.

But the influence of money should never be underestimated. Everybody's integrity is for sale if the price is right. So I knew that turning the information and the panties over to anybody else was risky.

I realized I was probably the only shot Kid had at justice.

I sat by the river, smelling the mud churned up from the bottom, but also smelling the perfume of the black-haired woman as it had come to me on the cool air from inside the big house. I couldn't stop myself from imagining what she wore under her dress. I could understand completely why Kid had been so eager and had disregarded the obvious dangers.

For a long time, I'd been telling myself I was happy with nothing. Give me a bedroll and a place to lay it, a decent meal now and then, and a few bucks for a bottle of booze, and what more did I need?

But the circumstances of Kid's death suddenly opened the door on a dark, attractive possibility.

I thought about the lovely house and its gardens.

I thought about that fine, beautiful woman inside.

I thought about the deceased Christine Coyer and all the money she'd left behind.

I thought about all that I didn't have, all that I'd fooled myself into believing I didn't care about—a set of new clothes, a soft mattress, something as simple as a haircut, for God's sake, nothing big really, but still out of my reach.

I was a starved man looking at the possibility of a feast. In the end the choice was easy. After all, what good did justice do the dead?

I got the telephone number from a friend still employed in the newspaper business. I kept calling until the rich man answered.

I identified myself—not with my real name—and told him I was a friend of Lester Greene.

He scraped together a showing of indignity. "I can't imagine what we have to discuss."

"A gift," I told him. "One your wife gave to him. Only she wasn't really your wife. She just pretended in order to lure Lester to your house to be murdered."

"I'm hanging up," he said. But he didn't.

"Ask the woman with the long black hair," I urged him. "Ask her about the gift she gave to Lester. Here's a hint. It's black and silky and small enough to be an eye patch for a pygmy. Ask your beautiful friend about it. I'll call back in a while."

I hung up without giving him a chance to respond.

When I called back, we didn't bother with civilities.

"What do you want?"

Justice for Kid is what I should have said. What came out of my mouth was, "One hundred grand."

"And for one hundred thousand dollars, what do I get?"

He sounded like a man used to wheeling and dealing. According to the paper, he was a financial advisor. I advised him: "My silence." I let that hang. "And the panties."

"You could have got panties anywhere," he countered.

"She's beautiful, your mistress. Who is she, by the way? Your secretary?"

"Christine's personal assistant. Not that it's important."

"But it is important that she's not very bright. She took the panties off her body and gave them to Lester. A DNA analysis of the residual pubic hair would certainly verify that they're hers. I'm sure the police would be more than willing to look at all the possibilities more closely. Do you want to take that chance?"

"Meet me at my house," he suggested. "We'll talk."

"I don't think so. Your last meeting there with Lester didn't end well for him. We'll meet on the High Bridge," I said. "I get the money, you get her panties."

"The panties I can verify. What about your silence?"

"I talk and I'm guilty of extortion. Jail doesn't appeal to me any more than it does to you. The truth is, though, you have no choice but to trust me."

"When?"

"Let's make the exchange this evening just after sunset. Say, nine o'clock."

I wasn't sure he'd be able to get the money so quickly, but he didn't object.

"How will we know each other?" he asked.

We'll have no trouble, I thought. We'll be the only cockroaches on the bridge.

The High Bridge is built at a downward angle, connecting the bluffs of Chero-kee Heights with the river flats below Summit Avenue. Although it was after dark, the sodium vapor lamps on the bridge made everything garishly bright. I waited on the high end. Coming from the other side of the river, the rich man would have to walk uphill to meet me. I found that appealing.

The lights of downtown St. Paul spread out below me. At the edge of all that glitter lay the Mississippi, curling like a long black snake into the night. The air coming over the bridge smelled of the river below, of silt and slow water and something else, it seemed to me. *Dreams* sounds hokey, but that's what I was thinking. The river smelled of dreams. Dreams of getting back on track. Of putting my life together. Of new clothes, a good job, and, yeah, of putting the booze behind me. I didn't know exactly how money was going to accomplish that last part, but it didn't seem impossible.

The evening was warm and humid. Cars came across the bridge at ir-regular intervals. There wasn't any foot traffic. I thought for a while that he'd decided I was bluffing and had blown me off. Which was a relief in a way. That meant I had to do the right thing, take the evidence to the cops, let them deal with it. Kid might yet get his justice.

Then I saw someone step onto the bridge at the far end and start to-ward me. I was a good quarter-mile away and at first I couldn't tell if it was him. When the figure was nearly halfway across, I realized it wasn't the rich man. It was the personal assistant. She stopped in the middle of the bridge and waited, looking up at the Heights, then down toward the flats, uncertain which way I would come.

What the hell was this all about? There was only one way to find out. I walked out to meet her.

I wasn't wearing the gray suit, but she recognized me anyway.

"You were at the house this morning," she said in that accent I decided was, indeed, French Canadian. Her hair hung to her ass and rippled like a velvet curtain. She wore an airy summer dress. The high hem lifted on the breeze, showing off her legs all the way to mid-thigh. Killer legs. Against this, Kid hadn't stood a chance.

"Where is he?" I asked.

"Who cares, as long as I have your money." Her lips were thick and red around teeth white as sugar. I smelled her delicate perfume, the same scent that had washed over me that morning. It seemed to overpower the scent of the river.

"Show me," I said.

"Where are my panties?"

I reached into my pocket and dangled them in front of her. "Where's my money?"

From the purse she carried over her shoulder, she pulled a thick manila envelope. "The panties," she said.

"The envelope first."

She thought about it a moment, then handed it over. I looked inside. Four bundles of hundreds bound with rubber bands.

"Want to count it?" she said.

All I wanted was for the transaction to be over with and to be rid of this business. "I'll trust you," I said.

She took the panties and threw them over the bridge railing. I watched them drop, catch the breeze, and cut toward the middle of the river, swift as a little black bat.

"Gone forever." She smiled.

"You didn't even check to make sure they were the ones. For all you know, I could have bought a pair just like them at Marshall Field's."

"They would never let a bum like you into Marshall Field's." She turned with a swish of her long, scented hair and walked away, her dress lifting on the breeze.

I watched until she'd grown small in the glare, then turned and headed back toward the Heights.

I was ten feet from a new life when he spoke to me out of the shadow of the squat pines at the end of the bridge.

"I'll take the money."

He'd probably come across in one of the cars during my meeting with the woman. I couldn't see his face, but he thrust a gun at me from the shadows and it glowed in the streetlights as if the metal were hot.

"I give it to you, I'm dead," I said.

His voice spat from the dark. "You were dead from the beginning."

I sailed the envelope at him like a frisbee. It caught him in the chest. The gun muzzle flashed. I felt a punch in my belly. I spun and stumbled into the street in front of an MTC bus that swerved, its horn blaring. I fled toward the dark, away from the streetlights.

The bus passed, and he came after me on foot, a black figure against the explosion of light from the bridge. I ran, making my way along the streets that topped the Heights. I cut into an alley, across another street, then into another alley.

Suddenly, inexplicably, my legs gave out. They just went limp. I sprawled in the gravel behind an old garage. A streetlamp not far away shed enough light that I could easily be seen. I managed to crawl into the shadow between two garbage cans, where I lay listening. I heard the slap of shoes hard and fast pass the alley entrance and keep going. Then everything got quiet.

My shirt was soaked with blood. My legs were useless. I'd hoped to make it to the river, but that wasn't going to happen. The end was going to come in a bed of weeds in a nameless alley. Nothing I could do about that.

But about the man and the woman who'd killed Kid, there was still something I could do.

I pulled the pair of panties from my pocket, the pair she'd given Kid and whose twin I'd found that afternoon at Marshall Field's and bought with money made by selling my own blood. I drew out my pen and notepad and wrote a brief explanation, hoping whoever found me would notify the police.

I was near the river, though I would never sit on its banks again. I closed my eyes. For a while, all I smelled was the garbage in the bins. Then I smelled the river. When I opened my eyes, there was Kid, grinning on the other side. Like he understood. Like he forgave me. I started toward him. The water, cold and black, crept up my legs. The current tugged at my body. In a few moments, it carried me away.

PART VI

STREET JUSTICE

VIC PRIMEVAL

BY T. JEFFERSON PARKER

Kearny Mesa, San Diego

(Originally published in *San Diego Noir*)

Y ou know how these things get started, Robbie. You see her for the first
time. Your heart skips and your fingers buzz. Can't take your eyes off
her. And when you look at her she knows. No way to hide it. So you
don't look. Use all your strength to not look. But she still knows. And anybody
else around does too."

"I've had that feeling, Vic," I said.

We walked down the Embarcadero where the cruise ships come and go. It
was what passes for winter here in San Diego, cool and crisp, and there was a
hard clarity to the sunlight. Once a week I met Vic at Higher Grounds coffee
and we'd get expensive drinks and walk around the city. He was a huge guy, a
former professional wrestler. Vic Primeval was his show name until they took
his WWF license away for getting too physical in his matches. He hurt some
people. I spend a few minutes a week with Vic because he thinks he owes me
his life. And because he's alone in the world and possibly insane.

"Anyway," said Vic, "her name is Farrel White and I want you to meet
her."

"Why?"

"Because I'm proud to have you as a friend. You're pretty much all I got
in that department."

"Are you showing us off, Vic? Our freak show past?"

He blushed. "No. But you do make me look good."

Vic was bouncing at Skin, an exotic dance club—strippers, weak drinks,
no cover with military ID. "I don't love that place," I said.

"Robbie, what don't you like about pretty women dancing almost naked?"

"The creeps who go there."

"Maybe you'll get lucky. You're lucky with the ladies."

"What do you know about my luck with ladies, Vic?"

"Come on, man. You've got luck. Whole world knows that."

More luck than I deserve, but is it good or bad? For instance, seven years ago Vic threw me out the window of the sixth floor of a hotel he'd set on fire—the Las Palmas in downtown San Diego. I was trying to save some lives and Vic was distraught at having had his World Wrestling Federation license revoked. This incident could be reasonably called bad luck.

You might have seen the video of me falling to what should have been my death. But I crashed through an awning before I hit the sidewalk and it saved my life. This luck was clearly good. I became briefly semi-famous—The Falling Detective. The incident scrambled my brains a little but actually helped my career with the San Diego Police Department. In the video I look almost graceful as I fall. The world needs heroes, even if it's only a guy who blacks out in what he thinks are the last few seconds of his life.

"Just meet her, Robbie. Tonight she goes onstage at eight, so she'll get there around seven-thirty. I start at eight too. So we can wait for her out back, where the performers go in and out. You won't even have to set foot in the club. But if you want to, I can get you a friends-and-family discount. What else you got better to do?"

We stood in the rear employee-only lot in the winter dark. I watched the cars rushing down Highway 163. The music thumped away inside the club and when someone came through the employee door the music got louder and I saw colored shapes hovering in the air about midway between the door and me.

I've been seeing these colored objects since Vic threw me to that sidewalk. They're geometric, of varying colors, between one and four inches in length, width, depth. They float and bob. I can move them with a finger. Or with a strong exhalation, like blowing out birthday cake candles. They often accompany music, but sometimes they appear when someone is talking to me. The stronger the person's emotion, the larger and more vivid the objects are. They linger briefly then vanish.

In the months after my fall I came to understand these shapes derived not so much from the words spoken, but from the emotion behind them. Each shape and color denotes a different emotion. To me, the shapes are visual reminders of the fact that people don't always mean what they say. My condition is called synesthesia, from the Greek, and loosely translated it means "mixing of the senses." I belong to the San Diego Synesthesia Society and we meet once a month at the Seven Seas on Hotel Circle.

Farrel had a round, pretty face, dark eyes, and brown hair cut in bangs, and one dimple when she smiled. Her lips were small and red. Her handshake was soft. She was short even in high-heeled boots. She wore a long coat against the damp winter chill.

"Vic tells me you're a policeman. My daddy was a policeman. Center Springs, Arkansas. It's not on most maps."

"How long have you been here in San Diego?" I asked.

"Almost a year. I was waitressing but now I'm doing this. Better pay."

"How old are you?"

"I'm twenty-four years old." She had a way of holding your eyes with her own, a direct but uncritical stare. "Vic told me all about what happened. It's good that you've become a friend of his. We all of us need at least one good friend . . . Well, guys, I should be going. I'd ask you in and buy you a drink, but it's supposed to work the other way around."

I glanced at Vic and saw the adoration in his eyes. It lit up his face, made it smarter and softer and better. Farrel smiled at him and put her hand on his sleeve.

"It's okay, Vic."

"Just so good to see you, Farrel."

"Vic walks me in and out, every night. And any other of the dancers who want him to. You're a cop so you know there's always someone coming around places like this, making trouble for the girls. But not when Vic Primeval is in the barnyard."

"I don't really like that name," said Vic.

"I mean it in a good way."

"It means primitive."

"It's only a show name, Vic. Like, well, like for a dancer it would be Chastity or Desire."

I watched the inner conflict ruffle Vic's expression. Then his mind made some kind of override and the light came back to his eyes. He smiled and peered down at the ground.

A hard look came over Farrel's face as a black BMW 750i bounced through the open exit gate and into the employees-only lot. It rolled to a stop beside us. The driver's window went down.

"Yo. Sweetie. I been looking for you." He was thirty maybe and tricked out in style—sharp haircut, pricey-looking shirt and jacket. Slender face, a Jersey voice and delivery. He looked from Farrel to Vic, then at me. "What's your problem, fuckface?"

I swung open my jacket to give him a look at my .45.

He held up his hands like I should cuff him. "Christ. Farrel? You want I should run these meatballs off? They're nothing to do with me and you, baby."

"I want them to run *you* off. I told you, Sal. There isn't a you and me. No more. It's over. I'm gone."

"But you're not gone, baby. You're right here. So get in. Whatever you'll make in a month in there, I'll pay you that right out of my pocket. Right here and now."

"Get off this property," said Vic. "Or I'll drag you out of your cute little car and throw you over that fence."

Vic glanced at me and winced right after he said this. When he gets mad at things he throws them far. People too.

Sal clucked his tongue like a hayseed then smiled at Vic as if he was an amusing moron.

"No more us, Sal," said Farrel. "We're over."

"You still owe me eight thousand dollars, girl. Nothing's over till I get that back."

I saw black rhombuses wobbling in the air between us. Black rhombuses mean anger.

"I'll pay you back as soon as I can. You think I'm dancing in a place like this just for the fun of it all?"

"Move out of here," I said. "Do it now."

"Or you'll arrest me."

"Quickly. It'll cost you forty-eight long cheap hours or two expensive short ones. Your pick."

"I want what's mine," Sal said to Farrel. "I want what I paid for."

"Them's two different things."

"Maybe it is in that redneck slop hole you come from."

The window went up and the car swung around and out of the lot, the big tires leaving a rubbery low-speed squeal on the asphalt.

"I'm coming in for a while," I said.

I had a beer and watched Farrel and the other dancers do their shows. They were uninhibited and rhythmic to say the least. Some were pretty and some were plain. Some acted flirtatious and others lustful and others aloof. Farrel seemed almost shy and she never once looked at either me or Vic from what I could tell. She had a small attractive body. Vic stood in the back of the room, lost in the lush plum-colored curtains, his feet spread wide and arms crossed, stone still.

After an hour passed and Sal had not come back, I nodded a goodnight to Vic and went home.

* * *

Two days later Vic left a message for me and I met him outside the Convention Center. There was a reptile show in progress and many of the people were entering and leaving the building with constrictors around their necks and leashed iguanas in their arms and stacks of clear plastic food containers filled with brightly colored juvenile snakes.

"Look at this thing," he said. He reached into the pocket of his aloha shirt and pulled out a huge black scorpion. "They don't sting."

Vic Malic had enormous hands but that scorpion stretched from his thumb tip to the nail on his little finger. It looked like it could drill that stinger a half inch into you anytime it wanted. In his other hand was a clear plastic bag filled with crickets. They were white with dust of some kind. They hopped around as crickets do.

"Scorpion food?" I asked.

"Yeah. And they dust them with vitamins for thirty cents."

He looked down at the creature then slid it back into his shirt pocket. "That son of a bitch Sal is stalking Farrel. That was the third time I've seen him. He shows up everywhere she goes."

"Tell her to come fill out a report. We can't do anything until she does that."

"Doesn't trust cops."

"She seemed proud of her dad."

"I'm only telling you what she told me. Sal loaned her ten grand because she totaled her car with no insurance, and her baby had to have chemotherapy. Darling little baby. I saw it. Just darling but with cancer."

"That is a shame."

"Yeah, and he was all charm at first, Sal was. She kind of liked him. Started paying with favors, you know, but the way he had it figured was he'd get anything he wanted for two years and she'd still owe him half. Plus he likes it rough and he hit her. Then he said he's got friends. He can introduce her to them, you know—they'd really like her. He's a Jersey wise guy, all connected up. Says he is. You heard him. He said he wants what's his and what he paid for."

I know who the mobbed-up locals are here in America's Finest City. Sal wasn't one of them. We've had our wiseguys for decades, mostly connected to the LA outfits. There's a restaurant they go to. You get to know who they are. I wondered if Sal was just a visiting relative, getting some R&R in Southern California. Or maybe a new guy they brought in. Or if he was a made guy trying to muscle into new territory. If that was true there would be some kind of trouble.

I watched the scorpion wriggle around in the shirt pocket. The pocket had a hula girl and it looked like the pincers were growing out of her head.

"I'm gonna get that eight grand for her," said Vic.

"Where?"

"I got a start with the book sales."

Vic has been hand-selling copies of *Fall to Your Life!*, which he wrote and published himself. It's about how "the Robbie Brownlaw event" seven years ago at the Las Palmas Hotel changed his life for the better. He does pretty well with it, mostly to tourists. I see him sometimes, down by the Star of India, or Horton Plaza, or there at the Amtrak station, looming over his little table with copies of the book and a change box. He wears his old Vic Primeval wrestling costume of faux animal skins—not fur, but the skins sewed together into a kind of bodysuit. It's terrifically ugly but the customers are drawn to it. To attract buyers, he also sets up an aging poster of me falling through the sky. He used to charge five bucks a copy for the book but a year ago it went up to ten. Once a month he still gives me a cut from each sale, which is twenty-five percent. I accept the money because it makes Vic feel virtuous, then turn it over to the downtown food pantry and ASPCA and various charities.

I did some quick calcs based on what Vic paid me in royalties for July—traditionally his best month due to tourists. My take was five hundred dollars, which meant that Vic pocketed fifteen hundred plus change for himself.

"It'll take you at least six months to get eight grand," I said. "Plus winter is coming on and you've got your own expenses to pay."

Vic brooded.

"Do you have any money saved up, Vic?"

"I can get the money."

"So she can give it to him? Don't give her anything. Have her file a complaint with us if he's such a badass. She can get a restraining order. You don't know her and you don't know him. Stay away, Vic. That's the best advice you'll get on this."

"What do you mean?"

"What about this doesn't scream setup?"

"A setup? Why set up a guy who doesn't have any money? She hasn't asked me for one nickel. She's the real thing, Robbie. That little baby. I don't have a world class brain, but my heart always sees true. Farrel passes the Vic Malic heart test."

"The best thing you can do is have her file a complaint."

"She won't. I already told her to. She said the cops can't do anything until they catch him doing something. What she's afraid is, it's gonna be too late when that happens."

Which is often true.

"But Robbie, what if you tell her? Coming from you, it would mean a lot more than from me."

The San Diego mob guys own and frequent a downtown restaurant called Napoli. It's an unflashy two-story brick affair not far at all from police headquarters. They have controlling interests in a couple of much swankier eateries here, but they do their hanging out at Napoli.

"Hey, it's Robbie Brownlaw," said Dom, the owner.

"Dom, I need a word."

"Then you get a word, Robbie. Come on back. How's San Diego's famous detective?"

He's a round-faced, chipper fellow, early sixties, grandson of one of San Diego's more vivid mob figures, Leo the Lion Gagnas. Leo and his LA partners ran this city's gambling and loan-sharking. Back in 1950, two men out of Youngstown tried to get in on the Gagnas rackets, and they both washed up in Glorietta Bay one morning with bullets in their heads. Leo and company opened Napoli back in '53. He was tight with Bebe Rebozo, who was a big Nixon fundraiser. Beginning in 1966 Leo did two years for tax evasion and that was it. He never saw the inside of a prison before or after.

We sat in his dark little office. There were no windows and it smelled heavily of cigar smoke and cologne. The bookshelves were stuffed with well-read paperback crime novels—plenty of Whit Masterson and Erle Stanley Gardner and Mickey Spillane. A floor safe sat in one corner and the walls were covered with framed photographs of Dom's ancestors and the people they entertained at Napoli—Sinatra, Joey Bishop, John Wayne, Nixon, Ted Williams.

I looked at the pictures. "Where's the new celebrities, Dom?"

He looked at the pictures too. "They don't come around here so much anymore. A time for everything, you know? It's good. Business is good. What do you need, Robbie?"

I told him about Sal—his alleged New Jersey outfit ties, his bad attitude and slick black Beamer, his fix on a young dancer at Skin named Farrel.

Dom nodded. "Yeah. I heard. My nephew, he's a manager at Skin. I got some friends checking this guy out."

"Ever had any trouble out of Jersey?"

"Never. Not any trouble at all, Robbie. Those days are long gone. You know that."

"What if he's what he says he is, trying to move in?"

"In on what?"

"On business, Dom."

"I don't know what you mean, *business*. But somebody blows into town and starts popping off about he's a made guy and he's mobbed up in Jersey and all that, well, there's fools and then there's fools, Robbie. Nobody I know talks like that. Know what I mean?"

"I wonder if he's got help."

"He better have help if he wants to shoot off his mouth. I'll let you know what I find out. And Robbie, you see this guy, tell him he's not making any friends around here. If he's what he says he is, then that's one thing. If he's not, then he's just pissing everybody off. Some doors you don't want to open. Tell him that. You might save him a little inconvenience. How's that pretty redhead wife of yours. Gina."

"We divorced seven years ago."

"I got divorced once. No, it was three times. You know why it's so expensive, don't you?"

"Because it's worth it."

"Yeah."

"You've told me that one before, Dom."

"And I was right, wasn't I?"

I met Farrel at Skin that night before she was set to perform. We sat at the bar and got good treatment from the bartenders. Dom's nephew, a spidery young man named Joey Morra, came by, said hello, told Farrel the customers were liking her. I took down Farrel's numbers and address and the name of her daughter and hometown and parents. And I also got everything she could tell me about Sal Tessola—where he lived and how they met, what he'd done for her and to her, the whole story. I told her she'd need all these things in order to write a good convincing complaint. We talked for a solid hour before she checked her watch.

"You going to stay and see me perform?"

"Not tonight."

"Didn't like it much, then?"

"You were good, Farrel."

She eyed me. "I don't want Vic trying to get me the money. I didn't ask him to. I asked him *not* to. He's not the brightest guy, Robbie. But he might be one of the most stubborn."

"You've got a point."

"How come you're not married? You must be about legal age."

"I was once."

"I'd a found a way to keep you."

"You're flattering me now."

"Why don't you flatter me back?"

"Center Springs took a loss when you packed it in."

She peered at me in that forthright and noncommittal way. "It sure did. And there's no power in Heaven or Earth strong enough to drag me back there."

I saw the black triangles of dread and the yellow triangles of fear hovering in the air between us.

I followed her from Skin. I'm not suspicious by nature but it helps me do my job. The night was close and damp and I stayed well behind. She drove an early-'90s Dodge that was slow and slumped to starboard and easy to follow.

She drove to a small tract home out in La Mesa east of downtown. I slowed and watched her pull into the driveway. I went past, circled the block, then came back and parked across the street, one house down.

The house was vintage '50s, one of hundreds built in La Mesa not long after World War II. Many of those navy men and women who'd served and seen San Diego came back looking for a place to live in this sunny and unhurried city.

A living room light was on and the drapes were drawn casually, with a good gap in the middle and another at one end. Someone moved across the living room then lamplight came from the back of the house through a bedroom window on the side I could see. A few minutes went by and I figured she was showering, so I got out and strolled down the sidewalk. Then I doubled back and cut across the little yard and stood under the canopy of a coral tree. I stepped up close to the living room window and looked through the middle gap.

The room was sparsely furnished in what looked like thrift-shop eclectic—a braided rug over the darkly stained wood floor, an American colonial coffee table, an orange-yellow-black plaid sofa with thin padding. There was a stack of black three-ring binders on the coffee table. Right in front of me was the back end of a TV, not a flat screen but one of the old ones with the big butts and masses of cords and coaxial cable sprouting everywhere.

I moved along the perimeter of the house and let myself through a creaking gate but no dogs barked and I soon came to a dark side window. The blinds were drawn but they were old and some were broken and several were bent. Through a hole I could make out a small bedroom. All it had was a chest of drawers and a stroller with a baby asleep in it, and I didn't have to look at that baby very long before I realized it was a doll.

Farrel walked past the room in what looked like a long white bathrobe and something on her head. I waited awhile then backed out across the neighbor's yard and walked to my car. I settled in behind the wheel and used the binoculars and I could see Farrel on the plaid sofa, hair up in a towel, both hands on a sixteen-ounce can of beer seated between her legs. She leaned forward and picked up one of the black binders, looked at it like she'd seen it a hundred times before, then set it down beside her. She seemed tired but peaceful with the TV light playing off her face.

Twenty minutes later a battered Mustang roared up and parked behind the Dodge and Sal got out. Gone were the sharp clothes and in their place were jeans and a fleece-lined denim jacket and a pair of shineless harness boots that clomped and slouched as he keyed open the front door and went through.

I glassed the gap in the living room curtains and Farrel's face rushed at me. She said something without looking at Sal. He stood before her, his back to me, and shrugged. He snatched the beer can from her and held it up for a long drink, then pushed it back between her legs and whipped off his coat. He wore a blue shirt with a local pizza parlor logo on it. This he pulled off as he walked into the back rooms.

He came out a few minutes later wearing jeans and a singlet, his hair wet and combed back. He was a lean young man, broad shouldered, tall. For the first time I realized he was handsome. He walked past Farrel into the kitchen and came back with a can of beer and sat down on the couch not too near and not too far from her. He squeezed her robe once where her knee would be then let his hand fall to the sofa.

They talked without looking at each other but I can't read lips. It looked like a "and how was your day" kind of conversation, or maybe something about the TV show that was on, which threw blue light upon them like fish underwater.

After a while they stopped talking, and a few minutes later Farrel lifted the remote and the blue light was gone and she had picked up one of the black binders from the pile at her end of the couch.

She opened it and read out loud. There was no writing or label or title on the cover.

She waved the binder at him and pointed at a page and read a line to him. He repeated it. I was pretty sure.

She read it again and he repeated it. I was pretty sure again.

They both laughed.

Then another line. They each said it, whatever it was. Sal stood over her then and aimed a finger at her face and said the line again. She stood and stripped the towel off her head and said something and they both laughed again.

He got up and brought two more big cans of beer from the kitchen and he opened one for her and took her empty. He tossed the towel onto her lap and sat down close to her, put his bare feet up on the coffee table by the binders and scrunched down so his head was level with hers. She clicked the TV back on.

I waited for an hour. Another beer each. Not much talk. They both fell asleep sitting up, heads back on the sofa.

It was almost three-thirty in the morning when Farrel stood, rubbed the back of her neck, then tightened the robe sash. She walked deeper into the house and out of my sight.

A few minutes later Sal rose and hit the lights. In the TV glow I could see him stretch out full length on the couch and set one arm over his eyes and take a deep breath and let it slowly out.

Two mornings later, at about the same dark hour, I was at headquarters writing a crime scene report. I'm an occasional insomniac and I choose to get paperwork done during those long, haunted times. Of course I listen to our dispatch radio, keeping half an ear on the hundreds of calls that come in every shift.

So when I heard the possible 187 at Skin nightclub I was out the door fast.

Two squad cars were already there and two more screamed into the parking lot as I got out of my car.

"The janitor called 911," said one of the uniforms. "I was first on scene and he let me in. There's a dead man back in the kitchen. I think it's one of the managers. I tried to check his pulse but couldn't reach that far. You'll see."

I asked the patrolmen to seal both the back and front entrances and start a sign-in log, always a good idea if you don't want your crime scene to spiral into chaos. You'd be surprised how many people will trample through and wreck evidence, many of them cops.

I walked in, past the bar and the tables and the stage, then into a small, poorly lit, grease-darkened kitchen. Another uniform stood near a walk-in freezer, talking with a young man wearing a light blue shirt with a name patch on it.

I saw the autoloader lying on the floor in front of me. Then the cop looked up and I followed his line of sight to the exposed ceiling. Overhead were big commercial blowers and vents and ducting and electrical conduit and hanging fluorescent tube light fixtures. A body hung jackknifed at the hips over a steel crossbeam. His arms dangled over one side and his legs over the other. If he'd landed just one inch higher or lower, he'd have simply slid off the beam to the floor. I walked around the gun and got directly under him and stared up into the face of Joey. It was an urgent shade of purple and his eyes were open.

"The safe in the office," said the uniform, pointing to the far back side of the kitchen.

The office door was open and I stepped in. There was a desk and a black leather couch and a small fridge and microwave, pictures of near-naked dancers on the walls, along with a Chargers calendar and Padres pendants.

There was also a big floor safe that was open but not empty. I squatted in front of it and saw the stacks of cash and some envelopes.

The officer and janitor stood in the office doorway.

"Why kill a man for his money then not take it?" asked the uniform. His name plate said *Peabody*.

"Maybe he freaked and ran," said the janitor, whose name patch said *Carlos*.

"Okay," said Peabody. "Then tell me how Joey got ten feet up in the air and hung over a beam. And don't tell me he did it to himself."

Carlos looked up at the body and shrugged but I had an opinion about that.

"What time do you start work?" I asked him.

"Two. That's when they close."

"Is Joey usually here?"

"One of the managers is always here. They count the money every third night. Then they take it to the bank."

"So tonight was bank night?"

"Was supposed to be."

* * *

I drove fast to Vic's hotel room downtown but he didn't answer the door. Back downstairs the night manager, speaking from behind a mesh-reinforced window, told me that Vic left around eight-thirty—seven hours ago—and had not returned.

I made Farrel's place eleven minutes later. There were no cars in the driveway but lights inside were on. I rang the bell and knocked then tried the door, which was unlocked. So I opened it and stepped in.

The living room looked exactly as it had two nights ago, except that the beer cans were gone and the pile of black binders had been reduced to just one. In the small back bedroom the stroller was still in place and the plastic doll was snugged down under the blanket just as it had been. I went into the master bedroom. The mattress was bare and the chest of drawers stood open and nearly empty. It looked like Farrel had stripped the bed and packed her clothes in a hurry. The bathroom was stripped too: no towels, nothing in the shower or the medicine chest or on the sink counter. The refrigerator had milk and pickles and that was all. The wastebasket under the sink had empty beer cans, an empty pretzel bag, various fast-food remnants swathed in ketchup, a receipt from a supermarket, and a wadded-up agreement from Rent-a-Dream car rentals down by the airport. Black Beamer 750i, of course.

Back in the living room I took the black binder from the coffee table and opened it to the first page:

THE SOPRANOS
Season Four/Episode Three

I flipped through the pages. Dialogue and brief descriptions. Four episodes in all.

Getting Sal's lines right, I thought.

Vic didn't show up for work for three straight nights. I stopped by Skin a couple of times a night, just in case he showed, and I knocked on his hotel room door twice a day or so. The manager hadn't seen him in four days. He told me Vic's rent was due on the first.

Of course Farrel had vanished too. I cruised her place in La Mesa but something about it just said she wasn't coming back, and she didn't.

On the fourth afternoon after the murder of Joey Morra, Vic called me on my cell phone. "Can you feed my scorpion? Give him six crickets. They're under the bathroom sink. The manager'll give you the key."

430 // USA Noir

"Sure. But we need to talk, Vic—face to face."

"I didn't do it."

"Who else could throw Joey up there like that?"

Vic didn't answer.

"Dom and his people are looking for you, Vic. You won't get a trial with them. You'll just get your sentence, and it won't be lenient."

"I only took what she needed."

"And killed Joey."

"He pulled a gun, Robbie. I couldn't thinka what else to do. I bear-hugged and shook him. Like a reflex. Like when I threw you."

"I'll see you outside Higher Grounds in ten minutes."

"She met me at Rainwater's, Robbie. I walked into Rainwater's and there she was—that beautiful young woman, waiting there for me. You should have seen her face light up when I gave her the money. Out in the parking lot, I mean."

"I'll bet," I said. "Meet me outside Higher Grounds in ten minutes."

"Naw. I got a good safe place here. I'm going to just enjoy myself for a couple more days, knowing I did a good thing for a good woman. My scorpion, I named him Rudy. Oh. Oh shit, Robbie."

Even coming from a satellite orbiting the Earth in space, and through the miles of ether it took to travel to my ear, the sound of the shotgun blast was unmistakable. So was the second blast, and the third.

A few days later I flew to Little Rock and rented a car, then made the drive north and west to Center Springs. Farrel was right: it wasn't on the rental-car company driving map, but it made the navigation unit that came in the vehicle.

The Ozarks were steep and thickly forested and the Arkansas River looked unhurried. I could see thin wisps of wood stove fires burning in cabins down in the hollows and there was a smoky cast to the sky.

The gas station clerk said I'd find Farrel White's dad's place down the road a mile, just before Persimmon Holler. He said there was a batch of trailers up on the hillside and I'd see them from the road if I didn't drive too fast. Billy White had the wooden one with all the satellite dishes on top.

The road leading in was dirt and heavily rutted from last season's rain. I drove past travel trailers set up on cinder blocks. They were slouched and sun-dulled and some had decks and others just had more cinder blocks as steps. Dogs eyed me without bothering to sit up. There were cats and litter and a pile of engine blocks outside, looked like they'd been cast there by some huge child.

Billy answered my knock with a sudden yank on the door then studied me through the screen. He was mid-fifties and heavy, didn't look at all like his daughter. He wore a green-and-black plaid jacket buttoned all the way to the top.

"I'm a San Diego cop looking for your daughter. I thought she might have come home."

"Would you?"

"Would I what?"

"Come home to this from San Diego?"

"Well."

"She okay?"

"I think so."

"Come in."

The trailer was small and cramped and packed with old, overstuffed furniture.

"She in trouble?"

"Farrel and her boyfriend hustled a guy out of some money. But he had to take the money from someone else."

Billy handed me a beer and plopped into a vinyl recliner across from me. He had a round, impish face and a twinkle in his eyes. "That ain't her boyfriend. It's her brother."

"That never crossed my mind."

"Don't look nothing alike. But they've always been close. Folks liked to think too close, but it wasn't ever that way. Just close. They understood each other. They're both good kids. Their whole point in life was to get outta Center Springs and they done did it. I'm proud of them."

"What's his name?"

"Preston."

"Did they grow up in this trailer?"

"Hell no. We had a home over to Persimmon but it got sold off in the divorce. Hazel went to Little Rock with a tobacco products salesman. The whole story is every bit as dreary as it sounds."

"When did Farrel and Preston leave?"

"Couple of months ago. The plan was San Diego, then Hollywood. Pretty people with culture and money to spend. They were going to study TV, maybe go start up a show. San Diego was to practice up."

"The scripts."

"Got them from the library up at Fayetteville. Made copies of the ones they wanted. Over and over again. Memorizing those scripts and all them words. They went to the Salvation Army stores and bought up lots of old-time kinda clothes. They both did some stage plays at the junior college but they didn't much care for them. They liked the other kind of stories."

"What kind of stories?"

"Crime stories. Bad guys. Mafia. That was mainly Preston. Farrel, she can act like anything from the Queen of England to a weather girl and you can't tell she's acting."

"Have they called lately?"

"Been over a week."

"Where do you think they are?"

"Well, Center Springs is the only place I know they ain't. I don't expect to ever see them out this way."

I did the simple math and the not-so-simple math. Eight grand for two months of work. Farrel dancing for tips. Preston delivering pizza and working his end of the Vic hustle. Vic caught between Farrel's good acting and his own eager heart. And of course betrayed, finally and fatally, by his own bad temper.

I finished the beer and stood. "Two men died because of them. Eight thousand bucks is what they died for. So the next time you talk to Farrel and Preston, you tell them there's real blood on their hands. It's not make-believe blood. You tell her Vic was murdered for taking that eight thousand."

"I'll do that."

"Thanks for your time."

"I can come up with a couple a hundred. It's not much, but . . ."

I saw the orange triangles bouncing in the air between us. I thought about those triangles as I drove away. Orange triangles denote pity and sometimes even empathy. All this for Vic Primeval, as offered by a man he'd never met, from his vinyl chair in his slouching home in the Ozarks. Sometimes you find a little speck of good where you least expect it. A rough diamond down deep. And you realize that the blackness can't own you for more than one night at a time.

Originally published in *Wall Street Noir*

PROMISED TULIPS

BY BHARTI KIRCHNER
Wallingford, Seattle
(Originally published in *Seattle Noir*)

I am floating between dream and wakefulness in my cozy treehouse nestled high in the canopy of a misty rain forest when he murmurs, "You're so beautiful with your hair over your face."

I smile and bid him a *Guten morgen*. Ulrich—I like the full feel of that German name in my mouth, the melodious lilt, and I definitely appreciate the warm masculine body, its sculpted hardness visible beneath the sheets. He stretches an arm toward me, as if about to say or do something intimate, then closes his eyes and allows his arm to drop. I snuggle up against him, savoring the musky sweet skin, on a morning so different from others. Usually I rise at dawn, slip into my greenhouse, and appraise the overnight progress of the seedlings.

If my mother were to peek in at this instant, she would draw a corner of her sari over her mouth to stifle a scream.

"Sin!" she'd say. "My twenty-five-year-old unmarried girl is living in sin!"

Fortunately, she's half a world away in India.

And I'm not in my treehouse, but rather in the bedroom of my bungalow in Wallingford, a.k.a. the Garden District of Seattle.

Next door the Labrador retriever barks. Never before have I invited a man home on the first encounter and I'm unnerved by my daring. If my friends could see me now, they'd exclaim in disbelief, *A shy thing like you?*

The silky, iris-patterned linen sheets are bunched up. He sleeps more messily than I, but for some reason I like the rumpled look. Last night's coupling, with its wild tumbling and thrusting—I wouldn't exactly call it lovemaking— has put me into deep communion with my body, and also taken me a bit out of my zone. My lips are dry and puffy from a surfeit of kissing.

The man beneath the blanket turns his blond head, nuzzles the pillow, regards me with his green eyes, then looks at the clock on the lamp stand. "Eight-thirty?" He throws the blanket aside and bolts from the bed. "*Ach*, I'm supposed to be at work by seven."

An engineer by training, he works in construction, a choice he's made to get away from "wallowing in my head." So, he happily hammers nails all day, fixing roofs, patios, kitchens, and basements. Siegfried, his German shepherd, always goes along.

I point out the bathroom across the hallway. He scrambles in that direction, mumbling to himself in his native tongue. A sliver of sun is visible through a crack in the window draperies. I can tell from its position that the morning has passed its infancy, the galaxy has inched on to a new position, and I've already missed a thing or two.

I hoist myself up from my nest. My toes curl in protest at the first touch of the cold hardwood floor. I stoop to retrieve a pair of soft-soled wool slippers from under the nightstand.

Then I look for my clothes. The long-sleeved print dress I wore last evening—a tantrum of wildflowers—lies on the floor, all tangled up with my bra and panties and Ulrich's charcoal jeans. Crossing the room, I rummage around in the closet, grab a pewter-gray bathrobe, and wrap it around me.

As I fluff the pillows, I hear the sounds of water splashing in the sink, and snatches of a German song. A peek through the draperies reveals a quick change of weather—a bruised, swollen April sky.

The jangling of the telephone startles me. Not fair, this intrusion. If it's Kareena on the line, I'll whisper: *Met a cool Deutsche last night . . . We're just out of bed. I know, I know, but this one is . . . Look, I'll call you back later, okay?*

Tangles of long hair drown my vision; I reach for the receiver. This is what a plant must feel like when it's uprooted.

"Palette of Color. Mitra Basu speaking, how can I help you?" Plants are my refuge, my salvation and, fortuitously, my vocation.

"Veen here." The downturn in her voice doesn't escape me. Vivacious and well-connected, architect by profession, Veenati is an important part of my social circle. "Have you heard from Kareena recently?"

"Not in a week or so. Why? Has something happened to her?"

"She didn't show up for coffee this morning. I called her home. Adi said she's missing."

"Missing? Since when?"

"Since the night before last. I was just checking to see if she'd contacted you. I'm late for work. Let's talk in about an hour."

"Wait—"

Click. Veen has hung up. This is like a dreadful preview of a hyperkinetic action flick. How could Kareena be missing? She's a people person, well respected in our community for her work with abused women. Although we're not related, Kareena is my only "family" in this area, not to mention the closest confidante I've had since leaving home. A word from my youth, *shoee*, friends of the heart, hums inside me. I'm badly in need of explanation to keep my imagination from roaring out of control.

A vase of dried eucalyptus sits on the accent table. Kareena had once admired that fragrant arrangement—she adores all objects of beauty. Now she, a beautiful soul, has been reported missing. Wish I'd pressed her to take the risks of her profession more seriously. Don't use your last name. Take a different route home every day. Always let somebody know where you are.

Ulrich is back. "Everything okay?"

"A friend is missing." I make the statement official-sounding, while glancing at the window, and hope he won't probe further. I'm of the opinion that intimacy has its limits. In the cold clarity of the morning, it discomfits me that I, a private person, have already shared this much with him.

Standing so close to me that I can smell the sweat of the night on his skin, he dresses hurriedly. I linger on his muscles. His large fingers fumble with the buttons of his muted blue shirt and a thin lower lip pouts when he struggles to insert a recalcitrant button in its hole. He wiggles into his jeans and throws on his herringbone jacket. Then he draws me closer with an eager expression and cups my face in his hands. I grow as still as I've ever been. He gives me a short warm kiss which softens my entire midsection. The hum in the air is like static electricity crackling.

Will I ever see him again? Coming from nowhere, the morbid thought slaps me on the forehead, but I recover quickly and my attention stretches back to Kareena. She could have gone somewhere for a breather from the daily battles she fights on her clients' behalf.

"I want to stay here with you," Ulrich says, "but . . ."

Modulated by his accent, the word want, or *vant*, hints at delicious possibilities for another time. I look up at his pale-skinned round face, and I really do have to look up, for he's a good nine inches taller. I struggle with words to convey my feelings, to put a lid on my concerns about Kareena, but stay mute.

"Catch you this evening," he murmurs.

As we walk to the doorway, our arms around each other, a yen to entice him to stay steals into my consciousness. I smother the impulse. Self-mastery is a trait I've inherited from my mother. (She denies herself pleasure of all sorts, refusing chai on a long train journey, and even returns bonus coupons to stores.)

Ulrich gives me one last look followed by another kiss, sustaining the connection, that of a conjurer to a captive audience. As he descends the front steps, his face turns toward my budding tulip patch—an exuberant yellow salutation to the coming spring—and he holds it in sight till the last second. Yellow is Kareena's color and I am growing these tulips for her. She'll shout in pleasure when she sees how gorgeous they are.

A Siamese cat from down the block watches from its customary perch atop a low brick wall as Ulrich lopes toward a steel-gray Saab parked across the street.

I shut the door, pace back to the living room, open the draperies. Ulrich's car is gone. Feeling a nip in the air, I cinch the belt of my bathrobe. Kareena and I bought identical robes at a Nordstrom sale. Despite different sizes—hers a misses medium and mine a petite small—we're like twins or, at least, sisters.

As I look down at my slippers, they too remind me of Kareena. A domestic violence counselor, she'd bought this pair from the boutique of a client who was a victim of spousal abuse. While I function in a universe of color, bounty, growth, and optimism, Kareena deals with "family disturbances." Hers is a world of purple bruises, bloodshot gazes, and shattered hearts huddling in a public shelter.

I look out at the long line of windows across the street. A blue-black Volvo SUV speeds by, marring the symmetry and reminding me of Kareena's husband Adi; a real prize, he is.

I met both Adi (short for Aditya, pronounced *Aditta*) and Kareena for the first time at a party they hosted. Before long, we began discussing where we were each from. Kareena had been raised in Mumbai and New Delhi, whereas Adi, like me, hailed from the state of West Bengal in Eastern India. Even as I greeted him, *"Parichay korte bhalo laglo"* ("How nice to meet you," in our shared Bengali tongue), Adi's name somehow brought to mind another word, *dhurta*: crook. The two words sort of rhyme in Bengali. That little fact I suppressed, but I couldn't ignore the insouciance with which he flicked on his gold cigarette lighter, the jaunty angle of the Marlboro between his lips, the disdainful way he regarded the other guests.

At just over six feet, he looked as out of place in that crowded room as a skyscraper in a valley of mud huts. He obviously believed that the shadow he cast was longer than anyone else's. He informed me in the first ten minutes that his start-up, Guha Software Services, was in the black; that his ancestors had established major manufacturing plants in India; that he'd recently purchased a deluxe beach cottage on the Olympic Peninsula. Then he walked away without even giving me a chance to say what I did for a living.

A chill has hung between us ever since. "Two strong personalities," Kareena has maintained over the years, but there's more to it. I don't know if Adi has a heart, and if he does, whether Kareena is in it. His smirk says he knows I think he's not good enough for her, but that he could care less. And, to be honest, they have interests in common. Both have an abiding love for Indian *ghazal* songs; both excel in table tennis when they can manage the time; both detest green bell pepper in any form. They make what one might call a perfect married couple—young, handsome, successful, socially adept, and with cosmopolitan panache. They look happy together, or, rather, he does. His attention to her is total, as though she's an *objet d'art* that has cost him no small sum. He professes to be "furiously, stormily, achingly" in love with her. *Every millisecond, I dream of you and you only*, he gushed in a birthday card I once saw pinned on a memo board in their kitchen.

Do the purplish contusions I saw on Kareena's arm attest to Adi's undying affection? I grit my teeth now as I did then.

Adi doesn't answer my phone call. I think about ringing another friend, but a peek at the red-eyed digits of the mantle clock stops my hand. Better to postpone the call and shower instead. Better to gauge what actually happened before I get everybody upset.

My nerves are so scrambled that the shower is no more than a surface balm. I towel myself but don't waste time blow-drying my shoulder-length hair.

In the mirror, my bushy eyebrows stand out against my olive skin. My nose is tiny, like an afterthought. Although I'm fit, healthy, and rosy-cheeked and my hair is long and lustrous, I'm not beautiful by either Indian or American standards. Friends say I have kind eyes. It has never occurred to me to hide the cut mark under my left eye caused by a childhood brush with a low-hanging tree branch. I don't like to fuss with makeup.

Dressed in a blue terry knit jacket, matching pants, and sneakers, I drift into the kitchen. Breakfast consists of a tall cool glass of water from the filter tap. I slip into my greenhouse and inhale its forest fragrance. The sun sparkles through the barn-style roof and the glass-paneled walls. I hope the fear signals inside me are wrong.

The plants are screaming for moisture. I pick up a sprayer and mist the trays, dispensing life-giving moisture to the germinating seeds and fragile sprouts poking up through the soil. A honeybee hums over a seed flat.

All around me, the life force is triumphant: surely that'll happen with Kareena too. Whatever the cause, her disappearance will be temporary, explainable, and reversible.

* * *

An hour later I call Veen. "According to Adi, Kareena was last seen with a stranger," she says. "They were at Toute La Soirée around eleven a.m. on Friday. A waitress who'd seen them together reported so to the police. I find it odd that Adi sounded a little jealous but not terribly worried over the news about this strange man."

I've been to that café many times. Kareena, who had no special fidelity to any one place, somehow took a fancy to rendezvousing there with me. Could that man have blindfolded Kareena, put a hand over her mouth, and dragged her into a car?

No, on second thought, that's impossible. A spirited person like her couldn't be held captive. Could she have run away with that man because of Adi's abuse? That's more likely. I ask Veen what the man looks like.

"Dark, average height, handsome, and well-dressed. He carried a jute bag on his shoulder."

"Oh, a *jhola*." In India some years back, *jholas* were the fashion among male intellectuals. My scrawny next-door neighbor, who considered himself a man of letters but was actually a film buff, toted books in his *jhola*. He could often be seen running for the bus with the hefty bag dangling from one shoulder and bumping against his hip. Tagore novels? Chekov's story collection? Shelley's poems? The only thing I ever saw him fishing out of the bag was a white box of colorful pastries when he thought no one was looking.

"But eleven is too early for lunch," I say, "and Kareena never takes a mid-morning break. Why would she be there at such an hour?"

"Don't know. And what do you make of this? I was passing by Umberto's last night and spotted Adi with a blonde. They were drinking wine and talking."

"He seems to be taking this awfully easy." I remind Veen that Adi has the typical Asian man's fixation on blond hair. According to Kareena, Adi's assistant is a neatly put-together blonde stationed at a cubicle outside his office. Veen and I discuss if Adi might be having an affair, but don't come to any conclusion.

As I hang up, my glance falls on my cell phone, the mute little accessory on the coffee table in front of the couch. Kareena and I get together most Fridays after work, and she often calls me at the last minute. No cause for concern, I assured myself when I left a message on Kareena's voice mail a few days ago and didn't hear back.

Silently, I replay my last face-to-face with Kareena at Toute La Soirée. On that afternoon two weeks ago, I was waiting for her at a corner table, perusing the *Seattle Globe* and reveling in the aromas of lime, ginger, and mint. It filled me with fury to read a half-page story about a woman in India blamed for her village's crop failures and hunted down as a witch. I would have to share this story with Kareena.

Sensing a rustle in the atmosphere, I looked up. Standing just inside the door, Kareena peered out over the crowd, spotted me, and flashed a smile. She looked casually chic in a maroon pantsuit (maple foliage shade in my vocabulary, Bordeaux in hers) that we'd shopped for together at Nordstrom. Arms swaying long and loose, she weaved her way among the tables. Her left wrist sported a pearl-studded bracelet-cum-watch.

As she drew closer, a woman in chartreuse seated across the aisle from me called out to her. Kareena paused and they exchanged pleasantries. The woman glanced in my direction and asked, "Is that your sister?"

Kareena winked at me. We'd been subjected to the same question countless times, uttered in a similar tone of expectation. Did we really look alike, or had we picked up each other's mannerisms from spending so much time together? At 5'1", I am shorter than her by three inches, and thinner. Our styles of dressing fall at opposite ends of the fashion spectrum. I glanced down at my powder-blue workaday jumper, a practical watch with a black resin band, and walking flats. My attire didn't follow current fashion dictates, but it was low-key and comfy, just right for an outdoors person. Fortunately, Seattle accommodated both our styles.

"*Kemon acho?*" Kareena greeted me with a Bengali pleasantry I'd taught her. "Sorry I'm late. First, I had a gynecologist appointment, then a difficult DV case to wrap up."

I pushed the newspaper to the far side of the table. DV—domestic violence—is an abbreviation that sounds to me more like a fearsome disease, less like a social thorn. Kareena likes to help women who are in abusive relationships and, as yet, unaware of their legal rights. She was named the top DV counselor in her office and has received recognition for her efforts.

"I really think you're overworking." I touched her hand. "Do you really need the money? Do you need to shop so much?"

She ran her fingers over her bracelet. "You don't resent my spending, do you?"

I shook my head, then stopped to ruminate. Well, in truth, there have been times. She likes to shop at Nordstrom, Restoration Hardware, and Williams-Sonoma, places that are beyond my means, but she insists on having my company. I have an eye for quality and she values that.

I got back to the subject at hand. "Was today's case one from our community, another hush-hush?"

"Unfortunately, yes." She mimicked a British accent: "A 'family matter, a kitchen accident.'" She paused. The waiter was hovering by her shoulder. We placed our orders.

Not for the first time, I agonized over the threats Kareena faces due to the nature of her job. Signs have been plentiful. She is frequently called a man-hater and, at least once in the last month, has been followed home from work. The spouse of one client even went so far as to publicly question her sexual orientation.

"You're the only one I trust enough to talk about this case," Kareena continued. "She's an H-4 visa holder, so scared that she couldn't even string together a few coherent sentences. I spoke a little Punjabi with her, which loosened her up. Still, it took awhile to draw out her story. Her husband beats her regularly."

I appraised Kareena's face. How she could absorb the despair of so many traumatized souls? Listen to songs that don't finish playing? Lately, her lipstick color had gone from her standard safe pink to a risky red. Brown circles under her eyes spoke of fatigue or, perhaps, stress, and I suspected the brighter lip color was intended to redirect a viewer's attention.

"Did you see bruises on her?" I asked and watched her carefully.

It was still so vivid in my mind, Kareena's last cocktail party a few weeks before and the freshly swollen blue-black marks on her upper arm. In an unguarded moment, her paisley Kashmiri shawl had slid off her shoulders. Through the billowy sheer sleeves of her tan silk top, I glimpsed dark blue, almost black finger marks on an otherwise smooth arm. The swelling extended over a large area, causing me to nearly shriek. Adi must have attacked her. Upon realizing that I'd noticed, she glanced down and repositioned the shawl. Just then, a male friend approached, asked her to dance, took her arm, and they floated away.

"Yes, I did see bruises on her forehead," Kareena now replied. "She'd be in worse trouble if her husband suspected she was out looking for help."

"The law is on her side, isn't it?" I allowed a pause. "You don't have problems at home, by any chance, do you?"

"What are you getting at?"

"Well, I happened to notice bruises on *your* arm at your last party. Who was it?"

I noticed the mauve of shame spreading on her face. "I don't want to talk about it," she said.

"Sorry to barge into your private matters, but if you ever feel like talking—"

Our orders came. Mine was a ginger iced tea and hers an elixir of coconut juice and almond milk. She raised her chin and lifted her glass to clink with mine, her way of accepting my apology.

I took a sip from my beverage; she drained hers with such hurried gulps that I doubted she fully appreciated the flavors. Typical Kareena; appearances must be maintained. Both of us looked out through the window and took in the sky-colored Ship Canal where a fishing vessel was working its way to the dry docks that lined the north shore of Lake Union. Sooner or later, I thought, I'd have to find out the truth about those bruises.

When the silver waves died down in the canal, Kareena spoke again: "But enough of this depressing stuff! How did things go for you today?"

I filled her in on the most interesting part of my day: consulting with a paraplegic homeowner. "Believe it or not," I said, "the guy wants to do all the weeding and watering himself. It'll be a challenge, but I'll design a garden to suit his requirements."

"You live such a sane life and you have such a healthy glow on your face. Just listening to you, I seem to siphon off some of it. " She gave me a smile. "Come on, Mitra. Let me buy you another drink."

She signaled the waiter. The room was emptier now, the sounds hushed, and a genial breeze blew through a half-open window. We ordered a second round.

"Before the alarm went off this morning," she said after a while, "I got a call from my nephew in New Delhi. He's seven."

"Does he want you to visit him?"

She nodded and mashed her napkin into a ball. I guessed she was undergoing one of those periodic episodes of homesickness for India, the country we'd both left behind. I, too, experience the same longing to visit people missing from my life. Whereas she can afford to go back every year, I can't.

I digressed from this aching topic to a lighter one by pointing out a cartoon clip peeking out from under the glass cover of our table. A tiny boy, craning his neck up, is saying to his glowering father, *Do I dare ask you what day of the week it is before you've had your double tall skinny?*

That got a spontaneous laugh from Kareena which, in turn, raised my spirits. I didn't have a chance to discuss the newspaper story with her. Well, the next time.

I go back to my living room. The airy tranquility has been transformed into a murky emptiness, as though a huge piece of familiar furniture has been cleared out but not replaced. I have an urge to confide in someone, but who could that be? The only person I can think of is the one who's gone away.

I wander into the kitchen, open and close the cupboard, rearrange items in the refrigerator, and fill the tea kettle with water. With a cup of Assam tea and a slice of multigrain toast, I sit at the round table. Bananas protrude from a sunny ceramic bowl within arm's reach. I fiddle with my iPod.

The tea tempers to lukewarm, the toast becomes dense, and the bananas remain untouched. It's difficult for me to stomach much food in the morning, and this news has squelched whatever hunger I might otherwise have. I stare at the *Trees Are Not Trivial* poster on the sea-blue wall. Even the cushioned chair doesn't feel cozy. I itch all over.

Could someone have murdered her?

I peer out through the western window. The Olympic Mountains appear stable, blue, and timeless. Somehow I doubt that Kareena could be the victim of a lethal crime.

How can I help find her? My career focus in art and landscape design— the study of the physiology of new growth, awareness of color and light, and harmony of arrangements—hasn't prepared me to deal with a situation like this.

I walk over to my side yard. Bluebells are pushing up from the winter-hardened ground. I notice a slug, pick it up with a leaf, and deposit it on a safe spot. Once again, spring is in the balmy air. I look up to the sky, out of a gardener's propensity to check the weather. It helps me see beyond the immediate.

Back to the living room, I sit at my desk, grab a notepad, and begin listing friends and acquaintances who I can call upon. The page fills speedily. The Indian population in the Puget Sound area, described recently by the *Seattle Globe* in a feature story as a "model" community, is some twenty-five thousand strong. The community's academic and professional accomplishments are "as lofty as Mount Rainier," the same article proclaimed. I'm troubled by such laudatory phrases, aware that we have our fair share of warts and blemishes. According to Kareena, the rate of domestic violence among our dignified doctors, elite engineers, and high-powered fund-raisers equals, perhaps even exceeds, the national average.

I consult my watch. It is ten o'clock, an hour when everyone's up and about, when the disappointments of the day haven't dulled one's spirits. This'll be a good time to ring Adi and draw him out. He loves to talk about himself in his Oxford-accented, popcorn-popping speech, which will give me a chance to tease information out of him, however distasteful the process might be, however potentially dangerous. Kareena is my best friend. When we're together, I'm fully present and my voice is at its freest. Day turns into twilight as we relax over drinks, gabbing, laughing, and trading opinions, oblivious to the time. We don't parse our friendship. It just is. We scatter the gems of our hours freely, then retrieve them richer in value.

With the phone to my ear, I pace back and forth in front of my living room window. Adi, at the other end, is ignoring the ringing.

The Emperor comes to focus in my mind—an impeccable suit, sockless feet (part of his fashion statement), and eyes red-rimmed with exasperation at some luckless underling behind on a project or the changeable Seattle sky. Adi takes any potential irritant personally. He snatches a ringing phone from its cradle at the last possible moment. The world can wait. It always does for Adi Guha.

The stand-up calendar on the mantel nags me about tomorrow's deadline for a newspaper gardening column. Yet, as I pace the cold floor once again, the phone glued to my ear, it becomes clear that such an assignment is no longer a high priority for me. My missing friend is my main focus now. All else has faded into the background.

Adi comes on the line, gasps when he recognizes my voice. I mention Veen's call, then get straight to the point. "What time did you get home that night?"

"Your core competency is gardening, Mitra. I'm not saying it's menial labor, but neither is it nuclear physics or private investigation. Go back to your garden and leave this situation in more competent hands, like mine."

I ignore the insult. "Do the police have any clues? Did they come to the house?"

"I gave them a photo which they looked at, then began to pepper me with questions. They gave me a song and dance about how many people disappear daily from the city. They assigned a laid-back cop, the only one they could spare. It's obvious they're not interested unless it's a blond heiress and television cameras are everywhere."

"What about the stranger she met at Soirée?"

"I'm not worried about that. She's a big girl. She can take care of herself."

"Have you talked to her gynecologist?"

Adi mumbles a no.

"Do you think she needed a break and decided to sneak away for a few days? There have been times, like at your birthday party, when she looked like she could use a break."

"Everything is fine between us, Mitra, just fine."

Everything's fine? What a laugh. About a year ago, Kareena and I were spending an evening at Soirée when a hugely pregnant woman waddled past our table. I shifted my chair to let her pass. Kareena put her fork down and gazed at the woman.

In a teasing tone I asked, "Could that be you?"

"Adi doesn't want kids." She returned to her voluptuous plum-almond tart.

Now I hear a staccato rumbling in the background, a car cruising. Adi has nerve, telling me everything was fine with Kareena. Kareena's everything and Adi's everything are obviously not the same.

"Did you check her closet?" I now ask.

"Looks like her clothes are all there."

Would he even recognize her alligator handbag, jeweled mules, flowing shawls she favored over the structured feel of a coat, or the new Camellia scarf? Would he be able to detect the nuance of her perfume? I believe he only remembers the superficial facts of her presence.

"Did you go to the safety deposit box to see if her passport is there?"

"No, yesterday I had to chair a three-hour offsite meeting. The market isn't as calm as it was last year. We need to get our cash-burn rate under control. It may be necessary to dehire some people."

I almost choke at the expression he uses for firing an employee. Then he begins to ramble on about market share, competitive disadvantage, and going public to raise new capital. In short order, his business-speak begins to grate on me.

I interrupt him by saying, "This is a life-and-death situation, Adi."

"It sure is," he replies. "This morning around five I got a call from the police. They asked me to go see a body at the morgue."

My vision blurs. "What?"

"A woman's body was found in Lake Washington. It wasn't her."

"Oh my God!" I shake my head. "Must have been difficult for you. I don't know what I'd do if . . ." I get a grip on myself. "Could we meet this morning? Put our heads together? The earlier the better. We need to mobilize our community. I'll be happy to drop by your office."

"Hold on now, Mitra. I *don't* want even my friends to get wind of this, never mind the whole community. You, of all people, should know how things get blown out of proportion when the rumor mill cranks up."

I sag on the couch. Losing face with his Indian peers is more important to him than seeking help in finding his wife. In a way, I get it. Our community is small. We have at most two degrees of separation between people, instead of the hypothetical six nationwide. Word spreads quickly and rumor insinuates itself in every chit-chat. Still, how silly, how counterproductive Adi's pride seems in this dark situation.

And that makes him more of a suspect.

There are times when I think Adi is still a misbehaving adolescent who needs his behind kicked. According to Kareena, he was an only son. Growing up, he had intelligence, if not good behavior, and bagged many academic honors. His mother spoiled him. Even on the day he punched a sickly classmate at school, she treated him to homemade *besan laddoos*.

Finally, Adi suggests meeting at Soirée at seven p.m.

How empty the place will seem if I go back there without Kareena. But I don't want to risk a change with Adi. It'll give him an excuse to weasel out of our meeting.

I ponder why he's so difficult. Rumor has it that his family in New Delhi disowned him when he married Kareena against their wishes. Not only that, his uncle sabotaged his effort to obtain a coveted position with an electronics firm by taking the job himself. Adi endured that type of humiliation for a year before giving up. Eight years ago, he and his new bride left India and flew to the opposite side of the world, as far away from his family as he could possibly go.

He landed in Seattle, where he found a plethora of opportunities and no one to thwart his monstrous ambitions. Before long, he formed his own software outfit. There was a price to be paid: long hours, constant travel, and a scarred heart. In spite of this, he persisted and ultimately succeeded. These days he flies frequently to India on business, and rings his family from his hotel room, but his mother will not take his call.

What is Adi doing to locate the woman on whose behalf he sacrificed the love of his family?

Would he really show up at Soirée this evening?

I walk over to my home office and dial Kareena's office number. Once transferred to the private line of the agency director, I leave her a message to get back to me a.s.a.p.

Then I wander into the bedroom where I confront the unmade bed, sheets wavy like desire building to a crescendo. Herr Ulrich floats in my mind, a man who appears so strong and unyielding, but who turns out to be tender and pliant. Right now, his taut body is pushing, lifting, and stooping in the brown-gray jumble of a construction site, the angles of his face accentuated by the strain. Did he stop for a split second, stare out into the distance, and re-experience my lips, my skin, my being?

It's a little too soon to get moony about a man, friends would surely advise me.

Just picturing Ulrich, however, warms my body. Not just the electric tingling of sex, but a kind of communion.

Muted piano music floats from the Tudor across the street. As I reach for the phone with an eager hand, my gaze falls on the bedside table. The pad of Post-it notes is undisturbed. Ulrich hasn't jotted down his phone number or his last name. He promised he would, but he didn't.

My dreamy interlude is sharply broken. With a drab taste in my mouth, I realize that a promise is an illusion and so is "next time." It's similar to hoping that your parents will never die, your friends will forever be around you, and your tulips will always sprout back the next year. This morning I've learned how untrue my assumptions can be.

These days I feel like I'm living in a ghost town. I don't know where to go, who to see, what to do next, or even what to believe. The last five days have coalesced into an endless dreary road. I've reached an impasse in my search for Kareena. Adi cancelled our meeting at Soirée at the last minute. From my repeated phone calls to him, I've gathered that Kareena's passport is missing, an indication she's left deliberately. It strikes me as odd that Adi seems so blithe about her being gone for so long. He even had the nerve to joke about it.

"You know what? I think she's flown somewhere for an impromptu vacation. She's punishing me for not taking her to Acapulco last February. Don't worry. She'll get a big scolding from me when she gets back."

Where might she have gone?

I've contacted the police and given them an account of the bruises I saw on Kareena's arm. Detective Yoshihama assured me he'd do what was necessary and gave me his cell phone number. This morning, I buzz him again, but he doesn't return my call. How high is this case on his priority list? To him, Kareena is no more than a computer profile of another lost soul, yet another *Have you seen me?* poster to be printed, whereas to me and our mutual friends she's a person of importance.

I'm not ready to give up. I call the Washington State Patrol's Missing Persons Unit, but am advised to wait thirty days.

I miss Ulrich too, even though he's practically a stranger. Everywhere I go, I see his broad face, neat haircut, wary green eyes. He appeared in my life about the time Kareena went missing. I haven't heard from him since he left my bed that fateful morning.

I have no choice but to get on with my life, except that the daily duties I took on happily before have become meaningless. I put off grocery shopping, misplace my car keys, and ignore e-mails from the library warning that three books are overdue.

Late this morning, I check the tulip patch. The buds are still closed and a trifle wan, despite the fact that the soil, sun, and temperature are just ideal for them to bloom, and there are still dewdrops hanging from them. Whatever the connection might be, I can't help but think about Kareena. Why didn't she confide in me?

What concerns me most is the nothingness, the no-answer bit, the feeling that the answer is beyond my reach.

I decide to make a trip to Toute La Soirée this evening. A voice inside has been nagging me to do just that, not to mention I have a taste for their kefir-berry cocktail. Kareena confided not long ago that she was saving the pricey Riesling for the next special occasion. Will her wish ever be fulfilled?

The café is located on busy 34th Street. To my surprise, I find a parking place only a block away. The air is humid as I walk up to the entrance. The stars are all out. I check my watch. Despite the popular spot's catchy name—meaning "all evening"—it closes at nine p.m., less than an hour from now.

Inside, the café pulses with upbeat, after-work chumminess. It is nearly full. A middle-aged man fixes me with an appraising look over a foamy pint of ale. I ignore him and survey the interior. The décor has changed since my last visit. The smart black walls sport a collection of hand fans. Made of lace and bamboo, they're exquisitely pleated. The new ambience also includes a wooden rack glittering with slick magazines and jute bags of coffee beans propped against a wall. I don't find this makeover comforting.

As I thread my way through, a speck of tension building inside me, I overhear snatches of a debate on human cloning. Ordinarily, I would slow down for a little free education, but right now my attention is focused on finding an empty seat.

The table Kareena and I usually try for is taken; how could it be otherwise at this prime hour? I was half hoping for a minor miracle, but finding a parking spot must have filled my evening quota. "Our" table is occupied by a couple whose heads are bent over an outsize slice of strawberry shortcake. Right now, I find even the thought of such sugary excess revolting. And the blood-red strawberry juice frightening.

Something about the couple nudges me and I give them a second look. Oh no, it's Adi and a blonde. He looks slightly upset. The overhead light shines over his copper complexion. He's dressed in a crewneck polo shirt in an unflattering rust shade—he doesn't have Kareena's color sense. The blonde wears crystal-accented chandelier earrings that graze her shoulders. I wouldn't bear the weight of such long earrings except on a special occasion. Or is this a special occasion for them?

Their presence so rattles me that I decide to leave. Besides, Adi might notice me and complain I'm spying on him.

On the way to the door, I knock over a chair, which I put back in its place. Then I almost collide head-on with an Indian man who has just entered the shop. Although he's young, dark, and devastatingly handsome, somehow I know he's not my type. Clad smartly in a silver woolen vest, this prince heads straight for the take-out counter. His impressive carriage and smoldering eyes have caused a stir among women seated nearby. A redhead tries to catch his glance. He touches the jute bag, an Indian-style *jhola*, dangling from his shoulder. Even Adi stares at him.

I slip out the door, too drained to absorb anything further, pause on the sidewalk, and take several deep breaths to cleanse my head. Please, Goddess Durga, no more intrigues this evening.

It's starting to drizzle, but the streets are mercifully clear. Within minutes, I pull into my garage and step out of my Honda. As I close the garage door, I flash on the enchanting prince from the café. Didn't Veen mention that Kareena was last sighted with a *jhola*-carrier at that very place?

A jolt of adrenaline skips through my body. Why couldn't I have been more alert? Stuck around longer to scrutinize another potential suspect and his belongings?

Should I drive back?

I check my watch: nine p.m. Soirée has just closed.

Filled with nervous excitement, I enter my house. Neither a hot shower nor a mug of holy basil tea tempers the thought racing through my head: what really happened to Kareena?

In a need to restore my spirit, I retire early. As I lie in bed, I can't help but run through the day's events, foremost among them being Adi's public appearance with a blonde. Suspicions about him blow in my mind like a pile of dry leaves in the wind. Eventually, the atmosphere settles; my mind clears.

I'm worrying too much about Kareena. Worry is a sand castle. It has no foundation.

Could my assumptions about Adi be wrong as well?

Assumptions, like appearances, can deceive, I tell myself. Adi's cheerful façade and his lack of concern about his wife's unexplained absence just might be more sand castle building on my part. I'm reading the worst in what might be a perfectly plausible and innocent situation.

You've been acting silly, Mitra, pure silly. You have no reason to fret. Pull your covers snug and get yourself a restful sleep. All will be well. The morning will come, the sun will be out, and Kareena will return, her bright smile intact, as surely as the swing of seasons.

I awake refreshed and invigorated. Last night's drizzle has evaporated, leaving behind a bright morning. The sun streams through a wide gap in the window draperies. A spider is building a nest outside the window, intricate but fragile.

I have the perfect task to usher in this new day. I shall tend to Kareena's tulip patch. The plants will soon release their full yellow blossoms as emblems of beauty and renewal and she'll cradle a bunch lovingly in her arm.

I don my gardening clothes—faded jeans and a worn black cardigan—gather my tools, and hurry outside. The morning light shines brilliantly on my front flower patch. An errant branch of camellia needs to be pruned. Its shadow falls over the tulips. I step in closer to inspect, an ache in my belly. All the tulip buds are shriveled and brown, as though singed by blight, their dried stalks drooping over to return to brown earth.

Why are they dying on me so soon? I fall to my knees and caress the tulip plants, lifting them up and squeezing their brittle stalks and wilted leaves. I roll each wizened bud between my fingers, but don't find a single one with any hope.

Holding a broken stem in my grasp, I think of Kareena, so vibrant, so full of life, and brood about the promise of these tulips.

THE EHRENGRAF SETTLEMENT

BY LAWRENCE BLOCK

Nottingham Terrace, Buffalo

(Originally published in *Buffalo Noir*)

hrengraf, his mind abuzz with uplifting thoughts, left his car at the curb and walked the length of the flagstone path to Millard Ravenstock's imposing front door. There was a large bronze door-knocker in the shape of an elephant's head, and one could lift and lower the animal's hinged proboscis to summon the occupants.

Or, as an alternative, one could ring the doorbell by pressing the recessed mother-of-pearl button. Ehrengraf fingered the knot in his tie, with its alternating half-inch strikes of scarlet and Prussian blue, brushed a speck of lint from the lapel of his gray flannel suit. Only then, having given both choices due consideration, did he touch the elephant's trunk, before opting instead for the bell-push.

Moments later he was in a paneled library, seated in a leather club chair, with a cup of coffee at hand. He hadn't managed more than two sips of the coffee before Millard Ravenstock joined him.

"Mr. Ehrengraf," the man said, giving the honorific just enough emphasis to suggest he rarely employed it. Ehrengraf could believe it; this was a man who would call most people by their surnames, as if all the world's inhabitants were members of his household staff.

"Mr. Ravenstock," said Ehrengraf, with an inflection that was similar but not identical.

"It was good of you to come to see me. In ordinary circumstances I'd have called at your offices, but—"

A shrug and a smile served to complete the sentence.

In ordinary circumstances, Ehrengraf thought, the man would not have come to Ehrengraf's office, because there'd have been no need for their paths to cross. Had Millard Ravenstock not found himself the subject of a murder investigation, he'd have had no reason to summon Ehrengraf, or Ehrengraf any reason to come to the imposing Nottingham Terrace residence.

Ehrengraf simply observed that the circumstances were not ordinary.

"Indeed they are not," said Ravenstock. His chalk-striped navy suit was clearly the work of a custom tailor, who'd shown skill in flattering his client's physique. Ravenstock was an imposing figure of a man, stout enough to draw a physician's perfunctory warnings about cholesterol and type-two diabetes, but still well on the right side of the current national standard for obesity. Ehrengraf, who maintained an ideal weight with no discernible effort, rather agreed with Shakespeare's Caesar, liking to have men about him who were fat.

"'Sleek-headed men, and such as sleep a-nights.'"

"I beg your pardon?"

Had he spoken aloud? Ehrengraf smiled, and waved a dismissive hand. "Perhaps," he said, "we should consider the matter that concerns us."

"Tegrum Bogue," Ravenstock said, pronouncing the name with distaste. "What kind of a name is Tegrum Bogue?"

"A distinctive one," Ehrengraf suggested.

"Distinctive if not distinguished. I've no quarrel with the surname. One assumes it came down to him from the man who provided half his DNA. But why would anyone name a child Tegrum? With all the combinations of letters available, why pick those six and arrange them in that order?" He frowned. "Never mind, I'm wandering off-topic. What does his name matter? What's relevant is that I'm about to be charged with his murder."

"They allege that you shot him."

"And the allegation is entirely true," Ravenstock said. "I don't suppose you like to hear me admit as much, Mr. Ehrengraf. But it's pointless for me to deny it, because it's the plain and simple truth."

Ehrengraf, whose free time was largely devoted to the reading of poetry, moved from Shakespeare to Oscar Wilde, who had pointed out that the truth was rarely plain, and never simple. But he kept himself from quoting aloud.

"It was self-defense," Ravenstock said. "The man was hanging around my property and behaving suspiciously. I confronted him. He responded in a menacing fashion. I urged him to depart. He attacked me. Then and only then did I draw my pistol and shoot him dead."

"Ah," said Ehrengraf.

"It was quite clear that I was blameless," Ravenstock said. His high forehead was dry but he drew a handkerchief and wiped it just the same. "The police questioned me, as they were unquestionably right to do, and released me, and one detective said offhand that I'd done the right thing. I consulted with my attorney, and he said he doubted charges would be brought, but that if they were he was confident of a verdict of justifiable homicide."

"And then things began to go wrong."

"Horribly wrong, Mr. Ehrengraf. But you probably know the circumstances as well as I do."

"I try to keep up," Ehrengraf allowed. "But let me confirm a few facts. You're a member of the Nottingham Vigilance Committee."

"The name's unfortunate," Ravenstock said. "It simply identifies the group as what it is, designed to keep a watchful eye over our neighborhood. This is an affluent area, and right across the street is Delaware Park. That's one of the best things about living here, but it's not an unmixed blessing."

"Few blessings are," said Ehrengraf.

"I'll have to think about that. But the park—it's beautiful, it's convenient, and at the same time people lurk there, some of them criminous, some of them emotionally disturbed, and all of them just a stone's throw from our houses."

There was a remark that was trying to occur to Ehrengraf, something about glass houses, but he left it unsaid.

"Police protection is good here," Ravenstock continued, "but there's a definite need for a neighborhood watch group. Vigilance—well, you hear that and you think *vigilante*, don't you?"

"One does. This Mr. Bogue—"

"Tegrum Bogue."

"Tegrum Bogue. You'd had confrontations with him before."

"I'd seen him on my property once or twice," Ravenstock said, "and warned him off."

"You'd called in reports of his suspicious behavior to the police."

"A couple of times, yes."

"And on the night in question," Ehrengraf said, "he was actually not on your property. He was, as I understand it, two doors away."

"In front of the Gissling home. Heading north toward Meadow Road, there's this house, and then the Robert Townsend house, and then Madge and Bernard Gissling's. So that would be two doors away."

"And when you shot him, he fell dead on the Gisslings' lawn."

"They'd just resodded."

"That very day?"

"No, a month ago. Why?"

Ehrengraf smiled, a maneuver that had served him well over the years. "Mr. Bogue—that would be Tegrum Bogue—was unarmed."

"He had a knife in his pocket."

"An inch-long penknife, wasn't it? Attached to his key ring?"

"I couldn't say, sir. I never saw the knife. The police report mentioned it. It was only an inch long?"

"Apparently."

"It doesn't sound terribly formidable, does it? But Bogue's was a menacing presence without a weapon in evidence. He was young and tall and vigorous and muscular and wild-eyed, and he uttered threats and put his hands on me and pushed me and struck me."

"You were armed."

"An automatic pistol, made by Gunnar & Swick. Their Kestrel model. It's registered, and I'm licensed to carry it."

"You drew your weapon."

"I did. I thought the sight of it might stop Bogue in his tracks."

"But it didn't."

"He laughed," Ravenstock recalled, "and said he'd take it away from me, and would stick it—well, you can imagine where he threatened to stick it."

Ehrengraf, who could actually imagine several possible destinations for the Kestrel, simply nodded.

"And he rushed at me, and I might have been holding a water pistol for all the respect he showed it."

"You fired it."

"I was taught never to show a gun unless I was prepared to use it."

"Five times."

"I was taught to keep on firing until one's gun was empty. Actually the Kestrel's clip holds nine cartridges, but five seemed sufficient."

"'To make assurance doubly sure,'" Ehrengraf said. "Stopping at five does show restraint."

"Well."

"And yet," Ehrengraf said, "the traditional argument that the gun simply went off of its own accord comes a cropper, doesn't it? It's a rare weapon that fires itself five times in rapid succession. As a member of the Nottingham Vigilantes—"

"The Vigilance Committee."

"Yes, of course. In that capacity, weren't you supposed to report Bogue's presence to the police rather than confront him?"

Ravenstock came as close to hanging his head as his character would allow. "I never thought to make the call."

"The heat of the moment," Ehrengraf suggested.

"Just that. I acted precipitously."

"A Mrs. Kling was across the street, walking her Gordon setter. She told police the two of you were arguing, and it seemed to be about someone's wife."

"He made remarks about my wife," Ravenstock said. "Brutish remarks, designed to provoke me. About what he intended to do to and with her, after he'd taken the gun away from me and put it, well—"

"Indeed."

"What's worse, Mr. Ehrengraf, is the campaign of late to canonize Tegrum Bogue. Have you seen the picture his family released to the press? He doesn't look very menacing, does it?"

"Only if one finds choirboys threatening."

"It was taken nine years ago," Ravenstock said, "when young Bogue was a first-form student at the Nichols School. Since then he shot up eight inches and put on forty or fifty pounds. I assure you, the cherub in the photo bears no resemblance to the hulking savage who attacked me steps from my own home."

"Unconscionable," Ehrengraf said.

"And now I'm certain to be questioned further, and very likely to be placed under arrest. My lawyer was nattering on about how unlikely it was that I'd ever have to spend a night in jail, and hinting at my pleading guilty to some reduced charge. That's not good enough."

"No."

"I don't want to skate on a technicality, my reputation in ruins. I don't want to devote a few hundred hours to community service. How do you suppose they'd have me serve my community, Mr. Ehrengraf? Would they send me across the street to pick up litter in the park? Or would they regard a stick with a sharp bit of metal at its end as far too formidable a weapon to be placed in my irresponsible hands?"

"These are things you don't want," Ehrengraf said soothingly. "And whyever should you want them? But perhaps you could tell me what it is that you *do* want."

"What I want," said Ravenstock, speaking as a man who generally got whatever it was that he wanted. "What I want, sir, is for all of this to go away. And my understanding is that you are a gentleman who is very good at making things go away."

Ehrengraf smiled.

Ehrengraf gazed past the mound of clutter on his desk at his office door, with its window of frosted glass. What struck him about the door was that his client had not yet come through it. It was getting on for half past eleven, which made Millard Ravenstock almost thirty minutes late.

Ehrengraf fingered the knot in his tie. It was a perfectly symmetrical knot, neither too large nor too small, which was as it should be. Whenever he wore this particular tie, with its navy field upon which a half-inch diagonal stripe of royal blue was flanked by two narrower stripes, one of gold, the other vividly green—whenever he put it on, he took considerable pains to get the knot exactly right.

It was, of course, the tie of the Caedmon Society; Ehrengraf, not a member of that institution, had purchased the tie from a shop in Oxford's Cranham Close. He'd owned it for some years now, and had been careful to avoid soiling it, extending its useful life by reserving it for special occasions.

This morning had promised to be such an occasion. Now, as the minutes ticked away without producing Millard Ravenstock, he found himself less certain.

The antique Regulator clock on the wall, which lost a minute a day, showed the time as 11:42 when Millard Ravenstock opened the door and stepped into Ehrengraf's office. The little lawyer glanced first at the clock and then at his wristwatch, which read 11:48. Then he looked at his client, who looked not the least bit apologetic for his late arrival.

"Ah, Ehrengraf," the man said. "A fine day, wouldn't you say?"

You could see Niagara Square from Ehrengraf's office window, and a quick look showed that the day was as it had been earlier—overcast and gloomy, with every likelihood of rain.

"Glorious," Ehrengraf agreed.

Without waiting to be asked, Ravenstock pulled up a chair and settled his bulk into it. "Before I left my house," he said, "I went into my den, got out my checkbook, and wrote two checks. One, you'll be pleased to know, was for your fee." He patted his breast pocket. "I've brought it with me."

Ehrengraf was pleased. But, he noted, cautiously so. He sensed there was another shoe just waiting to be dropped.

"The other check is already in the mail. I made it payable to the Policemen's Benevolent Association, and I assure you the sum is a generous one. I have always been a staunch proponent of the police, Ehrengraf, if only because the role they play is such a vital one. Without them we'd have the rabble at our throats, eh?"

Ehrengraf, thought Ehrengraf. The *Mister,* present throughout their initial meeting, had evidently been left behind on Nottingham Terrace. Increasingly, Ehrengraf felt it had been an error to wear that particular tie on this particular morning.

"Yet I'd given the police insufficient credit for their insight and their resolve. I've been completely exonerated, and it's their doing."

"Indeed," said Ehrengraf.

"They dug up evidence, unearthed facts. That housewife who was raped and murdered three weeks ago in Orchard Park. I'm sure you're familiar with the case. The press called it the Milf Murder."

Ehrengraf nodded.

"It took place outside city limits," Ravenstock went on, "so it wasn't their case at all, but they went through the house and found an unwashed sweatshirt stuffed into a trashcan in the garage. *Nichols School Lacrosse*, it said, big as life. That's a curious expression isn't it? Big as life?"

"Curious," Ehrengraf said.

"Lacrosse seems to be the natural refuge of the preppy thug," Ravenstock said. "Can you guess whose DNA soiled that sweatshirt?"

Ehrengraf could guess, but saw no reason to do so. Nor did Ravenstock wait for a response.

"Tegrum Bogue's. He'd been on the team, and it was beyond question his shirt. He'd raped that young housewife and snapped her neck when he was through with her. And he had similar plans for Alicia."

"Your wife."

"Yes. I don't believe you've met her."

"I haven't had the pleasure."

The expression that passed over Ravenstock's face suggested that it was a pleasure Ehrengraf would have to live without. "She is a beautiful woman," he said. "And quite a few years younger than I. I suppose there are those who would refer to her as my trophy wife."

The man paused, waiting for Ehrengraf to comment, then frowned at the lawyer's continuing silence. "There are two ways to celebrate a trophy," he went on. "One may carry it around, showing it off at every opportunity. Or one may place it on a shelf in one's personal quarters, to be admired and savored in private."

"Indeed."

"Some men require that their taste have the approbation of others. They lack confidence, Ehrengraf."

Another pause. Some expression of assent seemed to be required of him, and Ehrengraf considered several, ranging from *Right on, dude* to *Most def.*

"Indeed," he said at length.

"But somehow Alicia caught his interest. He was one of the mob given to loitering in the park, and sometimes she'd walk Kossuth there."

"Kossuth," Ehrengraf said. "The Gordon setter?"

"No, of course not. I wouldn't own a Gordon. And why would anyone name a Gordon for Louis Kossuth? Our dog is a Viszla, and a fine and noble animal he is. He must have seen her walking Kossuth. Or—"

"Or?"

"I had my run-ins with him. In my patrol duty with the Vigilance Committee, I'd recommended that he and his fellows stay on their side of the street."

"In the park, and away from the houses."

"His response was not at all acquiescent," Ravenstock recalled. "After that I made a point of monitoring his activities, and phoned in the occasional police report. I'd have to say I made an enemy, Ehrengraf."

"I doubt you were ever destined to be friends."

"No, but I erred in making myself the object of his hostility. I think that's what may have put Alicia in his sights. I think he stalked me, and I think his reconnaissance got him a good look at Alicia, and of course to see her is to want her."

Ehrengraf, struck by the matter-of-fact tone of that last clause, touched the tips of two fingers to the Caedmon Society cravat.

"And the police found evidence of his obsession," Ravenstock said. "A roll of undeveloped film in his sock drawer, with photos for which my wife had served as an unwitting model. Crude fictional sketches, written in Bogue's schoolboy hand, some written in the third person, some in the first. Clumsy mini-stories relating in pornographic detail the abduction, sexual savaging, and murder of my wife. Pencil drawings to illustrate them, as ill-fashioned as his prose. The scenarios varied as his fantasies evolved. Sometimes there was torture, mutilation, dismemberment. Sometimes I was present, bound and helpless, forced to witness what was being done to her. And I had to watch because I couldn't close my eyes. I didn't read his filth, so I can't recall whether he'd glued my eyelids open or removed them surgically—"

"Either would be effective."

"Well," Ravenstock said, and went on, explaining that of course the several discoveries the police had made put paid to any notion that he, Millard Ravenstock, had done anything untoward, let alone criminal. He had not been charged, so there were no charges to dismiss, and what was at least as important was that he had been entirely exonerated in the court of public opinion.

"So you can see why I felt moved to make a generous donation to the Policemen's Benevolent Association," he continued. "I feel they earned it."

Ehrengraf waited, and refrained from touching his necktie.

"As for yourself, Ehrengraf, I greatly appreciate your efforts on my behalf, and have no doubt that they'd have proved successful had not Fate and the police intervened and done your job for you. And I'm sure you'll find this more than adequate compensation for your good work."

The check was in an envelope, which Ravenstock plucked from his inside breast pocket and extended with a flourish. The envelope was unsealed, and Ehrengraf drew the check from it and noted its amount, which was about what he'd come to expect.

"The fee I quoted you—"

"Was lofty," Ravenstock said, "but would have been acceptable had the case not resolved itself independent of any action on your part."

"I was very specific," Ehrengraf pointed out. "I said my work would cost you nothing unless your innocence was established and all charges dropped. But if that were to come about, my fee was due and payable in full. You do remember my saying that, don't you?"

"But you didn't do anything, Ehrengraf."

"You agreed to the arrangement I spelled out, sir, and—"

"I repeat, you did nothing, or if you did do anything it had no bearing on the outcome of the matter. The payment I just gave you is a settlement, and I pay it gladly in order to put the matter to rest."

"A settlement," Ehrengraf said, testing the word on his tongue.

"And no mere token settlement, either. It's hardly an insignificant amount, and my personal attorney assures me I'm being overly generous. He says all you're entitled to, legally and morally, is a reasonable return on whatever billable hours you've put in, and—"

"Your attorney."

"One of the region's top men, I assure you."

"I don't doubt it. Would this be the same attorney who'd have had you armed with a sharp stick to pick up litter in Delaware Park? After pleading you guilty to a murder for which you bore no guilt?"

Even as he marshaled his arguments, Ehrengraf sensed that they would prove fruitless. The man's mind, such as it was, was made up. Nothing would sway him.

* * *

There was a time, Ehrengraf recalled, when he longed for a house like Millard Ravenstock's—on Nottingham Terrace, or Meadow Road, or Middlesex. Something at once tasteful and baronial, something with pillars and a center hall, something that would proclaim to one and all that its owner had unquestionably come to amount to something.

True success, he had learned, meant one no longer required its accoutrements. His penthouse apartment at the Park Lane provided all the space and luxury he could want, and a better view than any house could offer. The building, immaculately maintained and impeccably staffed, even had a name that suited him; it managed to be as resolutely British as Nottingham or Middlesex without sounding pretentious.

And it was closer to downtown. When time and good weather permitted, Ehrengraf could walk to and from his office.

But not today. There was a cold wind blowing off the lake, and the handicappers in the weather bureau had pegged rain at even money. The little lawyer had arrived at his office a few minutes after ten. He made one phone call, and as he rang off he realized he could have saved himself the trip.

He went downstairs, retrieved his car, and returned to the Park Lane to await his guest.

Ehrengraf, opening the door, was careful not to stare. The woman whom the concierge had announced as a Ms. Philips was stunning, and Ehrengraf worked to conceal the extent to which he was stunned. She was taller than Ehrengraf by several inches, with dark hair that someone very skilled had cut to look as though she took no trouble with it. She had great big Bambi eyes, the facial planes of a supermodel, and a full-lipped mouth that stopped just short of obscenity.

"Ms. Philips," Ehrengraf said, and motioned her inside.

"I didn't want to leave my name at the desk."

"I assumed as much. Come in, come in. A drink? A cup of coffee?"

"Coffee, if it's no trouble."

It was no trouble at all, Ehrengraf had made a fresh pot upon his return, and he filled two cups and brought them to the living room, where Alicia Ravenstock had chosen the Sheraton wing chair. Ehrengraf sat opposite her, and they sipped their coffee and discussed the beans and brewing method, and then gave a few minutes' attention to the weather.

Then she said, "You're very good to see me here. I was afraid to come to your office. There are enough people who know me by sight, and if word got back to him that I went to a lawyer's office, or even into a building where lawyers had offices—"

"I can imagine."

"I'm his alone, you see. I can have anything I want, except the least bit of freedom."

"Peter, Peter, pumpkin eater," Ehrengraf said, and when she looked puzzled he quoted the rhyme in full:

Peter, Peter, pumpkin eater,
Had a wife and couldn't keep her.
He put her in a pumpkin shell
And there he kept her very well.

"Yes, of course. It's a nursery rhyme, isn't it?"

Ehrengraf nodded. "I believe it began life centuries ago as satirical political doggerel, but it's lived on as a rhyme for children."

"Millard keeps me very well," she said. "You've been to the pumpkin shell, haven't you? It's a very elegant one."

"It is."

"A sumptuous and comfortable prison. I suppose I shouldn't complain. It's what I wanted. Or what I thought I wanted, which may amount to the same thing. I'd resigned myself to it—or *thought* I'd resigned myself to it."

"Which may amount to the same thing."

"Yes," she said, and took a sip of coffee. "And then I met Bo."

"And that would be Tegrum Bogue."

"I thought we were careful," she said. "I never had any intimation that Millard knew, or even suspected." Her face clouded. "He was a lovely boy, you know. It's still hard for me to believe he's gone."

"And that your husband killed him."

"That part's not difficult to believe," she said. "Millard's cold as ice and harder than stone. The part I can't understand is how someone like him could care enough to want me."

"You're a possession," Ehrengraf suggested.

"Yes, of course. There's no other explanation." Another sip of coffee; Ehrengraf, watching her mouth, found himself envying the bone china cup. "It wouldn't have lasted," she said. "I was too old for Bo, even as Millard is too old for me. Mr. Ehrengraf, I had resigned myself to living the life Millard wanted me to live. Then Bo came along, and a sunbeam brightened up my prison cell, so to speak, and the life to which I'd resigned myself was now transformed into one I could enjoy."

"Made so by trysts with your young lover."

"Trysts," she said. "I like the word, it sounds permissibly naughty. But, you know, it also sounds like *tristesse*, which is sadness in French."

A woman who cared about words was very likely a woman on whom the charms of poetry would not be lost. Ehrengraf found himself wishing he'd quoted something rather more distinguished than *Peter, Peter, Pumpkin Eater.*

"I don't know how Millard found out about Bo," she said. "Or how he contrived to face him and shoot him down steps from our house. But there seemed to be no question of his guilt, and I assumed he'd have to answer in some small way for what he'd done. He wouldn't go to prison, rich men never do, but look at him now, Mr. Ehrengraf, proclaimed a defender of home and hearth who slew a rapist and murderer. To think that a sweet and gentle boy like Bo could have his reputation so blackened. It's heart-breaking."

"There, there," Ehrengraf said, and patted the back of her hand. The skin was remarkably soft, and it felt at once both warm and cool, which struck him as an insoluble paradox but one worth investigating. "There, there," he said again, but omitted the pat this time.

"I blame the police," she said. "Millard donates to their fund-raising efforts and wields influence on their behalf, and I'd say it paid off for him."

Ehrengraf listed while Alicia Ravenstock speculated on just how the police might have constructed a post-mortem frame for Tegrum Bogue. She had, he was pleased to note, an incisive imagination. When she'd finished he suggested more coffee, and she shook her head.

"I have to end my marriage," she said abruptly. "There's nothing for it. I made a bad bargain, and for a time I thought I could live with it, and now I see the impossibility of so doing."

"A divorce, Mrs. Ravenstock—"

She recoiled at the name, then forced a smile. "Please don't call me that," she said. "I don't like being reminded that it's my name. Call me Alicia, Mr. Ehrengraf."

"Then you must call me Martin, Alicia."

"Martin," she said, testing the name on her pink tongue.

"It's not terribly difficult to obtain a divorce, Alicia. But of course you would know that. And you would know, too, that a specialist in matrimonial law would best serve your interests, and you wouldn't come to me seeking a recommendation in that regard."

She smiled, letting him find his way.

"A pre-nuptial agreement," he said. "He insisted you sign one and you did."

"Yes."

"And you've shown it to an attorney, who pronounced it iron-clad."

"Yes."

"You don't want more coffee. But would you have a cordial? Benedictine? Chartreuse? Perhaps a Drambuie?"

"It's a Scotch-based liqueur," Ehrengraf said, after his guest had sampled her drink and signified her approval.

"I've never had it before, Martin. It's very nice."

"More appropriate as an after-dinner drink, some might say. But it brightens an afternoon, especially one with weather that might have swept in from the Scottish Highlands."

He might have quoted Robert Burns, but nothing came to mind. "Alicia," he said, "I made a great mistake when I agreed to act as your husband's attorney. I violated one of my own cardinal principles. I have made a career of representing the innocent, the blameless, the unjustly accused. When I am able to believe in a client's innocence, no matter how damning the apparent evidence of his guilt, then I feel justified in committing myself unreservedly to his defense."

"And if you can't believe him to be innocent?"

"Then I decline the case." A sigh escaped the lawyer's lips. "Your husband admitted his guilt. He seemed quite unrepentant, he asserted his moral right to act as he had done. And, because at the time I could see some justification for his behavior, I enlisted in his service." He set his jaw. "Perhaps it's just as well," he said, "that he declined to pay the fee upon which we'd agreed."

"He boasted about that, Martin."

How sweet his name sounded on those plump lips!

"Did he indeed."

"'I gave him a tenth of what he wanted,' he said, 'and he was lucky to get anything at all from me.' Of course he wasn't just bragging, he was letting me know just how tightfisted I could expect him to be."

"Yes, he'd have that in mind."

"You asked if I'd shown the pre-nup to an attorney. I had trouble finding one who'd look at it, or even let me into his office. What I discovered was that Millard had consulted every matrimonial lawyer within a radius of five hundred miles. He'd had each of them review the agreement and spend five minutes discussing it with him, and as a result they were ethically enjoined from representing me."

"For perhaps a thousand dollars a man, he'd made it impossible for you to secure representation." Ehrengraf frowned. "He did all this after discovering about you and young Bogue?"

"He began these consultations when we returned from our honeymoon."

"Had your discontent already become evident?"

"Not even to me, Martin. Millard was simply taking precautions." She finished her Drambuie, set down the empty glass. "And I did find a lawyer, a young man with a general practice, who took a look at the agreement I'd signed. He kept telling me it wasn't his area of expertise. But he said it looked rock-solid to him."

"Ah," said Ehrengraf. "Well, we'll have to see about that, won't we?"

It was three weeks and a day later when Ehrengraf emerged from his morning shower and toweled himself dry. He shaved, and spent a moment or two trimming a few errant hairs from his beard, a Van Dyke that came to a precise point.

Beards had come and go in Ehrengraf's life, and upon his chin, and he felt this latest incarnation was the most successful to date. There was just the least hint of gray in it, even as there was the slightest touch of gray at his temples.

He hoped it would stay that way, at least for a while. With gray, as with so many things, a little was an asset, a lot a liability. Nor could one successfully command time to stand still, anymore than King Canute could order a cessation of the tidal flow. There would be more gray, and the day would come when he would either accept it (and, by implication, all the slings and arrows of the aging process) or reach for the bottle of hair coloring.

Neither prospect was appealing. But both were off in the future, and did not bear thinking about. Certainly not on what was to be a day of triumph, a triumph all the sweeter for having been delayed.

He took his time dressing, choosing his newest suit, a three-piece navy pinstripe from Peller & Mure. He considered several shirts and settled on a spread-collar broadcloth in French blue, not least of all for the way it would complement his tie.

And the choice of tie was foreordained. It was, of course, that of the Caedmon Society.

The spread collar called for a Double Windsor, and Ehrengraf was equal to the task. He slipped his feet into black monk-strap loafers, then considered the suit's third piece, the vest. The only argument against it was that it would conceal much of his tie, but the tie and its significance were important only to the wearer.

He decided to go with the vest.

And now? It was getting on for nine, and his appointment was at his office, at half past ten. He'd had his light breakfast, and the day was clear and bright and neither too warm nor too cold. He could walk to his office, taking his time, stopping along the way for a cup of coffee.

But why not wait and see if the phone might chance to ring?

And it did, just after nine o'clock. Ehrengraf smiled when it rang, and his smile broadened at the sound of the caller's voice, and broadened further as he listened. "Yes, of course," he said. "I'd like that."

"When we spoke yesterday," Alicia Ravenstock said, "I automatically suggested a meeting at your office. Because I'd been uncomfortable going there before, and now the reason for that discomfort had been removed."

"So you wanted to exercise your new freedom."

"Then I remembered what a nice apartment you have, and what good coffee I enjoyed on my previous visit."

"When you called," Ehrengraf said, "the first thing I did was make a fresh pot."

He fetched a cup for each of them, and watched her purse her lips and take a first sip.

"Just right," she said. "There's so much to talk about, Martin, but I'd like to get the business part out of the way."

She drew an envelope from her purse, and Ehrengraf held his breath, at least metaphorically, while he opened it. This was the second time he'd received an envelope from someone with Ravenstock for a surname, and the first time had been profoundly disappointing.

Still, she'd used his first name, and moved their meeting from his office to his residence. Those ought to be favorable omens.

The check, he saw at a glance, had the correct number of zeroes. His eyes widened when he took a second look at it.

"This is higher than the sum we agreed on," he said.

"By ten percent. I've suddenly become a wealthy woman, Martin, and I felt a bonus was in order. I hope you don't regard it as an insult—"

Money? An insult? He assured her that it was nothing of the sort.

"It's really quite remarkable," she said. "Millard is in jail, where he's being held without bail. I've filed suit for divorce, and my attorney assures me that the pre-nup is essentially null and void. Martin, I knew the evidence against Bo was bogus. But I had no idea it would all come to light as it has."

"It was an interesting chain of events," he agreed.

"It was a tissue of lies," she said, "and it started to unravel when someone called Channel Seven's investigative reporter, pointing out that Bo was at a hockey game when the Milf Murder took place. How could he be in two places at the same time?"

"How indeed?"

"And then there was the damning physical evidence, the lacrosse shirt with Bo's DNA. They found a receipt among the boy's effects for a bag of clothes donated to Goodwill Industries, and among the several items mentioned was one Nichols School lacrosse jersey. How Millard knew about the donation and got his hands on the shirt—"

"We may never know, Alicia. And it may not have been Millard himself who found the shirt."

"It was probably Bainbridge. But we won't know that, either, now that he's dead."

"Suicide is a terrible thing," Ehrengraf said. "And sometimes it seems to ask as many questions as it answers. Though this particular act did answer quite a few."

"Walter Bainbridge was Millard's closest friend in the police department, and I thought it was awfully convenient the way he came up with all the evidence against Bo. But I guess Channel Seven's investigation convinced him he'd gone too far, and when the truth about the lacrosse shirt came to light, he could see the walls closing in. How desperate he must have been to put his service revolver in his mouth and blow his brains out."

"It was more than the evidence he faked. The note he left suggests he himself may have committed the Milf Murder. You see, it's almost certain he committed a similar rape and murder in Kenmore just days before he took his own life."

"The nurse," she remembered. "There was no physical evidence at the crime scene, but his note alluded to 'other bad things I've done,' and didn't they find something of hers in Bainbridge's desk at police headquarters?"

"A pair of soiled panties."

"The pervert. So he had ample reason to pin the Milf Murder on Bo. To help Millard, and to divert any possible suspicion from himself. This really is superb coffee."

"May I bring you a fresh cup?"

"Not quite yet, Martin. Those notebooks of Bo's, with the crude drawings and the fantasies? They seemed so unlikely to me, so much at variance with the Tegrum Bogue I knew, and well they might have done."

"They were forgeries."

"Rather skillful forgeries," she said, "but forgeries all the same. Bainbridge had imitated Bo's handwriting, and he'd left behind a notebook in which he'd written out drafts of the material in his own hand, then practiced copying them in Bo's. And do you know what else they found?"

"Something of your husband's, I believe."

"Millard supplied those fantasies for Bainbridge. He wrote them out in his own cramped hand, and gave them to Bainbridge to save his policeman friend the necessity of using his imagination. But before he did this he made photocopies, which he kept. They turned up in a strongbox in his closet, and they were a perfect match for the originals that had been among Bainbridge's effects."

"Desperate men do desperate things," he said. "I'm sure he denies everything."

"Of course. It won't do him any good. The police came out of this looking very bad, and it's no help to blame Walter Bainbridge, as he's beyond their punishment. So they blame Millard for everything Bainbridge did, and for tempting Bainbridge in the first place. They were quite rough with him when they arrested him. You know how on television they always put a hand on a perpetrator's head when they're helping him get into the back seat of the squad car?"

"So that he won't bump his head on the roof."

"Well, this police detective put his hand on Millard's head," she said, "and then slammed it into the roof."

"I've often wondered if that ever happens."

"I saw it happen, Martin. The policeman said he was sorry."

"It must have been an accident."

"Then he did it again."

"Oh."

"I wish I had a tape of it," she said. "I'd watch it over and over."

The woman had heart, Ehrengraf marveled. Her beauty was exceptional, but ultimately it was merely a component of a truly remarkable spirit. He could think of things to say, but he was content for now to leave them unsaid, content merely to bask in the glow of her presence.

And Alicia seemed comfortable with the silence. Their eyes met, and it seemed to Ehrengraf that their breathing took on the same cadence, deepening their wordless intimacy.

"You don't want more coffee," he said at length.

She shook her head.

"The last time you were here—"

"You gave me a Drambuie."

"Would you like one now?"

"Not just now. Do you know what I almost suggested last time?"

He did not.

"It was after you'd brought me the Drambuie, but before I'd tasted it. The thought came to me that we should go to your bedroom and make love, and afterward we could drink the Drambuie."

"But you didn't."

"No. I knew you wanted me, I could tell by the way you looked at me."

"I didn't mean to stare."

"I didn't find it objectionable, Martin. It wasn't a coarse or lecherous look. It was admiring. I found it exciting."

"I see."

"Add in the fact that you're a very attractive man, Martin, and one in whose presence I feel safe and secure, and, well, I found myself overcome by a very strong desire to go to bed with you."

"My dear lady."

"But the timing was wrong," she said. "And how would you take it? Might it seem like a harlot's trick to bind you more strongly to my service? So the moment came and went, and we drained our little snifters of Drambuie, and I went home to Nottingham Terrace."

Ehrengraf waited.

"Now everything's resolved," she said. "I wanted to give you the check first thing, so that would be out of the way. And we've said what we needed to say about my awful husband and that wretched policeman. And I find I want you more than ever. And you still want me, don't you, Martin?"

"More than ever."

"Afterward," she said, "we'll have the Drambuie."

PHELAN'S FIRST CASE

BY LISA SANDLIN

Beaumont, Texas

(Originally published in *Lone Star Noir*)

Five past eight. Phelan sat tipped back in his desk chair, appreciating the power of the *Beaumont Enterprise*. They'd centered the ad announcing his new business, boxed it in black, and spelled his name right. The other ad in the classifieds had brought in two girls yesterday. He figured to choose the brunette with the coral nails and the middle-C voice. But just then he got a call from his old high school bud Joe Ford, now a parole officer, and Joe was hard-selling.

"Typing, dictation, whatcha need? She learned it in the big house. Paid her debt to society. What say you talk to her?"

"Find some other sucker. Since when are you Acme Employment?"

"Since when are you a private eye?"

"Since workers' comp paid me enough bread to swing a lease."

"For a measly finger? Thought you liked the rigs."

"Still got nine fingers left. Aim to keep 'em."

"Just see this girl, Tommy. She knows her stuff."

"Why you pushing her?"

"Hell, phones don't answer themselves, do they?"

"Didn't they invent a machine that—"

Joe blew scorn through the phone. "Communist rumor. Lemme send her over. She can get down there in two shakes."

"No."

"I'm gonna say this one time. Who had your back the night you stepped outside with Narlan Pugh and all his cousins stepped outside behind him?"

"One time, shit. I heard it three. Time you realized gratitude comes to a natural end, same as a sack of donuts."

Joe bided.

Phelan stewed.

"Goddamnit, no promises."

"Naw! Course not. Make it or break it on her own. Thanks for the chance, it'll buck her up."

Phelan asked about the girl's rap sheet but the dial tone was noncommittal.

Drumming his fingers, he glanced out his window toward the Mobil refinery's methane flare, Beaumont's own Star of Bethlehem. Far below ran a pewter channel of the Neches, sunlight coating the dimples of the water. Black-hulled tankers were anchored in the port, white topsides, striped flags riffling against the drift of spring clouds.

Or that's the view he'd have once his business took off—San Jacinto Building, seventh floor. Mahogany paneling, brass-trimmed elevator. Now he looked out on the New Rosemont, *$1 and Up*, where a ceiling fan once fell on the proprietress. The secretary's office had a window too, where sunlight and humidity pried off the paint on the Rosemont's fire escape.

8:32. Footsteps were sounding on the stairs to his second-story walk-up.

Wasn't skipping up here, was she? Measured tread. The knock on the door lately lettered *Thomas Phelan, Investigations* wasn't fast, wasn't slow. Not loud, not soft.

Phelan opened up. Well. Not a girl. Couple crows had stepped lightly at the corners of her eyes; a faint crease of bitter slanted from the left side of her barely tinted lips. Ash-brown hair, jaw-length, roomy white blouse, navy skirt. Jailhouse tan. Eyes gray-blue, a little clouded, distant, like a storm rolling in from out in the gulf. This one wouldn't sit behind the desk blowing on her polish. The hand he was shaking had naked nails cut to the quick.

"Tom Phelan."

"Delpha Wade." Her voice was low and dry.

Delpha Wade. His brain ratcheted a picture toward him but not far enough, like when a Mars bar gets hung up partway out the vending machine.

They sat down in his office, him in a gimpy swivel behind a large metal desk, both included in the rent. Her in one of the proud new clients' chairs, padded leather with regally tall backs.

"Gotta be honest with you, Miss Wade. Think I already found a secretary."

No disappointment in those blue eyes, no hope either. She just passed a certificate with a gold seal across the desk. The paper said she typed seventy words a minute, knew shorthand, could do double entry. The brunette with the coral nails claimed all that too, but she'd backed it up with a giggle, not a diploma from Gatesville.

"Your first choice of a job a PI's office?"

"My first choice is a job."

Touché. "What number interview would this be for you?"

"Number one."

"I'm flattered. Get off the bus, you come here."

The blue eyes let in a smidgen of light. "Course that doesn't count the dozen applications I wrote out 'fore they showed me the door."

No wonder Joe was pushing her. "Had your druthers . . . where'd you work, Miss Wade?"

"Library. I like libraries. It's what I did *there.*"

There being Gatesville. Now that she'd brought it up. "How many you do?"

"Fourteen."

Phelan quelled the whistle welling up. That let out check-kiting, forgery, embezzling from the till, and probably dope. He was about to ask her the delicate when she handed it to him on a foil tray. "Voluntary manslaughter."

"And you did fourteen?"

"He was very dead, Mr. Phelan."

His brain shoved: the picture fell into the slot. Phelan'd been a teenager, jazzed by blood-slinging, and reporters had loved the story. Waitress in a bayou dive, waiting for the owner to collect the take. Alone. Two guys thrown out earlier came back—beat her, raped her, cut her. Father and son, that was the kicker. That, and they went for the girl before the cash register. But surprise. Somehow the knife had changed hands. The father'd got punctured and son sliced. When the owner's headlights showed, dear old Dad ran for their heap and peeled. Delpha Wade had not let nature take its course. She finished off Junior in the oyster-shell parking lot.

The Gatesville certificate was being fit into a faded black leather clutch, years out of date. She gathered her feet under her. But didn't stand up. Those eyes got to him. No hope, no despair. Just a storm cloud back on the blue horizon.

The outer door tapped. A hesitant tap, like a mouse was out there. "'Scuse me," Phelan said and stood. His chair flopped its wooden seat upward like its next occupant would arrive in it via the ceiling. He wrenched it up; the seat surrendered again. "Gotta fix that," he muttered.

When he looked up, he saw Delpha Wade's straight back, walking out. Funny, he'd had the impression she wouldn't fold so easy.

"Forgot your purse, Miss Wade."

"No, I didn't." She shut the door between their offices—or rather, the door between his office and whoever got the secretary job's office—soundlessly. He heard, "Good morning, ma'am. Do you have an appointment to see Mr. Phelan?" Her dry voice was smooth as a Yale lock.

Phelan smiled. *I'll be damned.* He tipped the chair's seat into loading position and sat in it, like the boss should.

Mumbling.

"May I ask what your visit is in reference to?"

More mumbling, a lot of it. Then—Phelan hated this sound—sobbing. Not that he hadn't prepared for it. He'd bought a box of Kleenex at the dime store for the brokenhearted wives. Stashed it in the desk's bottom drawer next to the husbands' fifth of Kentucky. Had his .38 license in his wallet, PI license on the wall, newly minted business cards on the desk. An ex-con impersonating a secretary.

Delpha Wade entered, closing the door behind her. "Can you see a client now, Mr. Phelan?"

"Bring her on." He was rooting for a cheated-on society matron in crocodile pumps, her very own checkbook snapped inside a croc bag.

"You can go in now, Mrs. Toups."

A bone-thin woman in yesterday's makeup and rumpled shirtwaist took the doorway. Leatherette purse in her fists, little gold nameplate like a cashier's pinned over her left breast. The two slashes between her eyebrows tightened. "You're kinda young. I was looking for—"

"An old retired cop?" Delpha Wade said. On *cop* her neutral voice bunched. "Mr. Phelan has a fresh point of view."

What Mr. Phelan had was a fresh legal pad. He wielded a ballpoint over it. "Please, sit down, Mrs. Toups. Tell me what I can do for you."

Delpha Wade scooped an elbow, tucked her into the client chair, at the same time saying, "Can I get you some coffee? Cream and sugar?"

Phelan furrowed his own brow, trying to grow some wrinkles. *Coffee,* he thought. *What coffee?*

"Take a Coke, if you got one."

The inner door closed behind Delpha Wade, and he heard the outer door shut too. His first client stammered into her story; Phelan's ballpoint despoiled the virginal legal pad. The Kleenex stayed in their drawer. Caroleen Toups had her own hankie.

By the time his nonsecretary returned with a dewy bottle of Coke, Phelan had the story. The Toups's lived over on the north side, not far off Concord, nothing that could be called a neighborhood, more like one of a string of old wooden houses individually hacked out of the woods. Her boy Richard was into something and she didn't like it. He'd been skipping school. Running around all hours. Then last night Richard had not come home.

Gently, Phelan asked, "Report that to the police?"

"Seven o'clock this morning. They said boys run off all the time. Said been a bunch of boys running off lately. Four or five. Like it's a club."

Phelan silently agreed, having once woken up with two or three friends on a New Orleans sidewalk, littered, lacquered, and convinced somebody'd driven rebar through his forehead. "What does your husband think?"

"He passed last fall. Took a virus in his heart." Her reddened eyes offered to share that grief with him, but Phelan bowed his head and went on.

"Does Richard have a favorite item of clothing?"

"Some silly shoes that make him taller. And a Johnny Winter T-shirt he bought at a concert over in Port Arthur."

"Would you know if those are gone from his room?"

"I would . . . Mr. Phelan." Having managed to bestow on T. Phelan's callow mug that title of respect, Mrs. Toups looked at him hopefully. "They're not."

"Have a piggy bank?"

She snapped the purse open and took out a roll, Andrew Jackson on top. "Till about midnight," she said, "I read the *Enterprise*. That's where I saw your ad. After midnight I searched my son's room with a fine-tooth comb. This was in a cigar box under his bed. Along with some baseball cards and twisty cigarettes. There's $410 here. Ricky's in tenth grade, Mr. Phelan. He don't have a job."

The phone rang in the outer office, followed by the light click of the reconditioned Selectric. "You wouldn't a brought a picture of him?"

Mrs. Toups dug into the leatherette, handed over a school photo. Fair and baby-faced, long-haired like a lot of kids these days. Grinning like he was saddled on a Christmas pony. Ricky Toups when he still had a daddy.

The mother's tired eyes held a rising rim of water. "Why I wanted you to look old and tough—you find Ricky, scare him good. I cain't take any more a this."

Phelan was jolted by a gut feeling, a pact connecting him to that haggard mother. He hadn't expected it. "Okay," he said quickly. While Mrs. Toups sipped her Coke, he scrawled her address and phone number, then jotted an inventory of Ricky's friends. Make that friend, a neighbor girl, Georgia Watson. School? French High, Phelan's own alma mater, an orange-brick sprawl with a patchy football field. The legal pad was broken in now.

He wrote her name on a standard contract and slid it toward her. He'd practiced the next part so he could spit it out without blinking. "Fee is seventy-five a day. Plus expenses."

Nobody was blinking here. Mrs. Toups peeled off five Jacksons. "Could you start now?"

"First day's crucial on a missing-child case," Phelan said, like he knew. "You're at the top of the schedule."

He guided Mrs. Toups through the outer office to the door. To his right, Delpha Wade sat behind the secretary's desk, receiver tucked into her neck, typing. Typing what? And where had she got the paper?

"A Mrs. Lloyd Elliott would like to speak with you about a confidential matter. Says her husband's an attorney." Delpha Wade's dry voice was hushed, and she rubbed her thumb and fingers together in the universal sign for money.

She got that right. According to the *Enterprise*, Lloyd Elliott had just won some court case that paid him 30 percent of yippee-I-never-have-to-work-again.

Mrs. Toups stuck her reddened face back in the door, a last plea on it. But at the sight of Phelan taking the phone, she ducked her head and left.

"Tom Phelan," he said. Crisply, without one *um* or *you know*, the woman on the phone told him she wanted her husband followed, where to, and why. She'd bring by a retainer. Cash.

"That'll work. Get back to you soon. Please leave any relevant details with my . . . with Miss Wade. You can trust her."

And don't I hope that's true, he thought, clattering down the stairs.

The band was playing when Phelan pulled up to French High School. God, did he remember this parking lot: clubhouse, theater, and smoking lounge. He lit up for nostalgia's sake.

A little shitkicker perched on the trunk of a Mustang pushed back his Resistol. He had his boots on the bumper, one knee jackhammering hard enough to shiver the car. Phelan offered him a smoke.

Haughtily, the kid produced some Bull and rolled his own. "Take a light." Phelan obliged. "You know Georgia Watson?"

"Out there. Georgia's in Belles." The boy lofted his chin toward the field that joined the parking lot.

"What about Ricky Toups?"

The kid tugged down the hat, blew out smoke. "Kinda old to be into weed, ain't ya?"

"That why people come looking for Ricky?"

Marlboro-Man-in-training doused the homemade, stashed it behind his ear. Slid off the trunk and booked.

Phelan turned toward the field, where the band played a lazy version of "Grazing in the Grass." The Buffalo Belles were high-kicking, locked shoulder to shoulder. Line of smiling faces, white, black, and café au lait, bouncing hair and breasts, 120 teenage legs, kicked up high. Fondly remembering a pair of those white boots hooked over his shoulders postgame, he strolled toward the rousing sight.

After their routine, the girls milled sideline while the band marched patterns. Phelan asked for Georgia and found her, said he wanted to talk.

This is who Ricky Toups thought hung the moon? Georgia Watson had an overloaded bra, all right, and cutoffs so short the hems of white pockets poked out like underwear. But she was a dish-faced girl with frizzled hair and cagey brown eyes. Braided gold chain tucked into the neck of a white T-shirt washed thin.

She steered him away from the knots of babbling girls. Her smile threw a murky light into the brown eyes. Black smudges beneath them from her gobbed eyelashes.

He introduced himself with a business card. "Ricky Toups's mother asked me to check up on him. He got any new friends you know about?"

She jettisoned the smile, shrugged.

"C'mon, Georgia. Ricky thinks you're his friend."

She made a production of whispering, "Ricky was helping this guy with something, but I think that's all over."

"Something."

"Something," she hissed. She angled toward some girls staring frankly at them and fluttered her fingers in a wave. Nobody waved back.

"This guy. Why's Ricky not helping him anymore?"

Georgia shook her head, looking over Phelan's shoulder like she was refusing somebody who wasn't there. "Fun at first, then he turned scary. Ricky's gonna quit hanging out with him, even though that means—" Her trap shut.

"Giving up the green," Phelan finished. His little finger flicked out the braided chain around the girl's neck. Fancy G in twenty-four carat. "How long y'all had this scary friend?"

The head shaking continued, like a tic now.

Phelan violated her personal space. "Name. And where the guy lives."

The girl backed up. "I don't know, some D name, Don or Darrell or something. Gotta go now."

Phelan caught her arm. "Ricky didn't come home last night."

White showed around the brown eyes. She spit out a sentence, included her phone number when pressed, then jerked her arm away and ran back to the other girls on the sideline. They practiced dance steps in bunches, laughed, horsed around. Georgia stood apart biting her bottom lip, the little white square of his business card pinched in her fingers.

11:22. He drove back to the office, took the stairs two at a time. Delpha handed him Mrs. Lloyd Elliott's details neatly typed on the back of a sheet of paper. Phelan read it and whistled. "Soon's she brings that retainer, Lloyd better dig himself a foxhole."

He flipped the sheet over. Delpha Wade's discharge from Gatesville: *April 7, 1973. Five-foot-six, 120 pounds. Hair brown, eyes blue. Thirty-four. Voluntary manslaughter.*

"Only paper around," she said.

Phelan laid a ten on the desk. "Get some. Then see what's up in the Toups's neighborhood, say, the last three months. Thought this was a kid pushing weed for pocket money, but could be dirtier water." He told her what Georgia Watson had given him: the D name, Don or Darrell, and that Ricky brought other boys over to the guy's house to party. "I'm guessing Georgia might've pitched in with that."

Delpha met his eyes for a second. Then, without comment, she flipped through the phone book while he went to his office, got the .38 out of a drawer, and loaded it. Glanced out the window. New Rosemont's ancient proprietress, the one the fan had gonged, rag in hand, smearing dirty circles on a window.

When he came out, Delpha had the phone book open to the city map section. "Got a cross directory?" she asked.

Phelan went back and got it from his office. "Run through the—"

"Newspaper's police blotter."

"Right. Down at the—"

"Library," she said. She left, both books hugged to her chest.

Just another girl off to school.

The parole office nudged up to the courthouse. His buddy Joe Ford was in, but busy. Phelan helped himself to a couple donuts from an open box. Early lunch. Joe read from a manila file to two guys Phelan knew. One took notes on a little spiral pad. Phelan, toting the long legal pad, realized he should have one of those. Neater, slipped in a jacket pocket. More professional. Joe closed the folder and kept on talking. One guy gave a low whistle; the other laughed.

Joe stood up, did a double take. "Hey, speak of the devil. Tommy, come on down."

Phelan shook hands with Fred Abels, detective. Stuck his hand out to the other, but the man bear-hugged him. "Hey, Uncle Louie," Phelan said. Louie Reaud, a jowly olive-skinned man with silvered temples, married to Phelan's aunt. Louie boomed, "*Bougre, t'es fou ouais toi! T'as engage un prisonnier.*" Which meant Phelan was crazy for hiring himself a convict.

Who said he'd hired anybody?

Abels, sporting a Burt Reynolds 'stache and burns, only not sexy, studied Phelan like he was a mud tire track lifted from a scene.

Phelan zeroed in on Joe, who raised his eyebrows, pulled down his lips, shook his head to indicate the purity permeating his soul.

"Okay." Phelan set hands on his hips and broadened his stance. "All right. So my friend here appeals to my famous heart of gold. So I interview his girl. So she stuck some bad-doer. So what."

"Minced that one, yeah. I worked that case." Louie wagged a finger. "I'm gonna tell you, *cher*, lock up the letter opener." He punched his nephew's arm, nodded at Joe, and he and Abels ambled off, chortling.

"Loudmouth bastard," Phelan said to Joe. "Give me the dopers and perverts north side of town." Commandeering Joe's chair, Phelan reeled off some street names.

"That's confidential."

"Could have my secretary call you."

"Hand full a 'Gimme' and a mouth full a 'Much obliged'—that's you." Joe squinted, put-upon. "Not my territory, but old Parker lives in the can." Joe stalked over to his coworker Parker's vacant desk, the one next to his, and rambled through its file drawers.

Phelan phoned Tyrrell Public Library. Formerly a church—thus the arches and stained glass—it was a downtown standout, a sand castle dripped from medieval gray stone. He asked the librarian to get a Miss Wade, who'd be in the reference section, going through newspapers.

"This is not the bus station, sir. We don't page people."

Seems like, Phelan thought while locating his desperately-polite-but-hurting voice, *one bad crab always jumps in the gumbo.*

"I'm just as sorry as I can be, ma'am. But couldn't you find my sister? We're down at the funeral home, and our daddy's lost his mind."

Clunk. Receiver on desk. Joe was still pulling files.

Footsteps, then Delpha came on. "Hey, Bubba," she said.

Phelan grinned.

She told him she'd call him back from a pay phone. "Call Joe's," he said.

In three minutes Joe's phone rang, and Delpha read out what she had so far. "Check this one from last night." A Marvin Carter, eighteen, wandering down Delaware Street, apparent assault victim, transported to a hospital. Then, outside of husband-wife slugfests, thefts, one complaint of tap-dancing on the roof of a Dodge Duster, she'd found seven dope busts and two missing-boy reports. She gave him names and addresses, phone numbers from the cross directory.

Joe dumped files on his desk, said, "Vacate my chair, son." Phelan ignored him, boring in on each mug shot as he scribbled names on his unprofessional legal pad.

One of the names was a Don Henry. Liberated from Huntsville two months back.

Some D name, Don or Darrell.

There you go. Cake.

No mud, no grease, no 500-pound pipe, no lost body parts. Man, he should have split the rigs while he still had ten fingers.

2:01. He drove back to the office and hit the phone. Got a child at the Henry number, asked for its mother.

"She went the store. Git away, Dwight, I'm on the phone." A wail from the background.

"Honey, your daddy there?"

The child scolded Dwight. Dwight was supposed to shut up while the child had dibs on the telephone. But little Dwight wasn't lying down; he was pitching a fit.

"Honey? Hey, kid!" Phelan hollered into the phone.

"Shut up, Dwight! I cain't hear myself talk. They took Daddy back Satiddy."

"Saturday? Back where, honey?"

"Where he *was.* Is this Uncle Merle?" The child yelped. Now two wails mingled on the other end of the line.

A woman's harsh voice barked into the phone, "Low-down, Merle, pumping the kids. They pulled Don's paper, okay? You happy now? Gonna say 'I told you so'? You and Ma can kiss my ass." The phone crashed down.

Saturday was six days ago. Frowning, Phelan X'd Don Henry. Next, mindful of the gray-haired volunteers in pink smocks on the end of the line, he called Baptist Hospital and inquired feelingly for his cousin Marvin Carter. Strike one. Next was Saint Elizabeth, long wait, transfer, and strike two. Finally Hotel Dieu and a single to first.

He parked in a doctor's space in front of the redbrick hospital by the port. Eau de Pine-Sol and polished tile. A nun gave him the room number.

The face on the pillow was white-whiskered, toothless, and snoring. A pyramid of a woman in a red-flowered muumuu sat bedside. Phelan checked the room number. "Marvin Carter?"

The woman sighed. "My husband's name is Mar-tin. Cain't y'all get nothing right?"

Phelan loped back to the desk and stood in line behind a sturdy black woman and a teenage boy with a transistor radio broadcasting the day's body count in a jungle on the other side of the globe. The boy's face was lopsided, the wide bottom out of kilter with a narrow forehead. He nudged the dial and a song blared out. "Kung Fu Fighting." The woman slapped shut a checkbook, snatched the transistor, and dialed back to the tinny announcer spewing numbers and Asian place names.

"Jus' keep listenin'. 'Cause you keep runnin' nights, thas where you gonna be, in that war don't never end, you hear me, Marvin? What *you* lookin at?" She scowled at Phelan.

The boy turned so that Phelan verified the lopsidedness as swelling. He ventured, "Marvin Carter?"

The woman's eyes slitted as she asked who he was. Phelan told her, emphasizing that he was not a policeman. He told her that he was looking for Ricky Toups, kept his eyes on the boy.

The boy flinched. Bingo.

"Les' go." The woman pushed the teenager toward the glass doors.

Phelan dogged them. "Did that to you, Marvin, what's he gonna do to Ricky, huh? Want that on your slate? Could be a lot worse than the dope."

The boy tried the deadeye on Phelan. Couldn't hold it.

"We talking *dope* now?" The woman's voice dropped below freezing. "You done lied to me, Marvin Carter." Her slapping hand stopped short of the swollen jaw.

Marvin grunted something that was probably "Don't, Mama," enough so Phelan understood his jaw was wired.

"Ricky got you there promising dope," Phelan said, "but that wasn't all you got, was it?"

The boy squeezed his eyes shut.

"Wasn't white kids did this to you? Was some grown man?" Marvin's mother took hold of his skinny waist.

"Listen," Phelan leaned in, "if he said he'd hurt your mama here, I'll take care of that. It's just a line. But Ricky's real. You know him, and he's wherever you were last night. Help me find him, Marvin."

"Avy," the boy said.

"Avie? The street near the LNVA canal?"

Shake from Marvin said no. And he mumbled again, "Avy."

"Davy? That's his name?"

A shudder ran through the teenager.

Phelan scanned his list of parolees. Didn't have to be one of them, but he had a feeling. "Dave Deeterman? Concord Street?"

Shake from Marvin said yes. "Kakerd." Marvin muttered directions, minus lots of consonants. The mother glared Phelan away, and Marvin bent down and shook against her neck.

Phelan dashed back to the hospital's two pay phones, called Delpha, told her where he was heading, and if she didn't hear from him within the hour, to call Louis Reaud down at the station. "That's R-E—"

"Know how to spell it," she said. "Guess your second client brought over your retainer. Somebody left a wrapped-up box at the door."

"Hot damn. Why didn't she hand it to you?"

"Don't know. Just heard her on the stairs. Want me to unwrap the box?"

"No time. 'Less it's ticking, just hold on to it."

"Got time for one question, Mr. Phelan?"

"Shoot."

Throat clearing. "You think you might hire me?"

"Miss Wade, you were hired when you called me Bubba." He hung up the silent phone and jogged for the doors.

3:15. The house with the orange mailbox, painfully described by Marvin, was a dingy white ranch. It was set deep in the lot, backed up to tall pines and oak and magnolia, pockets of brush. Rusty-brown pine needles and dried magnolia leaves, big brown tongues, littered the ground. With oil shot up to twelve dollars a barrel, somebody'd be out here soon, hammering up pasteboard apartments, but for now wildlife was renting this leftover patch of the Big Thicket.

No car, but ruts in the grass where one had parked.

Phelan knocked on the door. Waited. Tried the knob, no dice. He went around the back to a screen porch that looked to be an add-on. Or it had been a screen porch before plywood was nailed over its large windows. A two-by-four had been pounded across the door; the hammer lying there in the dirt suggested that Dave Deeterman might be recently away from his desk. Maybe. Phelan could hear something. He beat on the door. "Ricky. Ricky Toups, you in there?"

He put his ear to the door. Something. Phelan pounded again, louder. "I'm looking for Ricky Toups."

A low creaking. Rhythmic. What *was* that sound? Like a rocking chair with serious rust.

He jogged back to his car, shoved a flashlight into his pocket, and snagged a pry bar. Ripped off the two-by-four. Opened the door. Directly across the porch was the door that led into the house. Phelan stepped over there, .38 drawn, and rattled it: locked. Already he was smelling piss in the hot, dead air. Then herb and cigarettes and some kind of dead-fish bayou stink. That creaky noise came from the far left, high up. He found a switch by the locked door and flipped it. Not a gleam.

He'd got the creaks figured now, and he shined the white circle up and left, to their source.

Christ Almighty.

Phelan's jaw sagged. On the top of metal shelves was a naked gargoyle, perched there. No, clinging. Haunches with a smooth, sheened back folded over them, fingers clawed around the metal, head cut sharply toward Phelan. Blinking eyes protruded from sunken holes; the downturned mouth wheezed.

"Asthma, right?"

An indrawn, "Yeah."

"Deeterman coming back?"

Ricky Toups's head bobbed loosely, flapping sweat-dark hair that had been dishwater-blond in last year's school photo.

"How long's he been gone?"

"Hour or—" The kid flung out a hand, pointing.

Phelan zigzagged the light downward over matted orange shag littered with marijuana debris, the arm of a bamboo couch, beer cans. He pivoted. The shaft of light from the door revealed the round edge of a black pile that blended into the darkness. What? Shit? Most of him failed to make sense of what he saw. But not his skin—it was crawling off his belly, his nuts squeezing north of nutsack.

The pile of shit shifted until only a tip remained. Then the tip disappeared into blackness.

That it was heading toward him told Phelan enough. Most snakes light out for the hills; cottonmouths come at you.

Phelan strode to the shelves and hauled Ricky down, shined the light till it hit the bamboo couch, and dumped the boy on it. "Keep your feet off the floor."

He scanned with the flashlight. Where the fuck was it?

Shag. Spilt ashtray. More shag.

Then the beam caught a section of sinuous black. He moved the light. There it was. Pouring toward him, triangular head outthrust.

Phelan fired.

The black snake convulsed but kept coming, tongue darting.

He fired again. Still the black form writhed in the orange grass. He blew its head off with the third round.

Phelan stepped wide of the quivering snake; wasn't dead enough yet to keep the head from biting. Ears ringing, he tossed the flashlight, looped the boy's arm around his neck, dragged him out of that room.

He saw the blue thumb-sized bruises on the boy's shoulders, a streak of blood on the back of his thigh, as he draped him in his own jacket and a blanket from his trunk. "It's the hospital, Ricky, 'less you got a full inhaler at home."

"Home," the kid panted, then turned the black tunnel of his eyes onto Phelan. "Book."

"What book?"

But the kid folded, struggling for air.

Phelan laid on the horn when they gunned into the Toups's driveway. In two seconds, Caroleen Toups busted out of the house, face lit up like stadium lights.

Phelan smoked in the Toups's pine-paneled living room that opened onto a pine-paneled kitchen. Except for the mention of a book, he had hold of the thing: Deeterman slipped Ricky cash and dope, Ricky steered him boys. Too stupid to know the son of a bitch would turn on him. *How many* ran in a loop through Phelan's brain. *How many you bring him, Ricky?*

After a while, wearing jeans and breathing, Ricky Toups stumbled out into the living room, trailed by his bewildered mother, her hands clasped at chest level. "There's a book," he said. "Told him I didn't have it. He didn't care, said he'd be back for me."

"What kinda book?"

"Like a diary. You gotta help Georgia." He hit his inhaler, and his jaw jittered sideways like his head was trying to screw off.

"She's got the book. Her idea to take it?"

Ricky's bluish chapped lips parted, like he was going to deny this point, but that was back when he had all the answers, before today. "She said we could get big money from him. That's where he went. To her house."

Phelan leapt up. "Call her."

Ricky mumbled into a phone on the kitchen wall then hung his head listening. The receiver fell to his side. "It's okay. He came to her house but she'd already took it to your office."

Phelan's stomach lurched.

Ricky slid down the wall, hunkered. Georgia'd told Deeterman he could go get the book where she'd left it, wrapped up outside this private eye's office. The guy wouldn't be there; he was out looking for Ricky. She'd talked fast, peeking through a latched screen door with Phelan's card taped to the outside of it.

4:55. Phelan burned up I-10's fast lane, swerving around truckers balling for New Orleans, cursing himself for wasting three rounds on a cottonmouth he could have outrun.

He took the stairs soft. Worked the doorknob soundlessly, hoping Deeterman was somewhere ahead of the truckers on I-10, not sitting in Delpha's chair watching the knob turn. Phelan eased into the still office, .38 out.

Delpha Wade's chair snugged to her desk. On top of it, the sheet with info on Client #2, typed on her release form. The door to his office stood ajar. Pressed against the jamb, Phelan pushed, swinging it open.

He stepped into a curtain of bourbon fume and quiet in the air, waves of it, wave on wave, quiet.

Until glass crunched under his shoe.

The client chair drifted around. Delpha said, "I put it away in your bottom drawer. Under the whiskey bottle."

Phelan slid the gun on his desk next to a wad of brown paper, sank down to her.

Her right hand hung behind the chair arm but her left lay on a small, worn ledger in the middle of a shiny darkness on her skirt. Different-sized spots stained her white blouse, spray and spatter, one red channel.

"'Fore I could get that box for him, he pushed me out of the way and grabbed it. He coulda left. I thought he would. But he had to do one of those things they do. Those extras." Her head lowered, shook once. "They just cain't resist."

He'd seen the legs on the floor by now, the rest of the body blocked from view by the big metal desk, and he needed to get Louie here, get an ambulance first, but he couldn't pick up the phone, couldn't get that motion going because he was listening to her, hearing it in the waves of quiet that rolled over him, quiet riding on waves of quiet, waves widening out from a center—the bayou, singing with insects and frogs, the surge-and-retreat, keening whir of it, the stir in muddy water, and her voice low as that chorus, he heard how she was still holding the bottle when the man licked the knife and cut her, and after he licked it again, she broke the bottle on the edge of the desk and shoved it up through his throat. Then she took the book and she sat down.

"You gonna find some boys."

"Delpha," Phelan whispered. The half of her face he could see wore a sheen of sweat. He laced his fingers through the brown hair, soothed it back.

Not a cloud in the gray-blue eyes that met his. The horizon inside them was clear.

A NICE PLACE TO VISIT

BY JEFFERY DEAVER

Hell's Kitchen, Manhattan

(Originally published in *Manhattan Noir*)

W hen you're a natural-born grifter, an operator, a player, you get this sixth sense for sniffing out opportunities, and that's what Ricky Kelleher was doing now, watching two guys in the front of the smoky bar, near a greasy window that still had a five-year-old bullet hole in it.

Whatever was going down, neither of them looked real happy.

Ricky kept watching. He'd seen one guy here in Hanny's a couple of times. He was wearing a suit and tie—it really made him stand out in this dive, the sore thumb thing. The other one, leather jacket and tight jeans, razor-cut bridge-and-tunnel hair, was some kind of Gambino wannabe, Ricky pegged him. Or Sopranos, more likely—yeah, he was the sort of prick who'd hock his wife for a big-screen TV. He was way pissed off, shaking his head at everything Mr. Suit was telling him. At one point he slammed his fist on the bar so hard glasses bounced. But nobody noticed. That was the kind of place Hanny's was.

Ricky was in the rear, at the short L of the bar, his regular throne. The bartender, a dusty old guy, maybe black, maybe white, you couldn't tell, kept an uneasy eye on the guys arguing. "It's cool," Ricky reassured him. "I'm on it."

Mr. Suit had a briefcase open. A bunch of papers were inside. Most of the business in this pungent, dark Hell's Kitchen bar involved trading bags of chopped-up plants and cases of Johnny Walker that'd fallen off the truck; the transactions were conducted in either the men's room or the alley out back. This was something different. Skinny, five-foot-four Ricky couldn't tip to exactly what was going down, but that magic sense, his player's eye, told him to pay attention.

"Well, fuck that," Wannabe said to Mr. Suit.

"Sorry." A shrug.

"Yeah, you said that before." Wannabe slid off the stool. "But you don't really *sound* that fucking sorry. And you know why? Because *I'm* the one out all the money."

504 // USA Noir

"Bullshit. *I'm* losing my whole fucking business."

But Ricky'd learned that other people losing money doesn't take the sting out of *you* losing money. Way of the world.

Wannabe was getting more and more agitated. "Listen careful here, my friend. I'll make some phone calls. I got people I know down there. You don't want to fuck with these guys."

Mr. Suit tapped what looked like a newspaper article in the briefcase. "And what're they gonna do?" His voice lowered and he whispered something that made Wannabe's face screw up in disgust. "Now just go on home, keep your head down, and watch your back. And pray they can't—" Again, the lowered voice. Ricky couldn't hear what "they" might do.

Wannabe slammed his hand down on the bar again. "This isn't gonna fly, asshole. Now—"

"Hey, gentlemen," Ricky called. "Volume down, okay?"

"The fuck're you, little man?" Wannabe snapped. Mr. Suit touched his arm to quiet him, but he pulled away and kept glaring.

Ricky slicked back his greasy, dark blond hair. Easing off the stool, he walked to the front of the bar, the heels of his boots tapping loudly on the scuffed floor. The guy had six inches and thirty pounds on him but Ricky had learned a long time ago that craziness scares people a fuck of a lot more than height or weight or muscle. And so he did what he always did when he was going one on one—threw a weird look into his eyes and got right up in the man's face. He screamed, "Who I am is guy's gonna drag your ass into the alley and fuck you over a dozen different ways, you don't get the fuck out of here now!"

The punk reared back and blinked. He fired off an automatic "Fuck you, asshole!"

Ricky stayed right where he was, kind of grinning, kind of not, and let this poor bastard imagine what was going to happen now that he'd accidentally shot a little spit onto Ricky's forehead.

A few seconds passed.

Finally, Wannabe drank down what was left of his beer with a shaking hand and, trying to hold on to a little dignity, he strolled out the door, laughing and muttering, "Prick." Like it was Ricky backing down.

"Sorry about that," Mr. Suit said, standing up, pulling out money for the drinks.

"No, you stay," Ricky ordered.

"Me?"

"Yeah, you."

The man hesitated and sat back down.

Ricky glanced into the briefcase, saw some pictures of nice-looking boats. "Just gotta keep things calm round here, you know. Keep the peace."

Mr. Suit slowly closed the case, looked around at the faded beer promotion cut-outs, the stained sports posters, the cobwebs. "This your place?"

The bartender was out of earshot. Ricky said, "More or less."

"Jersey." Mr. Suit nodded at the door that Wannabe had just walked out of. Like that explained it all.

Ricky's sister lived in Jersey and he wondered if maybe he should be pissed at the insult. He was a loyal guy. But then he decided loyalty didn't have anything to do with states or cities and shit like that. "So. He lost some money?"

"Business deal went bad."

"Uh-huh. How much?"

"I don't know."

"Buy him another beer," Ricky called to the bartender, then turned back. "You're in business with him and you don't know how much money he lost?"

"What I don't know," the guy said, his dark eyes looking right into Ricky's, "is why I should fucking tell you."

This was the time when it could get ugly. There was a tough moment of silence. Then Ricky laughed. "No worries."

The beers arrived.

"Ricky Kelleher." He clinked glasses.

"Bob Gardino."

"I seen you before. You live around here?"

"Florida mostly. I come up here for business some. Delaware too. Baltimore, Jersey shore, Maryland."

"Yeah? I got a summer place I go to a lot."

"Where?"

"Ocean City. Four bedrooms, on the water." Ricky didn't mention that it was T.G.'s, not his.

"Sweet." The man nodded, impressed.

"It's okay. I'm looking at some other places too."

"Man can never have too much real estate. Better than the stock market."

"I do okay on Wall Street," Ricky said. "You gotta know what to look for. You just can't buy some stock 'cause it's, you know, sexy." He'd heard this on some TV show.

"Truer words." Now Gardino tapped his glass into Ricky's.

"Those were some nice fucking boats." A nod toward the briefcase. "That your line?"

"Among other things. Whatta *you* do, Ricky?"

"I got my hand in a lot of stuff. Lot of businesses. All over the neighborhood here. Well, and other places too. Maryland, like I was saying. Good money to be made. For a man with a sharp eye."

"And you have a sharp eye?"

"I think I do. Wanta know what it's seeing right now?"

"What, your eye?"

"Yeah."

"What's it seeing?"

"A grifter."

"A—?"

"A scam artist."

"I know what a grifter is," Gardino said. "I meant, why do you think that's what I am?"

"Well, for instance, you don't come into Hanny's—"

"Hanny's?"

"Here. Hanrahan's."

"Oh."

"—to sell some loser asshole a boat. So what really happened?"

Gardino chuckled but said nothing.

"Look," Ricky whispered, "I'm cool. Ask anybody on the street."

"There's nothing to tell. A deal went south is all. Happens."

"I'm not a cop, that's what you're thinking." Ricky looked around, reached into his pocket, and flashed a bag of hash he'd been carrying around for T.G. "I was, you think I'd have this on me?"

"Naw, I don't think you're a cop. And you seem like an okay guy. But I don't need to spill my guts to every okay guy I meet."

"I hear that. Only . . . I'm just wondering there's a chance we can do business together."

Gardino drank some more beer. "Again, why?"

"Tell me how your con works."

"It's not a con. I was going to sell him a boat. It didn't work out. End of story."

"But . . . see, here's what I'm thinking," Ricky said in his best player's voice. "I seen people pissed off 'cause they don't get a car they wanted, or a house, or some pussy. But that asshole, he wasn't pissed off about not getting a boat. He was pissed off about not getting his down payment back. So, how come he didn't?"

Gardino shrugged.

Ricky tried again. "How's about we play a game, you and me? I'll ask you something and you tell me if I'm right or if I'm full of shit. How's that?"

"Twenty questions."

"Whatever. Okay, try this on: You *borrow*"—he held up his fingers and made quotation marks—"a boat, sell it to some poor asshole, but then on the way here it *sinks*." Again the quotation marks. "And there's nothing he can do about it. He loses his down payment. He's fucked. Too bad, but who's he going to complain to? It's stolen merch."

Gardino studied his beer. Son of a bitch still wasn't giving away squat.

Ricky added, "Only there never was any boat. You never steal a fucking thing. You just show him pictures you took on the dock and a fake police report or something."

The guy finally laughed. But nothing else.

"Your only risk is some asshole whaling on you when he loses the money. Not a bad grift."

"I sell boats," Gardino said. "That's it."

"Okay, you sell boats." Ricky eyed him carefully. He'd try a different approach. "So that means you're looking for buyers. How 'bout I find one for you?"

"You know somebody who's interested in boats?"

"There's a guy I know. He might be."

Gardino thought for a minute. "This a friend of yours we're talking?"

"I wouldn'ta brought him up, he was a friend."

The sunlight came through some clouds over Eighth Avenue and hit Gardino's beer. It cast a tint on the counter, the yellow of a sick man's eye. Finally, he said to Ricky, "Pull your shirt up."

"My—?"

"Your shirt. Pull it up and turn around."

"You think I'm wired?"

"Or we just have our beers and bullshit about the Knicks and we go our separate ways. Up to you."

Self-conscious of his skinny build, Ricky hesitated. But then he slipped off the stool, pulled up his leather jacket, and lifted his dirty T-shirt. He turned around.

"Okay. You do the same."

Gardino laughed. Ricky thought he was laughing at him more than he was laughing at the situation but he held on to his temper.

The con man pulled up his jacket and shirt. The bartender glanced at them but he was looking like nothing was weird. This was, after all, Hanny's.

The men sat down and Ricky called for more brews.

Gardino whispered, "Okay, I'll tell you what I'm up to. But listen. You get some idea that you're in the mood to snitch, I got two things to say: One, what I'm doing is not exactly legal, but it's not like I'm clipping anybody or selling crack to kids, got it? So even if you go to the cops, the best they can get me for is some bullshit misrepresentation claim. They'll laugh you out of the station."

"No, man, seriously—"

Gardino held up a finger. "And number two, you dime me out, I've got associates in Florida'll find you and make you bleed for days." He grinned. "We copacetic?"

Whatever the fuck that meant. Ricky said, "No worries, mister. All I wanta do is make some money."

"Okay, here's how it works: Fuck down payments. The buyers pay everything right up front. A hundred, hundred fifty thousand."

"No shit."

"What I tell the buyer is my connections know where there're these confiscated boats. This really happens. They're towed off by the DEA for drugs or Coast Guard or State Police when the owner's busted for sailing 'em while drunk. They go up for auction. But see, what happens is, in Florida, there's so many boats that it takes time to log 'em all in. I tell the buyers my partners break into the pound at three in the morning and tow a boat away before there's a record of it. We ship it to Delaware or Jersey, slap a new number on it, and bang, for a hundred thousand you get a half-million-dollar boat.

"Then, after I get the money, I break the bad news. Like I just did with our friend from Jersey." He opened up his briefcase and pulled out a newspaper article. The headline was: *Three Arrested in Coast Guard Impound Thefts.*

The article was about a series of thefts of confiscated boats from a federal government impound dock. It went on to add that security had been stepped up and the FBI and Florida police were looking into who might've bought the half-dozen missing boats. They'd arrested the principals and recovered nearly a million dollars in cash from buyers on the East Coast.

Ricky looked over the article. "You, what? Printed it up yourself?"

"Word processor. Tore the edges to make it look like I ripped it out of the paper and then Xeroxed it."

"So you keep 'em scared shitless some cop's going to find their name or trace the money to them. *Now, just go on home, keep your head down, and watch your back.* Some of 'em make a stink for a day or two, but mostly they just disappear." This warranted another clink of beer glasses. "Fucking brilliant."

"Thanks."

"So if I *was* to hook you up with a buyer? What's in it for me?"

Gardino debated. "Twenty-five percent."

"You give me fifty." Ricky fixed him with the famous mad-guy Kelleher stare. Gardino held the gaze just fine. Which Ricky respected.

"I'll give you twenty-five percent if the buyer pays a hundred Gs or less. Thirty, if it's more than that."

Ricky said, "Over one fifty, I want half."

Gardino finally said, "Deal. You really know somebody can get his hands on that kind of money?"

Ricky finished his beer and, without paying, started for the door. "That's what I'm going to go work on right now."

Ricky walked into Mack's bar.

It was pretty much like Hanrahan's, four blocks away, but was busier, since it was closer to the convention center where hundreds of teamsters and union electricians and carpenters would take fifteen-minute breaks that lasted two hours. The neighborhood surrounding Mack's was better too: redeveloped town houses and some new buildings, expensive as shit, and even a Starbucks. Way fucking different from the grim, hustling combat zone that Hell's Kitchen had been until the '70s.

T.G., a fat Irishman in his mid-thirties, was at the corner table with three, four buddies of his.

"It's the Lime Rickey man!" T.G. shouted, not drunk, not sober—the way he usually seemed. Man used nicknames a lot, which he seemed to think was cute but always pissed off the person he was talking to, mostly because of the way he said it, not so much the names themselves. Like, Ricky didn't even know what a Lime Rickey was, some drink or something, but the sneery tone in T.G.'s voice was a putdown. Still, you had to have major balls to say anything back to the big, psycho Irishman.

"Hey," Ricky offered, walking up to the corner table, which was like T.G.'s office.

"The fuck you been?" T.G. asked, dropping his cigarette on the floor and crushing it under his boot.

"Hanny's."

"Doing what, Lime Rickey man?" Stretching out the nickname.

"Polishing me knob," Ricky responded in a phony brogue. A lot of times he said stuff like this, sort of putting himself down in front of T.G. and his crew. He didn't want to, didn't like it. It just happened. Always wondered why.

"You mean, polishing some *altar boy's* knob," T.G. roared. The more sober in the crew laughed.

Ricky got a Guinness. He really didn't like it but T.G. had once said that Guinness and whiskey were the only things real men drank. And, since it was called stout, he figured it would make him fatter. All his life, trying to get bigger. Never succeeding.

Ricky sat down at the table, which was scarred with knife slashes and skid marks from cigarette burns. He nodded to T.G.'s crew, a half-dozen losers who sorta worked the trades, sorta worked the warehouses, sorta hung out. One was so drunk he couldn't focus and kept trying to tell a joke, forgetting it halfway through. Ricky hoped the guy wouldn't puke before he made it to the john, like yesterday.

T.G. was rambling on, insulting some of the people at the table in his cheerful-mean way and threatening guys who weren't there.

Ricky just sat at the table, eating peanuts and sucking down his licorice-flavored stout, and took the insults when they were aimed at him. Mostly he was thinking about Gardino and the boats.

T.G. rubbed his round, craggy face and his curly red-brown hair. He spat out, "And, fuck me, the nigger got away."

Ricky was wondering which nigger. He thought he'd been paying attention, but sometimes T.G.'s train of thought took its own route and left you behind.

He could see T.G. was upset, though, and so Ricky muttered a sympathetic, "That asshole."

"Man, I see him, I will take that cocksucker out so fast." He clapped his palms together in a loud slap that made a couple of the crew blink. The drunk one stood up and staggered toward the men's room. Looked like he was going to make it this time.

"He been around?" Ricky asked.

T.G. snapped, "His black ass's up in Buffalo. I just told you that. The fuck you asking if he's here?"

"No, I don't mean here," Ricky said fast. "I mean, you know, *around*."

"Oh, yeah," T.G. said, nodding, as if he caught some other meaning. "Sure. But that don't help me any. I see him, he's one dead nigger."

"Buffalo," Ricky said, shaking his head. "Christ." He tried to listen more carefully, but he was still thinking about the boat scam. Yeah, that Gardino'd come up with a good one. And man, making a hundred thousand in a single grift—he and T.G.'d never come close to that before.

Ricky shook his head again. He sighed. "Got half a mind to go to Buffalo and take his black ass out myself."

"You the man, Lime Rickey. You the fucking man." And T.G. started rambling once again.

Nodding, staring at T.G.'s not-drunk, not-sober eyes, Ricky was wondering: How much would it take to get the fuck out of Hell's Kitchen? Get away from the bitching ex-wives, the bratty kid, away from T.G. and all the asshole losers like him. Maybe go to Florida, where Gardino was from. Maybe that'd be the place for him. From the various scams he and T.G. put together, he'd saved up about thirty thousand in cash. Nothing shabby there. But man, if he conned just two or three guys in the boat deal, he could walk away with five times that.

Wouldn't set him for good, but it'd be a start. Hell, Florida was full of rich old people, most of 'em stupid, just waiting to give their money to a player who had the right grift.

A fist colliding with his arm shattered the daydream. He bit the inside of his cheek and winced. He glared at T.G., who just laughed. "So, Lime Rickey, you going to Leon's, ain't you? On Saturday."

"I don't know."

The door swung open and some out-of-towner wandered in. An older guy, in his fifties, dressed in beltless tan slacks, a white shirt, and a blue blazer, a cord around his neck holding a convention badge, AOFM, whatever that was.

Association of . . . Ricky squinted. Association of Obese Ferret Molesters.

He laughed at his own joke. Nobody noticed. Ricky eyed the tourist. This never used to happen, seeing geeks in a bar around here. But then the convention center went in a few blocks south and after that, Times Square got its balls cut off and turned into Disneyland. Suddenly Hell's Kitchen was White Plains and Paramus, and the fucking yuppies and tourists took over.

The man blinked, eyes getting used to the dark. He ordered wine—T.G. snickered, wine in this place?—and drank down half right away. The guy had to've had money. He was wearing a Rolex and his clothes were designer shit. The man looked around slowly, and it reminded Ricky of the way people at the zoo look at the animals. He got pissed and enjoyed a brief fantasy of dragging the guy's ass outside and pounding him till he gave up the watch and wallet.

But of course he wouldn't. T.G. and Ricky weren't that way; they steered clear of busting heads. Oh, a few times somebody got fucked up bad—they'd pounded a college kid when he'd taken a swing at T.G. during a scam, and Ricky'd slashed the face of some spic who'd skimmed a thousand bucks of their money. But the rule was, you didn't make people bleed if you could avoid it. If a mark lost only money, a lot of times he'd keep quiet about it, rather than go public and look like a fucking idiot. But if he got hurt, more times than not he'd go to the cops.

"You with me, Lime Rickey?" T.G. snapped. "You're off in your own fucking world."

"Just thinking."

"Ah, thinking. Good. He's thinking. 'Bout your altar bitch?"

Ricky mimicked jerking off. Putting himself down again. Wondered why he did that. He glanced at the tourist. The man was whispering to the bartender, who caught Ricky's eye and lifted his head. Ricky pushed back from T.G.'s table and walked to the bar, his boots making loud clonks on the wooden floor.

"Whassup?"

"This guy's from out of town."

The tourist looked at Ricky once, then down at the floor.

"No shit." Ricky rolled his eyes at the bartender.

"Iowa," the man said.

Where the fuck was Iowa? Ricky'd come close to finishing high school and had done okay in some subjects, but geography had bored him crazy and he never paid any attention in class.

The bartender said, "He was telling me he's in town for a conference at Javits."

Him and the ferret molesters . . .

"And . . ." the bartender's voice faded as he glanced at the tourist. "Well, why don't *you* tell him?"

The man took another gulp of his wine. Ricky looked at his hand. Not only a Rolex, but a gold pinky ring with a big honking diamond in it.

"Yeah, why don't you tell me?"

The tourist did—in a halting whisper.

Ricky listened to his words. When the old guy was through, Ricky smiled and said, "This is your lucky day, mister."

Thinking: Mine too.

* * *

A half hour later, Ricky and the tourist from Iowa were standing in the grimy lobby of the Bradford Arms, next to a warehouse at Eleventh Avenue and 50th Street.

Ricky was making introductions. "This's Darla."

"Hello, Darla."

A gold tooth shone like a star out of Darla's big smile. "How you doing, honey? What's yo' name?"

"Uhm, Jack."

Ricky sensed he'd nearly made up "John" instead, which would've been pretty funny, under the circumstances.

"Nice to meet you, Jack." Darla, whose real name was Sha'quette Greeley, was six feet tall, beautiful, and built like a runway model. She'd also been a man until three years ago. The tourist from Iowa didn't catch on to this, or maybe he did and it turned him on. Anyway, his gaze was lapping her body like a tongue.

Jack checked them in, paying for three hours in advance.

Three hours? thought Ricky. An old fart like this? God bless him.

"Y'all have fun now," Ricky said, falling into a redneck accent. He'd decided that Iowa was probably somewhere in the south.

Detective Robert Schaeffer could've been the host on one of those FOX or A&E cop shows. He was tall, silver-haired, good-looking, maybe a bit long in the face. He'd been an NYPD detective for nearly twenty years.

Schaeffer and his partner were walking down a filthy hallway that stank of sweat and Lysol. The partner pointed to a door, whispering, "That's it." He pulled out what looked like an electronic stethoscope and placed the sensor over the scabby wood.

"Hear anything?" Schaeffer asked, also in a soft voice.

Joey Bernbaum, the partner, nodded slowly, holding up a finger. Meaning wait.

And then a nod. "Go."

Schaeffer pulled a master key out of his pocket, and, drawing his gun, unlocked the door and pushed inside.

"Police! Nobody move!"

Bernbaum followed, his own automatic in hand.

The faces of the two people inside registered identical expressions of shock at the abrupt entry, though it was only in the face of the pudgy middle-aged white man, sitting shirtless on the bed, that the shock turned instantly to horror and dismay. He had a Marine Corps tattoo on his fat upper arm and had probably been pretty tough in his day, but now his narrow, pale shoulders slumped and he looked like he was going to cry. "No, no, no . . ."

"Oh, fuck," Darla said.

"Stay right where you are, sweetheart. Be quiet."

"How the fuck you find me? That little prick downstairs at the desk, he dime me? I know it. I'ma pee on that boy next time I see him. I'ma—"

"You're not going to do anything but shut up," Bernbaum snapped. In a ghetto accent he added a sarcastic, "Yo, got that, girlfriend?"

"Man oh man." Darla tried to wither him with a gaze. He just laughed and cuffed her.

Schaeffer put his gun away and said to the man, "Let me see some ID."

"Oh, please, officer, look, I didn't—"

"Some ID?" Schaeffer said. He was polite, like always. When you had a badge in your pocket and a big fucking pistol on your hip, you could afford to be civil.

The man dug his thick wallet out of his slacks and handed it to the officer, who read the license. "Mr. Shelby, this your current address? In Des Moines?"

In a quivering voice, he said, "Yessir."

"All right, well, you're under arrest for solicitation of prostitution." He took his cuffs out of their holder.

"I didn't do anything illegal, really. It was just . . . It was only a date."

"Really? Then what's this?" The detective picked up a stack of money sitting on the cockeyed nightstand. Four hundred bucks.

"I—I just thought . . ."

The old guy's mind was working fast, that was obvious. Schaeffer wondered what excuse he'd come up with. He'd heard them all.

"Just to get some food and something to drink."

That was a new one. Schaeffer tried not to laugh. You spend four hundred bucks on food and booze in this neighborhood, you could afford a block party big enough for fifty Darlas.

"He pay you to have sex?" Schaeffer asked Darla.

She grimaced.

"You lie, baby, you know what'll happen to you. You're honest with me, I'll put in a word."

"You a prick too," she snapped. "All right, he pay me to do a round-the-world."

"No . . ." Shelby protested for a moment but then he gave up and slumped even lower. "Oh, Christ, what'm I gonna do? This'll kill my wife . . . and my kids . . ." He looked up with panicked eyes. "Will I have to go to jail?"

"That's up to the prosecutor and the judge."

"Why the hell'd I do this?" he moaned.

Schaeffer looked him over carefully. After a long moment he said, "Take her downstairs."

Darla snapped, "Yo, you fat fuck, keep yo' motherfuckin' hands offa me."

Bernbaum laughed again. "This mean you ain't my girlfriend no more?" He gripped her by the arm and led her outside. The door swung shut.

"Look, detective, it's not like I robbed anybody. It was harmless. You know, victimless."

"It's still a crime. And don't you know about AIDS, hepatitis?"

Shelby looked down again. He nodded. "Yessir," he whispered.

Still holding the cuffs, Schaeffer eyed the man carefully. He sat down on a creaky chair. "How often you get to town?"

"To New York?"

"Yeah."

"Once a year, if I've got a conference or meeting. I always enjoy it. You know what they say, 'It's a nice place to visit.'" His voice faded, maybe thinking that the rest of that old saw—"but you wouldn't want to live there"—would insult the cop.

Schaeffer asked, "So, you got a conference now?" He pulled the badge out of the man's pocket, read it.

"Yessir, it's our annual trade show. At the Javits. Outdoor furniture manufacturers."

"That's your line?"

"I have a wholesale business in Iowa."

"Yeah? Successful?"

"Number one in the state. Actually, in the whole region." He said this sadly, not proudly, probably thinking of how many customers he'd lose when word got out about his arrest.

Schaeffer nodded slowly. Finally he put the handcuffs away.

Shelby's eyes narrowed, watching this.

"You ever done anything like this before?"

A hesitation. He decided not to lie. "I have. Yessir."

"But I get a feeling you're not going to again."

"Never. I promise you. I've learned my lesson."

There was a long pause.

"Stand up."

Shelby blinked, then did what he was told. He frowned as the cop patted down his trousers and jacket. With the guy not wearing a shirt, Schaeffer was ninety-nine percent sure the man was legit, but had to make absolutely certain there were no wires.

The detective nodded toward the chair and Shelby sat down. The businessman's eyes revealed that he now had an inkling of what was happening.

"I have a proposition for you," Schaeffer said.

"Proposition?"

The cop nodded. "Okay. I'm convinced you're not going to do this again."

"Never."

"I could let you go with a warning. But the problem is, the situation got called in."

"Called in?"

"A vice cop on the street happened to see you go into the hotel with Darla—we know all about her. He reported it and they sent me out. There's paperwork on the incident."

"My name?"

"No, just a John Doe at this point. But there *is* a report. I could make it go away but it'd take some work and it'd be a risk."

Shelby sighed, nodding with a grimace, and opened the bidding.

It wasn't much of an auction. Shelby kept throwing out numbers and Schaeffer kept lifting his thumb, more, more . . . Finally, when the shaken man hit $150,000, Schaeffer nodded.

"Christ."

When T.G. and Ricky Kelleher had called to say that they'd found a tourist to scam, Ricky told him the mark could go six figures. That was so far out of those stupid micks' league that Schaeffer had to laugh. But sure enough, he had to give the punk credit for picking out a mark with big bucks.

In a defeated voice Shelby asked, "Can I give you a check?"

Schaeffer laughed.

"Okay, okay . . . but I'll need a few hours."

"Tonight. Eight." They arranged a place to meet. "I'll keep your driver's license. And the evidence." He picked up the cash on the table. "You try to skip, I'll put out an arrest warrant and send that to Des Moines too. They'll extradite you and *then* it'll be a serious felony. You'll do real time."

"Oh, no, sir. I'll get the money. Every penny." Shelby hurriedly dressed.

"Go out by the service door in back. I don't know where the vice cop is."

The tourist nodded and scurried out of the room.

In the lobby by the elevator the detective found Bernbaum and Darla sharing a smoke.

"Where my money?" the hooker demanded.

Schaeffer handed her two hundred of the confiscated cash. He and Bernbaum split the rest, a hundred fifty for Schaeffer, fifty for his partner.

"You gonna take the afternoon off, girlfriend?" Bernbaum asked Darla.

"Me? Hell no, I gots to work." She glanced at the money Schaeffer'd given her. "Least till you assholes start paying me fo' not fuckin' same as I make *fo' fuckin'*."

Schaeffer pushed into Mack's bar, an abrupt entrance that changed the course of at least half the conversations going on inside real fast. He was a crooked cop, sure, but he was still a cop, and the talk immediately shifted from deals, scams, and drugs to sports, women, and jobs. Schaeffer laughed and strode across the room. He dropped into an empty chair at the scarred table, muttered to T.G., "Get me a beer." Schaeffer being about the only one in the universe who could get away with that.

When the brew came he tipped the glass to Ricky. "You caught us a good one. He agreed to a hundred fifty."

"No shit," T.G. said, cocking a red eyebrow. The split was Schaeffer got half and then Ricky and T.G. divided the rest equally. "Where's he getting it from?"

"I dunno. His problem."

Ricky squinted. "Wait. I want the watch too."

"Watch?"

"The old guy. He had a Rolex. I want it."

At home Schaeffer had a dozen Rolexes he'd taken off marks and suspects over the years. He didn't need another one. "You want the watch, he'll give up the watch. All he cares about is making sure his wife and his corn-pone customers don't find out what he was up to."

"What's corn-pone?" Ricky asked.

"Hold on," T.G. snarled. "Anybody gets the watch, it's me."

"No way. I saw it first. It was me who picked him—"

"My watch," the fat Irishman interrupted. "Maybe he's got a money clip or something you can have. But I get the fucking Rolex."

"Nobody has money clips," Ricky argued. "I don't even want a fucking money clip."

"Listen, little Lime Rickey," T.G. muttered. "It's mine. Read my lips."

"Jesus, you two are like kids," Schaeffer said, swilling the beer. "He'll meet us across the street from Pier 46 at eight tonight." The three men had done this same scam, or variations on it, for a couple of years now but still didn't trust each other. The deal was they all went together to collect the payoff.

Schaeffer drained the beer. "See you boys then."

After the detective was gone they watched the game for a few minutes, with T.G. bullying some guys to place bets, even though it was in the fourth quarter and there was no way Chicago could come back. Finally, Ricky said, "I'm going out for a while."

"What, now I'm your fucking babysitter? You want to go, go." Though he still made it sound like Ricky was a complete idiot for missing the end of a game that only had eight minutes to run.

Just as Ricky got to the door, T.G. called in a loud voice, "Hey, Lime Rickey, my Rolex? Is it gold?"

Just to be a prick.

Bob Schaeffer had walked a beat in his youth. He'd investigated a hundred felonies, he'd run a thousand scams in Manhattan and Brooklyn. All of which meant that he'd learned how to stay alive on the streets.

Now, he sensed a threat.

He was on his way to score some coke from a kid who operated out of a newsstand at Ninth and 55th, and he realized he'd been hearing the same footsteps for the past five or six minutes. A weird scraping. Somebody was tailing him. He paused to light a cigarette in a doorway and checked out the reflection in a storefront window. Sure enough, he saw a man in a cheap gray suit, wearing gloves, about thirty feet behind him. The guy paused for a moment and pretended to look into a store window.

Schaeffer didn't recognize the guy. He'd made a lot of enemies over the years. The fact he was a cop gave him some protection—it's risky to gun down even a crooked one—but there were plenty of nutjobs out there.

Walking on. The owner of the scraping shoes continued his tail. A glance in the rearview mirror of a car parked nearby told him the man was getting closer, but his hands were at his side, not going for a weapon. Schaeffer pulled out his cell phone and pretended to make a call, to give himself an excuse to slow up and not make the guy suspicious. His other hand slipped inside his jacket and touched the grip of his chrome-plated Sig Sauer 9mm automatic pistol.

This time the guy didn't slow up.

Schaeffer started to draw.

Then: "Detective, could you hang up the phone, please?"

Schaeffer turned, blinked. The pursuer was holding up a gold NYPD shield.

The fuck is this? Schaeffer thought. He relaxed, but not much. Snapped the phone closed and dropped it into his pocket. Let go of his weapon.

"Who're you?"

The man, eyeing Schaeffer coldly, let him get a look at the ID card next to the shield.

Schaeffer thought: Fuck me. The guy was from the department's Internal Affairs Division—the boys that tracked down corrupt cops.

Still Schaeffer kept on the offensive. "What're you doing following me?"

"I'd like to ask you a few questions."

"What's this all about?"

"An investigation we're conducting."

"Hello," Schaeffer said sarcastically. "I sort of figured that out. Give me some fucking details."

"We're looking into your connection with certain individuals."

"'Certain individuals.' You know, not all cops have to talk like cops."

No response.

Schaeffer shrugged. "I have 'connections' with a lotta people. Maybe you're thinking of my snitches. I hang with 'em. They feed me good information."

"Yeah, well, we're thinking there might be other things they feed you. Some *valuable* things." He glanced at Schaeffer's hip. "I'm going to ask you for your weapon."

"Fuck that."

"I'm trying to keep it low-key. But you don't cooperate, I'll call it in and we'll take you downtown. Then everything'll all be public."

Finally Schaeffer understood. It was a shakedown—only this time he was on the receiving end. And he was getting scammed by Internal Affairs, no less. This was almost fucking funny, IAD on the take too.

Schaeffer gave up his gun.

"Let's go talk in private."

How much was this going to cost him? he wondered.

The IAD cop nodded toward the Hudson River. "That way."

"Talk to me," Schaeffer said. "I got a right to know what this's all about. If somebody told you I'm on the take, that's bullshit. Whoever said it's working some angle." He wasn't as hot as he sounded; this was all part of the negotiating.

The IAD cop said only, "Keep walking. Up there." He pulled out a cigarette and lit it. Offered one to Schaeffer. He took it and the guy lit it for him.

Then Schaeffer froze. He blinked in shock, staring at the matches. The name on them was *McDougall's Tavern*. The official name of Mack's—T.G.'s hangout. He glanced at the guy's eyes, which went wide at his mistake. Christ, he was no cop. The ID and badge were fake. He was a hit man, working for T.G., who was going to clip him and collect the whole hundred fifty Gs from the tourist.

"Fuck," the phony cop muttered. He yanked a revolver out of his pocket, then shoved Schaeffer into a nearby alley.

"Listen, buddy," Schaeffer whispered, "I've got some good bucks. Whatever you're being paid, I'll—"

"Shut up." In his gloved hands, the guy exchanged his gun for Schaeffer's own pistol and pushed the big chrome piece into the detective's neck. Then the fake cop pulled a piece of paper out of his pocket and stuffed it into the detective's jacket. He leaned forward and whispered, "Here's the message, asshole: For two years T.G.'s been setting up everything, doing all the work, and you take half the money. You've fucked with the wrong man."

"That's bullshit," Schaeffer cried desperately. "He needs me! He couldn't do it without a cop! Please—"

"So long—" He lifted the gun to Schaeffer's temple.

"Don't do it! Please, man, no!"

A scream sounded from the mouth of the alley. "Oh my god!" A middle-aged woman stood twenty feet away, staring at the man with the pistol. Her hands were to her mouth. "Somebody call the police!"

The hit man's attention was on the woman. Schaeffer shoved him into a brick wall. Before he could recover and shoot, the detective sprinted fast down the alley.

He heard the man shout, "Goddamn it!" and start after him. But Hell's Kitchen was Bob Schaeffer's hunting ground, and in five minutes the detective had raced through dozens of alleys and side streets and lost the killer.

Once again on the street, he paused and pulled his backup gun out of his ankle holster, slipped it into his pocket. He felt the crinkle of paper—what the guy had planted on him. It was a fake suicide note, Schaeffer confessing that he'd been on the take for years and he couldn't handle the guilt anymore. He had to end it all.

Well, he thought, that was partly right.

One thing was fucking well about to end.

Smoking, staying in the shadows of an alley, Schaeffer had to wait outside Mack's for fifteen minutes before T.G. Reilly emerged. The big man, moving like a lumbering bear, was by himself. He looked around, not seeing the cop, and turned west.

Schaeffer gave him half a block and then followed.

He kept his distance, but when the street was deserted he pulled on gloves and fished into his pocket for the pistol he'd just gotten from his desk. He'd bought it on the street years ago—a cold gun, one with no registration number stamped on the frame. Gripping the weapon, he moved up fast behind the big Irishman.

The mistake a lot of shooters make during a clip is they feel they've gotta talk to their vic. Schaeffer remembered some old Western where this kid tracks down the gunslinger who killed his father. The kid's holding a gun on him and explaining why he's about to die, you killed my father, yadda, yadda, yadda, and the gunslinger gets this bored look on his face, pulls out a hidden gun, and blows the kid away. He looks down at the body and says, "You gonna talk, talk. You gonna shoot, shoot."

Which is just what Robert Schaeffer did now.

T.G. must've heard something. He started to turn. But before he even caught sight of the detective, Schaeffer parked two rounds in the back of the fat man's head. He dropped like a bag of sand. The cop tossed the gun on the sidewalk—he'd never touched it with his bare hands—and, keeping his head down, walked right past T.G.'s body, hit Tenth Avenue, and turned north.

You gonna shoot, shoot.

Amen . . .

It took only one glance.

Looking into Ricky Kelleher's eyes, Schaeffer decided he wasn't in on the attempted hit.

The small goofy guy, with dirty hair and a cocky face, strode up to the spot where Schaeffer was leaning against a wall, hand inside his coat, near his new automatic. But the loser didn't blink, didn't show the least surprise that the cop was still alive. The detective had interviewed suspects for years and he now concluded that the asshole knew nothing about T.G.'s plan.

Ricky nodded, "Hey." Looking around, asked, "So where's T.G.? He said he'd be here early."

Frowning, Schaeffer asked, "Didn't you hear?"

"Hear what?"

"Damn, you didn't. Somebody clipped him."

"T.G.?"

"Yep."

Ricky just stared and shook his head. "No fucking way. I didn't hear shit about it."

"Just happened."

"Christ almighty," the little man whispered. "Who did it?"

"Nobody knows yet."

"Maybe that nigger."

"Who?"

"Nigger from Buffalo. Or Albany. I don't know." Ricky then whispered, "Dead. I can't believe it. Anybody else in the crew?"

"Just him, I think."

Schaeffer studied the scrawny guy. Well, yeah, he *did* look like he couldn't believe it. But, truth was, he didn't look *upset*. Which made sense. T.G. was hardly Ricky's buddy; he was a drunk loser bully.

Besides, in Hell's Kitchen the living tended to forget about the dead before their bodies were cold.

Like he was proving this point, Ricky said, "So how's this going to affect our, you know, arrangement?"

"Not at all, far as I'm concerned."

"I'm going to want more."

"I can go a third."

"Fuck a third. I want half."

"No can do. It's riskier for me now."

"Riskier? Why?"

"There'll be an investigation. Somebody might turn up something at T.G.'s with my name on it. I'll have to grease more palms." Schaeffer shrugged. "Or you can find yourself another cop to work with."

As if the Yellow Pages had a section, *Cops, Corrupt.*

The detective added, "Give it a few months. After things calm down, I can go up a few more points then."

"To forty?"

"Yeah, to forty."

The little man asked, "Can I have the Rolex?"

"The guy's? Tonight?"

"Yeah."

"You really want it?"

"Yeah."

"Okay, it's yours."

Ricky looked out over the river. It seemed to Schaeffer that a faint smile crossed his face.

They stood in silence for a few minutes and, right on time, the tourist, Shelby, showed up. He was looking terrified and hurt and angry, which is a fucking tricky combination to get onto your face all at one time.

"I've got it," he whispered. There was nothing in his hands—no briefcase or bag—but Schaeffer had been taking kickbacks and bribes for so long that he knew a lot of money can fit into a very small envelope.

Which is just what Shelby now produced. The grim-faced tourist slipped it to Schaeffer, who counted the bills carefully.

"The watch too." Ricky pointed eagerly to the man's wrist.

"My watch?" Shelby hesitated and, grimacing, handed it to the skinny man.

Schaeffer gave the tourist his driver's license back. He pocketed it fast and then hurried east, undoubtedly looking for a taxi that'd take him straight to the airport.

The detective laughed to himself. So, maybe New York ain't such a nice place to visit, after all.

The men split the money. Ricky slipped the Rolex on his wrist but the metal band was too big and it dangled comically. "I'll get it adjusted," he said, putting the watch into his pocket. "They can shorten the bands, you know. It's no big deal."

They decided to have a drink to celebrate and Ricky suggested Hanny's since he had to meet somebody over there.

As they walked along the avenue, blue-gray in the evening light, Ricky glanced at the placid Hudson River. "Check it out."

A large yacht eased south in the dark water.

"Sweet," Schaeffer said, admiring the beautiful lines of the vessel.

Ricky asked, "How come you didn't want in?"

"In?"

"The boat deal."

"Huh?"

"That T.G. told you about. He said you were going to pass."

"What the fuck're you talking about?"

"The boat thing. With that guy from Florida."

"He never said anything to me about it."

"That prick." Ricky shook his head. "Was a few days ago. This guy hangs at Hanny's? He's who I'm gonna meet. He's got connections down in Florida. His crew perps these confiscated boats before they get logged in at the impound dock."

"DEA?"

"Yeah. And Coast Guard."

Schaeffer nodded, impressed at the plan. "They disappear *before* they're logged. That's some smart shit."

"I'm thinking about getting one. He tells me I pay him, like, twenty Gs and I end up with a boat worth three times that. I thought you'd be interested."

"Yeah, I'd be interested." Bob Schaeffer had a couple of small boats. Had always wanted a really nice one. He asked, "He got anything bigger?"

"Think he just sold a fifty-footer. I seen it down in Battery Park. It was sweet."

"Fifty feet? That's a million-dollar boat."

"He said it only cost his guy two hundred or something like that."

"Jesus. That asshole, T.G. He never said a word to me." Schaeffer at least felt some consolation that the punk wouldn't be saying *anything* to *anyone* from now on.

They walked into Hanrahan's. Like usual, the place was nearly deserted. Ricky was looking around. The boat guy apparently wasn't here yet.

They ordered boilermakers. Clinked glasses, drank.

Ricky was telling the old bartender about T.G. getting killed, when Schaeffer's cell phone rang.

"Schaeffer here."

"This's Malone from Homicide. You heard about the T.G. Reilly hit?"

"Yeah. What's up with it? Any leads?" Heart pounding fast, Schaeffer lowered his head and listened real carefully.

"Not many. But we heard something and we're hoping you can help us out. You know the neighborhood, right?"

"Pretty good."

"Looks like one of T.G.'s boys was running a scam. Involved some tall paper. Six figures. We don't know if it had anything to do with the clip, but we want to talk to him. Name of Ricky Kelleher. You know him?"

Schaeffer glanced at Ricky, five feet away. He said into the phone, "Not sure. What's the scam?"

"This Kelleher was working with somebody from Florida. They came up with a pretty slick plan. They sell some loser a confiscated boat, only what happens is, there is no boat. It's all a setup. Then when it's time to deliver, they tell the poor asshole that the feds just raided 'em. He better forget about his money, shut up, and go to ground."

That little fucking prick . . . Schaeffer's hand began shaking with anger as he stared at Ricky. He told the Homicide cop, "Haven't seen him for a while. But I'll ask around."

"Thanks."

He disconnected and walked up to Ricky, who was working on his second beer.

"You know when that guy's going to get here?" Schaeffer asked casually. "The boat guy?"

"Should be anytime," the punk said.

Schaeffer nodded, drank some of his own beer. Then he lowered his head, whispered, "That call I just got? Don't know if you're interested but it was my supplier. He just got a shipment from Mexico. He's gonna meet me in the alley in a few minutes. It's some really fine shit. He'll give it to us for cost. You interested?"

"Fuck yes," the little man said.

The men pushed out the back door into the alley. Letting Ricky precede him, Schaeffer reminded himself that after he'd strangled the punk to death, he'd have to be sure to take the rest of the bribe money out of his pocket.

Oh, and the watch too. The detective decided that you really couldn't have too many Rolexes after all.

Detective Robert Schaeffer was enjoying a grande mocha outside the Starbucks on Ninth Avenue. He was sitting in a metal chair, none too comfortable, and he wondered if it was the type that outdoor furniture king Shelby distributed to his fellow hicks.

"Hey there," a man's voice said to him.

Schaeffer glanced over at a guy sitting down at the table next to him. He was vaguely familiar and even though the cop didn't exactly recognize him, he smiled a greeting.

Then the realization hit him like ice water and he gasped. It was the fake Internal Affairs detective, the guy T.G. had hired to clip him.

Christ!

The man's right hand was inside a paper bag, where there'd be a pistol, of course.

Schaeffer froze.

"Relax," the guy said, laughing at the cop's expression. "Everything's cool." He extracted his hand from the bag. No gun. He was holding a raisin scone. He took a bite. "I'm not who you think I am."

"Then who the fuck are you?"

"You don't need my name. I'm a private eye. That'll do. Now listen, we've got a business proposition for you." The PI looked up and waved. To Schaeffer he said, "I want to introduce you to some folks."

A middle-aged couple, also carrying coffee, walked outside. In shock, Schaeffer realized that the man was Shelby, the tourist they'd scammed a few days ago. The woman with him seemed familiar too. But he couldn't place her.

"Detective," the man said with a cold smile.

The woman's gaze was chill too, but no smile was involved.

"Whatta you want?" the cop snapped to the private eye.

"I'll let them explain that." He took a large bite of scone.

Shelby's eyes locked onto Schaeffer's face with a ballsy confidence that was a lot different from the timid, defeated look he'd had in the cheap hotel, sitting next to Darla, the used-to-be-a-guy hooker. "Detective, here's the deal: A few months ago my son was on vacation here with some friends from college. He was dancing in a club near Broadway and your associates T.G. Reilly and Ricky Kelleher slipped some drugs into his pocket. Then you came in and busted him for possession. Just like with me, you set him up and told him you'd let him go if he paid you off. Only Michael decided you weren't going to get away with it. He took a swing at you and was going to call 911. But you and T.G. Reilly dragged him into the alley and beat him so badly he's got permanent brain damage and is going to be in therapy for years."

Schaeffer remembered the college kid, yeah. It'd been a bad beating. But he said, "I don't know what you're—"

"Shhhhh," the private eye said. "The Shelbys hired me to find out what happened to their son. I've spent two months in Hell's Kitchen, learning everything there is to know about you and those two pricks you worked with." A nod toward the tourist. "Back to you." The PI ate some more scone.

The husband said, "We decided you were going to pay for what you did. Only we couldn't go to the police—who knew how many of them were working with you? So my wife and I and our other son—Michael's brother—came up with an idea. We decided to let you assholes do the work for us; you were going to double-cross each other."

"This is bullshit. You—"

The woman snapped, "Shut up and listen." She explained: They set up a sting in Hanny's bar. The private eye pretended to be a scam artist from Florida selling stolen boats and their older son played a young guy from Jersey who'd been duped out of his money. This got Ricky's attention, and he talked his way into the phony boat scam. Staring at Schaeffer, she said, "We knew you liked boats, so it made sense that Ricky'd try to set you up."

The husband added, "Only we needed some serious cash on the table, a bunch of it—to give you losers some real incentive to betray each other."

So he went to T.G.'s hangout and asked about a hooker, figuring that the three of them would set up an extortion scam.

He chuckled. "I kept *hoping* you'd keep raising the bidding when you were blackmailing me. I wanted at least six figures in the pot."

T.G. was their first target. That afternoon the private eye pretended to be a hit man hired by T.G. to kill Schaeffer so he'd get all the money.

"You!" the detective whispered, staring at the wife. "You're the woman who screamed."

Shelby said, "We needed to give you the chance to escape—so you'd go straight to T.G.'s place and take care of him."

Oh lord. The hit, the fake Internal Affairs cop . . . It was all a setup!

"Then Ricky took you to Hanrahan's, where he was going to introduce you to the boat dealer from Florida."

The private eye wiped his mouth and leaned froward. "*Hello,*" he said in a deeper voice. "*This's Malone from Homicide.*"

"Oh fuck," Schaeffer spat out. "You let me know that Ricky'd set me up. So . . ." His voice faded.

The PI whispered, "You'd take care of him too."

The cold smile on his face again, Shelby said, "Two perps down. Now we just have the last one. You."

"What're you going to do?" the cop whispered.

The wife said, "Our son's got to have years of therapy. He'll never recover completely."

Schaeffer shook his head. "You've got evidence, right?"

"Oh, you bet. Our older son was outside of Mack's waiting for you when you went there to get T.G. We've got real nice footage of you shooting him. Two in the head. Real nasty."

"And the sequel," the private eye said. "In the alley behind Hanrahan's. Where you strangled Ricky." He added, "Oh, and we've got the license number of the truck that came to get Ricky's body in the dumpster. We followed it to Jersey. We can implicate a bunch of very unpleasant people, who aren't going to be happy they've been fingered because of you."

"And, in case you haven't guessed," Shelby said, "we made three copies of the tape and they're sitting in three different lawyers' office safes. Anything happens to any one of us, and off they go to Police Plaza."

"You're as good as murderers yourself," Schaeffer muttered. "You used me to kill two people."

Shelby laughed. "*Semper Fi* . . . I'm a former Marine and I've been in two wars. Killing vermin like you doesn't bother me one bit."

"All right," the cop said in a disgusted grumble, "what do you want?"

"You've got the vacation house on Fire Island, you've got two boats moored in Oyster Bay, you've got—"

"I don't need a fucking inventory. I need a number."

"Basically your entire net worth. Eight hundred sixty thousand dollars. Plus my hundred fifty back . . . And I want it in the next week. Oh, and you pay his bill too." Shelby nodded toward the private eye.

"I'm good," the man said. "But very expensive." He finished the scone and brushed the crumbs onto the sidewalk.

Shelby leaned forward. "One more thing: my watch."

Schaeffer stripped off the Rolex and tossed it to Shelby.

The couple rose. "So long, detective," the tourist said.

"Love to stay and talk," Mrs. Shelby added, "but we're going to see some sights. And then we're going for a carriage ride in Central Park before dinner." She paused and looked down at the cop. "I just love it here. It's true what they say, you know. New York really *is* a nice place to visit."

ABOUT THE CONTRIBUTORS

Drew Reilly

MEGAN ABBOTT is the Edgar Award–winning author of six novels, including *Dare Me*, *The End of Everything*, and *Bury Me Deep*. Her writing has appeared in *Detroit Noir*, *Queens Noir*, *Phoenix Noir*, the *New York Times*, and the *Los Angeles Times Magazine*. She is the author of *The Street Was Mine: White Masculinity and Urban Space in Hardboiled Fiction and Film Noir* and editor of *A Hell of a Woman*, a female crime fiction anthology. She has been nominated for various awards, including the Steel Dagger, the *Los Angeles Times* Book Prize, and the Pushcart Prize.

Arnold Lee

LAWRENCE BLOCK was born in Martin Ehrengraf's Buffalo, and has spent most of his life in New York City, where the greater portion of his fiction is set. For Akashic Books, he has edited *Manhattan Noir* and its sequel, cunningly titled *Manhattan Noir 2*. He has written a great many books and won an impressive number of awards, yet remains a humble and self-effacing fellow, although this short biography might lead you to think otherwise.

TIM BRODERICK is the creator of a graphic novel series featuring David Diangelo that originated as a webcomic on the Internet. He and his wife live in Chicago with their twin daughters, and all the women in the house are far smarter than he. He's currently president of the Midwest chapter of Mystery Writers of America and is working on his fourth book, *Children of the Revolution*, which can be read for free at timbroderick.net.

Martin Benjamin

JOSEPH BRUCHAC'S work, like the story in this collection, often reflects his Abenaki Indian ancestry and his deep interest in the history of the Adirondack Mountain region of upstate New York, where he was born—and still resides (in the house where his grandparents raised him).

Jerry Bauer

JEROME CHARYN'S most recent novels are *The Secret Life of Emily Dickinson* (2010) and *Under the Eye of God* (2012), the eleventh of his Isaac Sidel novels, which are being made into an animated television series. He is currently working on a novel about Abraham Lincoln and a study of Emily Dickinson.

Mary Reagan

LEE CHILD was fired and on the dole when he hatched a harebrained scheme to write a best-selling novel, thus saving his family from ruin. *Killing Floor* went on to win worldwide acclaim. His series hero, Jack Reacher, besides being fictional, is a kind-hearted soul who allows Child lots of spare time for reading, listening to music, and the Yankees. Visit www.leechild.com for information about the novels, short stories, and the movie *Jack Reacher* starring Tom Cruise.

REED FARREL COLEMAN, author of fifteen novels, has been called a "hard-boiled poet" by NPR's Maureen Corrigan and the "noir poet laureate" in the *Huffington Post*. He is the three-time winner of the Shamus Award for Best PI Novel of the Year and is a two-time Edgar Award nominee. He has also received the Macavity, Barry, and Anthony awards. Coleman is an adjunct professor of English at Hofstra University, and lives with his family on Long Island.

MICHAEL CONNELLY is the best-selling author of twenty-five novels and one work of nonfiction. With over forty-five million copies of his books sold worldwide and translated into thirty-six foreign languages, he is one of the most successful writers working today. In 2002, Clint Eastwood directed and starred in the movie adaptation of Connelly's 1998 novel *Blood Work*. In March 2011, the movie adaptation of his novel *The Lincoln Lawyer* hit theaters worldwide starring Matthew McConaughey as Mickey Haller. Connelly spends his time in California and Florida.

JEFFERY DEAVER, a former journalist, folk singer, and attorney, is an international number-one best-selling author. His novels have appeared on best-seller lists around the world, including the *New York Times*, the *Times of London*, Italy's *Corriere della Sera*, the *Sydney Morning Herald*, and the *Los Angeles Times*. His books are sold in 150 countries and have been translated into twenty-five languages. His most recent novels are *XO*, a Kathryn Dance thriller, for which he wrote an album of country-western songs; and *Carte Blanche*, the latest James Bond continuation novel.

BARBARA DEMARCO-BARRETT is author of *Pen on Fire: A Busy Woman's Guide to Igniting the Writer Within*. She has worked as an auto-parts runner, baker, crisis intervention counselor, and more. Her nonfiction has been published in *Orange Coast*, *Westways*, the *Los Angeles Times*, *The Writer*, *Writer's Digest*, and *Poets & Writers*. She teaches "Jumpstart Your Writing" for Gotham Writers' Workshop and hosts *Writers on Writing* on KUCI-FM. For more information, visit www.penonfire.com.

ELYSSA EAST is the author of the *Boston Globe* best-selling book, *Dogtown: Death and Enchantment in a New England Ghost Town*. A *New York Times* Editors' Choice selection, *Dogtown* won the 2010 L.L. Winship/PEN New England Award for best work of nonfiction and was named a "Must-Read Book" by the Massachusetts Book Awards. East's essays and reviews have been published in the *New York Times*, *San Francisco Chronicle*, *Boston Globe*, *Kansas City Star*, and other publications nationwide.

MAGGIE ESTEP has published seven books and recorded two spoken-word CDs. She has been a horse groom and a go-go dancer and is a pit bull advocate. Estep's books have been translated into four languages, optioned for film, and frequently stolen from libraries. She is presently working on two books and a TV show. Her short story included in this volume was adapted into a novel by the same name: *Alice Fantastic*. Estep lives in Hudson, New York.

Gianluca Gentiini

JONATHAN SAFRAN FOER is the author of the award-winning and best-selling novels *Everything Is Illuminated* and *Extremely Loud and Incredibly Close*, as well as two works of nonfiction: *Eating Animals* and *The New American Haggadah*. His books have been published in over thirty languages, and he was included in *Granta*'s "Best of Young American Novelists" issue as well as the *New Yorker*'s "20 under 40" list of the best young writers in the US.

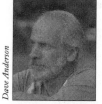

Dave Anderson

J. MALCOLM GARCIA is the author of *The Khaarijee: A Chronicle of Friendship and War in Kabul* and *Riding through Katrina with the Red Baron's Ghost*. His articles have been featured in *Best American Travel Writing* and *Best American Nonrequired Reading*.

Maggie Evans Silverstein

JAMES W. HALL is the author of four books of poetry, a collection of short stories, a collection of essays, and seventeen novels. His most recent work is *Hit Lit*, a nonfiction examination of the dozen most successful best sellers of the twentieth century and the common features they share. He was a Fulbright professor of literature in Spain and a professor of literature and writing at Florida International University for thirty-five years. Hall has won both the Edgar and Shamus awards. He and his wife Evelyn and their three dogs divide their time between South Florida and the mountains of western North Carolina.

Peter Foley

PETE HAMILL is a veteran journalist and novelist. He is the author of seventeen books, including the best-selling *A Drinking Life* and a new story collection, *The Christmas Kid*. His nine novels include the *New York Times* best sellers *Snow in August, Tabloid City*, and *Forever*. He has covered wars in Vietnam, Nicaragua, Lebanon, and Northern Ireland, as well as the domestic disturbances in American cities in the 1960s. In addition to his many years as a columnist, he has served as editor in chief of the *New York Post* and the *New York Daily News*. He divides his time between New York City and Cuernavaca, Mexico.

Yona Harvey

TERRANCE HAYES is the 2010 recipient of the National Book Award in poetry. His most recent collection is *Lighthead*. His other books are *Wind in a Box, Muscular Music*, and *Hip Logic*. His honors include four *Best American Poetry* selections, a Whiting Writers' Award, a National Endowment for the Arts Fellowship, and a Guggenheim Fellowship. He is a professor of creative writing at Carnegie Mellon University and lives in Pittsburgh.

Allyson Goudy

KAREN KARBO is the author of three novels, all of which have been named *New York Times* Notable Books of the Year. Her memoir, *The Stuff of Life*, about the last year she spent with her father before his death, won an Oregon Book Award. Her short stories, essays, articles, and reviews have appeared in *Elle, Vogue, Esquire, Outside, O, More*, the *New Republic*, the *New York Times*, *Salon*, and other magazines. Karbo is well known for her best-selling Kick Ass Women Series, the most recent of which is *How Georgia Became O'Keeffe*, published in 2011.

BHARTI KIRCHNER is the author of nine books—five critically acclaimed novels and four cookbooks. Her latest novel is *Tulip Season: A Mitra Basu Mystery*. Her essays have appeared in ten anthologies, and she has won numerous awards, including a VCCA (Virginia Center for Creative Arts) Fellowship and two Seattle Arts Commission literature grants.

WILLIAM KENT KRUEGER writes the *New York Times* best-selling Cork O'Connor mystery series, which is set in the north woods of Minnesota. His work has received a number of awards, including the Minnesota Book Award, the Loft-McKnight Fiction Award, the Anthony Award, the Barry Award, and the Friends of American Writers Literary Award. He does all his writing in a St. Paul coffee shop whose identity he prefers to keep secret.

DENNIS LEHANE is the author of the Patrick Kenzie and Angela Gennaro mystery series (*A Drink Before the War; Darkness, Take My Hand; Sacred; Gone, Baby, Gone; Prayers for Rain;* and *Moonlight Mile*), as well as *Coronado* (five stories and a play) and the novels *Mystic River, Shutter Island, The Given Day,* and *Live By Night*. Three of his novels have been made into award-winning films. He edited the best-selling anthology *Boston Noir* and coedited *Boston Noir 2: The Classics* for Akashic Books.

LAURA LIPPMAN has published eighteen novels, a novella, and a book of short stories, and she edited *Baltimore Noir* for Akashic Books. Her work has been nominated for virtually every award open to North American crime writers and has won most of them, including the Edgar, Anthony, Quill, Nero Wolfe, and Agatha awards. Lippman lives in Baltimore and New Orleans.

TIM MCLOUGHLIN is the editor of *Brooklyn Noir* and its companion volumes. His debut novel *Heart of the Old Country* is the basis for the motion picture *The Narrows*, starring Vincent D'Onofrio. His books have been published in seven languages, and his writing has appeared in *New York Quarterly*, the *Huffington Post*, and *Best American Mystery Stories*. He was born and raised in Brooklyn, where he still resides.

JOYCE CAROL OATES, who edited *New Jersey Noir* for Akashic Books, is the author of a number of works of fiction, nonfiction, and poetry, including the novels *Mudwoman, Little Bird of Heaven,* and *Blonde*. Her collections of short fiction include *High Lonesome: New and Selected Short Stories 1966–2006, Black Dahlia & White Rose,* and *The Corn Maiden*. She is the 2011 recipient of the president's National Humanities Medal, the 2012 recipient of the Norman Mailer Prize for Lifetime Achievement, and she won the PEN Center USA Award for Lifetime Achievement.

JOHN O'BRIEN was born in 1960 and grew up in the Cleveland area. He and his wife of thirteen years, Lisa, married in 1979 and eventually settled in Los Angeles. O'Brien published his first critically acclaimed novel, *Leaving Las Vegas*, in 1990. He died of a self-inflicted gunshot wound in April 1994, just weeks after signing over the film rights for *Leaving Las Vegas*. His posthumous publications include *The Assault on Tony's, Stripper Lessons*, and *Better*.

Randy Richardson

BAYO OJIKUTU is the critically acclaimed author of the novels *47th Street Black* and *Free Burning*. His work has won the Washington Prize for Fiction and the Great American Book Award. Ojikutu's short work has appeared in various collections, magazines, and journals. He has been nominated for a Pushcart Prize, and he has been recognized by the African American Arts Alliance for his contribution to literary fiction. Ojikutu and his family reside in Chicago.

Rebecca Lawson

T. JEFFERSON PARKER was born in Los Angeles and has lived his life in Southern California. He is the author of nineteen crime novels, including the Edgar Award–winning *Silent Joe* and *California Girl*. His first book, *Laguna Heat*, was made into an HBO movie. His latest novel is *The Famous and the Dead*. He lives with his family in San Diego County.

Ian Allen

GEORGE PELECANOS is the author of nineteen novels set in and around Washington, DC. He served as a writer and producer on HBO's *The Wire, The Pacific,* and, most recently, *Treme*. He edited both *DC Noir* and *DC Noir 2: The Classics* for Akashic Books.

PIR ROTHENBERG'S work has appeared in *Another Chicago Magazine, Dossier Journal, Harpur Palate, Juked, Makeout Creek, Overtime, Prick of the Spindle, Richmond Noir, River Styx,* and *Zahir*. He is currently pursuing his PhD at Georgia State University.

Ashley Gilbertson

S.J. ROZAN, born and raised in the Bronx, is the award-winning author of thirteen novels and three dozen short stories, and the editor of two anthologies, including *Bronx Noir* for Akashic Books.

LISA SANDLIN was born in the Gulf Coast oil town of Beaumont, Texas. She's the author of *The Famous Thing About Death, Message to the Nurse of Dreams, In the River Province, You Who Make the Sky Bend,* a collaboration with New Mexican santera Catherine Ferguson, and a coeditor of *Times of Sorrow, Times of Grace.* Her work has won numerous awards, including a Pushcart Prize and a Best Book of Fiction from the Texas Institute of Letters. "Phelan's First Case," included in this volume, was a finalist for the 2011 Shamus Award.

JULIE SMITH is the author of more than twenty mystery novels, most set in New Orleans and starring one or the other of her detective heroes, a cop named Skip Langdon and a PI named Talba Wallis. She is also the editor of *New Orleans Noir* for Akashic Books. Her book *New Orleans Mourning* won the Edgar Award for best novel. She has recently published her course on writing novels, *Writing Your Way,* as an e-book. Her digital publishing startup is www.booksBnimble.com.

ASALI SOLOMON is the author of *Get Down: Stories.* Her work has been featured in the anthologies *Philadelphia Noir, Heavy Rotation: Twenty Writers on the Albums that Changed Their Lives,* and *Naked: Black Women Bare All About Their Skin, Hair, Hips, Lips, and Other Parts.* She received a Rona Jaffe Foundation Writers' Award in 2006 and was selected as one of the National Book Foundation's "5 Under 35" in 2007. She is at work on a novel.

DOMENIC STANSBERRY is an award-winning novelist known for his dark, innovative crime novels. His North Beach Mystery Series has won praise in the *New York Times* and other publications for its rich portrayal of the ethnic and political subcultures in San Francisco. An earlier novel, *The Confession,* received an Edgar Award for its controversial portrait of a Marin County psychologist accused of murdering his mistress.

SUSAN STRAIGHT has published eight novels. Her latest, *Between Heaven and Here,* is the final book in the Rio Seco trilogy. *Take One Candle Light a Room* was named one of the best novels of 2010 by the *Washington Post,* the *Los Angeles Times,* and *Kirkus.* "The Golden Gopher," included in this volume, won the 2008 Edgar Award for best short story. She teaches creative writing at University of California–Riverside. She was born in Riverside, California, where she lives with her family, whose history is featured on susanstraight.com.

JOHNNY TEMPLE is the publisher and editor in chief of Akashic Books, an award-winning Brooklyn-based independent company. He won the 2013 Ellery Queen Award from the Mystery Writers of America; the American Association of Publishers' 2005 Miriam Bass Award for Creativity in Independent Publishing; and the 2010 Jay and Dean Kogan Award for Excellence in Noir Literature. He has contributed articles and political essays to various publications, including the *Nation, Publishers Weekly, AlterNet, Poets & Writers,* and *Bookforum.* He lives in Brooklyn.

LUIS ALBERTO URREA, Pulitzer Prize finalist and winner of the Edgar Award for the short story "Amapola" (included in this volume), is the best-selling author of fourteen books, including *Queen of America, Into the Beautiful North, The Hummingbird's Daughter,* and *The Devil's Highway.* Recipient of an American Book Award, a Kiriyama Pacific Rim Prize, a Lannan Literary Award, and a member of the Latino Literary Hall of Fame, Urrea lives with his family in Naperville, Illinois, where he is a distinguished professor of creative writing at the University of Illinois–Chicago.

DON WINSLOW is the *New York Times* best-selling author of more than a dozen novels, including *Savages, The Power of the Dog, The Kings of Cool, California Fire and Life, The Winter of Frankie Machine,* and *Satori. Savages* was made into a critically acclaimed film for Universal Pictures by three-time Oscar winner Oliver Stone. Winslow has received numerous awards for his writing, including the prestigious Raymond Chandler Award as one of the most significant figures in American literature.

ABOUT THE AKASHIC NOIR SERIES

Following are the full contributor lists to the original Akashic Noir Series volumes represented in *USA Noir*. Included are the author, title, and location for each story, and they are listed in the order they first appeared.

Baltimore Noir edited by Laura Lippman

LAURA LIPPMAN	"Easy As A-B-C"	Locust Point
ROBERT WARD	"Fat Chance"	Old Northwood
JACK BLUDIS	"Pigtown Will Shine Tonight"	Pigtown
ROB HIAASEN	"Over My Dead Body"	Fell's Point
RAFAEL ALVAREZ	"The Invisible Man"	Highlandtown
DAVID SIMON	"Stainless Steel"	Sandtown-Winchester
MARCIA TALLEY	"Home Movies"	Little Italy
JOSEPH WALLACE	"Liminal"	Security Boulevard-Woodlawn
LISA RESPERS FRANCE	"Almost Missed It By a Hair"	Howard Park
CHARLIE STELLA	"Ode to the O's"	Memorial Stadium
SARAH WEINMAN	"Don't Walk in Front of Me"	Pikesville
DAN FESPERMAN	"As Seen on TV"	Fells Point
TIM COCKEY	"The Haunting of Slink Ridgely"	Greenspring Valley
JIM FUSILLI	"The Homecoming"	Camden Yards
BEN NEIHART	"Frog Cycle"	Inner Harbor
SUJATA MASSEY	"Goodwood Gardens"	Roland Park

Boston Noir edited by Dennis Lehane

LYNNE HEITMAN	"Exit Interview"	Financial District
DENNIS LEHANE	"Animal Rescue"	Dorchester
JIM FUSILLI	"The Place Where He Belongs"	Beacon Hill
PATRICIA POWELL	"Dark Waters"	Watertown
DANA CAMERON	"Femme Sole"	North End
BRENDAN DUBOIS	"The Dark Island"	Boston Harbor
STEWART O'NAN	"The Reward"	Brookline
JOHN DUFRESNE	"The Cross-Eyed Bear"	Southie
DON LEE	"The Oriental Hair Poets"	Cambridge
J. ITABARI NJERI	"The Collar"	Roxbury
RUSS ABORN	"Turn Speed"	North Quincy

Bronx Noir edited by S.J. Rozan

JEROME CHARYN	"White Trash"	Claremont/Concourse
TERRENCE CHENG	"Gold Mountain"	Lehman College
JOANNE DOBSON	"Hey, Girlie"	Sedgwick Avenue
RITA LAKIN	"The Woman Who Hated the Bronx"	Elder Avenue
LAWRENCE BLOCK	"Rude Awakening"	Riverdale
SUZANNE CHAZIN	"Burnout"	Jerome Avenue
KEVIN BAKER	"The Cheers Like Waves"	Yankee Stadium
ABRAHAM RODRIGUEZ JR.	"Jaguar"	South Bronx
STEVEN TORRES	"Early Fall"	Hunts Point
S.J. ROZAN	"Hothouse"	Botanical Garden
THOMAS BENTIL	"Lost and Found"	Rikers Island
MARLON JAMES	"Look What Love Is Doing to Me"	Williamsbridge
SANDRA KITT	"Home Sweet Home"	City Island
ROBERT J. HUGHES	"A Visit to St. Nick's"	Fordham Road

Chicago Noir edited by Neal Pollack

DC Noir edited by George Pelecanos

Detroit Noir edited by E.J. Olsen & John C. Hocking

JAQ GREENSPON	"Disappear"	Sunset Park
JOSÉ SKINNER	"All About Balls"	East Las Vegas
NORA PIERCE	"Atomic City"	Test Site
CELESTE STARR	"Dirty Blood"	Pahrump
BLISS ESPOSITO	"Guns Don't Kill People"	Centennial Hills
FELICIA CAMPBELL	"Murder Is Academic"	Mount Charleston
JANET BERLINER	"The Road to Rachel"	Area 51

Lone Star Noir edited by Bobby Byrd & Johnny Byrd

LISA SANDLIN	"Phelan's First Case"	Beaumont
CLAUDIA SMITH	"Catgirl"	Galveston
DAVID CORBETT & LUIS URREA	"Who Stole My Monkey?"	Port Arthur
TIM TINGLE	"Six Dead Cabbies"	Ellington AFB
JAMES CRUMLEY	"Luck"	Crumley, Texas
JESSICA POWERS	"Preacher's Kid"	Andrews
JOE R. LANSDALE	"Six-Finger Jack"	Gladewater
GEORGE WIER	"Duckweed"	Littlefield
MILTON T. BURTON	"Cherry Coke"	Tyler
SARAH CORTEZ	"Montgomery Clift"	Houston
JESSE SUBLETT	"Moral Hazard"	Austin
DEAN JAMES	"Bottomed Out"	Dallas
ITO ROMO	"Crank"	San Antonio
BOBBY BYRD	"The Dead Man's Wife"	El Paso

Long Island Noir edited by Kaylie Jones

MATTHEW MCGEVNA	"Gateway to the Stars"	Mastic Beach
NICK MAMATAS	"Thy Shiny Car in the Night"	Northport
KAYLIE JONES	"Home Invasion"	Wainscott
QANTA AHMED	"Anjali's America"	Garden City
CHARLES SALZBERG	"A Starr Burns Bright"	Long Beach
REED FARREL COLEMAN	"Mastermind"	Selden
TIM MCLOUGHLIN	"Seven Eleven"	Wantagh
SARAH WEINMAN	"Past President"	Great Neck
JULES FEIFFER	"Boob Noir"	Southampton
JZ HOLDEN	"Summer Love"	Sagaponack
RICHIE NARVAEZ	"Ending in Paumanok"	Stony Brook
SHEILA KOHLER	"Terror"	Amagansett
JANE CIABATTARI	"Contents of House"	Sag Harbor
STEVEN WISHNIA	"Semiconscious"	Lake Ronkonkoma
KENNETH WISHNIA	"Blood Drive"	Port Jefferson Station
AMANI SCIPIO	"Jabo's"	Bridgehampton
TIM TOMLINSON	"Snow Job"	Wading River

Los Angeles Noir edited by Denise Hamilton

MICHAEL CONNELLY	"Mulholland Dive"	Mulholland Drive
NAOMI HIRAHARA	"Number 19"	Koreatown
EMORY HOLMES II	"Dangerous Days"	Leimert Park
DENISE HAMILTON	"Midnight in Silicon Valley"	San Marino
JANET FITCH	"The Method"	Los Feliz
PATT MORRISON	"Morocco Junction 90210"	Beverly Hills
CHRISTOPHER RICE	"Over Thirty"	West Hollywood
HÉCTOR TOBAR	"Once More, Lazarus"	East Hollywood
SUSAN STRAIGHT	"The Golden Gopher"	Downtown

RICHARD BURGIN	"Atlantis"	Atlantic City
ALICIA OSTRIKER	"August: Feeding Frenzy"	Jersey Shore
HIRSH SAWHNEY	"A Bag for Nicholas"	Jersey City
JEFFREY FORD	"Glass Eels"	Dividing Creek
B. MALZBERG & B. PRONZINI	"Meadowlands Spike"	Rutherford
ROBERT ARELLANO	"Kettle Run"	Cherry Hill
PAUL MULDOON	"Noir, NJ"	Paramus
JONATHAN SAFRAN FOER	"Too Near Real"	Princeton
E. WHITE & M. CARROLL	"Excavation"	Asbury Park
ROBERT PINSKY	"Long Branch Underground"	Long Branch
JOYCE CAROL OATES	"Run Kiss Daddy"	Kittatinny Mountains

New Orleans Noir edited by Julie Smith

TED O'BRIEN	"What's the Score?"	Mid-City
PATTY FRIEDMANN	"Two-Story Brick Houses"	Uptown
TIM MCLOUGHLIN	"Scared Rabbit"	Irish Channel
OLYMPIA VERNON	"Schevoski"	University District
DAVID FULMER	"Algiers"	Algiers
LAURA LIPPMAN	"Pony Girl"	Tremé
JERVEY TERVALON	"The Battling Priests of Corpus Christi"	Seventh Ward
JAMES NOLAN	"Open Mike"	French Quarter
KALAMU YA SALAAM	"All I Could Do Was Cry"	Lower Ninth Ward
BARBARA HAMBLY	"There Shall Your Heart Be Also"	The Swamp
MAUREEN TAN	"Muddy Pond"	Village de l'Est
THOMAS ADCOCK	"Lawyers' Tongues"	Gentilly
JERI CAIN ROSSI	"And Hell Walked In"	Bywater
CHRISTINE WILTZ	"Night Taxi"	Lakeview
GREG HERREN	"Annunciation Shotgun"	Lower Garden District
JULIE SMITH	"Loot"	Garden District
ACE ATKINS	"Angola South"	Loyola Avenue
ERIC OVERMYER	"Marigny Triangle"	Faubourg Marigny

Orange County Noir edited by Gary Phillips

SUSAN STRAIGHT	"Bee Canyon"	Santa Ana Narrows
ROBERT S. LEVINSON	"Down in Capistrano"	San Juan Capistrano
ROB ROBERGE	"Diverters"	Tustin
NATHAN WALPOW	"A Good Day's Work"	Seal Beach
BARBARA DEMARCO-BARRETT	"Crazy for You"	Costa Mesa
DAN DULING	"The Toll"	Laguna Beach
MARY CASTILLO	"2:45 Out of Santa Ana"	Santa Ana
LAWRENCE MADDOX	"Old, Cold Hand"	City of Orange
DICK LOCHTE	"The Movie Game"	Laguna Niguel
ROBERT WARD	"Black Star Canyon"	Dana Point
GARY PHILLIPS	"The Performer"	Los Alamitos
GORDON MCALPINE	"The Happiest Place"	Anaheim
MARTIN J. SMITH	"Dark Matter"	Balboa Island
PATRICIA MCFALL	"On the Night in Question"	Garden Grove

Philadelphia Noir edited by Carlin Romano

AIMEE LABRIE	"Princess"	South Philadelphia
SOLOMON JONES	"Scarred"	Strawberry Mansion
ASALI SOLOMON	"Secret Pool"	West Philadelphia
KEITH GILMAN	"Devil's Pocket"	Grays Ferry

DENNIS TAFOYA	"Above the Imperial"	East Falls
LAURA SPAGNOLI	"A Cut Above"	Rittenhouse Square
HALIMAH MARCUS	"Swimming"	Narberth
MEREDITH ANTHONY	"Fishtown Odyssey"	Fishtown
JIM ZERVANOS	"Your Brother, Who Loves You"	Fairmount
CARLIN ROMANO	"'Cannot Easy Normal Die'"	University City
DIANE AYRES	"Seeing Nothing"	Bella Vista
DUANE SWIERCZYNSKI	"Lonergan's Girl"	Frankford
CORDELIA FRANCES BIDDLE	"Reality"	Old City
GERALD KOLPAN	"The Ratcatcher"	South Street
CARY HOLLADAY	"Ghost Walk"	Chestnut Hill

Phoenix Noir edited by Patrick Millikin

JON TALTON	"Bull"	Downtown
CHARLES KELLY	"The Eighth Deadly Sin"	Hassayampa Valley
DIANA GABALDON	"Dirty Scottsdale"	Desert Botanical Garden
ROBERT ANGLEN	"Growing Back"	Apache Junction
LUIS ALBERTO URREA	"Amapola"	Paradise Valley
LEE CHILD	"Public Transportation"	Chandler
PATRICK MILLIKIN	"Devil Doll"	Tovrea Castle
LAURA TOHE	"Tom Snag"	Indian School Road
JAMES SALLIS	"Others of My Kind"	Glendale
KURT REICHENBAUGH	"Valerie"	Grand Avenue
GARY PHILLIPS	"Blazin' on Broadway"	South Phoenix
MEGAN ABBOTT	"It's Like a Whisper"	Scottsdale
DAVID CORBETT	"Dead by Christmas"	Tempe
DON WINSLOW	"Whiteout on Van Buren"	Van Buren Strip
DOGO BARRY GRAHAM	"By the Time He Got to Phoenix"	Christown
STELLA POPE DUARTE	"Confession"	Harmon Park

Pittsburgh Noir edited by Kathleen George

LILA SHAARA	"Atom Smasher"	Forest Hills
TERRANCE HAYES	"Still Air"	East Liberty
STEWART O'NAN	"Duplex"	Bloomfield
NANCY MARTIN	"Pray for Rain"	Highland Park
PAUL LEE	"A Minor Extinction"	Carrick
K.C. CONSTANTINE	"When Johnny Came Shuffling Home"	McKees Rocks
KATHLEEN GEORGE	"Intruder"	Schenley Farms
REBECCA DRAKE	"Loaded"	Fox Chapel
CARLOS ANTONIO DELGADO	"Far Beneath"	Morningside
HILARY MASTERS	"At the Buena Vista"	Mexican War Streets
KATHRYN MILLER HAINES	"Homecoming"	Wilkinsburg
AUBREY HIRSCH	"Cheater"	Squirrel Hill
TOM LIPINSKI	"Key Drop"	Lawrenceville
REGINALD MCKNIGHT	"Overheard"	Homewood

Portland Noir edited by Kevin Sampsell

KAREN KARBO	"The Clown and Bard"	SE Twenty-Eighth Avenue
LUCIANA LOPEZ	"Julia Now"	St. Johns
ARIEL GORE	"Water under the Bridge"	Clinton
FLOYD SKLOOT	"Alzheimer's Noir"	Oaks Bottom
DAN DEWEESE	"The Sleeper"	Highway 30
JONATHAN SELWOOD	"The Wrong House"	Mount Tabor

MARTHA C. LAWRENCE	"Key Witness"	La Jolla Cove
DEBRA GINSBERG	"The New Girl"	Cortez Hill
TAFFY CANNON	"Instant Karma"	Rancho Santa Fe
MORGAN HUNT	"The Angel's Share"	Hillcrest
KEN KUHLKEN	"Homes"	Newport Avenue
DON WINSLOW	"After Thirty"	Pacific Beach
LISA BRACKMANN	"Don't Feed the Bums"	Ocean Beach
CAMERON PIERCE HUGHES	"Moving Black Objects"	Mission Beach
GABRIEL R. BARILLAS	"The Roads"	Del Mar
GAR ANTHONY HAYWOOD	"Like Something Out of a Comic Book"	Convention Center
LUIS ALBERTO URREA	"The National City Reparation Society"	National City
MARIA LIMA	"A Scent of Death"	Gaslamp Quarter

San Francisco Noir edited by Peter Maravelis

DOMENIC STANSBERRY	"The Prison"	North Beach
DAVID CORBETT	"It Can Happen"	Hunter's Point
SIN SORACCO	"Double Espresso"	Russian River
BARRY GIFFORD	"After Hours at La Chinita"	The Bayview
KATE BRAVERMAN	"The Neutral Zone"	Fisherman's Wharf
ALVIN LU	"Le Rouge et le Noir"	Chinatown
MICHELLE TEA	"Larry's Place"	Bernal Heights
ALEJANDRO MURGUÍA	"The Other Barrio"	The Mission
PETER PLATE	"Genesis to Revelation"	Market Street
WILL CHRISTOPHER BAER	"Deception of the Thrush"	The Castro
JIM NISBET	"Weight Less Than Shadow"	Golden Gate Bridge
JON LONGHI	"Fixed"	The Haight-Ashbury
ROBERT MAILER ANDERSON	"Briley Boy"	The Richmond
EDDIE MULLER	"Kid's Last Fight"	South of Market
DAVID HENRY STERRY	"Confessions of a Sex Maniac"	Polk Gulch

Seattle Noir edited by Curt Colbert

THOMAS P. HOPP	"Blood Tide"	Duwamish
BHARTI KIRCHNER	"Promised Tulips"	Wallingford
STEPHAN MAGCOSTA	"Golden Gardens"	Ballard
ROBERT LOPRESTI	"The Center of the Universe"	Fremont
KATHLEEN ALCALÁ	"Blue Sunday"	Central District
SIMON WOOD	"The Taskmasters"	Downtown
PATRICIA HARRINGTON	"What Price Retribution?"	Capitol Hill
CURT COLBERT	"Till Death Do Us ..."	Belltown
PAUL S. PIPER	"The Best View in Town"	Leschi
R. BARRI FLOWERS	"The Wrong End of a Gun"	South Lake Union
BRIAN THORNTON	"Paper Son"	Chinatown
SKYE MOODY	"The Magnolia Bluff"	Magnolia
LOU KEMP	"Sherlock's Opera"	Waterfront
G.M. FORD	"Food for Thought"	Pioneer Square

Staten Island Noir edited by Patricia Smith

BILL LOEHFELM	"Snake Hill"	Eltingville
LOUISA ERMELINO	"Sister-in-Law"	Great Kills
PATRICIA SMITH	"When They Are Done with Us"	Port Richmond
TED ANTHONY	"A User's Guide to Keeping Your Kills Fresh"	Fresh Kills
SHAY YOUNGBLOOD	"Dark Was the Night, Cold Was the Ground"	South Beach
MICHAEL PENNCAVAGE	"Mistakes"	The Ferry

NOIR SERIES AWARDS, PRIZES & HONORS

Following is a list-in-progress of the various awards, prizes, and honors that Akashic Noir Series stories have either won or been short-listed for.

Boston Noir

EDGAR AWARD FINALISTS 2010
Dennis Lehane, "Animal Rescue"
Dana Cameron, "Femme Sole"

INCLUDED IN *THE BEST AMERICAN MYSTERY STORIES 2010*
John Dufresne, "The Cross-Eyed Bear"
Dennis Lehane, "Animal Rescue"

SHAMUS AWARD FINALIST 2010
Brendan DuBois, "The Dark Island"

ANTHONY AWARD FINALISTS 2010
Dennis Lehane, "Animal Rescue"
Dana Cameron, "Femme Sole"

MACAVITY AWARD FINALIST 2010
Dana Cameron, "Femme Sole"

AGATHA AWARD FINALIST 2009
Dana Cameron, "Femme Sole"

Bronx Noir

WINNER, NEW ATLANTIC INDEPENDENT BOOKSELLERS ASSOCIATION BOOK OF THE YEAR AWARD, SPECIAL CATEGORY 2008

INCLUDED IN *THE BEST AMERICAN MYSTERY STORIES 2008*
S.J. Rozan, "Hothouse"

Brooklyn Noir

EDGAR AWARD FINALIST 2005
Pete Hamill, "The Book Signing"

ROBERT L. FISH MEMORIAL AWARD WINNER 2005
Thomas Morrissey, "Can't Catch Me"

SHAMUS AWARD WINNER 2005
Pearl Abraham, "Hasidic Noir"

INCLUDED IN *THE BEST AMERICAN MYSTERY STORIES 2005*
Tim McLoughlin, "When All This Was Bay Ridge"
Lou Manfredo, "Case Closed"

ANTHONY AWARD FINALIST 2005
Arthur Nersesian, "Hunter/Trapper"

PUSHCART PRIZE FINALIST 2005
Ellen Miller, "Practicing"

DC Noir

INCLUDED IN *THE BEST AMERICAN MYSTERY STORIES 2007*
Robert Andrews, "Solomon's Alley"

Detroit Noir
> SHAMUS AWARD FINALIST 2008
> Loren D. Estleman, "Kill the Cat"

Kansas City Noir
> INCLUDED IN *THE BEST AMERICAN MYSTERY STORIES 2013*
> Nancy Pickard, "Lightbulb"

Las Vegas Noir
> INCLUDED IN *THE BEST AMERICAN MYSTERY STORIES 2009*
> David Corbett, "Pretty Little Parasite"
> Vu Tran, "This or Any Desert"

Lone Star Noir
> SHAMUS AWARD FINALIST 2011
> Lisa Sandlin, "Phelan's First Case"
>
> INCLUDED IN *THE BEST AMERICAN MYSTERY STORIES 2011*
> David Corbett & Luis Alberto Urrea, "Who Stole My Monkey?"

Long Island Noir
> INCLUDED IN *THE BEST AMERICAN MYSTERY STORIES 2013*
> Nick Mamatas, "The Shiny Car in the Night"

Los Angeles Noir
> SOUTHERN CALIFORNIA INDEPENDENT BOOKSELLERS ASSOCIATION WINNER 2007
>
> EDGAR AWARD WINNER 2008
> Susan Straight, "The Golden Gopher"
>
> INCLUDED IN *THE BEST AMERICAN MYSTERY STORIES 2008*
> Michael Connelly, "Mulholland Dive"
> Robert Ferrigno, "The Hour When the Ship Comes In"

Manhattan Noir
> EDGAR AWARD FINALISTS 2007
> S.J. Rozan, "Building"
> Thomas H. Cook, "Rain"
>
> INCLUDED IN *THE BEST AMERICAN MYSTERY STORIES 2007*
> Robert Knightly, "Take the Man's Pay"

Miami Noir
> INCLUDED IN *THE BEST AMERICAN MYSTERY STORIES 2007*
> John Bond, "T-bird"

New Jersey Noir
> INCLUDED IN *THE BEST AMERICAN MYSTERY STORIES 2012*
> Lou Manfredo, "Soul Anatomy"

New Orleans Noir
> SHAMUS AWARD FINALIST 2008
> James Nolan, "Open Mike"

Paris Noir
> EDGAR AWARD FINALIST 2009
> Dominique Mainard, "La Vie en Rose"

Philadelphia Noir
> MACAVITY AWARD FINALIST 2011
> Keith Gilman, "Devil's Pocket"

Phoenix Noir

        EDGAR AWARD WINNER 2010
            Luis Alberto Urrea, "Amapola"

        ANTHONY AWARD FINALIST 2010
            Luis Alberto Urrea, "Amapola"

        MACAVITY AWARD FINALIST 2010
            Luis Alberto Urrea, "Amapola"

        SHAMUS AWARD FINALIST 2010
            Gary Phillips, "Blazin' on Broadway"

Queens Noir

        ROBERT L. FISH MEMORIAL AWARD WINNER 2009
            Joe Guglielmelli, "Buckner's Error"

San Diego Noir

        SOUTHERN CALIFORNIA INDEPENDENT BOOKSELLERS ASSOCIATION
        AWARD FINALIST 2011

        INCLUDED IN *THE BEST AMERICAN MYSTERY STORIES 2012*
            T. Jefferson Parker, "Vic Primeval"

San Francisco Noir

        MACAVITY AWARD FINALIST 2006
            David Corbett, "It Can Happen"

Staten Island Noir

        ROBERT L. FISH MEMORIAL AWARD WINNER 2013
            Patricia Smith, "When They Are Done with Us"

        INCLUDED IN *THE BEST AMERICAN MYSTERY STORIES 2013*
            Patricia Smith, "When They Are Done with Us"

Toronto Noir

        ARTHUR ELLIS AWARD WINNER 2009
            Pasha Malla, "Filmsong"

        ARTHUR ELLIS AWARD FINALIST 2009
            Peter Robinson, "Walking the Dog"

Twin Cities Noir

        SHAMUS AWARD FINALIST 2007
            Bruce Rubenstein, "Smoke Got in My Eyes"

Venice Noir

        INCLUDED IN *THE BEST AMERICAN MYSTERY STORIES 2013*
            Emily St. John Mandel, "Drifter"

Wall Street Noir

        DERRINGER AWARD FINALIST 2008
            Twist Phelan, "A Trader's Lot"

        INCLUDED IN *THE BEST AMERICAN MYSTERY STORIES 2008*
            Stephen Rhodes, "At the Top of His Game"